Appassionato

Also by Gloria Vitanza Basile
THE GODSON
and published by Corgi Books

Gloria Vitanza Basile

Appassionato

VOLUME 1

CORGI BOOKS

A DIVISION OF TRANSWORLD PUBLISHERS LTD

APPASSIONATO

A CORGI BOOK 0 552 10910 X

First publication in Great Britain

PRINTING HISTORY
Corgi edition published 1978

This book is set in 9/9½pt Times

Corgi Books are published by Transworld Publishers Ltd.,
Century House, 61–63 Uxbridge Road,
Ealing, London, W.5.
Made and printed in Great Britain by
Hunt Barnard Printing Ltd., Aylesbury, Bucks.

For
my number two son, Robert,
and
the friendly Siculi demons
and
ghostlike apparitions
who
invaded my soul to keep me
company
while
writing this novel
and
to
the spirit of Salvatore
and
to
Louis A. Basile, Attorney
who
guided me
through endless
legal translations

TYRRHENIAN

Ustica Prison

Trapani
Mt. Erice
Castellamare
Partinico
Montegatta
Palermo
San Guiseppi
Monreale
Jato
Piana dei Greci
Portella Della
Rosa
Godrano
Corleone
Marsala
Castelvetrano
Villalba
Mazara
Selinunte
Mussimeli
Agrigento

kilometers

| 0 | 20 | 40 | 60 | 80 |

| 0 | 10 | 20 | 30 | 40 | 50 |

miles

MEDITERRANEAN

He was seven years old. His father had died. Confused by death's mysteries, he wandered off by himself to sort out the confusion in his mind. Standing at the edge of the broken clay floor at the Temple of Cats, above Montegatta, he stood gazing down at the scattering of villages strung together like broken and runted rows of teeth, spilled along the limestone slopes of the majestic mountains.

Flushed and elated at the new secret hiding place he had discovered earlier, he marveled at how an enormous stone between two pillars had moved easily for him, as if a power, not his, had induced it to budge and reveal an opening to an inner grotto. Inside the cool, mysteriously compelling cave, he had stared wondrously at the strange signs carved into the walls. And when voices, whispering and tunneled, rushed at him in a language he didn't understand, he had gazed about in awe, but he hadn't been frightened. He had made a vow to keep this place as his very own secret hiding place; not even to Vincenzo would he confide the discovery of such a place. He had left the grotto, replacing the stone with equal ease, still baffled that he could move such a stone. It was incredible.

Now, as he glanced at the valley below, it seemed to change before his eyes. Windswept plains no longer contained villages as he knew them. Ancient temples and edifices of another century, with marketplaces and bazaars, replaced the former scene. There came a distant sound of trumpets, a call to arms. He searched everywhere for the source of the sounds. In the distance came a charge of horses; legions of men on horseback converged from all directions like a splendid pageant of antiquity. Chiefs and subchiefs in scant, colorful dress, with breastplates, armor, and shields that glittered in the blinding sunlight; gaily dressed horses with bright feathers and gleaming bridle regalia; standard-bearers, with vivid banners waving in the wind, rode swiftly alongside the vast armies of Greeks, Carthaginians, and Roman soldiers, coming together as one force. Just as quickly, the rattling of wheels, clatter of horses, and eerie sounds of anguished trumpets faded and the scene restored itself to the present.

"Tori . . . Tori. . . ." He heard his name called, like the rustling of wind through bamboo thickets. Drawn seductively by the sirenlike voices, he stepped forward. God! He wanted to take that perilous step forward into the most exciting sight of his life. He hesitated, but not through any power of his own. His foot refused to obey his command. His energies tried to propel his foot forward, but it was useless. It was as if the same force that earlier had moved aside the rock now held him from pitching forward into eternity.

"Tori! Tori!" called Filippo and Marco. He turned to his older brothers with that same stunned expression of amazement on his face.

Filippo took one look at him and laughed. "The Siculis have called to him. See? It's written on his face. Don't be frightened, Tori. Legend claims they always call to their own."

"But I am not frightened," he told them. They paid him no heed. No one every paid much attention to boys his age. Except for his mother.

"The friendly Siculi demons won't permit you to be hurt, not if you listen to them," said Marco.

Taking his hands, they led Tori out the temple and back onto the winding road that led into their village.

"I wasn't really frightened," insisted Tori, his small face turned back to the scene as he stumbled along. His eyes compulsively searched the area, awe-filled, trying to understand all he'd been witness to. How could he tell his brothers he had wanted to go with whoever had called to him? They'd never understand—would they?

"You better tell Mamma, Tori," said Marco seriously. "It's time she taught him of more earthly things, Filippo. He's too impressionable at this age. He might have fallen to his death if we hadn't arrived in time. Now, with Papa gone, we'll have to devote all our time to the *campagna*."

Tori couldn't understand his brothers' concern. They didn't know what he knew. There was no way he could have fallen. Some force, something he couldn't begin to imagine, had held him back.

"Mamma, who are the Siculis?" he asked her one night weeks later.

"Where did you hear of them, Tori?"

"At the Temple of Cats. They called to me. Filippo told me."

2

"Did Marco also tell you?"

"Yes, Mamma, *bedda*. He said I should learn more of earthly things."

"I see. The Siculis, my son, were the first inhabitants of our island, whom God placed upon the land when he created it. Legend claims they call to their own."

"And what does that mean, Mamma?"

"It means—so claims the legend—that once upon a time you lived here before."

"I did?" he asked wonderingly. "Was I very good, Mamma?"

"Very, very good, Tori."

"Was I rich? As rich as the landlords?"

"Very rich, Tori."

"Was I important?"

"You were king!"

"Is that why they let me come back?"

"Perhaps."

"Will I be king once again?"

"You'll be whatever you picture in your mind."

"Are you sure, Mamma, *bedda*?"

"I'm sure."

"But—how do I make these pictures? Do I buy a camera?"

"The camera is already in your mind."

"Will I learn to use it?"

"You will learn. Be patient."

"Mamma—I already see pictures."

"Good. Then you already know how to use it."

"Mamma, if I see a splendid white horse, will I be a horse?"

"Tori. You are making jest with me."

"Or a tiger—a lion—or an eagle? What if I see them all?"

"And what if I see a broad paddle with which to warm your bottom?"

"Oh, Mamma, *bedda!* I truly love you."

"And I love you, Tori. Now run and play. But don't meddle with the Siculi. They are playful enough, but sometimes they don't know when to stop."

She watched him run out into the Sicilian sunshine to join his friends. Soon enough, he'd have to set aside these childish dreams and go to work with his brothers. Perhaps Marco is right, thought Antigone Naxos Salvatore. It's time to stop filling him with legends of his Greek and Roman heritage. He is growing up and is old enough to learn of earthly matters.

3

BOOK I

The *Mise en Scène*

Their national symbol is a funeral cortege. Their national anthem, a howling wail of soundless horror echoing in the blood-filled corridors of their minds. For seven years his existence on earth had proved threatening to them. His time had come. High officials in government, totally without conscience or humanity, had gathered to dispose of those who defied their edicts. An imperceptible nod, the slightest flickering of a power-saturated eye, a barely discernible movement in an upraised hand had decided it was time to put an end to a legend and bury his bones among the skeletons of the past.

CHAPTER 1

July 5, 1950
Castelvetrano, Sicily

At 2:30 A.M. on this Wednesday, there was no moon in the sky. No light of any kind flickered in the deserted streets. There was only a hollow silence in which there were no echoes, for the village at this time was dead, soundless. Villagers, exhausted and unable to sleep in the early evening hours, now entered their deepest slumber, unaware that ghoulish goings-on had already commenced in their village.

A three-day heat wave muzzled any breeze that might have escaped Mediterranean waters. It hung in a pall over the desperately hot village, where antiquated and delapidated houses with swan-breasted balconies jutted over narrow, cobbled streets, hardly more than alleys strung together by mean, sequestered courtyards, fetid and foul with the stench of animal excrement and waste waters.

But wait. There was a light after all, so faint it was barely discernible. In one of those shabby courtyards, at *numero* 54, Strada Sarina Madonna, two burly men worked feverishly against time, their faces dimly illuminated by weak, sputtering rays from a battery-powered hand torch lying on the ground at their feet. The men moved about their business with skillful dexterity, unaware that they unwittingly prepared the *mise en scène* for what would become the most bizarre drama ever to be enacted under the proscenium arch of Sicilian politics.

Earlier, a mule-driven lorry had deposited the body of a dead man with them. An aged driver with failing eyesight, amply paid for his services, was curtly dismissed. No one had to warn him not to breathe a word of his deeds on this satanic night. He knew full well the consequences: reprisal, even death.

Hampered by unabated heat, intolerable odors, and a deadline, the two men worked swiftly, as if prodded by Lucifer. The older man, dressed in shirtsleeves and trousers, propped the dead body up against the stone wall. For a split second, the faintest glimmer of triumph flashed in his intent dark eyes. He stared at the body, then he

7

brandished a submachine gun and fired several shots into the corpse.

The dead man didn't bleed.

Struck with amazement, the younger man marveled at the phenomenon. Damn! His captain was right. My, my, what skills one acquires in this line of work, he told himself. A profound respect shone in his eyes as he watched his superior officer scribble a name on a small card and press it into his hand.

"Run swiftly to this address," instructed the captain. "A man will give you what I ordered earlier. Make haste! We're fighting time."

As the aide left the courtyard, the captain glanced apprehensively at the pulsating eastern sky, at the fading, yawning stars, soon to be swallowed up in daylight. Shortly, peasants preparing for day labor at nearby feudal estates would be rising. *Vaccari* would fill the streets with their cows until all the milk in those swollen udders was sold. Bakers would fire their ovens. Goddamn! He had to move before the cocks crowed.

The captain, flushed with adrenalin, moved rapidly. Fleeting images came at him attempting to shatter his resolve. Methodically and meticulously, he shoved aside his scruples and adroitly blocked from mind all memories of the circumstances leading to this point. Four days ago, he'd made his decision. Despite certain drawbacks, he was fully committed to the act. It was too late to turn back.

Expertly, he turned the dead man over, sprawling him face down in the dirt, right knee drawn up slightly, right arm outflung to aptly display a large diamond solitaire on the third finger of his hand. He paused a moment to observe his handiwork. Everything had to be just right. There could be no errors—not at this point. He flashed the torch over the body, inspecting it against some inner design in his mind.

Probing dark eyes scanned the carefully creased beige Levis, spotless white undershirt, and spiffy dark mahogany sandals worn by the corpse. The four-day stubble on his face caused the officer a moment's consternation, but he had no time to worry over the incongruities. Perhaps no one will notice, he thought. Moreover, who'd contest the word of the Forces to Suppress Banditry, eh?

Satisfied for the moment, the captain wiped the rolling sweat from his face, moved closer, and with the aid of the flashlight attempted to read the inscription on the back of the golden scorpion amulet suspended on a gold chain around the dead man's neck. Unable to make it out, he cursed himself for not bringing his reading glasses. He carefully placed the amulet in the dirt, inches from the lifeless face. Next he slipped a leather gun belt under the inert hips and secured into place an open gun holster. Midway between the man's face and his outflung arm, he placed a German Luger. With painstaking precision, he placed a .38 calibre Beretta submachine gun two feet from the bent knee.

Behind the body, next to a broken stone wall at the rear of the enclosure, he casually dropped a beige rucksack and scattered at random a German-made camera, three rolls of undeveloped film, two packs of unopened Pall Mall cigarettes, two Breda machine gun cartridges, a freshly opened box of shells for the Luger, and the last item found in the dead man's pocket, a white toy soldier on a white horse which he partially buried in the dust.

By then it was nearly 4 A.M. His aide, Private Foti, reappeared with a tin container which he promptly turned over to his superior officer. Total bafflement filled the incredulous eyes of the dark-skinned private as he watched his mentor's busy, skillful hands. Unsure of many things at this moment, Foti was certain of one thing: He was going to be sick. The bloodless wounds inflicted earlier on the deceased—two bullet holes in the right rib cage; two in the upper right arm; one in the inner elbow; several at the mangled wrist—now oozed with bright crimson blood injected into the empty craters with a hypodermic syringe. The captain's expertise both confounded and repelled Private Foti, but it also evoked an expression of profound respect.

Scrutinizing his handiwork with hypercritical eyes, the officer, dissatisfied with the overall picture, frowned. It wasn't complete. Resetting the body into its former position, sprawled face downward, he poured the remaining goat's blood over the right shoulder, spilling a trail of carmine outward past the outflung arm until the container was empty. Again, he surveyed the scene. Satisfied, he shoved can and container at Foti. "Get rid of these."

Container and syringe in hand, the bug-eyed private nervously negotiated his way out the rear entrance into an adjoining, deserted, inner courtyard abutting a neighbor's house. As his eyes searched the darkness, he tossed the empty can into a bed of myrtle at the base of a solitary almond tree and shuddered involuntarily at the syringe in his hand. A thought struck him. Sprinting lightly on the balls of his feet, he reentered the first courtyard and moved along the far side of the widow Grissi's house where earlier he had noticed a recessed sewer drain. Lifting the crude wooden cover, he tossed the hypodermic into it, then dropped the lid gently into place. He grimaced with disgust and wiped his hands on the seat of his trousers to erase the blood stains. He couldn't wait to tell his new wife the things his eyes had seen this day.

The next phase of this bizarre scheme was entered into when the captain let loose a short volley of machine-gun fire into one of the narrow stone walls at the right of the archway entrance. A crash of fire and chipping stones, as ricocheting bullets pinged and zinged loudly, caused no stir in the sleeping village except to send a few cats and rats scurrying for cover.

In the shifting shadows made by lights breaking in eastern skies, Private Foti failed to notice the muzzle of the gun turn subtly toward him. Before he guessed his fate, the officer's trigger finger squeezed gently and a burst of fire cut the private in two. Propelled backward by the force of the missiles, Private Foti's face jerked wretchedly. Shocked dark eyes widened in surprise. He groaned, "Why? Why? My lips were sealed." He fell to the ground like a limp rag doll.

"Now there can be no doubt," muttered the *capitano*, talking to a dead man. His watch read 4:15 A.M. He gazed warily at the horizon, now ablaze with spectral lights, and swore under his breath. The last phase of his diabolical plot should have been completed by now.

Quickly he pulled the aide's body out of the enclosure and dumped him onto the street side of the courtyard. He moved swiftly. Already he could hear the creaking of the rickety carts rolling along the cobblestones, as the village started to come alive. He wiped the sweat from his face and neck, buttoned his shirt, yanked his tie into place, and ran his fingers through his short black hair. In the light, he looked more formidable, like a well-muscled athlete. His face, free of humor, was one which most people took seriously. From the short end of the broken rear wall, he picked up his beige tunic and slipped into it. He squared a visored hat on his head and allowed his fingers to slide down both sides of the braided uniform, out of meticulous habit. He finished not a moment too soon, for already the cocks were crowing.

Running to the house at the right of the courtyard, he pounded furiously on the wooden door with balled fists and shouting authoritatively, he commanded, "Open the door! Open in the name of the Italian government! Water! I need water for a dying man! Open I say! I'm Captain

10

Franchina of the Forces to Suppress Banditry! I've just captured the bandit Salvatore!"

Inside the shabby house, the widow Grissi and her lover had been in the throes of sexual ecstasy when Manfredo first heard the crackling gunshot sounds like distant fireworks. *"Managghia,* Giulietta," he whispered hoarsely. "I have always dreamed of hearing such sounds when making love, but I never dreamed I would experience such erotica!" He hugged her tighter and tighter, certain he had tasted eternal paradise.

"Ah, *che si beddu!"* she whispered. "Hold me tighter, *amore."*

"Can you feel me now?"

"What is it you do to me? I feel like an animal, a cat!"

"Si, my little cat, kiss me again."

"Oh, Manfredo, Manfredo," she sighed. "We must get married so we can do this every night. You have the balls of a bull and an appetite to match."

"And you, my Giulietta, have the balloons of a cow, but so much tastier, *cara mia.* Lie back now and take what I have to offer."

"I'll take it. I'll take it. Quickly, Manfredo, before I scream so loud the neighbors will hear me and know I have a seed bull in my house."

"Giulietta . . . ah, Giulietta. Giulietta!"

"Stop, Manfredo. Stop. Listen, listen. *Santo Dio,* will you stop for a minute!" She pulled away from him and placed her slender hand over his lips. "There's someone knocking on my door. I knew it! I knew earlier when I saw strangers moving about in the courtyard, I shouldn't let you in. Pray it's not police."

"To hell with them! Tell them to go away!" he cried hoarsely taking her hands from his lips. Wild-eyed and frenzied, holding his aching and enormously swollen tumescence in his hand, he tried to find her honey pot.

"Listen, you son of a whore! That idiot—whoever he is—is jabbering something about Salvatore! Listen!" Giulietta's eyes lit up with wild lights.

Faintly the captain's voice was heard. It came in clear and carried well in the silence. "I am Captain Franchina of the Forces to Suppress Banditry! Open up. I need water for a dying man! I've just killed Salvatore!"

The widow Grissi stiffened imperceptibly, for both names rushed at her out of her past to fill her with a vile and contemptible hatred. Firmly and with new-found strength, she told her lover, "You stay here—out of sight,

11

Manfredo—while I go downstairs to see what this is about. I dare not close my ears to such authority."

"And what do I do about this, my little *gatta?*" Manfredo held his slowly deflating weapon in his hand, a pain-filled, unsatisfied expression on his face.

"Unload the bullets," she said with a glint in her eye. "I shall return to help you fire at your target." She slipped into a flannel robe and left him.

Downstairs, her heart beating with unnatural excitement, the young widow peered through a narrow slit in the door and made out the khaki-colored uniform with shiny buttons. Even in five years, he looked the same. She remained in the shadows.

"I need your assistance, *signora*, for a dying man. Water, please, and a telephone," he told her. "I am Captain Giovanni Franchina of the FSB and I've just captured the brigand Salvatore."

Her face swollen with hostility as the face on the uniform came into focus, she scowled darkly and handed him the water jug. Beyond him in the growing light of dawn she saw a darkened form lying sprawled out in the courtyard. "Water, yes. *Telefono*, no. De Meo's house next door has a *telefono*." She moved back into the shadows so he wouldn't recognize her. Earlier, waiting for her lover, she'd seen strange goings-on in the courtyard. But it was not her business—or was it?

Grabbing the bottle from her hands, with a false expression of anguish on his face, Captain Franchina returned to the dead man's side and made a pretense of trying to elevate the man's head. Naturally there was no response. With a certain *panache*, Franchina removed his snap-brimmed hat, inclined his head briefly, and crossed himself religiously. From the corner of his eyes he saw the woman's darkened figure peering at him. He heard an audible gasp as she, too, crossed herself. A self-satisfied smile tugged at the corner of his lips. Unfortunately, the officer didn't see the smile of satisfaction on the widow's lips.

Bolting her door securely, Giuletta Grissi scurried upstairs to her lover's side. Dismayed to find him snoring, she shook him vigorously.

"Manfredo! Manfredo! Wake up! They've just killed Salvatore! His body lies crushed in de Meo's courtyard, killed by that black-hearted mercenary, Captain Franchina. Sweet Jesus, my prayers have been answered!"

"*Va, va,*" he told her sleepily, not fully hearing her. "Don't break my balls, woman! They'll never catch Salvatore. Never in a million years. He's in Brazil where he's been for nearly six months." He rolled over and commenced his snoring.

"Curse the devil, sweet Jesus. How sweet is the taste of revenge. How long I've waited for this. What justice! The memory of those men will no longer interfere in *my* life! Especially not my *love* life," she exclaimed, removing her robe and climbing back into bed. She began to prod her lover to renewed vigor. "Manfredo . . . Manfredo," she cooed lovingly.

By 5 A.M. a special squad of security police deputized by the FSB arrived at *numero* 54, Strada Sarina Madonna in response to the call made by Captain Franchina from the de Meo house. With them came the commander of the Forces to Suppress Banditry, Colonel Cesare Cala, a quiet, dignified, somber-faced man of forty-eight, with gray blue eyes and a perennial expression of apology carved into his features. His uniform was spotless, khaki-colored, with customary gold braid and buttons. His visored hat was tugged down over his expressive eyes. He stood to one side and watched without comment as the squad disposed of Private Foti's body—reported shot by bandits in the line of duty.

With official decorum, his hands clasped behind his back, the colonel lumbered through the stone arch into the courtyard, his keen, discerning eyes readily absorbing the scene. For the next twenty minutes he listened as Captain Franchina related the story of his successful coup against the redoubtable bandit Salvatore. He listened attentively as he usually did, asking no questions. This was not an unusual posture for the Italian intelligence officer who believed that listening, rather than talking, had paved the way for all his past successes.

The arrival of two police officers from the local office of the Security Police interrupted their tête-à-tête. Briefed on what had occurred and who lay dead in the courtyard, the duo were instructed to stand guard until men from the procurator general's office arrived to conduct their routine investigation.

"You are to guard this position, the body and all personal effects with your life, Corporal!" snapped Captain Franchina. "And button your tunic!" he added disdainfully. "Do you always dress so slovenly when on duty?"

"Yes, sir. I mean no, sir," retorted the corporal with a false brightness. Enmity between *carabinieri* and security police was a spreading cancer which the corporal tried to conceal in his response. Roused from barracks and a sound sleep, he and his companion had been shuttled off in haste to this address, hardly awake. Now both police-men stood at attention until the FSB officers disappeared in the shadowy haze of dawn in the functional black Fiat.

Deliberately unbuttoning his tunic in the wake of Cap-tain Franchina's stern admonition, the corporal glanced about the tricky shadows. His wary eyes met those of his companion and they both sensed silent, watchful eyes star-ing down at them from behind shuttered windows and sheltered balconies. With carbines held firmly in their hands, the two police officers moved slowly over the earth-en courtyard and stared long and hard at the youthful corpse sprawled in the dirt amid a lake of blood.

At 6:30 A.M. the Eternal City of Rome had already yawned twice as the capital came alive. In an elegantly furnished baroque bedroom at the Villa Belasci, the Minis-ter of the Interior, disturbed by the incessant ringing of the telephone, leaned over and reached for the raucous in-strument on the nightstand. Disrespectful bastards! Who dared call his private number at such an ungodly hour?

He mumbled, *"Pronto,"* softly into the mouthpiece, hoping not to awaken the sleeping form next to him in the oversized bed. In moments his emerald eyes blinked open in astonishment. He sat up quickly, swung his pajama-clad legs over the side of the bed, and turned on the table lamp. He listened attentively and nodded from time to time. "Yes, yes, Inspector Zanorelli. You did the right thing to call. Contact Colonel Cala. Have him call my of-fice at 9 A.M. sharp. Make sure all details are contained in the report." Belasci hung up.

Martino Belasci, cabinet minister in Premier de Aspanu's government, Minister of the Interior, and high-ranking political bigwig in the Christian Democratic Party, placed a hurried call to the villa of his premier. He blinked several times to force himself awake, reached for a cigarette from a decorative porcelain box, and lit it with a delicate, swan-shaped crystal and silver lighter. As Belasci inhaled deeply, his bright blue eyes betrayed an inner ex-citement.

When he had related the message to a joyous chief of state, Premier de Aspanu, he hung up and placed a second call to his personal secretary, Marcello Barone, and or-dered a press conference in his office at 10 A.M. sharp that morning. He placed a third call to Don Matteo Barbarossa in Monreale, Sicily. Unable to get his call through, he hung up.

14

Twenty minutes later, by the time his manservant appeared with a tray of steaming hot coffee. Belasci had showered and shaved and stood meticulously dressed in a dove-gray double-breasted suit. He took the tray from his man and shooed him away He poured the black beverage into a delicate bone china cup and gulped it down hurriedly. Satisfied with the image reflected in the gilt-edged oval mirror, the dark-haired, fair-complexioned state official, who wore custom clothing with a dashing flair, moved lightly toward the shadowy form under silken coverlets on the ornate bed, flushed with secret elation.

"Sorry to leave you, sweet. Important business. Everything we've been waiting for has just come to a stellar conclusion. I'll call you later for cocktails. Oh yes." Belasci adjusted his platinum and sapphire cuff links and gazed admiringly at them. "Thank you for the links. They are exquisite."

The sleeping form under the covers stirred slightly, opened a sleepy eye, and muttered huskily, "What is it this time? Hmmm?"

"They just got Salvatore. He's dead at last. Turn on the radio around 10 A.M. for the official announcement."

Prince Giorgio Oliatta sat up in bed wide awake. "Salvatore? Did you say Salvatore?" he asked wondrously. But Minister Belasci had already left.

At 8:30 A.M., under cover of an American diplomat, former U.S. Army Colonel Stefano Modica deplaned at Rome's airport. A compact fortnighter in one hand, olive green briefcase in the other, he limped noticeably through special customs provided for men with his credentials. In the deserted men's lounge, Modica paused to wash his hands, taking precautions to make certain he wasn't observed. He glanced casually at his watch just as the door opened and the shadowy figure of a man entered.

Morelli. former Italian aide attached to Colonel Modica's command during WWII, a man with the craggy countenance of a prize fighter, moved to the washstand next to him, nodded. and said, "It is done."

Modica heaved a relieved sigh. "His reply?"

"In this." Morelli placed an envelope on the briefcase.

Colonel Modica picked up both case and envelope and exited quickly.

Outside the terminal Colonel Modica was assisted to a waiting US Embassy Mercedes limousine, and in moments the auto sped easily through the morning traffic. He opened the envelope and read its contents:

SCORPIO AGREES. IT'S TIME WE HAVE DINNER.
FIVE YEARS HAVE BEEN TOO LONG. WILL MEET
YOUR PLANE IN PALERMO 7-5-50 AT 5 P.M.
AQUILO BRAVO.

By 9:15 A.M. Modica was seated at the large walnut
desk in a sequestered office at the American Embassy attempting to learn from special agents Matt Saginor, Renzo
Bellomo. and Len Salina what had gone sour on *Operation
Red Star,* a highly involved anti-communist assignment.

Modica synchronized his gold pocket watch with the
clock on the wall. He placed the timepiece open faced on
the highly polished walnut desk next to several thick
manila files spread open before him. He made a mental
note to conclude the session by 11 A.M. to give him ample
time to catch the 2:30 P.M. flight to Palermo. It was imperative that he make connections with Alessandro Salvatore, a young man for whose spectacular career Colonel
Modica felt, in part, responsible.

ORS, the anti-communist project, was secondary to his
purpose for being in Rome. Six months before, his support
was enlisted in a highly covert plan to smuggle Salvatore
out of Sicily. He had listened to Gina O'Hoolihan's proposal and in good conscience couldn't deny her aid. It
took diplomatic know how. sheer guts, political muscle,
plus a trunkful of special political favors owed him before
he could begin to assemble the plan. An unblemished
record of duty with the Office of Strategic Services, the Allied Control Council, and a stint as temporary legal
sidekick to General Patton helped push the project
through.

Colonel Modica, no stranger to the President, had
worked for two years under the Chief of State's guidance,
while the National Security Council was formed in 1947
to provide him with an advisory board on both foreign
and domestic policy. This obscene embryo, nurtured and
remolded by future administrations, would later become
refined and formally named the CIA.

Due to the sensitivity of the subject and despite their acquaintance, Modica was compelled to wade through time-
consuming protocol and reams of red tape before he could
approach the President. Two additional months had dissolved before he put the question to General Patton, and a
third month slipped by before General Eisenhower was
briefed. Still, no oval office appointment.

On May 15, five months to the date after the original
proposal had reached him, Modica, in a rush of excite-

16

ment, was ordered to "get his ass over to the oval office."

The President, familiar with Salvatore's anti-communist activities, which in spirit conformed to the Truman Doctrine, took into account the splendid work he had performed in crushing the Reds and his pro-American leanings. He recollected the letter sent to him by the Sicilian. Then he denied official sanction to Modica's "mad, mad plan" to slip Salvatore out of Sicily, with special reservations.

Before Modica deflated totally, Mr. Truman came to his rescue.

"Let me stress our position, Colonel. The White House can't overtly engage in plans which might alienate an Allied nation. Not now. Not at the height of the Cold War when we can't second-guess Russia's intent. However, you may—off the cuff—avail yourself of any government facility within your jurisdiction to bring your plans to fruition. But heed my words, bronc-buster. If this foolhardy plan fails and is exposed before its conclusion, any rumble from a foreign government will elicit a firm denial and formal statement disavowing our knowledge or implication in the matter. Is that clear? In short, Colonel, if your balls get burned, don't come crying home to Papa. Singed hair makes one helluva stink. Do you read me?" His Missouri accent thickened when making a point.

Ten minutes later, Modica, back in his office, had cranked gears and set his plan in motion. Gratefully, things moved ahead with amazing swiftness.

Now only one thing remained. He'd meet with Salvatore, provide him with necessary cover, passports and ID's, and together they'd fly to Rome, board an army transport, and fly to a pre-planned destination. Obviously, there was an alternate plan. Two fishing vessels, alerted to stand by in the Bay of Marsala, would on signal escort them to Lisbon, where another standby army transport would fly to a different destination.

Modica busied himself sifting through the bulky file containing a 400-page report, an update on ORS, including a dossier of photographs of certain high officials and their apparent involvement in the ORS project and frowned noticeably as he scanned the contents.

"Why have three top agents met with such obvious failure?" asked Modica, his eyes glued to the file's contents. "Is anyone on to you?"

"All right, Steve," began Matt Saginor. "You asked for it. We'll give it to you straight."

17

Slightly before 10 A.M. hordes of international and local news reporters, tipped off by highly paid collaborators who smelled newsworthy items miles away, milled restlessly through pillared halls and marbled corridors outside the office of the Ministry of the Interior like hungry pack rats, waiting to be fed the *official* version of Salvatore's death.

Minister Belasci finally emerged to address the reporters. Evasive in that maddening manner employed by politicians in making a point, his words brought smirks of disgust to the faces of seasoned pressmen. Minister Belasci's comportment, the self-containment of an overly ambitious man who'd do anything to attain his goal, after fifteen minutes of boring procrastination incited the reporters to press hard for answers. Belasci cranked out oratory considered to be the *official* statement. Some attentive newsmen, passionately provoked, began to scribble away in their note pads. Others, more astute, listened and stared unbelievingly at this audacious government official.

"Early this morning, at approximately 3 A.M., the bandit Salvatore was captured and shot to death in a skirmish with the Forces to Suppress Banditry while attempting to escape a stupendous dragnet deployed against him by Colonel Cesare Cala and Captain Giovanni Franchina, in the village of Castelvetrano," began Minister Belasci. "It is, therefore, with great pride that I announce the promotion of Colonel Cala to the rank of general. Captain Franchina, who inflicted the *coup de grâce*, is now promoted to the rank of major. I take this time to salute both these men, to whom we are indebted, the real heroes in our nation. The Forces to Suppress Banditry, initiated a year ago to combat this scourge, have served us well. Now that this mission has ended, Premier de Aspanu and I sincerely wish that you esteemed members of the press print no further reports to glorify that murderous and despicable criminal, Salvatore."

Minister Belasci posed briefly for photographers. Sensing their contempt, he curtly cut them off and retired behind hand-carved doors, aware that he left behind an assemblage of dissatisfied newsmen. There was no flurry of activity, no swift sprinting to locate phones in the usual race to scoop their competitors. These tough veteran reporters, most of whom were experts in their fields, felt terribly cheated. They had expected more from this heavyweight official who'd been at the center of a fiery controversy between Salvatore and the state, a controversy that had amounted to civil war for nearly seven years.

Within the hour their discontent took flight. Outraged

18

members of the fourth estate converged upon the airlines and all modes of transport that would take them to their hero—Salvatore. Dead or alive, one thing was certain, Salvatore wouldn't let them down. They'd get a story if it had to come from Salvatore's ghost.

It was 11 A.M. in Monreale, a suburb of Palermo. A gilded Roman warrior clock on the fireplace mantel struck the hour. Don Matteo Barbarossa, *capomafia* and the most influential feudalist in Sicily, numbly watched the six Roman warriors march out of a center door under the clock's face, rotate in a circle, and disappear inside the door by the time the last chime sounded. The Don had been sitting in the dimly lit study with drapes drawn against an inexorable sun all morning. He poured himself a stiff shot of whiskey from a decanter on the desk, threw it down in one swallow, and sat back listening to the soft sounds of music emanating from the small desk radio nearby.

Four days ago the Don had retired into a silence in his villa. Normally a vigorous, strapping giant of a man, on this day, he appeared haggard and aged beyond his sixty-eight years. White hair in wild disarray, shirt and trousers crumpled and unchanged in four days, face unshaven, he had the appearance of any old man, unloved, neglected, and unwanted. Where were the traces of the tough, two-fisted, hard, shrewd, and cynical Mazzarino bandit who once terrorized the entire island by killing his way to the top of the Mafia hierarchy? Would he ever pull himself together again to be *capomafia*? His dark eyes, swollen in their red-veined whites, had dimmed retractably.

Peppino Orafisso, a Palermo radio announcer and news commentator, interrupted the regular musical interlude to announce: *"People of Sicily! People of Italy! People of the world! Salvatore is dead! Long live Salvatore! This morning, before the break of. . . ."*

Orafisso's tremulous voice, overwrought with frenzy and emotion, began to describe the capture of the heretofore invincible Salvatore. Don Barbarossa, no trace of emotion on his heavy-jowled features, leaned forward in his chair and snapped off the radio. His face, lined with fatigue, paled noticeably. He turned off the desk lamp and sighed heavily, making audible grunts and groans as if something pained him terribly.

It had all worked out for the best, he told himself. Everything considered, he could have done nothing else. He reached for another bracer and gulped it down. He shoved his dark-tinted glasses to the top of his head and rubbed

19

his swollen eyes with his knuckles. Nothing eased his pain. Not even the whiskey coursing through to his intestines relaxed him. He fell like a sack against his chair, a giant tear spilling from his eyes. Angry that he couldn't take hold of himself, he groped in his rear pocket for a handkerchief and dabbed at his eyes as he tried to clear the thickness in his throat.

In that instant, the Don tensed. He cocked his head, as if listening to something. It was nothing outside himself he strained to hear. Something inside his brain nagged at him. His face screwed up reflectively. What was it the newscaster had said? An instant replay of the announcer's words tripped across his mind. He moved forward, turned the radio on, fumbled for several moments to erase the static, then picked up another newscast. He listened intently, his black lizard eyes staring motionless.

". . . *Captain Franchina of the Forces to Suppress Banditry inflicted the* coup de grâce *upon the dying Salvatore, who in his final moments begged the officer for water to sate his thirst. Utterly compassionate, the captain, out of the goodness of his heart and with deep sympathy for a dying man—even a bandit—obliged the mortally wounded man by supplying the water for which he desperately begged. . . .*"

In over sixty years of a life filled with indescribable crimes and violence, the *capomafia* couldn't recall when his senses had been so inflamed. Violent displeasure fired through him as he contemplated the man's words. So intent was he upon his hatred and loathing, he hardly heard the ringing of the telephone. It rang seven times before he moved to answer it. He lifted the receiver, and in a sudden transition, without emotion, he said, "Talk."

Chief Inspector Zanorelli's voice came over the phone, booming with melodrama. "Don Matteo—have you heard the news? They finally got that son of a bitch Salvatore! Goddamnit! That bastard is finally a thing of the past!" He was beside himself with the pleasure of his announcement.

The Don, who was not the *capomafia* for nothing, contained himself as if nothing had disrupted his composure.

"To whom are we indebted for such a service?" he asked with slow, measured words.

"But, of course, you must know? The FSB! They stalked him for a long time. Colonel Cala set the trap, Captain Franchina snared him, just as he always said he would. . . ."

"That's the *official* story?" The Don's deadly voice clearly transmitted foreboding.

Chief Zanorelli tensed. It wasn't the question that made him hesitate but the Don's cool, matter-of-fact tone. "*Mah*—sure. Sure it's official. No?"

"*Va bene, grazie*," muttered the Don as he hung up.

Startled by the curt dismissal and confused by the Don's attitude, the chief inspector was too cowardly to ring back and inquire why he should have been treated with such apparent lack of respect.

On the backside of the golden mountains, southwest of Palermo, in the village of Montegatta, Antigone Naxos Salvatore glanced up, wondering at the blatant invasion of her privacy. She sat in her garden, straining fresh tomato paste on bamboo trays. Two uniformed *carabinieri* had entered the rear terrace from a side entrance; two more had entered her house, strode boldly through it, and emerged at the rear door to join their companions.

Curtly, with no effort to disguise the triumph in their voices, they requested her presence in Castelvetrano to officially identify "the dead body of your son." Just like that! Without preamble, they had addressed themselves to her with skilled impertinence.

Hah! What will they think to do next, she wondered, watching them through hate-filled and contemptuous eyes. She told herself to be strong and defiant against these enemies. Inside her a small voice prayed, *it couldn't be true. Dear, sainted God, let it be a lie.* This was just another deception in a long line of lies and deceptions heaped upon her by these black-hearted mercenaries. She steeled herself against the bamboo frames on the wooden bench under the fig tree, pushed aside a few wisps of gray hair, blinked her pecan-brown eyes, and wiped her hands on the tomato-splattered apron.

She raised her eyes to meet the eyes of the spokesman, a young man about the same age as her son, hoping to read the truth in them. She saw only the official coldness of a man doing his duty.

"All I've been ordered to do is escort you to Castelvetrano to make the official identification," he told her without apology.

Ten minutes later, she had washed, changed into a black cotton shift, combed her hair, and draped a black mourning veil over her head. She picked up her rosary beads, a fresh white *fazzoletto*, and walked downstairs, hoping to disguise the sinking feeling at the pit of her stomach. Just to prove them wrong, she had capitulated, condescended to make the trip. Just to show them.

Outside her front door, Antigone noted with alarm the gathering of sober-faced villagers who watched with mixed emotions as she entered the car. She reconsidered the situation with trepidation. News had an uncanny way of reaching interior villages with frightening accuracy, before the official news was aired. In that instant she felt her world disintegrate. If only Athena hadn't departed. Or her son-in-law, Santino Siragusa. Even Vincenzo. Where was Vincenzo? Surely her nephew would know what had happened to her son.

Pausing only to pick up Antigone's personal physician who'd been treating her for a heart condition, the *carabinieri* hastily eased their car in a southerly direction toward Castelvetrano. Antigone's watch told her it was 10:45 A.M. Why, she asked herself, was she concerned with the time? Of what use was it to her anymore? Only that it would take approximately an hour or two to reach the southern village and learn this was just another hoax. *It has to be,* she kept telling herself, trying to keep calm. *Tori must be in Brazil—or America by now. Dear God—isn't he?* Her mind was afflicted with a whirlwind of memories of the past seven years as they drove down off the mountains.

Vincenzo de Montana took a mid-morning shower in a luxurious marbled bath at the Calemi villa. Rubbing his hard, lean body vigorously with an oversized bath towel, the handsome, dark-haired young man of twenty-nine years reentered the sumptuous bedroom, toweling his curly black hair and glancing casually at the naked brunette lying on the bed.

He had tired of her. After four days he could barely stand the sight of her. She had served her purpose and, while it lasted, had been most accommodating. He felt able to face the ordeal of the coming weeks without his cousin Tori Salvatore. Thoughts of Maria Angelica Candela, a flaxen-haired girl with emerald-green eyes and a voluptuous body, whom he once intended to marry, stirred him into asking himself what the fuck he was doing, here, with this whore.

At the sound of his footsteps, the whore opened one eye, then the other. She fanned her long black hair over her olive-skinned shoulders and smiled invitingly at him. She snaked seductively across the wide bed, transmitting sexual and erotic thoughts to him. Vincenzo forced an artificial smile, barely tolerating her presence. Oh, what the hell! In a pinch she hadn't been bad. Hadn't she satisfied his prurient longings? Why take out his frustrations on her, eh? She was only earning a living. All in all, if you discounted the dullness of perception brought on by the wine, in whose lights the whores of Lucifer would be appealing, she'd been pretty exciting.

What irked Vincenzo was the white powder she sniffed periodically. She had insisted it was balm for her hay fever. Fucking bitch! Did she think him a jackass, still suckling his mother's breasts? Her reaction to the powder was too immediate, too erotic, and for Vincenzo, a blow to his manhood. That a woman, any woman, might resort to stimulants to cope with his virility was shattering to his *maschiezzo*—his manliness. He recalled the effects of the powder had so inflamed her that within moments she became insatiable. His manhood taken into her hot, wet mouth began a series of wild and passionate responses in him; he could think of nothing else. In four days no thoughts of the outside world had penetrated his consciousness. Only the pyramiding excitement of her tongue, lips, and hands on his penis, inner thighs, and scrotum had pierced his awareness. Lost in this euphoric world, he'd thought of no one, not Maria Angelica or even his cousin Tori from whom he'd been inseparable for seven years.

Here at Calemi's villa where he temporarily hid from the world, he had truly been lost for a time. What the hell! She could—*hay fever*—him any time she wanted.

Yet, in the light of sobriety which always followed these sojourns, reality returned all too swiftly and with it came the agony of uncertainty. Wrapping the towel about his midriff, he moved across to the nightstand and reached for a cigarette. What the hell day was this? July 4? No, it was the fifth. He nodded to himself in reflection. Tori must be in Brazil by now. Or was it America? At the very last Tori hadn't been able to confide in Vincenzo except to say he'd be in touch with him. *Managghia!* Vincenzo looked for a match and thought, *I should have gone with Tori. It was stupid to remain behind. What is there for me, here, without Tori?* He lit the cigarette and inhaled deeply. He sat on the bed and lay back on the pillows.

Before he realized what was happening, the whore got to him again. At first he pushed her gently aside with a tolerant giggle. She persisted. As her hands caressed him, his insatiable flesh was aroused. He lay back without protest, listening to the soft romantic music coming from the the Palermo radio station. Well, damnit, why not? If it was up to Vincenzo, the whole world would be fucking every hour of every day. What else was there to do that was as pleasurable and worthwhile? He lay back contentedly, blowing smoke rings while the whore blew him.

Vincenzo swelled and grew harder, climbing higher and higher to that pinnacle of sweet forgetfulness. At that crucial moment, just before he began skydiving through fleecy clouds and came crashing to earth, the frenzied voice of Peppino Orafisso cut through the music to announce: *"People of Sicily! . . . Salvatore is dead! Salvatore, King of Montegatta, is dead! . . . Long live Salvatore!"*

Vincenzo's heart stopped. Wild-eyed and frenzied, he tried to swim through the euphoria. He cocked his head and strained to listen. Withdrawing from the whore, his manhood "plopped" out from between her lips like a soggy *cannolo*. He flung her from him roughly, sprang from the bed, and moved heavily across the floor to raise the radio's volume. Against the pouting protests of the slim-hipped prostitute, he listened with every nerve fiber in his mind, body, and soul.

". . . According to Minister Martino Belasci, the battle waged against Salvatore terminated before dawn in a bloody coup in which the Forces to Suppress Banditry emerged victorious. Salvatore is dead! Long live Salvatore!"

Vincenzo nervously pulled on his trousers, dug into his pockets, and peeled off a thick stack of lire from a healthy roll of bills. Stuffing them into the whore's hands, he told her to get lost. He'd learned never to disclose his true identity to such women. Always in the back of his mind lay the outside chance she could be a spy. He walked her to the door after she dressed, locked it behind her, and watched her drive off with her pimp who'd been waiting that morning for God knows how long. Giving them no further thought, he rushed back upstairs and listened as a newscaster described the capture of his cousin Salvatore.

He paced the floor, chain-smoked, wrung his hands, and slapped his thighs in nervous frustration until he was a total physical and emotional wreck. *Another trap,* he told himself. *Bastards! They'll try anything.* There was only one thing for him to do: beat it the hell out of there. He tossed a few articles into a duffle bag, and running downstairs into the butter rooms, he packed a few provisions and flung everything into the back seat of a dusty black Alfa Romeo parked in the courtyard. After a few bad moments in which the motor failed to turn over, it finally resounded with life. Breathing easier, Vincenzo kicked it

24

into gear, uncertain of his destination and headed away from Calemi's villa.

If it was true that Tori had been caught, he, Vincenzo, would be next. As cocaptain and second in command, he knew as much as Salvatore knew. *Think carefully. Plan your moves meticulously, step by step, until you hear from Tori or receive confirmation of his death.*

His enemies could be everywhere; at the moment he was uncertain as to just how many were involved. Past the Saracen Fort was another road off the coastal highway that few knew about. Vincenzo's decision to take this route away from Calemi Villa hadn't been made a moment too soon. Only a short distance from the villa, he noticed four squads of heavily armed security police pulling into the courtyard.

Very well, he thought, already he had been betrayed, just as Salvatore was betrayed. Only this time he had the jump on them. Accelerating quickly, he headed for the only place he could think of that might be safe: a deserted shambles of a Romanesque villa where Tori, Maria Angelica, and he had played as children. It had later been converted into a radio shack where the bandits had housed radio equipment for the past several years.

He almost missed the turn-off to the old villa, pondering what his Aunt Antigone might be thinking at such a time. What would she do? She had no one left. Guilt feelings took a stranglehold on him. How in God's name could he go to her without jeopardizing his own safety? There must be an all-out alert for him. The FSB had captured every other member of Tori's soldiers, hadn't they? The battery-operated portable radio on the car seat beside him squawked loudly with static interference, bringing him out of his reverie.

Fifteen minutes later, Vincenzo arrived at the old hideout and hid the car under straw matting in the old stable. As he walked toward the villa, mental images of Maria Angelica and his cousin Tori came at him, but he shoved them neatly aside until his plans for survival were intact.

Thoughts that these radio announcements might be a trap to flush him out into the open were uppermost in his mind, especially when he considered the many amateurish and fraudulent schemes they'd been subjected to over the past few years. Vincenzo shook his head in a gesture of frustration and ran his fingers through his curly crop of hair as he tried to collect his thoughts. Something vaguely familiar played hide-and-seek in his mind. He walked past the rear entrance of the villa and skirted along the time-eroded stone steps to the wildly overgrown and weeded area alongside the building. Gazing about, he finally located the entrance to a storage cellar beneath a layer of straw. He grinned with relief.

Goddamnit! That cousin of his was some man! He'd thought of everything! Stored in the cellar were enough provisions to last him a year. Tori had even thought to store fresh water! Vincenzo's spirits soared even higher when he located a cache of weapons and ammunition. If he'd uncovered a gold mine, he couldn't have been happier. And there was wine!

Moving cautiously about the shadowy interior, he sorted out a few tins of sardines, tuna fish, olives, artichokes, and other tasty morsels. Slinging an automatic rifle over each shoulder, he shoved two pistols into his belt, stuffed a few rounds of ammo into his shirt and several boxes of cartridges into his pockets. Then, gathering two blankets and a few candle tapers, he climbed the steps to daylight.

Depositing his booty inside the villa, he returned to secure and camouflage the cellar doors. Shading his eyes with his hands, he glanced cautiously about the area. No one could approach the villa without being spotted for a distance of at least 300 yards. What he needed now was an old hound to act as a watchdog. He made a mental note to acquire a dog somehow and returned to the house.

As he moved about the shabby interior trying to make it more livable, he uncorked a bottle of wine and began sipping it. Why hadn't he thought of this place before? Several such places of refuge, complete with stored provisions, had been provided by Salvatore in the event of unexpected emergencies. If he kept his head, he could survive for as long as he desired, or until he determined to show himself. He guzzled more wine. Next, he had to locate Salvatore's personal portfolio. Once before, it had bought time for Salvatore. It might do more for Vincenzo.

Spreading some hay for a makeshift bed, he turned on the battery-operated radio and zeroed in on a station from which an emotionally overwrought announcer described the famed bandit's seven years of glory. His bloodshot eyes began to well up with tears as the realization that his cousin was truly dead hit him. His swollen face engorged with blood and hatred and the tears spilled in a storm. "Goddamn them!" he moaned to the four walls. "Tori did nothing but good for his people! I tried to tell him! I told him not to trust those crazy bastards, but he wouldn't listen! By God their hour will come!" he raged aloud.

Convinced that his own life was in jeopardy, he

promised himself to be more careful, more calculating than Tori had been. There were many matters to be considered. He'd bide his time. He would trust no one! Certainly he'd not be as forgiving as Tori had been. Not by a damn sight! He, Vincenzo de Montana, would show these whoring sons of unchaste mothers they weren't dealing with an ignorant peasant dog!

Vincenzo fell into a drunken sleep, dreaming of the tasty nectars of vengeance.

Former U.S.A. Captain Matt Saginor, red-haired, freckle-faced and presently downcast, sat slouched in his chair with his polished boots propped up on the gleaming conference table. His right hand hung loosely over the arm of the uncomfortable wooden chair, absently twirling a golden eagle key chain. His dark probing eyes searched Modica's face, noting how his friend had changed over the past few years.

Modica's silent temperament kept him apart from the others. But it hadn't always been that way. Saginor, a captain with Army Intelligence during WWII, recalled many occasions when Modica's temperament had been more volatile than that of the Sicilians they'd been associated with. When Saginor noticed the decided limp made by the prosthesis Stefano wore in place of his left leg, he realized the change in Modica these past five years was irrevocable.

"This is serious, Matt. Nothing in a year?" asked Modica.

"Man, we're up against a slick combine, Steve," began Saginor in his thick West Texas drawl. "It's like an octopus with a hundred tentacles. "I tell you, man, no one knows where the orders originate."

"They're more organized then Luciano's drug army," said Renzo Bellamo, a craggy-faced, tranquil man in his thirties, recently transferred from Narcotics. "Whoever's at the helm of this gold slick is a mastermind first class!"

Len Salina, a sandy-haired, green-eyed former Marine commando with bushy brows over innocent but discerning eyes, shook his head. "Damn, we've planted good men in various agencies where official government documents are produced. Still the forgeries mushroom. No one will talk. They say the same thing anyway—like a broken record. They don't know where the orders originate. The small fry take their graft—peanuts compared to what the men higher on the totem rake in—and all are damned grateful for the dough!"

Len Salina moved his heavy bulk across the room,

27

turned up the volume on the radio, and dialed in some low-keyed music; it had been customary procedure since a microphone had been discovered hidden in the eyes of a golden eagle in the U.S. Seal hung decorously in one of the conference rooms at the Embassy.

"You can't believe how smooth things are run, Colonel. Too fuckin' smooth! There's not a rupture in the link, and I've tried finding a weak spot for nearly two years!"

Modica nodded mechanically. His watch read 11 A.M. He'd give it a few more minutes and then he'd wind it down to a lunch break. He had to make some excuses for not lunching with any of them today. Then, around 2 P.M., just before he boarded the Alitalia plane he would call Saginor and make some excuse to postpone their business until tomorrow. Tomorrow—well, he'd give that some thought after he had Salvatore safely out of Sicily.

He glanced at the men carefully. He knew them well and had recommended them for Project ORS. They were excellent. Top men in their fields. Tall, with athletic builds and crew cuts, all three agents were incessant gum-chewing, cigarette-smoking addicts who boozed a lot, loved a lot, and lived dangerously.

Modica, a handsome, well-tanned man with a touch of gray at the temples, looked much younger than his forty years. His startling azure-blue eyes dramatized his features vividly. A reserved intensity about him created a dynamic and forceful picture of a man who usually got what he went after. Once you met him you'd never forget him.

Saginor removed his boots from the desk, rose to his feet, stretched, and addressed himself to Modica. "From the moment orders for Cold War supplies are placed by Italian firms, everything follows strict procedure. Things grow uncontrollable when the materials arrive in port. To begin with, the country has too many rules, too many licensing procedures, and a crockful of senseless paper work that stretches to infinity. Just to secure a lousy permit! Add to our dilemma, poorly paid government employees who accept bribes as a matter of course to augment their shoddy incomes. For a lousy buck, they'll falsify, or sell, import and export permits, manipulate or ignore regulations—and we can't pinpoint any one of them. Men involved in narcotics traffic abandoned their work when they learned they could profit more by arranging for the false documentation of Cold War commodities behind the Iron Curtain."

Len Salina poured bourbon into his coffee cup from a slim silver flask. "Ever since America began pouring bil-

28

lions in economic aid into Europe, the racket has flourished," he told Modica. "Despite international agreements made by these companies to use the materials here, the practice persists. Incidentally, these same companies emphatically deny communist leanings."

Modica glanced uneasily at his watch. He had to wrap this up if he hoped to make connections to Palermo. Before he could bring the meeting to a conclusion, Saginor intervened.

"Man, just take a look at our inquiries. They're in the reports. We've conferred with the Embassy every step of the way. They pretend to be ignorant of the goings-on. 'No, no, no, no,' they tell us. To their knowledge there's been no infraction of agreements. Washington plays mute on laws governing foreign shipments. No one seems to give a coyote's hoot about what's happening. Isn't that a bust in the balls? It's a real *mishegass!* That the raw uranium moving into communist countries might one day be dropped on their heads as bombs doesn't disturb these larcenous and highly respected businessmen." Saginor's Texas accent thickened.

"Gotta admit to top cooperation from Belasci's office," said Renzo. He lit a cigar and grimaced. "Fuckin' cigars taste like camel dung."

Modica had listened intently. *Martino Belasci, Minister of the Interior.* He wrote the name and underlined it heavily with his pen. He clearly recalled the dapper, highly ambitious politician who had sat on the Palermo Grand Council with him in April 1945 and who had left to accept a position with Premier de Aspanu's government. He glanced at his watch. Just a few more minutes, he told himself.

Suddenly, something in the file caught his eye. A list of names, prominent men reportedly involved in this scheme to defraud the United States. The names of several Middle Eastern potentates—men who'd been driven from their palaces due to their immoral regimes—stood out. Learning these men were involved in such a corrupt affair incensed Modica; they were still receiving aid from both the State and Defense Departments! He read further, scanning the names of Greek shipping tycoons, French industrialists, and Italian diplomats. When he came across the names of two high-ranking American officials occupying two of the most important offices in the land, he gazed at Saginor with total disbelief in his eyes.

"You don't mean to tell me—" began Modica. He never got to finish his statement. At that precise moment, the music from the radio was interrupted by a special bulletin. The excited voice of a radio announcer, Peppino Orafisso, sliced through their conversation.

"People of Italy! . . . People of Sicily! . . . Hear this! Salvatore is dead! . . . I repeat, Alessandro Salvatore is dead! The King of Montegatta is dead! Long live Salvatore!"

His attention commanded instantly, Modica felt a chill sweep through him. He held up a restraining hand, gesturing for silence. He listened to each and every word as if it were a knife stab to his guts. The announcer's voice, tremulous and filled with emotion, continued:

". . . This morning, in the darkest hours of night, just before the dawn when fiendish demons prowl about the shadows and take earthly form, the Forces To Suppress Banditry encountered Salvatore. In a lengthy gun fight in which thousands of rounds of ammunition were expended, Salvatore fought valiantly against the hundreds of well-armed soldiers deployed against him. Finally felled and shot to death, his body riddled with bullets, he now lies in state at Castelvetrano. . . ."

Stefano Modica turned deathly white. His hands shook as he tried to light a cigarette.

"They got him!" Matt Saginor, listening intently, jumped to his feet. "The bastards finally got him! Damn!" he exclaimed. "I remember like it was only yesterday . . . newsmen from all over the world crammed into my office, demanding special passes to interview this Sicilian phenomenon! What a man!" Flushed with a curious exuberance, Saginor turned from the radio and caught sight of Stefano Modica's face. Noting the tight-lipped grimness, excessive paleness, the total incomprehension and shock etched into his features, he lowered his voice. "That's right, you knew him well, didn't you? Didn't Gina—" Saginor caught himself. He didn't complete the question, knowing it was a touchy subject with Modica. He just didn't know *how* touchy.

Bellomo's and Salina's interest piqued at the look of anguish on Modica's face as he nodded numbly and busied himself lighting a cigarette. Anything to keep from talking. Several moments passed before he was able to mutter, "I planned on flying to Palermo to renew our acquaintance this afternoon." He spoke economically, careful not to reveal his true intentions. Modica was crushed. He could feel his heart start up again as a series of mental images rushed at him.

The first time he had encountered Salvatore, at Allied

Command Headquarters in Palermo had been when the lad was twenty-three years old. Even at that age, Modica had recognized the greatness in him. Salvatore had exuded a compelling charisma, a peculiar naïveté, strong ethnic charm, and the most engaging smile he'd ever seen on a young man. This phenomenon, Salvatore, had risen out of the litter and rubble of a war-torn country to dominate the minds and imaginations of millions of people. In a land where bandits were held cheap and where thousands like him had passed unknown, unheralded, into obscurity, Salvatore had emerged a tremendously powerful man whose deeds would be recorded in Sicily's history.

In an unguarded moment, Modica muttered to himself, yet loud enough for the others to hear. "But why? Why now at this moment? Why, after all these years?" These were questions he hadn't intended for other ears.

His words drew surprised glances from the other three agents. Modica's background in politics and intelligence work precluded the asking of such unsophisticated questions. If anyone knew about the abrasive cunning and manipulative tactics employed in political coups, it was Stefano Modica.

Sensing his anguish, Renzo Bellomo said quietly, "Salvatore's been involved in political intrigue over his head for at least two years now—no, three. He's no match for that barracuda Belasci."

"You forgot to include the Mafia," said Renzo.

Modica glanced sharply at him, checked the impulse to say something, then busied himself collecting the papers spread before him. He shoved them inside the manila folder. God, he was numb from all this.

"You want to fly to Castelvetrano to see what's happening? Might be interesting to observe the end of a hero," suggested Bellomo.

That was all it took. Within the hour the Americans winged their way southward in a requisitioned U.S.A. army transport, never thinking their presence in the southern village would nearly cause an international incident.

Only when they were airborne did Colonel Modica realize he had inadvertently slipped the entire ORS file into his briefcase. About to mention this to the others, he changed his mind, telling himself he'd have to be careful with it and return it somehow.

31

CHAPTER 2

Castelvetrano, Sicily

Fifty miles south of Palermo, along the southwest shores of Sicily, shimmering Mediterranean waters wash up on the golden shores of Selinunte, where ancient empires once thrived and where Greek, Roman, and Carthaginian warriors who battled and died for the glory of their leaders now lie buried beneath the sands of time. Broken stones and a time-worn acropolis with pilasters and entablatures scattered on the ground covered with a mauve undergrowth are the only reminders of their existence. Temples erected to the worship of Venus and Apollo have long since disappeared; apathetic generations have permitted the area to become commonplace, a trap for tourists.

A little to the north of this oriental bazaar atmosphere of Selinunte lies Castelvetrano, a village that reeks of Arab ancestry and upon which has been applied a garish twentieth-century cosmetic to give the illusion that it belongs to modern day. Encouraged by the influx of tourists following the war, city fathers had built hotels and encouraged other accomodating businesses, but they were in no way prepared for the demands placed upon the town when, on July 5, the natives awakened to find the town's dull and monotonous routine interrupted. Long lines of traffic assaulted the desert oasis which was swollen beyond its capacity by international journalists, government officials, FSB brass, newly deputized recruits, and wide-eyed tourists. The middle-class village was baffled and conversely filled with dread when rumors spread that their village had been labeled *"Judastown."*

The American agents found disorganized chaos in that shabby, dried-up courtyard at numero 54, Strada Sarina Madonna. More than 300 people had jammed the narrow street, packed tighter than sheep in a branding corral. Renzo Bellomo dismissed the driver of their rented and immobilized Fiat a block away and the foursome snaked their way through the crowds to their destination. From the moment they were spotted, their presence brought immediate reaction from the Sicilians who parted the crowds to make room for them. Their towering bulk and imposing features precluded the anonymity they had hoped for and gave rise to rumors that American retaliation for Salvatore's death was imminent.

Much to the Americans' amazement, it became an easy matter for them to enter the well-guarded courtyard without identification. Their presence was accepted as procedural protocol and, for reasons unknown to them, was acknowledged by snappy salutes from the posted guards who restrained others and permitted them entrance. Not about to press their luck, they moved to the left of the courtyard and stood quietly along the wall of the de Meo house, observing the activities of the incompetent investigators, keeping their thoughts to themselves, and watching the busy activity around them.

Modica, staring interminably at the body of the dead man, meticulously searching it for some identifying clue. The face was concealed by dust and caked blood was splattered all over the body. The corpse could be anyone. Damn! Why hadn't he considered this before? The thought gave rise to hope. Was it possible this *wasn't* Salvatore? Had he been so caught up in the news broadcast and what the others had said about Salvatore that he had accepted the death as gospel? He knew better! Christ! He wasn't this naïve! Yet . . .

His eyes traveled to the faces of the somber men and women pressing in and about the crowded street, hoping to read the truth in their eyes. What he saw stirred his guts and filled him with foreboding and a sickening sensation.

Procurator General Maggio and his staff of investigators moved about with the clumsy theatrics of a neophyte disaster squad, taking endless measurements of the body. They inventoried everything in sight and huddled continuously over one apparent incongruity after another. Photographers had climbed the rear and front walls of the courtyard and balanced themselves precariously near the stone archway, shooting pictures from all angles.

For better than a half-hour the Americans scanned the all too perfect setting in disgust. They didn't utter a sound. The silent messages contained in their eyes as they exchanged glances indicated their awareness of the obvious inconsistencies existing in the scene laid at their feet. Unable to contain either his professional curiosity or the question he felt compelled to ask, Matt Saginor addressed himself to the procurator.

"Has this body been moved since the fatal bullet was inflicted?"

Procurator-General Maggio, a small wiry man with a cadaverous face, turned abruptly to Saginor and, with black squinting eyes under knotted brows, he shook his head. "My report indicates this is the position in which the deceased fell when he expired." He turned his back on the American.

Just as quickly Maggio reconsidered and once again turned to face the man of whose presence he'd been oblivious until the question had been posed. His bird eyes focused on Saginor, taking in the lightweight Brooks Brothers suit, the white shirt open at the neck, the rumpled red hair and inquisitive brown eyes. "Who are you?" he demanded to know. Blinking his eyes, he saw for the first time the three Americans lined up against the wall behind Saginor, intently absorbed in the goings-on.

Feigning wide-eyed innocence, Saginor glanced to either side of him and asked, "Who—me? I'm no one."

After a long hard look in which the procurator drew his own conclusions, he turned away from Saginor and harshly commanded his men to speed up their work. Periodically, however, Maggio would pause in his duties, glance uneasily at the Americans, and scowl darkly. No one had told him there might be American agents on the scene. He knew them all. Oh, not personally, but since the war he could smell foreign agents a lightyear away. He had had his fill of them when he had engaged in procommunist activities. "*Allesti te! Allesti te!*" he urged his men. "Hurry it up!" He liked less and less the expressions on the angry reporters around him.

Saginor sidled up to Modica, expressionless, and muttered without a glancing at him. "It's all wrong, Steve. All wrong. There's something too pat in this fucking mess."

Modica nodded. "Tell me."

"What do you make of that massive bloodstain, as contrasted with the darker, purplish blood dried up from the two bullet wounds below the left rib cage?" asked Matt Saginor.

Modica shook his head, unable to speak. There was something unreal, totally false in all this. Yet, weren't all his memories of Sicily the same? Everything done in this strange land of antiquity was exaggerated to a larger-than-life reflection, too theatrical. But this sham was too much. At this point, something sparkling brightly in a ray of sunlight caught Modica's eyes. Squinting, he moved closer to the body and caught sight of the familiar golden scorpion amulet. His heart stopped. In that split second he tried to shut out the possibility that it might indeed be Salvatore lying dead at his feet. Images rushed at him, vivid images of Salvatore on the day Colonel Modica had presented him with the golden scorpion amulet. They had said their farewells at the Temple of Cats. . . .

"You honor me much too much, Colonnello. I don't deserve such a tribute," Salvatore had told him. *"I truly wish I could be the man you see pictured in your eyes."*

"But you are, my friend," Modica had told him. *"You are a very special person. You have within you the power to lead your people out of bondage. You are Sicily's only hope."*

He could still see the flush of self-consciousness coupled with the ineffable delight on Salvatore's face when he received the golden scorpion. . . .

Modica opened his eyes now and discovered he had broken into a cold sweat. His fists were tightly clenched, his nails dug deeply into his palms. He felt terrible. Waves of guilt swept through him. He quickly lit a cigarette with shaking hands. He noticed Saginor on bended knees, touching the fresh blood with his fingertips. Renzo Bellomo moved in and did the same with the darker, caked blood. Both men exchanged noncommittal glances.

Noting the differences, they kept their thoughts to themselves. Too many discrepancies, they felt certain, but without tests they couldn't be sure. One thing was certain, they didn't believe the scene.

"Don't touch! Don't touch anything!" screamed the procurator.

Instantly the men jumped back. Every eye was on them.

It became obvious to Modica that Maggio had formed several conclusions that didn't coincide with the information given him by Captain Franchina. Bringing focus upon himself, Maggio was instantly besieged now with countless questions thrust at him by angry and impatient reporters whom he'd banned from the courtyard. Time and again he refused comment and, in so doing, found himself the subject of many sullen, uncomplimentary remarks. Hoping to silence the hungry tigers, he now declared for the third time, with a tone of finality, "I repeat, I'll make no comments until *after* the autopsy, and only after the FSB has released the official statement to you!" He then ordered the guards doubled at all exits.

Procurator-General Maggio sensed the Americans had discovered the jarring inconsistencies and he grew increasingly nervous. He cursed inwardly. Why hadn't someone found the means to bar *them* from the courtyard? They had no business here! From time to time he glowered at

35

them, hoping they'd take the hint they weren't wanted. As angry as he was at their presence, his ire was more heatedly directed toward the FSB. Why hadn't they posted their own men on this detail? Fucking smart of them! To make Maggio's office accept full responsibility for problems arising from this mess! Disturbed by discoveries made on this day, Maggio had let his mounting tension so cloud his judgment that he had forgotten this was *his* jurisdiction. He had but to open his mouth to deny entrance to anyone—including the Americans.

Speculation at their presence intimidated him more than the recriminating thoughts of his own participation in this distasteful conspiracy. The rewards? His cooperation would wipe the slate clean of all former procommunist activities enabling him to seek office with the Christian Democrats. Even this reward dimmed, however, when he learned that Private Foti had been shot with bullets from Franchina's machine gun, not by the Luger purportedly carried by Salvatore. Would his fate be the same as Foti's, he wondered? The thought provoked a rush of activity as he lit a rocket under his men. *"Avanti! Avanti! Subito!"* he prodded.

A cry arose from the men outside the courtyard. "An impostor lies here! The FSB lies! They can say what they will, but we know better!"

In Viterbo, a few miles from Rome, the trial of the People vs. Assassins at Portella della Rosa, held before a tribunal of judges, was in session. Presidente Umberto Ginestra, an impressive, highly polished aristocrat and presiding judge of the tribunal, glanced wearily at the clock on the wall opposite him. It was 11 A.M. In a half-hour he'd adjourn for lunch.

The prosecutor, interrogating Arturo Scoletti, one of the fifty bandits being tried for the Portella Massacre, glanced up at the sight of a federal courier entering the courtroom. He saw the slim blond court clerk accept a sealed envelope, and, signaling the *presidente* for recognition, the clerk approached the bench. He handed the envelope to the presiding magistrate.

The magistrate, a man with snow white hair and icy blue eyes, glanced down his slender nose to read the contents. He blinked several times, nodded to the clerk to rap for order, and, beckoning to the battery of lawyers to approach the bench, huddled with them for several moments. The president, with traces of irony, spoke to them in undertones, as spectators expectantly leaned forward in their seats.

The court was packed with prosecution and defense lawyers, as well as countless other *avvocati* who represented the fifty bandits individually to insure against a conflict of interest. Startled by the news imparted to them, the *avvocati* returned to their seats evidencing a variety of emotions, all colored by client interest.

President Ginestra now addressed himself to the entire court and to the *galleria* of spectators, most of whom were loyal to Salvatore and his men. He raised his head, lifted his voice, and announced without preamble, "This court is recessed. The bandit Salvatore has been captured and slain by the Forces of Suppress Banditry."

A hush swept through the stately halls of justice as the tribunal magistrates arose in a body and marched in single file out the courtroom into chambers. Fifty of Salvatore's men, all former brigands, sat deathly still in the witness cages without expression. A spectator's voice arose in a frenzied cry, *"Viva Salvatore! Long live Salvatore!"*

Tough, hard-nosed, and cynical, the exbandits exchanged silent glances, wondering and speculating over this latest development. Hah! What next? So many lies! So many betrayals! Who among them could express faith in this comedic arena of injustice where scapegoats were needed to satisfy the blood-lusting thirst of highly immoral, yet influential government officials?

Lawyers approached their clients and solemnly apprised them of the veracity of the president's words. "Word came direct from the Minister of the Interior. It's official all right," they were told.

Glaring in black silence, the exbandits spat contemptuously at the mention of Martino Belasci's name.

Fifteen minutes later, back in their cells, the men sat hunched over in their seats, ears glued to their radios, listening attentively to the bias of special commentators, the sad laments of the mourners, and the arrogant sarcasm of the celebrants. A few of the former brigands exchanged thoughts through the bars of their cells. Before lights went out that night, they told themselves that before they would believe this fable, Salvatore himself would have to appear in the flesh to tell them he'd been killed.

In Castelvetrano, Sicily, one of the American agents, Renzo Bellomo, overpaid for a camera and film and busied himself taking photos of the courtyard scene. He covered all angles. At one point, he nudged Saginor, unable to contain his contempt.

"I'd like to meet the dummy who staged this production. Look at this. A cartridge case of a Breda machine gun lying next to a Beretta .38 submachine gun. Shee—it! It's clear to see the cantaloupe-head who set this up was seedless."

"Patience," replied Saginor, tongue in cheek. "Let's not jump to conclusions. Let's wait for the official report."

At 1:30 P.M. Procurator-General Maggio gave the order to remove the body to the mortuary for autopsy. Instantly the stretcher bearers moved forward.

"Let's go," called Saginor. "This I gotta hear!"

Like most combat officers, Modica had seen many deaths during the war, but none had left him with the mounting guilt he experienced when he saw the men place the dead man's body on the stretcher. He felt wretched. The guilt continued to rise overwhelmingly. If only he hadn't urged Salvatore ahead. If only he had done as Matt Saginor suggested. "Let the fucking Sicilians play the game their own way!" he had advised. Why had Stefano interfered? If only he hadn't attempted to bring Salvatore into the twentieth century before he was prepared to tackle its complexities, the man might be alive today. If only he had arrived a week sooner—even a day. . . .

Modica, relentless in his self-persecution, was unaware that he had moved out of the courtyard. Somehow he found himself in the Fiat with the others. He had learned to mask his emotions during the hell of war, and later, in the agony that came ironically at war's end when he lost a leg by accidentally stepping on a mine in Berlin, he had wondered why God had permitted the accident to occur. For a time he believed it had been his punishment for interfering in another man's life. Intelligent enough to know a man's truth is ultimately what he believes it to be, he was just emotional enough to believe he wasn't guiltless in this monstrous tragedy. Behind that expressionless mask, he punished himself every moment.

Moving at a snail's pace, hampered by crowds on foot and the traffic jam at either side of them, the Americans removed their jackets and loosened their neckties, hoping for some relief from the prostrating heat.

"Craziest damn scam I've ever seen! The whole thing's staged like some demoniacal scenario. Someone's gone to a helluva lot of trouble to confuse the world—or else the corpse got up and messed things up," said Renzo Bellomo, wiping the sweat pouring off his face and neck.

"I'll lay odds on the corpse," said Saginor brightly.

"The Salvatore I knew wouldn't have fallen into such an obvious trap," murmured Modica half to himself, as he lit a cigarette from Saginor's.

The black sedan, heavily talcumed with layers of dust, traveled at moderate speed as it coursed along the narrow road winding down off the long mountain range. Antigone Salvatore noted the widening of the landscape. In the distance she saw the vast sweep of Mediterranean waters, sparkling and rolling like corrugated glass, mirroring the sun's glare. As stifling heat came at her, she stirred the air about her with a sweat-soaked *fazzoletto*. One hand speedily fingered her rosary beads. *Let them be wrong, dear God. Let them. It won't be Tori. I know.*

The mortuary at the Camposanto was overrun with disgruntled and morose members of the press, who cursed and damned the numerous delays. For a time the Americans cursed with them. Periodically a *carabiniero* appeared at the ornately grilled iron gates to issue bulletins. Entrance to the morgue had been denied them until the grubby little man they'd seen entering earlier had completed taking a death mask for the Palermo Criminal Museum. A variety of colorful expletives, articulated acridly by crusty press correspondents, echoed through the halls in a steady drone of dissatisfaction.

Irritated by the numerous delays and the conspicuous absence of the FSB officials, who they were told were being feted at a victory banquet held in their honor, Renzo Bellomo, who earlier advised his companions to underplay their presence, pressed them forward. "C'mon, let's use a little diplomatic clout!" He glided toward the khaki-clad *carabinieri* guards, flourished his ID, and beckoned to his companions.

"We'll be kicked out on our asses," said Len Salina.

Modica plowed on through, followed by Saginor and Salina, while Renzo Bellomo's voice bowled over the impressionable military police. Bowing respectfully, the *carabinieri* escorted them into the morgue, leaving behind an indignant horde of newsmen grumbling antagonistically over the preferential treatment accorded the foursome.

When the *carabinieri* returned to their posts, they were deluged with queries. Their lips, sealed until several dollars changed hands, mouthed a simple statement: "American agents with the State Department."

Their suspicions confirmed, the newsmen put two and

two together and came up with a highly explosive theory. A much-publicized letter written by Salvatore to President Truman, which had recently found its way into print in the communist press, was thoroughly discussed, and the reporters concluded there was some truth to the story of America's intention to support Salvatore in his anticommunist fight, after all. The story grew more explosive by the moment. Salvatore backed by the U.S.A.? When had the intrigue begun?

Inside, cool halls of marble lowered the temperature by several degrees. High-vaulted ceilings and *terrazzo* floors amplified sounds like an echo chamber. Under a concentration of spotlights, rigged like those in a surgical amphitheater, the nude corpse lay upon an oval slab of marble. The maskmaker, having completed his task, brushed away flecks of plaster from the deceased's hairline. The Americans approached the catafalque solemnly.

"My God! He was so young," whispered Bollomo.

"It *is* Salvatore, *isn't* it?" Saginor asked Modica. "They must be certain if they employed the services of a maskmaker."

Modica's hope sank. Saginor was right. "I'm not certain. It's been five years—longer than I thought. I never saw him in this position—" His sad eyes compulsively locked on the body. Five years *was* a long time. It was a crazy, wild affinity he felt with Salvatore, even with the dead body before him. From the first, there had been this same magnetism between them, an intangible, mysterious, and compelling force.

Reporters, finally admitted, swarmed like locusts and descended upon the raised dais without dignity. Light bulbs popped; cameras clicked with nerve-wracking monotony—without let up. Suddenly, without warning, the cavernous room became deathly still, as if the room's occupants realized they were in the presence of greatness. The youth of the dead man distorted the preconceived images of veteran reporters, who found it inconsistent with the reported ferocity of the highly lauded rebel whom most had written about but had never met. Recent reports of Salvatore had characterized him as a savage and ruthless murderer. Seeing him so young and handsome, bigger in death than in life, colored their reaction.

The Minister of the Interior's office had carefully spoon-fed them a sharply-defined prototype of a criminal. His terrifying and lawless nature had been grossly exaggerated, and this deception staggered them. Where was the Pancho Villa in him? How did he resemble Dillinger?

Which qualities could be likened to Al Capone's, they asked themselves? None of the hard-boiled correspondents who stood looking at the body in the cool marble room could hide their compassion or shock at the inexplicable tragedy. Irreconcilable contrasts made them study the body with microscopic intensity.

Attendants turned the body over and everyone saw that the right shoulder, from which the blood had seemed to flow endlessly, was devoid of injury. Not even a scratch could be found! A shocked hush swept through the room. They were ordered to stand back from the oval slab as attendants, under Dr. Alba's instructions, brought in large quantities of ice and began to pack the body. The coroner, a large-framed man noticeably intimidated by the hordes of newsmen, kept blinking at the persevering reporters, as if he didn't even see them. As they looked to the efficient man, who nervously cracked his knuckles as he directed his men, he seemed to sense what they were thinking and wanted no part of the questions he knew were coming. He was certain they'd pick up the flagrant inconsistencies—and he was right.

"Why all the need for ice," asked one reporter, "if, as the official report says, the corpse has been dead for less than twelve hours?"

Dr. Alba wiped beads of perspiration from his bald pate and deferred to the FSB officials. And when they persisted and asked why the blood seemed varying shades of red in the various wounds, Dr. Alba blinked his nervous eyes and ignored them. He waved all other questions aside.

While reporters harassed Dr. Alba, Modica sauntered by the table where the personal effects of the corpse lay with identifying tags. He studied the solid gold belt buckle with the Eagle and the Lion of which many ballads had been written. His eyes fixed on the golden scorpion amulet. His face flushed red with guilt. Sinking feelings churned his stomach. Picking it up, Modica turned it over in his trembling palms and read the familiar inscription: *To Salvatore: May the King of Montegatta rule Sicily wisely—Colonel Stefano Modica U.S.A. 4-12-45.*

Stefano turned to the body on the slab, sighed heavily, and closed his eyes. His hand clutched the scorpion tightly. When he reopened his eyes, he stared into the dispassionate, suspicious eyes of a *carabiniero*, who motioned to his clenched fist. Modica smiled weakly, opened his fist, and replaced the amulet. "Just looking," he said huskily.

At 2:30 P.M. Antigone Salvatore arrived at the mortuary only to be told with blistering candor that she couldn't enter the premises until Colonel Cala and Captain Franchina arrived from the victory banquet held in their honor for the killing of her son. It was the first of many humiliations this iron-willed matriarch would endure on this scorching hot day of bitter trauma.

Cameras, thrust into her face, clicked incessantly. Reporters anxious to solve the riddle of her son's death tugged and pulled cruelly at her for a statement. Bewildered and revolted by their brashness, she shied from them. The nightmare wouldn't cease. She tried to shut out the cyclopean lenses and retard the predatory swarm of vultures who posed threats to her existence. Nothing eased her heartache. and her vulnerability frightened her.

She felt pushed to the edge, hardly able to breathe. The smell of death's putrefaction was all around her; the unbearable odor of unclean, sweaty humans, nauseating cigar smoke, the malodorous stench of dead chrysanthemums from nearby waste receptacles wafted toward her sensitive nostrils and sickened her. Overhead in the tall. black cypress, branches bent with clusters of noisy cicadas protested the intrusion of strange humans upon their routine siesta. In the distance, Antigone saw the North African waters like a thin strip of glass drawing her hypnotically. She closed her eyes and retreated to safety behind the wall of her eyelids, away from all that threatened.

If it's true my son is dead, I am truly alone. . . . Take courage, she told herself. *Don't let anyone see you crumble. These vultures wait only to gloat when you disintegrate. Don't share your tears with anyone. . . .*

"Please take those cameras away," she pleaded. "They distress me." *It's so hot. I feel dizzy, sick to my stomach. Dear God, don't let it be my son in there. Not my last child.*

"No cameras, please." She raised her hands to shield her burning, swollen eyes.

The sea of faces melted into many more, none fully distinguishable to her. Antigone felt herself slipping into a pit of terrifying uncertainty. Everything became a blur.

She felt strong arms at either side of her in a firm grip. Through fluttering eyelids, she glanced into the faces of two strangers. and suddenly felt both frightened and safe with them. But the blinding lights of popping flashbulbs didn't cease. The vultures swarmed closer and closer

"Steady, *Signora,*" instructed the steady voice of Stefano Modica. "We'll get you out of this den of *animales.* Don't be frightened. We're friends of your son, Alessandro." he told her in well-schooled Italian.

Bellomo and Salina ran interference for them as Modica and Saginor, flanking Signora Salvatore, made for Dr. Alba's office. *"Fermate!* Stop!" shouted a guard. "Where the hell you going?" he asked in broken English. The *carabiniero's* rifle barred their entrance, until Bellomo and Salina shoved ID's under his nose.

"Go ahead, Colonel. We'll take care of this," snapped Bellomo in an authoritative voice.

Modica and Saginor propelled Antigone Salvatore through the iron gate and disappeared inside the open office where they helped her to a chair. She sank into it gratefully and studied them with questioning eyes.

"I can't thank you enough for rescuing me from those cretins. It took courage to brave that crowd. . . ." She lifted her wide brown eyes. "Is it really my son?" she asked softly of Modica.

"Only you can answer that, *Signora.* You must identify the body."

An enigmatic smile formed on her lips. "By now, my son is in Brazil, perhaps America. He'll laugh at the absurdity of these rumors. You'll see. He warned me something like this would happen. That I should be prepared. It's just that it came too soon. . . ." Her eyes glittered with anemic hope. "You'll see." Her breathing grew labored.

"Signora, are you all right?" Modica studied her intently.

"I tell you it's not him." She glanced from Modica to Saginor, wild-eyed. "But if I say it's him, identify the body as that of my son, they would stop hunting him down like an animal—wouldn't they?"

Saginor's eyes found Modica's. A trace of alarm flashed. "I'd better find her a physician. . . ." Leaning close to Modica, Saginor whispered, "She wouldn't do that, would she?" Modica shrugged and indicated he should find a doctor.

"I'm all right now," said Antigone, taking several deep breaths. A sudden Sicilian wariness crept into her eyes. She searched Modica's eyes for some sign of recognition. She felt certain she had seen him before.

"You said you are friend to my son, Tori?"

"Colonnello Modica. Stefano Modica. I was here during the war."

"Colonnello Modica?" She paled with excitement. *"Santo Dio,* you came, *Colonnello!"* She clapped her

43

hands together. "My son loves you like a brother. He talks of you always."

Concerned both by her peculiar choice of words and the possibility they might have been overheard, Modica gazed anxiously about the room. "I couldn't return at war's end to keep my promise to him. An accident—you see, I lost a leg." He waved his hands in the air aimlessly.

Out of curiosity, Antigone's eyes darted to his legs. A flush swept over her face, as she apologized for her rudeness and waved her hands in the air in a gesture of futility. As things jelled in her mind, she gave him an odd look. "But what are you doing here if you are supposed to be with Tori—"

Stefano, distressed by her abrupt question, frowned noticeably. "You know about that?" His voice was barely above a whisper.

She nodded. "Last year I confided my concern for Tori to a mutual friend. She wrote me months ago assuring me my deepest prayers would be answered the beginning of July. When you identified yourself, I assumed you were the man of whom Gina spoke."

Modica frowned again. *"Signora,"* he began, "it's important that you do not speak of this—" The look in Antigone's eyes arrested him. She wasn't listening to a word he spoke. He followed her line of vision.

Beyond him on the large desk, Antigone saw for the first time, several articles of clothing; a pair of beige Levi's, brown sandals, a beige rucksack, and the other items recovered in the courtyard on Strada Sarina Madonna. Her body sagged heavily forward and her fingers groped for her rosary beads tremblingly.

"Steady, *signora,"* said Stefano Modica in a hoarse voice. "Take courage. Take courage."

"Who the hell are you to disrupt our order of things?" bellowed Captain Franchina, directing his arrogance at Modica and Saginor.

The FSB officers burst into the room, followed by the sunken-faced procurator general, like ostriches hot in the pursuit of battle. Before either Modica or Saginor could respond, Captain Franchina addressed his anger at Signora Salvatore.

"—And who permitted you entrance to these chambers?"

Grossly offended by Franchina's manners and lack of taste at such a time, Modica, no slouch in handling these popinjays, leveled his blue eyes on the bombastic officer and asked icily, "And—just who are you?"

Watching Captain Franchina's discomfort, Antigone flushed with inner satisfaction, her memory vivid at their last encounter. She was certain Franchina hated her as much as he hated her son Tori.

Captain Franchina lost no time in introducing himself and his superior officer, Colonel Cala, to the Americans. He made certain that he explained with emphasis that Procurator-General Maggio was in charge of the investigation. These formalities over, he demanded imperiously, "Just who the hell are you and why are you here?"

Saginor moved swiftly. Bellomo and Salina had followed the uniformed peacocks into the room; now they all brandished their ID's. Saginor took the position of responding to Captain Franchina's queries himself, indicating they were Special U.S. agents on a security assignment in Rome. Then, with dashing aplomb, he introduced Modica to the anti-bandit detail's officers. In view of Franchina's pomposity, Saginor gave the introduction more importance than needed. "You may recall Colonel Modica was stationed in Palermo during the war," he began. "He was with the Allied Control Council—advisor to the Palermo Grand Council, wasn't it, sir?" He winked covertly at Modica.

Stefano merely glanced cooly at the officers, only the shadow of a nod coming from him.

The name struck Captain Franchina instantly. Flushing slightly, he conferred with Colonel Cala for several moments. The FSB chief listened with overt politeness, his blue eyes fixed on the cigar rolling between his tobacco-stained fingers.

"Consider us at your disposal, Colonel Modica. Accept my profound apologies for keeping you waiting." Cala, far more experienced in such matters, appeared overly cautious. He was uncertain of his position in this case. The presence of American agents in Castelvertrano intimidated him. He recalled vividly the headlines in the Communist press alluding to an American alliance with the anti-communist, Salvatore. Damn! What complications! He made a mental note to get to Minister Belasci in a hurry.

Modica, snuffing out his cigarette in a nearby ashtray, replied tactfully, "This is your case, Colonel. Your territory. Your country. Consider us merely as observers."

By minimizing the Americans' importance and their interest in the matter, Modica had unwittingly caused the FSB to interpret their presence on the scene as indicative of a subversive foreign plot. Prone to exaggerate their own importance at times, Italians, he knew, tended to assume foreigners would do likewise. In this case, foreign agents understating their position meant only one thing to the Italians—a cauldron of trouble.

Modica suggested to them that they see *Signora* Salvatore who, he stressed, shouldn't be kept waiting and put through intolerable and agonizing delays. This brought an immediate reaction from Captain Franchina. His face swelled to a livid purple hue as he angrily ground out his cigar. He had no recourse but to do his superior officer's bidding as Colonel Cala nodded to him. Franchina, in turn, gave the nod to Procurator-General Maggio.

"You heard the *Colonnello*. Proceed with the *Signora*."

Colonel Cala's face twisted with worry lines. Why else would the Americans arrive so swiftly on the scene if America weren't in some sinister way involved with Salvatore? If their presence didn't justify rumors of an alliance, he didn't know what did. Dammit! Why should destiny complicate matters, now that Salvatore was dead and no longer mattered? Why hadn't Minister Belasci briefed him thoroughly in this matter? These, plus countless other questions, remained unanswered in his mind. By damn, he'd get answers someplace, he promised himself.

CHAPTER 3

Antigone's dark eyes were fixed upon the body as it lay in deep repose on the oval catafalque. His features, as handsome in death as in life, appeared more relaxed, as if he were finally at peace. The accumulated bitterness of recent months was gone—erased as if it never existed on his face. In that instant, Antigone's body swayed and trembled, as a tremor shot through her; she felt herself crumble. She could hear his sweet voice, just as he had called to her in the past, *"Mamma bedda. Mamma bedda."* She closed her eyes for a moment and saw in her mind's eye an array of faces superimposed over those of Tori's. Filippo and Marco, handsome in their new soldiers' uniforms, appeared in her vision along with Athena's beautiful face. They smiled, but not as infectiously as their sister. It was as if they stood in judgement of her. "We told you,

46

Mamma, not to fill his head with legends of gods and godesses. We told you it was time you taught him of earthly matters. . . ."

Superimposed over this scene in her mind was the face of her husband Antonio. His face was a mask of stone, cold and disapproving. The voices grew, tunneled in the caverns of her mind; nevertheless they were loud and clear. "Come, Mamma. We're waiting for you," they whispered seductively. "Come Mamma *bedda*."

Antigone, overcome by grief, felt the blood drain from her. She fell heavily into the arms of Stefano Modica. From somewhere came the *strega*'s voice. *"He must be protected for seven years of glory."* Over and over, these words echoed in her brain until a merciful blackness enveloped her.

Instantly there was a flurry of activity around her.

"It's her heart," apologized her physician, who appeared from nowhere carrying a small black bag and a hypodermic needle which he quickly thrust into her arm. "Someone please bring a chair for the *Signora*," ordered the rotund and balding Dr. Raffa.

Five minutes later, Antigone, showing a surprising composure, requested that they get on with the business at hand.

"Is this your son, Alessandro Salvatore?" asked Procurator Maggio?"

Now, for the first time, Antigone's eyes came to rest on the massive amounts of crushed ice packed around Tori's body. She scooped up a handful, refreshed by its cool properties, and allowed it to sift through her fingers. A sudden mad gleam of denial crept into her eyes. It flickered—and died just as quickly. Sighing heavily, she nodded. Saginor, nearby, drew a steady breath of relief. Modica exhaled evenly and unclenched his balled fists. Now, he too, looked closer at the body on the catafalque, aware of the squirming mass of nerves that knotted achingly in his stomach.

"You must answer the question, *Signora*," said Maggio. "I can't accept the nod of her head as an answer."

"Yes," she said, throatily.

"Do you officially identify this body as that of your son, known as Tori, also known as Salvatore the bandit—the brigand?"

Antigone leaned in to stroke his face tenderly, brushing away a few particles of the plaster of Paris left by the maskmaker

"Signora?"

47

She drew herself up regally, head held high. "Yes I identify him. He is my son, Alessandro, hailed as king of Montegatta, born November 16, 1922." She turned to Modica and said softly, "You came too late, *Colonnello*."

Modica gave a start. Hadn't he made it clear she wasn't to say anything about his mission? His men gave no sign of having heard. He breathed easier.

In a room containing over a hundred sophisticated newspapermen, and photographers, not a sound could be heard. Only the tremulous voice of the Procurator-General, rising and falling in rhythmic cadence like a high priest reciting low mass, was heard as he continued to ask all the questions for which the law, required answers before the deceased could be pronounced officially dead.

The formalities had ended.

Antigone Salvatore looked up and around at the vast circle of faces she'd never seen before, and, after a long and dreadful silence during which every eye in the room was upon her, she flung herself down beside the corpse. She lifted his cool head and pressed it to her feverish bosom: hot flesh cooled by dead flesh. She seized his hands and pressed them to her lips with an abandoned passion. She kissed his cheeks; his cold unresponsive lips. "My magnificent son," she whispered in a broken voice. Her passionate whispers filled the room. She was a woman whose child had been murdered; a woman mourning the death of her son. She was all grief and despair. Yet, over it all, she managed to maintain a certain majestic dignity.

There were no maudlin histrionics; no beating of her breasts; no lingering lamentations of sorrow; no martyr's affectations. The crowd who moved in closer, anxious to document her final words, felt both cheated and astonished by her control. They watched as she released her hold on him and crossed his hands over his chest. These words they heard as she spoke clearly and firmly: "Now, my beautiful son, you truly do belong to the world, *Sanguo del mio sanguo* blood of my blood."

Hardly anyone there fully understood these cryptic words. Later they'd talk about this, talk and wonder and probe. But for now, they only watched this matriarch who appeared as invincible as her son had seemed. She was a magnificent woman of strength, courage and fortitude.

Suddenly there was pandemonium. A cry arose from the spectators, and the strangers moved in on her. The magic had ended. The legend had let them all down by being a mere mortal. Given priority, the reporters broke the spell. Earlier they had strained to hear her words, and now they asked one another, "What did she say?" They had to know if they intended to record her grief and loss for posterity. Once again the flashbulbs popped. Cyclopean camera lenses blinked incessantly all around her.

Antigone, shielding her raw, sensitive eyes from the flashes of blinding lights, asked the Procurator-General to be allowed a few moments alone with her son. Her request was denied by Captain Franchina. Recalling his initial encounter with the formidable matriarch, the arrogant officer glared at her with a perverse sense of triumph.

Undaunted, Antigone said," Very well, then, permit me to view my son's personal effects."

In Dr. Alba's office, Antigone seemed a different woman. Stronger, more composed and in full command of herself, she let her dark eyes scan the articles collected on the table in reflective silence. Watching her, Modica got the feeling that she was assessing the items individually with some diabolical plot in mind. He sensed something was wrong. But what?

He was right. Something caught Antigone's eye as she examined the articles, touching nothing for the moment. Catching sight of the golden scorpion, she glanced up at Modica. She picked it up tenderly in her hands and handed it to him. "It's made a complete circle. I'm sure he would want you to have it. *Colonnello.*"

The FSB Officers tensed and nudged each other. Modica caught their reactions, and mumbled a "thank you."

"But there was another amulet—" began Antigone.

Maggio handed her another, the *Eye of God.* "It was in his pack." He handed her the fabled gold belt buckle, the diamond ring, and the other articles.

". . . And his gold watch?"

Reporters, speedily scribbling down what they could hear of the conversation, moved in closer.

"There was no watch. . . ."

"He was never without it," she said firmly, fingering the toy soldier and horse.

The FSB Officers exchanged glances, and turned to Maggio for guidance.

"I tell you there was no watch." Maggio mopped his brow.

Antigone's eyes were on the leather holster and Luger. "My son carried *this* gun? In *this* holster?" she asked scornfully.

"I personally removed them from his person." admitted Maggio. "The gun lay alongside his body where he dropped it."

"I've never seen these items before in my life. My son carried a Browning automatic. He was never without it." She picked up the Pall Mall cigarettes and tossed them aside in disgust. "My son smoked Camels!" She turned to the FSB Officers to ask, formally, "When may I take my son home for burial?"

"That's impossible!" countered Maggio. "The time limit has expired. Now, he must be buried in Castelvetrano."

"Impossible? What time limit? What are you telling me, man? You still insist on playing the jackass? My son belongs to me. Tell me when I can expect to have him, and let's be finished with these disgraceful charades and infamy!" She tensed, prepared to battle to the end for her son.

Maggio looked to the FSB Officers for help. They were remote and impassive; it was up to him. "I regret, *Signora,* you cannot have him. The law clearly states—well, after so many hours, he must be buried here," he sputtered. "Besides, we haven't performed the autopsy yet. Our rules are explicit. . . ." Sweat poured off him.

Outraged, Modica intervened. He spoke evenly and slowly, so he wouldn't be misunderstood. "Are you saying, she can't have her son even *after* the autopsy?"

Antigone placed a restraining hand on Stefano's arm. "We'll see about these explicit rules," she said, directing her remarks as much to Captain Franchina as to Modica. "I shall return to claim the body of my son, after the autopsy, through the efforts of a man whose word will not be contested. They will not dare to deny me." She walked to the door held open by a mocking Captain Franchina, who, in bowing slightly, added salt to her wounds.

Burning memories of her first meeting with him, five years before, spurred him on. "Well, *Signora,*" he said, "It is finished. Now, who rides the ass?"

In Antigone's eyes burned the fires of a volcano. She stopped abruptly, lifted her dark eyes to meet his, and gave him a look that chilled him to the marrow. "But, *is* it over, *Capitano*? The final curtain has not descended." She moved on past him.

Outside, the desert heat rushed at her with its ovenlike intensity. Reporters converged upon her and hurled provocative questions at her while the Americans ran interference for her on her way to the waiting sedan.

"Have you nothing to tell us, *Signora*? What brought your son to Castelvetrano? Where has he been these past six months of silence? Did you expect him to be so brutalized by his enemies?"

Because she remained silent and unbending and comported herself with imperial dignity, the goading began. "Justice reigns at last, eh *Signora?* He finally got what he dished out for so long. The invincible Salvatore is no longer invincible—eh? What do you say to that, *Signora?*"

At the car door, Antigone turned and leveled her inscrutable eyes upon the assemblage. She stood before them, gaunt, gray-haired, but magnificent, a matriarch of power and dignity. Gazing at them, she spoke without preamble: "My son lies upon the marble *catafalco*, dead. You can simply say—he was betrayed."

She entered the car and it moved forward off the mortuary grounds, leaving a stunned mass of reporters, baffled and curiously moved by her provocative statement. *He was betrayed!*

Those three insidious words, like a lever, were to pry open the lid of a putrefying cesspool of political secrets and covert acts engaged in against the dead man, and swell in the minds of the newsmen like blistering boils to threaten the very network of the Belasci-Barbarossa-Christian Democrat combine.

Four hours later, the Coroner, Dr. Alba, made a limited statement to the press: "The missile causing Salvatore's death entered the heart chamber of the rear, directly under the left shoulder blade, perforating the heart itself. The lethal wound was inflicted by a .45 calibre revolver. Two bullets grazed his forehead, causing no serious damage. Frontal bullet wounds on right arm, wrist, hand and rib cage were made by machine-gun fire. Bleeding was comparatively slight." The gentle doctor spoke economically, and, visibly shaken, he evaded all further questioning under the usual shelter of "no comment." The FSB would release further facts later, he added before he disappeared behind closed doors.

There was enough ammunition in his words to pose a serious problem when the official statement was issued. This autopsy report, never printed in its entirety, disappeared shortly afterward from the coroner's office. Obvious to the reporters was the fact that both Coroner and Procurator-General had been forced into silence by the mounting discrepancies between the facts they uncovered in their investigation and those furnished them by Captain Franchina.

Alba and Maggio, in turn, brooded over the contradictory evidence. The most blatant inconsistency lay in the fact that the fatal wounds to the heart had been sustained several days before the bullet holes inflicted by a machine gun penetrated the body. The time span between these bullet wounds posed a serious problem. Why shoot a corpse *after* it was dead? Unless. . . Neither man dared to speculate. Both preferred living to dying.

Unable to believe what had been done couldn't be undone, Antigone wondered to whom she could turn for the strength needed to take her through these next few days? She ordered her driver to take her to the villa of the one man of power and influence who couldn't dare deny her the right to bury her son as she wished—the most powerful figure in Sicily, Don Matteo Barbarossa.

Four hours later she emerged from his villa in Monreale, white-faced, tight-lipped, agonized and shaking from the heavy burden inflicted upon her during her visit. No one had witnessed her terror, the black hatred she had felt, the crushed spirit she had endured in his presence. Yet, through it all, she had emerged victorious! She had gotten what she went after, the release of her dead son and the right to bury him where she chose.

Mah-Santo Dio at what cost? She had learned the identity of her son's murderer: his assassin! Bearing the heavy burden of this knowledge, she knew now that she could never reveal the assassin as long as she lived—if she wanted to live!

Don Matteo had been brutally exact, exceedingly precise in his assessment. "If this information leaks, who will the world believe? A deranged hysteric? A crazy, wild woman overwrought with the guilt of her son's criminal life? Or the official words of the Italian government? It would serve you little, *Signora*, and might even mar the image of the good deeds your son accomplished. My advice is to leave well enough alone."

Antigone had listened, dead inside. It was too much for her to contemplate, too much for her dazed, medicated mind to grasp. She knew he was right, and his power too formidable to contest. Slowly, as she made preparations to leave, she turned to the Don and said wearily, "There's one thing more, please."

He replied quickly. "Ask, and its yours."

Antigone picked up the bronze figure of a snorting bull from his desk. It was heavy and exquisitely carved. "I should like to have this, please."

"Consider it yours. Your, son, too, was fascinated by it," he said. "Has there always been such a passion for bulls in your family?"

She glanced sharply at him. Then, quicker than the eye could follow, she flung the bull from her, hurling it against the stone fireplace behind her where it struck with terrific force, cracking legs and horns and splintering the figure from its base, and fell to the hearth in several pieces. She removed the toy white soldier from her pocket and, having seen its companions on the large table behind him, she placed horse and soldier on the desk before him. She lifted her dark, anguished eyes to meet his.

"Now, Matteo Barbarossa," she told the startled *capomafia*, "it is finished!" She left him staring after her, confounded by her actions. She could hear his voice echoing through the halls as she took her leave.

"*Porco diaoro!* Devilish pig! Women! Always illogical! What the hell did she have against this poor defenseless bull? Where did she get this white soldier?" His eyes darted to the scale model she had left him. His eyes narrowed in thought.

Antigone returned to Montegatta, to her house where she bathed and rested and collected her thoughts. Tomorrow, she'd follow the Don's instructions to prepare for the burial of her son. For tonight, though, she wanted to mourn and release from her soul the grief collected over the past seven years.

However much Antigone had learned from Don Matteo, he, too, had learned a great deal from her—enough to force him to forego his personal despair and return to the business of *capomafia*. He had no doubt that he had aptly impressed Antigone with the need for secrecy, the need never to reveal the identity of her son's murderer.

He scribbled the names of two men on a slip of paper and rang for his personal bodyguard and emissary of confidential business. Mario Cacciatore, a frog of a man who bore a frightening air of malevolence about him, and who had been associated with the Don since their early Mazzarino days, entered the study and stood by until the Don finished his writing. The former bandit and cold blooded

53

killer, whose skill and dexterity in carrying out executions was second to none, watched his Don through gloomy, disturbed eyes. Armed with the knowledge of the past five days' happenings and what had caused Don Matteo to sequester himself, Cacciatore, a brute of a man, had sensed a moment of black foreboding when he had earlier denied entrance to the shrouded woman dressed in black who had sought audience with the *capomafia*. Given the usual brushoff, the woman who gave her name as *Signora* Salvatore, had refused to leave. Shrugging indifferently he had motioned her to a highback chair in the foyer.

An hour later, Cacciatore had approached her, to suggest that she leave, since the Don was granting audience to no one. At that point, the woman had caught the *sicario*—the assassin—off guard for perhaps the second time in his life: she brandished a pistol!

Che demonio! A gun in the hands of a frantic, emotionally overwrought woman could prove more dangerous than one in the hands of a trained killer: you could always, after all, second-guess the professional killer's move. In the split-second he had taken to determine how to humor her, she had shattered his composure with another surprising move. Antigone had turned the gun around, butt-first, and handed it to him.

"Here, take it," she had urged. "Go ahead. Take it and shoot me! It's the only way you'll get me to leave this villa without seeing Don Barbarossa. He must give me what I came for. He must. Do you hear?" Her voice, raised in acrimonious discord, had echoed through the cavernous villa and reached Don Barbarossa's ears. In moments, Cacciatore had heard the Don's voice calling, assuring him it was all right to show the woman to his study. Horns of the devil! Would anything ever right itself again?

Now, Cacciatore turned his attention on Don Matteo, who displayed a remarkable recovery of composure since the woman's visit.

"Take care of these two," ordered Don Matteo. He was composed now, and had regained his usual self-sufficiency. He handed a slip of paper to his body guard. "Understand, they are not to live long enough to enjoy their blood money. When you finish, return here to me. We may be busy again as in the old days, my friend. Call Ruggero's Funeral Parlor, arrange for a limousine to be at *Signora* Salvatore's disposal for as long as she needs. She is not to pay for her son's funeral. They are to bill me."

Cacciatore nodded dutifully and left the study. Pausing in the corridor long enough to read the instructions, he let a wicked gleam of satisfaction creep into his eyes as he read the names—Don Nitto and Natale Solameni. The perusal of instructions etched into his ugly features a look of diabolical glee.

"Is this Don Matteo Barbarossa speaking?"

"Yes, this is me."

"One moment please for Minister Belasci . . ." said the operator.

"Minister Belasci speaking. This is Martino P. Belasci, here."

"All right, I believe you."

"Ah—Matteo, how good to talk with you. I've tried to call you all day. Too many busy terminals. . . ."

"che se decci, Martino? What's going on?"

"Haven't you heard? They got Salvatore."

"Uh . . . *who* . . . got Salvatore?"

"The FSB. My sweet brainchild. Oh, yes, Captain Franchina."

The Don was silent.

"Matteo?"

"Ummmhum."

"What's wrong? Something's wrong, isn't it?"

"Do you buy their story?"

Belasci tensed. Something *was* wrong. "Shouldn't I?"

"Have you released anything to the press?"

"Yes. At approximately 10 A.M. today."

"What did you say?"

With measured words. Belasci filled the Don in on the press conference. Once again the lines fell silent.

"Why would four American agents from the State Department be interested in Salvatore?" asked the Don.

"American agents? I've no idea. Why?"

"They're in Castelvetrano, snooping around."

"Incredible! But—how? Is your source of information reliable?"

"The best."

"I'll look into it immediately. I can't understand. I've issued no special permits for Sicily in a long time. We've had agents looking into that . . . other matter, Matteo. But they know me as a strong anticommunist force, dead set against the Reds. What they could possibly want with Salvatore is. . . ."

The Don cut him off. "You remember *Colonnello* Stefano Modica with the Allied Control Council during the war?"

"From the Grand Council? Certainly."

"It's him, with three other agents, in Castelvetrano. Is Modica working on something special in Rome?"

"I had no idea he was here. I'll look into it immediately."

"Sure that no one in your office has issued special permits?"

"No, Matteo. I'm not sure. But our contacts at the U.S. Embassy have said nothing to me. Not a hint. You know there's been pressure from the U.N. about economic aid—that's all."

"I don't like it that Modica is in Castelvetrano. He was a *pezzonovante*—a big shot—in the war. He must have some position of high authority in his government. Modica's no fool, Martino. He was tough. A hard nut to crack in the Grand Council. If Roosevelt hadn't died when he did and if they hadn't transfered Modica to Rome. . . . He was too well informed, like a machine. Besides, he *knew* Salvatore! You know what must be done," said the Don.

"Yes, I know. You're sure he knew Salvatore?"

"I'm sure. Now, tell me what happened to Santino Siragusa? Is he to be deported from America?"

Belasci faltered. "None of our contacts through Genovese or Luciano located him in America. It was a false alarm. For all we know he might be dead."

"Martino, listen. For your sake he'd better stay dead."

"Calm yourself, Matteo."

"I'm calm. Tell me about Salvatore's personal portfolio. *Managghia!* Why didn't you tell me about Santino Siragusa sooner?"

"Matteo. I may have good news for you. It appears there is a duplicate portfolio in circulation. With Salvatore dead, we'll have no difficulty laying our hands on it. It may cost us a few *lire*, but once it's safely in our hands we shall ignite it. Then, we'll celebrate. *Va bene?*"

Don Matteo took time to light a cigar. He puffed on it hard until it was well lit. Listening to the inhalations at the other end of the line, Belasci took a moment to pour himself a stiff drink from a nearby decanter, grateful there was no one around to see him sweating.

The Don's voice was cold and contemptuous. "A duplicate, eh? Now, there's more?" He snorted. "What about Salvatore?"

"What about him?" Belasci's voice was guarded.

"They wouldn't permit his mother to claim the body," The Don's tone was deadly. Belasci recognized it and knew there was more to come.

"Why not?" he asked cautiously.

"You're asking me? I didn't hire those two *cappicolli,* Franchina and Cala. You did! Stupid shitheads? *Mah,* tell me something, Martino—where do you find these braying jackasses?"

"I'll take care of it immediately. . . ."

"No need. I just did. The mother came begging for her son's body. I made the necessary calls and finished it."

"Fucking idiots! I can't imagine what they were thinking of. . . ."

"*Allora,*" said the Don, unable to resist the snide remark, "read the newspapers and find out."

"What's wrong, Don Matteo? There *is* something else. . . ." Belasci tensed.

"Tell me, how much did you pay Solameni? Was the reward ample?"

Belasci's blood turned to ice. He forced bravado. "You are simply a genius, Matteo. I've always said so. You know everything before I make a move to do it. Can't I ever keep a secret from you? It was the usual—I forget how much."

"It's not necessary to be clever with me. Fifty thousand dollars you paid. You realize when the autopsy report is complete, you'll all look like asses tied to the sun. . . ."

"I'm not in swaddling clothes, Matteo. I've taken care of that."

"How? A payoff? Another murder?"

"Does it matter? You've handled things in the past."

"*Amico,* I put you where you are to use your head. If I wanted a butcher for your job I would have used Cacciatore. Murders will no longer cover your blunders. Perhaps I should have put Salvatore in your place—given him the advantages I created for you. He used the brains God gave him, with talent."

"It wasn't I who fouled up Portella Della Rosa," blurted Belasci. Instantly he contemplated swallowing his tongue. In person or on the phone, Belasci could feel the Don's menacing presence and it chilled him instantly.

"I see. I see. When the hawk grows old, even the sparrows mock him."

Belasci felt the earth move under him. Following a testy silence, Don Barbarossa made no move to hide the contempt in his subdued voice.

"It was your puppet, Chief Semano, who hired the men for the attempted assassination. Before their guns had cooled, the deeds were announced to the world. Both sides

5   57

sit in Viterbo ready to spill their guts. Now that Salvatore's dead—don't think they won't!"

Belasci froze. He couldn't speak. He couldn't move. The phone felt as if it had turned to dry ice that stuck to his hands, searing through the flesh. The past flashed before him. Here they sat, the boa constrictor and the mongoose, in silent challenge.

"*Allora*—are you there?"

"Yes. I'm here. Strange isn't it? We've waited a long time for the capture or death of Salvatore. Now, dead, he presents more of a threat than when he ever did alive." Belasci's voice dulled perceptibly.

"It displeases me to think that wherever he is he's laughing at us!" The Don's voice, usually devoid of emotion, took on color. "It wasn't enough you had him dead. You could have turned him over to his mother for burial and ended it! No! Your arrogance and pride forced you to concoct a stupid story just to justify the existence of that infernal FSB. You had to take credit and bask in false glory! Hah! *Porco Diaoro!* You expose yourself to the snooping of highly sophisticated foreign journalists whose worst reporter is more expert than any man on your staff. You construct a mountain of fables and expect the world to believe your bullshit? Martino . . . Martino! When will you face reality? How much longer can I extend my arms to cover your ceaseless blunders? I'm growing old. I'm no longer young enough to put up with needless errors. Humor an old man, eh? Take Cala and Franchina in hand, before their balls are hacked off and ground up for vultures' bait. Eh?"

"Yes. Yes, right away. Immediately. I'll fly to Castelvetrano. . . ."

"No, Martino, no," sighed the Don wearily. "You stay in Rome. Send for them. Coordinate your stories, before you all step hip-deep in your own stinking shit and sink in it."

"It shall be attended to immediately. Anything else?"

"There is no time left for cleverness, Martino. Only action. *Ciao!*"

"*Si, ciao,* Matteo."

The seeds of discontent, germinated, began to sprout rapidly.

Concerned with Antigone Salvatore's well being and even more concerned by the fact that she appeared to know his mission, Stefano Modica left his companions, rented an auto, and motored to Montegatta.

Stefano Modica found Antigone, seated in the solitude of an amethyst twilight in her garden, wretched with dry tears of despair as she reviewed the events of that day. She was astonished by his presence and, despite her heavy heart, she tried to be cordial.

"It's not necessary, *Signora*," insisted Stefano. "I didn't come here to be entertained. It's just that you shouldn't be alone at such a time. Is there no one else who can remain with you at such a time?"

"No. There is no one. I'm quite alone. *Natura aborret saltum*. Sudden changes are painful and this pain is greatly minimized by the appearance of a friend," she told him.

They chatted for a time, and Stefano, detecting a tremendous loneliness in her in addition to a desperate need to speak, allowed her to ramble in any direction.

"He was special, you know," she began. "How can I explain? Things meant more to him. He had more questions for me than I had answers," she smiled in reflection. "From the first, the mid-wife who delivered him prophesied his greatness. Oh, I didn't believe her," she blurted flushing with self-consciousness. "I'm too much of a realist to believe in potions and spirits and the supernatural even though she possessed real prophetic powers—"Her hands flew to her forehead. "I'm confused. Perhaps the medication is stimulating me to talk so much," she rambled.

"I had to make certain you were all right. There's something else, *Signora*," he began lighting a fresh cigarette from his butt. "Even though my original mission failed, I must impress upon you the importance of saying nothing to anyone."

Antigone lowered her eyes to her callused hands, picking on a hangnail, then smoothing it into place. "You came too late," she sighed.

"*Signora*. If the slightest hint of those plans get into the wrong hands, it could create severe problems for innocent people."

"Destiny is a cruel mistress. She has a voracious appetite," she muttered, hardly aware of his presence.

Modica, concerned, detected in her manner a suppressed hysteria that threatened to burst at any moment. She rambled about Tori's life. If only he, Stefano, hadn't encouraged Tori to pursue his destiny, he might still be alive.

"The *strega* warned me—but how could I have known for sure? Antigone began to rock to and fro, intent upon some inner vision." For twenty years there'd been no sign in his life to foretell the violence that would come in his seven years of manhood—of the glories that would come

59

to him—of the treacheries and betrayals for which his education hadn't prepared him. How could I believe that the *strega*'s prophecy would come to pass? That his impotency would be caused by a bull?"

Possessed by his own guilt and submerged in his own mortification, Stefano hardly heard her words, at first. "Your son was a spectacular man, *Signora*. He was both loved and feared by enemies and friends alike. He had personal power—enough to shake up the world." He sighed heavily. "One thing is certain. He left imprints on the sands of time and they'll not be washed away. His spirit will live in the hearts of his people." He inclined his head in a mark of respect for her grief.

Antigone shook her head sorrowfully. "No, *Colonnello*. Your emotions blind you. Powerful politicians won't permit his spirit to live. They'll take careful means to destroy his image. Those men, high in government—those men who intrigued to kill his flesh—will now annihilate his spirit."

Modica glanced at her, curious lights sparking his blue eyes. "Not if we keep him alive, *Signora*. Not if we keep the spirit of Salvatore alive."

As Antigone's eyes darted towards him in an effort to fathom his remark, Stefano became conscious of her earlier words as they replayed in his mind. *"Strega's* prophecy?" He turned to her. "What are you saying—witchcraft, black magic? How the devil could a bull influence your son's life?" Stefano was aghast. Surely she wasn't in her dotage?

Antigone kept her inscrutable eyes on the American for several moments, as if she were assessing him in a most curious manner. Then, rising to her feet, she asked him to follow her into the house, where she proceeded to bolt to the door. She led him upstairs into the modest sitting room. "Please be seated," she said cordially, gesturing to a comfortable sofa before excusing herself.

Modica's eyes instantly darted to the framed photograph that dominated an entire wall. Salvatore, seated on his white Arabian stallion, *Napoleono* was a spectacular sight. *By God, what a champion*, he thought; then, remembering what had happened to that magnificent beast early that afternoon, he felt as he had earlier, terribly saddened by the spectacle.

When Antigone returned she held in her hands the *Eye of God* amulet he'd seen earlier at the morgue and a frayed, yellowed folded paper. She set them on a nearby table and from a crystal decanter poured two *bicchierini* of anisette. She handed him one and took the other in her hand. They drank a silent toast to the dead man. Now, for the first time, she began to speak with coherence. *"Allora,* Stefano, please feel at ease. Don't be concerned that I possess certain information about the activities you engaged in with Tori. My lips are sealed. Because my son felt towards you like a brother—because you came despite the failure of your plans—and because of Gina, I shall entrust to you, certain explosive secrets. Let this be a legacy for Gina in her darkest hours of need," she said cryptically.

He didn't understand her words and couldn't guess where they were leading, so he remained silent, hoping to learn what her glittering eyes conveyed.

"I speak from love in my heart and through the memories of my son, be they bitter or sweet," she told him. "When you were here during the war, you knew a different man than the one he became in five years. *They* caused the changes in him. They made him what he became. They were afraid of him—those politicos in Rome and Palermo. If one—only one—of those men had kept their promises to him, he'd have been a king."

"I've never forgotten the potential greatness he possessed, *Signora.*"

"Va bene. I will start at the beginning. . . ."

CHAPTER 5

It would have been easier for Lucifer to enter the gates of heaven than for Minister Belasci, or anyone else for that matter, to place a telephone call to Castelvetrano in the next few days. In desperation the Minister sent a courier to the *"Judastown"* to order Colonel Cala and Captain Franchina to beat a hasty retreat to Rome for a regrouping of forces. Unfortunately for many concerned, the courier didn't arrive until well after the FSB Captain held the eagerly awaited press conference.

Baring their fangs like tigers at bay, an angry horde of reporters, waiting greedily for meat to be flung at them, refused to be pacified with milk. Mixed emotions surged through them as they awaited the "official" report. Gathered noisily in a special room set aside for them at the Selinus Hotel, the journalists, a heterogeneous lot, ignored the lavish display of wines and liquors set up for their benefit. For the most part they seemed short-tempered, incensed by unnecessary delays, and highly offended at the manner in which they had been treated. When finally Captain Franchina mounted the dais in the crowded ballroom, dressed in a brand new uniform with glittering brass buttons, and prepared to address the pressmen, their antagonistic presence was felt in overpowering waves of hostility. Undaunted, Captain Franchina got to the point.

"At approximately 3:15 A.M. on July 5, 1950, two armed men were seen walking along the Strada Sarina Madonna. Four specially deputized *carabinieri* went towards them and ordered them to halt. I was not far away when I heard the commotion, including the many shots they fired in their attempt to flee. One of the armed men took off in one direction, and evidently escaped. The second man ran in the opposite direction. I had a choice to make. Which man to follow? I chose the one who tossed aside his jacket, and made an attempt to escape in the narrow alleys off Strada Sarina Madonna. Apparently, I made the right choice, for as luck would have it, the man I followed turned out to be Salvatore. The other man is presumed to have been Vincenzo de Montana. But, this is not known for certain."

"Then, it was you who shot Salvatore, fatally?" asked one reporter. The others moved in closer to the dais. Perhaps they would get a straight story, after all.

"Yes, it was I, Captain Giovanni Franchina of the Forces to Suppress Banditry. It was a tough fight. Salvatore fought well, making use of a special invention of his that permitted him to keep an extra magazine of forty rounds in the butt of his submachine gun. The fight for his life lasted approximately thirty-five minutes. He zig-zagged in and out the many courtyards on that street, firing in excess of fifty-two rounds of ammunition.

"He was losing much blood from his many wounds, and I felt certain he couldn't last much longer. Finally, he threw himself into the courtyard at *numero* 54, Strada Sarina Madonna. Twisting and turning like a madman, he never noticed the machine gun set up to fire at him. With my own hands, I opened fire. He fell, riddled with bullets, before he could use the Luger he pulled from his holster. Salvatore didn't die instantly. He groaned and moaned and begged for water. Unable to stand by and watch his suffering, I knocked on a few doors. One woman, a saint, the widow Grissi, supplied the water. Even a dying bandit is entitled to mercy, to sate the terrible thirst that comes upon him. . . ."

The reporters pressed Franchina for more facts. "Why were you here in the first place? What tipped you off that Salvatore would be here, so far from his own territory?" they asked.

"Colonel Cala knew Salvatore's weaknesses—arrogance, egotism and women." began Franchina.

The disgruntled horde of reporters booed him loudly. Franchina raised his arms, gesturing for silence. When they quieted down, he proceeded to explain that the FSB had set a trap for Salvatore. They had circulated a rumor that a motion picture company from Cinecitta, eager to make a film on Sicilian life, wanted Tori for a starring role. "In addition," continued the Captain, "the bandit leader's favorite prostitute was in the area. Unable to resist passions of the flesh, he was easily lured to this area, and thus sealed his fate."

Discerning reporters ridiculed Franchina's last statement, verbalizing their discontent with loud boos. "What the hell do you take us for?" they shouted hostilely. When he was alive, even Salvatore's distrust of prostitutes had been legendary. He had punished his men for their lack of discretion in affairs of passion too frequently for the newsmen to believe such a story. Goddamnit! Was there no truth in this preening peacock?

Franchina raised his arms, hoping to stay the tigers. "And in addition," he said, "we were tipped off that an escape plan was under way. Colonel Cala had learned Salvatore was planning to leave Sicily, either from the old war airport here or through the fleet of high powered motor boats which mysteriously congregated near Selinunte and flee to America. . . ." Franchina gazed at them, perverse satisfaction glittering in his dark eyes.

A hush arose in the ballroom. So! America had come to Salvatore's aid, after all? The reporters pressed in closer, prepared to deluge Franchina with a barrage of questions. However, before they could pose the first of these, Captain Franchina's press conference was cut short by the arrival of Minister Belasci's courier, who quickly escorted the two FSB officers out of the Selinus in a whirlwind of secrecy, and flew them back to Rome without a hint of apology or explanation to the press.

The FSB's unexplained absence from the arena of action increased the discontent among the more scrupulous reporters, who were unable to fit together the distorted facts and downright lies spoonfed to them. They all agreed that a mere child could see through so flimsy a sham. It was a cover-up all right, they agreed. But why? Damned if they weren't going to find out!

Some reporters took off immediately for Viterbo to question former bandits. A few went directly to Montegatta to question the villagers. By late afternoon of the same day, Minister Martino Belasci's attempts to underplay and cover the facts of Salvatore's death boomeranged. Around the world, newspaper editors, hungrily awaiting the true facts of the story, were forced to reprint canned coverage of the famed bandit's seven-year career of glory, thereby bringing a spectacular rebirth to the legend and more prominence to Salvatore in death than he had enjoyed in life.

In Rome, Captain Franchina's "official" story was followed by a declaration from Belasci's office. There would be no further investigation in the matter of Salvatore's death: the case was closed. This should have satisfied the world and the international pressmen. But it didn't!

Banner headlines appeared in the Communist press:

WHO SPEAKS TRUTH? BELASCI IN LIFE OR SALVATORE IN DEATH?

INCONSISTENCIES IN SALVATORE'S DEATH BRAND FSB AND BELASCI AS LIARS!

"What is the grotesque secret behind Salvatore's death that Minister Belasci attempts to hide?" one newspaper demanded. "Reporters attest that the official version of the death of the Montegattan King is the poorest, most unbelieveable scenario written in Italian history, full of contrivances a child can detect and packed with blatant deceit. Why is the truth being withheld? The People of Italy and Sicily demand to know!"

Reporters remaining in Castelvetrano refused to abandon Salvatore to posterity, or to permit history to claim this as his final curtain. He had lent spectacular color to their dreary lives for seven years—should his death be less spectacular? *No!* they told themselves as they entrenched themselves firmly at the Selinus to organize a bit of team work to compare their findings. Certain there was treachery underfoot, aware that their presence would be met with stiff resistance, they watched and waited.

Then it came—subtly, with hinted innuendos. Six licensed prostitutes, imported to service the area, were suddenly withdrawn. Sex-starved newsmen, ready to give vent to the oldest and most primal of instincts, were told the women were for the exclusive use of the *carabinieri*, soldiers, and FSB.

Veterans among the press corps got the picture immediately. They sniffed out the procedure instantly, and, knowing their presence was no longer desired, they prepared themselves for that eventuality. Before the FSB closed down the liquor kiosks that day, the reporters had laid in a healthy stock of tobacco and liquors and a banquet of food. They offered to share their booty with the three American agents, who were cooling their heels, waiting for Modica's return.

"Damn!" griped Saginor to Renzo Bellomo, who sat cooling himself with a bamboo fan purchased in the Selinus lobby. "I wish we could stick our noses into *this* case."

"Yeah," retorted Renzo with a degree of preoccupation, moving the fan with rapid movements. They listened for a time to the excited chatter amongst the newsmen.

Saginor glanced casually at his friend, his eyes alert to the changes in him. "You're too quiet. You on to something?"

Renzo shrugged indifferently and accepted a drink thrust into his hand by one of the reporters. Saginor, unable to let it alone, guided Renzo towards the edge of the room close to the hallway, out of the hearing of the disgruntled newsmen. "Listen, pal, the *official* story stinks. You know it. I know it. They know it. Why didn't they just bury the poor bastard? Why all the *tsimmis?*"

Renzo stopped fanning himself. He stared at Saginor as if seeing him for the first time. "If I knew that . . . if I knew *that*—well, I could solve the riddle. The motive behind this is what baffles me." He commenced fanning himself, pausing now and again to punctuate his words with the woven bamboo.

"You that close to doping it out?"

"Franchina's version is a crock. How the bloody hell would he have time to set up a machine gun if, as he said, he was only out roaming the streets at that ungodly hour? And we both know a dying man with a bullet in him doesn't become thirsty until *after* fever sets in. And something else doesn't set right. Did you get a gander at Salvatore's sandals? There wasn't a speck of dust on them. Now how the hell could that be possible if, as Franchina says, he chased him through several courtyards? The dust would be that thick." He raised a hand, showing a wide space between thumb and forefinger. "Look, pal, let's get the hell outa here," he said impatiently. "I've had enough post-mortems and conjectures and repetitious allegations to last a lifetime." He guided Saginor out the door into the corridor, leaving the swarming hordes of reporters behind them. "Besides," he added. "I've had a bellyful of this hot box." He swatted angrily at the flies in the air with his fan. "Sonofabitching flies! These talk-filled jerks are gettin' to me. Whaddya say we beat it the hell back to Rome?"

Something else was itching Renzo, but he wasn't ready to scratch the itch yet. "Where the fuck is Modica—will you tell me?" he said sourly.

Saginor's attention was taken by a fresh gathering of news-hawks just alighting from the elevator. "So many leave, so many keep coming," he observed thoughtfully. "Why the hell do you suppose they're hanging around?" His endless fascination with the reporters had turned into morbid curiosity. "They got the official statement. What more do they expect from those jackals? The carcass has been plucked clean. Dead is dead; don't they know that?"

Renzo butted his cigarette on the tile floor with the heel of his shoe. "Ain't no more gonna happen here." He too was taken by another flock of journalists scaling the stairwell. "What else *can* happen?" he muttered weakly.

"Then why the hell don't the press get the hell back to where they came from?" commented Saginor.

"Beats me," muttered his companion. "Fuckin' reporters! That built-in radar of theirs can track a story across a fuckin' ocean." His heavy lidded eyes stared dourly at the men filing past him into the hospitality room. He plugged his ears with his fingertips to dim the tumult of conversation and busy drone of voices. "They're like a pack of buzzards watching a woodpecker chip away at a hangman's noose, waiting for the moment they can swoop down to their banquet and pick the carcass clean."

Matt Saginor nodded in agreement.

"Let's get outa here," urged Renzo in a voice that bordered on hysteria. "Look, buddy, do we have to be concerned with Modica?"

"He knows Sicily better than he knows the States. He'll find us."

Renzo rang for the elevator. In their absorption with the reporters, the lift had gone on to another floor.

"What do you make of Franchina's reference to an escape plan for Salvatore? Wouldn't we have heard a rumble if our side had planned it?" Saginor wiped the sweat rolling off his freckled face.

Bellomo's face turned a beet red. "Ya hadda bring it up, eh? I've been trying to ignore that ever since I heard it." He pushed the elevator button savagely.

"You *know* something." Saginor became intent. His eyes were riveted on the darker man. "You're on to somethin', aren't you? I can tell. When you get mad, good buddy—you're close to something."

"Does it matter? The poor bastard's dead. C'mon, for Christ's sake, elevator—work!" Renzo pushed the button again. "Let's take the fuckin' stairs! This elevator won't be here till Christmas!"

At *numero* 54, Strada Sarina Madonna, madness ensued. Bellomo, rushing ahead to observe the curious activity and milling crowds jostling each other, craned his neck to see over the heads of the people. Saginor, bewildered by the rush of activity, circled in behind his friend, and, making his way to the edge of the crowd, he saw the bent figure of a woman shrouded in a black shawl, sprawled over the body of what appeared to be a dead man lying in the position Salvatore's body had been in two days before. The woman appeared to be sucking up blood from the ground, in a reenactment of a scene in which it was claimed the mother of Salvatore had drunk his still-warm blood in an act of vendetta, swearing to be avenged for the death of her son—when, indeed, she had been nowhere near this courtyard at the time of his death.

Camera shutters clicked incessantly. Reporters scribbled in their note-books and the frenzied scene continued. On cue the woman got to her feet and stepped aside as photographers took photos of the young actor who played the part of Salvatore. Matt Saginor turned away in revulsion. He glanced about for Renzo, unable to find him. They'd been pushed apart by the swarms of curiosity seekers, and Matt, flung against the courtyard wall, scraped his nose sharply against the rough concrete. About to move away, he was struck with an idea. Turning, he searched the wall carefully in all directions. He heard Renzo calling to him, anxious to be leaving. Matt nodded, and, waving, acknowledged him over the heads of the mob.

Unable to press through the hordes of people, Saginor let his curiosity about the wall take priority for the moment. He continued to hug it closely as he followed a path along the outer perimeter of the courtyard, alongside the de Meo house, to the rear of the stone wall. Moving along, flush with the widow Grissi's house, he was unable to locate a bullet hole, except for those he'd seen to the left of the archway wall. Of the four possible places random machine gun fire could have hit, the least likely to have been struck by stray bullets was that narrow area of stone wall. *Man oh man!* Saginor, no dummy, reasoned these bullets had to have been purposely fired at the wall. His mind went back to Captain Franchina's words. How many rounds of ammo had Salvatore fired? What was it Franchina had said? He stopped himself. What the hell? Why get upset over the lack of bullet holes in the right places, when the whole fucking mess was an outright phony! Disgusted at himself for having even attempted to disprove Franchina's outright lies, he began to elbow his way through the crowds, with a grim determination to escape this insanity.

Flung back by the pressing horde, Saginor fell off balance, caught his boot on something, and held on to the drainpipe for support. The heel of his boot, caught between two wooden slats of the drain cover, wouldn't free itself. He gave it a kick and accidently dislodged the cover. In a shaft of light something glistening caught his eye. He ignored it until an after image flashed into his consciousness—something incongruous to the setting and unlikely to be found in such a setting distorted his senses.

The red-haired American shoved hard, pushed several people from him, and, falling to his knees, he saw lodged in the rim, between the crudely cut wooden frame and copper tubing of the drain itself, a bloodied hypodermic syringe. He reached into his pocket for a handkerchief, leaned in, lifted the syringe out, placed it on the white square of linen, and stared at it, unmindful of the glares and angry curses hurled upon him for his rudeness. On his feet, he continued to examine it with avid curiosity. Finally he wrapped it carefully, slipped it into his pocket, and pushed through the crowd to join Renzo.

They were some pair, these two. The most casual eye would assume they weren't acquainted with each other as they moved towards the *piazza*. Saginor grew introverted; Bellomo brooded, his mind intent on the morbid scene in the courtyard. They walked in the sultry heat, on antiquated streets too narrow for a car to traverse, past the better shops where business flourished. It became obvious there were now more arrivals in the village than departures, and everywhere hawkers had set up roadside stands to deal with the newfound prosperity the town had found in the vending of photographs and souvenirs. Photographers of the death scene in the courtyard had printed an enormous quantity of the photos and were selling them at dear prices. Women draped in black shrouds—women who bore little or no resemblance to *Signora* Salvatore—posed for tourists and sold amulets at prices dearer than gold. The American found the scene incredible.

At the edge of the *piazza,* they found a *gelateria* and seated themselves at a sidewalk table where they watched the ceaseless flow of pedestrians coming and going in the carnival-like atmosphere that descended on the village. Served their *gelato alle fragole*—frozen strawberry ice cream—in silence, they ate the cooling refreshment in silence, until Len Salina, having spotted them both from across the *piazza,* joined them, his face flushed with the relaxation of a sexual interlude. His companions brightened at his appearance and the mood broke.

By the time their coffee arrived, Saginor had taken out the hypodermic syringe and placed it before them on the table. "What do you make of this?" he asked quietly.

Bellomo stared at it with profound interest. "Where the hell did *that* come from?" He was perpetually angry of late.

Saginor explained.

"No sense asking Dr. Alba to run tests on it," said Renzo dryly. "It would probably disappear like the autopsy report."

"What do you *really* think, Renzo?" pressed the Texan. "I've never seen you without some theory to offer. Can't you make a guess?" Matt removed his jacket and lay it on a nearby chair.

"C'mon, supersleuth," urged Salina. "Make a guess. We ain't playing games."

Renzo felt wilted in the heat. His crumpled suit and sweat-soaked shirt didn't help his disposition. He liked things orderly, and he had a tendency to be skittish when they weren't. "Why pursue it, Matt? It won't do Salvatore any good. He's a dead man. Nothing will resurrect him. The days of miracles are long gone. Besides, who'd believe what we've stumbled on in this land of insanity?" Renzo stared off at nothing in particular.

Saginor shook his head regretfully. "Damn shame, when a man gets knocked off and no one gives a damn. . . . Steve knew Salvatore much better than he's led us to believe," he said thoughtfully. "I know him well enough to know something's eatin' at him."

"Is that why he went to Montegatta?" asked Salina, devouring the tasty strawberry cream.

Saginor lit a cigarette and inhaled deeply. "I suppose. The woman has no one."

"You don't think it strange that Modica chose this particular time to make this trip?" Renzo toyed with the melted cream running from his spoon. "Why Modica at this time? Nothing really pressed on ORS. Something else, good buddy. Something *Signora* Salvatore said bothers me. 'You came too late,' " she told him.

"What devilish brew is boiling your brains?" laughed Saginor. Then, he got the full implication. "You mean about that stuff Franchina refered to—boats in the harbor, a special plane awaiting Salvatore? All that mumbo-jumbo Franchina made up about an escape plan? C'mon buddy, you don't believe all *that* crap?"

Renzo merely raised his brown eyes and met Saginor's. Salina got the picture. He whistled low. Saginor sobered. His face screwed up with thought. "Nah," he scoffed. "You're off base. Even if you're right—what's the good of any plan, now? The operation's been snafued. . . . Besides, I'm more interested in learning for what devilish purpose this damned hypodermic was used." He was suddenly concerned for Modica.

"Only that I'd hate to be here if Italian intelligence has broken the case and it's learned that Modica is the key, *numero uno*, behind the plan.

"*Oy vey!*" muttered Saginor.

"*Oy vey*, my ass!" exclaimed Salina. "*Butana u diaoro* is more like it!" He rose to his feet, picked up the check. . . .

Saginor placed the syringe into his jacket pocket, slung the coat over one shoulder, and followed the others down the street. They turned off the square onto the Strada Vittorio Veneto, walking past delapidated houses and old buildings on whose peeled, faded and cracked walls were plastered electioneering posters touting *political* parties who had faded from prominence years before.

A poster of Salvatore dressed as a General, lauding the Partitionist Party, caught Renzo's eye a block away from the Selinus. He stopped, stared at it hard, and, wiping the sweat from his face and neck, opened up with a stream of consciousness. "Now, wait the hell until I'm finished before you burst the bubble. It's only a theory, from what I've observed, and without supportive data. I'm stretching it—believe me, you guys, I'm stretching it. Hear?"

Saginor brightened. "Listen, I only asked for an educated guess."

"O.K. How does this grab you? Dr. Alba stated death resulted from .45 calibre bullets entering a rear perforation of the heart chamber where we all noticed darker, caked blood. My theory is Salvatore wasn't killed the morning of July 5th. Probably not in Castelvetrano. Judging from the quantity of ice used to preserve the body, I'd say two—maybe—three days before. Got that? I think he was brought here and dumped into the courtyard, where someone then pumped extra bullets into him. Whoever killed him, whoever set the stage, came prepared knowing he wouldn't bleed. They bought fresh animal's blood. Goat's, or perhaps chicken's, blood isn't hard to come by. In Sicily such shops are open in the middle of the night. Then, with that needle you found, the bloodless holes were filled with crimson blood. . . ."

Saginor and Salina whistled low, trying to conceal their astonishment.

"The pool of crimson we saw concentrated over the right shoulder was probably made by pouring a moving container of blood over it into the dust. That explains the defiance to gravity—the uphill slant of the blood and the differences in the coagulation properties—and the variety of hues. It also explains the too-perfect positioning of the corpse. *Signora* Salvatore attested the guns were not her son's, that he smoked Camels not Pall Malls. So it proves someone hastily put the scene together. The weight of evidence that the murder was committed long before the official time is overwhelming in my eyes. . . ."

"You've got it narrowed down pretty well," Saginor said, "except for *why?* Why couldn't he have been found dead wherever he had been killed? Why manufacture so many obvious lies and distortions? It makes no sense at all, man!"

"It would if we knew all the facts leading up to the staging of the act. And we ain't gonna *get* no more facts," insisted Renzo. "So, we'd better haul ass back to the Selinus, pay our bill, and get the fuck back to Rome before we get our asses kicked in—or worse. Knowing you, Matt, I've already said too fucking much. That Jew head of yours will figure it too close!"

"Renzo"s right. We've got no business in this," said Salina, glancing cautiously over his shoulder. We've got more than we can handle with ORS."

"We can't leave the Colonel," protested Saginor.

"He's a big boy. He'll know where to find us. And you know something else?" said Bellomo, his dark eyes flashing. "I don't appreciate the sonofabitch not telling us what risks we might be taking down here."

71

"Christ! You don't know if it's even true!" admonished Saginor.

"Yeah. Maybe you're right." They picked up momentum as they walked back to the hotel. "Maybe I've been in the business too long."

"If Franchina didn't kill Salvatore, damnit, who did? And why would he admit to such a thing? Why would a man like Colonel Cala be a party to such a thing?" Saginor's perplexity alerted them.

"Oh! Oh!" lamented Renzo. "He's off and running. I knew I should have kept my big mouth shut!"

At the Selinus Hotel, mingling with the seasoned reporters up in their suite were a fresh batch of reporters who had arrived that morning. Fresher and shrewder in their questioning, they were echoing Saginor's thoughts. The grave conflicts at issue had caused such consternation among the men that they had gone out and interviewed twelve witnesses. All told the same story, and all disagreed vehemently with Captain Franchina's official story.

These reporters took a better look at the man—Captain Giovanni Franchina—professional soldier, injured in action, who had risen in the ranks of the *carabinieri* by promotion. Educated at Naples Police Academy. His thesis on Psychological Behavior of Criminals had earned him a special niche in forensic criminology. For establishing *modus operandi* in the behavior of certain types of elusive criminals, his opinions were sought after by several police units. The reporters could hardly believe such a man would string together such a flimsy story with so many loose ends. These actions were not worthy of such a man. Yet, on the other hand, this apparent carelessness on his part might have been deliberately planned to imply that he was an impostor, with the authority to claim the reward for executing Salvatore. If nobody believed him, this might ward off an onslaught of Sicilian vengeance.

The reporters now focused on Colonel Cala. Cesare Cala. Distinguished service in both World Wars. A long list of formidable successes throughout the world during his service with Italian intelligence, and every command a success. Slow, precise, painstaking and methodical, with an uncanny way of doing the right thing at the right time, Cala was a man who shied away from the kind of publicity in which Martino Belasci thrived. He hardly gave thought to the immense powers conferred upon him, which elevated him upon occasion to third man in a power structure of authority in the nation. Cala evidently lacked the inflated superego and flagrant audacity that commanded authority. Most of all he lacked that special quality of dishonesty that becomes requisite to overly ambitious politicians. He was at most a staunch Italian patriot, a man who took orders and executed them exceptionally well.

Why, then, would such a man be party to such obvious fraud? Promotion? A man who'd exposed himself to countless dangers all his life, who lived free of ostentation, needed no such encouragement. What then? The reporters were baffled. What was this crude conspiracy endorsed by these officers?

In Rome, both these men had emerged from their meeting with Minister Belasci, strained, red-faced, and filled with an inner turbulence which they held surprisingly in check. More surprising was the fact that the bombastic Capt. Franchina, whose pride and arrogance in the past had been a deterrent to his success, had refrained from mouthing off to Minister Belasci. How he wanted to tell the pompous ass what he could do with the FSB.

For hours they had kept silent while they pleasured themselves at the famed Madama Roulettini's bordello. Several weeks of pent-up emotions and self-denial had exploded in the aftermath of their visit with Belasci and they had to seek sexual outlets. But Franchina had continued to brood unrealistically.

It wasn't until they had retired to the Turkish baths and prepared themselves for the ordeal they both faced in Castelvetrano that Captain Franchina let loose a torrent of volatile expletives and a loquacious rhetoric to which even Cala hadn't been subjected to in the past.

"You should have told that cocksucker off, Cesare!" he began. "Where does that limp-wristed pansy come off, ripping our insides apart? Who does he think he is? Dandified asshole! He asks the impossible. When we deliver it, he sounds off like a harem of dissatisfied whores." Franchina craned his neck and struck vigorously at his nude body with a bouquet of birch branches tied together.

"He's our commanding officer in this special assignment," said the Colonel wearily. "That's who he is." Sitting hunched over on the wooden benches, naked, he appeared much older than his forty-eight years, and seemed completely cowed by the enormous burden carried on his shoulders. "We are simply good soldiers taking orders. Remember that. . . ." He pulled on a long cord at his side. Instantly, inundated by a forceful gush of steam, they basked in it for moments in silence.

"We're in it up to our necks. You know what'll happen if we get sucked under," said Franchina, trying to locate the Colonel in the vaporous air.

"Giovanni," said Cala patiently. "I've been an army man too long to change my ways. Wrong or right, I've taken orders all my life. In that time I've learned a lot. I've learned that no matter how much shit hits the fan, sweeping it up while it's fresh will only make one hell of a mess."

Franchina refused to be assuaged. "After the copious bungling and mishandling of our assignment and his constant interference with the press for his own self glorification, Belasci has a nerve calling us idiots!

"Bastard! Wasn't it he who demanded the blood of Salvatore? *Bring me the blood of Salvatore!*' he ranted that day in his office. Now we've done it, and *this* is the thanks we get? Hah!" He struck at himself with alarming brutality, until he winced at the welts raised on his body by the birch branches.

"What's done is done. We must go forward with what we have. No tears or laments over errors and wrongdoings. Next time we'll both know better. . . ."

"*Next time?* Are you insane, Cesare? There may never be a next time for us. I've seen what happens to people who know too much. They're shipped to a foreign land, where they evaporate into thin air—or are done in mysteriously by unseen forces in unforeseen accidents. Loyalty to these vultures earns no rewards!"

"You should know," said the Colonel. "The expiration of a certain Private Foti. . . ." He cut a reproving eye towards his companion.

"He knew too much!" retorted Franchina defensively. "He saw enough to crucify us."

"You mean *you;* to crucify *you,*" said the Colonel beating his body with birch branches to stimulate circulation.

Colonel Cala's point was well taken. Franchina's face became engorged with blood as waves of anger surged through him. Noting the mounting fury in his fellow officer, Colonel Cala tried to make light of the situation. "Come, come, take hold of yourself. You heard the Minister. Our main objective is to learn what the Americans are up to. Belasci assured us he can handle the press. In a month's time Salvatore will be forgotten. He guarantees this. Already he's requested the press to tone down their interest in the bandits. Their propagandists, the radio stations and the Christian Democrats' control over all such

74

platforms will insure his orders will be obeyed or they'll lose their licenses. Just think positive. Belasci will attain his goal. Remember he's an ambitious man who plans to be Premier. Let's look to ourselves. It pays to be on the winning side, eh, *Capitano?*"

Franchina nodded his head knowingly. "Come anything save an earthquake, we stick to our original story, is that it? What if the rumors are true—that the Americans represent President Truman?" he asked his superior officer.

Belasci will handle it," repeated the Colonel. "Look, our job is to make the Americans aware that they aren't welcome and are considered trespassers in our domain. To escort them out of town if necessary. Belasci has already lodged complaints against them with the American Embassy. You heard Belasci."

"Si," nodded Franchina, sullenly. "I heard that forked-tongued viper, all right. I also recall vividly that Salvatore warned you we'd be betrayed. He told us he'd neither be captured nor killed, and that Belasci intended to seduce us both and leave us as scapegoats, with both cock and balls exposed to the world. Cesare, I'm telling you now, I'll not stand for the same fate meted to *Il Duce* and his mistress! If I'm left alone in this, I swear I'll sing an aria that will straighten the Tower of Pisa!"

Precisely at that moment, the doors burst wide open and a blustery faced, irate madam, holding on to a waif of a girl, entered the *verboten* Turkish bath on the warpath. The young prostitute had been badly beaten around the face, neck and upper torso, and ugly swollen weals and bruises on her face had formed welts, half closing the girl's eyes. The madam confronted Captain Franchina. *"Signore!"* she shouted. "I demand restitution for the *infamia* you hurled upon this sweet, innocent bloom of youth."

The astonishment on his face turned to a blustery, red-faced embarrassment. Under heavy lids his eyes darted in the direction of his stunned superior officer. Colonel Cala, by nature a mild-mannered man, who had, in a career devoted to the military, probably strayed from the nuptial bed no more than a dozen times, and who, despite his reputation as a hard-driving man, was as gentle as a dove in bed, was shocked at what he saw. He averted his eyes, flushed with embarrassment for Franchina.

"It couldn't be helped," offered Franchina by way of explanation—not apology. "I was so furious—so fucking mad at Belasci. . . ."

". . . That you took it out on this poor child. Well, *Sig-*

nore," stormed the Madam. "For this you'll pay! I tell you you'll pay, or I'll go directly to the Minister and tell him what a devil he has on his hands!"

"*Va bene!*" shouted Franchina. "*Va bene!* I'll pay. As soon as I dress, and leave this damned establishment. . . ."

Colonel Cala reached up to pull the cord, to rid himself of these gawkers. Instantly the room filled with eddies of scalding steam, so hot that Franchina cried out indignantly.

"*Dio Malodetto!* Turn off the fucking steam! Aren't we in enough hot water already without you scorching us? *Butana u diaoro!* Whore of the devil! Come along and I'll pay you! Only for Christ's sake, shut your serpent's face!"

The Captain stalked out of the steam room, his mustache drooping like that of a giant walrus.

Colonel Cala shook with livid rage. *What else will go wrong?* he thought. *What am I teamed up with—a crazy psychopath, a sexual pervert?*

CHAPTER 6

Colonel Cala sat behind the hand-carved oak desk in the office of the Prefect of Police in a drab and badly-lit room of an ancient building. Captain Franchina sat next to him in a stiff high-backed chair, still intent on his reaction to Martino Belasci's excoriating effrontery and his own sadistic bent.

"Please come in, gentlemen," said Cala, rising as the trio entered. A glance at Saginor's red face and surly manner convinced him the American had been drinking.

"You wanted to see us?" asked Bellomo, with a tone of formality.

"Please be seated. But . . . aren't there four of you?" asked Cala.

"We've lost one. He's out sightseeing like a tourist," said Matt.

The Americans took the stiff high-backed chairs indicated and refused the English Ovals offered them. They lit their own cigarettes.

76

"What brings you to Castelvetrano?" Cala got to the point.

"Curiosity," replied Saginor.

"Official business?"

"No."

Cala and Franchina appeared to relax.

"You've no business in this area at all?"

"If we did, we'd have presented ourselves to the Prefect."

"How well do you know *Signora* Salvatore? You intervened on her behalf quite gallantly," Cala smiled tactfully.

"Correction, uh—*General*—Cala. It was Colonel Modica who intervened on her behalf. Not that we wouldn't have done the same for any woman given such shabby treatment by your men and all the ravenous reporters who clawed at her like vultures."

"Then it was merely an act of chivalry?" asked the Colonel tapping the tips of his fingers together, tentatively.

"That's what it's called? Funny you Italians get credited with chivalry. In America our women think we are grossly lacking in these graces." Saginor winked at his companions, both of whom refrained from winking back, uncertain where his impudence would lead.

"I hope you understand, uh—*Captain*—Saginor," said Cala clearing his throat apologetically. "There was no time for gallant behavior that day."

Sonofabitch, thought Saginor, *catching the reference to his past, the bastard probably knows the last time I took a healthy crap. Oooooh Kaaaay! He called me Captain!* From this Saginor deduced that Cala knew all about them.

"None of us has enjoyed a good night's sleep since the FSB was formed," continued Cala. "That loathsome bandit led us a merry chase. Our efforts finally ended his tyranny. The books are closed, once and for all. It's over," said Cala making his point.

"Over?" Saginor mocked scornfully. "It's only just begun—hasn't it?"

Bellomo and Salina angled their heads sharply towards Saginor. *Goddammit!* that Salina. *He's had too much to drink.* Bellomo cursed softly and inclined his head in disgust. As if there weren't enough problems already. Damn!

"What do you mean?" asked Franchina, rising to his feet. His craggy face was swollen with anger and he didn't give a damn if it showed. "Explain yourself, *Signore!*"

"Uh—what my associate means," interrupted Len Salina, shaken by Saginor's impertinence, "is that the difference between the way you perform the anatomy of a murder

. . . uh, death . . . uh, slaying, is, if you will, so diverse from our methods that your work appears to begin where ours would have already ended "

"Is that so?" Colonel Cala regarded Saginor with interest. "Since when do American agents with the State department concern themselves in the anatomy of murders, deaths, *or* slayings," he asked under a mask of polite affability.

"You'd be surprised, Colonel at the things we State Department ogres get involved in from time to time. . . ." Saginor beamed syrupy smiles at them.

Bellomo intervened. "Colonel Cala, We came only in curiosity, to examine the methods used by your law enforcement agencies. We've no personal interest in Salvatore. That *is* the reason for your questioning?" He wanted to get the hell out of town before irreparable damage had been done. As it was, they had stayed too long, said too much. . . .

"Oh come now, Renzo," Saginor smiled indulgently. "We wouldn't be hospitable if we didn't give the *General* and the *Major,* here, the benefit of some advanced techniques. Now, would we boy?"

Saginor had some balls! Here in Sicily where a man's life wasn't worth the clothing he wore, anything could happen, thought Salina. Renzo consoled himself with the thought: *they wouldn't kill Americans—would they?*

Saginor began his litany. Drunk, his accent thickened. His friends slunk down into their chairs, like whipped puppies.

"Well, sir, take the position of the body. Yes, that's as good a place to begin." He talked for several moments, pointing up all the weak spots and distortions and pitfalls. He directed his remarks more to Captain Franchina than to Cala. "You said Salvatore fired fifty rounds or more? Man, I looked and looked, and I couldn't find a bullet rupture in those walls, except in the southwest corner of the courtyard. But take the wounds of the deceased." He shook his head and clucked his tongue against his teeth. "That Salvatore must have been one super human being, to maintain such an unusual blood supply. More than two, perhaps even three types of blood poured from his veins and arteries, all with contrary properties of coagulation. Now, where we all come from, a man has only one kind of blood—red! But on Salvatore—man ,oh, man!—I saw red, purple, blue, some dried and caked and some bright crimson. . . ." His voice rose and fell in west Texas cadences.

78

Colonel Cala had paled to the color of paste. Captain Franchina's face had reddened deeply and his moustache twitched nervously. His eyes darkened with a scowl. "You were able to determine all that in a superficial examination?" he asked icily.

"I doubt the layman could discern the inconsistencies. But, you see, we're all experts. Well trained."

Some of the deathly pallor lessened on the Colonel's face. He recovered fully and grimaced distastefully. "You're drunk! Wine loosens the tongue. Sober, you wouldn't have the guts to fart in our presence. But since this is pure conjecture and since you seem to feel the need for catharsis, go on, if it suits your nature. You might provide us with enough imagination to convert this into a fairytale to tell our grandchildren on a rainy night."

Compelled to pause, Saginor wished he could tell them how he *really* felt. Sickened at the sight of such men, who simply followed orders and had no guts to speak the truth, he felt the trials at Nuremburg should have taught such men a lesson about executing orders for which they might have to answer. He made an instant transition, affecting a shyness, a rush of modesty. "I don't wanna appear presumptuous."

"I find your theory profoundly provocative. That's what it is, isn't it? A theory?" Colonel Cala's polite inquiry had an edge to it, now.

"Nope!" Saginor's brow wrinkled almost as apologetically as Cala's. Franchina considered Cala had lost his senses to pursue this. Bellomo groaned inwardly, and Salina inclined his head, to one side and propped it into his hand.

"If you insist, Colonel. But only because you insist. You take the deceased's skin tone. The degree of *rigor mortis*. We feel Salvatore was dead long before the alleged confrontation took place. With all due respects to your contrived story," he told Franchina.

Bellomo felt sick. His features suffused with mortification and dread. Salina paled and remained speechless. Captain Franchina seemed turned to stone, a look of offended dignity frozen on his face. Colonel Cala stared intently at Saginor, testing his many years experience against the brassy American.

"Then, there was the question of so much ice. When does a freshly-killed body have to be packed in so much ice? Not as soon as you did to Salvatore, if he was dead at 4 A.M. that morning. . . ."

"You've gone too far!" Franchina kicked back his chair.

79

With burning rage and humiliation, he turned to face his superior officer. "How dare he suggest that I'm falsely proclaiming to the world to be . . . It's too much! This is too much! To take these insufferable comments from a—"

"I'm sure you misunderstood my good friend, Captain Franchina," interrupted the cold and formal voice of Stefano Modica as he entered the room. He turned to Saginor. "Matt. Apologize, instantly!" he ordered.

All heads turned to him. The Americans breathed in relief. Saginor affected to be crestfallen. "Apologize? For an educated opinion?" He walked to Franchina and jabbed him playfully in the ribs. "I could be wrong, but I'm not. Am I? Between us cops, I'm not wrong, eh?"

Captain Franchina pushed Saginor's hand aside as if it were contaminated. "Colonel Cala! I demand an immediate apology from this foreigner. . . ."

"Matt! This has gone far enough." Modica, appearing strained, addressed himself to Colonel Cala. "I regret my associate has seen fit to be utterly thoughtless. Totally without sense and decorum. To intrude upon a matter of no concern to us is appalling to me. I can't apologize enough, Colonel."

Matt Saginor spun around and studied Modica askance. Was this the same man who had promoted eyeball confrontations with the voracious General Patton? Bellomo and Salina breathed easier. Saginor sulked.

"We've all been drinking a bit too much, sir," apologized Salina.

Modica nodded to Bellomo, who began to guide Saginor out the door.

"He meant no disrespect," said Modica, slipping a pair of binoculars around his neck.

"Oh, yes I did!" shouted Saginor. "You goddamn well betcha I did." He shrugged off Bellomo's restraining arm, adjusted his seersucker jacket, and, mustering a bit of dignity, he walked towards Captain Franchina. A moment's reflection might have saved Saginor from committing his greatest folly. But he didn't reflect. He reached into his pocket and handed the Captain the linen-wrapped hypodermic. "A parting gift. Just for you—*Major!*" Saginor was elated and exquisitely amused at the menace he saw in the other's face, as he wagged the object under the other's nose.

At a quick nod from Modica, Len Salina and Renzo Bellomo moved in. Saginor felt both arms in a vise-like grip as he was lifted bodily off the floor and whisked out the room, his toes barely touching the floor. Saginor turned his head back toward Franchina, eyed him reprovingly and clucked his tongue at him. He broke free of one arm and wagged his fingers reprovingly at the FSB officer.

The Americans left with the echo of Saginor's zany laughter ringing through the halls of the old building.

"He's crazy! That sonofabitch is crazy!" shouted Franchina with blood-engorged veins pulsing over each temple. He opened the linen square and stared dumbly at the bloodied hypodermic syringe. A red flush crept up his neck into his face.

"No, he's not crazy," said Colonel Cala simply. "How can a man be crazy when he speaks the truth?" He leaned wearily back in his chair and glanced up at the thunderstruck figure of his captain. "What's wrong? What do you have there?" He leaned forward and glanced into Franchina's outstretched hand. When he saw the syringe, he sat back in his chair heavily, as if the life had been drained from him. He shook his head and his eyes grew maniacal.

"Colonel! This is no time to show weakness. No time for second thoughts! We're in this up to our necks and you sit there moralizing. We had no other choice!" insisted Franchina.

"It's beginning to appear that Salvatore reigns supreme even from the grave. . . ." reflected Cala.

"*Va! Va!* Don't hand me that shit. He's dead! What does it matter how he died?" stormed Franchina tossing the syringe on the desk angrily.

"Salvatore was right, after all. I'm the scapegoat, just as he told me I'd be. Why didn't I leave well enough alone?"

"You know why! We'd have been left holding the bag. Belasci would have made *cafone* of us. We followed *your* plans, didn't we?"

"And *your* suggestions," countered Cala.

"Still, we took orders. We have no reason to fear. Our superior, the Minister of the Interior, commanded us and we obeyed!"

They stared at each other in a grim silence.

"Why? Why are we talking to each other like this? Some stupid meddling American dared to insinuate. . . ."

"*Basta! Basta!*" interrupted the Colonel. "You and I know the truth! Don't try to convince me of your innocence, nor of your notion that the American is stupid! He's not. The blood of Salvatore is on *our* hands—not because we're guilty of his death, but because we insisted on taking credit for it! Belasci must be told of this incident so he can control it from Rome." Cala was all business. "Now, we'd better get on to the mortuary. Someone signed the necessary papers for Salvatore's mother to claim his body and I, for one, want to know who dared defy our authority!" snapped the FSB Chief. He was unusually upset. His usual calm had evaporated.

"You stupid bastard! What the fuck's wrong with you? If you think nothing of your own neck, you could have considered Len's and Renzo's," admonished Stefano Modica, trying to contain a smile.

Renzo drove at breakneck speed until the Fiat sputtered and wheezed.

"Sorry," grinned Matt. "Couldn't resist it." He sipped from a container of black coffee they had insisted on to sober him up. "You don't know the half of it, Steve. You should have been there to hear what I told him . . . ugh, this coffee is awful! Goddamnit! You trying to poison me? . . . Hey, did you get a good look at Franchina's face when I gave him the syringe?"

"Yeah, sure—hero—at the expense of our fucking lives!" smirked Salina bitterly.

"What syringe? What's he talking about?" asked Stefano Modica.

The men explained their findings, Renzo's theory, and all that had transpired in Stefano's absence, while Modica sat in an attitude of remote contemplation. Antigone Salvatore's words began to make sense, he thought as he listened.

Stefano Modica had come away from the Salvatore house with dynamite in his possession—the personal portfolios of Alessandro Salvatore. Bound by his solemn promise not to share his findings nor his plans with another soul. Modica had, as a matter of wise judgement, stopped off in Palermo to pack and mail the explosive material including the ORS file to Gina O'Hoolihan in the USA. He had also sent her a wire. Simple and direct, he hoped it would explain his failure: *"I could have taken on any power—even God's—but never destiny. Package to follow. Keep safe for me."* It was signed, Steve."

"Pull that shit again, Matt, and I swear I'll put in for a transfer! I hate to think what's waiting for us in Rome!" yelled Renzo Bellomo, piercing Modica's thoughts.

"Aw, go to hell!" mumbled Saginor. He felt awful. The heat, the alcohol, and the criticism filled him with nausea. Coffee hadn't helped. Low laughter formed deep in his throat and he smiled mischeviously. "What I'd give to wire those two FSB's for sound. They sweat bullets up there. Their skins blistered under the strain of my words. . . ."

Renzo impatiently sounded the horn on the rented Fiat. Milling traffic had thickly congested the area of the mortuary, next to the *camposanto*. "Bastards! *Avanti! Avanti!*" he shouted to the pedestrians who blocked their way.

Absorbed with angry thoughts over Saginor's outrageous behavior, the agents had forgotten about Modica's prolonged absence. Grateful for the diversion and knowing he'd found the means to be evasive, Stefano glanced out the car window, wondering at the milling crowds.

"Can't you go faster, Renzo?" He prodded impatiently.

"There's a bottleneck up ahead . . . packed with people. . . ."

Saginor stuck his head out the window, shaded his eyes, and peered about the area. Bellomo sat on the horn. The raucous sounds made no dent in the converging masses up ahead. They could feel the electric vibrations in the sultry air.

"Kill the motor," ordered Modica. "We aren't moving. Might as well park it, and we'll walk to the mortuary up ahead. Something's happening."

Bellomo complied instantly. He locked the car and left it standing and followed the others who'd begun to carve a path through the congestion. The Americans glanced at either side of them as they snaked forward. Lines of people having spilled off the road had fanned out into the open fields for as far as Modica could see. It was impossible not to sense that something exceptional was about to happen. On the faces of the people were fixed expressions of reverence or awed superstition. Men reverently uncovered their heads. Shawled women knelt on both knees. They blinked their eyes from time to time, muttering incoherent prayers and rocking to and fro. Brown fingers formed the sign of the cross in vigorous repetition, their words gibberish, unintelligible.

The whole thing began to resemble a giant pilgrimage as people chanted indiscernible mantras, but every now and then the word *Salvatore* was clear and audible.

Modica's point of focus was directed to the top of a grassy hill, ringed a quarter of the way up by marble headstones of the cemetery opposite the marble halls in which Salvatore's body lay in repose.

Outlined against a fiery blue sky, there stood a magnificent, riderless snow-white Arabian stallion, adorned with a black leather saddle studded with a profusion of silver ornaments which splintered in the blazing light into myriads of brilliant colors, so bright in the sunshine that people were forced to avert their gaze from time to time.

From the saddle dangled a pair of shiny black boots. It was an electrifying scene, and a moving one

"What's going on?" Salina asked of a genuflecting peasant. "What is it? What's happening?" He received no answer he could make out.

"Follow me," said Saginor, gazing at the strange reaction at either side of him as he followed Modica through the mob. "I don't know what the hell's going on."

"Paesano," Bellomo asked of an elderly man. *'Che c'e?* What's happening?" He slipped several lire into the man's trembling hands.

Tugging off his beaked cap, white hair standing on end like snowy pine needles, the old man crossed himself religiously time and again.

"The Spirit of Salvatore! The spirit of Salvatore and his Napoleono!"

They all heard. Instantly the Americans turned their attention on the spectacular sight of the stallion standing in an attitude of uncertainty on the hill. They watched with mixed emotions for several moments, then wound their way through to the mortuary in full view of the spectacle, leaving behind them hordes of supplicating Sicilians.

Several squads of *carabinieri,* ordered to disperse the immovable hordes, gave up and watched, in open-mouthed fascination, the awesome sight and its effect on the masses.

"What's going on out there?" shouted Captain Franchina, emerging from the mortuary. "What's the trouble?" he asked the guards, who pointed to the scene at the top of the hill. Shading his eyes, Franchina peered at the proud and stately stallion, whose arched tail and long silky mane fluttered slightly in the breeze.

"Looks like Salvatore's ghost has returned to haunt you, eh, Captain," needled Matt Saginor standing a few feet away, unable to resist the urge.

Bellomo and Salina groaned internally and gave Modica a helpless look.

Livid with rage, Captain Franchina bridled indignantly and scowled at him. "You six men," he called to a squad of *carabinieri.* "Go up there and bring that damned animal down to me!"

Shuffling awkwardly on the pebbled walkway, the men individually resisted his command and glanced uneasily at each other, each reluctant to be the first to move Unsure of what was happening, they obeyed the instinct which told them not to budge. Enraged at their insubordination, Franchina, frustrated, snorted like a charging bull.

"Sniveling cowards! Understand this, you're on report!

Very well, then, come with me! I'll fetch him!" He called to another squad. "You six men over there. and you six here, all of you accompany me!"

Flanked on either side of the Captain, a total of twelve men moved in a body across the narrow road, past the courtyard, beyond the tricolor flag of Sicily set on a standard at the center of the compound.

"*Avanti! Avanti!*" shouted Captain Franchina as they began the ascent past the gravesites and the wooded area onto the denuded breast of the hill.

Modica, in adjusting his binoculars, observed the activity of the reluctant soldiers without comment. He raised the powerful lenses to his eyes, focusing on the stallion. He saw candy-glazed eyes of ebony flaring instinctively at the approaching strangers. The stallion's powerful head angled sharply in a nearly human response as he warily watched these uniformed men. Suddenly he reared on his hind legs, his velvet-pink nostrils pulsating as he clawed the air with his forepaws. He whinnied. flinging his head from side to side, snorting several times as if he sensed these enemies.

Light refractions bouncing off the glittering silver saddle momentarily blinded the advancing officers, obliging them to shade their eyes.

Forced at one point to avert his head from the glaring brightness, Captain Franchina lost his footing on the rocky terrain, stumbled. slipped back and fell several yards, rolling down the hill, landing with a hard fall against a marble headstone, totally disheveled, in what was perhaps the luckiest fall in his life.

One *carabiniero* braver than the others, cooed to the stallion who had resumed his original, silent and unmoving pose. His arms outstretched, the officer moved in closer, beckoning the animal. *Napoleono* eyed him hesitantly. Reaching him at last, the *carabiniero* triumphantly grasped the reins firmly, pulling the animal towards him.

Suddenly, the earth exploded! The booby-trapped stallion and twelve *carabinieri* shot up into the air, to the accompament of loud explosions!

CHAPTER 7

Stunned! The American agents were stunned when, with the setting of the sun on July 10, blistering orders arrived from the American Embassy, demanding the immediate return of the agents to Yankee soil. The very network of the Christian Democratic Party had been visibly shaken by their findings in Castelvetrano, and the lives of the American agents, now worth less than the price of a shoestring, had to be protected to avert an international incident.

The next several months brought about a series of events explicable only to those deeply involved in the matter of Salvatore. Major Franchina accepted with pompous affectation the quasi-martyrdom accorded him by the loss of one arm, together with the national acclaim as a hero who had brought about the demise of Salvatore, thus hopefully ending banditry in Sicily.

General Cala, with modest reservations, showered consolation upon the convalescing Major and both men basked in the glorious limelight afforded them by a grateful Premier de Aspanu and fawning Minister Belasci who demanded, with his usual panache, the need to bask in the spotlight alongside his victorious officers of the Forces to Suppress Banditry. He made what he hoped would be his final words in the Salvatore matter: *". . . I fully confirm the version of Salvatore's death as reported by General Cala and Major Franchina, and can state with authority there was no conspiracy involved in the bandit's death other than routine business expended in the normal course of FSB operations. Once again, it is the profound wish of Premier de Aspanu and myself that the people of this great nation put Salvatore behind us and allow us to move forward to more important business. . . ."*

In the United States, things moved swiftly for the agents. Following time for proper indoctrination, Bellomo, Salina and Saginor were transferred to Japan, where it had been learned that American currency was being counterfeited in abnormal sums. Stefano Modica, greatly distressed by both the course and coincidence of events, grew incensed and more introverted over the dastardly affair. However, both Bellomo and Salina, well aware of how close they had come to giving up the ghost, welcomed the transfer, feeling safe only when they heard the reassuring sounds of Japanese music and Geisha girls.

Matt Saginor, taking transfer in his stride and accepting his new role with vigor and daring, paid little attention to those dark and sinister shadows accompanying him wherever he went. If he had, he might have been spared the agony of a bloody and gory death meted him while relaxing in the indolent luxury of a geisha house. So that his death would be recognized for exactly what it was—a silent warning to others—Saginor, slaughtered by means of a butchering knife thrust into the jugular by unknown assailants, was found floating in a bath of crimson, his face blown off by a shotgun. At the far end of a carmine pool, a portion of his face, upon which had been placed a dead, withered hummingbird, was found adrift, affixed to a slab of cork.

But, on August 28, months before this atrocity took place, Stefano Modica's disillusionment with the State Department had reached the breaking point. Having sent his letter of resignation four days before, he sat, sober, suspicious and hard eyed, in the air-conditioned halls of the State Department in Washington D.C., waiting to be heard, at a meeting of the National Security Council advisory board, by the very men who'd given birth to his functions with the bureau.

Their quick departure from Rome—shuttled off like criminals—and the swift transfer of his men out of his jurisdiction had thoroughly rankled Modica. In addition to the countless unanswered questions plaguing him, there lay deeply imbedded in his mind the remotest possibility that he'd been done in by his own government. God knew how he tried to dispell such nagging thoughts, how he fought to reject them from mind. Why would his own country be a party to such fraud? he asked himself. He knew he'd done his best in the Salvatore matter, yet something had come apart. What? How? Where? Each time he dissected every step of his involvement, he came up blank. Modica was about to learn he had overlooked the most obvious factors in the appalling treachery.

"Colonel Modica?" Summoned by a nattily-dressed page, Modica nodded, picked up his briefcase, and followed him into an oval-shaped room where twelve men sat comfortably around a mirror-polished oaken conference table against a stately decor of Colonial stuffiness. Tight-lipped, Modica seated himself at the end of the table, barely acknowledging the others.

Two hours later, Modica, ready to commit murder, emerged from the room, revolted by what he'd heard and incited to the point of madness. In all his life, he'd never come as close to doing physical violence as he had while seated in that austere office, where everything dovetailed and added up to a stinking mess of political immorality, with himself—him, Stefano Modica—at the center of the contemptible betrayal of Salvatore.

Washington, D.C. sweltered in the stifling August heat wave. Yet Modica, seated in his broiling apartment, killing off the best part of a pinchbottle, felt nothing except the dull uncertainty that he'd been sold out by his own government. Nothing, not their words, the scotch, or his own attempts to minimize the situation eased his pain or re-moved the guilt. Yes, he thought, that's what it was—guilt. His personal guilt in the Salvatore matter would never be assuaged, and he might have to live forever under its strangling weight. Stretched out on the sofa, he chain-smoked and watched the disintegrating rings drift off into nothingness as he reflected on the previous few hours—two and a half hours he'd never forget.

Earlier, Richard Bixby, an obnoxious, self-righteous, prissy-assed Presidential aide, had attempted to explain the vast complexities of international politics. Even the Council, in refusing to accept Modica's resignation, had told him, "Reconsider. Take a long rest. Gain a new per-spective. Then reassess your position."

Modica, no fool, sensed their rejection. Most of the consortium had resented his appointment because he was commonly referred to as a "hyphenated American of Italian descent." Before the war the bigotry had been in-calculable. But since so many sons of Italian parentage had fought for America and returned as heroes, these WASPs couldn't be as obvious in their hatred of Italians as they had in the past. However, in their sly, subversive and covert ways, they nipped any promising political careers in the bud if the aspirant was of the Italian-Ameri-can persuasion.

He paid little heed to their false expressions of florid patriotism; he knew all of them too well, with their empty chatter and redundant rhetoric. But as they spoke, and while Stefano listened, there began to form between the lines a hidden message, which at first he rejected as ridiculous, unfounded and without basis. They offered him scraps in appeasement, and he saw through them.

When it came together in Modica's mind, a wave of shock swept through him. Yet, there it was—proof to corroborate his deepest suspicion. He, Stefano Modica, had been set up in the Salvatore matter! Salvatore's planned expatriation had been a sham! Uncle Sam's protective umbrella had collapsed under a hailstorm of betrayals that led from the Italian High Command to the White House and that had ended with Stefano buried neck-deep in the putrefaction of their corrupt seduction.

The way Modica figured it, even *Operation Red Star* had been a sham! Tremendous interest in the de Aspanu-Belasci-Christian Democratic Party had been heightened in the past two years, especially since the war. American Ambassador J. H. Steele had been keeping the White House and certain Wall Street interests well informed on the internal business affairs and growing conditions in Italy. Modica's costly file on ORS confirmed his government's apathy in the matter; their reluctance to take necessary action to retard the cancerous spread of graft in Italy was indicative that some—or many—were profiting enormously . . . and the trail of bloody dollars led directly to the White House.

There was more. Stefano asked himself, what could possibly be the interrelationship of these various far-flung interests? Viewing it internally, Modica could see the emblem of the Christian Democrats, the cross itself, standing upright with the Presidential seal atop it; upon it, in his mind's eye, was superimposed the American dollar sign. The shadow of this ignominious cross fell across a bloody background of stinking politics and insatiable ambitions, beneath which had been buried, in hopeless obscurity, the seven-year reign of Salvatore.

The appalling, manipulative chain linked Ambassador Steele to the President; the President to Wall Street; and Wall Street to de Aspanu, Belasci and the papacy. The last three would insure the nation would remain in capitalistic hands, where Wall Street would find Welcome mats spread over the wealth of Sicily. A capitalistic nation had no use for the rebel Salvatore. He had served his purpose. All their loyalties to him had ceased. As the only link left to their bloody misdeeds, Salvatore had become expendable. Bloodstained hands of the government officials had been scrubbed lily white, leaving no trace of their gross misdeeds.

But Salvatore, that enigma of redoubtable power, hadn't

been an easy mark. Three thousand soldiers, sent to liquidate him, had failed. What was left for these trembling, ambitious politicians? If they convinced him to expatriate and promised no further action against him and his mother, would Salvatore believe them? There had been so many false promises. . . . But . . . suppose a skilled agent of a cooperating government, sworn to uphold his duties for the glory of his country, a man with a stellar background, and one who could be trusted in such circumstances, could be found? And suppose this man was the only man whom Salvatore would trust? What then? Only one such man would fit the bill—one man, whom the outlaw Salvatore would trust, Stefano Modica! *Colonnello Stefano Modica!*

What a fool he'd been not to recognize this at the outset! With Salvatore out of the way there'd be no further threat to the Christian Democrats. No further strife and complications for these sanguinary and overly-ambitious vipers. Having created Salvatore, their monster, they now had an obligation to remove him from their midst.

But how, if everything else had failed? Of course, with the cooperation of a powerful and protective nation, how could they lose? They didn't. Biding their time, they moved decisively, using Stefano as their pawn.

Within this sphere of machinations, when it was learned that Modica had conceived the lofty ambition of secreting Salvatore out of Sicily, there arrived through another arm of the National Security Council, unknown to Modica, information that certain foreign diplomats sought the annihilation of Salvatore. Certain officials, then, arranged for both ideas to flower simultaneously, yet, out of necessity, to remain independent of each other. In mid-May, red tape suddenly swept aside, Modica was permitted license to set his plans in action.

"Bastards!" cursed Stefano jumping to his feet and pacing the floor in a sorry limp. "I should have known! I should have guessed when things moved ahead so swiftly," he said aloud as if to convince himself. He had killed off the rest of the pinchbottle, and, reaching for a fresh one from his back bar, he peeled off the foil, lifted the snap spring of the tightly fitting cap, and poured himself a stiff shot without ice. He gulped it down, made a wry face, and continued to whip himself for the next few hours. His subjective involvement had precluded his second-guessing the real reasons behind the abnormal velocity with which the operation moved in mid-May.

Well, there it was. Modica, fall guy personified, had

been had! In a life filled with uncertainties, rotten politics, death and the dangers of war, even the loss of his leg hadn't made him feel as impotent as he had in that moment of truth when, earlier, he had faced Bixby and the other devils of deception. Modica had been admonished by Bixby when he clearly indicated his gross displeasure at having become an unwitting ploy to entrap an old and trusted friend, and at the dangers to which he and his co-agents had been subjected. He could still hear that insufferable dolt's stinging words: "What does the life of one man matter when the security of our grand and glorious nation is at stake?"

Modica, unable to contain his anger, had countered savagely," Would you be so charitable if your life was the one to be expended?"

He'd listened to these State Department ghouls with a sense of death hovering over him. Arguments, offered as balm to soothe his fierce reactions of shame and humiliation, had only increased his agony. None of the flimsy, glossed-over cliches or patriotic euphuisms compensated for the terrible loss he felt. Judas Iscariot would have hanged himself on the first available tree instead of delaying the act as long as he had, if he felt what Stefano felt in those moments.

Very well. He'd been the Judas goat! But it hadn't ended. Modica would have his victory. It might only be a microdot of victory, overshadowed by the unwarranted death of Salvatore. Nevertheless, it would be a victory to show these supercilious whoremasters, wrapped in their cloaks of respectability, that they couldn't continue to manipulate and expend human lives for their own self-serving purposes. Stefano Modica had promised himself such a victory when he had addressed the twelve-man council brass earlier.

"You have my resignation, gentlemen," he'd said. "Accept it. But before I go, I want you to know your deceit is transparent. You think I need explanations for the complex and diabolical manipulations of men in government who, in their god-like superiority, snuff out lives needlessly, bury their heroes in disgrace, and hail with hallelujahs the vicious criminals in their midst? The shroud of political expediency and ruse of government security no more deceive me than do the files stamped *confidential* or *top secret* when they in fact mark the cover-up for greed, graft and immorality prevailing among power-hungry, salacious and self-serving men in office—men whom an unsuspecting public place on pedestals next to gods!" Stefano had to catch his breath before he bombarded them with his wrath.

"I've seen it all, from the unique position I held—the power plays and mad struggles for supremacy when nation pitted against nation in the stinking cancer of war play corrupt games. But when my own nation takes part in such vile practices, knowing in advance the rules of the game have been rigged, and they condone wrongdoings—well, I grow appalled! I shan't be a party to such action. I refuse to serve a government for whom I feel disrespect!"

Reflecting bitterly as he left the conference room, he noticed several of the room's occupants were red-faced, speechless and sputtering with indignation. Those hard-nosed politicians might have suffered a momentary setback due to his caustic remarks, but Modica knew them all too well. Before he left the austere building those twelve men would clear their aristocratic throats, light fresh cigars or cigarettes, guzzle from bourbon-spiked water carafes and make recommendations for his replacement. He suffered no delusion that he'd be missed, or that the council would suffer from the loss of his expertise and experience.

Modica was unaware there was one exception amidst this covent of political ghouls—Roger Cutter. This man, who would one day be President and gain prominence as the most corrupt public official to hold public office of such magnitude, read the contents of Modica's file with profound interest. His beady eyes scanned the contents and held at the following passage:

Stephen Modica, L.L.B. Born Palo Alto, California. Educated: Stanford University. Entered U.S. Army in 1941, commissioned Captain. Transferred to Army Intelligence. Attached to Office of Strategic Services. Served under General George Patton in North Africa. . . .

Roger Cutter, an ambitious party man, briefly read the information dealing with Modica's OSS activities and those with the Allied Control Council. It was impressive, and his service record was outstanding. He'd been recipient of the Silver Star and Purple Heart and other high citations and recommendations. However, it was the medical reports compiled by Orthopedic, Neurosurgery and Psychiatric chiefs at Letterman General Hospital that caught his attention. These reports he read more critically:

Emotional trauma as result of BKA (Below knee amputation) considerable. Patient shows signs of acute depression. Extensive therapy, both physical and psychological, recommended."

He read a fourteen-month progress report indicating it had been slower than expected. Cutter's eyes stopped at the word, *Prognosis:* "Favorable if patient can be remotivated and guilt syndrome reduced."

Further notation indicated that all charts and X-rays had been transferred to one Bartholomew T. Baines, M.D. in Georgetown.

The man who'd one day become President smiled internally. Who'd believe the wild rantings of a former mental patient if he did elect to talk? He could be discredited by any neophyte lawyer. Half way through a self-satisfied smirk, Cutter gave a start. In his hand was a resumé: a subsidiary file on the *Operation Red Star* project. Included were the names of those men, both here and abroad, who had either promoted communism or fought against these forces during the wartime and postwar period. Cutter studied these names with undisguised interest. The far-reaching implications in these papers was enough to jolt him.

Always a wheeling-and-dealing man, Cutter wasn't about to miss an opportunity that could springboard him to national attention and public acclaim. Ambition dripped from his greedy jaws. Hadn't Dewey had his Tammany Hall and Lucky Luciano battles to elevate him to prominence? Why couldn't Cutter find his ladder to help him scale those slippery slopes to political fame? Buried in this file was enough ammunition to shoot down many potential competitors. *Goddamn!* As excitement mounted in the presidential aspirant, sweet visions of political persuasion winked out at him from that pregnant file in total seductiveness.

He pored through the file. Suddenly he tensed. There was enough in the file to send him into borderline shock! The extensive probe on the Italian affair revealed enough ammunition to hammerlock certain political enemies of his, all right. But, in addition, the file contained weaponry that could shoot him down as well, and deter his own progress. He mopped the beads of perspiration forming on his forehead, hoping the others wouldn't notice his discomfort. By damn! If this subsidiary file contained dynamite—what would the *original* contain? Roger Cutter didn't know how or when he could pull it off, but he had to have access to the original ORS file before it got into the wrong hands. With the original tucked away into his private vault, he'd be free to drape himself in saintly robes and impart his knowledge and guidance to the man who'd next occupy the presidential office. Time now to collect on a large debt owed him by his Roman friends. Hadn't he just done them an immeasurable service? They'd get that file for him—or else!

On September 30th, after Modica had floundered about, infected by a growing depression, he leased an apartment in Sausalito, overlooking a colorful bay of sloops, yawls, yachts and other seaworthy craft in California waters. He joined the reputable law firm of Bally, Bowls, Baccardi and Schwartz hoping to bury himself in trials and the tribulation of others.

Nothing eased his conscience or removed the guilt he felt in the Salvatore affair. Nights spent in seclusion in the labored perusal and tedious translation of Salvatore's personal portfolios intensified Stefano's guilt feelings, Modica's continuous impression that he'd sent an unsuspecting victim into murky waters, where voracious *piranha* thrived, refused to abate.

On December 5, word of Saginor's brutal murder arrived. Confusion swirled around Stefano like black storm clouds. Uncontrollable outrage and a venomous anger took possession of him and Modica felt waves of insanity engulf him as his self-assigned guilt multiplied. The death of two friends worked on his conscience to drive him like a powerful dynamo. Unconsciously there began to form in his mind a plan, one of which he wasn't fully aware and wouldn't be for a while.

Driven by that inescapable urge that grips a man of conscience, a man who finds life intolerable until he makes amends, he took time to have the Salvatore portfolios microfilmed. These he placed in a bank vault along with the original manuscripts, retaining the transcribed copies for himself. On the previous advice of Antigone Salvatore, he'd written letters to specific people, taking the precaution to cover his actual whereabouts. Answers to these inquiries began to arrive periodically.

Shortly before Christmas Stefano knew what he had to do, and presented his empty-sounding excuses of resignation to Bally, Bowls, Baccardi and Schwartz. His special knowledge helped him acquire the necessary passports and IDs for the new identity he intended to assume. No shelter of diplomatic immunity would protect him if he were found out. The risks were immense; the reward—his sanity. For security he held fast to the ORS file. It received the same treatment as had Tori's portfolios.

Modica reasoned that the clandestine operation to smuggle Salvatore out of Sicily had failed. Very well, his next move was to make certain Italian officials hadn't learned who authored the script. At top-level priority, it would be no problem for them to obtain the information. He had to work fast.

He contacted a loyal friend in the Bureau in Washington, asking him to pull the Salvatore file and delete his names from any portion of the operational proposal. A few days later Stefano got his reply. His friend was unable to comply with the request, due to the fact the entire file was missing. Despite the ramifications and complications this discovery presented, Stefano forged ahead with his plans. In response to an inner compulsion he could no longer ignore, he returned to Italy to learn more about Salvatore's involvements. The jaws of deception, firmly locked on its prey, had to one day open and release its victim. Then, the truth would out, Modica reasoned. He planned to be there when it happened.

He was, and it did—up to a point.

CHAPTER 8

Viterbo, Italy

This medieval village north of Rome, once the home of Popes, now the judicial seat of a military tribunal where the trial of *People vs. Assassins of Portella Della Rosa* was in progress, rocked with the latest development in the Salvatore affair.

On December 5, 1950, six months to the day after Salvatore's demise, Vincenzo de Montana, first cousin, blood brother, and former co-captain to the bandit, shocked an entire nation of citizens and police officials by surrendering himself into custody. A month later on January 7, 1951, banner headlines appeared in every major newspaper in the nation, above this astonishing text:

"I, Vincenzo de Montana, assassinated Salvatore in his sleep. This act was done by personal ar-

rangement with the Minister of the Interior, Martino Belasci, in the government of Premier de Aspanu."

Was that all there was? wondered Modica as he read the news account. Was it purely and simply a matter of betrayal by his most trusted companion—his blood relative? Modica was baffled. Viewed without its fullest implications, it was a statement of simple betrayal. Examined against a background of political intrigue among crafty Sicilian mentalities it carried ominous and serious implications.

If it were taken at face value as a true statement, Vincenzo de Montana had just signed his own death warrant. Unwittingly he had slipped into the same position held by Salvatore before his questionable demise. Why? Now why would de Montana kiss his life away?

Three months later in March 1951, Stefano saw Vincenzo de Montana enter the courtroom for the first time, where he remained under a gag order imposed by the Tribunal, restraining him from speaking. As he studied the handsome young man, Stefano still wondered why. Why had he put himself into so vulnerable a position? He'd have to wait and see it out.

The daily excitement of personality clashes between tribunal magistrates and the battery of lawyers fighting for their clients stretched into tedious, repititious testimony, encased in reams of denials and accusations bordering upon boredom. The dull testimony, moving at the pace of a tortoise, wore at him and Modica began questioning his sanity at coming to Viterbo. It began to appear that the truth would never be told.

In August 1951, Modica returned to San Francisco on pressing business. When he returned Viterbo was in festival. The Santa Rosa *festa* had attracted thousands of tourists in addition to the galaxy of news reporters who attended the trial. Since they had appropriated every available hotel room in the ancient city, Stefano was forced to seek lodgings at the Villa Etruria, at the outskirts of the city, where he remained until the trial's end in October. Countless times he had considered interviewing Vincenzo, but to do so would blow his cover and expose him to unnecessary dangers.

Modica slept badly on the night after the trial ended. Early next morning, before dawn, he ordered breakfast sent to his room as he packed and prepared the next leg of his journey. He'd shaved, showered, and rubbed soothing ointment on his knee stump before slipping it into his artificial limb. Built into the prosthesis was a small compartment containing his real ID and a small firearm, a single-shot derringer, used in WW II by the OSS. He checked the firearm, replaced it, and finished dressing. He wore beige khakis with a short sleeved bush jacket. A wide brimmed Aussie-style hat with a leopard band lay on a nearby chair.

Bags packed, ready for departure, Stefano waited for his breakfast. He moved across the room, flung open the French doors, and inhaled the fragrant aromas of the sweet-smelling countryside as he walked into the patio. His azure eyes veiled in thought. Something in addition to the trial results nagged at Stefano and provoked his decision to meet with Antigone Salvatore before leaving Europe. The only way of saving the remaining bandits, including de Montana, from the kangaroo-court edicts which sentenced them all to life at hard labor was to persuade the *Signora* to permit him to publish Salvatore's portfolios before the time previously agreed upon.

There was more. Modica was troubled by something more personal. Experience in clandestine operations had conditioned him to know instinctively when he was under surveillance. Certain that Minister Belasci had recognized him one day in court when their eyes locked, Modica knew there'd be a tail on him sooner or later. It came sooner than expected. Immediately following the tragic and mysterious death of *Principessa* Gabriella Rothschild, proprietress of the Villa Etruria, an incident which left him shaken, he began to experience the familiar feeling of being watched. He had expended considerable caution to avoid bringing attention to himself. He wore dark glasses wrapped around his eyes and dressed in the garb of a local citizen. He'd even adopted several ethnic mannerisms. In court he remained in the background, swallowed up by the hordes, as he attempted to take notes in his high-school shorthand. Nightly, in the confines of his hotel room, he'd transcribe his notes and mail them the next day to a post office box in northern California.

Three weeks before, the faces of two strangers had appeared at the Villa Etruria. Was it coincidence they kept the same hours he did? That they entered the dining salon when he did, and left when he did? From time to time he had spotted one or both men in the previously deserted courtyard, under a domed archway or behind a stately pillar. It had occurred to Modica he might be overly sensitive, so he'd pushed them out of his mind for a time.

One day, after court, he had stopped at his favorite tobacco kiosk. The sight of their faces peering into the shop window had filled him with annoyance. He'd remained in the city that night, taking dinner at Zia Giulia's on the Via Tuscanese. Was it coincidence that these swarty-faced brutes had also picked the same night to dine on spit-roasted game? Still coincidence when he'd seen them in court, never too far away, observing with increasing curiosity the notes he took? Stefano thought not. For him it had stopped resembling coincidence after the first four days. He'd taken precautions to avoid them and confuse them and, on several occasions, he'd gone out of his way to lose them in traffic. Only yesterday, after outfoxing his watchdogs, Stefano had managed to smuggle the last of his writings out of the villa and mail them safely back to the United States.

Why hadn't they approached him to make their business known? Under normal circumstances, Modica would have taken the offensive. Confronting them, he'd have extracted from them their reasons for tailing him. But, without a backup crew or an aide, it would have been suicidal for a BK amputee to jump the gun. He wasn't ready to kiss off his life—not yet.

Absorbed in these thoughts when a soft knock sounded at the door, Modica called from the patio, *"Avanti."* It would be the room steward with his breakfast. "Set the tray on the table, please," he called out in Italian. "I'll serve myself."

The instant he sensed his error and started to turn around, he felt his arms gripped in a vise-like grip. A black hood was slipped over his head. He struggled. A coarse hand chopped him across the nose. He heard the soft crunch of bones and a warm flow of blood as it gushed from his nose and ran down his lips and chin. Another hand struck a severe blow to his solar plexus, and he doubled over. A knee rammed into his groin. Modica felt little after that. A pressure exerted at a vulnerable point on his neck rendered him unconscious.

But Modica was lucky. He was still alive.

He heard voices, faded and tunneled. His eyes, speckled with blood clots across their whites, refused to focus, and he thought he was blind. His body ached excruciatingly in the hour it took a physician to motor in from Viterbo. Modica felt like he'd been crushed by one of General Patton's former Iron Ladies—those turreted, creeping crawlers of the desert that destroyed everything in their path. Uncertain of anything, Stefano slipped in and out of consciousness for several hours, unaware that silent eyes watched over him.

It was 4 P.M. before he regained consciousness. Trying to pierce the haze before his eyes until they focused, he felt the room spin beneath him. As focus returned to him, he could see his luggage ripped apart, its contents torn to shreds; the room lay in a state of wild disorder, a total shambles. His briefcase, picked clean, was damaged beyond use.

"*Signore*, are you all right?"

Modica recognized the voice. Now, if only he could see the blur standing over him. . . . Images blended into several before they formed one figure. He recognized *Avvocato* Luigi Basile, de Montana's lawyer.

"The entire hotel speaks of nothing save this disgraceful *infamita* done to an American citizen, *Signore*. How can we apologize for so deplorable an act done to you?" asked the dapper young lawyer, indicating his grave concern.

Stefano winced with pain and, trying to pull himself up to a sitting position unsuccessfully, fell back against the pillows, groaning with pain. His hands flew to his face. His nose, swollen beyond its size and magnified far more in his mind, dazed and distorted his perception, creating a problem in breathing.

"You'll be fine in a few days," consoled Basile. "No doubt you've suffered a broken nose. The doctor gave you morphine and left you several pain tablets. You're a fortunate man, *Signore*, lucky, as they say in your country."

"Yeah," muttered Stefano through pain-filled jaws. "Damned lucky."

Basile appeared superficial for several moments as he explained, "I was leaving for Rome when I was apprised of this calamitous and most regrettable affair. In good conscience, I couldn't leave until I assured myself you didn't need some assistance." He leveled his perceptive hazel eyes on the blue-eyed American; then, suddenly, dropped his defenses. "Look, who the hell are you, eh? What interest do you have in the trial—in my client, de Montana? Don't bother to deny it," he wagged a finger at the bedridden man. "I've seen you constantly for many months. Now, after all this, I'm more than curious."

Modica, silent and sullen, didn't reply.

Basile nodded his head tentatively; then he shook it, his teeth biting his lower lips contemplatively. "Was this

Belasci's handiwork?" he indicated the disordered room, Modica's.

"Belasci who?" asked Stefano superciliously.

Basile shook his head tolerantly. "All right, play your games. It's your life. I've instructed the local *questura* to post an officer at your door and afford you protection until you're well enough to leave. We Italians can't permit such reprehensible treatment to our American allies. Or is it Irish?"

"No! Stefano shouted, trying to raise himself again. "Send them away." He sank back on the pillows, prostrate with pain, his face reflecting his agony.

Avvocato Basile moved in swiftly, forcing him to stay down. "Is there anyone I can summon for you?" he asked with concern. He lit a cigarette and slipped it between Modica's lips. Stefano acknowledged it gratefully.

"I'll be fine." said Modica. "Thanks."

Basile glanced anxiously at his watch. "I'm due in Rome—overdue. Won't you reconsider talking to me about my client? I'll need all the help I can get if I'm to save Vincenzo's life before the next trial comes due."

"What makes you think I can be of help to you?" Modica tried not to be obvious. A thousand aches and pains shot through him, and he grimaced sharply.

Basile smiled enigmatically and paced the floor like a man driven by time. "Someone thinks you know too much to remain alive. You think they won't try again?" scoffed Basile. "By the looks of this place and your face, they nearly finished the job. What the hell were they after?" He regarded the disorder in silence. "Salvatore's personal portfolio—is that it?"

Modica feigned innocence. "What gives you the idea I had anything to do with Salvatore?"

Basile laughed good naturedly. "If you'd been on this case as long as I, you'd be paranoid. To enumerate a few curious entanglements, my office has been broken into, my wife and children threatened with bodily harm. I've even been offered a handsome bribe to abandon de Montana. Lately, I've come to maintain a stable of bodyguards. . . . Basile paused. "Speaking of bodyguards, I insist on the loan of two of my most trusted men, until you leave Italy—or at least until you can handle yourself." He stared at Stefano's game leg, prone on the bed. "You must be mad to engage in whatever you're engaging in without benefit of an aide—with *your* handicap. And I refuse to take no for an answer."

In the time *Avvocato* Basile left the room, Stefano

raised himself with great effort and retrieved the Derringer from his prosthesis. He slipped the small weapon under the coverlet at his side just as the dapper young lawyer re-entered the room in the company of two burly men built like Primo Carnera, with faces that contained a hundred different twisted curves and angles and deadly eyes that could send chills up your spine.

"Borsini and Morelli will remain with you until you no longer need their assistance," said Basile. He glanced at Modica's rumpled trousers—at the partially exposed prothesis—and a glimmer of distortion flickered in his eyes. "You've got guts, my friend."

Modica hardly heard the lawyer's words. His eyes were fastened on the man, Morelli. Morelli's black eyes, rounded to steel points, registered surprise when he recognized Modica. The man, Morelli, Colonel Modica's Italian aide during the war—an undercover agent, the same man whom he had met at Rome's airport and to whom he had entrusted the special job of delivering a letter to Salvatore on July 5, 1950—stood before him, staring in astonishment. Before Modica could signal him into silence, he blurted,

"*Colonnello* Modica! *Managghia*! It's you? What the hell have they done to you?"

Observing this new development through cautious and alert eyes, *Avvocato* Basile instructed his men to wait in the corridor for him. Alone he confronted the American.

"So!" exclaimed the lawyer. "It's not *Signore* O'Hoolihan, but *Colonnello* Modica. "Please explain the charades."

"Nothing to explain," said Modica evasively. "Very well," he added, noting the chagrined expression on Basile's face. "I'm using an alias for personal reasons."

"Suit yourself. I can either be a friend or your worst enemy," retorted Basile. "You think it will be difficult to inquire at the Embassy?"

Modica cocked an eyebrow. "I wish you wouldn't. I'm not here officially. If it's bandied about that I'm using an alias, my presence will be misconstrued."

"Then tell me, so I won't be prompted to jeopardize your position."

Modica wondered how far he could trust Basile. He'd seen the stuff the lawyer was made of in court. His style, fearlessness, and astute legal tactics had impressed Stefano. Despite this, there was always that old guarded instinct which precluded Stefano from babbling freely. Using the utmost discretion and speaking with measured words, he stated only that he'd met Salvatore during the war and had been taken with him; that his presence in Castelvetrano at the time of Salvatore's death was purely coincidental; and that his interest was only one of simple curiosity. The closest expression of truth were the feelings he imparted about the sham—and the attempted conspiracy to cover up the facts—that surrounded Salvatore's death.

Avvocato Basile, no fool, sensed the avoidance of truth. He smiled tightly. "Yet, you've attended the trial from the outset, *Signore?* Very well, will you answer at least one question? Do you believe de Montana killed his cousin?"

"You don't believe the admission of your own client?"

The lawyer gave him a look that could have meant anything. "If it's only Salvatore you knew, what brings you here? Why is your curiosity so stirred? You'll forgive me, but I feel compelled to ask this."

"I had hoped to uncover the mystery surrounding Salvatore's death. Perhaps one day I might write a story about the brigand's life. . . ."

"You intend to pursue such a goal—after all *this?*" Basile waved his arms in the air about him. It was too incredible to him.

"If anything, this demonstration has only reinforced my determination."

The lawyer rose to leave. "I wish you good fortune, *Colonnello*. Guts, you have in surplus. *Pero*—I would reassess my capacity for brains, if I were you. A man would have to be crazy to pursue the course you've embarked upon." They shook hands.

"Good luck in your coming trial, *Avvocato*," said Stefano. He reached into his shirt pocket. "Here's my card. One day in the near future, I might like to converse with you about your client. Presently my hands are tied." The morphine was taking its toll.

Basile took the card, glanced at it and raised his hazel eyes in surprise. "You're a lawyer, also?" He shook his head regretfully. "I'd have considered it an honor, Colonel, if you had approached me prior to this. We could have exchanged a few experiences . . . but I forget, you are here *incognito*. Well, again, accept the apology of a humiliated Italian at the treatment you have received in our country. I'd enjoy remaining here. Unfortunately, I am already late for many appointments in Rome. *Buona fortuna*—good luck, to you. *Ciao!*"

After Basile left, Stefano made an attempt to sit up. He could not. He sank back against the pillows and closed his eyes. For a time he wafted in and out of a drugged euphoria.

102

Only vaguely did he become aware of another presence. His sixth sense, forever at work, nudged him, and he blinked his eyes and focused on the shadowy form of Morelli.

"I am distressed to find you in such a state. Tell me what I can do to ease your pain, *Colonnello*." The former aide moved in closer to the bed.

"Ah, it's you, Morelli," sighed Stefano relaxing. "I'm tired, my friend. Exhausted. Done in. Good to see a friendly face, though." The drug haze thickened. "So many times I've tried to reach you. So many times. At least you saw him. At least that, eh? Did the 'brave eagle' say anything to you? Anything at all to indicate what might have happened?"

"Rest, *Colonnello*. Rest. *Allora*—it took many weeks to reach him. Such complications. Phew! Those Sicilians are too clever. They guarded him well. He said nothing to me. Nothing. I gave him your message. I delivered his reply to you in Rome, remember?

Stefano turned his face away from him and sighed once again. "He was so young, Morelli. So young. What a waste." He couldn't keep his eyes open.

"Si, *mi colonnello*. He was young."

"I tried to save him. You know I did." He fought the drug, unsuccessfully.

"Si. You tried."

Modica grimaced in pain. His eyes took on unusual bright lights. Feverishly he cried out, "You'll tell no one, Morelli. I have your word! You're the only link between Salvatore and me. I can't impress how vital your silence is in this case!" His words were slurring and his mouth turned cottony.

"I will say nothing, *mi colonnello*." Morelli moved in closer to the bed. His right hand moved forward to pat Stefano's lean shaking hands reassuringly. In his left hand, behind his back, he held a .45 with a silencer affixed to it. "You have my word, and, out of respect for our former alliance, my lips are sealed."

Stefano fixed his drug-dazed eyes on his former aide and blinked them several times. Something he saw reflected in those piercing black orbs coming closer to him made him slowly grope for the gun beneath the coverlet. But his will dissolved, his strength dissipated. Before Morelli could bring his left hand around to fire point-blank at Modica, before Stefano discerned the intent, and before his hand touched the pistol at his side, the dull *pppphhhffffttt* of a gun fitted with a silencer pierced the room. Morelli's body jackknifed, then fell back. A startled expression was frozen on his craggy face. His gun hand jerked up and the weapon bounced out of his hand, falling to the floor with a dull thud. He pivoted in a startled daze, crashed into a chair and went reeling uncontrollably into the wall before falling to the floor, dead.

Enveloped by a drugged stupor, unable to move a muscle, Stefano allowed everything to wind down into slow motion before he blanked out entirely.

He awakened in strange, shabby surroundings, in a dark, shadowy room barely discernible to him. Recollections of what had transpired earlier, mirrored intermittently in his mind came to him now in bits and pieces.

"Do not be alarmed," a voice said. "You are among friends. We transported you to a safe place until you can travel. I am Santino Siragusa. My friend here is Angelo Duca. Will you trust us? Place yourself in our hands?"

The voice came from a small man of medium build—a man dressed in the garb of a Franciscan Monk—who hovered over him.

Stefano elevated himself on one elbow, shook his head, and winced painfully. "I've no choice, have I?" The priest, a man with bushy, curly hair, had kind grey eyes and an expression of grave concern on his face. The other man, smaller more wiry, seemed familiar to him, but Modica couldn't place him. Memory returned slowly.

"What happened to Morelli?"

"I killed him," said Duca.

Modica blinked his eyes hard. "How easy you say it. Why?"

"It was you or him. He intended to kill you. The gun in his left hand was promised to your heart."

Modica, speechless, lay back on the sofa, stunned, shattered, distraught. "Not Morelli. I trusted him with my life . . . with—" He stopped. He had trusted him with *Salvatore's* life! "Oh God! Sainted God!" he moaned.

"Listen, *Colonnello*. Since the war a man does anything for money." said Santino. The subject was closed. A betrayal was so easily accepted by them!

"Where has loyalty, honor and fidelity gone?" asked Stefano rhetorically.

"To the man with dollar-lined pockets. Where else?" reflected Santino, bitterly. "Morelli has been Minister Belasci's man for some time. When we saw him acting as Basile's bodyguard, we had him checked out. His days were numbered. Now it's over for him."

Stefano watched Siragusa, the former "priest," removed

104

his cassock and busied himself making fresh coffee. Duca removed his jacket to reveal a shoulder holster with a .38 Beretta slung into it. On the table close by lay a Colt automatic and a German Luger. He studied the smaller man and something jelled in Stefano's mind. "I was instructed, if we encountered each other to mention *Terra Diavolo*," he managed between painful spasms.

"Who gave you such words to speak?" asked Santino moving in closer. He nodded to the man, Duca, assuring him it was all right.

"*Signora* Salvatore."

Nodding, Santino pulled up a chair, sat closer to him and spoke in subdued tones. "One can't be too careful, *Colonnello*. For five months we've seen you in court. Word from *Signora* Salvatore verified that you were in Viterbo. Behind those dark glasses and the clothing you wore, we couldn't spot you, and I only had a vague memory of your face seen on the day of my betrothal to Salvatore's sister. Through the *Principessa* Rothschild, we made the connection. Duca took a job at her hostelry and learned where you were quartered, and from that moment you've been under our protection, watched by our friends. We picked up on your recent escorts from the moment they tailed you, and kept them under surveillance. This morning Duca attempted to deliver your breakfast. He forgot to remove the sleep balls from his eyes. Caught off guard, he was hustled into a broom closet. Very fortunately, for all of us, the custodian discovered him within moments following the assault upon you. They rushed into your room in time to frighten off your assailants, who, sad to say, escaped through the open courtyard."

Duca reached into his jacket pocket and placed a thick, bushy false moustache under his lip and grimaced humorously at Stefano. Modica recognized him and smiled wanly. "I'm grateful for your help."

"What are you doing here in Viterbo?" asked Stefano. "Aren't you concerned that someone will recognize you? Do you still maintain contact with the other members of Salvatore's gang?" He addressed himself to Duca.

"Who me? How is it possible to communicate with them? You saw them in court. They wouldn't complicate our lives by writing to us. Our being here, in their time of need, gives them moral support. Santino and I have racked our brains to determine a way we can help them escape. There is none. The security is too tight. Why do you think they moved the trial out of Sicily—eh? They suspected that someone might be tempted to help them escape.

Besides, I only know a few of these men. I was with Tori only a year before I got too many of these." Duca opened his shirt, bared his chest. "See! Fourteen bullets! Go ahead, count the scars," he said proudly, showing off his battle wounds.

He went on. "Fearing the fifteenth might prove fatal, Salvatore, our chief, insisted I was more valuable alive than dead. I was never enamored of guns, you see. Me, I'm a lover. *Capeeshi?* The men who joined Tori after 1945, only Santino knows. When they needed a job from Duca only the paladins approached me. Vincenzo, Santino or the Scoletti brothers. I'm here only because Santino needed me. How did you know me?" Duca arose to see if the coffee was ready.

"From the History of the Bandits," Stefano told the expert forger.

"History of the Bandits? Where did you obtain such documents?" asked Santino, guardedly. Duca paused frozen to the spot.

Modica explained.

Only then did Duca move to the small stove to get the coffee. Santino lit a pipe and puffed on it evenly. "Why are you really here, *Colonnello?* After what happened in Castelvetrano and later in Rome, we never considered you'd return."

Stefano sighed and fixed his pale blue eyes on the former priest. "To find Tori's murderer. I swore an oath to write the truth about him and his men."

Duca almost dropped the boiling hot coffee pot. It was hot! But not as hot as the words he'd just heard from the lips of the *Americano*. "Whores of the devil! You will write the truth? The real truth? Colonnello—are you some crazy man! Tell him, *padre!* Tell him he's crazy! *Pazzu! Demonio!*" Duca shook one hand as if it was on fire. "If word leaks out that you're here for such a purpose, you'll never see your country again. You'll be given a house of Sicilian concrete, a mausoleum, six feet above the ground! You saw what happened to the men at the trial," exploded Duca. "They were railroaded, *amico.* See how equitable is our justice? Hah! Those men were as innocent of the charges as I am. See how it is? The Mafia is everyplace. They see everything, they know everything, and they bide their time to strike. One has no chance with them."

Before Stefano could ask what the Mafia had to do with the trial, Santino asked, "Do you know the identity of your assailants?"

"I can only guess. Please call me Stefano." He accepted the steaming cup of black coffee from Duca.

"Belasci or the Mafia?" asked Santino.

"Belasci or the Mafia?" exclaimed Duca. "What's the difference, *padre*? They are one and the same. Barbarossa is Belasci's benefactor, and Barbarossa is Mafia." His array of hand gestures fascinated the American.

"Barbarossa? Is that old goat still around?" Modica forced a tight smile.

Duca regarded the American with awe and stupefied curiosity. "You call the most powerful man in Sicily an old goat?" He swallowed hard and glanced at the noncommittal former Jesuit. "You must be crazy!" he said in a voice above a whisper. "Listen, Barbarossa knows everything. Even when a cockroach relieves himself that is known to the *capomafia*. Nothing escapes him." Duca wiped the sweat from his brow. "But, why do I chatter like a machine—*puta boom, puta boom?* It's Santino who knows everything. What I know is but a thimbleful compared to the barrelful Santino has written in his lifetime."

"My guess is your assailants were hired by the Minister of the Interior," said Santino, taking his cue. "The Minister and the *capomafia* disagree rarely, although there have been times when they are not in accord. Don Barbarossa, the perfectionist, creates political masterpieces. Minister Belasci, the 'reasonable facsimile.' the bungler, is a strange, crazy man. For instance, Don Barbarossa's men wouldn't have left you alive. *Capeeshi?* But, then, he wouldn't have been so foolish as to make an attempt on your life. You think he would have chanced killing an American in Sicily or Italy? Never! If you posed a threat to him, their arm would reach across the oceans to your country, *mi siente?* You hear?"

Stefano got the picture. "I wasn't aware that Don Barbarossa held the Sicilian sceptre in his hands. I recall vividly, however, that one can't play the fool with that devil." He reached for a pain pill on the table near him.

"Are you feeling badly?"

"The pill will help."

"Why are you really here, *Colonnello?*"

"I thought I made myself clear. To write Salvatore's memorial—the truth. Will you help me, Santino? I had hoped for your cooperation."

Santino aghast, reacted passionately. "You know what you ask? The death of all who remain. No," he shook his head emphatically. "No, you ask too much from me. I don't want the deaths of my former companions on my conscience!"

He doesn't want *their* deaths on *his* conscience, thought Stefano, listening. *If you only know how I feel, Santino Siragusa.* He cleared his throat. How could he explain? "Their deaths are what I hope to prevent," he began. He explained further his intent to contact Antigone Salvatore and secure a release from his promise to wait twenty-five years before publishing the portfolio. "If I can arrange to make public the contents of the portfolio right away, all those who were badly railroaded at the trial can be saved. Don't you see, Santino? Only the truth will save them now!"

Santino stared at him in disbelief. "The truth will kill them! Their only hope is escape. If you published the truth in the papers, tomorrow—that is if you knew the real truth—I guarantee those men would be dead in less than a week. The government would find some way to discredit you and deny the story, even if it meant producing another set of false documents. They could confuse and distort the truth until even you wouldn't recognize their handiwork. Believe me, Stefano, they wouldn't hesitate resurrecting your past, including the fact that you spent time in a mental hospital."

"I what?" Modica was stupified that Santino should know this.

With that, without waiting to hear more, Santino excused himself, retired to the next room, and returned moments later with a photostatic copy of a report, which he handed to Stefano. The American's stupefaction grew at the sight of the medical report from Letterman General Hospital. Underlined particularly was the report by the psychiatrist.

"How did you come by this?" he asked with insatiable curiosity.

"What does it matter how we got it? We got it, all right?" He saw the stony-faced expression on the American's face. "All right, one of our men works in the Minister's office in Rome. This is how we learned of Morelli's treachery. He arrived in Viterbo in the stable of *Avvocato* Basile—"

"You mean *Avvocato Basile* is part of this infamous conspiracy?"

"No, no, no, no. I doubt Basile knows about Morelli's double—or was it triple?—life."

"What a sweet setup, infiltrating the camp of the defense counsel. A possible assassination scheduled for Basile if he didn't stay in line? And God knows what else?" Modica's mind shifted into high gear.

A clear mental image of the twelve-man security council rushed at him. One of these men was linked directly to Martino Belasci. Which one? How could they have known about Morelli? Had they known all the time? Even to the sending of the message to Salvatore? Morelli—had he been a double agent during the war, too? The only way the civil government could have tied Morelli to Modica, had been through U.S.A. Army files; the OSS or ACC. Someone had leaked Top Secret information. Goddammit! Modica had taken such pains to button down every possible connection to him—except the one through Morelli!

Modica felt sick. He wanted to scream out at those conniving, double-dealing bastards in Washington who had craftily steered him towards these ends—and at Morelli, the man who, ironically, had once saved his life. The insurmountable guilt of his own culpability tore at him. Through his own negligence he had led Salvatore to slaughter. God! Where would he begin to sift through this labyrinthian maze of intricate scheming? Where?

He began by explaining to Santino that he wasn't mentally deranged, that mental trauma is a natural by-product of the kind of injury he sustained.

Santino nodded his head knowingly. "But, you see, Stefano, how much the information could be used against you? With such documents, they could brand you insane, and insist you concocted the story you want to publish, for self-glorification or for whatever reason they invent to discredit you with."

"Not if I release the story in America. I have influential friends—honest, God-fearing men that despise conspiratorial politicians who plot to elevate themselves to power and fill their coffers with blood money. I've more reasons to promote the truth about Salvatore."

"And they are? . . ."

Modica didn't reply. He grew wary and, uncomfortable.

Santino glanced at Angelo Duca. "We're getting into deeper waters, *amico*. Perhaps deeper than you should involve yourself."

Duca took the cue. "I have no ache to know more than I know. It's not my affair. Already I've stayed too long." He packed a duffle bag in the corner of the room. "I will go to my house in Bagheria, Santino. You know where to reach me if the need arises."

Duca held up a restraining hand. "Please don't get up, Stefano. We say, *Ciao. Va bene?*" They shook hands. "I make only one request. When you write your book—it would please me if you forget my name. I wish to live long enough to read this story, by some *crazy* man, so I can smile and recollect those early days. It is not necessary for my children to inherit the sins of their father and forever live under the fear of exposure or possible *vendetta.* I've grown accustomed to breathing, and at my age a man shouldn't have to change his habits too abruptly." He embraced Santino. After glancing out the window several times to see if it was safe, Duca left.

Santino bolted the door after him and moved to the window, to peer cautiously behind the blinds at the street below until Duca was safely lost in the crowd. He stoked a pot-bellied stove in the corner of the room, slipped into a heavy coat sweater, and prepared a dish of cheese, bread and tomatoes for them to munch on. In no time Santino began to ramble, just as Stefano hoped he might.

"There was no one like him, Stefano. Salvatore was a giant among men. Men loved him and feared him. Women throughout the world fantasized over his sexuality. People from all walks of life sought his favor. There were those who sought to emasculate him. Sheer distortions of the truth have been written about him since his death. But—only his mother and I know the real truth. Right up to the very—" He sighed. "It *hasn't* ended yet, has it?" Santino puffed thoughtfully on the cigarette he had lit moments before.

"It's plain to see you loved him."

"It was more than love—and in a way I cannot explain. When I had to suffer all the lies and distortions told about this man, I wanted to go out and kill every last sonofabitch responsible for his death. Why is it, Stefano, that the best are always cut out of the flock and destroyed? They even dared intimate that Russia was behind him, that all the coups he'd perfected against the Reds had been a put-on—that he'd worked for them all the time! The nerve of them! The Reds had the audacity to accuse America. *They* spread the rumor that America planned to expatriate him! What a laugh that was! With Belasci and the *Mafia* so close to those politicians in Washington—how could that have been possible, eh?"

Stefano Modica's heart stopped. He moved stiffly forward on the couch, towards his host, his thin voice cracked. *"Belasci and the Mafia, linked with Washington politicians? How?"* He tried not to show his stupefaction.

"Ahhh. *That* you won't find in Tori's papers, only because *he* didn't know the truth. Or maybe he learned the truth too late to be recorded in the portfolio." Santino paused. "I never considered this, Stefano. I've been perplexed, wondering why, after such lengthy negotiations, after the expenditure of so much money and men, they took his life? You see what I mean? Well, in any event, I learned much during my stay in America. Much in the same way I came into possession of your medical report, I also stumbled on the name, Cutter. . . ." Santino stopped. *"Pero*, I'm getting ahead of myself. Perhaps between us, Stefano, we can find the truth, eh?"

Stefano didn't hear him. His mind stopped earlier at the mention of Cutter. *Roger Cutter!* His throat thickened with bitter bile. He couldn't swallow. The man about to occupy one of the highest offices in the land—he was in collusion with the *Mafia?* How was this possible? His senses reeled. Unfortunately, Modica knew little about this sanctimonious, double-dealing snake. Modica found himself saying, "Why don't you begin at the beginning?"

"Yes, of course. Between my Italian, Sicilian and broken English, if I don't paint the proper picture, please stop me and I shall try to make myself clear." Then, in an almost laughable cloak-and-dagger manner, Santino rechecked his pistol and automatic weapons, rebolted the door and tested it several times. He went into the adjoining room, returned with a blanket which he wrapped around Stefano, a box of .38 cartridges which he placed on the table, and a thick manila file. He blew the dust off it and wiped it with a cloth, then opened it. Inside, among many loose papers, lay a foolscap notebook like the ones in Stefano's vault in Sausalito. He handed it to Modica.

"It's the personal diary of Salvatore."

Modica frowned. "I already have it—don't I? How the hell many more are there?"

"Perhaps you have his personal portfolio, the one explaining his political involvements. This contains a personal biography, encompassing all phases of his life as written and set forth in his own hand. The date of the last entry is June 30, 1950. Without this, Stefano, the story can never be told."

While Santino refilled an oil lamp and set out a few more candles to accommodate his temperamental eyesight, Stefano, book in hand, was hesitant to open it. Perhaps it would be best not to stir up the hornet's nest. Who knew the nature of this explosive? Already, many lives hung in the balance—even his own. He didn't relish the thought of

111

living the life of a recluse as Santino did, or living with the pervasive fear Angelo Duca felt. It was possible they might find something better left buried with Salvatore. Yet, there was still the score of settling Matt Saginor's death—and Salvatore's. The attempt on his own life couldn't be ignored, either.

Stefano drained his coffee cup, sat back on the sofa and with trembling hands turned the page. In Salvatore's handwriting, he read: *The Biography of my Life. A. Salvatore.*

For an instant, he paused. This was different than the previous manuscripts. He could sense it. There could be no turning back. Committed, he could only go forward, despite the contents—or perhaps because of them. His eyes dropped reluctantly to the page. He swallowed hard.

"Thus begins the story of Salvatore," said Santino. "It's all there in the book. Go ahead, read it. But bear in mind, not until after the trials have ended can you hope to know the full story. Then again, perhaps the full story will never be known."

"Oh, but it will, Santino. I've just made a covenant with myself. I promised myself I'll find out and I will. You have my word. But—I'll need your help. Do I have it?" he asked somberly.

Santino Siragusa, former priest, Jesuit, scholar, and historian to Salvatore, paced the floor, his pale face creased with furrows of thought. It took several moments before he replied. Finally he said, "Yes. God help us both. I'll try to explain things only a Sicilian could understand. But first, Stefano, you must firmly fix in your mind an understanding of the complex political system in Sicily—or you will never understand Salvatore enough to write about him. Understand this also. Its been nearly two years since his demise, no? *Va bene*, the spirit of Salvatore endures. Most of the purposely distorted rumors about Tori were circulated with the intent of discouraging the legend of Salvatore from perpetuating itself in the hearts and minds of our people. Iron-fast rules of the Mafia, Church, nobility and government—the people who set themselves up as paragons—had been violated by Salvatore's power. God forbid any young men should take it upon themselves to emulate Salvatore! None of them, *mafiosi*, landbarons or politicians, is prepared for another Salvatore to spring up and proliferate the gnawing cancers in their bellies planted by Salvatore himself."

Santino sipped a glass of wine, refilled his glass, and poured one for his guest. "*Capeeshi*, Stefano?"

"*Capeeshu*, Santino."

112

"Very well, my friend, I shall begin by telling you there has never been a Sicily without bandits. Sicily has always been the dumping ground their slaves, who were put to work in the sulphur mines, in the building of underwater conduits, and in farming by conquerors.

"Those persecuted slaves who escaped the jaws of oppression took to the many grottos in the honeycombed mountains and became brigands to survive. Over the centuries these brigands, supported by a strong conviction that breaking the law was a respectable activity, never cooperated with the police, and between them prevailed a strict code of silence—*omertà*. Soon the Feudalists, the landlords, enforced the practice of hiring bandits to settle their disputes with the peasants and among themselves.

"Banditry came to be known as national character of the island. No conquering nation has ever succeeded in wiping out the existence of bandits. The governments most successful in dealing with the situation were those who suppressed their indignation and came to terms with members of the underworld, underground and bandit leaders. Setting a thief to catch a thief achieved some success, but it set a precedent which reached far into the 20th century. Notorious criminals—men for whom the people had no respect—were employed by police forces. Men, I might add, for whom the people had even less respect. Thus, a regard for law and order diminished rapidly."

"I see," said Stefano. "Then the problems faced by successive governments were not necessarily the isolated gangs of highwaymen, but rather a way of life shared throughout the society."

"Exactly," replied the former Jesuit. "Sicilians evolved into a tribal society, where the relationship of patron to client was more important than the State—and where the family counted most of all. You see, almost everyone carried arms in those early days and was prepared to use them in an underground conspiracy against the law. Later, these lawless forces, bandits, brigands and criminals were refined into what today is known as the Mafia.

"You have to take into consideration, Stefano, that Sicily's foreign invaders left behind them uncodified legislation extremely difficult to understand or apply. Many laws contradicted each other. For this reason public justice was disobeyed, even derided. In a world of overlapping and contradicting jurisdictions, of privileged exemptions from ordinary courts, of judgeships being sold and of witnesses intimidated, frequently the local boss or landowner was

113

more important to law enforcement and law making than a central government."

Santino paused momentarily and, moving towards the window, glanced cautiously about the street area below. Satisfied there were no imminent dangers, he stoked the fires and refilled the wineglasses. "Even viceroys complained then that the law was positively discredited by its deviousness. Its complexities and delays forced individuals to seek other means of redress. The poor were ruined by protracted lawsuits, and this put a premium on gangsterism for everyone. Peasant or landlord, priest or business man, even criminals had an added incentive to commend themselves to quasi-legal organizations which proved more practical and effective than the regular forces of law.

"The courts imposed harsh and deterrent penalties on any action they settled—penalties which included branding, public torture, and the strangling and disembowling of criminals. But, all this, including a permanent display of severed heads hung on hooks like so much meat, was a futile effort to conceal the ineffectiveness of these same courts in supporting law and order.

"Believe me, Stefano, this was the situation in 1600—and in 1700 and in 1800. There had been little change except for the burgeoning poverty of the peasants and the increasing wealth of the Feudalists. By the end of the 1800 the Mafia controlled most of the bandits, and crime became just one method of obtaining wealth and power. Political revolution was another."

Modica popped a pain pill into his mouth and gulped it down with water. He said, "I suppose each nation has had such a history to contend with, a way of life to guide them. But why hasn't any attempt been made to better the life here?"

"We are an old, old nation. All of Europe is old, for that matter. It isn't easy to teach the people a new way of life. Even Fascism, which Mussolini introduced and which promised so much, was greatly lacking. The most corrosive legacy of Fascism to Italy was World War II, which it strenuously advocated and finally brought about, but for which few preparations had been made. Sicily, especially, suffered gross hardships, as you very well know, Stefano."

"How well I know," said the former colonel." Reflective, he lay back to let the opiate take effect.

Santino's voice grew wistful as he recalled. "Once Montegatta, the village of Salvatore, an inland mountain village with an imposing Norman tower that lights up like a citadel of fable at night, had been noisy and colorful by

114

day; romantic and melancholy by night. Along its cobblestoned streets and from the antiquated houses, there echoed mournful songs saturated with a special poetry of a haunted, spectral breed of Sicilian. Over the centuries this remote village became a refuge for a strange and oppressed people of Greek, Arab, Saracen, Spanish and Norman heritage: women with thickly fringed lashes over dark smoldering eyes that can kill, with wit that can blister or please, with love phrases that can infatuate or assassinate: men who became either young gods or nonentities. You've seen what's become of it. They are a people without hope.

"In the summer, an inexorable enemy, the sun, afflicts them with a prostrating force which Montegattans greet with remorseless and resolute silence. There follows a suffocatingly hot time when the tumultuous *sirocco* arrives. This sweltering North African wind gathers momentum from across the sparkling waters of the Mediterranean and with unbearable, pulsing, raw heat, blows gales of dust—blinding dust, as white as milk and powdery as ground glass. When the *sirocco* erupts, it scatters a devastating dust whimsically; sometimes gentle and insidious; sometimes in surly white clouds that snake and writhe with a vengeance only Boreas, God of the North Wind, could have created when he abducted Orithia, daughter of the King. . . ."

Santino paused to nibble on some cheese, then continued, "Spawned by the equatorial heat in this land of desolation, the people fall into a total despondency with their lot in life and the struggle for survival is usually no more than a day-to-day existence." He slapped his thighs with an air of finality. "*Va bene*, this was Tori's life. Montegatta was his village. Amid these surroundings and against this background of human misery, this exceptional Sicilian, Salvatore, was born. No man in contemporary history was so influenced by his environment as was Salvatore. He belonged absolutely to Sicily, was as much a part of her as if he had sprung from her loins. I tell you this, so you will better understand him.

"And now for the more pertinent facts. . . ."

CHAPTER 9

Two weeks later Modica came away with more information than was stored in his vault in California. Would the story never end? Wherever he turned, a new branch sprang from the tree—a branch on which new blossoms sprouted into a complicated maze of design. It was exhaustive work marking time, and compiling such data, but he felt certain in the not too distant future this labor would produce enormous results. He had one more stop in Montegatta to see the *Signora* Salvatore, and then—home. God, would he be glad to get back to the U.S.A.!

Modica, on the flight to Palermo, caught a few hours sleep and by the time he arrived in Palermo and checked into the *Albergo-Sole,* he felt refreshed and invigorated. Modica wasn't in his room ten minutes before the phone rang. A man's low voice, speaking meticulous accented English, came over the instrument.

"If this is the American *Colonnello* Stefano Modica who was stationed here in the war, would he join Don Barbarossa for lunch at his villa? For the *Colonnello's* convenience, a car and driver awaits him at the hotel entrance."

It was a subtle request, one which precluded refusal.

Moments later Stefano Modica, American citizen, sat in the back seat of the vintage Mercedes someone had kept in mint condition, trying to assure himself that he wasn't intimidated by the expressionless, scarred face of Mario Cacciatore. Earlier, when he'd caught sight of this gargoyle-faced man, he had instructed the desk clerk to convey his regrets to the deputy from the American Embassy. He made it a point to convey that he was lunching with the Don at his villa. Of course, Modica had no appointment with the Embassy deputy. If he'd known that the *Albergo-Sole* was a sacred Mafia institution, he'd have saved his breath.

On the silent ride to Monreale, Stefano found himself focusing on the rights of the American citizen abroad, something he'd never paid heed to before and to the com-

116

ing meeting. In moments he'd come up against an indestructible force, a titan, a giant, the formidable overlord of Sicily—a man who'd given him many bad moments seven years ago, a man who, he hoped, would no longer intimidate him.

Don Matteo Barbarossa stood casually at the entrance gates of his villa awaiting Stefano's arrival. In his customary garb—shirtsleeves, his trousers held up by suspenders—and with three frisky English hounds playing at his feet, he looked exactly as Stefano had remembered him: a man much like any simple, hillside peasant found everywhere in Sicily. It was difficult for Stefano to reconcile in his mind, that here, indeed, was a power broker extraordinaire.

"Benvenuto, Colonnello! Welcome to Villa Barbarossa. Come. Come into my house," the Don spoke up with unexpected hospitality. "It is yours for as long as you wish to remain." He was the quintessence of cordiality, a perfect host, an amiable, warm and gentle man who prepared an excellent repast for a long-lost friend. He spoke his thick Sicilian dialect as usual.

They reminisced for more than an hour, following a superb luncheon of hot sausage, a variety of fresh, garden grown vegetables, and the pride of any Sicilian table, eggplant *parmesan,* and freshly baked bread as light as angel's hair.

"Let us do away with the many years in which we've not seen each other," began the Don. "Do you recall those exciting days during the war? Truly, the pulse of Sicily pounded with great excitement and hopeful promises as the tempo set by you Americans spread throughout out land." He sighed despondently. "When you left, it became the Sicily of old—antiquated, a bit stodgy, and without life." The overture had ended, Don Barbarossa went straight to the aria.

"I should be offended by your quick departure, *Colonnello.* You didn't take the time to say *adieu* when you left. But the war with its uncertainties was the culprit, so I forgave you. *Allora,* what brings you to Palermo?"

"I'm travelling. Unable to settle down after the war, I thought if I revisited Italy and other parts of the European theater I might find my lost years and glue myself back together again."

"Your leg, does it complicate your life?"

"Not physically." Stefano tapped his forehead.

"Ah. *Capeeshu.* That pain can be more complicating."

117

Without preamble he asked, "Did you find the trial at Viterbo enlightening?"

"You know I was there?" Stefano affected to be surprised. "Were you there? You should have made your presence known to me. It was rather lonely all those months."

"What kept you there if it was lonely?" The bull tiger bared his fangs.

"Why would the presence of an old friend—anywhere—interest you?"

"It pleases me to know where my friends are and what they are doing. I can offer better protection. Don Barbarossa permits no casualties to occur to his friends."

"Protection, Don Matteo? Ah, I see. Too bad you weren't around when I was attacked by unknown assailants. See—they broke my nose. Oh, it will heal in time. It's just damned inconvenient. I'm puzzled why they picked me. I carry little of value, if robbery was their motive." He played his part well.

Don Barbarossa sniffed out the game Stefano played. In addition, his memory served him well. Modica, his own man, wasn't an easy man to convince. During the war he had had to play a crafty game with the American. But, then, he had been only a newly resurrected Mafia Don. Today he was *capomafia* of all Sicily, with far reaching influences in Rome and abroad. At that time Modica had been the illustrious conqueror, the American colonel, the power. Today he was a plain American citizen, Stefano Modica. Even in this pose, too many complications could be reaped, if he didn't proceed with caution.

"Listen, *Colonnello*, out of respect to each other for our former association, let's be straight with each other. *Va bene?*"

"*Si, va bene*. Very well."

"In July 1950, you and three American agents, in Castelvetrano when Salvatore died, caused a big noise—eh?"

"You know that, too?" Stefano's blue eyes twinkled, dimming his indignation.

"You were difficult to convince in 1944. You haven't learned much since then, eh?"

Modica burned in silence.

"I'm getting old, *Colonnello*. Humor an old man. I have no time for games, symphonies or concerts—*capeeshi*? No longer do I dance the tarantella, either with my enemies or my companions. I no longer fox-trot to a fast-paced tune as I did in my youth. Now, I'm lucky if I can mark time to a funeral dirge. But, mind you, in my head there are no spider webs. There is no softness, no faded memories. My pictures are quite clear, as sharp as they were during the war, and I remember you perfectly. *Colonnello* Modica of the Grand Council was direct, concise, and to the point. I liked you. Admired you. Never mind the differences between us. Never mind the difficulties my irrational companions caused you. With me you were straight. You spoke your mind. That's the way I remember you. Please permit this old man to hold such a picture of you now, even if we speak of disagreeable things."

"Perhaps I haven't learned as much as I should have learned, Don Matteo. I, too have clear recollections. Tell me, did you realize all your ambitions?"

Don Barbarossa nodded his head, and regarded the American through his darkly tinted glasses. "My observations have offended you? Please, take no offense. It confuses me to see you in such a light. Perhaps the *Colonnello* has indeed changed. In a uniform you were a real *pezzenovante*—a big shot who knew everything. Why you insist playing the man who is ignorant of my sovereignty amuses me. Tell me, my friend, did you permit me all those extravagances—all those privileges—without knowing for *whom* they were granted? They were not concessions accorded *every* man in the street," he said indulgently.

"During the war I took orders. My superior officers directed me to give Barbarossa whatever he required. Operation Redbeard—your code name—was a valuable asset to the Allies, and they simply reciprocated," said Modica.

"You asked no questions?"

"Question my superiors?" Modica laughed. "If they didn't know what the hell they were doing, I shudder to think what the war's outcome might have been." He managed a small rush of laughter.

"*Va bene. Va bene.* That's how it should be. One *capo*—the rest take orders." The Don made a sudden transition. "How long did you know Salvatore? You worked close—under Truman's orders, no?"

By now, Modica had had it. It hadn't been his posture during the war to be cowed by the Don, and he couldn't gracefully assume a different attitude now. He spoke crisply. "What's on your mind, Don Matteo? Sicilian intrigue has never been my cup of tea—or did you forget? Ask me what you wish to know, and if I can I'll try to answer. Now, what's this nonsense about Salvatore?"

"Why are you here?"

"I told you. I'm not a repetitious man."

"You have no interest in Salvatore?"

"In a dead man? Why? Should I?" Modica lied with a pleasant expression.

"Only you can answer."

"I've no interest in the dead. What must I do to convince you? Only the living can influence my life."

"Did you find Salvatore to be—special?" The Don meticulously unwrapped a foil covered cigar, careful not to tear it.

"You mean when he was alive? Of course. He was exceptional. You knew him much better than I. Didn't you find him an exceptional man?" Modica temporized. "As a matter of curiosity perhaps you can tell me what went wrong? What circumstances brought about his death? In 1945 he held much promise." Stefano continued to play the game well.

The Don grew silent and thoughtful, fully absorbed in twirling the red and gold cigar band around his finger. He nodded. "*Si.* He was exceptional. He deserves that much. *Pero*—he was stubborn. Unfortunately, he knew too much. And *caro mio*, death is the inevitable fate of men who know too much, and use the knowledge unwisely."

If Modica detected the silent warning couched in the Don's words, he shrugged them off. Impulsively, he affected a bright smile. "By the way, while I'm here I wish to pay my respects to the *Signora* Salvatore. Why not come with me, Don Matteo? Having such an important man visit her might help cheer her up. I understand she is quite a lonely woman since the death of her last son."

His words, expressed with such innocence, caused the Don to temporarily set aside his warring armor. *Perhaps,* he thought, *the Colonnello doesn't know as much as we give him credit for knowing. Would he have asked so foolish a question if he were in possession of the truth?*

"Permit a gesture of friendship, *Colonnello*. I shall have my driver escort you to Montegatta. It's been rumored there are a few desperate men in the hills, who might prey upon you, if you travel alone."

"Bandits, Don Matteo? *Still?* My, my, I thought Captain Franchina had put an end to banditry in Sicily."

The Don removed his dark glasses and glanced at Stefano. In that moment, all the things he'd ever heard and what he'd learned from Santino about this formidable *capomafia* rushed at him. If he'd been incautious, he regretted it instantly. "But of course how can I refuse your gesture of friendship, Don Barbarossa?"

They left the dining salon and the Don ordered coffee and wine brought into his study by his servant.

"Sit a while before you leave. It is seldom that I receive guests." He indicated a chair opposite his desk and sat down heavily in his leather chair. Stefano sat down.

He glanced about the room, gave a slight start. Perhaps the Don had forgotten. It might have slipped his mind. Or having lived with it, he might have grown used to it, never thinking it could set another man to thinking. Perhaps the Don had no reason to concern himself with the thoughts of others. Whatever it was, he failed to consider that the wall behind him contained a rash of faded newspaper clippings and worn photos of Salvatore astride his stallion. Modica tried to suppress his astonishment, until he recalled that this man was Salvatore's Godfather. Why wouldn't he have collected such trivia on his Godson?

Drawn blinds kept out the early afternoon sun, and shadows shifted frequently about the cluttered room. They sipped coffee in silence. Finally the Don began to talk.

"What decided you to write about Salvatore? And don't bother to deny it." He tossed a bundle of papers at his guest across the desk. "Work sheets collected from your trash bins from both hotels in Viterbo."

One thing in Modica's favor, the bundles had contained a mass of shorthand scribblings, for which only he knew the code. Affecting distress that his privacy had been violated, he confronted his host squarely. "Why are you pressing me? You should know I don't make a move without the full approval and sanction of my government," he bluffed.

"Bullshit! You resigned your post in August, 1950. Four months later you arrived in Viterbo, rented a writing machine, and proceeded to beat the hell out of it, stopping only to attend the trials, eat, sleep, and relieve yourself. It will be a simple matter to turn these over to Italian intelligence. But, listen, *Colonnello,* out of respect, I don't wish to boil the hairs off your ass, *pero*—its best you speak truth with me. Every minute of your time since you arrived in Italy has been documented. Now, suppose we talk, man to man, and cut out the bullshit, eh?"

Tense, stiff backed and doing a slow burn. Stefano pulled his prosthesis into a better position, then lit a cigarette. What else could he do, seated before this formidable tiger?

"*Va bene. Va bene.* I knew you as a man of understanding, good sense and reason. Where is Salvatore's portfolio?" The Don spoke easily as he began to decant two bottles of wine in Stefano's presence. "Which do you prefer? Red? White?"

"With your permission, white." Stefano couldn't pretend to know nothing of the portfolio. Any man attending the trials would have had that subject shoved at him three times a day. "What makes you think I might know?"

"Do you know who has it? Into whose hands it was left?"

"No." Stefano watched in utter fascination, the steadiness of the Don's hand, the manner, like an artist's, in which he prevented the sediment from mixing into the new crystal decanter.

"I thought we decided to be straight with each other?" Finished with the red wine, the Don proceeded to decant the white. "You saw what happened to its author, his associates. Ah—it is finished." He placed the old bottles on a sideboard and opened a *credenza* to remove two glittering wine goblets with a flourish.

"Certain powerful men would pay substantially for the return of this damaging document. Not because it rings of truth, understand." The Don used the decanter stopper to punctuate his words. "When malicious propaganda in the wrong hands causes too many complications. And you remember how Don Matteo dislikes complications? Consider my words, *Colonnello*."

"Please, call me Stefano. *Allora*, Don Matteo, is this your doing? Do I detect a hint of a threat towards me?—or—are you merely the voice for other men?" Stefano watched the artistry as the Don chilled the glasses in a bucket of ice.

"Never chill the wine, Stefano. You see? I teach you a long known art. Only the glasses. I speak for a number of men who will protect what they have, with anything it takes to silence the words of Salvatore." He poured a little red wine into a glass, picked it up, swirled it and tasted it. "Ahhh! *Che bello sapore!* What exquisite flavor. You sure you don't wish the red wine?"

"The white, please. Even if I had the portfolio, it wouldn't be for sale. Is that why you invited me to lunch and question me relentlessly?" Stefano clucked his tongue against his teeth. "Why didn't you ask me straight?"

"You *know* where it is?" The Don paused in his labors, feigning surprise.

"No. Not directly. At the trial, I heard rumors."

"Yes, yes, what rumors?"

"The portfolio has been microfilmed and remains in a vault, safe, someplace in America."

122

Don Matteo glanced at him through tilted eyes. The room grew silent.

"How do you know this—and don't be clever with me."

"Sorry. It's privileged information."

"What is this—privileged?" The Don glanced suspiciously at his guest.

"It means I can't reveal the source of my information."

"Or . . .?"

"Or I could be disbarred for breaking the confidentiality between lawyer and client. I'd not be permitted to practice law," he added at the Don's questioning glance.

"A client of yours has Salvatore's portfolio?"

"Possibly."

"Who is this client?"

Stefano laughed lightly. "You know I can't reveal such information."

"Or you'd be disbarred, eh?"

"Exactly."

"What if you don't live long enough to be disbarred? Oh, not by me, Stefano." He wagged a finger at him. "No, no, no, no. You have nothing to fear from me. It's been a long time since I've done the job of a hired killer. Others should concern you. I heard they almost did a first class job on you in Viterbo."

"All this for a portfolio?" Stefano's words were spoken slowly and clearly.

"All this." Having finished his decanting and pouring, the Don wiped his hands on a towel, and made no move to serve Stefano the glass of wine, yet.

Stefano, raging internally, grew braver. "Earlier you asked if I intend to write about Salvatore. Very well—straight as an arrow—yes. I plan to write a suitable memorial to him. The pity of it is, I've given my word, my solemn promise, not to publish it for twenty-five years. Uncertain of where my loyalties lay, up 'til now, I've quarreled with myself in assuming so large a burden. But, suddenly Don Matteo, your words have convinced me, stirred me into making a decision." Hs eyes grew electric.

The Don lit his cigar, puffed on it to conceal his rising anger. "My words—eh, Stefano? *Pe d'vero?*" *Before this stubborn mule is finished, my words will seal his tomb.*

The game grew interesting. It became the Don's move to estimate just how inculpating were these papers Salvatore had written and how much Modica really knew. In the next half hour, he asked a series of seemingly irrelevant questions. When Stefano, on guard, responded by purposely placing too much importance in some replies, and not enough in others, the Don concluded there were many truths in the Salvatore affair of which this cunning fox and slick American lawyer was totally ignorant. And without these truths, there could be no story, no memorial, no book. He kept these conclusions to himself.

"How long do you estimate such a memorial will take for you to write?"

"Two—perhaps three years. Why?"

"And if you shouldn't live so long?"

"Another threat, eh Matteo?"

The Don wagged a finger at him, "*Allora,* you know the entire story?"

"With Salvatore's death, the story ended. No?"

Don Matteo held the wine goblet containing the white wine in his hand, ready to set it before Stefano. He paused, glass in midair, and studied his guest. It was at this moment that Don Barbarossa made a decision.

Modica, sensing the immediate change in him, wasn't certain what had brought about the transition. His keen eyes fixed on the Don skeptically.

"It *is* over with—ended, is it not?" queried Modica.

The Don made a fumbling move; the glass slipped from his hand and fell crashing on the tiled floor. Stefano moved to retrieve the pieces, only to be stayed by his host.

"No. My servant shall attend to it. Here, I shall pour you another.

Fully aware of how quickly the Don bounced back, and that he poured the white wine from another decanter without the previous panache, Stefano accepted the wine and raised his glass along side the Dons, in toast.

"*Cento anni,* Stefano.

"*Cento anni,* Don Matteo."

During this time spent in mental gymnastics, neither man sold the other short. Having once engaged in very secretive matters of State, both men knew each other well. But it became apparent that Don Barbarossa held the trump card in this display of skill and technique. His demeanor changed, and so did his speech.

"Too bad we do not see eye to eye in this affair, *Colonnello.* It appears I cannot convince you of the folly in pursuing such a risky task, so I wish you well." Inwardly the Don felt a sense of relief. *This pezzenovante is spinning his wheels. He knows nothing,* he told himself. Then he said something inconsistent to his character, which might have given Stefano more insight on what would follow, if he'd known the key to his thinking.

"This story is one worth telling, and if it could be told

in its entirety it would be most spectacular. *Pero*—you will never write it, because you do not know it."

Sonofabitch! How easy he says it. Well, he won't get a rise out of me, thought Stefano as he steeled himself against a sharp reply.

"Humor an old man, eh?" the Don continued." Tell me why you, an American, with no business in our country or our culture, should wish to champion Salvatore after his death?" An expression of interest, rather than one of cunning or duplicity, shone in his eyes.

Stefano hesitated, uneasy at the change in him. "You wouldn't understand. Men of your stamp could never hope to understand a great man like Salvatore."

The Don wanted to say, "If you only knew. If you only knew." Instead he said, "Ahh. Now insults. Is that it?"

"I don't give a fig if what I do sits well with you or not. As an American citizen, I resent your intimidation. When I return home, I shall write the story of Salvatore, and neither you nor anyone else will prevent it. Just so you and your unholy coterie of holstered gunmen don't make the mistake of thinking you're dealing with a prize jackass, you tell your *compares* that the personal portfolio and all relevant papers of that remarkable Sicilian have been microfilmed, and lie in a vault to be opened if I don't arrive at my destination within a specified time. This information, which includes my personal observations, will be viewed critically by both American State and Defense departments. Such information, in the hands of scrupulous men, can cause repercussions that will break down the machinery of economic aid from the U.S.A. to Italy and cause it to shut down tight. Then where will your government be?"

"That's straight?" asked the Don, chewing his cigar benignly as if all this really made no impression on him. "Are you such a *pezzenovante*?"

"You can believe it!" retorted Stefano checking his temper at the Don's mocking tone.

"*Allora*—you have me by the short hairs, Stefano. The first round is yours. Once in awhile, like a wounded virgin, I must retreat into a corner, hoping no one learns of my *pecato*."

This transition left Modica speechless—and incensed.

"As long as we understand each other, Don Matteo, I'll take my leave. Thank you for your hospitality, especially for the use of your car and driver."

The Don merely nodded and watched Stefano leave.

After Stefano left, the Don, no fool, reflected on his meeting with the American. He had no reservations about putting out a contract on Modica. He'd do it in a moment if it would reap rewards. The consequences of killing an important American on Italian soil, however, were too numerous. In addition, such an act would be most imprudent and foolhardy. No way would he jeopardize the accomplishments of an entire career. Everything they had worked for could blow up in their faces and take them along with it. Hadn't he painstakingly explained this to the emotionally overwrought Belasci? That thoughtless, alcohol-crazed asshole had almost wrecked his own chances at the Premiership when his men had attacked Modica in Viterbo. No. Once Modica was safely back in his own country, means to erase him could be taken, *if* he still posed a threat. The arm of the Mafia had stretched across oceans before this, and would continue to do so.

But what was this crazy ambivalence? This hesitation? Scruples? Doubts? This inclination he had to become immortalized?

By the unholy sperm of Satan! Had he lost all perspective earlier? What the hell was he thinking to present the American with the white elixir of death? It had been a long time since he used his decanting skills to prepare a cup of instant eternity for a man, eh? *Allora*—no sense crying over spilled wine, eh? The Don laughed aloud. That was a good one: 'crying over spilled wine.' He'd have to tell Martino that the next time they spoke.

Something else nagged at the Don, causing a violent itch he couldn't scratch. And knowing he wouldn't have to wait very long before he could relieve the infernal itching, he made certain preparations, then lay back on his sofa and took a short nap, hoping as he did to resolve many conflicts.

An hour and a half later, Stefano Modica returned to the Don's villa, ready to commit murder if provoked. Tossing all caution to the wind, he raved at the Don in a manner quite inconsistent with his own character.

"You fatuous son of a bitch! You set me up. You knew what would happen if she saw me in your car, with your driver. And you let me destroy the woman! Hasn't she suffered enough indignities? You black-hearted son of a reprehensible whore!"

Stefano Modica paced the floor of the Don's study, not fully certain of why he had returned except that he had to

126

get the last word in. He shook with rage in recollection of the catastrophic encounter.

Antigone Salvatore, that stalwart matriarch, both pleased and gravely disturbed by his presence in Montegatta, yet ready to accord him her most cordial hospitality, had caught sight of the familiar car and driver in her courtyard and recoiled. Her reaction, instant and complete, had struck her into insensibility. Shattered at what she misconstrued to have been a unification of forces between the American and Don Barbarossa, she had lashed out at him like a wounded tigress.

Unprepared for the burst of hostility and suspicion, Stefano Modica had been rendered impotent by her reaction. There had been no way for him to assure her of his fidelity, of his innocence, in this well-calculated and provoked encounter. And because he didn't know all the facts, there was no way he could hope to understand.

His attempts to secure her permission to publish her son's papers before the specified time had sent her into hysterics. She had damned herself for having trusted him, for having been so imprudent in turning the papers over to him at the outset. Highly emotional, she had ranted and raved like a madwoman, and when she had begun to hyperventilate, Stefano, fearing she might have another stroke, had been at a loss to know what to do for her. Nothing he had said could assuage her hysterics and he had made little of her thick, garbled mountain accent. The gist of her concern had been that, in a moment of weakness, she had entrusted the fate of all who survived her son to a double-dealing, black-hearted viper who was certain to betray them all. This much he had grasped.

He'd been helpless, stunned into full bewilderment by such erratic behavior, unsure of what he'd done to deserve such treatment. He had intended asking so many questions—about Vincenzo's testimony, about Santino's statements, about many other things. He had left, shaken and saddened. He'd ordered the driver to return to Palermo, where he could pack and leave this land of hopeless insanity.

He had ample time to consider why the sight of Don Barbarossa's car and driver had turned Antigone Salvatore into a madwoman. His brain roiled with suppositions. Sure, several parts of the puzzle were missing; he knew this. Hadn't they all told him so? Siragusa had made this apparent right off. Don Barbarossa had implied the same thing. What had eluded him? What? Everyone concerned knew more than they were telling—he knew it.

Goddamnit! Here he was at the center of a seemingly insoluble puzzle, straining to build an edifice with which to support it. What to do? What to do?

During the ride through the arid saffron mountain desolation, portions of the puzzle had come together in his mind and dovetailed to a logical conclusion. Instantly, Stefano had rejected these as being forcefully contrived, too fanciful and highly imaginative. He had concluded he was just groping for straws. Yet, he'd come this far, and having already risked a great deal including his life, why not press for the right answers? What could he lose? He had instructed the driver to return to the Don's villa. He had dealt with this self-inflated, high-and-mighty cock o' the walk before and won. Why not now? So here he was, more courageous perhaps than at any other time in his life, a bit too incautious, but still determined to do combat with this imperturbable feudal overlord.

Seated in a meditative, impenitent silence, watching Modica give vent to his fury, the Don let his face relax into lines of fatigue. It seemed he aged ten years. The Don raised his hand, gesturing for silence, but Stefano wouldn't comply.

"There's nothing you can say to me, that will excuse your lack of humanity and inconsideration for a poor woman pushed to the end of her rope!" he bellowed. "I wanted you to know that I understand what you did. And I shall keep this foremost in my mind when I do my writing—*Don* Matteo!"

"Sit down, Stefano, eh? When you were here earlier—we exchanged words. Now, we talk, man to man. *Va bene?*" His entire demeanor altered.

"You have nothing to say to me. I'll never forgive such brutality. Suppose the woman had died of a stroke? Would you have wanted this on your conscience?" he demanded hotly.

"We talk—eh? So that you understand me better, you should know that I made an attempt on your life earlier. It was easy. You were totally unsuspecting." He indicated the broken glass still on the tiled floor. "It would have been so easy. A few drops of strychnine. . . ."

Stefano faltered a moment in total disbelief. "I don't believe you."

The Don opened a drawer, withdrew a small vial and tossed it at him across the desk. Stefano hesitated before fixing his eyes on the label. *Strychnine!* His stomach gurgled uncomfortably. He lifted his eyes to meet the Don's.

128

"Why are you telling me this? What curious quirk in your character made you reluctant to snuff out another life?" he snorted contemptuously.

"It's not necessary to insult me. Once I permitted you to leave, I knew you'd return. All my moves are carefully plotted and with good reason. *Allora*, I want you to sit down and listen. I want no interruptions until I am finished. This is not easy for a man of my calibre, *capeeshi?*"

Don Barbarossa commenced. He talked into the hours of the night, and when he finished, he stood before Stefano, stripped of all pretense, totally without guilt, free from duplicity, a simple, vulnerable old man.

If Stefano had been moved by what he heard, he gave no outward indication. Because he was stunned, because the information had staggered his imagination, because he felt confusion,, torment and an inner wretchedness, rolled into one—a wild compulsion urged him to go out and get blind, staggering drunk. He wanted to leave. He craved to return to America, to leave this crazy madman's land behind and retreat into some sanctuary where he could think straight. Dear God! He'd been better off before a portion of the riddle was solved for him!

"Understand, Stefano. Certain machinery which I am unable to halt has been set into motion. You must guard yourself, take every means to protect yourself at all times, from the moment you leave my villa.

Numb, still unable to grasp all his mind had recorded, he prepared to leave the Don's villa. Totally out of character, Stefano found himself saying, "When you visit America, I'll be offended if you do not visit me in San Francisco."

The Don wagged a finger at him. "San Francisco? No, no, Stefano. Don Barbarossa will not leave this villa. I am nearly seventy years old, now—I am no longer a young buck. In my lifetime I've seen and learned many things. These things, not the years, have aged me. I've been powerful, invincible, and unbreakable. I was fortunate. Having sprung from the loins of Sicily, I knew all its secrets. Destiny, my tenacious mistress, that most clever of clever matriarchs, will never permit me to leave. She will cling to me, clutch me to her bosom, until I draw my last breath. The pity of it all is there is no one to whom I can leave such a legacy. You see what irony?"

The Don removed his glasses, lifted his swollen, red-rimmed eyes, and fixed them piercingly on the American. "You understand all I've told you? There will be—can be—no further communication between us. Your gesture

129

of friendship will be remembered the rest of my days. I accept your word, my friend. Nothing for twenty five years. *Capeeshi?* I wait for only one more achievement. In February, Martino Belasci will hold the highest office in the land. Only then will I retire in my beloved *Sicilia*, away from public life. I will tend my horses and grow my roses, and smell the fragrance of orange blossoms again, in the season of planting. You know, next to harvest time it's the most romantic time in the year." His eyes grew soft.

Under the spell of his power-saturated eyes, Stefano was unable to avert his eyes, until the Don reset his glasses into place and broke the connection. For the first time since he'd first met the Don, he no longer resembled a marble institution of power.

They shook hands in parting. The Don startled him by embracing him warmly; a rare gesture on the part of this iceberg of a man. Precisely at this moment, distracted by something he saw on a mahogany console along one side of the wall, Stefano caught sight of a Belgian-made Browning lying next to a leather holster. Next to it, covered by a glass dome on an elevated base, he saw a gold calendar watch displayed. He gave a start, sucked in his breath, then, as quickly, breathed out.

Why wouldn't a Godfather cherish such memorabilia— eh? Why wouldn't he? Oh God! What a crazy bit of intrigue was this!

"I will see that *Signora* Salvatore doesn't fret over the misunderstanding of this day," Don Barbarossa told him in parting.

In Rome, Stefano suffered through a two-hour stopover before he could make connections to San Francisco. He paced the airport terminal, smoked incessantly, stopped in the bar for a few belts, and finally, bored with the delay, retired to the men's lounge to take care of a few physical needs, hoping to relieve his mind of the churning thoughts running rampant.

A peculiar feeling swept through him. He peered about the confines of the semideserted lavatory. There it was again—that inescapable feeling of being watched. Damn! He'd packed his gun away—hadn't thought to hide another on him. Taking the usual precautions, he failed to detect anything unusual. He finally convinced himself he was imagining things.

Bent over the washstand, washing his hands, he reached for a towel. A dull thud at the base of his skull turned on an array of colored lights in his head. Under the impact of the blow, he went reeling against a concrete wall, and everything became an enormous blur. A powerful fist struck the side of his head. From then on everything happened in split-second timing. He became aware of a confrontation between four men, who, ignoring him, commenced to exchange blows. In the scuffle, his assailants, immobilized, were left bloodied and brutally beaten on the tile floor.

He felt himself pulled up bodily off the floor. Apologies and concern for his well being, expressed sincerely by his benefactors, only added to his mental confusion. Between these burly brutes, he was eased out of the men's lounge. He became clearly aware that as one man hastened to steer him out of the area, the second man fumbled with a container the size of a match box and tossed it inside the men's room—then ran like hell in the opposite direction, through the lumbering crowds.

A loud explosion shook the airport terminal. Hysteria prevailed, as people scattered in every direction. Glancing over his shoulder, Stefano saw the outer lavatory wall crumble into rubble, smoke and debris. Joined by the second man, he was steered to the terminal gate where his plane was readied for departure. His benefactors tipped their fedoras politely.

"To whom am I indebted for saving my life?" he asked shakily.

"Don Barbarossa wishes you a safe journey and imparts a word of advice. Stay in your own country, *Signore, Colonnello*. It is not safe for you here. It matters not who nearly did you in. Only that we arrived in time to retard their efforts—only this should concern you. Outside this country, the Don's protection ceases. The Don wishes to impress this upon your mind, and he urges you to take proper precautions."

Between their valiant rescue and the silent threat couched in their message, Modica got the point. He thanked them, nodded and boarded his plane. Seated on the starboard side, nursing his lumps and bruises, he peered out the window and noticed his benefactors watching the plane. They remained until the plane was airborne.

Almost two years had passed.

Incredibly, he was home. More incredibly, Stefano was still alive.

His first impulse, when he had arrived safe in the confines of his Sausalito home had been to gather up all the

131

files on Salvatore—the portfolios, the diaries, the biography and all similarly explosive material—and toss it into the fireplace—to burn every last shred of Salvatore's existence on earth, along with his own bad dreams and nightmares. But, judging from the condition of his house, he had felt sure someone had beat him to it.

He had found it a total shambles.

Whoever had desecrated his property had known his business; not an item was left untouched. Thank God, he had forwarded all materials to a special post office box in San Mateo, miles south of San Francisco on the Peninsula. For a time he had moved about in a daze, staring at the interior of his house in full dismay.

How much more violence, how many more deaths would be forfeited before this snowballing force of depravity could be stopped? Modica had seen enough violence and death in the war, enough to leave him fearless of the things he could perceive. Fear of the unknown was what eroded his guts. Never certain of when an unseen hand in the darkness might reach out and strike, or when a swift bullet aimed at him from some remote hideaway when he passed along the street might find its mark, he had reasoned this was no life for a man as vital as he.

He leased another house overlooking the sea in Marin County, under a fictitious name, and for the next three months, as he furnished the place, he entered into a heated debate with himself. On the one side was honor, respect, integrity, and a firm resolve which rebelled at the liars, traitors and cold, hard, ambition-driven hypocrites who'd shown him their true colors. Someone had to let them know they couldn't get away with their corrosive and corrupt politics. Someone had to stand up to them.

On the other side was the accumulation of all that had happened, and the concern that even more could happen. The deaths of his friends, the brutality, the torment, the lack of justice done at the trials—all of it, having grown to phenomenal proportions in his mind, simply couldn't be swept aside and forgotten. He couldn't remain blinkered and silent the rest of his life and let his overwhelming hatred and resentment grow. He couldn't. He wouldn't. He, Stefano Modica, had the ammunition with which to crush them all, balled tightly in his fist, ready to hurl.

With no one close to him to suffer the consequences of his acts, he reasoned, he could lose nothing—save his own life—if he pursued the task he set for himself. Modica knew such a mission might prove suicidal, and that he stood alone; one man against a two-nation, political criminal cabal.

A newborn cynicism and a growing resentment prodded him to show contempt for those men who had betrayed his trust and now sought to annihilate him. In Stefano's mind, there was only one way to match the treachery of those self-righteous, self-serving jackals who had used him to entrap Salvatore, those satanic louts who had made a Judas out of him: *extinction!* Oh, not by aiming a weapon at them and slaughtering them as they so justly deserved. Nothing so simple for them. Uprooting their diabolical plots and plans, their selfish ambitions and foul lives, that was the ticket. Political slaughter of these treasonous bastards by the most public and efficient means. Exposing their deeds to the world so they could be seen in their true light. Regardless of which side of the Atlantic the chips might fall, the President's Palace in Rome or the White House in Washington, he was convinced that those who were culpable of the recent crimes must be exposed. This was his dream, his hope, his reality.

God plagued Stefano with an unrelenting conscience and increased his own personal guilt to a point where the pain became unendurable. It was enough to drive him mad. For Stefano the pain would grow, until, out of necessity to preserve his sanity, to absolve his guilt, he'd be forced to move in the right direction. It wouldn't take a day, a week, a month or a year. It would take time. It would take another death, another near-successful attempt on his life, before he would be moved to decision.

On a foggy day in the Bay Area, as the mist rolled into the bay in thick banks, a telephone call to Stefano from Fred Chall, deputy director of the Security Council's archives division, elicited a polite exchange of words before Chall zinged in with the real reason for his call. The entire ORS file had been missing from the Rome office since 1950. Did Modica know anything about it? Where the hell had he been all this time? Incessant calls to him—calls which failed to reach him—had gravely worried the bureau. Could he enlighten them on the possible whereabouts of this Top Secret file? Modica couldn't. Len Salina and Renzo Bellomo indicated the files had been seen last in Modica's possession. Modica expressed his regrets. He personally had turned over the file to Matt Saginor. *Let them go either to hell or heaven for verification of this,* thought Modica. He hung up the phone before bothering to ask how they had got his new telephone number or tracked him down.

Firmly entrenched in his new quarters with ample provisions to last a while, he kept at his side a newly purchased Browning and an old service pistol, plus an army surplus M-1 rifle, which he'd field-stripped, cleaned meticulously, oiled, and loaded. Having already microfilmed the entire ORS File and locked it in his vault with the rest of his treasure, he retrieved the original file and began an immediate, detailed and systematic perusal of it, never having previously had the opportunity to critically assess its contents and familiarize himself with them in the past.

Somehow, somewhere in all this mess, Modica would find the tie-in with Martino Belasci's office, someone willing to pawn one life for another to satisfy his own greed. Who was the logical man? Was it Roger Cutter, as Santino Siragusa had unwittingly mentioned to him? If so, he would need a complete make on the man—and, for additional insurance, one on every man in the Council. Chall had dropped the information that Len Salina and Renzo Bellomo, back many months from the Japan detail, were in the San Francisco area. He would trust them with his life—and did.

Five days after the call from Chall, Stefano Modica lay in the intensive care unit of the University of California Hospital in San Francisco, more dead than alive. He was alive due only to his ability to sense danger. A split second before Modica had been shot through the head by unknown assailants, he had been sitting at his desk immersed in his work. He made an instinctive move as the bullet sped along the trajectory and tore into his cranium at an angle striking the left temple and exiting the upper portion of the skull, missing the optic nerves and vital grey matter. A second missile punctured his left rear shoulder and exited through his throat, miraculously missing vital parts.

Simultaneous to the shots, the phone on his desk rang. Somehow, he managed, as he fell over the desk, to jar the phone from its cradle.

Salina's filtered voice came through the phone. "Steve! Steve! Be careful. There's a contract out on you!"

Modica tried to mouth the words, "Too late!" as he toppled over in a heap and fell into a coma.

Len's voice, frantic came through the instrument. "Steve! Steve! Are you there?"

He wasn't; and Salina, less than a block away when he decided to impart to Stefano the volatile information he had received an hour before from Bellomo, left the phone dangling from a hook in the public telephone booth and dashed to Stefano's house. Unable to enter the well-secured house, he used his gun to blow off the front door lock and ran up the cantilevered steps that hugged the glass-walled house to search the rooms until he located Stefano's body.

Salina had no way of knowing that whoever had gained access to the house had wiped the desk clean of the entire ORS file. During the month Stefano remained in a coma, Salina and Bellomo went over every possible reason for the assault of their former chief. Renzo Bellomo decided—it had only been speculation on his part up to now—that this was still part of the retaliation extending from the Salvatore affair. What else would have brought about such desperate ends? Neither agent had forgotten Saginor's fate, and often wondered why they'd been spared. Was it only a delayed time bomb? Would they taste the bite of vengeance, too? One thing, they sure as hell weren't about to waste their time worrying about it. Too many things needed doing.

Their skillful training and their long-standing friendship for Stefano made their next steps easy. They transferred Stefano to the University of California hospital, obscured his whereabouts, and gave him a new identity. Obvious to both agents was the fact that someone wanted Modica dead. Very well, dead he'd be. His death, reported to the San Francisco *Examiner* as the result of a mysterious malady, was posted in the obituary column. A coffin was ordered and a burial took place, so the world would believe him dead.

Prognosis for Stefano's health wasn't promising. For a time his life would be touch and go. His friends took turns staying with him, until Salina returned to Washington or until they could find a suitable, trustworthy nurse or companion.

Modica regained consciousness on the morning scheduled for Salina's departure. Dazed and partially confused by the time gap, he was still unable to speak coherently, and it took several moments before his brain started up and worked with enough efficiency to absorb what Salina told him about that fateful night. Questioned about the nature of his involvement, Stefano only shook his head. He couldn't tell Len Salina.

"Never mind. Don't overtax yourself, Stefano. Relax. Renzo will be here soon. Talk with him. I gotta go, pal." He glanced at his watch. He reached over and gripped Stefano's frail hands. "You'll be okay. Next time we see each other we'll have a few blasts and thumb our noses at death. There's a gun under your pillow, if you need it."

Len Salina left just as a rush of nurses and doctors entered the room, excited about Stefano's return to consciousness, and set about an exhaustive examination of their patient.

Salina stepped out the door of the hospital into a dazzling daylight, and descended the steps to the concrete pavement. He ambled down Parnassus Street to where he had parked his rented black sedan. It was quiet this time of the day, before visiting hours. He paused to stretch his large frame, yawned and shook himself to wakefulness. He'd lost a lot of sleep this past month, he thought as he unlocked the car door. He sat down in the driver seat, lit a cigarette, and puffed on it for a few moments, hoping he might see Renzo before he left. Inserting the key into the starter, he thought, *Renzo had better learn what the hell Stefano was involved in before it was too late.* He turned the key, stepped on the accelerator, blowing himself to kingdom come.

The explosion knocked out windows in several of the nearby buildings. What was left of Len Salina; both arms severed from his body, his intestines splattered on the nearby pavement, decapitated and decimated beyond recognition, was growing cold by the time the hospital crew arrived to search for all his remains.

Renzo Bellomo, whistling happily and blinking his eyes against the bright sunlight, made a right turn on Parnassus Street and drove up the incline to approach the hospital area and the crowds gathering at the parking lot. He parked his car a block away and snaked through the crowds as the stretcher bearers loaded sections of the battered body into a canvas receptacle. Gazing away from the ghastly sight, Renzo let his eyes focus on the remains of the black sedan. His eyes narrowed with clinical detachment. Wasn't that the car Salina had driven away from the motel this morning? God, no! Not him!

Reluctantly his eyes moved towards the canvas where portions of the body were being fitted grotesquely together as into some obscene jigsaw puzzle. Only a long-ingrained discipline and years of training prevented him from collapsing over the state to which his dearest friend had been reduced. He turned a chalky grey and crumbled internally. He glanced about uneasily and peered at the horrified faces of the shocked onlookers, who instructed to leave by the police, had refused to budge.

When the homicide squad infiltrated the area, Bellomo

exchanged a few words with the officer in charge, showed him his credentials, and waited patiently until they located Salina's ID. The identity substantiated, Bellomo requested they keep the information under wraps until he was contacted later in the day, either by Bellomo or by the Bureau Chief. God! How would he explain to Salina's wife? How?

"Before there are none of us left, Stefano, you'd better tell me what the hell you've been involved in," insisted a brittle-voiced Bellomo, evidencing immeasurable sorrow at the death of their friend. He faced him in the hospital room.

"Not Len! Goddammit! Not him!" yelled Modica hoarsely in a violent reaction. He turned his face from Renzo and tortured himself for several moments. Hands, balled tightly into fists, struck at the bed at either side of him. "How can I tell you what I'm doing after this? It would only mean trouble for you."

Bellomo laughed sardonically with harsh overtones. "Len *didn't* know, and it seems to me he reaped plenty of trouble."

Stefano's bloodshot eyes and his swollen face contorted into a look of diabolical hatred. "You'd better leave, Renzo—while you're in one piece. Damn them! Damn them all! They think they can kill and maim and cheat and twist the minds of men because they sit in lofty positions and construct laws to make themselves immune to prosecution for the crimes they commit, while lesser men pay with lives and property. Have they no human decency? No respects for the rights of others?" he cried.

"Stefano! Stefano! What the hell's wrong with you? What the hell are you talking about? Calm down, man. You aren't home free yet!"

"Why the hell did we fight that fucking war? We paid a helluva price—the blood of innocent young men—just so we could perpetuate a breed of inhuman politicians who pile up mountains of gold and oil and riches for themselves, made available to them by the blood, sweat and tears of fools like us!" His eyes glowed unnaturally and he sat up in bed, shaking uncontrollably. He ranted on.

"I swear, Renzo, I shall light burning crosses for Salvatore, Matt Saginor, and Len Salina and I'll plant them on the White House lawn, so they can see what they've done!"

Bellomo rushed to his side, to hold him down. "Stefano, stop talking, man. You're raving!" He shook him. "Cool it. You're in no condition to work yourself up like this!"

Modica, spent, fell back on his pillows, his face wet

with perspiration, unable to control his shaking. Bellomo lit a cigarette and placed it between Stefano's lips. He lay back smoking, trying to calm himself. "This is my doing," he said, at last. "I'll make restitution for their deaths and these brutal atrocities. They can't stop me now!" His voice, deadly, was without expression. "How far do these tentacles of power reach? Between the ORS and the Salvatore story lie a dozen hangmen's knots, waiting to be stretched around the necks of the guilty. Those knots stretch from the White House to the Italian High Command, and I swear, Renzo, on the deaths of all three, Salvatore, Saginor and Salina, I'll find those nooses and prepare them for those men whose necks are tailored to fit them, if it kills me."

"You're already a dead man, Steve," said Renzo who pointed out how Len Salina had planted Modica's obituary and held a mock funeral.

Stefano glanced swiftly at his friend. "Good," he said after a moment. "Now perhaps I can work in peace."

"Can you use a partner?"

"No, no, no, no. *No!* I can't ask you to subject yourself to all this!"

"So don't ask. I volunteer. Besides, you need someone with my talents."

"You're right. I do need your talents, friend."

And so it went. Stefano Modica, a dead man, working diligently with Renzo Bellomo for several years, was finally ready. Bellomo resigned from the Bureau.

In a remote fishing village off the shores of Baja, California on the Bay of California, a few miles south of Palmia, a tall, distinguished American with piercing blue eyes stood on shore with his wife. an attractive brunette with pale lavender eyes and a soft smile, dressed in casual jeans and a shirt. watching as their son waved to them from the decks of Grand Banks fishing scow. Standing close by him, Renzo Bellomo watched as the huge prize marlin was loaded on a dinghy headed for shore.

Native fishermen, stripped to the waist, their skins sunbaked to the color of clay pottery, with toothless grins and straw hats, wearing pants wrapped like diapers around their lean hard. well-muscled bodies, moved into the water towards the approaching dinghy.

"Every day he grows. he looks more and more like his father," said Stefano with an undisguised smile.

"I hope we've done the right thing, Stefano," said his wife with worry lines creasing her forehead.

"We've done the right thing, Gina," he said turning to her. "It's the only legacy he'll have. A son should know his father."

That evening, as they sat in the open-aired portico of the Spanish hacienda. Renzo Bellomo handed Gina and Stefano their usual after-dinner drinks, *Damiana* on the rocks. Stefano sipped the silent toast made by his friend, placed it on the nearby rattan table and opened the manuscript on which both men had labored for so long and for which so many lives had been expended.

"Appassionato," began Modica. . . .

BOOK TWO

1943

The Beginning of a Legend

CHAPTER 10

September 27, 1943

. . . Before this day ends, tragedy will strike and effect the lives of countless people. My life will take an irrevocable turn and I will no longer be the same person I was when dawn broke on this day. Nothing in my childhood could have predicted what was to be in the early days of my manhood. For me, it all began on this day, shortly before my twenty-first birthday.

—Alessandro Salvatore

It was desperately hot. The *sirocco*, blowing aprons of white dust, fine, sharp as ground glass, had darkened the day, sealing off all vestiges of sunlight. At 1:30 P.M. it seemed like dusk. Early this morning Tori Salvatore and his friend Pallido, a bridegroom of two weeks, had hiked 20 miles to Jato to buy cheese with their hard earned money. Taking the usual precautions not to be caught, they found themselves nevertheless trapped only moments from home. They had no weapons, knowing if they were caught it would go hard on them.

To make matters worse they were surrounded on all sides by *Guardie Campestre* (Agriculture Police) and *carabinieri*, who promiscuously shot their Mannlicher-Carcano rifles at random into nearby wheat fields and bamboo thickets, hoping to flush out the culprits—or kill them. What did it matter which? Hot on their heels from Borgetto and from the dry waterways marking provincial borders, the police were rapidly converging upon them.

They tried to tell themselves not to worry, that it only made matters worse. But, as bullets pinged and zinged overhead and at either side of them, so close they felt rushes of hot air whizzing past their ears, they knew they could be easily killed, and they were crazy out of their heads thinking what to do next.

They asked themselves why they were treated like ferocious beasts and escaped murderers. Why? Hunted by police, shot at, because they bought and paid for food with

143

their own money to feed their families? What irony was this? What mad scheme had the devil conjured up this time? They could understand an intensive manhunt if they'd been vicious killers who robbed and murdered for profit. But all this for buying food? Was it to be believed?

The sound of shrill police whistles split the air overhead. The shooting suddenly stopped. Tori and Pallido froze. They didn't breathe. They didn't move. What miracle had happened? Voices shouting in the wind, muffled and barely discernible, suddenly rang loud and clear.

"*Firmate! Firmate!* Stop firing! We've caught them!"

They exchanged startled, confused glances. Moving forward under the weight of their cumbersome packs, they saw through a clearing countless policemen waving rifles over their heads in a gesture of capitulation. Now, nodding to someone beyond their view, the policemen retreated into their jurisdictions.

Santo Dio! Their present and immediate danger far from over, and fully aware that much had to be negotiated before they arrived safe in their village, Tori and Pallido still expressed relief at the sudden reprieve. Sweat poured freely from Tori's handsome face. He wiped it with a red kerchief, then tied it Indian-fashion about his forehead to keep the salty sweat from running into and stinging his eyes.

He took stock of their situation. To the north lay terraced buckwheat fields, affording no cover. Directly east, running north and south, the winding, corkscrewed road from Castellammare Valley snaked through villages all the way to the summit of Monte d'Oro, where graft-filled *carabinieri* scouted the area, prepared to extort bribes from submissive peasants. Less than twenty feet from them, across the road, stood a straw hut—a *pagliao*—converted into a *carabiniero* checkpoint.

Peering from behind a thick cluster of cactus and bushes, Tori recognized two young lads from their village. Johnny and Joey Russo, ages eleven and twelve, had been caught by two khaki-clad *carabinieri* dressed in summer shorts and shirts, wearing desert forage caps and neck protectors.

The youths, both wearing beige shorts, shirts and ankle boots, were arguing heatedly with the *carabinieri* over the meager backpacks they carried.

Tori and Pallido, a small, wiry, dark-eyed youth of eighteen, with sun-baked features the color of mud, stared at the activity without feelings of personal involvement. It wasn't their affair. Their only concern lay in finding an

144

avenue of escape. There was none. Stuck, unable to move, they watched the activity, unaware that these two obscene *carabinieri* were Gucci and Molino, the swinish sons of whores who had maimed and killed half the youth in Montegatta.

Gucci, a swarthy-faced brute with owlish eyes, the nose of a killer hawk, and the toughened skin of a behemoth, pressed the lads. He asked where they had come by the food they transported. In true Sicilian style, the lads professed ignorance. Threatened with jail, the eldest boy, Johnny, protested that his family had no money with which to buy their release from jail.

"Then we take half your goods," said Gucci. "Mind you, I'm fair!"

"The boys protested loudly. "No. Our family needs the food."

"No, eh?" roared the gargoyle whose powerful torso and upper arms set into the misfitted body of a bandy-legged gnome bordered on the grotesque. "You'd like it better, I suppose, if we took all your goods and clapped you in jail as well."

"All right," said Johnny, reconsidering. "I'll permit this injustice."

"Now, there's a smart peasant dog," said Gucci grinning evilly. His grin quickly dissolved and he commanded his partner, "Take it! Take it all!"

Molino, a bland looking man under whose face lurked the brain of an imbecile, did as he was told, while his companion Gucci raged aloud.

"I'll teach you misbegotten sons of a pig-eyed rhinoceros not to be so greedy. It doesn't pay to be so insolent to the *carabinieri*!" He struck the lad a powerful backhand blow and knocked him off his feet.

Tori's apathy disintegrated. He lunged forward, jolted by a spurt of rage. Encumbered by his back pack and unable to sprint forward fast enough, he found himself held in check by the bantamweight Pallido, who in an instant developed the strength of an ox.

"Fool!" he hissed. "Do you want to get us killed? This isn't our affair! Those trigger-happy sons of two-holed cunts would like nothing better than to cut us in two before we crossed the road. What purpose would our deaths serve, eh?"

Tori strained hard against him. Oh, how he wanted to give that bastard a sample of his own fare! Pallido was right. Knowing this only angered him more. His left ear began to throb like a giant kettle drum. Since he knew

145

what caused this phenomenon, he paid it little heed. His attention, caught by the strange lights in Pallido's eyes, shifted back across the road.

"You said *half*," came a storm of protests from young Johnny, who, for no apparent reason fell into a crouched position opposite the crazy brute as if he intended to do *mano a mano* combat with him.

"What's this? What's this?" snarled Gucci. Raising his gun butt high, he brought it down, full force, and struck the boy, catching the side of his head. Stunned by the blow, the boy reeled back with an insensible and idiotic look in his eyes. Blood spurted from both his nose and mouth. Holding his head between his hands, he twisted and moaned. Judging from the sounds he made, his pain must have been excruciating.

His younger brother, Joey, frozen under the gun of Molino, stood by helpless. Once again Gucci brought the gun butt down heavily upon the shoulders of the hapless victim. He struck him time and again, without mercy, until the lad no longer screamed, or moaned, or moved. Or breathed.

"Let me go, goddammit!" gurgled Tori hoarsely. "I said, let me go!" Pallido's strength, from wherever it came at that moment, increased. By now, he fairly sat on Tori and placed a hairy hand over his friend's mouth.

"Stay here!" he hissed. "I said, stay here! They'll kill you before you come within a yard of them! Goddammit! Calm down and I'll take my hand away," he told the wriggling squirming mass under him. "You know who I think they are? Gucci and Molino!"

Tori stared at him in disbelief. Held down by the damnable backpack and Pallido's leverage, he stopped struggling. Angry at Pallido, angry at the weighty backpacks, angry at the two beasts across from him, and angrier at his sudden impotence, he felt sick. Pallido cautiously removed his hand, ready to clamp it back on Tori's lips if he were to yell. For all his eighteen years, the lad showed wisdom.

"*Va bene,*" he said softly. "There are other ways to handle such matters, *amico*. Now is not the time."

There's a *bastinada* you won't forget!" yelled the bull moose, Gucci. He turned to the younger lad. "Now, move! Move! Get your brother out of here! Move before I do the job on you! And if you're thinking to report me, remember, I know your name and your face and I'll come looking for you!"

Startled by their sudden reprieve, Joey Russo pulled, and tugged at his brother's deathlike form. Dragging him by the arms, legs, or anything he could grasp firmly in his young hands, he stumbled, fell, tripped and lost his footing, only to scramble compulsively to his feet again and labor breathlessly along the dusty road until they were mercifully swallowed up into the eye of the *sirocco*.

Salvatore felt wretched. His ear throbbed relentlessly. He continued to ignore the built-in device God had given him to alert him of impending dangers. What good was it? Pallido and he had brought no weapons. If caught, they'd be helpless. "Bastards!" he muttered, followed by a string of curses that expressed his feelings towards these black-hearted mercenaries infecting their land—the *carabinieri*. His ear wouldn't let up.

Shame-filled for not having aided the Russo boys, he took out his wrath on Pallido. "You should have let me go! Why did you hold me back? They were young babies," he hissed bitterly. "Goddammit! We should have brought a *lupara*—handguns—anything!" He reached up to worry his earlobe, as if that might stop the throbbing, and, unable to control his rage, he cursed aloud. "*Botta de Sanguo!* Why, God?" he supplicated, "Why do you see fit to warn me of trouble when you give me no wisdom or strength to combat the evil? You provided Moses with a staff containing your power. Me, you provide with a sensitive ear that plays a minuet. What good does it do a man to know of such things if he can't alter the conditions?"

Pallido's head swivelled around to stare at his handsome friend as if he'd lost his senses. Before he could ask why the hell Moses had entered their conversation, they were propelled forward by an unexpected shove from behind, and they both landed unceremoniously, scrambling forward into the middle of the road.

Alerted by a glimpse of Tori's red neckerchief, spotted when the winds blew through the thicket, Officer Molino had craftily crept in behind them and caught them off guard.

Towering over them stood that demon, Gucci. Tight lips pulled back fiendishly over yellowed teeth; scornful, hating eyes that could challenge a herd of charging bull elephants without flinching; everything about him told Tori that Gucci was capable of killing them both.

"Your identity cards!" bellowed the bull moose.

Tori took his time in pulling himself off the ground. He assisted his friend, who'd been thrown off balance by the backpack weight. He dusted off his trousers, clenched his teeth until his jaws ached, and, against his will, complied with Gucci's order. They both handed him their cards.

147

"What the hell is it with you ignorant Sicilians? Can't you read or write? Haven't you seen the notices? It's against the law to transport food over provincial borders. What's in your packs? Goddammit! Move! Move, I said, and remove those packs. We haven't got all day!"

"Cheese," said Tori, his eyes intent on the guns of their obstructors.

"Where did you buy the cheese? I suppose some vendor just happened along the road," snorted Gucci. "You all tell the same story." He studied their identity cards with marked interest.

"That's right. That's just the way it happened," replied Tori with a false brightness that drew a dumb look of surprise from Pallido's face. They slipped off their backpacks. Where the leather straps had cut into Tori's arms, angry welts had blistered and opened. He ached all over. Every muscle and nerve in his body felt swollen and he was consumed with thirst. He uncorked his goatskin. "Mind if I sip some water?" he asked pointedly.

Gucci hated handsome men who reminded him of his own ugliness. His eyes burned into Salvatore's and slowly assessed the peasant's physical potential. In his prime, suntanned and in perfect physical condition, Tori stood a hair under six feet. Broad shoulders, strong arms and thickly muscled thighs strained through khaki colored trousers and shirt. One strong hand held the goatskin to his lips; the other, thumb hooked through his belt, gave him the appearance of a relaxed, fearless man, one unconcerned with the presence of an obstructor. Warm brown eyes masked the inner fury of a man bent on destruction. Nostrils at the end of his straight nose flared, and his jaw line rippled as he clenched his teeth.

Gucci saw all this and more. None of it was in Tori's favor. He growled wrathfully. "Impertinent bastard! Be quick with those packs!" Gucci fingered his gun a little too eagerly. ". . . Or do I need my trusty little friend to persuade you?"

"There's two cheeses in each pack," volunteered Pallido.

"I didn't ask for an inventory, you son of a humpbacked turtle. I gave you an order!"

There came a sound of fast riding. Through clouds of dust came a squad of seven riders and their horses—raspy-throated, coughing men who braved the sweltering North African winds. The riders, coming to a stop, pulled up sharply on their reins. Their leader, a well-muscled officer flamboyantly-dressed in the *Napoletano* style, yanked hard on the reins of his lathered horse and let it dance a

148

bit. Birds of such rare plumage, rarely seen in the interior villages, drew instant attention. Even Tori and Pallido seemed impressed by such a uniform.

"I'm Lt. Franchina of Bellolampo," he shouted at Gucci who saluted him smartly. Molina quickly stood at attention and saluted. "We're looking for two young lads carrying backpacks. . . ."

Lt. Franchina, a sharp bird, glanced at the Montegattans as if they were something utterly abhorrent to him. He inspected the *carabinieri* with discerning eyes, silently taking note of the lorry full of confiscated foods. His eyes assessed with more curiosity the large cache of weapons stacked against one wall of the straw hut. This, he surmised, was dirty business.

As the *carabinieri* exchanged words, Tori paid them no heed. More intent on watching the brutal Gucci, he wondered at his and Pallido's fate. The guns enticed him. Should he make a dive for them? If he were fast enough, he might bag both his obstructors. Pallido's earlier words deterred him: *There are other ways to handle such matters.* Tori bided his time.

"Is there another entrance to the village?" asked Lt. Franchina, shouting above the wind to be heard. He ignored the man's obvious salute of dismissal.

"Only along the dry waterways guarded by those ferreteyed *Guardie Campestre*," answered Gucci. "I tell you those *birbanti*—those sharpies—don't let a flea escape. Nothing gets past them, *Tenente*, hear?"

"*Va bene,* I believe you," replied the peacock Franchina, who couldn't resist adding, "If they get through, then, it shall have been through your negligence, eh?"

Preoccupied with his own thoughts, Tori heard none of this conversation between the peacock on horseback and the vile obscenity, Gucci. Obviously something the peacock said had angered Gucci. By the time they had exchanged salutes and the officer and his squad of men had disappeared into cornucopias of dust, Gucci, tense, irritable and seething, was ready to turn his wrath on the men he detained. For a moment he listened to his partner make small talk.

"Is this good cheese?" asked Molino. "I've not seen anything worthwhile in these times," he added, his mouth watering for a taste of the cheese.

"We've had no opportunity to sample it," said Tori in the manner of a dandy. "Our auto broke down, you see. We sent our man for help—" He stopped abruptly, sobered by the name-tag on Gucci's shirt which came into

149

clear focus. So! *This was Gucci!* He lifted his inscrutable dark eyes slowly, fixing them steadfastly on the brute.

Instantly Tori got the distinct impression that his testicles had exploded. He jacknifed forward to catch his breath. He'd been struck front, and nearly bull's-eye, by Gucci's rifle. Tori was lucky. Gucci had missed his manhood by a hair. That's not to say he wasn't in pain. He took his time drawing himself up to his full height. Without the weight of his backpack he towered over Gucci. He saw little else now, except the devil in his path.

One look at the menace in Tori's dilated eyes spurred Pallido into action with the antics of a court jester. He grinned broadly: "Here! Take a look! See what *fantastico* cheeses! Twenty pounds each, and orange as a harvest moon. Go ahead, take one and let us be on our way." He put on a good show, avoiding Tori's contemptuous glare, and moved about the area like an agile dancer. What did he care if Tori was angry? He had a new bride waiting for him at home, and he aimed to get there in mint condition. For now, he was all gaiety. He smiled falsely and did a side-stepping cakewalk to distract the police.

"You want us to look the other way and let you pass. Is that it?" asked Gucci. "Very well—two." He held up two grubby fingers.

"Take one and be satisfied," bargained Pallido. "We don't mind if you wet your beaks as long as there's enough to go around."

Gucci drew his service pistol. "Two—or jail for both."

"*Allora*—two," said the crestfallen bridegroom, with no help from Tori.

"Go on, move. Move!" yelled Gucci. "Move before I change my mind. I said move, mules, move. *Move!*"

Food in Sicily, more precious during wartime than money, could buy anything, even life. Food had become a vital weapon to ward off the sword of Damocles and death's invincible warriors. Which atrocity affected Tori most—the brutal *bastinada,* or the loss of their food—was hardly important now.

"I should peel you like a prickly pear for being so generous," he told Pallido as they scaled the rocky incline to their village. "Chop you at both ends and slit you down the middle!"

"*Allora*—that was really Gucci? That ruthless obscenity who's cut the lifeline of our youths? *Managghia!* And did you see all the artillery? Rifles, handguns?"

"I saw them. Do you realize the back-breaking sweat

150

that paid for those cheeses? How long we saved to buy them?" Tori wouldn't ease up.

"Whores of the devil! They have no feelings except for themselves. What do they care for us, eh?" Pallido, on his own tack, hardly heard his friend.

"They had no right to confiscate our cheese. I hope they choke on them."

"Listen, *professore*, be grateful we're alive—eh?" Pallido was exasperated.

"Be grateful we're alive?" Tori repeated in scornful mimicry. "Thieving bastards! Instead of bringing us relief, the Allies and their goddamned laws brought us doom. We cross borders, risk our lives for food paid with our own money—*our own money*, mind you—and we become felons. Is that justice? Blood sucking *carabinieri!* They bleed us dry with tributes we're forced to pay, then they steal our food and capriciously shoot us down. Next they'll steal our lands!"

Pallido lost all patience. "*Cazzu!* Did you want to go to jail? End up like your cousins, murdered in cold blood? You forget the de Montanas?"

"They'll never steal or cheat Salvatore again!" he glowered angrily.

"*Cafone!* Goddammit! There was no other way!" shouted Pallido, infuriated by the other's stubborness. "*Allora*—you go ahead. Be a hero! Anytime! *Pero* not with me around. I don't ache for a bullet in my belly. . . ."

Ping! Zing! Ping! Ping! Cracking sounds of rifle fire burst around them in small explosions.

"Get down, Pallido!" shouted Tori in warning.

Pallido, a look of insane bewilderment in his eyes, pitched forward and fell into his friend's arms.

"Pallido! Pallido!" Tori fell to the ground over his friend's body, searching frantically for the source of gunfire. In the distance, he saw those murderous monsters, Gucci and Molino, firing at them. He ducked, but not before a bullet creased his skull. Instantly blood dripped down on his forehead. He reached up, touched the warm sticky fluid, and stared dumbly at the crimson splotches in his hand. A surge of madness crept through him as he dove to the side of the road and shed his backpack. Crawling forward in the dust bowl, he grabbed Pallido's body and, pulling him closer, he prayed Pallido's wound would be as superficial as his own. He tore off his friend's backpack, flung it savagely aside, loosened his shirt, and placed his ear over the lad's heart. Heartbeats, faint and irregular, worked hard to keep him alive.

Out of range of those gun-crazed devils, he uncorked Pallido's goatskin and forced wine through his pale lips. Only when he removed his hand from Pallido's back and felt the warm blood oozing from an open wound did his hatred for those butchers multiply, and his concern for his friend intensify. He stroked the dirt-smeared face, pushed Pallido's hair off his forehead. "Talk, Pallido. Talk! Sonofabitch, you can't die! You hear? You can't die!"

Pallido's eyes fluttered opened. He smiled wanly. "It will pass, *professore*. It will pass," he said, and died.

Tori leaned over, feeling dead inside, and picked up Pallido's body in his arms. He lumbered through the *sirocco* towards the village, and with every step he told himself, *Pallido is wrong. It will not pass. Things will get worse. A wrathful Lucifer has entered Montegatta, bent on holocaust. Things won't right themselves without help and for all appearances there is no help for his people.*

He kept telling himself it wasn't his affair. Why should he court trouble? He was a pacific nature, that of a young scholar who had rightfully earned the title of *professore*. He had plans. After the war he intended to become a senator, a legislator, a lawmaker. This was his dream, his hope, his life. He was not, and never had been, a violent-tempered juvenile delinquent who'd go off half cocked to support a cause not his own.

Yet, Alessandro— "Tori"—Salvatore, who was not twenty-one years of age on this day when he first was feeling the irrevocable stirrings of his destiny, found himself, thirty minutes later, huddled across the road from Gucci and Molino's Checkpoint Two, where earlier he and Pallido had hidden. Pallido was dead; but Tori wasn't alone. His companions were a trigger sharp wolf gun—a *lupara*, a deadly weapon—and two loaded Beretta pistols—just in case.

Watching the vipers divide their collected graft from the lorry, Tori was uncertain what he'd do or how he'd do it. For a time, forced to wait until several villagers passed Checkpoint Two and paid their tributes to those dishonorable swine, Tori wondered if Destiny was attempting to dissuade him from his intended task.

At last, when the roads appeared deserted and he was readying himself for a move, he was once again deterred when Molino disappeared behind a roadside shrine and reappeared, holding two young lads by the scruffs of their necks. Tori, his blood boiling, watched them like a hawk.

He recognized the Giunta lads from his village, cousins

to the lads he and Pallido had seen stopped only that morning when they left Montegatta. Caught, the boys were made to part with a kilo of pasta. Like others before them, they protested the unfair treatment. Then, as the remorseless Gucci had done in the past—and would continue to do unless he was stopped, Tori reflected—he bullied the lads and threatened them. Their refusal to back down to him brought on the officer's specialty with the butt of his rifle. Time and again, he struck the impertinent child until blood ran freely and the lad reeled like a crazed animal.

A gust of wind rolled across the valley at them, lifting dust from the ground and swirling it about into a congested mass. When the dust settled, Tori stood at its center, *lupara* held firmly in hand, poised like a young god out of hell. He crept forward stealthily. His eyes, the wary eyes of a golden eagle, veiled the angry volcanic fires that maddened him.

Officer Molino saw him first. He froze. Young Frankie Giunta, a quick-witted lad of twelve years, saw Tori and made a fast grab for Molino's gun, but he wasn't fast enough for Gucci, who paused in his destruction to draw his service pistol and fire point-blank at the boy. The bullet caught the lad between the eyes. He gasped in surprise, screamed loudly, and fell back onto Molino, clutching his face and clawing at the officer with his last ounce of strength. He left a trail of carmine on the *carabiniero's* shorts. Blood gushed from between Frankie's horrified eyes. Tori couldn't believe what he was seeing.

Molino had turned into a dumb statue of immobility. Gucci neither saw Tori nor sensed him until he followed the inert expression on the face of his partner, and his line of vision. Recognition filled Gucci's eyes. Tori could almost see the wheels turn in the *carabiniero's* mind as he extended his pistol in a gesture of submission and permitted it to fall off to one side of his hand where it swung impotently from his trigger finger. His other hand let go the rifle. It fell to the ground at his feet. Tori nudged Gucci back a few steps to enable him to kick the weapon out of the way.

Gucci, collecting his wits, began to argue his case. "Listen, you don't hold all this against us, do you? Your people have been warned. Look, I don't make the laws. The Allies are the conquerors."

He was a cold, unfeeling, self-inflated ass, and his words rasped across Tori's nerves like a knife scraping the bottom of a kettle. Another gust of wind came at them. The neck protector on Gucci's forage cap flapped savagely against his shoulders. In that instant Gucci might have had an opportunity to twirl the revolver back into place and fire at Tori; but the definitive menace with which the Montegattan held his ground precluded any foolishness on Gucci's part. He smirked, shrugged, and tossed the gun forward into the nearby lorry with an attitude of resignation.

With the tip of his *lupara*, Tori motioned Molino in closer to Gucci. The man, rigid and embalmed with fright, was unable to move.

"What do you want, eh?" asked Gucci with false benevolence. "You'd best lay that elephant gun aside before someone gets hurt. I know you're a good lad. If you had intended to kill us, you'd have done it before this. What do you want, eh? Your cheeses? Go ahead, take them. No hard feelings, eh? Listen, take all you want from the lorry. And don't say we aren't generous."

Tori stared at him murderously, unable to express either his thoughts or his feelings, as the brute bargained for his life. Tori's outward calm and silence concealed a storm of inner rage and turbulence. Mistaking his silence for a reluctance to shoot, Gucci took courage and continued to bargain, obsequiously. "Listen, I've collected a handsome bundle of lire today. You want it? Take it all." He made a furtive effort towards his hip pocket, halted only by Tori's compelling voice.

"I wouldn't be that foolish," he said slowly and deliberately, so as to leave little doubt as to his intent. "Make one more move and you'll be dead before I permit you to make peace with the devil who spawned you. Now, move, both of you. To your knees. You've one minute to ask forgiveness for the butchery you've done to the youth of my village. One . . . two . . . three . . . four. . . ."

"You're going to shoot us in cold blood?" Molino, coming to life, accosted his partner. "Do something, you child-molesting son of a whore! You've been so big in the past. So brave! Where's your guts, now that you face a real man?"

"Be quiet, you sniveling son of a horned-toad whore," snarled Gucci.

"Thirty five . . . thirty six . . . thirty seven. . . ."

"In God's name, be human," shouted Gucci, his parched voice cracked.

"What's that? What did you say?" asked Salvatore, brightly.

"I said, in God's name, be human!"

154

Tori thought for a moment. "Very well. That seems a reasonable request. *Va bene,* Gucci." He nodded in seeming agreement. "I'll be as human as you've been. Can that be more equitable? Fifty-nine . . . sixty. . . ." Tori pulled the trigger and blew off Gucci's head.

The blast of a *lupara,* diffused by the sounds of the howling *sirocco,* sounds much like the discordant blast of a small cannon; its effects equally as devastating. Tori watched Gucci's face disintegrate and leave a gaping hole exposing portions of splintered bone fragments on the skull. Shreds of flesh hung like rent fabric. Gucci's body, propelled into the air from the force of the blast, sailed back and fell several yards from them.

Molino urinated in his shorts, unaware that the yellowish fluid soaked through him and ran down his hairy legs. Frightened, he fixed his eyes on Tori, staring like a raving madman. He began to rant and rave and methodically curse Gucci, the *carabinieri,* the day he had accepted duty in Sicily, and the blackest day of all, the day when he had gone against his wife's admonishments and warnings: "You told me not to be a party to Gucci's corruption, Maria Rosa. Did I listen? 'What you do to others will be done to you,' you told me. *Santo Dio!* Why didn't I listen? Why didn't you make me listen?" he squealed like a freshly slaughtered piglet. "Now, it's too late. *Arrivederci, mi amore.*" Molino closed his eyes and clasped his hands over his heart in a deathlike pose. *Carabiniero,* Antonio Molino waited—and waited—and waited. At last, one eye cocked open, he squinted at Tori.

"On your feet, dog!" commanded Tori. "Today is your lucky day—one you'll remember as long as you live you misguided son of a cross-eyed buzzard. You may deserve to die, but not at my hands. Now, hurry, load the lorry with the bodies of those two young innocents. *"Move!"* Tori borrowed Gucci's words and liked their effect. "Move!" he repeated, finding satisfaction in the way Molino moved his tail to the tempo he set.

When he finished, Tori ordered him to remove his service revolver and his boots. He pointed him in the direction of Borgetto with the admonition to run like hell and keep his mouth shut about the incident. "If I as much see your shadow I'll blow you apart as I did Gucci!"
Gucci!"

"I promise. I promise never to return. I swear! I swear. You hear, Maria Rosa? This Sicilian isn't an animal after all." His hope, thus reinforced, strengthened his thoughts of reprieve.

And Tori strengthened his warning. "If I see your face in my village, I'll not take time to count. *Butana u diaoro!*" yelled Tori. "Move!" And Molino moved. Before he was out of sight, Tori did to him what he and Gucci had done to Pallido. The second pellet in his *lupara* blew off the back of Molino's skull.

"This is Salvatore's brand of justice!" he said aloud. "You've been avenged, Pallido!"

Twenty minutes later, he deposited the bodies of the Giunta lads at the house of Doctor Raffa, where earlier he had left Pallido. Tori, unable to speak, made a gesture of hopelessness. Understanding, the doctor patted Tori's shoulder and promised to handle everything.

Outside, Tori welcomed the bleakness of the *sirocco* and the deserted streets which darkened by the moment. On a borrowed mare, he rode swiftly to the Temple of Cats to hide the weapons in his secret hiding place.

Having dumped the bodies of Gucci and Molino over a precipice into a deep ravine like a seasoned murderer, he realized only later that his lack of experience in such mattrs had precluded the removal of their identification. Because he felt no different after the killings, than before, he examined his conscience now, asking himself what it felt like to be a murderer. He had no answer. Inwardly he nursed a sense of secret joy, knowing that unless Gucci was reincarnated, the youth of the village would be no longer molested, abused, maimed or killed.

The clock in the Norman tower at the *piazza* of Montegatta struck the half hour. It was 3:30 P.M., and yet it seemed like midnight. He couldn't go home, yet. Not now. How could a man announce to his mother and sister that he'd just killed two men?

CHAPTER 11

Tori found her where they usually met, in the loft of the stable at the deserted Romanesque villa to the north of the village. He'd never killed a man before, let alone two. The soul-searching experience began to tear at him about a

156

half hour after he had performed the deed. On this unforgettable day he didn't feel his usual self.

Maria Angela Candela—medium brown hair, green siren's eyes, a voluptuous and most desirable body—had just turned eighteen. She was in her prime. Reaching for Tori, she pulled him eagerly towards her throbbing body. "You promised to be here sooner," she pouted. "Five minutes more, I'd have left and you would have found the place empty and the straw cold."

Mistaking his silence for a rebuff, she caught sight of the tight, hard lines on his face. "What is it? Is something wrong? What's happened?"

Unable to reply, he clutched her to him roughly and they both lay back on the matted straw, searching, greedily for each other in the silence. Only their heartbeats sounded above the force of the *sirocco*. The skies continued to darken until they could barely make each other out in the shadows.

Sensing his need, Maria Angelica clung to him even more tightly than usual. She guided his hands over her breasts until she felt him harden against her. It always gave her a sense of power to feel a man respond to her femininity. Tori felt a strange excitement, unlike any he'd experienced in the past with her. He kissed her as the savagery in his soul unleashed. Always, always in the past, he'd been gentle with women. His touch, tender and light as if they were fragile porcelain dolls, was like a whisper of love. Now he ravaged her, tore at her, lifted her breasts from her low-cut blouse, kissed them and sucked greedily as if he never could get enough of them. Tense, he generated a fierce excitement in himself as well as in her.

Maria Angelica moaned and groaned in ecstasy. Never had she been so alive and filled with passion. They didn't recall how or when they removed their clothing, but there they were, suddenly a tangle of arms and legs wrapped about each other. He prepared to enter her, and she strained upward to meet him. Her eyes, like those of a bitch in heat, luminous, lust-filled, rolled upward. They both made those low-voiced animal noises as they tossed and tumbled in ecstasy.

They moaned, writhed, and twisted deliriously, filled with erotic pleasure. Fifteen minutes later, fully spent, exhausted and incomplete, Tori slipped out of her broiling loins, his mind filled with perplexing curiosity. Impotence in any form was frightening. If Tori's puzzlement was profound, the hurt and disapointment in the girl's eyes was more devastating to him. Red-faced and embarrassed, he sat back, filled with burning humiliation and lit a cigarette.

"What did I do wrong ,Tori?"

"It's not your fault. I'm tired. Exhausted from the trip." How could he tell her he'd just killed two men, or that he'd seen Pallido killed before his eyes, or that he'd witnessed the brutal beating of the Russo and Giunta lads?

She didn't believe him. He saw the frustration and self-blame in her eyes, so he looked past her, through the broken walls, out at the dark skies, and tried to shut out the events of the day. Her fingers on his upper thigh traveled upward until she found his manhood, limp and as lifeless as a honey-soaked *pinolatto*. Determined, she moved her hands rhythmically until he responded. He felt a tingle, and a surge of excitement swept through him again. He felt her move silently over him, place her cool, feverish body between his legs. His eyes closed. New sensations rushed at him. He still held a lit cigarette between his fingers during this period of uncertainty. New hope sprang to life. Alien feelings of impotence melted under the fluttering of her hot tongue, and his erection responded in a confused excitement.

Straining forward, he lifted himself on one elbow, and watched her head bob up and down. In that instant he filled with both revulsion and ecstasy. Before he could do anything about either, he felt a surge of power spring from his loins and shoot out through his manhood. For what seemed an eternity of painful pleasure, he sighed and moaned with uncontrollable orgiastic release.

Pleased with her newfound powers, Maria Angelica sensed a strange inner excitement as she watched Tori's face during his release. She wiped her lips on her petticoat and snaked towards him, removed the dead ash from between his fingers, tossed it aside, and snuggled against him, unprepared for the stinging blow of his hand across her face, or for his caustic tongue.

"*Butana!* Whore!" he said, savagely. "Where did you learn to do a thing like that?" Shaken by her brazen sexual act, he rose to his feet and gazed down at her as if she were a vile animal. He couldn't believe what she'd done. "Only the whores in Palermo know of such things!" He let loose a string of expletives, followed by a rash of accusations which sprang from feelings he had harbored for too long, he realized later. But, at the moment, he was revolted. Her tears left him unmoved.

"I've never done such a thing before. I just thought— well, I thought when you love someone the way I love you. . . ." Maria Angelica paused. She didn't understand.

158

She knew he had felt a strange excitement—knew he had experienced orgasm; then why did he strike this attitude? "Oh, Tori, I love you so much. Can't you see? That's why I did it. You were hurting, and I wanted you to feel better." She couldn't have felt worse.

He didn't believe her. She was too well-practiced. In that moment he felt betrayed, defeated. Yet, even as he asserted his mid-Victorian *maschiezzo*, something inside him chanted a different lyric. Confusion overwhelmed him. And in this confusion he grew protective of her. Under this blanket of protection he told her, "You mustn't be in love with me, Maria Angelica. I can love no one. I regret slapping you. And I thank you for sensing my need." He drew her close to him, held her affectionately in his arms. "But you must never do that for a man unless he is your husband, and only if he instructs you to do such a thing. . . ."

Her brain stopped at his previous statement. "Why can't you love me? All this time I thought you felt about me as I feel about you. . . ."

"I don't know why I can't, only that I can't."

"There's someone else. You love another. Oh, I'm so ashamed now. Why didn't I see it before? No wonder you're impotent with me. You love someone else. You do!" she repeated incredulously.

"There is none other, Maria Angelica. Not in the way you think."

"Then, how, Tori? Tell me so I can understand."

"Since I don't know, how can I explain?"

"There's another woman, I know."

"Perhaps you're right," he said in an attitude of remote contemplation. Outside the howling winds abated. The *sirocco* would soon leave them.

"Who is she? Tell me. You owe me that at least."

He lit a cigarette, inhaled the smoke deeply, and exhaled it with a resigned sigh. Tori turned to her. "If you insist, I'll name her. But you won't understand what I say, and you won't hear what I tell you." He reached over, kissed her forehead lightly, sprang to his feet, and pulled on his pants.

"Her name is Destiny. . . ." he said.

Tori left Maria Angelica to the self-destruction that ravages a woman scorned.

Outside he battled the winds all the way back to his house. He mentally regarded Maria Angelica and his cousin Vincenzo de Montana, as they had been three years ago, before Vincenzo had left for the army. They had used the old villa for their numerous escapades. Maria Angelica, a hot little bundle of enormous passions whom no one, including her parents, suspected of entertaining prurient longings, had exuded sex from every pore the moment she blossomed into womanhood.

Calf-eyed, love-struck, and possessed of rampant emotions, Tori had worshipped the girl as one might a goddess. Each night during his adolescence he had serenaded her with love songs of his own creation, accompanied by friends he'd cajoled into assisting him musically. Marriage might have been the next step. However, Tori quickly came to learn that the intoxication of youth, stronger than the intoxication of wine, grows less addictive with time.

He thought back to the time, not long ago, when he and Maria Angelica had taken their pleasures in this same villa, when suddenly Tori heard the voice of his cousin, Vincenzo de Montana, call to him. As he'd been about to withdraw from the girl, Maria Angelica had protested loudly and vehemently. "Don't go, Tori. Not now. Don't leave me in the middle—like this."

Tori had laughed aloud, good-naturedly. They'd been at it for nearly two hours and she wanted more? She had clung to him fiercely. There'd been little he could do except continue with those well-practiced movements familiar to lovers since the beginning of time, until he could detect familiar overtones of impending orgasm. He had waited until she had quieted down.

"Now can I go?" he had asked tolerantly as she came out of the euphoria.

One eye had cracked open, then the other. Focusing on his expression of amused patience, she had become enraged at his total discipline and control. She had jackknifed her legs, shoved them hard against him, and pushed him off balance and he'd fallen, laughing against a bale of hay. That he found the whole thing humorous had brought forth a series of expletives from her lips. "I hate you! I hate you!" she had cried. "Always so smug! You act like you're doing me a favor!" She had pointed to the hardness between his legs. "Look at you—still hard! Why aren't you like the others?"

Tori had risen to his feet, pulled on his trousers, and gently stuffed his erection into them and buttoned his fly. He had patted the sizable bulge affectionately. "Why? Because I'm not a rabbit? *Cara mia,* when Salvatore attends

160

a ball, he is a star who gives unforgettable performances," he'd grinned proudly.

"Vincenzo can keep me happy for hours!" she'd pouted.

"*Va bene*. Then, go fuck Vincenzo."

"But it's you I want, Tori. Can't you show me the excitement, emotions and affection Vincenzo shows me? Must you always be so calm? So studied?"

He'd walked to where she lay, taken her hand, and placed it over his tumescence. "Does this hardness indicate I am calm, without emotions?" Her greedy hands had grabbed at him and began to unbutton his fly.

"Oh, no you don't, you hot little whore. You've had your share for the day. I need my strength. I've work to do."

"You make me so mad! You're like a frozen statue," she'd said with spite. "Who wants to fuck a statue?

Tori had left her in the hay, pouting and angry.

That day, Tori hadn't been gone five minutes when he filled with remorse at having left her so abruptly. Returning to the loft with apology on his lips, he had been arrested by the sight of two shadowy forms thrashing about in the hay.

By God! There they were, both of them, engaged in those familiar frenzied erotic movements. He'd been able to see that Maria Angelica and Vincenzo were really enjoying themselves. Momentarily startled as he'd been at the sight of them, there had been a split second when Tori considered he should be angry—that he should demonstrate his artful manliness with a sudden outburst of temper and utter a string of violent curses upon them both. But, at the sight of such abnormal vigor expended by his cousin Vincenzo, he hadn't been able to contain his laughter. Vincenzo, a sexually insatiable lad with only one thing in mind, would have been content if the walls in his house had consisted of a thousand cuntholes. His craving for what lay between a woman's thighs had been more enslaving than an addict's to drugs.

Sounds of Tori's laughter had startled the lusty couple. Maria Angelica's stifled cry of shame had had no effect on Vincenzo, who, at the point of no return couldn't and wouldn't stop, and, in his frenzied erotic state, every struggle against him had only heightened his arousal. Tori's face had creased with laughter, infecting Vincenzo with a need to prove his *maschiezzo* and his staccato thrusts had accelerated. Turning her face away from him, the girl had made the best of the situation, for, in Tori's mask of laughter, Maria Angelica told him later, she had clearly seen the end of her affair with him.

161

As it happened, she had been psychic, afterall. Their relationship had eroded. Vincenzo had left for the war. Tori had seen little of her. Recently in July, one night, after learning of the deaths of his two older brothers, he'd gone to the villa alone, never thinking he might encounter anyone. But, there she'd been. In a nostalgic moment he had surrendered to her sexuality. He had made it clear there could never be anything more between them than the fulfillment of baser needs. She had agreed to those terms.

One day she had confessed to him that it was easier to pretend affection for a man who fulfilled her sexually, even if her tortured soul longed for another—whom she loved.

"You see, Tori, I'm insatiable. There's a name for someone like me, for someone who indiscriminately craves for sex. All my life I'll be compromising. . . ." She had added also that when Vincenzo made love to her, she closed her eyes and pretended it was Tori. "Skillful and rewarding as my imagination can be, I wasn't prepared for the devil who punished me. You see, I couldn't transform the touch, taste and feel of Vincenzo into the touch, taste, and feel of you, Tori. It's true, one can't have everything."

Lately, Maria Angelica had begun to hope again. Tori knew he had to cut it off with her for good. He promised himself now that it would be the last time he'd be with her sexually. Grateful to have cut it off without the usual false expressions of mutual affection and slim promises, he had made it back to his house wading through the *sirocco*.

No sooner had Tori arrived at his house than his mother, Antigone, informed him he was wanted at the workshop of Candela the cooper. Annoyed at the prospect of having to brave the *sirocco* again, and still not at peace with himself over the tumultuous emotions he'd experienced on this day, he dreaded the thought it might have something to do with Maria Angelica. He needed no such domestic tribulations on this day. "Is it necessary?" he asked his mother. "Can't it wait?"

"For me it matters not if you go. It must be important, else who on his right mind would venture outside in this weather?"

"Yes, Mamma. Who in his right mind?" had been his reply.

Antigone Salvatore must have remained at the door staring out at the rear terrace for a hour after Tori returned from Candela's with the shocking news that Don Matteo Barbarossa, the man she'd so foolishly palmed off

162

on Tori as his Godfather, wasn't dead these many years! Instead he was more alive than before—and a hero at that. She'd been outside in the yard, rearranging trays of drying figs when Tori had come home and exploded that bombshell. If Tori had noticed his mother's sudden pallor, he hadn't remarked over it. His own excitement over the news superseded all else.

She had entered the modest kitchen at the moment Athena, her extraordinarily beautiful daughter, had entered the room. The girl suffered from a mysterious malady which caused a rash of severely painful migraine headaches in recent months, rendering her helpless for days. Then, as mysteriously as the symptoms appeared they'd vanish. Attracted by Tori's joyous voice, she had come in search of him.

Athena, an enchantress with wide and exotic dark eyes and a flawless ivory skin, had been instantly swept up in her brother's arms. He had planted an affectionate kiss on her lips as he'd twirled her around. They'd begun chattering like clucking chickens while their mother scanned the contents of the newspaper article Tori had brought with him, substantiating the fact that Don Barbarossa still lived.

The article bore a glowing account of the unquestionable aid Barbarossa had given to the Allies during the Sicilian invasion. For these special services the Don had been the recipient of many favors and courtesies extended by the Allied forces.

If Antigone had ever been strong-willed in her life, it was at this moment, when she had been forced to conceal the growing disturbance she'd felt at this new development. Moreover, she had been greatly distressed at the near hero-worship she'd seen in her son's eyes when he had rushed out to tell her the stunning news. She'd begun to feel pangs of remorse over the grotesque lies she had perpetuated these many years. In addition to these shaky feelings, a native wariness provoked her next remarks.

"Tori, for the love of God, you didn't mention to Candela or the others that Don Barbarossa is your Godfather?" It had been a painfully posed question, to which she had quickly added, "I mean with all the *fascisti* lurking around we don't need added problems. We must be cautious these days. . . ."

Tori would have had to be obtuse now, not to notice the changes in his mother. Just as he'd observed the aggravation and concern etched into the faces of the men gathered at Candela's when he read them the article of

163

Barbarossa's resurrection, he saw the disturbance in his mother. "I said nothing," he told her. He noticed the remark had brought approval to her face. He told himself he might be too sensitive this day, for many things had happened to color his outlook. Yet despite this, something nagged at him.

"How is it, Mamma, you were so misinformed about my Godfather?"

Antigone shrugged. "After the Mori holocaust, when Mussolini purged the island of the *Mafiosi*, I presumed him dead. That butcher was intent on killing all of them. There was so much carnage and confusion in those blood-letting days. Who knew from anything?"

"What will happen now that he's powerful again? What was his political persuasion?" he asked, chomping on a piece of cheese.

"I'd hesitate to speculate on the politics of Matteo Barbarossa," she said, feeling her stomach churn. "A man can change. It's been many years. . . ." Antigone's eyes narrowed in thought as she moved about the kitchen. She paused to light a gas burner on the stove to warm the coffee, her thoughts roiling with the sudden changes in her village. Perhaps she should have kept her thoughts to herself, but she didn't. "I wondered how it was that suddenly from nowhere, Don Florio becomes mayor of Partenico. Those rumors about Don Russo in Piana dei Greci must also be true."

"Why should such things concern you?" asked Tori, studying her inscrutably.

She shrugged indifferently. "I thought it peculiar that these hard-core *Mafiosi* should move so swiftly back into power. After twenty years in obscurity? Only Barbarossa could have effected such a coup." She clapped her hands together in a gesture of sudden awareness. "*Allora!* Now it begins!" she said cryptically. Then, as it all came together in her mind she exclaimed, "Those foolish Americans! *Pezzi de shekki!* Jackasses is what they are." She continued to upbraid the Allies with stinging rancor, shouting uncomplimentary expletives in a voice loaded with irony as she moved about the kitchen, preparing a small snack for her children.

She paused a moment, breaking her concentration, and glanced at Tori and Athena. "Don't you see what I'm driving at? They've been duped. The Allies have been duped, *figghiu beddu,* my beautiful son."

Tori straddled the chair next to Athena, fully bewildered, unsure of what had set his mother off. "Truly, Mamma, you have me confused."

"Confused? You don't understand?" Antigone paused. "Why can't you see—" Again she paused, suddenly recalling that her children, like the rest of their generation, really knew nothing tangible about the Mafia. Why would they? The past twenty years of fascism had been devoid of *Mafiosi*. The Mafia was to them like a bad dream that never existed. She calmed down and set the coffee pot on the table, and tried to explain. "If the Americans allowed the Don Matteo to aid them in this conquest, the price they'll have to pay in return for his special services will have made their victory worth less than—uh—*merede*," she said flatly.

Tori laughed. "Mamma, no one dictates to the United States."

"No one dictates to the United States, eh?" scoffed Antigone. "No one? Hah!" she smiled tightly. "You'll see. Just give him time. Just give him time, *caro mio*."

The room hung heavy with uneasy silence. Somewhere in the neighborhood an old Victrola played a Neapolitan love song. Shadows lengthened in the dimly-lit kitchen. Tori exchanged confused glances with his sister; then he raised dark, chaotic eyes to study his mother's face as she sat pouring coffee.

"Why do you attack my Godfather?" he asked in a crushed voice, dazed by the inexplicable vindictiveness by his mother.

"Because I know them—all of them!" she retorted in a rash moment. Incited by fires neither of her children could know about, she halted only when she saw the silent questioning in their eyes. Antigone faced a terrifying dilemma. How could she tell Tori? He was no longer an impressionable child. He'd grown up, and only expected the truth from her. She made a disorganized gesture. "Forgive me. I forget you never lived in those times. Perhaps it's as you say, no one dictates to America. I allowed foolish, womanly emotions to cloud sound judgment."

Tori's dark eyes lost their intensity. His face flooded in relief. In moments he and Athena, filled with youthful exuberance, pored over the newspaper article and were lost to their mother. Antigone retreated into the pantry, leaving her children to talk. She leaned her head against the cool concrete wall as tears sprang into her eyes. *Matteo Barbarossa, alive after all these years!* How was it possible, sainted God of the universe? How? She felt like a caged animal, silent, frenzied, hesitant to give rise to the muffled

165

screams lodged in her throat, afraid to claw her way out of her inner torment.

Subtle changes in her village as old *Mafiosi* were restored to their former positions of power should have indicated something to her—and it did. But, never in her wildest dreams could she have guessed that Don Barbarossa had been resurrected! More than the rebirth of the Mafia instilled stark fear into her heart. That Barbarossa himself was alive terrified her.

What was she to do? Now that Barbarossa lived, she couldn't permit Tori to equate him as a hero with the godlike qualities she'd painted so vividly over the years. If she were to tell Tori the truth—he'd have every right to hold her in contempt. He'd be lost to her forever. Once she'd lied to her children—once for the love of God. Hadn't she paid the penalty? One husband and two sons dead! Wasn't that enough penance for one indiscretion, for an involuntary act done when the lives of her children were at stake?

Antigone took out her frustration on the risen bread dough. She punched savagely into the aerated mass, deflated it with her fists, pounded it, and kneaded the clumpy mass until it was reduced considerably in size. Finished, she slipped it back into the pan, covered it, and told herself to stop worrying. It was not for nothing she was considered an iron woman by her neighbors. Hadn't she always said that worrying never helped matters? She told herself to take courage. The chances of their ever meeting were remote. *God, let it be so. . . .*

For some strange reason she kept getting fresh images of Dona Sabattini, the village *strega*. The old woman was a seer, a prophet with an uncanny talent for prophecy. Antigone was too intelligent, too well educated, to give credence to such obvious fakery, despite the compliments bestowed on the *strega's* ability by her neighbors. Under no circumstances would she revive that old prophecy the *strega* had prepared for *Tori* at his birth. Not Antigone, not her. Recently, giving in to a weakness following the deaths of her two older sons in July, she'd given in to an urge and revisited the old sorceress, only to have Tori's prophecy resurrected along with the old uncertainties, fears and anguish of the past. She had received no balm. Why, then, should she even consider the old crone?

The sound of her son's voice calling to her stilled her thoughts. She skillfully erased all traces of her tears and moved back into the kitchen. "Yes, my son?"

Her paleness and distraught appearance was obvious and Tori asked himself how he could conceal the deaths of the

Russo and Giunta lads. There was no way to spare her, so he explained what had happened to the lads, adding only that he was leaving to pay his respects to their families. He told her about Pallido and how he met his death.

"Tori," she addressed him calmly looking him in the eyes. "Are there any other surprises you've forgotten to mention?" she asked in all candor.

He blinked to avoid her piercing gaze and reached over to the table to pick up a *biscotto* and began chomping on it. He shook his head. How could he mention Gucci or Molino? How would she take it when she heard he'd killed them? She was shaken enough over Pallido's death, and how it left his new bride a widow.

"Be careful, Tori," cautioned Antigone. "If you're caught aiding and abetting others it will go equally as hard for you and us."

"Can I turn my back on children trying to be men in the absence of their fathers and older brothers?" he asked.

"We must look to ourselves, Tori. This is the beginning of the end for a soil-tilling people. It's best we don't delude ourselves into thinking times will improve.

"We must be patient. The Allies will do something. It just takes time," Tori insisted.

"Like the laws they enforce to kill off our men? We can't permit you to take more chances, Tori. You expose yourself to too many dangers. One day—" Antigone's voice cracked. "One day, you may not return. We value your life more than a sack of flour or a tin of olive oil. God!" she agonized. "I feel we are all poor lambs in a field, disporting under the eyes of a fickle butcher who chooses, first one then another, until we are all gobbled up."

Athena and Tori had never seen their mother so distraught. She turned to him, her eyes fired with peculiar lights. "No! I won't let it happen. You mustn't allow anything to interfere with your dreams, my son. You must educate yourself, involve yourself in politics. The future of our world rests in the hands of young, strong, thinking men like you. Help restore to our people our God-given rights. *Misericordia!*"

Tori slipped off the chair he'd straddled. He stretched and yawned and patted his hard stomach at the waist. "Destiny decrees the war must end before the future of this *giovanotto* can be decided upon." He forced a weak smile. "Until the schools are rebuilt, Mamma, what can we do, eh?"

"I can go to work in Palermo," said Athena defiantly.

167

"Many girls are there working and making good money. It's important you go to school, Tori."

Confusion struck at him. He stared at them outraged and pulled himself up to full height. "Stop!" he shouted. "Stop this minute .Are you crazy? Have you both taken leave of your senses?" He stormed about the kitchen with the emotional outrage of a proud Sicilian male, directing his fury at Athena.

"Get this straight, sister dear. If the day ever came that you sold yourself on the streets like a common whore, I'd put a bullet through my head after killing you, first. I promise! Never let me hear such disgraceful words again!" He turned to his mother, angrily. "Not from you, either. It's not worthy of you and what you've taught me all my life. As head of this family I'll provide for you both. My future can wait until the war ends."

Antigone shrank away from him, and felt the worse for mentioning such a foolish plan. "Very well, my son," she said resignedly. "Speaking of plans, you'd best prepare yourself for an encounter with Don Pippinu Grasso."

Tori's dismay was readily apparent. "Not again? How much in arrears is he this time?"

When she replied, "Six months," her son asked why she'd waited so long before telling him. She explained that she'd expected to see the payment in the mail each month, and suddenly time had flown. She added, "But we can't wait for his convenience any longer."

"Are we in such dire straits?" he asked pouring a fresh glass of water.

Antigone nodded. "I have no heart left to nag at you— to remind you of our predicament."

He assured her she needn't worry, that he'd manage and he'd attend to Don Pippinu. "I'll go tomorrow to Mt. Erice and straighten him out." Tori's face took on a peculiar expression, one his mother couldn't hope to understand. To have explained what was in his heart would have brought her face to face with a stranger at that moment.

She watched him leave the house with a heaviness in heart that grew unbearable. In the last three months things for the Salvatore family had significantly collapsed. Inflation, sky high prices and a toppling economy had drained their savings to nearly nothing. The fragmenting of her world began in July with news of Filippo's and Marco's death. Now news about Barbarossa had caused an erosion to set in and she grew fearful—fearful that all would be lost soon. And then there was this crazy malady of Athena's! Dear God, what else could happen to the Salvatore family?

For a time she remained framed in the doorway, glancing at the valley beyond the terrace. Swirls of cloudy dust in abstract shapes and form moved across the open sea at Castellammare in the far distance, giving pale illumination to the sun-scorched wastelands. The *sirocco* was leaving at last. She watched the raw, hot lights of a beginning sunset filter through the grey-white mist flooding the land with an incandescent glow, giving a fertile appearance to the broken clay of her back yard where little life had imposed itself in years. Once a few chickens ran around clucking their silly heads off. Now there was no sign of them—nothing.

At forty-five, the petite, gray-haired matriarch looked older because she had neither the interest in cosmetics nor the time or money to support the vanity. Her hair was worn pulled back into an unbecoming bun, speared through with tortoiseshell hairpins. Her high, wide forehead and piercing pecan-brown eyes, set wide, gave character to her spectacular bone structure. Her nose was straight and turned up slightly, complementing her strong, honest face. The beauty of her youth was indelibly stamped on these classic Greco-Sicilian features.

Being a sagacious woman, she'd wasted little time in grief, for the chaotic duties of raising her children, after the death of her husband, had been fulfilled with the matriarchal fervor of a woman intent on a vital mission; this was something she couldn't have accomplished if her time had been wasted in maudlin martyrdom. She was an iron woman all right, but none of these qualities were at her disposal in these next moments, as she reflected on her earlier behavior. Her dark eyes, filled with brooding, stared out at the panorama.

Whatever had possessed her to blurt out her feelings to her children earlier? She'd never lied to them. She had bent the truth, but never lied intentionally. There's a difference, she told herself. One day she'd have to reckon with the truth, consider the consequences. *Oh, God it isn't fair!* she thought. Why did he have to be alive after all these years? Why?

She had no one to talk with—no one to whom she could pour out her heart. She shivered involuntarily as if struck by an icy wind. Her mind began to settle slowly. *So, you struck a sensitive chord for which only you are responsible. So what? Get back inside and prepare your family's supper,* she told herself firmly. She closed the door and returned to her mundane chores.

Outside the winds continued to tear at him, blowing gales of dust—that insufferable dust that stiffens clothing to cardboard consistency, enters your nose and eyes and ears until it parches your brain, refusing to let up. The perennial smell of Sicily, *Stratto,* a tomato paste concentrate, clung to his nostrils, stimulating Tori's appetite. Why didn't he think to wait until after supper to break the news to the unfortunate parents? About to heed that inner voice, Tori was arrested by the crackling sounds of *carabinieri* rifle fire, followed by muffled sounds of scurrying feet at the far end of the deserted street.

He cocked his head to listen. Dust stung his eyes and Tori, drawing his head in like a turtle and turning his back on the inexorable winds, continued to walk in that manner, wondering if he'd actually heard rifle fire or if his imagination had been overworked.

Turning left off Via de Grande onto a narrow, worm-like alley, Tori cocked his head once more to listen. His left ear throbbed with dull precision and he shook his head despairingly. Not again! Damnit to hell! Three quarters of the way into the alley he stopped dead in his tracks. Black clouds drifting overhead created a mass of shifting shadows. *But there!* He heard it again—rifle fire: *rat-a-tat-tat-tat rat-a-tat-tat-tat.* Moved by intense curiosity, he hugged the buildings and slowly crept forward cautiously, his dark, furtive eyes everywhere. Muffled voices grew more distinct. The sounds of horses, snorting and wheezing, came at him. Somewhere there was trouble.

He flattened himself against a shabby building, peering ahead of him into the swirling density of dust at the end of the *cul de sac,* edging in closer. Moments later he came upon the devastating scene. The bodies of two young lads, sprawled face down in the gutter, turned his stomach. He felt a rising nausea, his body sagging heavily against the doorway of a house. Touching his forehead, he found it ran cold with sweat. His dark eyes moved slowly around at the circle of somber-faced men standing over the bodies, reading the horrifying effects at the senseless deaths at their feet.

Would it ever stop? Would this limitless design of death never cease? cried Tori internally. He had shot Gucci and Molino just to end this continual killing. How many more Guccis and Molinos were there? He felt like vomiting.

Finished with their killing, the *carabinieri* stood to one

side of their prey like triumphant hunters flushed with the success of a fresh kill, while sobbing, wailing and grief-stricken parents picked up the lifeless young bodies and sober-faced neighbors, resigned to such a fate, assisted them and carried them into their house. Behind them, left lying in the street, two small backpacks, slit open by bayonets, were strewn about, spilling a handful of corn meal and flour. For *this*, thought Tori, two young lads, yet to reach manhood, had been slaughtered?

Moving in closer to the crowds to observe the goings-on, Tori gave a sudden start when he recognized that sleek, well-preened vulture, the dark-haired predator with the fancy uniform he'd already encountered twice that day; first at Gucci's Checkpoint Two and then later he'd been stopped by this same Lt. Franchina, who had demanded he produce his identity card. Asked by the officer if he knew anything about a black market ring operating in these parts, Tori had replied, *no*. Had he encountered anything unusual that day? *No*. Had he seen lads with backpacks in the past hour? *No*. Those questions, superficial enough, had given Tori a few bad moments. Had the deaths of Gucci and Molino been discovered? he asked himself.

Volunteering no information, Tori had been permitted to pass, but not before the officer had studied him carefully and asked if he hadn't already encountered him that day. Tori had shook his head indifferently and gone on his way before the carabiniero recognized him.

Now, less than ten feet away, the preening vulture raised his voice to the solemn gathering in stern reprimand. Authoritatively, Lt. Franchina asserted himself. "Let these deaths be a warning to one and all. You can't continue to defy the Allied laws without suffering the consequences. The laws are clear. Whoever breaks them shall be punished to the fullest. . . ."

Lt. Franchina turned from the stony-faced villagers, whose hatred of him and men like him was masked by a bland passivity, and all at once he caught sight of Tori's fiery eyes, arrested by the pure venom in them. Glittering dark eyes—eyes that spelled compelling messages—and a firm jaw line caught Franchina's casual glance and held.

"You again, Salvatore?" his eyes narrowed thoughtfully. "What business brings you here? Your card states you live on Via de Grande. . . ."

Tori, noting the man's retentive memory, tried to conceal his own hostility. "Is it now against the law to go

171

visiting in my own village without being questioned by the *carabinieri?*"

"I suppose you will know your rights," retorted the officer, bowing slightly.

Tori, resenting the attention brought to him, frowned and fixed his eyes on Lt. Franchina, who, without comment, mounted his horse. From his saddle, the officer turned to study Tori with intensity. Perceiving the silent menace in the young man's eyes, he retreated wordlessly. He had no real desire to tangle with him. He permitted his mare to dance a bit; then, wheeling her about, he called to his men, *"Avanti! Avanti!"* He spurred his horse on and, in passing Tori, he took another long, meaningful look at the lad. It wouldn't be difficult for Franchina to remember this young man: "His face stood out among the other villagers like a princely white panther in a den of black mice," he would tell the distinguished members of a Tribunal nearly seven years later.

At the right of the *piazza*, Lt. Franchina directed his tired, sweaty and thirsty squad of men to a *birreria*. After such a day they were entitled to refreshments before the long, nerve-wracking ride back to Bellolampo Barracks.

He stretched his legs after he dismounted before the tavern. Placing his hands in the small of his back, he arched it and stretched it as his men filed into the tavern. For a brief second, he felt a chilling tremor shoot through him as a clear mental image of their being served strychnine flashed through his mind. What a perverse flight his imagination had taken on this, his first day in western Sicily!

For Salvatore this day hadn't ended. For Lt. Franchina the nightmare was about to begin, one that would haunt him until his dying day.

CHAPTER 12

Tori had just sat down to a Spartan supper a half hour after his encounter with Lt. Franchina when the hair-raising blasts of a *lupara* shook their house. The blasts, known to literally crumble the walls of houses, were followed in rapid-fire order by the unmistakable staccato of *carabinieri* rifles.

"Stay here," Tori commanded his mother and sister as they exchanged terrified glances. "I'll see what it is." Kicking back his chair, he ran through the house and out the front door, which bore a bright purple mourning band with gold letters reading: *For Our Beloved Sons and Brothers.*

Across the street, at the house of his uncle Gianna de Montana, crowds of curious male neighbors had formed. Women, not permitted on the streets after dark in keeping with ancient customs inherited from the Moslems, stared out from shadowy doorways, their dark, inquisitive, terror-stricken eyes peering through shuttered windows, their lips moving soundlessly in prayer. Even the noisy, boisterous street *ragazzi* were subdued in the presence of death.

"Keep back, all of you," ordered a haughty, Turkish-looking *carabiniero,* wielding his rifle like a Lacrosse stick, "or we'll arrest the lot of you."

At that moment the bodies of two dead *carabinieri* were carried out of the de Montana house, much to the gloating satisfaction of the aged spectators.

"At least Gianni got two of those bastards," cursed the father of Maria Angelica, spitting hard into the dust.

Tori moved forward. "Permit me to pass. This is the house of my uncle," he told Lt. Franchina who turned sharply at the sound of the familiar voice. Surprise was etched into the officer's features as he recognized Tori.

"No one's permitted inside," growled another officer, obstructing Tori.

"If you're as intelligent as is rumored," said Tori, subduing his rage, "You'll not obstruct me."

At a nod from Lt. Franchina, the officer lowered his rifle and let Tori pass. Inside, sprawled face down in a pool of blood on a spotless kitchen floor, lay the inert body of his uncle. Tori, kneeling on one knee, stared solemnly at the motionless form. He couldn't believe what his eyes registered. *Demonio!* What violence this day had wrought. Filled with a mixture of flaring emotions, Tori turned the body over gently, closing the sightless staring eyes, and for several moments he watched the older man turn into an effigy of waxen features. A peculiar isolation gripped him. Tears spilled from his eyes onto the face of his uncle. He reached in and wiped the dead man's face off tenderly and whispered huskily, "For all the good it does, you've been avenged, *Ziu* Gianni."

Tori wondered how he could explain any of this to his cousin Vincenzo, when he returned from the war.

In this house one month had seen the death of four people. Two cousins, his aunt, and now his uncle. It just wasn't possible! Only last week he'd begged his uncle to ignore the constant harassment inflicted upon him by these despicable *carabinieri* who had made his life unbearable after he lodged complaints against the butcher, Gucci. Gianni had gone to the security police over the brutal, unprovoked attack on his sons who were obstructed for carrying food across provincial borders. "One day they'll tire of their persecution and give up,' he had told his uncle.

"Today, they came," rasped the voice of Tomasso de Montana. Tori looked up at the bleary-eyed brother of his uncle. "Like they have each day for the past month, just to torture my brother. *Annunca*. Today he was ready for them. When they broke in the front door, your uncle, *lupara* in hand, gave it to them. Poor soul! How could he have known that another son of a demented whore would enter the rear door and blast him from behind? Oh, if only Vincenzo were here. He'd show them!" Tormented, the brother of Tori's uncle shuffled about the room as his neighbors filed in to view the spectacle of death.

"Goddammit! The man never hurt a fly!" Tori's fists balled tightly and he pounded the nearby wall, hurting his hand. Hardly noticing the pain, he turned to Tommaso and spoke gruffly. "Get a blanket. Cover your brother. Let him lie in the dignity he deserves until the mortician arrives." He picked up the *lupara* at his uncle's feet and stroked the weapon lovingly. Countless happy hours spent at *caccia*—hunting—with his beloved uncle, a second father to him, were carved into the shotgun. He set it aside as he took the blanket from Tommaso's hands and covered the bullet-riddled blood-splattered body. For a moment he watched the older man pour wine for the others in true Sicilian fashion so that Gianni de Montanna's friends could drink to his departed soul.

"Bloody assassins murdered my brother!" cried the brother of Tori's uncle wailing and sobbing with torment.

Tori could hear the tremulous voice pitched high out in the street as he made his way through the crowd to his house .

"Salvatore!"

He turned abruptly in the direction of Lt. Franchina's voice.

"It's incredible to me that I've seen you so many times in one day. If I were a superstitious man I'd begin to think

174

it an omen. You see I don't happen to view these encounters as mere coincidence," said the officer reeking of whiskey. "I'm beginning to think——"

"Goddamnit to hell, man! I don't give a shit what you think!" Tori turned his back on the red-faced, blustery *carabiniero* and strode boldly across the cobblestone street to his house, where for a few moments he stood talking with his mother and sister. He didn't give a damn if the entire army of *carabinieri* obstructed him, at this point. Tori was incensed; he was crazy with hatred as he'd never before felt in his life.

"He's dead," said Antigone. No one had to tell her.

"*Si.* He's dead," replied Tori, checking his emotions. "Four deaths in the family, because like all humans they couldn't escape the habit of eating."

"Now, all our cousins are dead," said Athena sotto voce, her sorrowful eyes searching her brothers.

"Not Vincenzo!" Tori turned to his mother. "Don't tell me that, Mamma. Not him!" He was visibly shaken, his momentary anger replaced by stark fear at the prospect.

"We've had no word from him in two years."

"But no word came from the Ministry like it did for my brothers——"

"No."

Tori sighed. "*Allora,* there's hope. We must believe Vincenzo will return safe from harm. We must." He lit a cigarette, his eyes moving across the street towards the bustle of activity. He had quieted down a notch, but his voice was empty and dead. "Look at us. Have we no tears left to shed? Are we all damned here in Montegatta? Is this decaying village truly the house of Lucifer?" He made a disorganized gesture. His throat thickened and, unable to hold back the burning tears, he went into the house followed by his mother and sister.

Lt. Franchina glanced at his watch. It was nearly 7:30 P.M. "How soon before this mess is cleared up, Marino?"

"It's not your mess, *'tenente.* You're free to leave. I can give you a brief run down, however, if you feel obliged to make note of this in your report."

"Suppose you brief me tomorrow?" Franchina wiped the sweatband of his snap-brimmed hat and his forehead before resetting it on his head. "God Almighty, I've felt heat before, but this is more like the bowels of hell. Is it always this hot in the interior?"

"Always. You get used to it in time." Marino saluted the officer and watched him idly as he mounted his mare and gave orders for his squad to follow him.

Lt. Franchina led his squad back along Via de Grande in a brisk canter, as the horses' hooves assaulted the cobbles and led them out past the winding road above the Camposanto which led to the summit and Rigano Pass. On the return trip he brooded inwardly, hardly aware of the magnificent twilight of amethyst ribbons, shot through with white fire as the sun slipped behind a mass of electrifying colored clouds. The violent *sirocco* had finally spent itself over the Tyrrhenian Sea.

Lt. Giovanni Franchina had no way of knowing that, through a curious twist of fate, his squad of men would be totally demolished before the clock struck ten, or that he'd be the sole survivor of an ambush directed at them. Nor did he have any inkling that his life, from this day forward, would be inextricably caught up in the life of one exceptional Sicilian, Salvatore, or that for the next seven years, perhaps for the remainder of his life, he'd come to know little peace. If he'd known in advance the hand that destiny had dealt him, he might have recharted the course of his life by fleeing Sicily. But then this hardnosed, seemingly indestructible bulwark, a man possessed of driving ambition, might not have heeded the danger signs even if they were spelled out for him in large block letters. Enroute to Bellolampo Barracks, Lt. Franchina concentrated his mind on the events of the day and how they'd figure into his report.

At 10 A.M. that morning, acting as second lieutenant of the Italian military police presently under the jurisdiction of AMGOT (Allied Military Government of Occupied Territories), Franchina had stepped out into the sun-bleached courtyard of the command post at Bellolampo, a military *caserne* some 2,000 feet above Palermo to the southwest. He had mounted his mare and waved his squad of six men forward heading for the summit at Rigano Pass. A backward glance at the vast sweep of sapphire waters in the bay and at the golden basin of fertility known as the Conca d'Oro in which Palermo nestled reenforced his courage. He could always return, coudn't he?

The contrast between what greeted him and what he had left behind had transported him back into the Middle Ages. The heat had been stifling. Outlined against a brash sun, slowly fading from sight in the path of an impending *sirocco*, an eagle whirled arcs in an empty sky; he had filled with premonitiion at the time, but shook himself out of it. It would be nearly twelve hours later before Franchina would learn the merits of trusting to his intuition.

Once through the narrow pass, they prepared for the steep descent on the rear slopes of the limestone mountains. He'd noted where portions of the road, destroyed by Allied bombs, ended abruptly and the alien terrain grew harsh, rugged and unpredictable, the vegetation scant. Approximately an hour out of Bellolampo, Franchina had risen in his stirrups and turning in his saddle observed his men. Both horses and men had projected a marked inner turbulence. No one had to tell him; he could tell by the uneasy manner in which his men surveyed the area that they were in bandit country. Franchina had paused to mark these events in his notebook. He was a stickler for reports and their accuracy.

As their skittiness continued, Franchina unconsciously felt for the security of his service revolver. He also fingered his Mannlicher-Carcano rifle nervously. The feeling persisted. He felt that hundreds of eyes stared out at them from behind white boulders and the countless grottos nestled in the honeycombed mountains, watching, waiting, silent and hating; he grew wary of every second spent in this guerrilla paradise where boulders took on the shapes of men and the prickly pear cactus leaned over the narrow, impassable roads in silhouette and became ominous and threatening.

The horses, spooking, and rearing at the presence of porcupines, had trampled over *esparta* grass so sharp it could cut through horseflesh. It was at this point that Lt. Franchina had shouted to his men. "*Avanti! Avanti!* Forward—on the double!" He was anxious to move on to some form of civilization—anything but to remain here, in this living cemetery, where death was a heartbeat or two away from every turn in the road.

His discerning eyes made note of every possible area that could germinate an ambush. From time to time, he'd make further notes in his small book, much to the annoyance of his men who were even more anxious than he was to escape this treacherous land.

His first glimpse of Montegatta, as they passed a Greco-Roman ruin identified as the Temple of Cats, lay beyond the buckwheat terraces at the end of a narrow, corkscrew road which dove precariously into a series of right-angled turns and emptied into the mean poverty-stricken village. He couldn't help recalling his first impression that it resembled a giant centipede, with its tangle of narrow, squiggly streets running the hump of one main *strada* that stood silent, incubating in malignant concrete. By the time their clattering horses' hooves cleared the deserted streets of the village there was no life, no activity to be seen. It hadn't occurred to him that earlier, when they'd heard a bleating of oxhorns, it might have been a signal to herald their coming. He couldn't wait to leave this village of brooding concrete, where sullen people had hidden from his sight.

At noon, the clock in the Norman tower had struck the hour. The sweating, agitated *carabinieri* left through the south entrance and rode into the eye of the *sirocco*, shielding themselves as best they could from the tempest, eager to arrive in Borgetto. He had completed his business in the small village and by 2 P.M. they were riding swiftly back towards Montegatta in pursuit of the alleged black marketeers. It was then he'd encountered Salvatore and Pallido at Checkpoint Two where they were being detained by Gucci and Molino.

Lt. Franchina had paid little attention to Salvatore then; he had been interested in the activities of the two corrupt *carabinieri*. He had disliked Gucci on sight, and when he saw this pretentious, ugly man wink slyly to his partner, Lt. Franchina had sensed these two were involved in some immoral activity. There was no question he intended to put them on report for retaining an enormous amount of contraband with no visible prisoners in sight. And that cache of weapons! Certainly it hadn't all been collected that day.

He'd gone about his business and in Montegatta at approximately 5 P.M. he'd encountered Salvatore walking along Via de Grande in a fresh change of clothing. Then later, he had confronted him at the *cul de sac* where the two youngsters had been apprehended and shot, and, of course, at the house of his uncle, de Montana. Although Salvatore's activities that day had piqued his interest, he still had no reason to suspect the lad of anything subversive or illegal.

Yet, for inexplicable reasons, his thoughts had centered on Salvatore. He'd been so concentrated on Tori that he failed to take normal precautions before advancing his men through the bottleneck at Rigano Pass.

It happened so swiftly. Suddenly they were halfway through an unprovoked ambush, with bullets zinging and pinging all around them, and all around him he saw his men falling like ducks at a shooting gallery. Stunned by the chaotic order of events, with no time to order his men into a counterattack or a retreat, Lt. Franchina had spurred his horse and galloped swiftly through the fusillade of bullets and miraculously escaped. Riding a whirlwind, he had arrived at Bellolampo and recruited a relief squadron, but

178

by the time he returned to the bloody scene the ambushers had fled, taking with them all the horses, weapons and men's clothing, leaving the denuded bodies of the dead *carabinieri* floating in lakes of their own blood.

Lt. Franchina, solemn, somber-eyed, the very life drained from him, sat low in his saddle, observing the deathly scene. Pale shafts of moonlight illuminated the area between two mountain peaks, adding an eerie quality to the wooded basin as he pondered the reason destiny had spared him. He found no solace to comfort his wildly beating heart.

Later, in the confines of his meager office at Bellolampo, he paced his small room with the ferocity of a wounded tiger, appalled and incensed at the utter disregard Sicilians displayed for law and order. Finally, he sat down at his desk and began to write his report. He guzzled from a whiskey bottle periodically, and when he finished he glanced over the report.

Underlined several times was the name: *SALVATORE*. Even as he read the name he wasn't aware of why he had underlined it—only that he had. He was too upset to contemplate the reason for this. He was anxious to lay all this before his C.O., Major Carrini, immediately—regardless of the late hour.

Major Carrini, a lusty, physical man of medium build, was furious. Was this Franchina out of his mind? It was nearly midnight when his orderly had interrupted his sojourn with a prostitute imported from Neptune's Daughters in Palermo. And at a most inopportune time. *Sonofabitch!* Had he no regard for his superior officers? Major Carrini had no intention of leaving his warm bed, where the woman had been servicing him in a way that made him forget this lousy duty in a land of barbarians. His aide, however, insisted and when he mentioned that six men had been killed in an ambush, he put the girl off, whispering he'd return in moments.

There was another reason why Major Carrini decided to talk with Lt. Franchina. He disliked the man intensely, and itched to get something on him. Even at their first encounter, Franchina had recognized the gross resentment in the Major's eyes. The hard-bitten, scrappy officer pulled on his trousers and a shirt now, recalling how rankled he'd been by Franchina's natty appearance when they met. The preening peacock dressed meticulously, bringing into focus his own sloppiness, to which his apathy and conditions of the war had reduced him. He wasn't used to a man of Franchina's breed, whom he branded instantly as a stuffy, stodgy social climber, an ambitious fanatic, highly dangerous to the regulars because such men with their social notions couldn't be trusted.

He was grumpy and out of sorts when he entered his office to find Lt. Franchina seated in the cramped quarters chain-smoking. For all his libertine persuasions, the Major knew his duty, and he listened patiently to Franchina's impassioned report, trying to suppress his yawning boredom. Finished, Franchina waited to hear the Major's reaction. Carrini shrugged indifferently.

"Listen lieutenant, don't get your ass kicked out of shape. Here in Sicily you don't always follow the letter of the law. You give a little, you take a little, *capeeshi?*" He yawned and scratched his crotch, anxious to get back to that bundle of dynamite warming his mattress.

"Just so I don't misunderstand you," said Franchina stiffly, "Tell me more so I understand you." He refused the drink offered him.

The Major glanced impatiently at his watch. *Managghia! Is this prick to be believed?* He lit up a cigar and puffed on it with agitation. "Look, these Sicilians are strange birds. They resent outsiders. Why? Who knows. They consider us their mortal enemies. There's no way, no way at all, we can make them obey laws unless we shoot them. And I mean every last accursed son of a whore in sight! It's either that or we jail them. *Pero*—who has enough jails? We can't justify shooting them—so, we join them. *Capeeshi?* When we catch them violating our laws, we play their game and make them divvy up the booty. This way we go about our business and they go about theirs. Everyone is content."

Franchina didn't like what he heard. "You mean you condone felons? How the hell can we enforce Allied laws if we become a party to the torts? Major, by condoning these offensive practices, you're endangering the life of every *carabiniero* who does duty in this island. We're sitting on a time bomb that could explode without warning. How long do you think these people will tolerate such shabby treatment?" He then proceeded to relate to Carrini the reactions of the people he'd seen that day, the vile hatred in their eyes, the loathing and contempt and murder in the air. He mentioned the lorry filled with confiscated weapons he'd seen at Checkpoint Two. "Then all the undercurrents of pure vitriol I felt from them had some basis after all," he shouted angrily.

Major Carrini's face turned a ghastly purple. "Goddammit, Franchina! What the hell song are you singing? You're no cherry. You know the ropes. Don't give me that shit. You can't tell me you haven't wet your beak. In these times you're telling me this is all new to you?"

Franchina saw it did no good to repudiate Carrini's statement. Indignant at the suggestion he'd be party to the abominable acts, he pulled himself to his feet, boiling with resentment. In his mind it all fell into place. The laxity at the checkpoints, the general apathy of the mounted police, all of them. Why should they arrest a wrongdoer when they could share in the thriving graft, sit back, and live off the blood, sweat, and terror of another man's plight?

As he saw it, the ambush in which his men had been slaughtered could be justified when viewed through the peasants' eyes. Since these lawmen, sworn to uphold the law, were more lawless than the brigands who roamed the hills, how in the name of the Lord Jesus could they command respect?

Franchina said tersely, "I haven't wet my beak, Major, but I understand more than I did this morning. You should have explained things to me before you placed me and my men in such jeopardy. I hold you personally responsible for the deaths of those six men. You didn't squeeze the triggers. You didn't fell them with your own gun. You didn't even plan the ambush. But, by the soul of Satan, you're as guilty of their deaths as I am for not acquainting myself with such rank conditions beforehand."

A volcano erupted in the Major. He jumped to his feet, kicked back his chair, and snarled fiercely, his face swollen to a black-hued purple. "Where the fuck do you come off being so high and mighty—so disrespectful to your superior officer? You stupid sonofabitch! These are hard times, man! With the war on, we don't even know who's side we're on, you brainless orangutang. You dare spout morals and ethics to me? We're goddamn lucky the Allies chose us to enforce their laws. They could have tossed us into the *gaoletto*—jail—and declare us their enemies. We could have been left there to rot during the occupation. Tell me, omnipotent one—do you know what's happening on the mainland? I don't. We've not been paid in months. How do we live, eh? How do we feed ourselves and our families? Look! You don't like it here? *Va bene.* Then transfer the hell out of here, and don't bust my balls! Don't look down that supercilious, holier-than-thou nose of yours at us. Wait until you've been here a year like the rest of us. You'll play the game soon enough."

"With your permission," said Franchina bracing himself. "I'll put in for a transfer.

Major Carrini picked his chair off the floor and set it

back into place. He growled, "Put in for a transfer. What the hell do I care? Don't play the fucking game. See where it gets you. You'll be here for at least three weeks until the transfer comes through. Make the best of it."

"With your permission I'll make arrangements for the bodies of my men to be shipped home to their families."

Carrini's head swiveled towards the other. "You'll do what?"

Franchini repeated his statement and was cut off in mid-sentence.

"Never mind," exploded the major. "I heard you. I heard you but I don't believe you. You're a real *citrollo*, Franchina, you know that? A real cucumber. Where the hell do you come off thinking we offer first-class ac-comodations in wartimes, eh? Goddammit, we're under Occupation! Have the burial detail dispose of the dead in the customary manner. Now we've six mouths less to feed."

"But—"

"Yes, lieutenant?" the Major's voice was deadly.

Franchina saluted him, a protest dead on his lips. "With your permission, I'll withdraw."

"So, withdraw." muttered his C.O., flinging his soggy cigar into a nearby spittoon. "Meanwhile you take the same detail tomorrow. And don't go around infecting the other men with your crazy ideas, or, so help me, I'll write you up for subordination and dereliction to duty, and by the unholy balls of Satan, I'll make it stick."

All the way back to his quarters, Lt. Franchina was thinking that his superior was probably capable of anything. If he'd been a mere fanatic, he surmised, he'd have been no threat to Carrini. Long ago Franchina had learned to adjust to outside conditions while inwardly retaining his own principles. Never a joiner, he was his own man, a prodder, someone who kept books and profited from his mistakes, but always preparing methodically for some future day when he would receive his own command and reach the goal he had set for himself.

Still stinging from the Major's words it was the last thing the major said to him that stirred his *cuglione*. "You don't belong here," the Major fired at him. "You belong in Rome, Florence or Naples with the rest of the *carabini-eri* snobs who articulate anemic policy that we red-blooded men put our lives on the line for. All you holier-than-thou, self-righteous men, out to save the world, never take into consideration that the world was fucked up by men like you in the first place!"

Franchina was filled with countless doubts as he undressed for bed that night, but one thing was certain. As his commanding officer, Major Carrini called the shots, and he had to obey. Before he fell asleep that night, he put in for a transfer, unaware that destiny had already begun to formulate other plans for him.

The next morning, stuck on this detail until his transfer was approved, Lieutenant Franchina awakened to a bright, clear and sunny world devoid of *siroccos*. The temperature, having dropped several degrees, brought some relief to the west. Given command of a new squad of men, he left the military barracks for Borgetto, where he was required to fill out several reports.

The day was uneventful until they passed Montegatta and Checkpoint Two, where they found no officer of the day. Gucci and Molino were nowhere about. Making a note to report this oddity at Borghetto, the *carabinieri* contingent proceeded south at a leisurely pace.

Lieutenant Franchina noticed, as they descended the narrow twisting roads towards Castellammare Valley, the eastern sky filled with several buzzards, wheeling arcs over a lonely gulch. Fascinated, he watched these flesh-eating predators through binoculars, wondering what tasty tidbits these sable-plumed gourmets had spied. Somewhere in these time-eroded mountains, beneath them, they sensed a banquet of death had been spread for them. He watched them slowly, very slowly descending to the feast, spiralling lower, lower, until they disappeared behind limestone ridges out of sight.

Lieutenant Franchina galloped ahead swiftly to catch up with his men, who were already at the entrance to Borgetto by the time he closed the distance between them. At HQ's he handled the lengthy red-taped reports of the previous day, had lunch, and after reporting the absence of a detail at Checkpoint Two, he and his squad of men headed back up the mountain towards the summit.

Converging towards them, at a slow pace over a lonely mountain road from Piana dei Greci, several *carabinieri*, escorting two horse-driven lorries over the tedious, rutty roads, waved to Lt. Franchina. He ordered his men to halt, and with an aide rode forward to greet the newcomers. Exchanging salutes, Lt. Franchina introduced himself asking, *"Che passa?"*

Young Corporal Greco raised his arms, halted the lorry drivers, and introduced himself. He explained that the lorries contained dead bodies found in a ravine where his men had seen vultures circling overhead and pointed to the area where Franchina had seen the predators earlier.

Lt. Franchina spurred his horse and rode to the end of the lorries to inspect the bloodied carnage, mutilated beyond recognition from the long fall against the jagged rocks and from the pickings of vultures. "Who were they?" he asked as the corporal rode up alongside him.

Corporal Greco reached inside his tunic and pulled out several identity cards. Two of them—I'm not sure which—were fellow officers: Gucci and Molino," he read from their IDs. "The others, the young lads must be those missing from Montegatta these many months. Listen, Lieutenant, will you take the lads to Montegatta? We'll take the officers to Borgetto. Their deaths will have to be investigated. They were both shot with a *lupara*, an ethnic firearm, according to the nature of their wounds."

"You surmised that in their condition, Corporal Greco?"

"My specialty, Lieutenant. One day I hope to transfer to Naples to work in Intelligence."

"My, my," commented Franchina. "I wish you good fortune."

He accepted the identity cards and watched as the men transferred the bodies of the dead youths to one lorry. Once again the officers exchanged salutes and each contingent went its separate way.

It was dusk by the time Lt. Franchina deposited his lorry of death with the security police in Montegatta and returned with his men to Bellolampo without incident. That night, he was totally exhausted and unwilling to fraternize with the other officers. He retired to his room and slept like a baby, unaware that in other parts of the land there brewed bits of intrigue that would give him many a sleepless night for the rest of his life.

CHAPTER 13

The very same day that Lt. Franchina reluctantly began his second day of duty in western Sicily, Tori had arrived in Mt. Erice. Having scaled the spotless stone pavement up the hill to the quaint village from Trapani on his horse, he dismounted, tethered it to a hitching post, and strode boldly into the Naxos Weights and Measures *negozio*, ready for his encounter with Don Pippinu Grasso. He was annoyed to learn that the Don was out lunching with Allied officials and wouldn't return until after the noon siesta.

A toad-faced clerk directed him to a small table to partake of a cup of *espresso* or whatever suited his appetite while he waited. He chose instead to wander about the *negozio*, fully irked by the delays. *Managghia!* He'd intended to take care of the pressing business and return with the overdue payments owed them by this cousin of his mother. The chore, distasteful enough because this distant cousin had a penchant for making him feel like a poor relative who came begging for something to which he wasn't entitled, further aggravated him when he caught sight of the phenomenal amount of food stores stocked in the shelves. *Porco Diaoro!* Damn the devil! Where were the food shortages here? Black market goods abounded in this place. Most Montegattans hadn't tasted or seen pasta in years. Here, boxes of that precious commodity were stacked from floor to ceiling. This very fact set Tori to wondering about such special privileges. His senses were assaulted by the appetizing aromas of the soul-stirring foods. His mouth watered at the sight of the *prosciutto*, cheeses, salamis, and other delicacies; yet he felt compelled to swallow his hunger pangs and avert his eyes, lest he give in to temptation. Who in Montegatta would believe him when he described such a display of food? The prices were prohibitive; nonetheless the food was sold openly. Imagine—sold openly!

Earlier, when he had arrived in Trapani, the sight of the recent aerial bombardment given the city had shaken him into a fit of depression. Yet nothing had astonished him more, when he had ridden among the Greco-Spanish and Norman-influenced village of Mt. Erice, than to see it had escaped unscathed by Allied bombs. His spirits had been elevated considerably because he loved the birthplace of his mother, where, she'd always assured him, "the most beautiful woman in Sicily come from Mt. Erice." It was a game they played. Tori would respond to this declaration by telling her, "Since they are all descended from gods and goddesses, isn't it fitting they should come from Mt. Erice?" Tori had yet to encounter these creatures of legendary beauty, and he teased his mother about this. Always ready with a reply, Antigone would insist that the men of the village kept their women hidden, and with good reason. With such hedonistic stallions as Tori and Vincenzo around, she would say, the women had to be safeguarded. Then Tori, with sparkling deviltry in his eyes, would laugh, insisting it wasn't necessary to see them, because to him *she* was the most beautiful woman in the world, Athena included.

He laughed internally now, for he always recalled these anecdotes each trip he made to this quaint village. He sauntered over to a counter and picked up a newspaper, growing more restless by the moment, the puzzle of so many foodstuffs sticking in his craw like bitter bile. Later he was to learn why this village had earned such privileges not granted to his province. It seemed that the Mafia, under the able guidance of his godfather, Don Barbarossa, assisted by those members of the Honored Society, had been instrumental in assisting the Allies by painting the tops of buildings housing Axis arsenals, strategic stronghold, and ammunition dumps with luminous paint to facilitate the aerial bombardment. For these services, Mt. Erice had been spared and an abundance of food had been released. A neat exchange, he thought when he heard this story. It had also set him to thinking about the wheeling and dealing that went on.

The sound of a young woman's voice, cool and disdainful as she crisply ordered the toad-faced clerk about, caused him to glance up from the newspaper into the face of the most beautiful creature he'd ever seen. Dressed simply in a navy blue skirt with a pale blue sweater that revealed a body of voluptuous curves, she was purchasing what to him seemed an abnormal amount of groceries, for which she overpaid with a staggering amount of *Am-Lire* (the new occupational currency) She appeared to take perverse delight in flaunting the money.

Toadface moved in closer to Tori and, with whispered innuendo and animated gestures, indicated she was a member of the world's oldest profession. "*Managghia!* Does this whore make money! Phew!"

Tori noticed the forced, sullen respect for money indicated by the clerk's attitude. He also noticed that the faces of a few inquisitive shoppers had screwed up with a superior attitude: here and there a raised eyebrow, envious stares, bold and haughty attitudes, while others stood by quietly with prudent reserve, avoiding the girl as if she were a leper. For some unknown reason Tori had to check the sudden impulse he had to change the sniggering expression on the toad's face with an upraised fist. Just as quickly, he asked himself why he should feel personally

186

affronted. After all she wasn't his girl—or his property. *What's the matter with me?* he asked himself, shrugging in annoyance.

Yet when she brushed by him, accidentally dropping a parcel, he didn't back off or mind his own business as he'd been taught to do all his life. He gallantly retrieved the parcel and bowed in a cavalier manner. "Permit me to assist you *Signorina*," he said, hoping to disguise a rising excitement. Before she could refuse him, he relieved her of another parcel. The girl flushed with a mixture of pleasure and self-consciousness at his gracious manners. Her eyes caught sight of the eye-popping stares of those around her who gawked openly at them.

With a toss of her coppery gold hair, she gave them a *go fuck yourself* look and, fixing her electric green eyes alluringly on the accommodating man, she smiled dazzlingly. "*Signore*, how kind of you. I'd be most grateful for your assistance," she purred with an angel's voice that caused his heart strings to quiver.

"Tell Don Pippinu, Salvatore will return," he told Toadface as he left.

Good God! Is she beautiful! Tori felt a sense of pride as he walked alongside this angelic beauty, despite Toadface's candid observation. Her skin, the texture of a baby's, was soft and white, with a tinge of pale blush to her cheeks. Her red-gold hair, worn cropped in a mass of curls, danced glowingly in the sunlight. Her eyes, incredible to behold, looked unreal, more like precious jade and turquoise jewels. Within them, he saw unfathomable emotional depths; perpetually haunted, like those of so many female victims in a war-ravaged country.

Tori wondered, could she be a love goddess of legend his mother had told him about? The idea titillated his senses, caused his heart to beat faster, and filled him with indescribable joy.

They stopped before a run-down apartment, and he appeared dismayed that such a beauty should live in a place short of a palace. He was unaware that his thoughts were scrawled boldly, across his face, like graffiti.

"What did you expect, the palace of a queen?" she asked defensively.

"Why—uh—I—er—uh," he stammered at her perception. "I didn't mean to appear impolite or unmannerly, *signorina* . . ."

His eloquence of speech threw her off balance and she glanced hesitantly at him.

"May I carry these to your apartment?" he asked pleasantly.

"No!" she grew defiant. "No one comes to my house—unless they pay." Her voice, no longer soothing and angelic, turned acrimonious.

Salvatore smiled indulgently. "Even the delivery man?"

His tone and manner forced a smile upon her lips, which suddenly bloomed into a sunshine of laughter and infected him with her spontaneity. . . .

"My name is Apolladora Felice," she told him later. "I'm eighteen. Until three months ago, I lived in Jato with my parents, four sisters and three baby brothers. My family had always been poor. The war made us destitute. My friend, Concetta, sent me a bus ticket and told me I could earn more money than my family would need to survive. Could I stand around watching the children die of starvation and other illnesses? Knowing what I had to do, my father refused to talk with me or kiss me goodbye. I cried all the way to Mt. Erice.

"A week later, when I returned with food, medicine, and clothing, I no longer cried. Into my father's hands I pressed enough money to support them for months. Weekly I make the trip to bring them food and money. My parents never ask, 'Do you have a place to sleep? Enough to eat?' They just ignore me. My father turns his back on me. He eats the food I bring, drinks the wine, and smokes the cigars like a royal pasha. But he doesn't talk with me. I'm a stranger to them. It's as if Apolladora Felice no longer exists for them. I'm a phantom who comes weekly to attend to their needs.

"I'm an outcast because I sell my body to the British and American soldiers to keep my family alive. I no longer try to convince my family that if what I do keeps nine humans alive and well-fed, could it be so wrong? . . .

"It wasn't all sunshine and morning glories for me, Tori. My first night was a nightmare. What drove me were the haunted faces of my younger brothers and sisters. Even my cherished dreams of being deflowered by the man I love—these, too, dissolved. In the wake of poverty, how quickly one learns to adjust. The feel of so much money in my hands and knowing the good it could do erased all sentimental thoughts of my virginity. . . .

"Three times a week, I go to Naxos Weights and Measures to buy groceries, which I take to Jato each week. Something compels me to make those weekly visits, like a penance I must pay for the life I lead.

"One Saturday, an American GI drove me to Jato to save petrol costs. Everyone on our street noticed the American machine. Filled with shame, my father wouldn't come into the sitting room. His caustic voice, shouting vile names at me, echoed through the streets. *"Disonorata! Butana!"* Oh, the things he called me!

"The American, furious, wanted to tell my father a thing or two. I implored him to pay the old man no heed, and assured him it didn't bother me. But in truth I felt dead inside. My friend boiled at the shabby treatment I had received. But how can a foreigner hope to understand the fierce pride of a Sicilian father? The disgrace at having a prostitute for a daughter? Such stigma too deeply planted in their minds can never be erased.

"And so it was that today, when I went to Naxos and met you, I felt sure it was Destiny that pushed me. Earlier I had awakened with such a headache I told myself I'd not go shopping on this day, that tomorrow would be as convenient. But something prodded me, pushed me into getting up, and I ended up at Naxos. When I saw you standing there, looking at me in that special way, I felt a warm flush inside me. I am not so eloquent with words that I can describe what I felt, but it seemed I'd known you all my life. Did you feel what I felt? That we might mean something to the other? *Allora*—I dropped my package. Then I heard you ask in that voice that sent shivers in me, " 'May I assist you, *Signorina?*' "

Apolladora giggled like a naive child and sat up in bed. The sheets fell from her milky skin and her full breasts trembled slightly from the excitement that swept her body. "So, I said in my most seductive voice, 'I'd be grateful for your assistance, *Signore*,' and here we are, three hours later, as if we'd known each other all our lives." She was breathless, vibrant and trembling.

"Yes," he said huskily. "Here we are."

"So!" She sprang from the bed and returned with a fresh pot of coffee she'd made during her oratory, and pouring a cup for him and one for herself, she said, "Tell me about yourself. Are things bad in your village?"

"Yes." His eyes devoured her nakedness and he was delighted at her lack of embarrassment. He was as breathless as she was, and equally astonished by his own actions. Such women were to be used—not revered.

"From where do you come ?"

"Montegatta."

"Are you married?"

"No."

189

She smiled at that. "Are you here on business? Do you come often?"

"Yes, business. No, not often."

"I love it here. To me Mt. Erice is like a fairyland. Do you like it here?"

"Do I like it here?" He rhapsodized. . . . "I am enchanted with it. Part of my ancestry lies in Mt. Erice. Do I like it here? Ah, *Signorina,* besides being the birthplace of my mother, it was here that Hercules challenged the King. Here Venus arose from the sea and, with a legion of cupids, built her temple high on the rocks, 2500 feet above the sea. And it was here that I meet you. What's not to be enamored of Mt. Erice?" he whispered, trying to subdue his own excitement.

She listened with wide-eyed wonder as he told her of the lore connected with this village. For a while they made small talk, none of which mattered. What did matter to Tori were the strange and unique feelings that shot through him when he set eyes on her copper-colored hair, the color of an amber sunset, and her jade-green eyes that gazed right into his soul, it seemed. She had a voluptuous body, unlike any he'd ever seen, with everything worked into the right places. Just to feast his eyes upon her left him with a strange and peculiar breathlessness. *"Cara mia,"* he cooed softly. "I'm happy you dropped your parcel . . ." he told her huskily, pulling her close to him again.

Before they got around to drinking their coffee, they melted into each other's arms as if it was the most natural thing to do. For Apolladora, the experience with Tori was fascinating and terribly rewarding. For the first time in her sexual life, she hadn't exacted a fee from her lover, and it gave her an entirely different outlook on the sexual act. She found the passive role profoundly exciting and unendurably delicious. Later, the breathlessness and trembling and shaking wouldn't cease.

"You like it?" she felt impulsed to ask.

"Apolladora—Apolladora," he replied huskily. "What's not to like?" His greedy young body swelled and strained against her softness, and she giggled self consciously, filled pleasurably by his soft caress. He cupped her breasts gently, ever so gently, and with the faintest touch flicked his hot moist tongue over her nipples. Apolladora sighed, delirious with ecstasy, and wondered what else she had been missing.

He had a marvelous way of teasing her by rubbing his large erect penis against her vagina in soft light touches, until she felt she was losing her mind. Gently, lightly, like the touch of a feather, he caressed her until the juices ran freely and she climaxed time and again until she seemed unable to endure the precarious heights to which he propelled her. Clutching at him she begged him to enter her. "Please! Please!" she cried hoarsely.

She raised her body up to meet his. "I can't wait any longer, Tori. I'm begging you. I'm going to burst wide open if you don't enter me!" She pleaded, frenzied and wild-eyed.

Slowly, like an artist creating a masterpiece, Tori entered her a bit at a time, teasing, until she gasped and grew more frenzied by the moment. Slow, sensual thrusts brought alive every nerve in her body, and suddenly they both tensed. Like bursting rockets, time and again they soared into space, until smaller rockets burst from these into a fan of tiny explosions. Their heads pounded, and their hearts—their delirious hearts—could no longer endure the delicious strain. Finally, in the gigantic stillness, they lay back, breathless and motionless.

Faint sounds of a radio playing in another apartment, filtering through the thin, shabby walls for several moments, became their first awareness of reality. Slowly, moving forward through the erotic euphoria of sex, other natural sounds became discernible.

"I've never known such feelings," whispered Apolladora. "When I began my work, I promised I'd never feel anything. It's only a job, I told myself, a job to support my family. I would save my feelings for the man I'd one day marry, God willing. But, now, Tori, all that is finished. I'll not be able to keep my promise, for you've stirred up in me such feelings I shall never forget. With you I feel no shame. You make me feel like someone very special. Very very special."

"You are special," he told her. "Truly, like no other I've met." he found himself saying, almost against his will. "I've never been with a woman who had the power to make me forget everything except being here with you." He wasn't being dishonest, as men were prone to be with whores. He had never felt the love, the tenderness and erotic feelings, he had experienced with Apolladora. Not with Maria Angelica, not with anyone!

Apolladora melted against his lean muscular body and breathed in deeply, inhaling the clean, fragrant smell of his body. This in itself served to arouse her erotically. Tenderness, the key to her soul, made her highly vulnerable. She experienced an overwhelming desire to reciprocate his love, to make him feel as he'd made her feel.

Totally without inhibitions, throwing all modesty to the winds, she exposed herself to him by engaging in highly sensual movements he'd never permitted the girls at Neptune's Daughters to do to him.

She moved her body sensuously over his and began to caress his manhood and inner thighs until he quivered under her expert touch. In the past he'd been indifferent to oral copulation, and on occasion, as with Maria Angelica only yesterday, he'd been terribly offended by the act. He could take it or leave it, and Tori, who loved as sensually as he lived, still preferred the feel of a woman's loins. Now, as Apolladora performed the act, he was consumed by an overwhelming feeling of love; a tenderness shook him deeper than the astounding force of the subsequent orgasm, which rendered him prostrate for more than a half hour. He wanted to reciprocate her love, but couldn't. He was spent. He was replete.

Side by side they lay, naked, silent and unmoving. He reached for a cigarette, lit it and lay back on the bed. She hadn't moved. He looked down on her face and pushed a damp curl off her forehead. He thought about all she'd told him, and, recalling all he'd told Athena yesterday, wondered what he'd do if she ever turned to prostitution; an involuntary shudder passed through him. Apolladora stirred in his arms. He straightened the slim silver crucifix around her neck and stroked her face tenderly. Life was hard. Life was very hard, he thought.

Her spectacular green eyes fluttered lazily and opened. She smiled indolently at him. In a wonderously inspired voice, he whispered, "Apolladora, where did you learn to make love so exquisitely? With you it's an inborn art. Truly you must be descended from all the nymphs of Venus. Here, in Mt. Erice, where her temple still stands, have you come to me as the reincarnation of all the love nymphs she kept at her side . . . ?" As he spoke a flush of warmth flooded his loins, and once more he felt himself give rise to the feelings of sexual exigency.

He also felt Apolladora stiffen and pull away from him. On her marble-like face he saw the same cold defiant shield of protection he'd seen at Naxos when she was bargaining with hostile clerks.

"Where?" she asked icily. "Working at the *fattoria* canning tuna fish! Where else?" Profound hurt surfaced into her eyes at what she mistook to be an insult. Unfamiliar with the gods and goddesses of mythology that were commonplace to Tori, she didn't understand his words.

Needless to say, the mood splintered. Nothing Tori

could say would appease her. He stopped trying and grew silent. She ranted on. "You had me believing you were different than the other men I've met. But I was wrong. *Managghia!* Was I ever wrong! Animals—all of you! You lie and cheat and deceive and flatter until you get what you want, and then it's *Va Futta!* Go fuck yourself! No?"

Tori's face blanched with indignation. Tight-lipped and livid, he'd gone to the bathroom, cleansed himself, then returned in silence to finish dressing. "How dare you classify me with all these promiscuous, lust-filled soldiers? How dare you? No matter what you think, I'm unlike any man you'll ever meet. But don't fret. Knowing how you feel, I shall not see you again." He had to have the last word. His Sicilian *maschiezzo* was at stake. There was nothing left for him but to leave.

"Hah! As if I care!" she retorted indignantly.

"If I did, you'd never see another man but me!" said Tori, unhearing.

"What makes you think I'd want to see you again?" she countered hotly.

He smiled enigmatically and walked to the door. "Goodbye my love goddess," he said softly.

Her aim was expert, and Tori barely ducked in time to avoid colliding with a bottle of French perfume. It connected with the door, broke, and spilled over his clothing. He smiled and closed the door behind him.

Long after he left, Apolladora cried bitterly and berated herself for allowing Tori to walk out of her life, for not making some move to stop him. No one had ever touched her as he'd touched her. For all time he was committed to her memory, for he had taken with him the best part of Apolladora Felice. Why hadn't she stopped him? But how? She was a whore!

Try as he did, he couldn't remove the fragrance of her perfume from his clothing. He hastily returned to Naxos to keep his appointment with Don Pippinu Grasso. As it was he had lingered too long with the girl.

Don Pippinu Grasso, heavily paunched and, with a wide, flat nose set deeply in swollen flesh and nostrils resembling a pig's snout, sniffed the air gingerly at the reeking aroma of perfume and grinned lasciviously.

"Ah, Salvatore! What a strong young stallion you've become!" He grinned revoltingly. "I see Apolladora has serviced you, also. . . ."

Tori froze. She couldn't have! Not with *this* pig of a man, who stank of garlic, wine and strong Romano cheese, and of the putrefaction of male uncleanliness. He wanted to retch. Speechless, shattered, dazed by the pulsating venom boiling his blood and searing his soul, he took hold of himself. *What the hell's wrong with me? She isn't my property. Why do I take this so personally? Hadn't she admitted being a whore?*

"She knows her stuff, eh?" suggested the snorting lump, never knowing how close he came to having his face smashed in.

Mental images of Apolladora lying naked in the arms of this uncouth brute rushed at Tori. He fought for control. *Goddammit! Stop this,* he told himself. *She's a whore! A whore! Stop acting as if she were Sheba reincarnated!*

"*Allora*—what brings you to Mt. Elice?"

"What always bring me here?" he asked tightly.

"Ah, *si*. Payment on the leases. You will tell that generous and most understanding of cousins, your Mamma, an angel if I ever saw one, that I shall be late with the payments. Business is bad. With the war it's intolerable!" He shook his head in a woebegone manner.

"No, no, no, no." Tori's sudden hatred for the man fell into organized articulation. "I shall tell her no lies. I've seen the business you do. One look at the prices you charge tells me the entire story. If it hadn't been for the weights and measures leased to you by my mother, you'd be what you were twenty years ago, a mere beggar without enough backbone to do an honest day's work! Now, I've come to collect what's legally hers by virtue of the agreement you made with her." Never had Tori spoken so boldly before.

"How dare you?" Don Pippinu's fat lips hung open, in indignation. The cigar had fallen from between his lips, spilling ashes down his vest. "How dare you?" He shook with rage. "You the son of a pitiful sheepherder, dare come to my house and treat me, Don Pippinu, with such disrespect!"

The power-saturated glance transmitted to the young man remained totally ineffectual, for Salvatore had been raised to fear no man, not even a *Mafioso*.

"This pitiful son of a sheepherder happens to be the man to whom you are presently indebted" he said mockingly, taking a step towards the *Mafioso*. "But, you misjudge me," cooed Tori with cunning. "I speak with more respect than to which you are entitled. If I didn't respect you . . ." he paused within inches from the fat man's face and averted his head at the distasteful odor reeking from him. He placed his hands on the man's grimy lapels, grasped them firmly, and pulled the Don in towards him. ". . . I would have smashed your face in long ago. Are we in accord?" His dark fiery eyes sent clear messages to the Don.

Instinctively Don Pippinu averted his head and flinched as if to ward off an imaginary blow. "You're crazy, you know—crazy in the head. No one dares treat Don Pippinu with such foolish craziness! You must be insane. Perhaps the desert *sirocco* has broiled your brains, eh?"

Tori continued to sniff and squint as if he'd stepped on something distasteful and backed away. The stench emanating from the man was intolerable. The Don, meanwhile, glanced apprehensively at the son of his third cousin, related to him through marriage, and, with nicotine-stained fingers clasped to his chest in supplication, he decided to tread carefully. Something about the lad. . . .

"Because I cannot meet my payments, am I to be treated so disrespectfully?" he wailed. "In these trying times, even Satan would extend credit to a man unable to keep up with payments."

"I'm not interested in the ethics of Satan, only my own," temporized Tori. "*Allora*, I don't like coming here any more than you like having to be reminded what a *schifoso* you really are. What do you say we strike a bargain? Make me a flat offer of six thousand American dollars for an out-and-out sale of the weights and measures. Then we won't have to see one another again."

"You're crazy! I knew it, you're crazy! Demented! Out of your head! You must have fucked yourself crazy and drained the brains from your head!" roared the Don. He paced the floor with mounting agitation.

"Where the fuck will I get six thousand dollars?" He turned the pockets of his trousers inside out in a gesture symbolic of poverty. "What money do I have, eh? I have no money. I can barely support my family, and you ask me for a fortune. You're crazy! Like I said before, crazy!"

Tori's mind functioned with an adroit cleverness that surprised him. "Very well," he said in a deadly calm. "The weights and measures go up for sale in—what's customary—three, five days, a week? Can you vacate the premises by then?"

"For sale? What the hell are you saying? What is this 'for sale'?" The Don, stunned, had never contemplated such an eventuality. He should have—but he didn't, because he had decided long ago to somehow cheat Antigone Salvatore out of the business and property as well.

Yesterday, Salvatore had learned his Godfather was

alive. Contemplating this now, he grew bolder, bluffing his way. "I've been assured by Don Matteo Barbarossa of Godrano that his people are willing to pay a great deal more for the lease than you are paying now. When approached, I indicated, out of respect to you, that I'd be obliged to give you first refusal in the matter."

"Don Matteo Barbarossa?" The Don's obesity in no way interfered with the swiftness with which he pivoted on one foot, did an about-face, and stared with utter disbelief. Black pig eyes narrowed to slits, glittered insanely. "Your Godfather?" The wheels turned swiftly in his mind.

"Yes. My Godfather."

"Mah—how the hell is he your Godfather?" scoffed the obnoxious Don.

For a second Tori faltered. "How many ways are there for a man to become a Godfather?" he asked evenly.

They locked eyes. Don Pippinu read the truth in Tori's eyes and made an impatient gesture. He poured himself a glass of wine, gulped it down, and wiped his lips with the back of his wrist. He made a half-baked gesture at the wine, indicating Tori should help himself.

Standing in a careless pose, thumbs hooked into his belt, he watched the high-strung *Mafioso,* who hadn't thought enough of the encounter to keep a muscle man at his side, and smiled internally, at the other's distress and at his unmanly comportment.

Don Pippinu's pig eyes jumped here, there and everywhere with erratic intensity. As he waddled about the *negozio* he shouted, outraged, "Six thousand dollars! Where the hell will I get that sum in these impoverished times?" He stopped abruptly and, in a quick transition, struck a bargaining note. "Oh, no you don't! Not a cent over five thousand—and that's tops!"

Tori remained steadfast. "Six. Take it or leave it. Where you get the money isn't my concern." He glanced at his watch. "You have an hour to decide. If it's not ready then, I'll deal with Don Barbarossa. One hour," he said firmly. "And another thing, Don Pippinu, don't plan anything clever if you desire to live," he said lightly as he might have said a greeting.

Ten minutes later Tori walked among the temple ruins of centuries past, high above Mt. Erice where the fabled Rock of Venus had materialized and where legends claimed that over 200 soldiers once guarded the fabulous treasures given as gifts by the many enchanted visitors who had enjoyed the ingenious and amorous rites performed by the sacred, nymphlike prostitutes, those constant companions of the goddess Venus. Hitching his horse to a nearby post, Tori looked about for the caretaker he usually encountered when he came here. He lit a cigarette and for a time glanced out from these Cyclopean Phoenician walls at the magnificent spread of ocean—at the Egadi Islands at his feet, overrun with countless medieval castles and picturesque grottos, at the magnificent panorama of antiquity.

Never in all his youth had Tori felt such explosive forces within him. He felt as if a sleeping Hercules in his subconscious mind, aroused, had been born in these past few hours spent with Apolladora. This plus the events of the past twenty-four hours had caused an emergence of some inner force he'd never recognized before. He was a different man. Forceful and cunningly direct as he'd been in his dialogue with Don Pippinu, he now found that the change in him both confused him and intrigued him.

Quaint salt-grinding windmills turned in the wind below him along the shores of Trapani, and for a time he watched them absently. As he turned about, gazing at the Rock of Venus, his imagination ran rampant. Before his very eyes everything seemed transformed back in time to the era when Venus had been worshipped. The ruins had disappeared and the temple had been restored as it had been when the Greeks ruled the island; resplendent with mosaic water fountains, marbled pillars, graceful statues and friezes of dancing nymphs—and one added delight; the face of Apolladora took form on the faces of the dancing girls.

Wherever he looked he saw Apolladora; he saw her face, her body, heard her laughter and felt her presence. His clothing, saturated with her perfume, continued to stir his senses. Earlier, in the presence of the despicable Don Pippinu, the aroma had so engulfed him that he could hardly concentrate on the business at hand. Now, as he fought off the impressions the girl had left behind, he found there was no escaping her. She'd taken possession of him. *What the hell's wrong with me?* he asked himself. Closing his eyes and turning from the pulsating scenes of the floating, gyrating dancers around him, all replicas of Apolladora, he shouted internally, 'She's a whore! A common whore! Whores have their place in the world—but not in mine!"

Despite every logical reason Tori formed in his mind to turn from her, there was no escaping her or the overwhelming feelings taking possession of him. He'd never felt such sensations. He was in agony; he was in pain; he was in a confusing world of new excitement—but he also felt ecstasy, joy and a lightheaded, wondrous feeling that could fly him into Venus and back if he but willed it. *What to do? What to do?* he asked himself, over and again. A glance at his watch told him he was due back at Naxos.

Tori's disillusion with Don Pippinu amounted to distrust and active dislike. He hated duplicity or impropriety, and he abhorred men who made stupid and improper remarks without foundation. But to his surprise, when he arrived back at the end of the hour and found the money waiting for him, all these negative feelings dissolved.

Tori, astounded, had expected an excuse, a temporary payment—anything to appease the serious default, but, never six thousand dollars! No question that it was the best possible solution to a nagging situation, but the sight of so much money dimmed Tori's usually excellent judgment. In his entire life he'd never seen so large a sum of money at one time.

Don Pippinu, craftier than Tori, watched him, urging, "Go ahead, count it. It's all there. I know I overpaid you," he lamented. "To show you my heart's in the right place, I wish to make further reparations."

"And what does that mean?" asked Tori, too engrossed with the money count to pay him much mind.

"Only that I took the liberty of having my men saddle your horse with a few extra tokens of my respect for that angelic mother of yours, my wife's third cousin. All prewar stuff, *capeeshi?* Oil, sugar, flour—you know, a few extra tidbits, to show we're in accord. . . ."

Tori completed the money count. He lifted his eyes to meet those of the fawning man. He said politely, "I assure you that whatever you send will be accepted with sincere appreciation. It will bring tears of joy and happiness to the eyes of my mother to think that the husband of her third cousin would be so generous and thoughtful. She has always held Don Pippinu in the highest esteem." He gave the Don a bit of his own kind, then packed the money into his saddle bags as the Don watched him through veiled and sinister eyes.

"She's an angel, that woman—an angel!" The Don's oratory, loaded with all the venom collected in a serpent's tooth, burned him like a malignant infection as he studied the assured *Mafiusu* attitude, that arrogant cocksure manner ascribed only to such *men of respect*. Unquestionably, beneath Don Pippinu's fat face lay a vicious brain, a petty man with overinflated ambitions. Burning at the fact that he'd been bested by a *montanaro*—a peasant hillsman, he

198

cursed inwardly. *Fucking upstart! I'll get the sonofabitch yet. Insolent dog!* Words stuck in his throat like impassable gall stones. Acid sprayed his intestines as he watched the proud young eagle, born under the sign of Scorpio, proudly tuck away the money in a money belt.

Exquisitely delighted at the unexpected victory and more possessed each moment with thoughts of Apolladora, Tori failed to detect in the Don the obvious signs of craft, guile, and hatred fermenting in his bowels. Amid strained farewells he departed, leaving the Don staring after him in the night.

In minutes he was knocking at Apolladora's door.

"You came back," she cried joyously with abandon. "You came back to me!"

"Did you really think I wouldn't, Apollodora?" he asked hoarsely, his eyes boring into hers, causing the excitement to begin inside her all over again. She fell into his arms. "I'll never let you go, *cara mia*," he said breathlessly with the impetuosity of a youth struck through the heart by a love dart from Eros.

"Yes," she cried. "No. Oh, I don't know. What matters is that you're here."

They clung together in silence, adoration and a rising desire. Tori had to push her away from him reluctantly. He walked to the balcony and drew the blackout drapes.

He made certain the door was locked. Opening the saddle bags, he removed all the money, counted out five hundred dollars, and set it aside. On a small white card, he scribbled the name of a priest in Palermo and instructed the girl to go to the Church of St. John and present herself to Father Capellino. "Tell him you'll need shelter. In three days I shall come for you to take you to the house of my mother. Then we'll be married." He handed her the five hundred.

"All this money? It's a fortune," she explained flabbergasted. Ecstatically delirious over his proposal, she muttered, "You're crazy, *caro mio*. Completely crazy!" Tears of joy blurred her vision, and she trembled rapturously.

"I know. I know I'm crazy in love with you. I've never known such joy," he confided passionately. "Never!"

"Knowing what I am—what I've done—you still want to marry me?"

He placed his strong hand over her trembling lips tenderly. "You are my *adorata*—my beating heart—my life. We've never lived before today, when we both came alive in the magic of our love." He pressed her close, and Apolladora uttered a low cry and melted in his arms.

199

"Carissima, my time is limited. I must leave you for now," he said softly.

"Oh, Tori. If we never saw each other again I'd die content to know that at least I've known your love, *amore mio,"* she whispered huskily. "I will go to Jato on Saturday. From there I will go to Palermo."

He nodded in agreement and explained that he needed certain items. Did she have any tissue paper, envelopes, stamps and glue? She did. Moving about the room collecting the items, Apolladora brought them to him, then sat and watched in total fascination as he counted out the balance of the money. He wrapped three thousand dollars carefully in tissue paper, slipped it into an envelope, sealed it, stamped and addressed it to himself. He then counted out four hundred more, which he placed into the toe of his sock before slipping his foot back into his boot. He placed a hundred into his pocket and divided the remaining two thousand into three stacks. He then wrapped them in tissue paper and glued them to the inside of his belt.

Glancing into the puzzled and enthralled eyes of Apolladora, he smiled and explained. "Bandits would make short order of me if they caught me with so much money. They'd never think to look here," he said, fastening the belt into place.

"Tori—you didn't—" She hesitated. "What I mean is— you didn't—"

"Steal it?" He laughed amiably, nibbling on the sandwich she'd made for him. "No, *Cara mia,* I didn't steal it." He told her the story and for a time, they both laughed.

Apolladora sobered instantly and reflected. "You must be careful in your dealings with Don Pippinu. He's a demon, that one. An evil animal. He's not to be trusted, Tori. He's in league with the old Mafia. Even the Allies detest him, yet treat him with much respect. Among the girls who work the streets, it is rumored that his enemies disappear mysteriously. Recently one of his *sicarii* attempted to extract compensations from the girls. Several who were approached refused, protesting the unfairness of such demands. Three that I know of, Tori, will never earn another lira as they did in the past. They were so badly mutilated, they can only beg on the streets as side-show freaks. . . ."

Tori stared at her in disbelief, then gathering all his *maschiezzo,* he drew himself up and in bold *pronunciamento,* declared, "He wouldn't dare harm me. I am Salvatore!"

The logic of his words was lost in the pomposity of his

200

attitude. His departure saddened Apolladora and filled her with pangs of dismay. Only their renewed vows to meet in Palermo, no later than the following Monday, brought a smile to her lips and happiness to her jade eyes.

Tori rode swiftly to the post office in Trapani, deposited the envelope containing the money, and headed out into open country.

At midnight, at Bellolampo Barracks, a desk orderly ran into Lt. Franchina's quarters and awakened him from a sound sleep. A military warrant issued at Allied HQ in Mt. Erice for the arrest of one Alessandro Salvatore of Montegatta, necessitated the lieutenant's immediate attention. The charges: grand larceny, and the transport of stolen and illegal goods.

Pulling on his trousers, a sleepy-eyed Franchina made a quick telephone call to Officer Nino Marino in Montegatta. Salvatore, it was reported on good authority, should be approaching Montegatta shortly before sunrise. Therefore Marino was instructed to prepare an ambush with a special detail to insure the felon's capture.

"I knew it! I knew it all along!" Lieutenant Franchina's excitement was transmitted to Nino Marino. "It *wasn't* sheer coincidence that I encountered the blackguard so many times on Monday," he bellowed. "I should have followed my intuition and locked the bastard up!"

"What the hell are you saying, Franchina?" Marino yawned sleepily, but he hadn't missed the self-accusatory remark. It would take more than Franchina's say-so to convince him that Salvatore was a felon, and he spoke out and said so. "Salvatore's no criminal. He's a straight young man who possesses morals you or I might fall short of."

"Listen, Marino," boasted Franchina. "I've a good nose for criminals. They can't fool me. The sonofabitch might just turn out to be head of the black market ring that's plagued Borghetto. Hell, now that I consider it, he might even be guilty of murder—perhaps two. I've nothing to go on except a policeman's hunch. . . ." Franchina thought about Gucci and Molino. Hadn't he seen Salvatore in their company that first day?

"*Va! Va!* With all due respect, *'Tenente*, you can shove that theory up your ass. I've been here a long time. I know these people. This young Tori is a religious acolyte whom the villagers respectfully call, '*il professore*'. Goddammit, man, he doesn't involve himself in criminal activities. There's not a dishonest bone in his body. Look, it must be another man with the same name. So many people are named Salvatore in these mountains."

201

"Listen, Marino. You think your way, I'll think mine. I tell you there's more than meets the eye here. We'll know soon enough. You just make sure the ambush is set up. I want no excuses. If he's innocent, he'll have enough time to prove himself. We'll compare notes later."

"Yeah, sure," said Marino under his breath. "Fat chance."

"What's that, Marino? Speak up. I can't hear you."

"I said, yes sir! I'll attend to it immediately."

CHAPTER 14

P—i—n—g! . . . *P—i—n—g!* The whistling, cracking sound of rifle fire burst all around him. A bullet, then another, and still more whizzed overhead and around him. Tori's stallion spooked, bolted, and reared uncontrollably for several moments until he managed to check rein the beast. Wheeling him around, Tori's eyes squinted in the bright sunlight of dawn, but he saw them. Every last one of them came at him. He was at the center of a circular ambush, and *carabinieri* converged on him from four points on the dial. They came at three, six, nine and twelve o'clock, with rifles aimed at his heart.

"*Firmate!* Stop!" shouted officer Nino Marino, galloping swiftly to Tori's side. "Dismount and identify yourself!"

There was no time to think. His hands were raised over his head in submission. Once again Marino shouted to him.

"I said, dismount!" commanded the feisty *carabiniero*.

Tori was in a daze. He listened to Marino snap out orders to the rest of them, dismissing them and keeping with him only another officer named Fabrizio. "This man is known to me. Two of us can handle him. We'll meet at Bellolampo, later," he told his men. To Tori he shouted even louder. "Goddammit! I said dismount!"

Tori complied. He was ordered to turn over his identity card. "And no funny stuff! One false move and you'll find yourself separated from half your body," added Marino.

All of this seemed false to Tori. Even as Marino walked to the rear of his stallion, identity card in hand, it seemed to Tori he was playacting. With the tip of a knife, Marino

202

slit open the ropes tying the foodstuffs to his saddle and sliced away the tarp exposing the goods. Marino snorted contemptuously.

"Black marketeering too, eh? Don't bother to explain. You can tell it to Lt. Franchina at Bellolampo. In case that lawyer's head of yours questions my orders, I've a warrant for your arrest. Now make it easy on yourself—tell me where you've hidden the money."

"The what—?" In all this confusion Tori hadn't given it a thought.

"Stop stalling. Turn it over, Salvatore. It'll go easier for you in my report, you hear?"

Tori was stunned as it all came together in his mind. So this was the game Don Pippinu played! The bastard reported him to the police. Now he'd get his money back and jail Tori on a trumped up charge. He should have known better.

"Listen, Marino," he began, "I can explain all of this—" He was so intent on his hatred for the despicable Don that he wasn't prepared for the next jolt.

"I said tell it to Franchina. Now hand over the belt!"

For Tori this would be the blackest moment of his life. He could only stare dumbly at Marino. *Santo Dio!* Only one person knew of the belt. *Apolladora! Apolladora! Sweet merciful God tell me I'm wrong.* Don Pippinu and Apolladora working together! His legs turned to water. Shaken, disorganized and stunned by the sequence of events, he moved as if in a dream; his stiff, cumbersome hands fumbled with his belt buckle, unhitching it and handing it to the officer. His mind had stopped, gone blank.

He vaguely heard Marino's words of chastisement. Something to the effect that he'd argued with Lt. Franchina about the question of Salvatore's involvement, certain the lad wouldn't have been involved in a reprehensible crime. "My faith in you is shattered, Sicilian," said Marino. "Grand larceny and black marketeering!"

Tori, numb from shock but not too stunned to berate himself, waded through the mental fog that enveloped him. What a jackass he'd been! *Un pezzu de shekko!* Trusting two people that an idiot of three years wouldn't have given the time of day! Moving robotlike, bewildered by the deception foisted upon him, Tori vaguely heard Marino's words: "Get on your horse and don't try anything funny or I'll give it to you through the head!"

Five minutes later they were mounted and climbing the narrow corkscrew road to the summit. Confusion blistered

Tori's mind, yet in this confusion he caught sight of the *lupara* in his saddle holster, which Marino had failed to remove earlier. The treacherous road was narrow, and they were approaching a tortuous hairpin bend in the road where his keen eyes discerned that, judging from the distance between him and his captors, as soon as he made the U-turn, he'd be facing the officers. He had to make a split second decision, and he did. Once past the U-turn, Tori moved fast. He pulled up on the *lupara* and got the drop on the *carabinieri*, taking them by surprise. And then, the unexpected happened—a freak accident.

Pursuant to regulations when escorting a prisoner, Officer Marino carried his Mannlicher-Carcano slung under one arm. The sight of the *lupara* aimed at him had caused him to rein his horse; the antique rifle misfired and sent a bullet spiralling through Tori's left shoulder. The sudden impact of the perforating missile, ripping into Tori, caused an involuntary reflex action as his trigger finger squeezed tightly exploding the *lupara*. A blinding ball of white fire caught Marino between the eyes, and with a loud, agonized groan of pain he went flying off his saddle, toppling to the ground, his hands clutching blindly at his head where blood oozed and spurted like a fountain. Marino's horse, an army mare, spooked for a moment, then retired to a distance a few feet away from the scene.

Fabrizio's horse, a squeamish, quivering mass of animal flesh, shuddered under him as the neophyte took random shots at Salvatore before he panicked and rode off in a whirling cloud of ocherous dust. Most of the shots went wild, but one struck Tori's left arm inches below the shoulder wound.

Wincing at the pain in his upper arm and shoulder, Tori clutched at the area of shooting fire and saw a thick glob of warm blood seep through his fingers. Despite his injuries, he rode to Marino's side, and springing from his saddle, sickened by the ghastly sight, he stared numbly at the faceless mass where portions of the skull had exploded, exposing sections of the cranium and the skeletal structure of bones and teeth. There was no mistaking it, the man was dead.

Tori reeled unsteadily as the faces of Gucci and Molino superimposed themselves over the bloodied mass of Marino's body. Sickened by the rapidly evolving order of things, he couldn't believe his senses. He felt dizzy, flushed with burning sensations and considerably weak. Dimly his eyes made out a cloud of dust riding at him from the distance. How many were there? Four. Four uniformed *carabinieri* approached him.

Without thought of the moneybelt or his identity card, he mounted his stallion, wheeled him about, and rode off the road beyond several large boulders. He found a secluded grotto and hid from sight.

He could hear their voices dimly. Too weak to scale the boulder that overlooked the scene, he lay his head on the cool stone and remained motionless.

"Where's the money?" asked a voice vaguely familiar to Tori. "The six thousand." Lt. Franchina's voice rang loud and clear.

"I swear, it's all he had on him," insisted Fabrizo.

"Take Marino's body back to Bellolampo. Go to Salvatore's house and wait for him. Bring him back with the rest of the money, or *you'll* be swinging from the nearest tree. The charge in addition to grand larceny is murder, now."

Tori couldn't see them, but he heard this portion of their conversation. Moments after he heard their horses ride off, he returned to the cool grotto and sat down. He removed his shirt, ripped off the sleeves, and bound his upper arm as best he could. He found a twig and made a tourniquet to halt the flow of blood. Using a torn sleeve to stuff the bloodied hole in his shoulder, he tried to find something to bind it and couldn't. Sweat rolled off his face as the pain intensified. It being so early in the morning, he didn't dare chance an escape in broad daylight, only to be picked off by roaming *carabinieri*. No. He'd have to wait until nightfall before chancing it. He lay back against a cool rock, his head roiling with violent and uncontrollable thoughts.

The effect on Salvatore of this bewildering and rapid succession of events struck him with a sequence of alternating reactions. First, blind fury and outrage at Apolladora's betrayal and Don Pippinu's obvious treachery. Then came concern over his family. What must they be thinking? Would his mother believe the charges of grand larceny—the murder of Nino Marino? God! What had happened to him these past forty-eight hours? Had he suddenly been possessed by a demoniacal monster? He didn't recognize these strange emotions coursing through him. From where had they sprung? Had they always been there inside of him, lying dormant waiting to be unleashed?

Only last night, after he had left Apolladora's apartment he'd been like a man returning to a warm hearth after a long and glorious journey to far and wondrous places he'd never forget. He'd galloped with the speed of a meteor along the winding roads, through barren orchards, past olive groves older than those in biblical Babylon with their gray whorled trunks like spiralling goat horns. Thoughts of Apolladora had saturated his mind, body and soul, and love had oozed from every pore in his body. The tableau of love he'd created with Apolladora had dazzled his senses and occupied most of his thoughts, diffusing all thoughts of that devil, Don Pippinu.

It was his own fault for trusting in a whore. Yes! That's what she was—a whore! How could he have been so blind? He had even pushed aside the nagging thoughts that had attempted to pierce his mind, trying to warn him. What could happen to him? Just before midnight, he had paused at the Greek ruins at Segesta to rest his horse and nibble at the *companaggio* prepared for him by Apolladora. Seated at the base of one of the enormous pillars of the temple, Tori had felt his left ear throb. It had come to him at the time that the matter with Don Pippinu had been too easy.

Moving quickly, he had pulled the *lupara* from his saddle holster and loaded it with pellets. He'd slipped it back into place, then checked his Beretta automatic. At least he'd had the good sense to take the warning in good stead. He had even detoured to Castellammare, where he'd awakened a keeper of stables and bargained for the black stallion, which he had exchanged for the chestnut mare by adding a few lire to the bargain. He had thought if anyone lay in ambush for him they wouldn't be looking for a black stallion. . . . Well, a lot of good it had done!

The sun had just been rising when Tori had paused in the plains of Partenico to water his horse from the cascading crystal waters spouting from the jaws of open-mouthed serpents constructed by the Romans centuries before. Back on his horse, he had galloped through wheat fields, suddenly very tired, hungry and saddle sore and unduly irritated by the creaking bridle paraphernalia—a sound that he found grating on his nerves. The familiar throbbing in his ear had commenced once again, causing Tori to become wary and edgy. Even the snorting, labored breathing of the stallion had alerted him, as if he, too, sensed the impending dangers. In the distance Tori had seen vultures circling overhead against the eastern skies, and he had suddenly recalled the deaths of Gucci and Molino. Just before the shots rang out, he had felt the beast quiver under him and snap his powerful head from side to side, his nostrils flaring and ebony eyes darting wildly about. He had grown skittish, resisting Tori's control.

Hah, thought Tori reflecting on this. Even the beast had been more intelligent than he'd been when he rode into the ambush.

By mid-afternoon, Tori became increasingly feverish. He needed water to slake his thirst. Hunched over, he let his head fall heavily into his right hand. He felt miserable, defeated. Worse, he was sick. He'd smoked incessantly and had no more tobacco left. The pains he felt were sheer agony. His eyes grew swollen and distended, his bloodshot eyes frenzied and maniacal. In the raging fever his madness increased. His heart shriveled at Apolladora's deception.

"Don Pippinu!" he shouted with satanic exhaultation. "Watch yourself carefully. Your days are numbered. And you, Apolladora, to whom I gave my love, my heart and soul, there's a place for traitors. You'll not live to enjoy the fruits of this day's treachery. By, God, I shall be avenged for the betrayal you wrought upon me this day, you Delilah!" Tears of humiliation stung his eyes as he recanted his misery aloud.

"How you must have laughed at me! I stood before you, a simpering shadow of a boy, parading his tumescence like a badge of honor! A jackass is what I was. A foolish adolescent! All cock and no balls! A foolish joke of a boy, trying to impress the world with his manliness. *Cafone! Cafone!*" As bitterness and self-condemnation eroded his guts and sapped him of strength, he succumbed from sheer exhaustion, slipping in and out of fretful consciousness.

Dreams. Nightmares. Recollections came at him. The events of the past two days wouldn't quit in his mind. The faces of Gucci and Molino were etched sharply on each eyeball. He'd never killed before. Not from squeamishness or fear, but because he'd felt this a violation of human dignity. Yet in three days he'd killed three men. The faces of those brutalized youngsters, helpless at the hands of Gucci—even Pallido who had died in his arms and his uncle Gianni dead at their hands—faded into the recesses of his mind while the faces of Gucci and Molino remained vivid in his memory to torment him. Finally he fell mercifully unconscious.

Tori awakened in high fever. Shaken by chills, consumed by fire and unable to hold to a clear thought, he struggled to his feet holding his head in his hands in an effort to unscramble the chaos in his brain. A dullness of

207

perception struck him. Memory came and went with alarming frequency. He staggered and stumbled about in the darkness, confused by a body that refused to do his bidding. Yet somehow, miraculously, he managed in this confusion to strap himself onto his horse and head out into the night towards a destination he had never dreamed would be his home.

Irrevocably drawn by unseen forces towards a particular place and a specific people to fulfill some predestined plan, he slumped over the saddle of his satiny stallion and, guided by an instinct older than time, he moved slowly over the craggy terrain of boulders and stones of antiquity.

A swarm of stars hung over the desolate land with fierce intensity, as if they'd purposely been turned on to illuminate his path and guide him forward into the blackness. No matter how he tried to retain consciousness, he found himself outwitted by a raging infection and an all-consuming fever which broke down his resistance. Through the murky haze he vaguely heard a voice calling. "Apolladora . . . Apolladora. . . ."

Lieutenant Franchina had had no time to compare notes with Nino Marino. The next time he saw the younger man, Molino was dead at Salvatore's hand, and this had been attested to by an eyewitness, *carabiniero* Fabrizo. Franchina needed no further proof. He had in his possession Tori's identity card and a belt containing only a portion of the six thousand dollars allegedly stolen from a Mt. Erice merchant, and the dead body of Nino Marino. In his eyes, now, Salvatore was guilty beyond a shadow of a doubt. He'd turned all this evidence over to Major Carrini at Bellolampo late that afternoon, and to his astonishment was instructed to charge Salvatore only with the murder of Nino Marino and the stolen foodstuffs. He was instructed under oath to say nothing about the money or grand larceny charges. He complied with the orders of his superior, keeping his thoughts to himself.

For the next several days Lieutenant Franchina launched an exhaustive search for Salvatore. Nothing turned up. It was as if those infernal mountains had swallowed him up. On Sept 29 he presented himself at the Salvatore house. Greeted by Athena who was ill with one of her nagging headaches, he asked to speak with her mother.

As he departed, leaving the woman and her daughter shaken and distraught over the information he had imparted to them, he requested their cooperation in the matter of apprehending Tori. He was annoyed by the unusual strength and fortitude the woman displayed. Earlier when he had thrust the warrant into Antigone's hands and told her he was looking for 'that murderer, Salvatore,' Antigone had insisted he must be mistaken. He assured her they had an eyewitness to the felony.

"Who?" Antigone had queried. "Another *carabiniero?*" She had displayed her contempt.

"When will you peasants learn you can't continue to violate the laws?" he'd asked.

"The same time you learn that we Sicilians have stomachs that need feeding as regularly as yours," she had replied scathingly.

By then his aides had searched the Salvatore house thoroughly and returned, announcing they'd found no one. "He can't have gone too far with two bullets pumped in him," he said aloud, watching the reaction on the women's faces.

Lieutenant Franchina touched his cap politely and informed them the police and *carabinieri* would be watching their house with the eyes of hawks. "When a man needs shoes he goes to a cobbler," he told them in parting. "And when a man needs his family—well, we'll be here to grab him." He and his men left immediately, leaving the women to their despair.

"Mamma, oh Mamma," cried Athena. "Our world has collapsed. First, Filippo, then Marco, now Tori." She buried her face in her mother's shoulder. "Two bullets shot into him! *Two!* How will he live? Who'll care for him?"

"Don't cry, *cara mia*," said her mother soothingly. "Don't cry. If crying helped, I'd be the first to shed tears. Don't believe their lies. Tori's no murderer."

"I can't help it. I'm not as strong as Tori or you."

"All right then, cry if you must, dear heart."

Athena pulled away, blew her nose, and dabbed at the tears.

"That's my girl. Dry your eyes. You'll only aggravate your pain if you cry. Wherever Tori is now, God watches over him. He's fully protected now—" Antigone gave a start. She had stopped in mid-sentence, horror-struck. She blinked hard as if to help sharpen her mind.

"Mamma, you're truly made of iron," said Athena, impervious to the changes occurring in her mother until she glanced at the terrified expression on her face. "Mamma? What's wrong?"

Antigone ran from the kitchen with the frenzied eyes of

a woman possessed. She ran up the stairs and groped along the wall of her bedroom until she located the key to her hope chest. She moved across the room, inserted the key, and turned it in the lock. She lifted the cover and removed from the chest both the prophecy and the amulet, sinking to her knees in a crumpled heap. Sighing deeply, as if to catch her breath, she read and reread the *strega*'s prophecy, her eyes spotlighting certain portions: *"He musn't be without this protection. Already there are strange webs of entanglements in the fires of his life. . . ."*

She told me there'd be trouble," wailed Antigone softly. "I didn't listen. Oh God of all that's sacred and holy, what have I done? *Santo Dio*, what have I done?"

Athena stood at the door watching her mother, wondering at this peculiar behavior. Who'd told her there'd be trouble? What had she done by not listening? She caught sight of the glittering disc in her mother's hands, and, unable to make it out, she decided it was the wrong time to invade her mother's privacy. She retreated back to her room and placed a vinegar-soaked cloth over her forehead. The fumes in some way helped to alleviate the pain.

On October 3, a Saturday, Lieutenant Franchina, filled with an inner restlessness and an increased loathing for Bellolampo and the growing apathy he discerned in his fellow officers, gathered together a squad of men and ventured forth in the direction of Rigano Pass, where only five days before his men had been massacred. Drawn back to the area by a profound curiosity and a desire to avenge the deaths of his former companions, he was eager to find those responsible for the atrocity.

During the course of the past few days, Lieutenant Franchina, on his own initiative, had sought the services of a special breed of man who for a price would spy for him and report their findings. Most of these leads, however, turned up without the much sought after results. However, the knowledge that such men existed among this clannish withdrawn society was filed away in his mind for future reference.

For three hours the weary, overheated *carabinieri* wove in and out of the few accessible grottos and came up with nothing. Finally, from the southern-most point of the pass, Lt. Franchina gave his men the signal to remount and return to Bellolampo.

Bandits approaching the Pass from the north had the advantage of spotting their enemy first. Had any *carabini-*

ero at Bellolampo Barracks been walking idly about the military *caserne* and glanced up in the distance, they might have wondered at the small puffs of smoke rising in the distance. Even the faint popping of rifle fire might have captured their attention. If any of them might have been discerning enough to realize what was happening and thought to ride swiftly to Rigano Pass, they might have caught up with the bandits and finished them off.

But unfortunately it was Saturday, a day most officers already in Palermo had begun to wind down in preparation for a gala weekend, partying with the British and American soldiers and the influx of prostitutes abounding in the city. What few remained on duty at Bellolampo were playing cards and drinking sociably, never once thinking about their foolish companions whom that crazy Franchina had encouraged to go out scouting on a Saturday. A Saturday—imagine!

In the bottleneck at the Pass five bandits picked off Franchina's men, one at a time, felling a man with each bullet they expended. Once again Lt. Franchina's star must have been in the ascendancy. He escaped death in the ambush. But this time he felt no stirrings of immortality surging in his loins. He wasn't as fortunate as he'd been on September 28. A heartbeat or two away from death's greedy claws, he hung on desperately to his saddle, his body riddled with bullets and spouting rivulets of blood. He reached the barracks miraculously and was rushed to the Palermo Hospital, more dead than alive—but still alive

CHAPTER 15

An early Sicilian sun splintered through a webbed network of upper branches on tall pine trees. He saw portions of a fiery blue sky in a cross-illumination of light outlining dark foliage. He had awakened to such profound weakness that he thought for an instant he was paralyzed and blind until he blinked his burning eyes and the milky film over his vision cleared and lightened enough for him to discern familiar objects, like trees, leaves and branches. Forced to blink time and again, he stretched his eyelids until his vision cleared entirely.

Life first came to his mind in short electric bursts while his body lay immobile. But for Tori, it was enough to know he was alive! The smells of clean earth, pine needles, and fresh coffee invigorated him and he knew he was coming to. Slowly, his eyes gazed about the confines of his shelter. He wondered where he was. The shadowy form of an older man with wrinkled skin the color of smoked leather, propped sleepily against a tree trunk, caught his eyes. Wearing a brown beaked cap with flaps tugged down over his ears, the old man made grumbling noises as he snored. Intermittently, he'd nod as one did in fighting off sleep. Beyond him, through a small clearing, Tori saw a scattering of idle men, moving about a camp-fire sipping hot coffee.

Perplexed, he tried to wade through his mental confusion, and found to his dismay that his memory wasn't anxious to obey him. As more life stirred in him, he grew aware of bandages around his left shoulder and a sling around his neck in which his left wrist lay supported. A blanket wrapped warmly about him to ward off the early morning chill fell away as he moved. Then, like a rolling fog bank, a tunneled voice cut through his numb and hazy brain and pulled him back into reality.

"Buon Giorno. Buon Giorno, aquilo bravo. I see the brave young eagle has returned from the mountain," grinned a toothless old man, before he hawked up phlegm from his throat and spat it into a nearby bush. He cast off his poncho-shawl, and Tori saw a curiously misshapen man, bent from a crippling form of arthritis, move with remarkable agility and approach him. He helped to sit him up, and propped Tori against a tree trunk.

Tori glanced warily at him. He wanted to ask a thousand questions. He felt his lips move, but no sound came for several moments. Finally he asked with difficulty, . . . What day is this?" Tori leaned forward as pain spasms tore at him. He winced, gasped, and grimaced painfully.

"Santo Dio!" shouted the old man. "Mother of Satan! Lie still! Two bad bullets were pumped into you! Might as well have been a dozen, for all the trouble they caused. Don't you remember? *Managghia!* What the hell hit you—a *carabiniero's* relic of a gun?"

Instantly, Tori froze. He disliked questions. He became suspicious of anyone prying into his business, and drew away from the old man with an animal wariness.

"Don't worry, you're safe with the rest of us, here in the

212

macchia. I've had enough experience with *carabinieri* bullets to know their story. If the shot doesn't get you, infection from their rusty bullets will destroy you. Imbeciles! Haven't the sense to use proper bullets in their guns. You'd think Mussolini would arm his soldiers correctly, no? Imagine—they use World War I relics! They deserve to lose this goddamn war! Junk is what they use. Junk! 1891 Mannlicher-Carcano's and ancient Vetterli Vitale's, rebarreled for 6.5 mm rifles. What a disgrace, eh? *Allora,* would you believe these same guns are used for .22 calibre training rifles by the *carabinieri?*"

As the old man spoke, he peered critically under the dressings in Tori's arm and shoulder, and nodded in satisfaction. *"Molto bene . . . molto bene. . . ."* He replaced the bandages. "One day, *Il Duce* will wake up to learn he lost this fox trot with Hitler because those goddamn weapons blew up in the faces of those soldiers who accompanied him in the grand ball of war. I am called Giacomo. What are you called?"

"Alessandro," he began, surprised at the weakness of his voice. "Alessandro Salvatore. My friends call me Tori."

"Benvenuto, Salvatore. Welcome to the Mountain of Cats. This is Thursday. For two days, you've been embraced by the arms of death, *aquilo bravo.*"

"Aquilo bravo? Me?" Tori forced a smile. "I doubt that I resemble a brave eagle. I feel more like a plucked goose." *So,* thought Tori bitterly, *I ended up in the bandits' camp.* He grew more guarded until he realized that in his condition there was little he could do to defend himself.

"Listen," confided the old man, rubbing his hands together to warm them, before he lit a cigarette, which he handed to his patient. "When I found you, fighting to sit tall in the saddle, in the darkness, where only the whites of your eyes and those of your valiant horse's were visible, and your body raging with fever as the angels of death fought over your bones, you brought to mind a magnificent golden eagle I once saw felled by hunter's bullets. It was too dangerous to approach, and I was forced to keep my distance. Daily I brought food and water to that king of flying creatures. He lasted eight days. If only I could have gotten closer without him savagely clawing me to death I might have saved his life. You reminded me of this *aquilo bravo,* for you too, fought me off. In your delirium you cried out, 'Let me die! Let me die!' Just as quickly, I told God he'd better not listen to you, that you were crazy out of your mind. That if he listened to you, he'd have to reckon with me. So, knowing my wrath, he

213

wouldn't argue with old Giacomo. I told God, 'This time I think we saved an even more magnificent eagle than before.' " The old man became a symphony of hand gestures.

Touched by the man's words, Tori nevertheless felt bitterness at his plight. Thoughts of Apolladora and Don Pippinu seared his soul. He glanced about the wooded area, beyond the makeshift campsite, noting the many unsightly and bearded men in their midst.

"You want to meet the others?"

"No." Tori's prompt reply brought a questioning look from the other.

"Later, then. Don't be concerned if there comes upon you a peculiar dizziness. I have medicated you with the wondrous sulpha drug I stole from the American dispensary in Palermo. *Allora*—rest for now. Soon I will bring you first class coffee. Phew! What I found in your saddle bags! *Managghia!* Such luxuries. But, do not worry. I shall not permit these thieving buzzards to steal them. What a joy to taste real coffee—" He rambled.

About to protest the brazen appropriation of his precious cargo, Tori shrugged it off. Who was in a position to argue? He neither possessed the strength or the desire to challenge a flea. In his misery he watched as Giacomo limped off towards the campfire, shuffling and dragging his arthritic leg behind him.

Tori's outward calm masked an earthquake of *vendetta* and vengeance. Unshaven for days, weak and far from healed, he'd made his plans. On Saturday when Apolladora arrived in Jato to bring food to her family he'd be there to greet her—unless that, too, had been a crock of deception! He didn't think so, though. Armed with the knowledge that he'd be settling the score shortly, Tori tried to get to his feet in Giacomo's absence. The earth suddenly moved from under him, and the sky whirling above him changed color. He lost his footing, and, falling heavily against a tree, he remained there until Giacomo returned with the coffee.

"Are you crazy?" shouted the old man. "By the balding black balls of Satan, are you trying to kill yourself? Get back down and stay put. Crazy fool!" He set the steaming mugs of coffee on the ground nearby and helped steady his patient.

"I want to walk," insisted Tori weakly. "It will make me stronger. Just a few feet. I have to—I must."

"All right. I'll walk with you," said Giacomo sensing the other's resolve. "But, by the beard of my sister's husband twice removed, you're a stubborn mule! *Testardo!* Lean on me, fool. I've ten times your strength."

"Thank you for taking care of me," said Tori as they walked.

"Balls! You'll thank me by getting off your feet—not by empty words. Why do you push yourself? You'll walk in time."

"Tell me—who are all these men?" Tori tried to change tack. It worked.

For a time he listened in courteous silence as Giacomo pointed out first, one then, another. Most were petty offenders who had run from the *carabinieri* for transporting food over provincial borders. The old man's eyes lit up suddenly as if possessed with a mighty secret. "These are only a few men," he added. "See those men up there—high on the ledge?" He pointed to a wooded area overhead, against the great mountain. "Up there are hundreds of men I've not met as yet. Prisoners of war, they say. Dangerous men, young eagle. True criminals. Damned tough, I hear. I tell you straight, *aquilo*," he whispered conspiratorially. "Those men have an arsenal of guns that could run the Allies out of Sicily. I do not lie!" he exclaimed crossing his heart. I personally have seen these weapons.

"Are they in the Grotto Persephone?" asked Tori sparked with interest.

"You know this place?"

"I know it." Tori paused to light a cigarette from a burning stick in the campfire. Finished, he tossed the twig back into the heart of the fire and inhaled deeply on the cigarette. "Listen, *amico*," he said, *sotto voce*. "If I desire to get a message out of the *macchia*—"

"Leave it to me, *aquilo bravo*," Giacomo interrupted boldly as if he read the other's thoughts. "It shall be done."

"Not now. Soon, perhaps, but not now. I'm tired. For now we sit down, eh?"

A few heads turned in their direction, most of them apathetic, paying them no importance. Tori felt better. Weaker, but better. He could feel his senses come alive, and that was better than the insensitivity he'd felt these past days. In an hour he'd take another walk. For now, he lay back against the trunk of a tall cypress, bundled warmly against the cool mountain air.

Still searing his heart and soul were the burning images of Apolladora and Don Pippinu. Until their fate was

215

settled in his mind, Tori was determined never to forget the infamy done against him.

A few days rest and concentrated exercise would work wonders for him. On Saturday—in Jato, he'd settle the score. He'd killed before, this time it would be easier. The time passed swiftly, with revenge firing his emotions.

CHAPTER 16

"Padre!" called Tori for the fourth time.

The bent figure of a middle-aged parish priest, working vigorously in an unprolific garden, finally glanced up. *Padre* Francesco Voltera, a craggy-faced man with grey streaks in his wiry dark hair, possessed dark, angry eyes, smoldering under a shelf of bushy brows that expressed his outrage and the dark, brooding thoughts he harbored. Without thinking the uncordial man cursed aloud. *"Ma che cazzu voi?* Speak up! Speak up! I haven't all day."

Startled by the tart language uttered by priest at the Church of Santo Crocifisso, Tori stared at him in silence, aghast at the holy man's comportment.

Sensing his error, the priest lowered his shovel, dropped his anger a notch or two, and squinted up at the stranger who wore a sling around one arm. He sighed aloud, set aside his garden tool, tugged at a handkerchief from his rear pocket, and commenced to wipe the sweat from his face and neck. He ambled to the gate, grumbling and scolding himself for both his uncalled-for rudeness and his damned lumbago. He rubbed his back, gingerly.

"Come, come, my son," said the scowling priest. "Come. Sit down." He walked, leading the way to the *pergoda*, and continued his compulsive oratory. "Yesterday, our village was struck with the most deplorable atrocity in its history. Horrifying! Simply horrifying! Who can preach piety or turn the other cheek from the pulpit tomorrow—eh? Not after this. Please, take a seat. See?" He made a wide sweeping gesture with his arms. "Nothing grows here. Our people die from unproductive lands and intolerable *siroccos*. Nine months out of each year we pray for rain. When it comes it washes away half the village. Now—the

216

abrasiveness of war with foreigners once again. Most inhuman. Most inhuman! There's no hope for Sicilians, I tell you. No hope at all." He broke wind without apology.

"Uh—I—uh, Padre," interrupted Tori, in no mood for long-winded speeches about centuries-old grievances and inequities. He knew them by rote.

"Forgive me. I've come on an urgent matter. I'll not take your time if you will kindly direct me to the house of Felice, to the family in which there's a daughter, Apolladora."

The priest, suddenly aloof and suspicious, asked, "Who are you?"

Tori avoided the cleric's eyes. "A friend of the family," he replied.

"Ah, then you're here for the funeral. I tell it straight," said the priest relaxing somewhat. "It's unbelievable. Poor Abruzzi. What a job for the mortician. It'll be a closed casket, of course," rambled the agitated priest.

"Please direct me to the proper house," insisted Tori impatiently, as he pressed a stack of *Am-lire* in the man's hands. "For the poor box," he added.

Reacting to the money, Padre Voltera replied eagerly. "Better still, I'll take you there, personally." He was instantly cordial and obsequious.

"No, no, no. It's not necessary," said Tori, visibly irked.

"Nonsense. It's my duty. I want to apologize for my rudeness. . . ."

Before Tori's voice raised in protest, he found himself guided through the most depressed area he'd ever seen. They passed through narrow alleys, past hovels unfit for animals, yet occupied by humans. He sidestepped filthy gutters, gurgling with fetid waters. He saw dull, half-starved faces peering at him from behind dirty curtains: hungry children, brown from the sun, standing on thresholds dressed in rags. In the air was a feeling of doom, desperation and depression.

Revolting odors of animal excrement, heat and dust thickened the air. Stale foods, sickness, disease and the putrefaction of death appalled him. Was there no humanity in this wretched village? He could scarcely breathe. Tori reached for his handkerchief to cover his nose.

"I hardly notice the foul odors any more. One gets used to them," said the priest.

Tori wondered, as he'd wondered many times in the past, what good were priests? Was their role directed to the sole purpose of hypnotizing people into accepting such miseries in life without encouraging them into something better?

The alleys became more littered with refuse, and he felt the awareness of pain, fear and starvation pulsing in the atmosphere. Here and there a solitary figure approached them and paused to stare, then passed on, nodding to the priest. There was something ominous in their silent presence, and when he looked into their eyes they seemed not the eyes of humans, but more like those of wary animals, hating, suspicious and hostile.

He wondered: *Why are they like this? Is this why Apolladora had left this land of hopelessness?* Had all the interior villages crumbled to such decay? In his village, shabbily dressed men roamed the streets, but there the resemblance ended. Or was this the first time he had taken a good look at his country? Had the dreams and fantasies been suddenly stripped from his eyes, permitting him to see things as they'd always been, revealing X-rays of the shabby and deplorable life to which his fellow man had been reduced over the ages? He asked himself candidly if his sensitivity to these conditions had been heightened by his own inescapable dilemma. No answer came to ease his torment.

They stopped before a grubby, run-down shanty, generously called a building. A hand-lettered sign, in bold script, graced the door: *"Abruzzi's Funeral Parlor—A. Abruzzi, Mortician."*

"Be a good lad, stop with me for a moment. I must bless the body," urged the frocked man giving Tori no time to refuse. He disappeared inside.

Before Tori could grope for an excuse, there was no one left to listen. *Damn it to hell!* he cursed inwardly. His wounds pained him; his stomach felt queasy, nauseated from the lack of nourishment. He wanted to complete his mission and get the hell out of Jato. Reluctantly he followed the priest's footsteps inside the dismal and intolerable building. Odors of bland paraffin, intermingled with formaldehyde and death, clung cohesively to the air and mixed with the decaying stench produced by the dead, humans as well as flowers; Tori felt more nauseous. His eyes, adjusting to the interior, took in the familiar scene.

Death and God! God and Death! Always the immaculate white altar, upon which was displayed a profusion of statues; the Virgin with Child, Santa Rosalia, St. Anthony, St. Sebastian. Floral offerings, burning candles, incense— all of it stood in complete incongruity to the earthen-floored room with its leaky walls and leprous ceilings, where open sections of the roof allowed an ample view of the sky. Bowled over by the stench, Tori's first impulse was to run.

From the back room came the fat-jowelled, owlish mortician, wearing bloodstained rubber gloves, and a rubber apron, splattered crimson, around his rotund belly. Telltale lines of irritation creased his sweaty face. Recognizing the priest, the mortician Abruzzi took license to express himself and beckon them both inside.

"Ah, it's you, *Padre*. I can do nothing! Nothing!" he pushed his bifocals into place over the bridge of his nose.

"Abruzzi, this is Salvatore. Friend of the family."

The men nodded to each other. A protest lay on Tori's lips, unspoken. Death appalled him. His line of vision, partially obstructed by the priest's body, enabled him to see only a portion of the nude body lying on the marble slab, next to the bloodstained sewer drain. Quickly Tori turned his attention out the window, unsure of which sight was worse; the lifeless, skeletal structures abutting the buildings, or the lifeless cadaver on the slab. He heard an exchange of words between mortician and priest.

"You see? The heart's completely excised. See the gaping hole? The worst cadaver I've ever seen. Who'd do such an infamous job in these civilized days, eh, *padre*? Is there no more morality in our world?"

The priest, tight-lipped and grim in the presence of such atrocity, was speechless and visibly shocked. A swarm of black flies, attracted by death's stench, zeroed in through open windows and buzzed peskily about Tori's ears. Annoyed, he brushed them aside, dabbed at the air, and turned to avoid them. In that instance the priest moved aside, affording Tori a better view of the cadaver. He caught sight of the pale, waxen corpse, covered with a mass of swollen, discolored welts and purplish bruises. The body, barely recognizeable, did allow Tori to see instantly the mortician's dilemma. A rusty pipe two inches in diameter protruded from between the legs of the cadaver, from the vagina. Sickened at the sight, Tori turned away. God Almighty! What an obscenity! Who in his right mind would do such a brutal, inhuman thing? Who, indeed?

"That's how they found her, my son. Impaled upon this pipe, stuck into the ground, outside her parents' house like a slaughtered baby lamb skewered through for roasting. Fiendish devils! Did you know Apolladora well?"

Tori's agonized eyes snapped open. Everything converged into a wild moment of disbelief. "Apolladora?" He

219

could barely mouth the name. *"Apolladora?"* Horror turned him into a frozen statue of ice.

He forced himself to gaze upon the fragile, mutilated remains. Steadying himself upon the priest's arm, he uttered a low gasp, a savage moan at the incomprehensible violence done to the remains on the marble slab. His eyes lingered on every inch of the body and came to rest upon the silver crucifix at her neck, as if this symbol could finally make it all real for him, make him believe this to be Apolladora. *Apolladora! Oh My God!* A thousand images of their intimacy flashed before his eyes. It was incredible, this. Too grotesque, and unreal, too horrendous to be believed.

He moved in slow motion towards her. He felt as if his stomach had been ripped open and his guts lay sprawled upon the floor. Pressures in his head and chest wanted to explode with his feelings. Gently, he reached in and pushed aside tendrils of blood-clotted hair off her swollen and distorted face, unaware that the priest and mortician watched all this with mounting curiosity. Tori wanted to gather her in his arms, kiss her, and blow the breath of life into her lifeless body. Her last words echoed through his mind: *"Caro mio, if we never saw each other again, I'd die content—"*

"Who did this to her?" he asked the priest later at the rectory.

"You think I know? Only Satan keeps books on these malevolent acts. Did you know her long?"

Tori couldn't reply. His throat had thickened and felt parched, and he felt the violence of the past days rush at him like a cancer. He listened to the cleric as the man rambled.

"She was to have been married soon. She had sent her parents a tidy sum of money. There was a letter from her. But, come, we'll go to the house of her parents."

"No. Not now." Tori's voice trembled. He couldn't pull himself together. "You mentioned a letter. What sort of a letter?"

Father Voltera studied the young man, whom he'd have cause to remember in the not too distant future. There was something about him. . . . "I have the letter here. The family is illiterate. Wait here," said the priest. He disappeared inside his house and returned in moments with the letter and handed it to the grief-stricken Tori.

The letter was simple and written in a childish scrawl. It explained that she was to meet her future husband in Palermo, where they'd be married. It told Salvatore she hadn't willingly betrayed him. How then did the *carabinieri* learn of the moneybelt? Don Pippinu knew they had spent time together. Had Tori been followed to the apartment of Apolladora? Had they tortured her to reveal the hiding place of the money? Had she been forced to betray him? The answers to his questions lay dead on the marble slab in Abruzzi's mortuary. He reread the letter, bit the back of his hand, and fought off the impulse to scream.

There came upon him the relentless urge to kill; to strike back at those murderers. How much longer could he control this unfamiliar voice of violence and destruction which threatened to rise out of him? *God help me!* He sagged forward and stared at the letter in his left hand. His right hand fell limply between his legs in an attitude of utter futility, all the strength, courage and manliness, drained from him. Tears fell from his eyes.

"Do you wish to make a confession?" asked the priest.

At the very heart of Tori, a voice warned. *"Trust no one, not even a priest.* "I'll confess to my confessor in my village, *Padre.* With your permission, I'll be on my way," he said with stiff politeness. *Sainted God of the Universe! God of all that's merciful and just!* Apolladora didn't deserve such a fate! No one had to tell him at whose hands the atrocity had been effected. Tori felt like bursting.

Father Voltera studied the man as he lit his pipe. Surely it wasn't all grief he thought. *He's too somber. His face and angry eyes fill with too much menace.* He puffed on the pipe and extinguished the match.

"If I didn't offer a few words of solace I'd be remiss in my duties," he began. This isn't my affair. True, you haven't solicited expostulation. Yet, I feel compelled, at the risk of being called a meddling hypocrite, to tell you that vengeance belongs to God."

I've no idea why Apolladora was subjected to these atrocities, and I don't burn with a desire to know. My son, close the book on this shocking act, turn away from it and forget it," he held up a restraining hand. "What I'm trying to say is that was no ordinary death. This form of torture, reserved for prostitutes and other women who through their sexuality earn a living by collaborating with an enemy, is typical Mafia atrocity dating back to the days of the Sicilian Vespers. The bloodiest massacre in all Sicilian history. Sicilians, summoned at the first stroke of—"

"—a vesper bell," interrupted Tori. "Arose en masse to massacre all the French on the island, dethroned Charles I of Anjou, that tyrannical king who overburdened the citizens with unjust taxation and oppressed them, beyond all endurance. The underground's battle cry was *"Morte a Francia Italia Anela: M.A.F.I.A.* Mafia! And so it was born!"

Unable to hide his astonishment, Voltera said, "What a strange young lad you are. My bones shudder at the savagery of your soul. You seem so intelligent, different than most young peasants—" He sighed. "I see it's futile to talk. You've not heard a word I've spoken."

Stimulated by Salvatore's silence, the priest flung off his cassock, removed his cleric's collar, rolled up his sleeves, and trudged back to his garden and, with his shovel, picked up where he had left off earlier. He resembled a wind-up toy gone haywire as he dug, turned over earth, and repeated the process with short, jerky, uncoordinated movements.

"Would the family object if I kept the letter?" Tori asked him.

"Take it! Keep it! If it helps your pain—it's yours!" snapped the irrate priest. He didn't pause in his work, because he saw death reflected in Tori's eyes.

"Perhaps, *padre,*" said Tori as he moved towards the gate. "If I might suggest—"

"Yes?" growled the laboring cleric.

"—if you poured love into the earth instead of working out your hostilities, the land might prove more prolific."

Voltera straightened up, placed a hand in the small of his back and grimacing peered at Tori. "That's a strange suggestion coming from you. All I see in your heart is burning hatred, violence and pure vengeance," he retorted.

Salvatore shrugged. "Until a few days ago, there was only love in my heart. What you claim to see in me is of recent birth, caused by all this inhumanity I see around me. Something inside me rebels at all this. Stirs me with alien forces. . . ."

The priest set aside his shovel, wiped his brow and spoke. "We're all born with base feelings of hatred, an urge to do violence—even murder. Only through the power of love which God pours through our hearts can those demons of evil remain asleep in our subconscious. Remove that love and demons will spring forth, unchecked in their malevolency, to conquer and be conquered. . . ."

Tori turned back to the priest. He took a cigarette from his pocket and, holding a match box in his left hand, struck a light with his right and brought it to the tip of his smoke. After a few puffs he exhaled thoughtfully.

One day, Tori would recall this conversation with this *padre*, who was soon to become a vital part of the Palermo Grand Council; but, not as much as this priest, who would rise to be Archbishop, would recall with clarity every moment spent with this phenomenon that the world would come to know as Salvatore.

Tori groped for the words, the proper expression to put his thoughts across.

"If that's the case, I haven't the strength to keep these feelings buried. God's love has gradually thinned, paled and diminished by these foul conditions. Where was God's love when he permitted Apolladora to be brutalized? And don't insult me by trying to tell me she was punished for the way she earned money to feed seven hungry mouths!"

"Look, *Padre* . . . Look around you, here in your garden? Is it God's love that strips it of nourishment and renders it barren? Is God responsible for a government which refuses to bring water inland to the people? Oh, *Padre*, we are indeed a forsaken people!"

The sweaty priest studied him in a somewhat comatose state. Too much had happened this day. Too much. "Young man," he began. "If I were your father, of the same flesh and blood, I couldn't offer you more solace in your grief than what you are prepared to accept, more suggestions than your mind is willing to embrace. Every man is the seeker of his own destiny. Don't lose sight of God's love, or the sleeping demons within you shall rise to consume you as they have every other man in history who has ignored God."

Tori turned from him, somberly, and mounted his horse.

On this day, this unforgettable day carved out of the life of Apolladora, Alessandro Salvatore left in San Guiseppe Jato the soul and spirit of his adolescence to be buried with her, the *inamorata* of his destiny.

Facing the worst predicament of his life, Tori detoured to the Temple of Cats, his refuge in a storm. Seated astride his horse, he stared out at the stunning panorama, his brain churning with thoughts of the day's events—of Apolladora, of Don Pippinu, of the despicable events leading to this day.

That Apolladora's death would be avenged was a foregone conclusion. The liquidation of the Mt. Erice Mafia Don was inevitable—only the time and place of the *Mafioso's* demise hadn't been firmly fixed in Tori's mind. There'd come a time for him to set the ball in motion, and when he did, he'd seek the cooperation of one special person, his Godfather, Don Matteo Barbarossa.

Below him the lights went out on Montegatta, Montelepre, Borgetto and Alcalmo. He filled with an unendurable melancholy. He strained to hear the familiar sounds of the ancient trumpets announcing the presence of the *Siculi*. Hearing nothing only multiplied his sadness. He thought: *here in the temple among the caves and high cliffs and brooding mountains of timelessness, I must find and come to terms with my destiny.*

Giacomo had upbraided him like an errant child in the tone of a scolding father when he had discovered Tori's wounds reopened, pus-filled and bleeding with infection. Despite his patient's uncooperative nature and marked depression, the faithful old man's diligent care, the laborious cleansing of the wounds and the application of sulfa revived the eagle. In the coming weeks, Tori came to miss his mother and Athena more than he could bear. When he could no longer endure the melancholy, he sent a messenger to his mother with a note. Upon the lad's return, he anxiously asked if his mother had sent word. The boy shook his head. Never had Tori felt so despondent until he considered, she might have prudently exercised caution. Yes. That was it. His mother was no fool. He'd wait.

During his convalescence Tori grew keenly observant; his eyes and ears went everywhere, and his keen interest in the character and idiosyncrasies of these men forced together into similar circumstances intrigued him. He missed none of the goings-on in the camp.

Sharpened by the recent fever, his mind brought all these men into clearer focus. All of them—bandits, brigands, murderers, thieves, petty criminals alike—wore haunted expressions, all despondent at their lot in life, bitter towards an uncaring, unfeeling government which had turned them into hunted criminals. The inescapability of their common predicament and its effects upon those dear to them weighed heavily on their conscience, just as it did on Tori.

Dimly he began to see these men as a contingent force of power that might conceivably cause a decentralization of the present political system—such as it was—and through them, the liberation of his people.

The metamorphosis in him came gradually, not overnight. Embryonic stirrings of the sleeping Hercules he had felt in Mt. Erice continued to disrupt his tranquility. The more he considered the predicament of the men confined to the grottos, the more feasible became his plan. Was it possible that together they could minimize inequities, even stabilize the economy in some indirect way, until such time as reparations could be made to his people for all that had been taken from them? It stood to reason that a more sympathetic government would come to power. The way Tori viewed the political turmoil and unrest in his nation, everything was up for grabs. Only dimly in his mind did an idea begin to form—a powerful idea, through which he could equalize or reduce the problems that beset his people.

In coming days, Tori grew more critical and discerning. He studied the men, mentally selecting those who, he felt, would work into his plans. For a time he stared at those men on the upper ridges who remained shadows to him, and he wondered: Were the men in the Grotto Persephone a different breed of men than those in the lower grottos? What Giacomo had told him about those escaped prisoners intrigued him. As soon as he felt up to it, he intended to amble up there and look around.

Of late, burning thoughts of his cousin Vincenzo de Montana nagged at him. How many times he'd wondered, trying to imagine where that rascal could be.

"Vincenzo! Vincenzo," he'd cry out into the night. "Tell me where you are—that you're safe. . . ."

CHAPTER 17

Little did Tori know that his cousin, Vincenzo de Montana, was physically less than ten minutes away from him in the upper reaches of Grotto Persephone. Tall, slender, badly emaciated, his features pale from prison pallor, Vincenzo bore little resemblance to the army conscript who, in 1941, had left Montegatta as a handsome, proud and gallant cock o' the walk whose bulging biceps, staunch vigor and endless vitality had resembled that of a Roman centurion. His large, dark eyes, sunken in their deeply shadowed hollows, retained few traces of their former laugh-lines. Like that of other *Terra Diavolo* inmates, his dark curly hair had been shorn close to retard body lice. Look close, and you'd detect a peculiar hardness in him, the bold, cynical shrewdness of a man who'd seen too much and experienced untold horror.

Prison, for Vincenzo, had been an endless round of nightmares. Beaten half to death for his repeated attacks on the sadistic prison guards and starved when he had aired grievances on behalf of the other prisoners, he'd emerged from *Terra Diavolo* during an Allied bombing raid and miraculously escaped with other inmates possessed of a morose phobia, a fear of enclosed places and defiance to authority. He vowed repeatedly that he'd never be caught alive, if it meant he had to be returned to such a place—even if it meant his life and the lives of those who dared to obstruct him.

It was from this that Vincenzo had developed a form of paranoia which had triggered off a curious behavior in him. In addition to a tubercular lung, contracted in prison, it was his mental attitude that perplexed his friends now. He hallucinated at times, and displayed a perverse hostility towards those very men who he considered to be his obstructors, considering them his mortal enemies. Yet his friends understood. They held him in high esteem, and viewed this strange behavior as something which would pass as soon as he was back in his home.

And why wouldn't they revere Vincenzo? He was a hero! True—a real hero. If it hadn't been for his clear thinking, his wits, and the latent forces of which heroes are made, none of them, including Vincenzo, would have been alive or in Sicily, today.

God! Good God! How anxious he was to see his home. He knew nothing of the tragic catastrophies that had plagued his family. Standing at the edge of the Grotto, staring down at the lights in his village, he felt his heart and thoughts center around a deep longing to be with his dear ones. Deeply ingrained in his mind was a stark fear of leaving the bandits' sanctuary. In his condition, in these perilous times, it was unthinkable. If he were caught—well, he wouldn't think about this.

To contemplate the future at this time was difficult for Vincenzo. Uncertain as he was of the present and unable as he was to handle the past, his ambivalence disconcerted him. Yet, on this evening, early in October, if Vincenzo could have gazed into a crystal ball to see what destiny, working hand in hand with his cousin Tori, had in store for him, that together they'd make their mark in the nation's history, he might have done much to expedite such a fate.

Wrapped warmly in a sheepskin jacket, collar pulled

high around his neck, Vincenzo stomped the ground with his thick mountain boots and shoved his trembling hands into fur-lined pockets to ward off the oncoming chills produced by his erratic body temperature. One moment he'd sweat bullets; the next moment, those beads of sweat would turn into icicles.

He moved back towards the mouth of the grotto, now, and sat down on a boulder. Behind him, straggled about the reflecting fires, hundreds of men, desperate and haunted, made up a weird spectacle which could have been a scene designed by Federico Garcia Lorca. Closest to the fires sat the *Terra Diavolo* escapees, who never seemed to get enough warmth.

Two years had changed him drastically. Two years had changed Tori, too, so that when he walked among the men in the upper grotto, no one recognized him, not even Vincenzo. As was the custom, each man kept to himself, unless he was fortunate enough to have formed a coterie of friends or had the distinction of belonging to the *Terra Diavolo* fraternity. And on this night Tori was perhaps ten feet away from his cousin, jotting down names in his foolscap notebook as he'd taken to doing of late. Giacomo was at his side, as usual. He'd become Tori's mascot, a fountain of information and knowledge, he seemed to know nearly all the men in the camp, and if he didn't, give him a few hours and he'd return to Tori, fully oriented on the others in question. At times he possessed startling revelations.

Tori's tablet contained the names of several men whom he'd observed lately, noting a few of their characteristics and habits, he'd wanted to learn more about them. He'd remain quietly in the background, and, from time to time, he'd ask Giacomo about this one or that. On this night he'd paused slightly and, for the first time, took a good look at the scrawny-faced, skeletal man who sat at the mouth of the upper grotto, dressed in such heavy garments.

How could he know this was Vincenzo, when the man didn't bear the slightest traces of resemblance to the cousin he remembered and missed so much? When he nudged Giacomo to ask him who he was, the old man shrugged in vexation.

"Don't bother with him. He's crazy—that one. *Managghia*, I was told he was their chief in prison." He shuddered and moved forward along with Tori, dismissing the strange haunted fellow from mind—as did Tori.

Seated on a boulder, with his knees drawn up for a time, Tori leaned back to resume his observations.

Arturo Scoletti moved towards the grotto entrance in an apelike fashion, carrying a cup steaming coffee to Vincenzo. He was accompanied by Santino Siragusa, who leaned over and asked Vincenzo solicitously, "Feeling better?" He accepted a light from a burning stick in the hairy, apelike hand of Arturo Scoletti, then stood for a time watching him wrap his brother Miguel in a blanket.

Suddenly for no apparent reason Vincenzo jumped to his feet and accosted Santino. "Goddamnit! Leave me alone! Stop busting my balls, *padre!*" he shouted in what seemed an irrational moment of confusion.

All eyes including Tori's turned in his direction. Others jumped to their feet, gawking, straining to get a better view of the activity. They saw Vincenzo fall to a crouch position, like a cornered animal, and back away from Santino. His dark, glazed eyes, shining unnaturally in the reflected firelight, were fixed on the former cleric as if he were some underworld demon. On a signal from Santino, Arturo moved in swiftly, pinning Vincenzo's body against the grotto wall, until Siragusa moved in from behind with a thick blanket to wrap around their friend.

Observing all this, Tori marvelled at their loyalty. He glanced at the others. They were tough and cynical and trained to mind their own business, yet they shook their heads regretfully. He listened to the comments among them. Apparently they'd seen this strange behavior before, wondered at it, and refrained from commenting on the patience demonstrated by this man's friends.

Reluctantly he agreed with Giacomo's observation—the man, whoever he was, did seem crazy out of his mind. As Tori listened, it seemed that the crazy man had subjected his friends to vile and contemptible language and constantly shouted obscenties at them. Tori learned even more. Ever since these prison escapees had arrived in the *macchia*, looking like haunted skeletons—and there were hundreds of them—they'd kept to themselves. Little was known about them except that they'd brought a formidable cache of weapons with them and guarded them zealously. When the "crazy bastard" had moments of lucidity, he seemed to be in command. Imagine, taking orders from a crazy loon! Oddly enough, although many of these men weren't escapees from the prison, they had somehow gravitated towards each other as if an affinity of a predestined nature bound them together.

They had begun to converse now, wondering why the

man Santino Siragusa, a former *priest*, had given up the cloth and found himself in the company of brigands.

"Ask the *padre*, himself," spoke up Arturo, a pint-sized titan who once had broke chains with his biceps in a carnival he and his brother had owned before the war. "It's best you get the word straight from the horse's mouth."

"Are you crazy?" asked Bastiano Terranova, a handsome young man. "It's not our business. Besides such talk can be dangerous with the Reds and anticlerics around. Are you sure he isn't a communist?" he asked dubiously.

"Not our business!" Arturo snorted contemptuously. A shock of black hair, straight and wiry, grew low over his forehead, giving him an apelike appearance. His nose, like a bird's beak, was sharp and hooked, and a slight protrusion to his jaw line accented his primate appearance. "Listen, you porcupine, when this business of war ends, things had better be different for us or there *will* be revolution. I don't know about communists, and I don't care. Up north, where men aren't afraid to speak out, there's talk of labor unions. Labor unions and strikes. Up there the men are getting smart."

"Labor unions? What hell is that? Labor unions and strikes?" Fidelio Genovese, a dark, Moorish-skinned Sicilian with compelling black eyes that intimidated most men, was perplexed. Perhaps the most politically oriented of the lot, he knew the score. In this young man, as with most of the men gathered here, was the desperation of the illiterate who felt deeply the urge to speak out, but hadn't mastered the articulation of these feelings. It was enough to drive a man crazy!

With the superior aloofness of one possessed with great knowledge, Vincenzo, suddenly in perfect control of his faculties, spoke up. "Unions are organizations where the men think and act as one body. Fifty men, even a hundred, agree on one thing and fight for their rights in an organized way."

"Fifty men agree on one thing?" Fidelio Genovese's face knitted into a scowl. "*Mah*—how the hell is that possible? I've heard of everything, now!"

Tori leaned forward eager to listen to this strange young man, who now seemed as normal as the others.

"It works like this," began Vincenzo. "The landlords and peasants sit down and discuss their problems. Once the workers agree on certain terms, they tell the landlord straight out what they want." Crazy or not his words commanded their full attention.

"It's that easy?" asked Dominic Lamantia, another young, very handsome lad with startling green eyes.

"Let me put it this way," responded Vincenzo, lighting a cigarette. "If the landlord disagrees with what they want, he offers alternatives. Somehow it all works. One man alone, can't instigate changes, but many men, united together, become a powerful force."

"I don't know what the hell you're talking about," insisted Fidelio Genovese, impatient with all this talk. He pulled out his holstered gun. "See this gun?" He patted it suggestively. "This is my labor union. With this little piece I can make everyone agree with me. So, who needs these goddamn labor unions?"

Turridu Nuliano, another handsome young man, outrageously ostentatious in manner of dress as well as behavior, twirled his six-shooter in the air before him. "That's the way it is, here. Power is the man with a gun. *K'pow! k'pow!*"

Terranova addressed himself to Vincenzo. "Your words stir my stomach to disquiet, and I find them too fanciful to give them importance. You're sure these things are possible?"

Vincenzo nodded. Arturo bobbed his head up and down.

"By the unholy balls of Satan! What wonders there must be on other lands. Labor unions, eh?" Terranova was impressed.

"If the peasants and landlords fail to agree, the peasants don't work—not until the landlord and they come to terms," said Vincenzo growing more articulate.

"Now I know you're crazy!" Fidelio Genovese shouted in rebuttal. "You know what would happen here? Landlords would import workers from other estates, then where would we be? We'd starve. Are you so crazy not to see such perils?" He wagged a finger at Vincenzo in reprimand. Then as his eyes narrowed suspiciously, he asked, "Listen, you aren't a political agitator—a communist, are you?"

Ignoring Genovese, Vincenzo turned to the others. "If all the workers on the island agree not to trespass on any lands under protest, it's possible. It works elsewhere."

Genovese holstered his gun and shrugged when he saw the expressions on the faces of his companions seated around the campfire. "*Allora, amico*, Genovese is no fool. He'll listen to such ideas if they are possible. Labor unions, eh? It makes sense, saying that one hundred voices, saying the same thing, make a bigger noise than one voice. But by the belly of a sterile whale, tell me how so many can agree on one thing? Here each man is for himself. *Carabinieri* come to arrest a man. You think his neighbors help? *Mah—quando?* Afraid their own families will suffer or go hungry or that they'll be punished in other ways, they keep to themselves. Their neighbor's business isn't their affair. So tell me how so many long-eared men can agree on one thing?" The contest was between him and Vincenzo.

"They take a vote and the majority wins."

"What if my voice isn't one of the majority?"

"Your voice will be caught up in the majority."

"*Buttana u shekko!* We're back to guns again. See,—it wouldn't work!"

"Believe me, Genovese, you'd be convinced."

"How—with guns, bombs and artillery?" He scoffed openly.

"No. With words and common sense."

"What of my common sense? Why should another man's common sense be more prominent than mine? If I think the majority is wrong, why should I go along with them? You see, it wouldn't work." He patted his holstered gun affectionately. "I'll make my unions with my gun. My strike is my gun. This way we'll all be content."

This time the men's laughter was complicated by thoughtful speculation. Vincenzo had given them food for thought. What to do with this food was another matter *Demonio! Why be cursed with such brainwork? Such crazy ideas are dangerous,* the men told themselves. Uneasy in the midst of revolutionary concepts, they glanced uneasily about the fires. Who knew what enemies lurked around them?

Tori glanced about, noting the reaction of the men and the kind of thinking they were used to. Some of the men got up and moved about, getting coffee or talking in groups. Giacomo indicated he wanted to return to their campsite. He was bored with such rhetoric. "Only action counts," he grunted. "You'll see, *aquilo bravo.*"

A few minutes later, Tori, shivering in the wind, considered he'd better leave. His attention was caught by the "crazy young man" who'd been struck with a coughing seizure. He began to bark and rasp and hawk convulsively and, rising to his feet, he swept past Tori, heading for the ledge on the rocks. For a split second their eyes met without a glimmer of recognition.

Tori decided to return to the comfort of his own fires, giving no importance to the coughing young man, who

231

sounded as if his insides would burst. Just as he began to descend the rocky incline, Tori stopped, uncertain of what it was that had deterred him. Turning to glance over his shoulder in the darkness at the prison escapee, Vincenzo's plaintive cry reached him.

"Tori! Tori! Where are you? Don't you know I'm up here in the mountains? Can't you hear me calling you?"

Tori's heart stopped. Had he heard correctly—or was the whispering wind deceiving him like the *Siculi* often did? *Dio Buono!* Could this shadow of a man be Vincenzo? He retraced his steps, slowly, inching towards him, careful so as not to startle him. When he was within two feet of him, he called to him softly. "Vincenzo—"

His cousin turned around, a fierce scowl on his face, ready to pounce, his hand on his knife worn in a sheath at his waist. His eyes had turned into those of an animal's, his body into a low crouch.

"It's me—Tori. I heard you calling. By the sainted balls of Christ, I heard you calling me."

Vincenzo searched the other's face, in disbelief and wonderment. "It's you, Tori? *Pe d'avero*—it's really you?"

"It's me. It's me," shouted Tori excitedly as the two cousins embraced. They slapped each other on the back and stared in wonderment at each other. In moments Vincenzo seemed a new man. They jabbed at each other playfully with broad swipes and rough caresses. Incredulity and disbelief were followed by gestures of affection. Then they sat back and talked for a while, until Vincenzo dragged Tori back towards the grotto to introduce him to his friends.

Inside, the men were discussing present conditions in Sicily. Most of the men wore dark trousers and shirts, with leather and sheepskin jackets. All wore one or two guns at their hips, with a knife or two in sight. They looked up when Tori and Vincenzo entered, aware of the change in the "crazy" man.

Tori let his cousin make all the introductions and he sat down to enjoy the comfort of men and their idle talk. It was Marco Genovese, Fidelio's younger brother, who started the ball rolling. Marco contrasted his brother's swarthy looks with his round, cherubic face, smooth as a baby's buttocks. Marco was a man who believed in no order except his own. His blue-eyed expression of innocence belied his true nature. He was a born thief, who laughed a lot and cried convincingly if it suited his purpose. This consummate actor, under whose face there always lurked some ulterior motive, some scheme, was as shrewd as they

232

came. He didn't believe most of these Terra Diavolo inmates, and thought that since they were all together he'd
put the question to them.

"How did you all escape? How did you get through the
Italian and German lines? Better still, how did you cross
the seas, crawling with Allied battleships and marine patrols? *Managghia*, the whole of the British and American
fleet lie warming their bellies in the water surrounding us
since the Occupation—"

"Yes," echoed the others, "Tell us how."

Tori's presence had sparked Vincenzo with new life, and
his friends were the first to see these changes. He drew
himself up and, taking center stage, he began to speak.

"The first week in September, I filled with premonition.
I was nervous, edgy, short-tempered, and I must have
driven my cellmates crazy. I awoke one night when a
vision of my aunt came to me in a dream so real I could
feel her presence. *Mizzica!* I can still feel my flesh crawl
the way it did that night. No, not the way those lice who
made such short order of my body crawled. This was different. I leaned over to wake up the *padre*. Santino didn't
want to hear my *baccano*. 'Listen,' he told me, 'in the
middle of a good dream you have bust my balls!' But I insisted that I heard strange noises. Again he cursed me.
'You crazy fool,' he told me. 'Each night for a week it's
been the same with you. Goddammit! Roll over and go to
sleep.' I suppose I should have been mad at him. But who
had the strength to challenge him, eh? I closed my eyes
and told myself I was dreaming. But, then, suddenly there
it was again. This time I didn't have to awaken Santino.
One by one, all the men in our complex came alive,
asking what had happened.

"Then, there came a rumbling, groaning sound like an
earthquake. It shook the walls and caused tremors under
our feet. *Maronna!* The men screamed. They yelled and
cried for assistance. We could see nothing through the
barred windows except a patch of black sky. 'Earthquake!
Earthquake!' cried the men. It was Santino who fell to the
ground, his ear glued to it listening. 'No,' he screamed.
Not an earthquake! *Bomba! Bomba!*"

Vincenzo paused and, looking at Tori, said solemnly,
"You know what it's like to be in such a place, knowing no
one would come to save us?" His voice dropped in volume
and he stared hauntingly into the fires. "I can still hear
their voices, calling the guards to come and help them.
'For the love of God, don't let us die,' they cried. 'Not
like this!'

"Then came the bombs. From the bowels of those flying machines they erupted. *Boom! Boom! Boom!* Flame, like lightning, struck all around us, as the heavens opened up and reined its fury on us.

"*Allora, caro mio*, the earth roared, buckled and trembled, exploding everything in sight. The walls of the prison crumbled in a shower of rocks as devastating as the bombs themselves. They wouldn't stop, those bombs. *Dio Maledetta!* All around were the dead bodies of the men whose time was up.

"So many things to be negotiated in the dark! Dead and dying bodies, the broken rubble, the bombs themselves. We ran. God Almighty, did we run! We scattered like lizards, every which way. Then, through it all I heard Santino, the *padre* here, call to me. He told me to follow him to the arsenal. *Va bene.* I could hardly make him out in the congestion of dust, but I did the best I could. It was the same all over. More bombs. Explosions that shattered our ear drums and confusion! *Managghia*, none of us knew what to do. The men awaiting execution in death's row had been freed too. Liberated, they ran every which way, like ferocious animals, picking up weapons from the dead guards and shooting their way out when obstructed.

"As for us, the Sicilians in our complex managed to dance our way through that tarantella of hell! So many were killed. You know what it's like to see a man's leg or arm torn off before your eyes? *Ayeee*," he sighed.

"One of the men—" he paused and glanced towards a hulk of a man built like a bull tiger, with the muscle-bound look of a Samurai warrior—Ross Rizzuto, nicknamed *Sporcaccione*. "*Allora*," continued Vincenzo. "He led some men from another building and we all converged on the arsenal. With a Beretta submachine gun I took from a dead guard who had no further use for it, I sprayed the lock with bullet fire. Sporcaccione kicked in the door and the men poured in. I shouted, 'Grab all the weapons you can carry!' *Managghia!* They went wild, strapping on automatic rifles, carbines and submachine guns—all they could carry, including small arms, which they shoved into every inch of their clothing.

"I ordered the men to run swiftly across the courtyard through the openings in the broken walls as they rushed out the door past me.

"While they were running for their lives, clearing the marble quarries some distance from *Terra Diavolo*, another load of bombs fell. We suddenly faced another enemy,

234

more lethal than the bombs. The air rained pellets of marble, slag and sharp stones. Then, having dropped their loads, the bombadeers moved on into the darkest of skies. Behind this came ear-splitting explosions, one after another, until what remained of the arsenal, ammunition and warheads blew up, including what remained of *Terra Diavolo*.

"For a time we all stood on the lower slopes of the Tuscany hillside, weak from hunger, exhaustion and overexposure, to observe the spreading fires. *Demonio*! The stench of burned flesh, with its sickeningly sweet odor, fairly knocked us out. With the light of dawn came the realization that we couldn't stay in open country and risk being spotted by enemy patrols. So, I led them to another location, a spot cradled between the breasts of two hills where we could spot any approach. In prison we'd heard little of the outside world, so we didn't know what to expect.

"To tell the truth," continued Vincenzo, somberly, "I was dismayed by the number of escapees who clung to us, refusing to run off to the many avenues of freedom. I made my thoughts known to the *padre* here, wondering how we'd fare with so many men. There were at least six or seven hundred. *Managghia*! The *padre's* answer was, as usual, 'God will show us the way!' *Allora*, I didn't have the *padre's* faith. . . ."

Vincenzo paused at this point, weak and without energy to continue the story. He urged Santino Siragusa to finish the tale so that his cousin Tori would know all the facts. He rose to his feet and, walking to the water cistern, sprinkled his face with cool water. He returned and sat down next to Tori and lit a cigarette with shaking hands. Then all eyes were riveted on the former Jesuit as he relit his pipe. Pushing his glasses on the bridge of his nose, Santino ran his fingers through his thick, curly dark hair, corkscrewed like little mattress springs, settled himself more comfortably, and picked up the story where Vincenzo left off. In perfect Italian, his gentle voice grew reflective. It rose and fell with dramatic pauses. "We knew absolutely nothing of the war's status, not even that the Allies had landed in Sicily, or that on July 25, King Vittorio Emmanuele had ordered Mussolini's resignation and formed a new government with Marshal Badoglio at its head, or that the liquidation of the fascists had followed. We certainly didn't know that the peace negotiations were already underway between Italy and the Allies, or that on September 3 a secret armistice had been signed with Italy."

"What has all this to do with you ex-prisoners?" asked Tori, eager for hm to get along with the story.

"Just this," said Santino patiently. "It meant that a furious race had commenced between the Germans and Allies for possession of territories, bases, arms and supplies, communications, and other war facilities under Italian control. Where we suddenly found ourselves—in Northern Italy—the land, unbeknownst to us, was overrun with Nazi patrols. Those bloody Nazis could have been anywhere. Behind every boulder, curve and bend in the road, and in all the villages not burned down by partisan guerillas.'

The men sucked in their breaths. They listened to this man with every nerve-fiber in their bodies. Marco Genovese and Bastiano Terranova interrupted at this point, to relieve themselves just outside the grotto, and returned anxiously to their places. These were the kind of stories Sicilians loved and could recount for generations to anyone who'd listen.

"None of use was free from the terror we experienced," continued Santino. "It's not to be believed that we finally arrived here in Sicily after the nightmares were endured. . . . *Allora*, as I was saying, six hundred of us trudged through Tuscany. We wondered at the flooded fields, frowned at the idle valleys, despaired at the fallow lands and stared solemnly at the ruined *fattorias*. We were outraged at the deserted farmhouses. *Misericordia*! Not a morsel of food to be found any place. Only God and Vincenzo could have seen us through what was to follow.

"Starved, weakened from exposure, we needed something to inspire us—some life—something to assure us all wasn't lost! No life greeted us anywhere; not a bird, a lizard, a dog, a rabbit—not even an insect. We covered ten miles in what seemed to be the stillness of death. Finally, below us, in a fork in the road, we caught sight of a road sign. Vincenzo ordered the men to rest on the slopes of the hill while he and I went below to investigate. The sign read: *Cecina—4km*. I knew then exactly where we were: a few miles from the Ligurian Sea. Elated at the prospect of reaching the water after the stunning effects of the near-desert lands we'd crossed, I attempted to infect Vincenzo with my optimism. By then the lice began attacking my body and to alleviate the aggravation I began scratching myself. Watching me, Vincenzo laughed good-naturedly, 'They got no respect, even for a man of God, eh, *Padre?*' "

The men laughed at this. Santino tapped his pipe alongside him on the boulder and continued, "Wrapped in my discomfort, I trudged on ahead of Vincenzo, still scratching at my body, only to be pulled back by my shirttails. Annoyed, I turned to Vincenzo, ready to challenge him, only to be arrested by the look in his eyes. That man with cat's ears had angled his head sharply, listening to something that hadn't penetrated my ears. All at once he raised his rifle high above his head signaling the men on the hill to halt. His fingers over his lips silenced what protests I might have offered at this point.

"Then Vincenzo loudly shouted, 'Take cover, men. Take cover, *Padre!*' He waved the others off the road and back up into the hills. 'Pass the word, *Padre*. Tell the men to take cover and be ready for anything I might do. And tell them to stay out of sight, goddammit!' I moved swiftly to obey his instructions, scrambling up the nearby slopes, passing the word to anyone and everyone in my path. *Allora*—the men moved! *Managghia*—how they moved. They came to life and hid behind bushes, stone walls, tree stumps and any blade of grass that offered protection. They crouched down on all fours, out of sight. Along the sloping hillside, the newly liberated men lay still as death, with rifles, submachine guns, hand pistols and grenades, clutched in one or both hands, ready for anything. I saw the sweat pour off their faces, necks and underarms. Their dilated pupils reflected the terror in their hearts. Their tongues darted over parched, cracked lips, and it seemed their heartbeats, mine included, pulsed as one giant heartbeat. Sitting and crouching like wooden puppets, hunched over in fatigue until our muscles ached and our legs twitched from being in one position so long, we all prayed that whatever had disturbed Vincenzo would either cease or erupt.

"Those moments for us were an eternity. Then, suddenly, it all happened. We all heard what had penetrated Vincenzo's ears earlier. Approaching us was the sound of motors, straining and shifting gears—muffled at first, then more audible. It was the erratic sputter and cough of motorcycles in the distance. Then, there they were, pouring into the basin below us.

"From around the bend in the worm-like road came the largest detachment of Nazis we'd ever seen—even in the height of battle. More than five hundred—many more! They came in open touring cars, containing high-ranking Nazi officers, followed by countless trucks, supply wagons and other vehicles in a full troop train. So many—who took the time to count? Motorcycles zoomed up ahead and

237

at either side of the train and several brought up the rear.

"Vincenzo, meanwhile, never took his eyes off this stunning display of military strength. His mind worked swiftly, with rare perception and know-how. As they stretched out before him, filling the flatlands, Vincenzo became aware that we were in a perfect ambush position to annihilate the Nazi convoy. With no time to speculate, he quickly shouted orders to me: 'Tell them to get the grenades ready, *Padre*. When I move—they move! They are to hurl the grenades into the convoy, without hesitation.' Naturally, I bridled at the orders. 'You're crazy! We'll all be wiped out to the last man!' I shouted. Whereupon Vincenzo countered, 'Impossible! They're outnumbered. Move your ass, *Padre*, or we will be slaughtered!'

"*Allora*. I pulled in my neck and snaked along the slope repeating my orders to the Scoletti brothers, who were now securely entrenched. 'Watch for Vincenzo's signal and do what he does,' I told them.

" 'That crazy bastard has lost all senses,' Arturo shouted, but he moved. He and the rest of the men—they moved their asses right on down the line. On and on they went until the hillside came alive, charged with the electricity of their fear and excitement. Below us the Nazis began to gear down, pacing the rest of the convoy, until, suddenly, there it was, both ends of the convoy spread out across the valley. . . . The unsuspecting Nazis never knew what struck them. Nearly three hundred grenades hurled into their midst exploding them straight to hell. Trucks, cycles, autos and troops shot up into the sky taking half the countryside with them. Gasoline exploded and caught fire. It was an incredible sight, a scene so shattering to us that none of us will forget it until our dying day."

Santino wet his lips with a tankard of wine and continued. "When the dust settled we saw that what had been a flatland was now filled with enormous craters, and the road had vanished completely. Landslides occurred all around us, throwing our men off balance, some of them sliding down the hill, luckily unhurt. A few Nazis who had miraculously escaped the holocaust were instantly felled by blasts of machine gun fire from our men. The ambush was a total success—not one Nazi was alive to boast of his luck. Never have we seen such carnage. The land was littered with bloody, screaming, kicking, torn and dying bodies. For a moment we all stood in dumb stupefaction as silence descended upon us. For a second only—then there was bedlam. Desperate, hungry men, all who had been in prison for so long, rushed forward like a swarm of ravenous locusts to salvage what we could out of the rubble. Anything for survival! It was a ghastly sight. Decapitated bodies, whose severed heads lay close by attached by bleeding tendons and bearing expressions of demonical horror, arched brows, popped eyeballs and leering grins, with wet teeth glistening in the sunlight—these hardly intimidated the scavengers. Survival was all that counted and the men looked everywhere for food—rations—anything to fill their swollen and empty bellies. Unable to stomach their reactions I expressed my feelings to Vincenzo. 'Wild savages! Have they no respect for the dead? What an atrocity!'

"For a time Vincenzo's black, burning eyes jumped from one point to another as the predatory scene unfolded, and with an astonishing and mystical power of recuperation he replied vigorously, 'Better them than us!' "

The men came to life after listening to Santino's story. They reacted vigorously to Vincenzo's assessment of that scene, as Santino wrapped up the final portion of the story.

"Shortly after that, Vincenzo split the men into four groups with instructions to meet at the most southern point on the beach at Piombo. By the grace of God we all met again and crossed to the Island of Elba where, with the aid of some friends, we gained passage on fishing boats. In October, at intervals of a week, less than four hundred of us landed along the northern and western shores of Sicily, disguised as fishermen. And here we all are," said Santino wistfully, "here in these honeycombed mountains we met, and are unable to conceal our disappointment over the wretched conditions we find in our beloved Sicily."

Tori turned to observe his cousin Vincenzo, who had come to life, revived by the contents of a wine bottle. "A real hero, eh?"

Vincenzo flushed with a mixture of embarrassment and pleasure at his cousin's assessment.

"What are your plans, now?" asked Fidelio Genovese with a newfound respect shining in his eyes for the "crazy" man. "You don't intend to stay in these mountains until the war ends?"

Vincenzo didn't answer. He felt a self-consciousness permeate him, a sickening paranoia, a need to hide from them.

Santino came to his rescue. "He'll let you know. He must get well, first. In his condition—" he paused. He

239

didn't have to explain. They all knew and understood. Hadn't they seen his strange behavior?

"It's not the way it was three years ago, *padre,*" said Dominic Lamantia.

Santino nodded. He'd seen these conditions and detested them.

"And the Americans—what of them?" asked Arturo, whittling on a piece of wood. "Is there no help from them?"

"What can they do? Besides, what the hell do they want with us? All they want is to waltz on to Berlin, to the tempo of a fox trot, and finish with Hitler."

Tori listened as they talked—and noticed there was a better *camaraderie,* now, than there'd been earlier. As the natives described the shabby conditions in Sicily, a few of the *Terra Diavolo* escapees, whose homes were in various other parts of Sicily, grew disconsolate, and when Dominic Lamantia told them that Sicily had become a free-for-all, a lawless and chaotic land where every man was for himself and where the women of the villages had taken to the streets, whoring to keep their families alive—whoring for the benefit of foreigners—they grew restless and angry. Jumping to their feet to express their Sicilian *maschiezzo,* they huddled in small groups talking among themselves.

The next morning, several approached Santino Siragusa, expressing their desires to leave for their villages. The shocking and distressing news of conditions in their homeland tore at their emotions. They were incensed and, physically, nervous wrecks. It was then that Tori suggested that an expert forger whom someone had mentioned might prepare identity cards for these troubled men, to facilitate easy travel to their villages. The idea so intrigued them that they looked to Tori, questioning him about several matters and finding his answers satisfactory, and left their names and addresses with him in the event they were ever needed—for anything.

Tori, in a manner that seemed easy and natural, turned the names over to Santino, and, although no words were spoken, it was as if he relegated to the former Jesuit the duties that were later to be given him officially.

For the next few days Vincenzo and Tori bridged the gap between them. Tori had waited to find the right time to break the news to Vincenzo. How did you tell a man that his entire family had been murdered by men whose duty it was to uphold the law and enforce it? It didn't come easy to Tori, but in accepting the responsibility he was only grateful that he was there for Vincenzo to lean on in his heartbroken moments of anguish.

Fiery tears escaped Vincenzo, and cries of savage vengeance burst from his swollen and engorged lips. The loathing and violence he felt was like the unleashing of a tempestuous storm. Only after Tori confided that he'd personally taken the lives of the brutes responsible, did Vincenzo calm himself. Consoled by his friends, he remained in a debilitated state. They left him alone for a while, to mourn in silence. If the bond between Tori and Vincenzo had been strong once, it was now like steel.

There remained little emotion to be wrung from both Vincenzo and Tori. Thoughts of the injustices in Sicily infuriated them both to borderline madness; yet Tori took it entirely different than Vincenzo. The difference between them was to become quite apparent in the near future.

CHAPTER 18

"Will you forgive me for bringing disgrace upon our house?" Tori asked his mother after their reunion was over.

She stroked Tori's face lovingly. If she harbored dismay at her son's predicament, she covered her feelings and became solicitous of his wounds, his pale and wan appearance. "You did what had to be done. What matters is, you're alive! We prayed for you—Athena and I were crazy out of our heads after we learned what happened. To think you were forced into a gunfight over food!"

You don't know the extent of the charges against me?" he asked. "Aren't you concerned? They're true, you know."

"What charges?"

"What charges?" Tori stared at her. "What precisely did the *carabinieri* tell you?"

Up ahead of them, Giacomo trundled the mule-drawn cart she'd ridden up the mountain to the Grotto Persephone as she and her son walked the short distance to the campsite. Antigone stopped in her tracks. "That you were stopped for transporting food over provincial borders. You were obstructed by Nino Marino, and in a skirmish, you killed him. In my heart I know you bore him no malice. It was an accident, no?"

"What about the money? Didn't they mention the money?" Veins at his temples pulsed like writhing eels. "The charges of grand larceny?"

She was flabbergasted. "What are you saying? What money?"

Very quietly Tori led her to a felled tree and sat her down some distance from the others. He wasn't ready to share her with his cousin, not just yet. He lit up a cigarette and told her the whole story from beginning to end, including the deaths of Gucci and Molino. He especially told her about Apollodora, omitting nothing, not even the fate meted her. Antignone listened in stupefaction. If she felt one way or another about her son's adverse circumstances, she gave no sign. Reaching over, Tori took both her work-worn hands into his forcing her eyes to gaze into his.

"Mamma, I've sworn vengeance on him. I vowed to kill Don Pippinu."

"No!" she retorted, hastily withdrawing her hands from his. "You've not been raised in the ways of *vendetta*. If he's brought no further charges against you, his feelings may have been softened."

He was appalled. "He cheated us out of money. Because of him, my world has collapsed—yours too. He murdered an innocent person—and you say, 'let it be!'"

Antigone studied her son inscrutably. "You've punished yourself too much," she observed. After a moment's silence she added tersely, "*Mafiosi* don't go to the authorities with their grievances."

"This one did," countered Tori hotly. "He reported me to the Allied military police and they to the *carabinieri*. I walked into a planned ambush!"

She shook her head adamantly. "Let it be, Tori. I want no trouble—not for you, not for me, not for anyone. Certainly not from a *Mafioso*."

"It's too late. I've pledged my vow of vengeance," he said with finality. Then, as an after thought, he scoffed with indignation. Hah! *Mafiosi* don't go to the authorities. Where did you hear such goat dung?"

"Don't scoff. It's true. They don't violate the code of silence."

"*Omerta* or no *omerta*, Don Pippinu violated the code."

Antigone shrugged. She couldn't believe her ears. It was legend that the Mafia settled their own matters. "What do you make of this deception? Why would the *carabinieri* re-

242

frain from making formal charges against you? It makes no sense."

"No sense, eh? To line their own pockets—what else?"

Antigone gasped. "For this?"

"Now they can shoot me on sight and keep the money they found by eliminating all traces of me." After explaining the hard and bitter facts to his mother, Tori instructed her to claim the letter he'd sent from Mt. Erice containing the money. "Those protected thieves would sell their souls for so much money. By damn, they shan't have it!"

She stared at her son in a confused silence. In a short space of time her son had become a man she didn't recognize. Words of retribution and vengeance pained her, for in her mind the laws of *vendetta* were as alien as her son's present predicament. A twinge of sadness exploded her heart at the ends to which her son had arrived. When he had first confessed to the slaying of those two obscenities, Gucci and Molino, she had exclaimed, "Good! They deserved it." This was the justice of her people—the only kind they'd ever known. Inwardly she'd experienced a tinge of pride that it had been her son who had put an end to those two evil creatures. With this knowledge locked in her heart, she could approach the Lord in her nightly prayers to beg His forgiveness. She'd point out to the Deity that He must take into account that it had been a just killing, before He sat in judgment of Tori.

So caught up in her thoughts was Antigone that she hardly noticed Tori had left her side and returned with a tall stranger with a pale and gaunt countenance. She shuddered inwardly as she glanced about the camp—at the desperadoes who'd become her son's companions.

"Now for a surprise, Mamma," said Tori with Vincenzo at his side.

"I doubt I need any more surprises," she said tersely.

"Don't you know me anymore, *Zia?* I'm Vincenzo," he told her with a sheepish grin on his face.

After a hailstorm of emotional greetings subsided, Antigone's role became a motherly one as she plied them with the banquet of food she brought with her in the cart. From time to time Antigone's hands would fly to either side of her face and cupping it she'd shake her head in disbelief. "Look, Tori, look what they did to him—those beasts! How thin you are, Vincenzo. Eat. Eat, my nephew."

"I'm not the bull Tori is," exclaimed Vincenzo, admiring Tori's physique. Tori's upper torso, covered only with a sheepskin vest cut deep in the armholes, revealed two livid scars healing on his shoulder and upper arm. "Is that where the *carabinieri*'s bullets hit you?" he asked his cousin.

"Eat," urged Antigone. "You can talk later." She leaned in closer to them. "First tell me who are those strangers staring at us?" She indicated to Santino Siragusa and the Scoletti brothers, who stood a short distance from them with eager-eyed expressions on their faces waiting to be drawn into their circle.

"Demonio!" cursed Vincenzo. "I forgot about them. He signalled to his friends and drew them closer. Vincenzo made the introductions. Antigone nodded at them, barely hearing the names "Well, what do you think, *Zia?*" said Vincenzo, trying to make light of a serious situation. "Imagine, now Tori is a fugitive and, like us, is hiding from the law." It was a bad joke, and he realized it too late.

Antigone glanced sharply at her son. The statement stunned both of them. It was Tori's turn to become aware of this truth. At first he thought, *me, a fugitive?* It was still new to him. Whether or not it agreed with him, one thing was certain: the sooner he got used to this truth, the better off he'd be. In these next moments, Tori told himself, *forget your dreams,* caro mio. *You're a fugitive with a price on your head—and there's no mistaking it.* Tori retreated into a silence, mulling over this startling revelation, and for a time he sat back and watched the others, solemnly.

Arturo Scoletti kept his eyes on his brother Miquel as he hungrily devoured three plates of food. *"Prego, Signora,* excuse my brother's gluttony," he apologized. "Some men can take the horrors God keeps tightly clenched in his left hand. Others can't. My brother's been very ill." He reached over and slapped his brother's thigh playfully. "You see, Miquel? Didn't I tell you to have faith? Didn't I tell you the *Signora* would cook for us again one day?"

Antigone, as well as her son, raised an inquisitive eyebrow as Arturo, noting their astonishment, hastened to explain. Apparently Antigone had once bargained with them to play their carnival at an orphanage by promising to cook a banquet of food for them.

"You are Arturo and Miquel?" she exclaimed in astonishment. "I would have never known you. *Dio buono,* you are thin as toothpicks. Here," she pushed more food at them. "Eat. Eat all you want."

Then, beginning with Vincenzo's next few words, a strange story began to unravel. He'd expressed his joy at his reunion with her and Tori and added. "I knew we'd see each other again, like this. I knew it. I kept seeing your face in visions, *Zia*," he told her. "Just before the bombing at *Terra Diavolo*, your face came to me in a vision. It was an omen, *Zia*. An omen that we'd be together—don't you see?"

Santino Siragusa's face blanched as he set aside his plate of food. A strange expression crossed his face. "*E a verida*? Is that the truth?" The former priest turned to Antigone. "Will you believe it I, too, saw your face before we encountered the Nazi's. I used to speak to you from the pulpit, *Signora*—Padre Siragusa—do you recall?"

Before she could respond to all this, Arturo chimed in. "—And I, also saw the *Signora*." He turned his ape like head towards her. "Just before the bombing at *Terra Diavolo*, before we crushed the Nazis." His voice dropped to a whisper.

"What can it mean?" she asked, as confounded as the others. Sicilians, predisposed to visions, omens and superstitions, didn't take lightly to them, for in them, they felt, lay their destinies. They must decipher them early in their existence, or life might pass them by and make of them another army of mankind who just didn't count. "It must be destiny, no?" she whispered, half afraid to speak aloud.

It was at this point that Tori came alive. From wherever it came—the power, insight and courage—Tori grasped the moment. His mind shifted into high gear, and when he broke the austere silence, no one, not his mother, or his cousin guessed at the awareness he possessed. They had no idea of the ingenious ability he had to perceive situations and make the sound judgments he'd shortly come to demonstrate. When he opened his mouth to speak, his opening words captured their attention and held it through sheer animal magnetism and a sharp articulation they'd never forget.

"Yes," he began. "It's Destiny's doing. Why else would she have sent you all safely back to me? I listened to your harrowing adventures—all you endured before returning to Sicily—to me." The magic commenced with these outrageously bold words, and he melded them all under a spell for over an hour.

"The fate of our people is in our hands. You—you— you . . . and me," he gestured to several men. "It's our responsibility to lift Sicily out of this evil lethargy. Men like us, men of the soil, of the mountains, of the plains, we are the oppressed. We must unite as one and fight for our rights and rid our lands of these black hearted mercenaries. You've returned to your homes only to find them robbing, stealing and arresting our people and if we resist or protest, throwing us into jail. What can we to do to help our starving families? Nothing. Our hands are tied because we never had a voice."

Moved by profound curiosity and drawn by his princely posture and burning words, a small group of eavesdroppers began to gather about him. His voice had reached them. The more he spoke of conditions in their lands and because he spoke the truth, the more magnetic he seemed to them. He was one of them—a peasant! He knew of what he spoke. He didn't resort to florid patriotism; he didn't march them through fields and into battle with raised colors; he didn't hark back to Garibaldi's fame and triumphant conquests. No. He spoke little of history, and spoke instead of man's human rights.

"The time has come for us to break the chains of our desperate past. We must bring new ideas to this, our land. Let our voices be the voice of the future!"

The power of Salvatore's words and the contagious excitement he generated held them in rapt fascination. He strutted before them boldly, with precise animal movements, strong and sure of himself, without arrogance or the conceit that usually afflicted self-serving men.

Before Tori had finished speaking, hundreds of men, lured by the activity at first, had gathered around him, held only by the honesty and straight-forward manner in which he spoke. He had spoken to them, man to man—Sicilian to Sicilian—in a way none other had done before.

"Who is he?" asked many of the men. "What's his name? Is this brave young man running for public office—what? From what village does he come?" They muttered wondering and marvelling at him.

"His name is Salvatore," said Giacomo, proud as a jaybird as he circulated among the crowd, his chest inflated with a stirring excitement. "He is Alessandro Salvatore, *un' aquilo bravo.* . . ." They turned their attention back on the young "brave eagle" to hear his next words.

"It's true the Allies and their abortive attempts to control prices have succeeded in making criminals of every decent Sicilian. I can understand farmers holding back their grain to take advantage of higher prices. But I ask, why isn't the graft stopped higher up, where it starts? The Allies or lawmakers could certainly consider this. But do they? No! What's worse, the Allies employ *carabinieri* to enforce their laws. Having worked for the *fascisti,* these men have become nothing but unscrupulous mercenaries, to be bribed and outsmarted according to the capacity of those who are obstructed." Tori paused dramatically then continued.

"I resent living in an atmosphere where violence is the order of the day. Where shooting, coupled with unnecessary brutality, prevails. Where youngsters are shot for transporting a pound of butter or a kilo of pasta, or are jailed if they can't pay a bribe. I resent, most of all, the fact that a Sicilian cannot walk his land free from fear, where strangers have always and still continue to walk our lands with more authority than we who are born to the soil." He hooked his thumbs into his belt and moved among them.

"If there's any man among us who doesn't feel the resentment *I* feel at having become a criminal due to forces beyond my control, let me hear from him. Let him step up here to tell us where we have erred and I'll listen." He glanced earnestly into their knowing faces, watching them nod in agreement.

"Is our crime simply that we have become habitual eaters? Drinkers? Let someone show us how to survive *without* food in our bellies and *without* water to nurture us, and I'm willing to bend to his will. But, until such a time, no one tells Salvatore he's a criminal for struggling to survive in these extraordinary circumstances of war!"

This exceptional young man, who commanded the attention of hundreds of men that day, continued to outline a plan. As he talked, they came to realize this plan wasn't a spur-of-the-moment, wild figment of his imagination, but, a well-planned and clearly articulated blueprint of hope—by a man who was one of them, a *paesano,* a compatriot, a Sicilian.

From across the campfire, Antigone stared at her son in marvelous wonder. Never had she seen him in such a pose. Vincenzo de Montana angled his head from time to time, unable to convince himself that this young man, speaking with silver tongued oratory, was his young cousin, with whom he'd grown up and played with not long ago. Santino Siragusa, perhaps the most literate man among this group of men, assessed him critically. He lit his pipe with lingering inhalations, studying Tori's comportment and evaluating his words. Arturo Scoletti tapped his brother's shoulder and commented, "You hear, Miquel? Listen to this *picciotto*, he has plenty to tell us. He makes sense—no?"

"Well, what do you think?" asked the calculating Marco Genovese of his brother Fidelio, feeling the electricity in the air.

"What do I think of what?" Fidelio replied with a tinge of annoyance.

"About this man—this Montegattan."

"What should I think, eh? He makes sense, no?"

"Phew," whistled Marco shaking his hand limply. "He makes much sense, *caro mio*. Just like those labor unions make sense." Marco stared at the cigarette he rolled between his fingers. "You know what I see, Fidelio?" he asked quietly. "I see a man who lights fires in the eyes of the men. I see a chance for us to make a lot of money for our nest egg, *capeeshi*?"

Salvatore paced about with long, striding movements. His thigh muscles strained against his khaki pants. His thumbs were hooked into his belt. His back was to the sun at the edge of the grotto. The late afternoon sun splintered through the tree tops, and where shafts of light converged, curious patterns of light of a bright intensity heightened the supernatural effect of power emanating from him.

Santino Siragusa, spellbound by the Montegattan and as captivated by his words as the others around him, felt certain that Salvatore possessed some magic of communication in that he articulated what the others had felt and hadn't been able to express in words. He turned his full attention on this young prince.

"If we unite," temporized Salvatore, "and strategically plan all our maneuvers, travel together, and become of one mind, not only will we outnumber the *carabinieri* and the security police, we can send them packing! We'll become our own police force and end this blood-sucking graft and corruption. If we don't unite, *amici*, we'll be picked off, one at a time and jailed, or killed by any thieving sonofabitching *carabiniero* who roams the hills."

"You see, Fidelio? What did I tell you? I see good times for us!" Marco's green eyes gazed over the thickening crowds of men. "Flies to honey, brother. Flies to honey," he muttered in exquisite delight.

"Be quiet, you crazy bastard! You've been drinking too much wine!" cautioned his brother hotly, gazing about uneasily for eavesdroppers.

"Not as much as I *will* be drinking, brother. Not as much."

The men moved in closer. Now nearly three hundred men had gathered, to listen to the "brave eagle."

"I have a plan, my friends, one as ancient as the laws and basic principles of feudalism afford us. In the situation we find ourselves, in times of war, anyone who can seize power has the right to govern. The ruler isn't restricted in his right to judge or interpret the law. Laws will be made to meet the situation at hand, with no concern for permanency, and those subject to our laws must obey, regardless of any other circumstances. When the war ends and our government is reestablished, we shall turn over the reins of our province to the State. Meanwhile we drive the *carabinieri* from our lands—or we dig our own graves."

"Caspita!" murmured Marco Genovese, delighted and chuckling with immense approval. "It's our lucky day! I can see it all! We drive out the *carabinieri* and we collect the loot. Think of those rich barons who'll tremble on their chamber pots when they see us coming! The tide is turning!"

"Shut up!" glowered Fidelio, grabbing his brother's arm roughly. "Goddammit! Go sober up! Get some coffee in you. Stop drinking the grape. For once start thinking with your brains instead of your balls!"

". . . If we unite," continued Salvatore, oblivious to the scenario enacted between the Genovese brothers, "I'll put an end to the starvation among our people. Foodstuffs will no longer be hoarded among our people until prices are suitable for higher profits. I'll make sure the Allies understand our problems. If they don't, I promise not to be as ineffectual as they. We shall protect ourselves until a proper government is formed, one which will treat Sicily with justice and restore to her the lands, livestock, and years the Italians have stolen from us. A Sicilian shall no longer endure the humiliations of the past!"

"Bravo, Salvatore! *Bravo! Bravo!"* shouted Santino Siragusa, cheering the loudest of all. He removed his sunglasses and studied Salvatore inscrutably. *He speaks like a revolutionary,* he told himself. *Per larme dio! This is what the people need! A revolutionary!*

They talked of arms and ammunition. And while Vincenzo took his cousin to the upper grotto to inspect the cache of arms, Antigone Salvatore remained at her son's campsite, besieged with alien thoughts.

Earlier, when Tori had moved across the rocks and stood with his back to the sun in a penumbra of power, in a play of golden lights, he had resembled a magnificent golden idol. She had felt the electricity generated by her son's words and his presence and found the whole thing incredible. Yet hadn't he grown in stature since she last saw him? He appeared much taller, loomed larger than life. Was it merely her imagination? Sainted God, everything was moving too fast. She didn't know anyone or anything, anymore. Her world had suddenly become a world of strangers, she told herself sadly.

Tori had seen the cache of arms before, and had acknowledged them mildly. But this time, when he reexamined the wealth of weapons through different eyes, he was delighted at the array of Lugers, Mausers, snub-nosed carbines, M-P 38's and .40 calibre Beretta submachine guns. There was an abundance of cartridges, and grenades, and ammo belts, enough to fire him with encouragement.

He picked up a few of the weapons, examined them critically, manipulated them expertly, and held them in firing positions. He even checked the gun sights, reversed them and peered into their barrels. He tested triggers, pulled back on bolts, and, slipping them back into place, he glanced excitedly at his cousin. He was impressed. Pausing momentarily he took notice of a Belgian-made Browning automatic, a 9mm weapon containing fourteen bullets. Such a gun with so many bullets? *Phew!* Awed by such a weapon, Tori laid claim to it. Later it was to become the symbol of Salvatore, an instrument immortalized by balladeers.

Tori grinned and addressed himself to his cousin. "What no Messerschmidts? Guns and horses must be given more consideration than you give yourself. They can be your friend or your worst enemy. . . ."

In these few moments, Alessandro Salvatore became their uncontested leader. Readily apparent was the fact that he knew, more intimately than they did, the problems they faced, and because he was a born leader the role suited him well. He struck a pose of bold authority.

"When we're ready we'll move on the prison at Monreale to liberate the prisoners. . . . We'll need all the manpower we can find to liberate our people!"

Everything moved forward with such staggering momentum, Antigone Salvatore wasn't prepared for it. This hadn't been the future she had planned for Tori. But then, death hadn't been the future she had planned for either Filippo or Marco, either. . . .

On this day, her son proclaimed his plans to reshape their world, Antigone had watched the phenomenal conversion of defeated men into super-charged warriors, infected by the words of Salvatore. The rosary beads in her brown, work-worn hands sped rapidly to the accompaniment of countless *Our Fathers* and many more *Hail Marys*.

That night, in the confines of her bedroom, she read

and reread the *strega*'s prophecy, hoping to make some sense out of it. Sainted God! It had taken her twenty years to work up the courage to visit the *strega*. Could she now set aside her foolish pride and present herself again, to ask the witch to explain the prophecy?

She sat rocking to and fro, holding both the prophecy and the Eye of God amulet clenched in both her hands. Let Tori laugh or ridicule me, she thought. She had never used feminine wiles or maternal ploys upon him in the past, and she had enough tears tucked in reserve to influence her son to humor her. He'd *have* to listen to her. *Dear, sainted God! Show me how to make him listen, to make him understand*, she prayed.

She closed her eyes and reflected upon her life. . . .

CHAPTER 19

Antigone's great grandfather, Plato Naxos, had come from the island of Naxos—midway between Greece and Turkey, one of the Cyclades—and settled in the romantic medieval village of Mount Erice where he had perpetuated farming skills and raised a fine family. One of his sons, Aristotle, had resisted farming. Through his personal ways, political inclination and enterprising spirit he'd managed to secure the highly prized Weights and Measures license in his village. Once secured, the Weights and Measures would remain in the family in perpetuity, or until such a time as they might be sold, leased or forfeited. There was the possibility of enriching oneself, and the tremendous prestigious benefits were far reaching. Through these means a less scrupulous man might make a fortune, just as Don Pippinu was now doing ever since the business had been leased to him.

Antigone's three brothers had joined the priesthood, and because she'd been a precocious child and displayed a bright intelligence, they'd convinced their father to educate her. She had become a school teacher, teaching privately for a year, before she'd met and fell in love with Antonio Salvatore, a husky, well-developed young man, a handsome shepherd from Montegatta who had come to Mt.

Erice to sell his wool. The dark-eyed, flamboyant mountaineer had lost his heart to her instantly.

Their sudden chemistry had turned to magic, and their love had broken her father's heart. He'd had visions of marrying her off to a wealthy nobleman who'd have provided her with an easy life crowned with an abundance of culture; but this dream had evaporated for Aristotle. Nevertheless, with a father's love and pride, he had provided Antonio with a handsome dowry which had helped them purchase more cattle. The happy couple had married and moved into the Salvatore house in Montegatta, on Via de Grande, and had planned a rosy future. Things had been simply marvelous at first for the enchanted couple whose lusty appetite for one another had turned Antigone into a prolific mother. They'd been so in love. . . .

The birth of each son had added to their joy, and Antonio had burst with pride at his good fortune in having so fertile a wife, for nowhere in civilized lands were young boys adored by adults as they are in Sicily. Boys were treated like gods and were treated to unrestrained emotional worship by their parents. In this idolatry came the strength needed for them to mature into a relationship that colored their entire life. Beauty in the male, considered a double blessing, invoked a near reverence from their neighbors, and as the lads grew into exceedingly handsome adults they had been critically assessed by eager mothers hoping to make good marriage contracts for their daughters. The fourth child, a daughter, hadn't been deprived of beauty. Doted on by her brothers, she had in turn became devoted to them.

How wonderful it had all been for so long—until the war. The boys had learned things of the farm, and manly ways, from their father. They had looked to their father for the development of their bodies, to their mother for the development of their minds. After all she'd been a schoolteacher—no?

Each night on their return from the farm where they went daily after school they'd become Antigone's to feed, pamper, and make over. She would gather them about the hearth with their cousins, the de Montana children, and spin tales of their Greek and Roman heritage until these mythological gods and goddesses and masterful earthlings had occupied their daily lives with as much ease as their everyday companions.

Perhaps she'd been wrong to teach her sons the philosophies that kept their heads in the clouds. She'd stimulated their mentalities and caused their imaginations to soar beyond the environs of Palermo, into the world beyond Sicily itself, instilling them with an intensive restlessness. How disillusioned her oldest sons had been to discover their real world lacked the idealistic concepts given birth to in their minds! The death of their father, when Tori was seven, had contributed in part to their rude awakening into a world of grim reality. Her sons, industrious farmers, had conformed to their mundane world until *Il Duce*'s power interrupted their lives to show them what little control they'd had upon their own destinies.

"How generous of *Il Duce* to leave me a son and a daughter," Antigone had told the officers who conscripted Filippo and Marco. "After taking all our sheep, every last head of cattle, all our crops, to feed alien soldiers, they take our blood, too!" There were many times when Antigone had wished she'd been born a man. She'd have made some politician, this woman, this bulwark of strength, this matriarch of wisdom.

Her sons, named Filippo for Philip of Macedonia and Marco for Marcus Aurelius, had taken their Greco-Roman heritage in stride. Once past their adolescence, they'd occupied their minds with healthy masculine longings until their stint in the army had turned them into statistics as casualties of WWII.

Alessandro, named for Alexander the Great, unique to begin with, had displayed an exceptionally bright and curious mind. In his formative years a squabble had ensued between his schoolteacher and parish priest in an unending rivalry over Tori's future. "He must become a priest," the Catholic cleric had insisted. "No," the school teacher had urged, "he must become a scholar." Neither realized there had already formed in Tori's mind the nucleus of a life's ambition, one their restricted intelligence couldn't have hoped to grasp.

At age twelve, Tori had been introduced to the incredible feats of the great Alexander, his namesake. Overwhelmed by the conquests of this ancient leader, he wondered how a man living in so primitive an era could have engendered loyalty from the vast armies he commanded. He had asked his mother this question one day. "Truly, he must have been a supernatural being. They *should* have declared him a god!"

Antigone had attempted to explain. "Only a man educated in the ways of men, one who understands their passions, comprehends their mentalities and can measure both the good and evil in them, one who's driven by a force superseding that of the gods can become such a leader."

Tori had stared at her, uncomprehending, until his mother hastened to add, "Bear in mind, Tori, that Alexander had for a tutor Aristotle himself. From this great scholar and master philosopher, he amassed a vast knowledge of history, literature and rhetoric. He created for Alexander a thirst for science, medicine and philosophy, all of which dovetailed into his own unique system for inspiring his men to follow him in battle. As he conquered, Alexander spread his ideals."

Because Tori had dared to dream a dream his contemporaries hadn't, he had immersed himself in a solitary world of ancient greats and, for a time, lost touch with the real world. During his adolescence, his cousin Vincenzo had pulled him away from his studies long enough to enjoy the real world. Following Vincenzo's conscription into the Italian Army, Tori was lost and turned more and more to books.

But with the war and the changes occurring in his land, there had begun to form a new awareness. Daily his subconscious mind had stored a warehouse of injustices he'd seen perpetuated against his people. One day he'd boldly announced to his family that he wanted to be a lawmaker, a *senatore* perhaps, someone high in government. He had feverishly declared that there should be equal justice for all men, something greatly lacking in his own environment. He had grown ardently impassioned over the works of several American authors—John Steinbeck, for example—and one book, *In Dubious Battle*, had held his interest at length.

In July the deaths of his brothers had caused him to take another look at the horror of war—at his environment, and at what the results of war had wrought upon his people. He had felt lost again, like a man poised between two worlds, shackled to one, while aching for another; one which remained as elusive as a faraway dream. Tori had expressed his concern to his mother numerous times since July, but she had nothing left to say to him. All her hopes for her sons had been shattered by influences over which she had no control, and she had withdrawn in near panic from external involvements. . . .

Nothing she'd ever intended for Tori, she thought now, could compare with the display of power she'd seen on this day. She was still stunned by his comportment, his strength and his silver-tongued oratory.

Antigone sighed. She stopped rocking and reexamined the articles in her hand. How long had it been since she'd

254

first encountered Donna Sabattini? Twenty years? As long as she lived she'd never forget that night of November 16, 1922 when the *strega* officiated as midwife. How could she have known what was about to explode from her womb?

Every facet and event of that night stood out now in her mind as if endowed with some mystic significance, for on that night, at the birth of her third son, Antigone had been highly impressionable. On that night of unusual twilight, pulsating skies the color of blood had been streaked with white and gold fires. Radiations of a crimson-tinged purple had fallen like congealed blood in vast blanketing shadows over the desolate village. The wind, having risen, had whispered through the nearby trees with increasing momentum while she, Antigone, having drunk from a copper vessel filled with a drugged potion concocted by the *strega* to ease her troubled soul, had fallen off into a labyrinth of disturbing dreams.

In one of these dreams the fate of her unborn son was being determined by two redoubtable powers, Destiny and History, who, majestically draped in ethereal robes hotly contested claim over him until a third and more powerful force, Sicily, appeared in a blinding radiance of light to voice protestations. Dulling the luster of the golden-robed History and dimming the brilliance of the argent. Destiny, Sicily claimed jurisdiction over the unborn child. Antigone could still hear the seduction of Sicily's voice as it filled the room. "Interfere with my plans for him and no one will claim him. I will end this charade once and for all."

Antigone had awakened from that dream, soaked through with perspiration, screaming, "He's mine! He's mine! None of you shall have him. He's mine, I tell you!" So intense had her memory and that dream been that she had opened her eyes expecting to see the three throned monarchs before her. In the flickering candlelight she'd seen only the face of Donna Sabattini staring at her with those burning black eyes. Terror gripping Antigone, she had shouted hoarsely, as one in a raging fever, "They can't have him, you hear? He belongs only to me. He's all mine!"

She had remembered nothing after that until she had awakened to the sounds of howling winds and peals of thunder erupting against black skies as lightening split and cracked drunkenly across the skies. Her eyes had fluttered and her gaze fell upon the newborn baby squirming wet and hot on her pulsating belly; a tangle of squirming legs

255

and hands. The *strega*'s eyes, reflected in the oil lamp, had shone like two black suns.

"Your son, born in a caul, will be someone special," she had prophesied. "One day—he will be Sicily."

Antigone's eyes fell upon the mass of bloodied caul. As lucidity had returned to her it had all registered. Why *wouldn't* this son be different? She'd had plenty of time to calculate the time on the calendar, now there'd been no mistake. She'd shook her head in near panic, and the word "no" had tried to form on her pale, parched lips. Her eyes had met those of the *strega* and the rare smile on the older woman's lips had dissolved. Arrested by the terror reflected in her patient's eyes and the wild-eyed denial transmitted to her in that instant, the *strega* had turned from her, for in that moment, Antigone had unwittingly communicated to the mind of the clairvoyant the full extent of her *peccato*. The one sin she'd kept locked tight in her bosom and dared not tell another soul, not even her confessor, had been communicated to Donna Sabattini!

She had not been the village *strega* for nothing, this strange, mystic woman who mixed love and death potions on request and whose powers of perception brought respect and reverence to her from the superstitious villagers over the years. On that night she had learned Antigone's secret.

Antigone, a well-educated woman with an intelligence beyond that of most men, disputed the supernatural powers attributed to the *strega*, and anything that hadn't fallen into the pattern of logic and reasoning had cast aside the strega's words giving them no importance. Yet, something that night, when Tori was born, had filled her with portents of impending disaster. For a long time afterwards she had continued to experience a tangle of hazy dreams and burning prophesies which left her in a state of unrest. For this reason she had refused to see the *strega* again after Tori's birth, and, when Athena was born, she had deliberately selected another midwife to assist in the birth.

"*My son will 'be' Sicily!*" she had scoffed. "*Indeed!*"

Yet, with every scoffing denial there had remained in Antigone a inner brooding, and, as Tori grew into manhood without incident, she had begun to breathe easier. Certainly if any prophecy were to come to pass, it would have shown up in twenty years. Antigone reasoned, if the *strega* knew her secret, she hadn't revealed it to another soul in all these years, or there would have been rumors and these rumors would have been certain to find their way back to thwart her. . . .

And so it was, because she had had no other recourse that fatal night Tori had come home with the earth-shattering news that Don Barbarossa was alive, Antigone had had to once again trust the *strega*—or go mad. The need for prophecy, never greater, had had to offset the insurmountable pressures and uncertainties and the heartaches caused by the death of the de Montana family and of her own sons. Pushed beyond the realm of reality, she had needed assurance that this stark terror facing her wasn't true. That Matteo Barbarossa wasn't alive!

Donna Sabattini, considerably changed in twenty years, with a heavy, cartilaginous face and snow-white hair, had sat crosslegged before an open brazier at the center of her shabby, one-room, dung-odored house, staring with turbid eyes under heavy lids into the fires. Considered by most not to be of this earth, the *strega* had used her amazing powers of prophecy judiciously, and her reputation had grown immeasureably. She hadn't resorted to sham or trickery and hadn't frightened the simple-minded peasants with fakery or sorcery although she was an expert in the art. Yet Antigone's presence after all these years stirred a perverse wickedness in the old crone. She experienced a diabolical desire to shake up this unbeliever.

Cackling through the distortion of a distended goiter, the *strega*'s voice, parched and brittle, had cut through Antigone's thoughts: "Why do you come now, after all these years? Once I could have saved your husband—even the lives of your sons."

The statement had struck Antigone between the eyes. Yet, not daring to speculate on her meaning and with more intent desire to reenforce her own courage, the matriarch had replied coolly, "I came not in mourning for the dead, but with grave concern for the living."

"For prophecy?"

"For prophecy."

Once again the old crone had cackled in a voice that sent shivers through Antigone.

Donna Sabattini, bent on tormenting the woman, had caused the fine hairs on Antigone's neck and arms to stand on end; her flesh had begun to crawl when, suddenly out of the fires there had come a hissing serpent. Slithering, slimy, with evil green eyes shining opalescent in the firelight, it had flicked its tongue between open jaws in short, darting movements, staring at her transfixed. Rooted to the spot, Antigone had stared, spellbound. Whether actuated by sheer chicanery or by the phenomenon of reality, she had been unable to circumvent the paralytic fear gripping her as she held her ground. Through it all she had reminded herself that the *strega*, a sorceress, could mesmerize her into seeing what she willed her to see. Was this the catechism for which she'd come? *Demonio!* It had taken superhuman strength to force her eyes away from the apparition. It had been hell in those few seconds, but Antigone fought against the sorcery, valiantly.

Finished with her playful torment, the *strega* had got down to business. She'd made no mention of Antigone's deep, dark secret, and in the wake of what followed, Antigone had nearly forgotten what initially had compelled her to visit the *strega* in the first place. She had come away from the old crone's house gravely troubled and filled with a deeper ambivalence than before the *strega* had handed her the prophecy she'd fought against for twenty years.

The prophecy, set forth on yellowed paper so many years ago, was heavily couched in a jargon that made little sense to her. In addition she had been given an amulet of exquisite proportion, a spectacular piece of metallurgy referred to by the *strega* as the Eye of God—a circular disc, sightly larger than a silver dollar with a fireballing sun at its center surrounded by lightning bolts. Within the sun's center was carved an eye.

Stubborn pride had foiled her attempts to make herself ask the *strega* to interpret the prophecy. Even after the witch had asked emphatically if she had understood the contents of that yellowed paper, Antigone had simply nodded and left the woman's house.

How could she have discussed either with Tori or Athena the things she'd seen and heard in the *strega*'s house? How? Could she have offered them an explanation of either the prophecy or amulet without creating the impression she was in her dotage? After all her teachings and admonishments against belief in the supernatural, they'd have teased her unmercifully and shamed her into silence. She'd taught them too stringently. That night she had crept soundlessly into her room and undressed for bed, and fought every sensible reason in her own mind for not throwing the items away. Yet, she had no intention of discarding them, and before she'd placed them in her hope chest out of the reach or sight of her children, she had reread the prophecy.

Seated in her rocking chair, in a chenille robe, her long hair unpinned and hanging loosely around her shoulders, Antigone lit the candles before the wall portraits of her late husband and sons. She turned up the oil lamp on the table next to her and commenced to read:

Mother of the child, the one child, you are for-
given. For he shall belong to the world. The chil-
dren of one father shall soon cease to be. The
double sting of the scorpion gives flight to the
eagle and power to the lion. Beware. Beware!
The eagle is rendered impotent by the fury of
the bull. Beware the scorpion, keep the fires of
heaven and earth to protect you. The Eye of
God shall forever be upon you. Only this shall
be your invisible protection in the Seven Years
of Glory. There shall be a white horse, reined in
silver profusion, which must be protected. The
amulet must never be rendered impotent. After
the third year, it must be crafted in solid gold
for added protection—for SEVEN YEARS OF
GLORY. Son of the World must never be with-
out the Eye of God.

Antigone had permitted the paper to fall to her lap.
She'd held the Eye of God amulet in her hands, staring at
it in fascination, unable to break her gaze. She had felt a
strange, tingling sensation, as if it, in some mysterious
way, generated an energy of its own. She had refused to
accept so precious an amulet, because she hadn't the funds
to pay for it.

The *strega* had retorted with an offended dignity: "Who
speaks of money? He can't afford to be without it. Already
there are strange webs of entanglement in the fires of his
life. You do understand what I've told you? It's of dire importance to the Son of the World." At that moment,
Donna Sabattini had raised her enormous black eyes and
fixed them on Antigone. And the mother of the Son of the
World had shuddered and felt as she had the night Tori
was born, as if the *strega* had reached into her soul and
held it up for scrutiny and with her gnarled old hands
dissected it, piece by piece.

The prophetic clairvoyant had continued her litany, and
the words still burned vividly in Antigone's mind: "The
prophecy as I repeated this night, written twenty years
ago, hasn't changed. In all these years, I'd hoped you'd
swallow a most stubborn and foolish pride and come to
me, where working together we might have been able to
dissuade Destiny. Now it's too late. He's been seduced by a
voracious mistress, a designing Destiny, and stands deeply
entrenched in the path chosen for him. Pray we're in accord. You understand all I've said . . ."

Before Antigone could reply, the *strega* had commenced her meditations and stared into the fires in a gesture of dismissal.

If she'd wondered once, she'd wondered a thousand times what it all had meant. On that night the line in the prophecy reading *Mother of the Child, you are forgiven* had struck her. A surge of blood had shot through her veins as the warmth of guilt spread through her. "I'm forgiven," she had shouted, as if these very words had suddenly lifted a burden from her shoulder. "I'm forgiven!"

That Tori belonged to the world was something she had neither understood nor given credence to at that moment.

On this day, Antigone had seen her son become another person before her very eyes. The *strega* had predicted he'd *be* Sicily—hadn't she? What did it all mean? she asked herself over and over until she was nearly crazy with worry. All those references to the scorpion—the eagle— the lion and bull! What was this mention of Seven Years of Glory? Did she dare sit quietly with Athena and sort out these seemingly insoluable bits and pieces and put them in some order she could understand? Did she dare show Tori the prophecy? Certainly not now. To whom could she turn, then? The *strega?* If she could only swallow her stubborn pride of intellect. . . .

She reflected a moment. *Santo Dio*—what power Tori generated among those men in the mountains! *Managghia*—was this her son, the young, gentle lad she'd raised? She hadn't had time to discuss his actions with her daughter yet, uncertain as she was how to describe the magic that had taken place in the *macchia* that day. Besides, how would Athena believe the picture she'd describe, of a magnificent young prince with spectacular oratory? Her own sweet, loving brother? Never!

Antigone fell asleep that night, replaying all those scenes she'd seen that day and wondering more about this girl Apolladora whose influence, it seemed, had been the turning point in her son's life.

CHAPTER 20

The next six weeks saw a metamorphosis taking place in the Mountain of Cats. That whirlwind, Salvatore, let no grass grow under his feet. He became a brilliant organizer, with the keen ability to place the men in the positions to which they were best suited—and with ease. It wasn't easy. There were times when another man might have thrown in the towel and given up. But Tori's resolve was unshakable. His cousin Vincenzo, voicing his cynicism, thought Tori to be daft for attempting to unify the men. One day when he could no longer hold back his anger Vincenzo cursed aloud.

"You expect loyalty from such *cafone?*" he exploded one day. "To make these mules follow orders will take the power of an earthquake. They don't understand unity. They all want to be boss, but lack the balls to organize. That day, Tori, you lit fires under us and in that instant we were ready to move heaven and earth. *Allora,* it's already tomorrow and it's another day, *capeeshi?*"

They were seated around the fire, Vincenzo, Santino and the Scoletti brothers, drinking coffee after an exhaustive day. Santino softly added to Vincenzo's comments. He studied a troubled Salvatore, watching with fascination the smoke curling from his cigarette.

"Make no mistake, they're rough and tough men, self-centered and cynical, and they make no apologies for themselves. Brother fights brother in decades of *vendetta.* Some would sell his neighbor to put food on his own table. It's true, their loyalty is to themselves and they trust no one. What can you expect from such men? To hear an agreement reached between them is a matter for a tribunal."

"Listen," began Tori. "I reject your cynicism. It's natural that men should differ in opinions. As for a lack of trust, who blames us—any of us—for distrusting the men that have been shoved down our throats as leaders, eh? To whom could we go to air our grievances—to ask for justice? Our mayor? That insipid rabbit who hides behind the skirts of women? Our Parish priest—that spineless Victrola who plays the same words over and over and says nothing?" Tori laughed and glanced beyond the men at the setting sun melting into a flaming twilight of orange pinks, ribboned with white and golden fires. "Enough for such talk—we have important business," he exclaimed.

"You four men, Vincenzo, Santino, Arturo and Miquel, I name as my trusted paladins. To you, I, Salvatore, will incline myself and entrust the gravest responsibilities. You first duty will be to help me unify the men."

"What you propose is a helluva tough order," temporized Vincenzo.

"What in life isn't tough, cousin? And while I'm at it, you I name my co-captain. Any man who has the balls to evaporate the Nazis with such quick thinking shall be my right hand, *capeeshi?*" Vincenzo flushed pleasurably. "But first," added Tori, you go to Palermo—to the doctor. I have a friend, a most discreet physician."

"And take the chance of being recognized? Oh, no," retorted his cousin.

Tori glanced sharply at him, concerned by the alarm in his voice. Santino, striking his pipe against the palm of his hand to empty it, hastened to explain.

"You see, Tori, none of us could survive if we were caught and sent back to prison."

Tori rolled the cigarette between his thumb and forefinger thoughtfully. "You said the prison was destroyed. Files, records, all else must also have been destroyed. Why then are you concerned? The war is still going strong. Who will question your presence here? With no records to substantiate that you deserted the army and were jailed— why do you keep a frog up your ass, eh? You mentioned the expertise of, uh, what's his name, the forger?"

"Angelo Duca."

"Si, him. *Allora.* He'll make up identity cards for you. You could have been injured and sent home—"

Vincenzo was aghast. "All the time we've been hiding in these hills for nothing?" He slapped his thigh in a mixture of vexation and delight.

"At least until the war ends, and some *birbante* decides to check the central records in Rome. Even then, who pays attention to the Italian army?" He laughed easily. "Who'll know you didn't die in the bombing, unless your ghosts walk around to tell the others what happened?"

"Why the hell didn't we figure this out? You, *padre*—you should have figured this with your intelligence."

Before Santino could react, Vincenzo gave his cousin a bear hug. "*Managghia!* Not only have you grown into a roaring stallion, but, *caro mio*, you don't lack for brains. What a ball-buster! My cousin! Imagine, my little cousin with such brains!"

Tori laughed at his cousin's antics and took the compliments in his stride. Once again he got back to business. "In addition to you paladins, I will select from among the men twelve men to become my Inner Circle. To them shall be entrusted the responsibilities that the five of us can't accomplish without their support. *Va bene*. The task isn't simple. I'll work you all until your asses drop in exhaustion. To be Salvatore's men means they'll have to be the best goddamn fighters and soldiers on the island. Shirkers and troublemakers are to be weeded out from the beginning. When Salvatore plants sweet corn, he doesn't intend to reap bitter husks."

The paladins fell silent and reflective. He was tough, this Salvatore. And demanding. How the others would take to this thunderbolt after the tinsel of his oratory wore off would be something to see, thought Santino Siragusa, repacking his pipe with tobacco, his gray eyes intent on the human dynamo before him.

"Is this man, speaking with such powerful persuasion, my cousin Tori, who only a few years ago ran around with his head in the clouds, composing love sonnets and musical ballads? Has that passionate young cock, who sent the girls of our village into rapturous tailspins, turned into a powerful young god whom I recently saw seducing thieves, murderers, brigands, and army deserters into pledging their allegiance to him?" extolled Vincenzo in a picturesque manner. "Imagine! My cousin, Tori! *Managghia*, you're something else, *professore. Professore?* To hell with that nonsense. *Generale* is more like it!'

They all laughed heartily at his antics. He was a clown, this Vincenzo. A real clown. A *pagliaccio*, a court jester.

"Enough. Now, tell me, who among all these men have you observed to be the possessor of much *fegato—guts?*" asks Tori.

"Besides you? . . . Me," replied Vincenzo mischievously. Then he sobered. "What I might see in a man might not equal your idea of guts."

"What about *Sporcaccione?*" asked Santino subtly. "You considered him most capable once." This drew a deep scowl from Vincenzo.

"Why do you call him *Sporcaccione—*the filthy one?"

263

asked Tori, catching the look of annoyance that crept over his cousin's face.

Vincenzo didn't reply immediately. His eyes traveled across the campsite searching the faces of the men until he came upon the solitary figure of the man, Ross Rizzuto, the convicted murderer, that bull tiger of a man from whom the others shied away.

Tori's curious eyes fixed critically on the bronzed skin of the Samurai, who sat chain smoking and staring into the fire's embers. He turned in fierce profile, unaware he was the object of attention for several men,

"I suppose you couldn't pick a better man—to follow orders." He began, explaining *Sporcaccione's* background. "With partisan guerrillas in Trieste, he plagued the Nazi's, retarded their progress, and did heavy damage to supply depots. Some high ranking German officer—or an agent, I'm not sure who got on to him—set a trap. Somehow the tables were turned, and it was the Nazi who ended up at the end of *Sporcaccione*'s garrote." Vincenzo shuddered involuntarily.

"Trouble was," added Santino, "Rizzuto was caught—*flagrante delicto,* in the act. Jailed and tried, he was sentenced to death. Rumor has it, he's killed three or four hundred men. If he feels remorse, he doesn't show it. He's cool. Never talks about it . . . only Lucifer knows the fires of hell that burn inside him. . . ."

Salvatore felt a stirring in him. He liked the bull tiger, fangs or not.

"He's a master at commando tactics," marveled Arturo. "You should see, him, Tori. Goddamnit, he's got the strength of ten bulls! A real Hercules." Arturo's zeal communicated itself to Tori instantly.

"Is that straight?" Tori's fascination mounted incurably.

"Sometimes he and Gambo Cusimano do *Mano a mano* combat for exhibition to keep the men entertained. *Lotta Giapponesa*—Japanese wrestling, they call it. It's something to see!"

The smell of fresh earth and fire, of sweating men and horses, of wines and various foods cooking over several campsites permeated the twilight. At the center of the Grotto Persephone, in the bright illumination afforded by the giant fire, two men prepared themselves for a wrestling exhibition. Salvatore leaned over a saddle slung over a boulder and kept his attention on the two men.

"Who's the elephant with *Sporcaccione?*" he asked, watching the two men stalk each other like animals.

"Gambo Cusimano, a deserter like the rest of us. He

was in charge of small arms and ammunition in my unit. I tell you he was a real talent."

"You say he knows guns? Well?"

"As well as I used to know the whores at Neptune's Daughters!"

"And probably treats them the way same way! Screws up real good! I'm not interested in amateurs, Vincenzo. Old Giacomo really knows his business."

"Listen, Tori. This man is first-class. He was in the service with me. I saw how he complicated war for the Germans and Italians. He's changed the course of many a bullet by realigning the barrels; he's made duds of many a godless bomb; he's jammed the bolts of thousands of rifles. And cousin, if he can do that, he could perfect our weapons to hit bull's-eyes!"

"He did all this, eh?"

"And more. . . ."

"And more?"

"And more! But don't take my word. Talk with him. He can make bombs from bottles. The powers of which would amaze you!"

Their attention was drawn to the arena of action, not far from where they stood.

"*Ayiiiieee yi yi!*" shouted Vincenzo, joining the excitement of the others. "Did you see that, Tori? Did you see the way he tossed the elephant? Look! There! He did it again!" A murmured wave of astonishment swept the campsite. No matter how often they witnessed the feat, they still felt amazement as if it were some sleight of hand, a trick, an illusion.

Both men stood, stripped to the waist, their sweating upper torsos gleaming like copper satin in the fire's glow. Cusimano, a man twice the size of *Sporcaccione*, wore a red kerchief around his forehead, Indian style. They seemed totally mismatched for such a contest. Vincenzo whooped and yelled with gusto.

More than a hundred men clustered about them, watching the combatants, shouting their approval or disapproval depending on where their loyalties lay. Tori grew more fascinated by the moment. He found the exhibition incredible. Bound with insatiable curiosity over what appeared to be a battle of wits, skill and artistry, it became apparent that physical strength was secondary. Three times in succession, Rizzuto, the smaller of the two, felled his opponent in swift, deliberate moves employing the principle of leverage. Gambo took his time in premeditating every move; yet once he reached a certain point, he became powerless to ward off the other's incredible attack. No matter what strategy he employed, he was unable to bring it to a conclusion, and ended up victimized by a thrust or fall that came before his eyes could discern it.

"Amazing," muttered Tori. "Incredible!" He called out to that powerhouse *Sporcaccione*: "Rizzuto—can you show me commando tactics?"

Sporcaccione nodded. Quicker than the eye could follow, he slipped behind the unsuspecting Turridu Nuliano, held his upper torso in the viselike grip of a half-nelson hold and, wrapping his right leg around his victim's left leg, immobilized him. A sharp stiletto appeared from nowhere, nearly puncturing the skin of Turridu's throat. Nuliano, a strong, crafty, quick-witted fighter, was unable to move or struggle free. *Sporcaccione* released him easily, helping him restore his equilibrium. Scowling and rubbing his neck gingerly, Turridu stretched his left leg and arched his back in a less than bemused manner. "Bastard!" he muttered, his ego sorely wounded.

Before Arturo Scoletti realized *Sporcaccione*'s intention, a garrote had been slipped around his neck and his body had been manipulated to a position where, with little effort, his back could be easily broken. Slowly, he, too, was released and helped to his feet, as the men watching sucked in their breaths with wonder.

Sporcaccione, pausing in his demonstration, placed a cigarette between his lips and asked Uccidato for a light. The other obliged, and as he did he observed the champion with an animal wariness. However, *Sporcaccione* moved with such swiftness and dexterity, with both hands raised over his head, that he managed to pull the other man's head down to his chest, and connect with a knee to Uccidato's groin. The victim doubled over in mortification rather than pain, allowing time for Rizzuto to grab his wrist and flip him expertly to the ground. Instantly his thick black boot moved into place at the man's neck, nailing him to the ground. Then he reached down and helped Uccidato back to his feet. Stunned by the display, Uccidato moved away from him, a frown on his face, unsure of what to make of the other's prowess.

Now the others, too, backed away from him, sullen, angry and somewhat frantic, almost like clucking chickens hoping to escape the axe. Their mouths hung agape at such cleverness demonstrated before their eyes, and they reflected a healthy respect for this hulking loner of a man. His felled victims vigorously rubbed their sore spots and, blinking their eyes at him, were uncertain of the steam-roller's next move.

"Bravo! Bravo!" shouted Tori clapping his hands in appreciation.

The others hesitantly eyed both the victims and their assailant and slowly acquiesced that they'd witnessed something special in those few moments. *"Si, bravo,"* they muttered with mixed feelings. *"Va bene. Va bene."*

"Basta," shouted Tori, good naturedly. "Stop, *amico,* before you put our men into the hospital." Moving closer to the arena of activity, Tori patted one of the victim's back consolingly. "It was for a good cause," he told him.

He called to Rizzuto. "Come with me, my friend. We have many words to exchange."

Calo Azzarello picked up his flute, and in moments the air filled with sweet, haunting sounds. Vincenzo picked up a mandolin and Duca a guitar, and soon a mood of gaiety filtered through the wooded area where Tori and *Sporcaccione* sat on a felled tree trunk, talking.

"You're pretty damn good, you know that, Rizzuto?" he told the former commando. "You think you could teach me and about fifteen men what you know?" He offered him a cigarette.

"Perhaps, if they are not too stubborn, *mi Capitano.*" he said in a surprisingly gentle voice, filled with profound respect.

"How long would it take for them to learn enough to get by with, say in the event of a surprise attack?"

"It depends on how much they have up here." He touched his forehead. "Force is secondary to a man's wits."

"I see. I see, *amico.* A practised skill, eh?"

"—And an art. *Pero*—you can kill your opponent too easily. It is very, very important to know how far you can go to merely disable a man."

Salvatore took to *Sporcaccione* instantly. He was big and tall and straight and tough. A real sonofabitch of a man! Short on humor, but long on action. He could do with his hands and brains what others did with a cannon. "Tell me, who among those men would you select to learn this *como si chiama*—what do they call it? Hand to hand combat?"

Rizzuto studied the men across the campfires and, without hesitation, he named his choice. "The Genovese brothers, the Nuliano's and Gagliolo's."

Salvatore smiled internally, for he had already selected

these same men, plus a few others. "Why these above the others?"

"Why? Because they think with their heads like foxes instead of their balls."

"What about de Montana, Siragusa and the Scoletti's?"

"De Montana?" *Sporcaccione* shrugged and made a vague gesture.

"Why not?" Tori tensed. He experienced a slight sinking sensation.

"That one's been sick a long time—plagued with consumption."

"How long?" asked Tori glancing with concern across the fires at his cousin.

"A year—perhaps longer. I do not keep records."

"Then, we must see to it that he gets to a doctor, eh *amico*?"

"Why? It is no concern of mine if a man wishes to die, *capitano.*"

"It should be the concern of all of us," he said quietly. The other shrugged noncommittally.

"Back to business—what about Gambo Cusimano, Terranova, Azzarello and Lamantia? What do you say to them?"

Sporcaccione quietly considered these men. *"Va bene, mi capitano."*

"There's one more, *amico*." Rizzuto raised an inquisitive eye. "Me," added Tori, grinning.

The ex-guerrilla flushed with pleasure. "You, *mi capitano*, I'll teach privately, and with the deepest of honor." And he did.

From that point forward, Tori's interest in anything this bull tiger had to teach him would become his strength. They shook hands that night and the former commando returned to his campfire, where the men, previously kept at a distance, suddenly converged upon him and engaged him in conversation.

"Whores of the devil!" exclaimed Vincenzo at the amazing spectacle. "That's the first time the others had considered him one of them."

"Then, it's a beginning," Tori smiled. "See how unity is born?"

And so began the thunder over the mountain. Deep in the heart of the golden mountains an idea, once born, began to stir and come alive amid the utmost secrecy. Tori organized things swiftly once he shifted into gear. First, came a special squad of carefully chosen men, selected to procure food supplies and clothing. They accompanied Tori on carefully planned raids, and never returned empty-handed. The other men were separated into squads of twelve men and put under the command of expertly trained soliders who knew their business; these special leaders took orders directly from Salvatore.

Amid a perilous and most provocative situation in which a rash of daily uncertainties and unique challenges thwarted the men, the most frustrating chore of his life was to convince them of the necessity of unity. He expected the best from these men and fought with every trick he could devise to exact it. Subjecting them to a rigid discipline, he aimed at separating the men from the boys in a hurry. It was the greatest education Tori could have had about human nature, one which would serve him well in the coming years.

At the *campagna* belonging to the Genovese brothers, abandoned by the police who had once confiscated it when the brothers had been involved in smuggling of contraband, the men were run through additional maneuvers performed under simulated battle conditions. Once the grounds were properly staked out, the men were ordered to crawl, slide, snake or weave their way across a predetermined area while squadron leaders shot live ammo expertly around their bodies.

Immediately the men voiced their indignation with shocked resentment against such suicidal practices. Dominic Lamantia sputtered indignantly at his superior officers, de Montana and Gambo Cusimano who meticulously enforced the maneuvers! "You're all a bunch of crazy bastards! That's what you are."

Uccidato, better known as Giovanni Gagliolo, glowered fiercely. He was a stocky, well-paunched man, hulking and beetle-browed and built like a bull moose. This man nicknamed Uccidato—killer—was all the name implied. In his eyes could be seen the history of Sicily. On this day he was at his fiercest. "If you think we'll let you shoot us like pigs led to slaughter, you've another guess coming," he snarled angrily.

Pietro Gagliolo, his brother, at fourteen a red-haired lad with a face peppered with freckles and a laughing, happy go lucky disposition, pulled his beaked cap down over his forehead and agreed with his brother. "This is fool's play. We'll all get killed. *Cazzu!*"

"Get back to your positions," ordered *Sporcaccione* with fiercer intimidation. "*Subito*—right now."

269

"Subito, your ass!" shouted Marco Genovese, accompanied by an obscene gesture.

"You'll have to kill us first. This is crazy, you know? Idiotic," said Lamantia, planting his feet firmly into the ground and pointing his rifle at Sporcaccione's heart.

This foolish performance continued for an agonizing and frustrating half hour before Vincenzo lost all patience. Hadn't he told Tori it would be useless? To convince these arrogant and egotistical infants the merit of conforming to rigid army training had become a feat worse than extracting venom from a serpent's tooth. "Better call Tori," he growled. "Sonofabitches! If it was up to me I'd let the cowards have it, right now."

Dressed in American combat fatigues like his men, Salvatore arrived and stood nearby on a small cluster of boulders a bit higher off the ground so they had to look up at him. For a time he listened as they aired their grievances. All the remarks made earlier to Vincenzo and *Sporcaccione* were repeated with more added.

"Either you shoot blanks at us or we quit and go home," called one of the men.

"Why should we play this silly game and risk getting shot up for nothing?"

On and on went the complaints. When they finished Tori spoke up. "What do you think the *carabinieri* will shoot at you—cotton balls?" He gave them no quarter. "Anyone who thinks this is fool's play had better pick up his toys and return to his mother's suckling breasts. There's no room for cowards or Mamma's boys alongside Salvatore. This is a job for real men."

He waited. No one moved. He stared at them inscrutably until they began to shuffle about, uncomfortable and ill at ease under the sweltering brash sun. "If you've nothing to say, then, quit wasting time. Get back to your business."

They didn't like it. Nevertheless, the grumpy, sullen and resentful men returned to their places soaked with sweat, dirt smudged, keeping their humiliation to themselves. They sprawled out and, hunkering down, they began their belly crawling bivouac as *Sporcaccione* and Arturo shot live rifle fire all around their moving bodies. Tori watched them quietly for nearly an hour inwardly pleased for, despite such protestations, they had become more cautious, more concerned and remarkably agile, their senses honed appreciably. They had hardened up in that space of time and become stouter of heart and more vigorous in their participation. Even *Sporcaccione* noticed the improvement.

"They'll do anything you ask of them, *mi capitano*. It's as if they need reassurance from you—no matter what *we* tell them."

When next Tori ordered a rectangular pit to be dug, cemented, and filled with water and the squadron leaders ordered the men to jump in and maneuver their way across the pool with live ammunition exploding about them, the men rebelled again. It was highly perilous, to say the least. This time the men decided, while preparing their protest, they'd outsmart Tori by offering a foolproof argument against the continuance of such folly.

When Tori was once again called before the striking men, Uccidato became their spokesman. "Show us where there's water like this any place in Sicily—where we'll be required to fight over a box of cement—and we'll continue with these foolish and dangerous exercises," he challenged, the livid scars on his face shining like pink fire in the sunlight. He glanced smugly at his fellow conspirators.

Tori countered, "Show me where it's written that men like us should be shot down for trying to feed our families and I shall turn myself in to the authorities. I'll ask all you men to join hands with me and follow me to jail."

"You have an answer for everything, don't you?" retorted Fidelio Genovese.

"Would you think more of me if I had no answers?" He held Fidelio's power-saturated stare with his own dark eyes. "Would you follow such a man who offered no explanations except to command you blindly to follow his rule?"

The men had been bested again. Antagonistic over their lot, they retired to their tasks with continued sullen behavior. Tori sighed resignedly. It began to look as if Vincenzo and the others were right. It would have been easier to move the golden mountains than to convince these men of the intelligence behind these tasks. These men, bright, quick, with the ability to comply skillfully with these rigorous routines, also possessed the willful stubbornness of spoiled adolescents who wanted their way and refused to risk anything in return for promising rewards.

Two weeks later, at the end of a gruelling day, the men fell exhausted, eager to partake of their evening meal. Sporting an adhesive bandage over his left temple, Turridu Nuliano, a man with mocking brown eyes who was perpetually dismayed that he wasn't able to keep up his meticulous peacock appearance, threw himself down at the edge of the fire and devoured the rabbit stew hungrily. "Tough bastards! Those Terra Diavolo devils must have

271

sprung from the loins of an iron tank! Ball busting seeds of Satan!"

"You mean *Sporcaccione*—don't you?" glowered his brother Calo, better known as "the fox," due to his strong resemblance to the animal as well as his skill in avoiding the *carabinieri*. He was boiling mad. "Incestuous fucking son of a whore has no nerves at all. Nothing scares him!"

Uccidato had had it. "You jackasses can take all this spoonfed horseshit all you want, but no one's gonna make Giovanni Gagliolo less than a man. I'm no *mammalucco* who intends to hand over his sword to another conqueror." His scarred left hand, run through with a pitchfork by a landlord who had caught him stealing a few oranges, brandished a cup of wine, which he guzzled noisily and in prodigious gulps. He wiped his mouth sloppily and resumed eating.

"You don't intend to do anything foolish, do you?" asked his kid brother the red-haired Pietro. "You swore loyalty to Salvatore," he said hesitantly. "A Gagliolo never goes back on his word," insisted the lad, who'd begun to display an idealistic worship for Tori.

"*Sta zitto!* Shut up!" ordered his brother. "I'm still boss in our family, *capeeshi?*"

"Working under live rifle fire has its hazards," remarked Terranova, the *Casanova*, who'd been sneaking off nights for romantic interludes with hot-blooded peasant girls. "*Pero—*" he grinned. "The food's great."

"What's the good of food if we aren't around to enjoy it?" complained Lamantia.

"Trouble is, Tori tries to run us like a bull runs a pasture," said Turridu.

"Why don't you all shut up, eh? Either stop complaining or do something about it! All you do is talk, talk talk, *putapoom putapoom putapoom*," complained Calo Azzarello, the handsome shepherd lad who had confessed to copulating with sheep, "For the past two weeks I've heard the same record played over, and over, and over. Yet every day you get up and do exactly what you say you won't do each night. Stop your griping so we can get someplace or change the fucking record!" He tossed aside his food and grabbed his guitar. He began to play and sing loudly to drown out the other voices of protestations. "*Io sono nu maritu fortunato . . . Io sono un marito con amore. . . .*"

He grinned and adopted a lighter tone, and in moments the men forgot their laments and began to sing along with him. And as the spirit moved them they began to clap their hands and stomp their feet. Vincenzo and Arturo leapt into the circle and began to dance feverishly with abandon, bringing smiles to the onlookers. There was a sudden change of tempo as other men joined in with guitars and mandolins and a *tarantella* began. The dancing grew frenzied and ended abruptly an hour later when Vincenzo, the wind knocked out of him, fell to the ground in a faint, and began a coughing seizure.

He was taken inside the small farmhouse, where Tori was speaking with the Genovese brothers and carried to a bunk where his coughing seizure finally abated. Tori studied his pallor with stern reprimand. "Goddammit! Tomorrow, without fail, you go to the doctor *Capeeshi?* This is the final time I tell you. Next time I'll toss you on a horse and take you in myself."

It was almost over. The men entered the final phase of training. The final maneuvers consisted of the simulating of actual ambush tactics in which two sides would oppose the other.

Pietro Gagliolo was struck right off; a bullet grazed his forehead. Another grazed his right arm. Instantly he flung his rifle into the air. Seeing this, the next man followed suit. On it went until they all lay down their arms in submission.

"Get back to your posts, and be quick about it," ordered *Sporcaccione* gruffly.

The Genovese brothers grabbed their M-1 rifles, aiming them at the Samurai's heart. "Who the hell do you think you are—Salvatore's enforcer? You gonna make us play this comedy if we refuse?" growled Fidelio resentfully.

Vincenzo and Arturo stood by helplessly, unsure of their next move. They didn't want to hurt any of the men. Yet they didn't want Rizzuto to be hurt. They tensed as *Sporcaccione* inched closer to the Genovese brothers.

What the hell was he thinking of walking into that trap? they wondered. The Genovese's egged the Samurai on. These were tough, hard men, intimidated by no one. They'd reached the end of their rope in patience. As the paladins watched, they wondered at *Sporcaccione*'s daring. Was he so fearless that two rifles aimed at his heart by two expert shots didn't deter him? The others moved in closer, intent on the scene, some with smug grins, hoping the two-fisted guerrilla would get a sample of his own fare, others eager for blood; the rest wondering where all this would lead.

"Come closer and you'll taste the bite of our bullets," threatened Fidelio.

Sporcaccione pressed forward as if he'd heard words of

encouragement instead of threats, until he reached a point equally distant from each man. He dropped his Beretta sub machine gun in a gesture of submission, taking his assailants off their guard for a split second. Triumph glittered in their eyes. Then, quick as a flash, *Sporcaccione* disarmed Marco on his right by pushing up on the man's gun while simultaneously shoving down on Fidelio's, dislodging the weapons from both their hands. Next in a surprised move, he drove a swift kick into Marco's groin, bringing him to his knees. Another rapid-fire movement and he had caught Fidelio from behind, wrapping one leg around him and felling him before he knew what struck him. He scooped up the weapons and tossed them to Miquel Scoletti, who, grinning wickedly, watched in exquisite amusement.

Before the other sympathizers could move into action they were covered by Tori's paladins. "No, you don't," warned Arturo sternly. Two against one was bad enough. *Sporcaccione* isn't finished yet."

With another body twist *Sporcaccione* released Fidelio and helped his brother off the ground. "Now, we're even.

With no guns, I'll take on the two of you, by myself," he told them. He stretched out his hairy arms in a wide gesture beckoning to them. "*Allora*—for why do you wait, eh? You wanted action—and here I am."

The Genovese brothers rubbed their aching spots with sullen and withdrawn faces, at the same time they backed off away from the ex-commando. Fidelio cursed bitingly. "Enough. This is the end. *Basta e fine!* Over and done with, You'd best call Salvatore. We'll tell him to his face."

Sporcaccione straightened from his crouch position and looked with distaste and disgust at the small crowd of dissenters forming a ring around the brothers. He nodded resolutely, signalling Miquel Scoletto. "It's best you call our *capitano*. Even I grow weary of changing diapers and wiping the noses of these spoiled, snot-nosed adolescents."

When Tori stood before them, he allowed himself to be verbally assaulted by their emotionally charged voices, knowing it was best to let them air their feelings.

"Dictator! You're worse than Mussolini. How do you justify exposing us to such dangers? Black-hearted despot! You want to kill us off, don't you? I'll bet you're in league with the *carabinieri*. You'll probably claim a reward for killing us off!" 'The fox' wasn't called that for nothing. His brain roiled with a complication of intrigues. If one didn't work, he'd think of another dart to aim at Tori.

Only the ruffling of an early winter wind was heard whipping through the bamboo rushes and the heavy scent of lemon and orange blossoms permeated the crisp air. Tori remained silent, in his usual pose, until they all had their say. Damn it! Why didn't this strange Montegattan get mad at them? Why didn't he yell at them and shout obscenities, so they could get angry at him and expurgate the acid that churned and twisted their guts. They'd never known anyone like him. In the silence, they began to shuffle about with disquiet.

They weren't likely to forget his words this day. "You're tired, overwrought, and need a rest," he said quietly. He took off his pith helmet and tossed it on the ground nearby. "Perhaps it's as good a time to get everything out in front so you all understand, eh? Because of what we've been through, I felt all of us had become men with a purpose—to rid Sicily of its blood-sucking enemies." He unstrapped his Beretta automatic rifle and dropped it with a dull thud in a careless gesture, too careless for even these men to understand. They stared, ill at ease and raised their eyes from the fallen weapon to Tori's impassive face.

He extended his arms in a helpless gesture. "I was wrong. It's not easy to admit, but when you are—you are. *Allora*—it's ended."

The men were stunned. They had expected an argument, a protest—not capitulation.

"You think we can discuss it?" suggested Fidelio Genovese. "It's little the men ask. Just that no live ammunition is used on maneuvers. Isn't there a half way place—some middle ground at which we talk?"

"There's no middle ground in war," snapped Tori. "Make no mistake, *amico*. Once we declare ourselves to our enemies it's out and out war. With Salvatore, nothing is half-assed. I know what's out there, what to expect. If you think I'd send anyone into combat without preparation, you're crazy, half-witted cretins who deserve to be shot up. If you don't care enough to protect yourselves in every way, I'm damned if I accept the responsibility for your stupidity! I want no part of such idiocy!"

He paced before them with bold strides, his thumbs hooked into his belt. "You think I've spent my time training a suicide squadron? If I permitted you to think that fighting our enemies is a game—it *would* be suicide. I'll take no part in a comedy of errors where one life is sacrificed for another."

"But be reasonable, Tori," protested Lamantia. "We can outshoot anyone." He looked to the others for support. Hadn't they all killed at least one *carabinero* in their lifetime?

275

"Si," agreed Terranova blinking his green eyes in the bright sunshine. "We're expert shots. We can shoot the balls off a bull at a hundred paces."

"Ahhh," said Tori nodding as if he understood. "I see. Because you can shoot a gun makes you powerful, eh? Is that your measure of a man? The gun he carries?" He stared at them with contempt.

"It's the only talk our enemies understand," spoke up Uccidato.

Again the men's voices murmured their approval.

"Because our enemies are imbeciles—you wish to be classified as such?"

From the start, these brooding men knew they were powerless to match wits with him. This was logic and reasong you couldn't dispute. He had a way with words. They felt Tori's seduction all right, yet they all felt it was an honest seduction in which they'd all share and share alike. For this reason they had listened to him as they'd never listened to another man. They watched him as he lit a cigarette and smoked a few minutes, with one leg raised up on a boulder. "We've banded together to preserve life, not snuff it out," he continued. "You think because we possess enough guns and ammunition to blow us all to hell and back we'll do it? It's best you learn the power behind the gun, *cari amici*. A gun in the hand of a coward makes no hero of him. A man is what he is, with or without a bullet stinging machine. A gun in your hand doesn't mean you should shoot up your enemies at will. A gun is merely a symbol of strength, not strength itself."

"Symbol or not, Tori, it comes in goddamn handy when a *carabinero* aims his rifle at you," said Turridu Nuliano.

"What will you do if you find yourself in a position where you've been disarmed? Give up and surrender meekly, because you've been relieved of your strength? Any jackass can find a gun and run off half-cocked to shoot his fucking head off in battle, to the end. A real man is one who wants to live, not die. If he keeps his wits about him, trains himself to become fearless, and uses his brains to think, he'll know when he's been disarmed, he has lost merely a firearm, not his power."

"If a gun isn't power, what the hell is?" snarled Fidelio. "In my lifetime, the man with a gun has been the most feared." These were strange and alien words to his ears. Tori confused them made them feel uneasy, even though they sensed the truth in them.

Tori grew weary. They were indeed children, who lived by instinct alone. It was hard to reeducate them in so short a

276

period of time. "We were drawn together for a purpose and must stay together as a team. If one man fails, we all fail. Which among you wants it on his conscience that he's responsible for the downfall of his people? Speak up. Tell me now and I'll excuse you. Any of you. Return now to your villages. Risk the chance of being captured and imprisoned. Or if you escape capture you can accept the oppression of our people without contest and live forever with a yoke around your neck, thinking of the glorious days when you might have been responsible for promoting a needed change in your country and were too chicken-livered to take that chance."

Tori's words, like the sting of a scorpion, were sharp and infectious. "I repeat, all you defanged and declawed tigers who think your stripes alone will paralyze an enemy are excused. The rest of us are in to the end—and victory."

The men lowered their shame-filled eyes and, walking off the rolling hills of the *campagna*, retired to their temporary housing along the side of the ancient farmhouse, a ghost of a centuries-old villa. The men cursed. They flung their weapons from them like petulant adolescents resentful of authority. Bullheaded and obstinant, as they were, they let their fiery tempers clash to explode their reasoning.

"Why should we get killed playing silly games for that power-crazed madman? Who made him our leader? Did we take a vote, eh? Who does he think he is?" came the genre of remarks.

After an hour of this, young Pietro Gagliolo jumped to his feet in disgust. "I've never seen anyone like him! If you beat me up you won't get me to abandon Salvatore," he told his brother with audacious bravado.

Uccidato gave his younger brother a withering look that normally would have sent shivers down his spine. This time, the young redhead picked up his gear and strutted across the dirt yard. With the tip of his bayonet, he drew a line down the center of the confine. "I'm with Salvatore all the way. I'll sit on this side of the line. Anyone who wishes can join me," he announced boldly.

For a time the fiery-headed youth remained by himself. The older men, those in their late teens or early twenties, ridiculed his youthful zeal and loyalty. The next day the men awakened and went about their usual routine, conforming to the rigid schedule imposed upon them. The end of each day, for the next week, found them vowing each night would be their last. Then, the very next morning they'd report to their squadron commander. This frenzied on again, off again behavior lasted a week. They went

277

through the frightening ritual of bivouac, not sure of why they complied and angry at themselves for not punching Tori in the mouth. At the end of the week Pietro Gagliolo had been joined by twenty-six men.

Finally it was over—the six weeks had ended and a miracle had taken place. The men felt a deep sense of achievement, and it reflected in their behavior. A new *camaraderie* sprang up between the men, and an expression of care and concern for one another manifested itself. It was a good feeling, they told themselves, to know someone cared what happened to them.

The men Tori chose for his inner circle turned out to be those same men to whom he'd entrusted *Sporcaccione* to teach commando tactics. Of these twelve men, two were placed on probation. Terranova, with his hazardous collection of paramours and excessive promiscuity in sexual matters, had given Tori cause for alarm. He had explained his feelings to the Castellamarese and wasn't surprised that the young stallion hadn't taken too kindly to his ultimatum. Dominic Lamantia was the second man, and his probation came about due to his excessive drinking.

"Women," argued Tori, "can innocently, unintentionally, or if provoked, bring about the betrayal of any man. Wine loosens the tongue and causes the strongest of men to boast and do foolhardy deeds they wouldn't consider doing when not under the influence. I can't afford to take chances with such men who haven't the will power to control their weaknesses."

Terranova and Lamantia both protested the points of their probation but Tori remained steadfast in his decision. They complained and argued that Calo Azzarello should be placed on probation. That sonofabitch fornicates with sheep!"

Tori shrugged. "Sheep are less treacherous than women. They can't betray a man," he retorted walking away from them, leaving them with his thoughts.

Tori appointed Santino Siragusa his personal historian and the biographer of the bandits. He stressed only one thing. "You are to keep the records accurate. In years to come, I don't want some half-crazed historian to distort the issues at hand, nor the work we do. No matter what our involvement, Santino, I insist you record it in truth. And you can be certain I'll check on your work periodically to insure this, understand?"

At the time, the former holy man took all this in his stride, but in days to come he'd have time to think heavily on these prophetic words from Tori. They would one day return to haunt him.

And so it was that Santino Siragusa, the Scoletti brothers, the Genovese, Nuliano and Gagliolo brothers, plus Lamantia, Terranova, Azzarello, Rizzuto, Duca, Cusimano—and, of course, Vincenzo—became the nucleus of Salvatore's band, which would later grow into an army of three thousand men. All were to remain close and well-protected through the most unusual and complex political situation—only Sicily could have produced in its day—and were to remain as such to the very end of Salvatore's miraculous seven-year reign.

Tori had instructed his men patiently and groomed them with considerable care. Now, he was ready to see if they had absorbed anything besides *pasta fazule*.

CHAPTER 21

It was 4:15 P.M. the following Friday. In a faint drizzle of rain, a modest crowd of villagers gathered before the ancient jail in Monreale, a few miles from Palermo. They stood by silently, watching as *carabineri* locked chains on the ankles of twenty new prisoners who'd been recently apprehended for minor infractions of the law—stealing food to keep their families alive. The prisoners ranged from 12 to 23 years of age and were covered by two officers holding rifles aimed fiercely at them, while four more sat about swiftly clamping on the locks and chains about their ankles. Something in the air—something intangible—caused a restlessness among the *carabinieri*. From time to time they'd gaze about with apprehension, without comment, and subdue the rising nervousness they felt as their guts churned. Nearby a large truck waited to transfer the prisoners to a Palermo jail.

Overhead a mass of storm clouds drifted in a congealed mass of darkening gray mist, threatening a long-overdue rain. The stony grey limestone mountains in the distance reflected the somber black moods of the peasants, who stood motionless and staring at the officers. It was all too pat, too much like a stage setting where anything could happen—most likely the unexpected, one of the officers told himself as he scanned the area with guarded and suspicious eyes.

Four men who blended easily with the crowd stepped forward, not too noticeably so as to bring undue attention to themselves, but enough so that six additional men who cautiously inched forward, moving into a preplanned position at both sides of the low stucco building, would know they were in readiness. The air was charged with electricity, and none sensed it more than the agitated police officers, who asked themselves what in hell was happening.

From out of the crowd, Salvatore stepped forward, wearing a white trenchcoat with its collar pulled up around his neck in a debonair fashion. Under it, and concealed at the moment, he wore the elegant riding habit of an English Lord; breeches, gleaming black leather boots, a black turtleneck sweater and a tweed patch-sleeved jacket. He grinned easily tossing the *carabiniero* nearest him a mock salute. For a moment the crowd moved forward with him.

"Get back, *contadino* pigs!" snarled the nervous officer.

"Are you addressing such vile language to me, my good man?" asked Tori in the manner of a dandy.

"No, excellency, not you," said the *carabiniero* speaking politely to the clothing Tori wore. "It's these filthy beasts. Go on, get back with the rest of the dogs," he snarled savagely at them, poising the rifle with menace.

"Pigs? Dogs?" said Tori playing with him. "My, my, there's a difference." Meanwhile his eyes were everywhere, taking in the entire scene.

"Excellency, I beg of you, get back. With your permission I beg you not to toy with me. I've work to finish here with these *bruti cani—dirty dogs*."

Tori recognized officer Fabrizio, the one who had shot him when Nino Marino had fallen accidentally under the blast of his *lupara*. A kneeling guard glanced up, shaken by the peasants unusual behavior, only to be admonished by Fabrizio. "Mind your business. *Fa presto!*" snarled Fabrizio. anxious to get these prisoners out of his jurisdiction as swiftly as possible.

Tori let his coat fall open. He hooked his thumbs into his belt, standing well-braced with a benign look on his face. Officer Fabrizio was coming unglued by Tori's steady gaze. When Fabrizio's eyes were leveled on him, Tori elected to stare at a point above the officer's head. Certain that this move had been duly noted by Fabrizio, he moved his eyes a few feet to the right and fixed his gaze at a distant point. Tori repeated these movements twice after that.

Less sure of himself, Fabrizio took a firmer grip on his Mannlicher-Carcano and gazed beyond Salvatore's head; he saw the peasants move their eyes now in the same manner Tori had done. Fabrizio, sweating bullets, wouldn't take time to wipe his face. Some inner sense warned him of impending danger. The arrogant, cocksure pose of that damnable man with a grin on his face alarmed him. *What devil's game is this?* he asked himself. His stomach continued to churn. He'd never seen anything like this. Usually the stinking peasants yelled and screamed in a display of histrionics designed to break a man's heart as they cried for mercy and the release of their loved ones. Now that Fabrizio recalled it, this was the first time since he'd begun duty on the island that none of them had offered him a bribe. That alone should have tipped him off that something unusual was underfoot.

He disengaged his attention from Salvatore and, under the pressure of all those stares, he turned to observe what they were so interested in, almost afraid of what he'd see. His jaw opened in astonishment as he counted four men dressed in combat fatigue of American soldiers complete with pith helmets. They stood on the roof of the jail aiming guns. Slowly, Fabrizio released his grip on the rifle, and as it rolled out of his hands Tori reached in to retrieve it.

Things moved swiftly after that. Fabrizio's partner released his hold on his weapon, and on cue Tori's men moved in quickly from out of the crowd and, in sure-fire order, discarded their coats and set to work unlocking the chains from around the prisoners' ankles.

Vincenzo and Santino and a few of the other men ran swiftly inside the jail to unlock the cells and release the ecstatic inmates, who rushed out past them as fast as they could run, yelling and shouting triumphant yells. Arturo and his brother, Miquel, together with the Nuliano brothers, began the destruction of the prison files. In a matter of moments the file drawers had been emptied and the desk compartments torn open, and, together with every chart, official paper and wanted posters in sight, the men heaped them into the center of the room where Michele set fire to them.

Marco and Fidelio Genovese had rounded up all the *carabinieri* and, after snapping chains around their ankles, marched them into the jail where they proceeded to lock them into the cells. The Gagliolo brothers and *Sporcaccione* had broken into the arsenal and confiscated every weapon and box of ammunition in sight.

Outside, the prisoners hugged and kissed their family

281

members and loved ones, wondering to whom they owed such a debt of gratitude for their freedom. They searched with curious and inquisitive eyes to find the leader of this motley group. They stared at Salvatore, noting his impeccable dress and manners. Some approached him with marked respect, coupled with great puzzlement for his deed.

"Who are you? From where do you come? Why do you take it upon yourself to save us?" they asked at random.

"I am Salvatore," he replied. "I come from Montegatta to liberate our people from their enemies."

An older man, more wise in life's ways, peered at their savior with suspicious eyes. "What do you propose to extort from us in return for your valorous deed?"

Tori's eyes on the man, filled with icy disgust—until he realized the poor man, robbed all his life, cheated and unprotected by his government, swindled by feudal landlords and kept in bondage, wouldn't recognize a kindness if he saw one and moreover he'd be suspicious of such an act.

In a princely manner, Tori addressed the gathering.

"Salvatore takes nothing from civilians. Ours has been a cause for survival for centuries. Until now, we've not had an opportunity to stand up and be counted. Any man among you who wishes to join our cause against a government who has abandoned its people can sign up with my men. With Salvatore you'll earn a small salary, plus the ability to feed your families and yourselves. . . ."

"*Bravo*, Salvatore! *Bravo*, Montegattan!" the people cheered, pledged their support.

"If we join you and become bandits we are as good as dead!" spoke up another concerned citizen. "You know the penalty imposed upon bandits! They'll kill us all!"

"We are not bandits, *paesano*!" proclaimed Salvatore with the majesty of a king. "Rebels, yes. Rebels who've united to fight a tyrannical and ineffectual government which must be made aware of our existence. Hear me well. Only the bravest of men are wanted. Those who still suckle their mother's breasts need not join. Return to the jails where you'll remain in the comfort of servitude, like animals chained to the ground!"

The villagers cheered with bravado. As he moved among them, the crowds parted to let him pass. They grabbed at him, kissed his hand.

"*Dio de benediggi*," they shouted. "God bless you!"

"Salvatore? Who is this Salvatore?" they asked themselves as he passed among them. From that day forward they were never to forget the name.

The Genovese and Gagliolo brothers remained behind

to recruit volunteers for Salvatore's army. An hour later, Tori put into action his second surprise attack. He and his men rode to the government granaries at the edge of Palermo and pulled off a daring coup in broad daylight. Leaving the premises with truckloads of flour, wheat, pasta, olive oil, and a few food staples they hadn't seen in ages, the men returned to their bandit's lair.

From this point on, Salvatore struck with the speed of a meteor. Before the *carabinieri* could recover from the blow dealt them at Monreale, Tori and his men working in clockwork precision attack the jails in Partinico, Alcamo, Borgetto, Castellammare and other villages in the interior. Finished with the jails, where he had freed the prisoners and burned all records as he had done in Monreale, Tori selected as his targets the government granaries and warehouses, where he politely removed the foodstuffs to fill the warehouses of Salvatore with the precious commodities.

"Strike while the iron's hot!" he instructed his men, and they did just that. Their unanticipated moves began to unnerve the police network throughout western Sicily.

"Who can he be?" asked the titled landlords, appalled that the police offer no aid.

"Who is this Salvatore? How dare he defy law and order?" asked Chief Inspector Semano of the security police in Palermo when reports flowed into his office of the daring deeds perpetrated by this unusual band of brigands.

"Who dares strike at the heart of the *carabinieri?*" the head of the Sicilian Division of the Italian military police, demanded to know. "Who is this outrageous outlaw who dares set himself above the law?" demanded General Brancuso. "How dare he defy the laws of the Church?" asked Cardinal Rumalino.

On and on came the queries. The more people asked, the less they knew of this phantom who began to resemble a gallant Robin Hood. Salvatore's ostentatious generosity to the poor and his stern sense of justice, coupled with his handsome *maschiezzo* and his uncanny flare and sense of publicity, caught the attention of an admiring press, who succeeded in making a hero of him.

If it appeared that Salvatore took special care to set the stage and judiciously select his cast of players to act out in the most intriguing drama ever played in Sicily's political history, he did so as if gifted with insight. It began to appear, when he took certain precautions, as if he knew

283

years in advance the ending of the script and the forces which might one day betray him.

From the first, Salvatore and his men were unique, distinct from all the other brigands who roam the countryside. Considerable care, taken to mold his men into something special, prepared them for the role they were to play. The untenable position held by the *carabinieri* as they perpetuated the greed and corruption made them the target for Tori's wrath. It was against these black-hearted mercenaries that he aimed his rebellion and directed his hostilities, hoping as he did that someone in Rome's government would take note of the intolerable conditions in Sicily.

His manner of food distribution was adopted by his people as being most equitable and increased their dedication to him. Soon the cause of Salvatore became the cause of every Sicilian in his province. Vital to this young renegade's purpose was the importance he placed on not being hailed as a self-serving brigand, or a common thief. God forbid he should be equated on par with the *carabinieri!*

Salvatore never doubted the support of the people. He was one of them. He cried their tears, felt their pain, talked their talk. He identified with them. They were the men he knew, loved and needed as much as they knew, loved and needed him. They, both of them, were the people of Sicily: the despicable and destitute peasants; the landless *contadini*; the old men begging in the slums of the cities; the poverty-stricken; the needy; the laboring peasant who'd hardly known a moment's rest from birth; the women whose bellies were swollen with growing embryos whom they couldn't feed; the *ragazzi*, begging in the streets, yet filled with a peculiar pride and arrogance—the infinite throngs of Sicilians, exploited, cheated, browbeaten, shunned, trampled on, degraded and submissive. They were all Salvatore and he was all of them.

In the next two years, if he needed reassurance, he received it from the people. He would become a genius in the art of guerrilla warfare, unequaled as yet in the history of man. Salvatore would also come to the attention of a most scurrilous sect of feudalists, politicians and government officials, a genre of bloodthirsty men who had written the history of the ages with the blood of their fellow man. From their festering bowels will come the hatefilled battle cry—*Bring Me the Blood of Salvatore!*

All this because he will not bend to their whirlwind.

BOOK III

Two Years Later
February 1945

CHAPTER 22

Allied Command HQ
Palermo, Sicily

The island of Sicily trembled with excitement and a keen awareness, knowing something fresh and daring had come alive in these ancient lands. Without a doubt this awareness struck the feudal land barons first, since they were the ones who had the most to lose. They had gathered this day to discuss their grievances with the only man capable of resolving the issue of Salvatore.

Don Matteo Barbarossa sat at one end of the oval table in his penthouse suite at the *Albergo-Sole*, a hotel commandeered by the Allies as their headquarters for the duration, trying to act civilized. Once, as the most dreaded of *Mazzarino* bandits, he'd have found other means to deal with these laughable members of Sicily's nobility. One swift bullet for each man would have ended the idiotic small talk and then, by hell, decisions would be made. However, since the Don had become *civilized*, he had been sentenced to suffer the delays and compromises to which all civilized men were committed.

By design rather than choice the Don was quiet, attentive, soft-spoken, and restrained in the face of dangers, to the point of being impervious. He was ordinary of face, with no outstanding facial characteristics to distinguish him from most white-haired men in their sixties, and could walk the street unrecognized as the redoubtable *capomafia* of Sicily. Unrecognized, that is, until he removed his dark tinted sun glasses and the people saw his eyes; black burning fireballs, dilated and power-saturated, Matteo Barbarossa's were the eyes of Sicily.

He'd been a spectacular-looking man in his youth, with a flaming red beard and coal black hair the color of anthracite, as startling a contrast as it took for this tyrannical barbarian with the glittering jet eyes of Lucifer to terrorize the countryside. Barbarossa had perpetuated a legend of violence that no one, including all the baronial feudalists gathered in this room, had ever forgotten—and which, of course, was tactfully never discussed in his presence. Don Barbarossa's crude, coarse and illiterate peasant's voice had once thundered through the hills and valleys in the stony mountains of Sicily, shaking up the ancient skeletons of his forefathers buried under the substrata of the land. The Don could roar, did so on occasion, but only as a last resort, when he lost all composure at his wit's end.

He was a tough, hard-hitting, shrewd manipulator of men, a born predator, a man who made and broke his own rules, an exponent of Machiavellian politics who ruled absolute. He had but to flicker an eye, and one man, or a hundred men, would die; he had but to cough apologetically and a nation would legislate his slightest desire. A power-saturated glance from him inspired nations to march to his tempo. Because of Don Barbarossa, men had been elevated to great power. Because of him, these same men could be crushed before tasting the fruits of this power. Formidable political giants with the balls of a bull stood impotent before him when he held them by the testicles and squeezed until his will—not theirs—was done.

Since the Don had become refined in manners and social graces, no hint resembling a threat passed his lips now. There was no need. A reputation, a legend unlike that of any Sicilian before him, stood on its own merit with few daring to contest him.

This implacable power broker moved behind the scenes like a giant, omnipotent shadow. No longer the ignorant peasant of his birth, he grasped many things long ago when Destiny turned a light on in his mind. Stumbling about in the darkness of life was not a role to be played by this chosen son of Destiny. Yet, with all he'd accomplished, the Don was not replete. Something, he felt, was lacking in these winter years of his life.

Don Matteo Barbarossa, who had maimed, killed and murdered in a bloody path of violence all the way to the top of the political totem pole, had no doubt sired many a bastard in his day—none of whom ever came forward to claim kinship. His procreative powers, as an indifferent spouse in a marriage of convenience to a woman he could scarcely tolerate, had brought forth three issues—all daughters—for whom he'd contracted excellent marriages and who now lived many miles in the north with husbands of refinement and social prestige.

This widower of nearly eighteen years had sought no other companionship. Except for the torrid love affair he maintained with power, his *inamorata* was Sicily. Saddened by the fact there was no son of his seed to whom he could leave a legacy of omniscience and power, no one to carry on his teachings or further his powerful acquisitions Don

Barbarossa was satisfied knowing he was the only man of his kind, that Sicily's history would document him as such. He invested in several proteges periodically, out of a need to promote and extend his own ego.

So on this afternoon, early in February, at this gathering of the Palermo Grand Council, a group of formidable politicians selected by the Allies upon the recommendation of their advisor, Don Barbarossa, to restore some semblance of governing order in the chaos of war, it became evident the men were bent on discussing a subject alien to Grand Council business, one hot on the lips of nearly every Sicilian on the island—Salvatore. Much to his consternation and annoyance, he permitted the tiresome chatter, only because this was the *civilized* way.

He indulged this coterie of dignified nobles and politicians, knowing well in advance that his word would be adhered to in the end. *Santo Dio!* He detested these time-consuming moments. Valuable time could be better spent attending to matters of consequence. However, if the Don had learned anything during his twenty years of impotence under fascist rule, he had learned patience. Twenty years of being less than a nothing, during which time he hadn't raised his voice even to a chicken, had taught him that patience was the greatest of all virtues. Twenty times a day, for twenty years, he had practiced patience.

And with considerable patience, he masked a rising frustration in permitting these petulant nobles and ecclesiastic princes to voice their grievances.

"Just who is this impertinant upstart? This—uh—what's his name?" asked Duke Federico de Gioia, a corpulent giant of a man weighing close to three hundred pounds. As one of the wealthiest nobles, the Duke figured prominently to be crowned King in the future Monarchy of Sicily.

"You see?" shrugged the Don, making his point. "This Salvatore is a nothing. He's no one. Outside his province, he's unknown. Why do we waste our time discussing this *capo comedia*?"

"You call him a comedian when he controls the land west of Palermo?" asked Cardinal Rumalino. "A man who controls the people as he wishes?" The red prince expressed mild surprise at what he considered a rash statement. He sipped water from a delicate crystal goblet held between slender, jewelled fingers, while his lime-green cat's eyes moved furtively under a shelf of knotted brows and lingered longingly on the wine enjoyed by the others seated around the oval table.

"He's a champion to his people and he wields frightening and abnormal influence for so young a man," added the Archbishop, blinking his dark eyes. He'd never forgotten that strange brooding man he met in San Giuseppe Jato.

"My dears," sighed the obese Duke de Gioia, "Don Matteo is right. Why waste time discussing an annoying peasant—a mere passing phase who must be tolerated in these troublesome times."

"Exactly. My words exactly," echoed Mayor Cesare Tedesco, an egg-shaped man whose bald pate glistened like the freshly oiled buttocks of a baby, a man who hadn't expressed an original thought all his life.

"I don't agree with you, Excellency," interrupted the Archbishop, addressing himself to the Duke. "Two years of a man's life don't constitute a passing phase. Salvatore has become a god to his people. Never has an outlaw inspired such love and superstitious worship and profound obedience as had this—uh—passing phase."

"Are you personally acquainted with this upstart, Francesco?" asked the Don quietly, glancing at the black prince behind his dark tinted glasses.

"Matteo," interrupted the Cardinal, "it's come to our attention that Salvatore commands legions of men, armed better than the Italian Army, who don't blink an eye unless Salvatore nods." He watched Voltera refill his water glass. "Inspector Semano's been ineffectual in controlling this menace. He and his security police are a laughing stock. . . ."

"No more than the *carabinieri*, Eminence," muttered the Don, tightly.

"We learned Salvatore has formed some alliance with the bandit Barone, from Caltanisetta. Would revolution be a possibility? In a matter of hours they could march in unison, nearly a thousand strong, and take Palermo, if they had a mind," suggested the Cardinal coolly.

"Is this why you insisted we meet before the Grand Council convenes, Eminence?" The Don tried to hide his contempt. What was wrong with these idiots? Didn't they realize the Allies could crush a revolution in less time than it took to speak the word? A wall of reserve veiled his thoughts. The others present, leaned in closer to watch these figureheads lock horns.

The Cardinal shrugged imperceptibly. "The Vatican, concerned with his growing influence against the background of rising anticlerics in Rome who, under the very nose of the Church, promote communism, feels impotent while conquerors patrol our lands. Already in Salvatore's province the vibrations of anticlerical sympathies are heard. We requested this meeting, to present a clearer picture of the nation's pulse," said the Cardinal tactfully. "Strange rumblings have been heard beyond the mountains."

"If that's all that disturbs your Eminence," began the Don, drumming his fingers on the table in a manner that belied his easy voice, "forget it. It's not possible. You think my people are sleeping? I guarantee, if such rumblings were taking place in the belly of Sicily, I'd be the first to know and offer bicarbonate of soda, to remedy the belching. Take my word. Perhaps fantasy dims your judgment in this—eh? No offense meant, Eminence.

"*Annunca*, who the hell gives a fig about this—uh—Salvatore? Few victories hang from his trophy belt. What is it he's called by the foreign press? Robin Hood? A man who steals from the rich and gives to the poor? Hah! If this is his story—why do you permit acid to spill into your bellies? Only a demented man would pursue such folly in our lands. I should know, eh?"

The Don paused dramatically. "Have we finished with this pesky, insignificant fly? Shall we progress to more important business? Or must I take measures to destroy the honey pot? Crush the house to kill the fly? Is that what you'd have me do?"

Within this melting pot of impatient ambitions, steeped knee-deep in political intrigues, every man seated at this austere gathering harbored secret, personal aspirations. Sketching grand designs of enormous power, prestige and riches in their imaginations, no matter how corrupt or illicit their involvements might prove, each man held hope for holding offices of high esteem and dominion in the Sicily they all dreamed of owning and controlling.

First among such schemers and undoubtedly the most ambitious was the Don's protegè, Martino Belasci. Smooth, slick and bombastic, this colorful man, glib of tongue, skillfully employed his legal background.

"With your permission, Don Matteo," interrupted Belasci in a well-modulated voice reeking of oratorial pretentiousness. He addressed himself quickly to the Cardinal and asked in respectful tones, "Do you have proof to substantiate such allegations, Eminence?"

"Surely *you* place no stock in such nonsense, Martino," asked the Don.

Belasci shrugged slightly; his aquamarine eyes were fixed on the red prince, whom he saw nod to the black prince. On cue Archbishop Voltera recited as if by rote:

"In 1943, Alessandro Salvatore, known as Tori to his

men and people, released over seven hundred prisoners from jails surrounding Montegatta. In 1944, that figure doubled. He burned prison records. Put the *carabinieri* out of commission. Recently, it's learned, he gives himself airs of omnipotence. He grants pardons! He places himself above the law, as if none exists. Don't you call this setting a precedent? What if this idea catches hold and spreads across the land? What will we do, then?"

"Are you really concerned about this nonsense, Eminence?" asked the Don, directing his attention only to the Cardinal.

"My concern is not the issue, Matteo," replied the Cardinal with dignified patience. These Allies are a strange breed of men, who turn Italy into a land of dubious intrigue. The Papacy grows uneasy. If the Vatican is concerned enough to make inquiry they must know something. Would that worry you?"

"Eminence, Don Barbarossa worries over nothing. *Pero*—on this desk are vital issues to be settled before we meet with the American *Colonello* Modica. The end of our long negotiations; the control of Sicily is at hand. Only because I, Matteo Barbarossa, have worked at great length, with much fatigue, for the past two years, against all odds and with much fervor, under enormous pressures, is it possible to navigate this crazy ship. Need I tell you what's at stake? We must play our chosen roles with great artistry—in perfect tune with one another, in full accord. *Capeeshi?*"

Aghast at their shortsightedness, the Don puffed with exasperation, "And you giants sit there stewing over a mere *contadino* whose life can be erased at the nod of my head. I do not understand such thinking." He clucked his tongue impatiently, as if to chastise a child.

Martino Belasci shrugged skeptically. "You must admit, Salvatore has succeeded in doing for his people what the government's failed to do. He's kept them well-fed and alive. I hear crime in his province has vastly decreased since he eliminated all *carabinieri* from his province."

"Don't tell me you've heard of this punk as far as Rome?" snorted the Don glancing at the sleek, well-polished politician seated next to him.

"The papers write of nothing else. Even the Communists champion him. I hope this isn't an ominous prediction, Matteo." Belasci's handsome face grew taut and grim. "Of late I can't open a newspaper without the image of Salvatore staring out at me." He leaned in closer to the Don and spoke in hushed tones. "Tell me, Matteo, what's really going on with this audacious renegade? What a Sicilian—

eh?" He selected a choice cigar from the humidor extended him by the Don. He sniffed it appreciatively, then unwrapped the tinfoil, savoring it each step of the way.

"Believe me when I tell you, he's a nothing," whispered the Don. "A nothing! Outside his province he's unimportant except to these *cafone!*" he glanced dourly at the others. "For some reason our associates are impressed with him, like obstinate children by a new toy."

Belasci lit his cigar as clouds of blue-white smoke spiralled over head and drifted towards an open window. "Rome is outside his province, and we've heard of nothing else but Salvatore, Salvatore, for months." He clicked shut his lighter.

"Propaganda, my dear Martino. You should know how that works."

Belasci, presently employed in the Office of Propaganda, smiled knowingly and, turning his head towards the Archbishop, he listened intently as that wiry, energetic and compulsive talker spoke.

"If Salvatore succeeds where the government has failed, shouldn't the government intervene to set the score straight, before this brigand's worth increases far more in the eyes of his people, to the point where he can do no wrong?"

"An excellent point, Francesco. An excellent point," said Belasci drawing on his cigar. "Unfortunately at this time I must ask—*what* government? We are still in utter chaos in Rome. Ferrucio Parri's government recently formed the National Liberation Committee from a coalition of all parties. *Pero*—without peace settlements on matters such as frontiers and reparations and the status of the colonies, his government will become a little more than a stopgap regime. Parri is unable to grapple with the economic, social, and political problems that beseige him daily. Truly, I don't envy his task. Poor fool! Wrong timing will do him in."

Don Matteo took his cue. He placed his cigar in the ashtray and leaned back in his chair, leveled his eyes on them. "Of *course* the Parri government won't last! Listen—I'll try to explain. Right now, we are small fish, grabbing for a few crumbs. But they are *our* crumbs, *amici*. *Our* crumbs! Not crumbs the Allies toss up out of kindness and respect for our cause. These are crumbs I've had the balls to take. Crumbs for which I ingratiated myself, for which I even risked my life to grab and cling to. From these crumbs will come the land, the power, and the riches that spring from our beloved Sicily—and she will be

293

ours. Bought by my blood, sweat and brains," said the Don, without the slightest hint of modesty or apology. "And your cooperation of course," he added.

They recognized the bitter truth. No one contested the Don's words. He winked slyly, with the confidence of one possessed with an enormous secret, and stated their position firmly and with a tone of finality. "For the present we shall keep the people happy playing with their toy hero. This—uh—Salvatore will content them with his vainglorious escapades, while we complete our business and victory is secure in our pockets.

"Once we succeed in forming a separate Sicily with full autonomy and the Monarchy of Sicily is firm with the Duke De Gioia as king, and when finally the premiership of Italy is handed to Martino Belasci, this Salvatore can be crushed. Meanwhile he serves an excellent purpose by diverting the interest focused upon us."

Unmindful of his rumpled trousers or the ill-fitting suit jacket he was forced to wear during these *civilized* affairs, Don Matteo rose to his feet with his wine goblet clutched firmly in his hand. "To the Monarchy of Sicily," he toasted, hoping to end the talk of Salvatore.

"To the Monarchy of Sicily," came the echoes, one at a time, as they rose to their feet to drink.

The room swelled with a comforting silence. Then, like a plague, talk resumed.

"They say Salvatore has an arsenal of weapons double what the Italians used in the war," reflected Mayor Tedesco, a real Humpty Dumpty of a man.

"Yes," agreed Archbishop Voltera nodding. "That's confirmed in my report."

"Managghia!" exploded Don Matteo. "It appears you are bent on boiling this issue! What is it? Is there some personal grievance that needs a quick solution?" he asked the Archbishop.

"Double the arsenal of what Italians used in the war doesn't say much," interrupted Belasci. *"Pero*—if you suggested double what the Nazis used. . . ." Belasci winked playfully at the Archbishop, who saw no humor in his facetiousness.

The Cardinal, fond of his assistant, recognized the den of foxes closing in on the rabbit. He gave the black prince the business with his cat's eyes. Voltera, his face tinged in color, sat back in silent submission.

None of this interplay was missed either by Don Barbarossa or Martino Belasci. More curious than cautious, Belasci persisted, unabashed. "On the contrarly, Eminence.

If Francesco has become fanatical over this *contadino*, Salvatore, and has something to report, let him do so. If, at some future time, problems evolve over this peasant, Francesco will have every right to tell us, You wouldn't permit me to speak when I tried to warn you. . . ."

Voltera asked himself why he bothered with these smug, arrogant, power-crazed men. Were it not for the confidence inspired by Cardinal Rumalino, he'd tell them all to become guests of Satan, where they were certain to fit into the design of things.

Don Barbarossa fumed inwardly and wondered why Martino persisted in this *tarantella* of controversy. He twirled a red and gold cigar band aimlessly around one finger, and told himself there'd better be a good reason for such idiocy.

"Don't be disturbed, Francesco," soothed Belasci with purring tones, at the black prince's silence.

"For now, Salvatore may be an annoying fly in the honey pot, but, in truth I share Don Matteo's feelings. This peasant and his activities are nothing compared to the issues at stake before the Grand Council. We're involved in matters far greater than the life of any one man, an outlaw at that. Within our grasp is the future fate of Sicily—and of ourselves, too. It's essential we remain diligent and do the right thing. Don Matteo's reasoning is not only intelligent, as usual, but wise. Let the people be content with their toy. We can take their pleasures from them—*after* we're in control."

Archbishop Voltera turned livid. As usual this compulsive talker couldn't resist the opportunity to assert himself. "Of course, you're right," he said silkily. "I keep forgetting that Jesus Christ was never looked upon as a prophet in his own land. He was merely the lowly son of a poor carpenter. The Sadducces and Pharisees were too busy in more important matters of the government to concern themselves with the brazen upstart son of a mere handyman's son." His voice dripped sarcasm.

"Francesco!" reprimanded the Cardinal. "Surely you don't equate our Lord Jesus Christ with this—uh—this Salvatore!"

Voltera made a disorganized gesture. "Forgive me, Eminence. The plots are so similar, I get carried away."

Mayor Tedesco poured garnet Valpolicella over crushed ice, and reflected. "Inspector Semano has offered rewards in these hard times that would have tempted the Angel Gabriel to betray Salvatore. This fact alone instills him with a sense of immortality."

"Such audacity," muttered the Duke de Gioia, fingering his gold watch fob in the manner of a coffee-house dandy.

"It's my understanding that the Chief Inspector came to some understanding with this brigand," spoke up Prince Giorgio Oliatta, a handsome, grey at the temple, *avant-garde* progressive who'd been silent and reflective for the most part. Dressed impeccably in a dove-grey flannel suit, he fingered his waxed moustache. "What was it—oh yes, 'The security police will not bother' Salvatore if Salvatore permits them to go about their other business."

With the exception of Don Barbarossa, the room's occupants suppressed smiles. The Don's patience had thinned considerably, to the point of losing his patience.

"If anyone says Salvatore to me once again I shall dismiss this council! *Porco Dio*! Enough is enough! By the tainted whores of Satan!" He waved an apologetic hand at the Cardinal and flushed with annoyance he subdued his anger. "Forgive such disrespectful words, Eminence. But, I refuse to permit this farce to continue. Why do we waste valuable time discussing this sheepherder?" He drew a bead on the gathering and addressed himself to them. "Once and for all time, understand that *nothing* happens in Sicily without my sanction or approval. *Capeeshi?*"

They should have known better than to be concerned, each man there told himself after the Don's outburst. In truth, the Don was right. Nothing *did* go on without his knowledge and permission. The rudest awakening came to Archbishop Voltera who, up until that moment, hadn't known the true identity of Sicily's real ruler. Now he knew. Why hadn't the Cardinal seen fit to explain such matters? he wondered.

In a more civil tone, Don Barbarossa continued. "Who can tell? in time we may need Salvatore and his rebel army. I'm watching . . . I'm watching, you can be sure. Nothing is settled yet with the Allies, nothing." The Don wanted to say—and of course didn't—that if he were to wait for *this* nest of capons to fertilize the eggs nothing would get done. He glanced at his watch, noting the time, and, slipping it into his pocket, he pushed his tinted glasses into place.

"In a few moments we convene with *Colonnello* Modica. Are we agreed on the points to stress? Complete separation from Italy. Full autonomy. We can't risk allowing another nation to rule us and pass new land reforms. His Eminence is correct about the growing threat of communism spreading like a pox in the north." He paused, sipped his wine and continued with the cunning of a fox. "In the

East, our people toss kindling on the fires of insurrection in a rebellion of loyalists opposing nationalism under Italy's skirts. Oh, don't concern yourselves yet. Everything is under the control of experts in such matters. The man, Canepa, is not my choice, you understand. You all chose him, you and the Allies. Just remember my admonishments regarding this man, eh? *Annuncia*, for now we sit, we wait, we watch like the great bird circling overhead watching a stray baby lamb. When the time is right—" *Wham*! He struck the table a hard blow with his fist "—Sicily will be ours!"

Twelve startled heads, including Martino Belasci's, shot up and stared inquisitively at their redoubtable leader. The Don was up to something. What? He leaned in closer, in a movement noticed by the rest. They leaned forward in their seats, eyes on the Don. Enjoying the attention, the Don continued.

"Massive spread of communism distresses our Allied friends *more* than it annoys us. *More*, in recent days," The Don paused, searched their faces, surprised they didn't pick up on the point he made. "You don't see eh? If Italy goes communist, America will be forced to support Sicily's separation from Italy, if only to keep an ally in the Mediterranean. You see what a big stick Sicily carries? A real weapon is in our hands."

Belasci uttered a low, knowing gasp. *"Ahhhhh."* Profound respect and admiration shone in his bright blue eyes. Lucky was the day when destiny had brought him to Don Barbarossa's attention, he told himself.

Needless to say the Don's words weren't lost on the others. Recognizing as they did the far-reaching power they would soon wield, they now let visions of personal involvements and future rewards transport them to another world of dreams, in which they could envision themselves a sovereign power, a new autonomous nation.

This Sicily had been Matteo Barbarossa's dream. By his own hand he'd carved and shaped its future and soon, through means of a supreme ego and sheer political genius, Sicily would become his monument for all eternity. These feudalists were certain to share in the power and its glory and all the profits. *Well, Well*, they told themselves. This Sicilian mongoose has gone and done it! *Mizzica!* Who would have believed it possible?

Twenty years stuck back in the womb of obscurity had sharpened his wits, heightened his ambitions and recharged him with a greater power than they had imagined. *Va bene*, Don Barbarossa! *Viva Sicilia! Viva Don Matteo! Managghia!* He was beyond belief!

Salvatore and his band of brigands, immediately expunged from mind, dwindled and shrank in importance in a wave of omnipotency that permeated the room and occupied the minds of each man on the Palermo Council. Don Matteo smiled internally as he watched their reactions.

The Don rose to his feet and waved them on. "Go into the Chambers ahead of me. Explain to *Colonnello* Modica that Don Barbarossa will arrive in five minutes."

"Is there anything wrong, Matteo?" asked Belasci solicitous of the Don, remaining behind after the others exited the sumptuous suite.

"Why is it so difficult to find intelligence among the nobility—eh, Martino?" asked the Don, sighing. "Such children. Always used to having things handed to them. Not one among them possesses an ounce of brains."

"Because they've not had to scratch for their bread, the dust collected in their minds has dulled their perception. Who knows?" Belasci shrugged, anxious to catch up with Prance Oliatta. "I'll see you downstairs, Don Matteo."

The Don nodded and waved him on. Alone, he gazed about the penthouse suite, nodding to himself as if to convince himself of his worth. For his monumental contribution to the Allied War effort, Don Barbarossa had been appointed official advisor to AMGOT—Allied Military Government of Occupied Territories. No one, not even the American gangster Vito Genovese who'd backed Mussolini with his American racket dollars until it became obvious Il Duce was drowning in his own semen, could match the honors bestowed upon the Don by the Allied High Command. Nick Gentile, a deported gangster who had professed loyalty to King Victor Emmanuel, had never reached the heights to which the Don had been elevated in postwar Sicily.

There was more. In the days before fascism, Don Matteo had been the most powerful feudal overlord and *capomafia* in Sicily, whose mighty power reached across oceans and made itself known. Mussolini's war on the Mafia and the subsequent holocaust orchestrated by his hatchet man Cesare Mori, brought about expert maneuvers on the part of the *capomafia*.

Secretly he'd imprisoned himself in Palermo's Ucciardone Prison, a Mafia stronghold. One day, a few years later, no one the wiser, he disappeared, his criminal file tucked under his arm. If you had viewed the situation through the eyes of government officials who searched in vain for him, you'd have thought no such man as Don Matteo Barbarossa ever existed.

Twenty years later, in paving the way for a successful Occupation for the Allies, the Mafia was reborn. Don Barbarossa was to enjoy a power greater than any he had imagined in those hard years of struggle up the ladder of the Mafia heriarchy. Historians, analyzing the man and these circumstances, would swear Destiny had brought about the Second World War simply for the convenience of this super power broker. As advisor to AMGOT, he recommended, for putting into key positions as Mayors in all principal cities and villages in Sicily, men whom he guaranteed to be antifascist; these were favorably accepted by the Allies. Probably the only truthful statement he had ever uttered was when he faced his Allied benefactors, American and British top brass officials, in an eyeball confrontation and passionately declared, "I swear by God and on the dead bodies of all those loyal Sicilians sacrificed in this ungodly and monstrous war, that the names of the men I submitted for these important political posts are all antifascists! No one could be more anti-Mussolini than these men and myself, who suffered grave injustices under fascism."

"We believe you. We believe you," admitted the Allied Officials, noting the prison pallor on the faces of those who stood humbly before them on that fateful day. Their belief was so profound, they bestowed limitless powers on this power broker.

Through the efforts of an intricate underground network of Mafia spies whose talents had been perfected over the many past years into a slick, well oiled machinery, Don Barbarossa had learned almost immediately of Salvatore and his activities.

Bandits abounded in Sicily, prior to and during World War II in greater quantities than in Sicily's history. Under normal circumstances Don Barbarossa might have controlled these mushrooming hordes, but not now. Not when he might need them. . . . Not since visions of a new Sicily took priority in the Don's mind. He couldn't be bothered with such petty offenders who'd never reach the glory of his Mazzarino days.

Rumors of Salvatore's philanthropy hardly fazed him. His credo was, take care of *numero uno*, first. He reasoned that while this idiot, who hadn't the sense to line his own coffers, first spent time feeding a thankless, worthless people in his province, he, Don Barbarossa was involving himself in the creation of an empire. It was purely a matter of priorities. Which came first? Salvatore's prominence diminished in the Don's mind.

A soft knock at the door brought the *capomafia* out of his reverie. "Matteo?" Belasci opened the door, intruded in his privacy, concerned with his well being. "Are you all right? Is something wrong? Colonel Modica awaits your presence."

Don Matteo sipped the remainder of his wine, rose to his feet and nodded. "I'm fine, *excellency*. I'm coming."

Martino Belasci faltered. Puzzled, he leveled his eyes on the Don. "*Excellency*? Why do you call me *Excellency*?" Confusion scrawled on his face.

"Didn't I mention it? Hummmm," said the Don nonchalantly tapping his forehead. "Confirmation of your appointment as Minister of the Interior arrived this morning." He spoke as if it were an everyday occurrence. "You'll be in the cabinet of the new Premier when he assumes office. Well, well, come along, *Excellency*. Let's not erase the smile from *Colonnello* Modica's face, yet."

Astonishment on Belasci's face was indescribable. Jesus Christ! He trembled at the prospect. In a few years the nation would be his! Martino Belasci! All this at the hands of this super powered *mafioso* who stood before, him looking like a simple *contadino* himself. *Managghia!*

Archbishop Voltera burned with indignation throughout the Council meeting. He hardly heard the words being spoken, either by the American Colonel Stefano Modica or by the redoubtable Don Barbarossa.

He glanced at the others, felt an extravagant desire to shake them and awaken them to the vigorous rumblings echoing from the hills of Montegatta, where, from the bowels of the earth, came emanations proclaiming the coming of their savior Salvatore. What supercilious conceit these foolish men contained within their addlepated brains!

Their actions proved them foolhardy and immune to storm warnings. They were like cocky, confident sailors, foolish enough to think they could outsmart Poseidon, without knowing first his contradictory and unpredictable nature. Very well, he told himself, let them drown in the juices of their own masturbations.

Right now, in those connecting grottos of the honeycombed, golden mountains Salvatore claimed as his own, there must be cauldrons of intrigue boiling, with Salvatore himself stirring the brew, thought Archbishop Voltera. *God! Good God!* What he would give to make himself the size of a fly so he could watch and listen and know what they were plotting. When he found himself praying that Salvatore would as usual emerge victorious, he felt uncomfortable, like a traitor. He glanced anxiously about at that moment, wondering if anyone had read his thoughts.

At that moment, he caught Don Barbarossa's glance and shuddered inwardly. He swore in that instant, the Don's eyes had focused on his thoughts and read them clearly.

CHAPTER 23

The very man whose name was bouncing off the tongues of Palermo's most formidable politicians was riding swiftly towards the Grotto d'Oro high above the golden mountains. Tori sat taller in his saddle than did his companions, Vincenzo de Montana and the Scoletti brothers. He rode with a quiet pride, for something unmistakably primitive was demonstrated as horse and rider fused into one unbroken rhythm. Tori was enroute to meet the rest of his men, and now, having crossed the shimmering topaz wheat fields in the plains of Partenico, they galloped up the twisting road towards the summit, turning off the road at a certain point where they slowed down to a canter in their approach to the grotto.

Overhead and behind them a glittering of mirrors flashed in a cross ray of blinding lights across azure skies, signalling their approach. Shepherds scattered here and there on the grazing lands, only a few in that vast, silent army of many in Tori's employ, sounded ox horns and waved excitedly to him in passing. There were more armed sentries standing like lonely sentinels on the ledge above the grotto, waving their rifles overhead in greeting. Santino Siragusa left the grotto to run down an incline to greet the approaching riders. A few men appeared from the lower meadow to take their lathered horses, and, when the riders dismounted, steered the animals to water troughs.

Vincenzo ambled towards his cousin Tori, slapping him

on the back affectionately, pleased at the outcome of their mission.

"How did it go?" asked Santino.

"How do you think it went?" asked Vincenzo, strutting to the nearby water cistern to slake his thirst and wash down the dry dust collected in his parched throat after the long ride. "If you hear the loud croaking bellowing through these mountains, you can bet your ass it'll be that crocodile, Chief Inspector Semano, when he learns the outcome of Tori's meeting with Director Umberto Rocca, today."

"You mean," interrupted Miguel Scoletti, jiggling his Adam's apple effectively, "He'll *maaaaaaahhhhh* like a judas goat!"

Arturo laughed like hell, slapping his thighs. "That's more like it. A judas goat. That's what that sonofobitch was—a judas goat! He thought he had you, eh, Tori?"

"You can bet that jackass Director Rocca will never pull another stunt like that," laughed Vincenzo, stimulated by his memory. "*Managghia*, you should have seen Tori. He is something else, *amici*. Something else." As he led the others back into the grotto, Tori laughed tolerantly at his cousin's generous praise and walked towards Santino's makeshift desk in the grotto to glance through the accumulations of bulletins and messages.

Once Tori had laughed with gay and infectious humor; now he smiled occasionally, and then with a sort of impatience. These past two years had taken their toll on him. He was in the prime of his manhood now, not quite 23 years old, and he'd matured into the handsome Apollo of his Greek ancestors with the physical beauty of Michelangelo's *David*. His forehead was broad and high, his nose straight with just enough of a curve to make him exceedingly handsome. His full lips, turned up at the corners, were set into a firm jaw line. His broad arms and upper arms bulged muscularly through his olive drab pinwale corduroy jacket and his thighs under the slim breeches bore an unmistakable *maschiezzo* about him. He stood in a nonchalant but power-packed pose, his thumbs hooked securely into his belt, his hands never far away from the holster encasing his fabled Belgian-made Browning. His mirror-polished boots at the moment tapped an impatient staccato against the flat stones of the earthen-floored cave as he glanced through the collection of memos—none being of great importance.

Tori's large velvety eyes, more cautious of late, were careful and cynical. He was a man in every sense of the word, always in command of emotions; rarely losing his temper. He believed with conviction that a man unable to control himself was a nothing, just as he believed that a man who boasted of his virility was without loins.

As Vincenzo related to the eager men the course of events that took place that morning, Tori sat on the edge of the desk to listen.

"Listen—will you tell us what happened?" asked Fidelio Genovese. "Or must we wait until the wheat is harvested before we taste the bread?"

"All right. All right," said Vincenzo, puffing expansively on a cigar. "Yesterday two thousand workers were dis missed without reason from Prince Oliatta's lands. *Alora*, this morning two hundred of these men arrived at Tori's house, pleading for his help. *Va bene*, we rode to the Prince's estates to find Director Rocca in his office. A more surprised man couldn't have existed. He was a pleasant enough chap, and when Tori asked politely, after introducing himself, what had happened, the bloke told us the story right off. 'Look,' he tells us. 'I want no trouble, not for the Prince or myself. But, what am I to do when Chief Inspector Semano orders me to cancel the work contracts with your people, eh? I was ordered to starve Salvatore and his people off and out of those infernal mountains that offer him sanctuary.'

"*Allora*, then he tells us that if he didn't cooperate with the police inspector, things would go rough on him. 'And believe me, that porcupine throws plenty of quills,' he told us. Semano demanded his cooperation, and the fool agreed to go along with him."

Vincenzo grinned wildly. "Then what do you think our *capitano* did, eh? I'll tell you," he said with pure delight and a flair for storytelling. "Now picture this, this fat slob seated at his desk as Tori walks towards him nonchalantly. To begin with, seeing Salvatore in person nearly caused him to wet his pants. . . ." Vincenzo laughed as the others joined in. "*Allora*, then, Tori took out his Browning and politely and quite easily shoved it into Rocca's ribs until his fat shaking belly did a dance with nervousness. Then in a soft voice to soothe a baby he said, 'With your permission, *Signore Direttore*, there are many moral reasons why I could insist that you alter your decision and resume business relations with my people. However, time, unfortunately, doesn't permit our entering into dialogue, so I'll limit myself to the fourteen solid arguments contained in this gun. Are we in accord?' "

A mixed reaction of astonishment, pride and gay laugh-

303

ter echoed through the grotto. Tori's men grinned with pleasure; their eyes twinkled in amusement and they filled with a fierce pride for their chief. They glanced at him, nodding in approval as if they had anticipated victory. Hadn't he always uncannily been victorious?

Tori flushed with a modest self-consciousness and shook his head tolerantly at the overblown antics of Vincenzo. Subconsciously, his hand slipped under his open jacket to pat the holster of the Belgian Browning.

Vincenzo's voice cut through his thoughts. "The director's belly shook like jelly. His beady eyes never left the gun in his gut, and sweat rolled off him like the hot piss of a dog. He agreed to revoke the order immediately. 'You think I'm crazy to go against the word of Salvatore?' He promised to honor the original work contracts instantly. *Mah—*" interjected Vincenzo, with appropriate hand gestures. "You should have seen that pig's face when Tori said, 'No, *direttore*, the original contracts shall not be honored. It now becomes necessary for you to increase their compensation to allow for time lost. Let's say by one third more than that originally agreed upon. *Va bene*?' What could the old bastard do, but agree?"

Delighted, Tori's men chuckled and voiced their approval at his astuteness.

"How's that for swift justice?" asked Vincenzo.

"It beats legislation," retorted Santino Siragusa, his eyes twinkling in amusement.

Tori acknowledged Santino's compliment and moved outside the grotto. Earlier he'd been disheartened when so many peasants had gathered at his house with their problems. Having listened to their laments, he had instructed them to go home and eat a hearty dinner and leave the rest to him. The men had cheered and applauded him as smiles formed on their fearful and hard-lined faces. They knew Salvatore's promises weren't empty. His word to them was like iron—like steel—as strong as God's.

Demonio! Tori had brooded for a long while after that. No matter how difficult he'd made it for his enemies to harass his people, they kept up the farce, which only made matters worse. Filling his life with petty complications, it succeeded in only taking up his time, preventing him from going on to more important work. This act, however wasn't a petty one. It was the first time his people had been directly targeted for wrath and to Tori this became a point of concern.

Whose deviltry had planned so crafty a move? If suspicion lurked behind Tori's smoldering eyes, it wasn't with-

304

out foundation. His distrust of men who spun empty promises like intriguing spiders had become strong in him. It was enough to cause him to lose faith in all mankind. Tori, however hadn't reached that plateau of immunity, yet. He'd learned to deal with each treachery, one at a time, as he'd done on this day.

Inwardly he felt contented at the outcome of this confrontation; a deep, glowing inner satisfaction surged through him for the first time in two years. He'd finally done something significant for his people. He wasn't simply putting bread on their tables, as he'd done in the past. Today he'd succeeded in buttering that bread. His action today had given them hope for the future.

Santo Dio, it had taken two years of his life to accomplish a feat that now took but a few moments to put into operation. Now, the mere mention of his name permitted bargaining in the right direction; with a little help, of course, from his trusted Browning. It was times like these, that his heart took wings. Perhaps with willingness, arms, and the force of justice behind him, Salvatore might stir this drowsing giant, Sicily, awake to take its true place in the world.

Tori moved out along the ledge of the cliff, gazing out at the magnificent panorama. In his eyes was a vast shadow. By now there should have been some word, he told himself, on another matter, quite vital to him and his companions. He retraced his steps past the grotto's entrance to where his horse grazed contentedly and, swinging to his saddle, he wheeled the beast around and rode swiftly to a point closer to the summit, absorbed in thought. Seeing him take off, Vincenzo followed suit. Wherever Tori went, his cousin was right alongside him.

Watching them ride off together, Santino grew thoughtful. Between those two was a vast difference, he concluded. Vincenzo, the eldest of Tori's fraternal aunt, bore only a superficial resemblance to his first cousin. The marked difference between these two grew more distinct each day. Vincenzo's mentality, however complex and intelligent, was superficial compared to the labyrinthian compulsions which were to propel Salvatore to soar to fantastic heights and rise above his fellow man. More at home on the ocean floor of intrigue and negotiations, Vincenzo was totally unencumbered by the plaguing conscience, the morals and ethics which periodically handicapped Salvatore. Having lived by his wits for several years, Vincenzo had learned well what benefits lurked behind a facade of smiles. He was a natural born actor, who with the *degage* of a moth turning into a butterfly could adjust easily to quickly evolving circumstances.

Where Salvatore had become the King of Montegatta to his people—the strategist, the greatest exponent of guerrilla warfare in history, their prince of justice, and for a time their Messiah—Vincenzo, the administrator of Tori's planning, became the facile politician, the temporal handler of internal complaints within the organization—and their treasurer. Vincenzo was darker-skinned, more exotic in appearance, and wore his neatly-brushed, curly black hair off his face like a lion's mane. His nose was straight and well-formed; his lips, full and sensual like a woman's, were covered by a thick moustache. Two years of good living had erased the former prison pallor. Now, he stood tall and straight and strutted about with unmistakable Sicilian *maschiezzo*. He was addicted to well-tailored clothing and ostentatious gold jewelry, and when not on duty he dressed impeccably. He and Marco Genovese were nicknamed 'movie stars' by the others.

Vincenzo laughed a great deal, and was more prone to view the world through rose-colored glasses. The attitude wasn't necessarily inborn; rather, it was one he'd adopted after his stint in prison and embellished by the self importance he'd engendered as Tori's co-captain. Things for Vincenzo couldn't have been better, except for the recurring ailment of a tubercular lung which at times knocked him flat on his back, into a period of insensibility and pain.

Between Salvatore and Vincenzo, there was a fraternal closeness, a bond renewed with fresh loyalties, which no one or nothing could tear asunder. Vincenzo never failed to humor Tori, who always laughed the hardest and loudest at his clownish capers and humorous antics.

All these revelations, Santino Siragusa had duly noted and documented in his History of the Bandits, which was growing to sizeable proportions over these past two years. His thoughts were interrupted by the sound of Fidelio's voice as the man approached him on the bluff.

"Well, Santino, what do you think, *padre?*" asked Fidelio.

"About what?"

"About what? About us, of course. See that bull in the pasture below us? I tell you that bull has more excitement than we do, anymore," muttered Genovese, gazing down on the rocky slopes at the focal point of his remark.

Santino laughed. "You don't like living the life of a

gentlemen anymore? Wasn't it you who said all he wanted to do was live in his house like decent folk?"

Fidelio turned to gaze into Santino's eyes as he twirled a straw shaft between his lips. He tried to see behind Santino's tinted glasses. "Look, *padre*, there's a whisper in the wind. Talk of a big revolution. Things are happening in Sicily and I feel we should be a part of it. We should all participate before we're castrated, *capeeshi?* How much longer can this existence remain tranquil for us? Something is ready to bust wide open, and I, for one, prefer being the propeller rather than the propelled."

"Tori knows what he's doing," insisted Santino. "He'll be back soon. Talk with him. Ask him. He'll tell you straight." He ran his fingers through a mass of curly brown hair that stuck out like untied mattress springs, and began to walk back to the Grotto Persephone, skirting past the spiny thistles planted at the mouth of the cave to deceive interlopers. Fidelio, not to be dissuaded, fell into step alongside of the former Jesuit.

"There's talk of insurrection," he blurted.

"Yes, I know."

"Will Tori drag us into it?"

"Ask Tori."

"But he must tell you something. You're historian to Tori."

"Listen," retorted Santino impatiently. "In two years when has he confided in any of us? He's brought us through terrible times, so why should we change his ways?" Santino lit his pipe, drawing on it deeply. He hated questions for which there were no immediate answers.

"He's obsessed with pardon, *padre*, and that should be all our business. You think when this mazurka of war ends, the central government in Rome will thank us for all we've done? Hah! Fat chance! They'll throw us into jail or shoot us. I'm for taking all we can, while we can, and skipping the country with our necks intact. Brazil—perhaps. We could live like kings."

Tori has something else in mind," said Santino tersely. "Pardons for all, in addition to several hundreds of acres for each man. Then we can live in our own country, on our lands, with our own kind of people. It's not as farfetched as you might think, Fidelio."

"You know something, *padre?* You're crazy. Just like Tori. You're both *pazzi*—crazy out of your heads! The world that Tori dreams up doesn't exist," exclaimed Genovese, fully exasperated. "But since I'm here, I'll have to stick around to prove you both wrong." He wagged his finger at Santino and entered the grotto to join his companions, who were just beginning a card game.

The grotto no longer looked homey or lived in. It was merely a place of convenience now. In two years little had changed. The men had grown more civilized. They no longer lived in the wilderness without a roof over their heads like ferocious animals. The headhunting expeditions once engaged in by the *carabinieri* no longer affected them, nor did the thought of getting shot intimidate the men. Salvatore had changed all that. Now, the men ate well and fed their families and kept them alive and clothed. They no longer dreaded awakening to each dawn with the fear they might be dead by nightfall. They drank a lot, laughed too much, fornicated like rabbits in heat, and otherwise led complacent lives, while the grinding gears of Rome's central government slowed down for re-tooling during war time and floundered amid the complexities of restoring law and order throughout a war-torn nation.

You'd think they'd be satisfied, reflected Santino. But no, the men grew more restless each day. A potpourri of intrigue was brewing erratically in Sicily's political arena. Conditions changed so swiftly, in the confusion of war, that one couldn't be certain of the day-to-day reports they received. Santino was certain that Tori planned something. But—what? Tori, always a private person, permitted no one to become privy to his thoughts—not even Vincenzo, who knew him best, knew what went on inside his head. They'd have to wait until Tori made up his mind before they learned his plans.

Santino began to make entries into his notebook behind the makeshift desk, as the voices of the men chattered incessantly. The feverish excitement of those early days, filled with uncertainties, when they had matched wits with their enemies had leveled off into a dull routine of boredom, creating an incurable itch in these young men, an itch relieved only by continuous story-telling, and this they did in colorful profusion of animated hand gestures and a body language all their own.

Santino glanced at his watch. Tori should have been back by now. The voices of the others interrupted his thoughts.

"You tell me how he does it—Tori never sleeps," said Fidelio.

"With what he has on his mind, would you?" muttered Lamanita, guzzling his wine.

"Damn!" muttered Terranova, the hedonist. "How does

he do without the warmth of a woman's buttocks? *Marrona!* I'd end my life if denied this pleasure."

"You would," grunted Lamantia. "Women, to you, are like drugs. You think the gates of heaven lies between their thighs. By now, Lothario, you should own all of Neptune's Daughters."

"Goddammit!" shouted Fidelio, pausing in the card game. "No wonder I've been losing every hand. We're missing an ace in the deck." He slammed down the card on the rickety table and began sorting through the cards.

"Speaking of Neptune's Daughters, have I told you what new innovations have been made since the British and Americans soldiers have become *Madama*'s best clients?" asked Terranova rolling his eyes suggestively. "*Madama* Neptune has converted her house into a real League of Nations!"

"League of Nations? Now, what the hell is that? Goddammit! You always come up with something or another. Next you'll tell us she's a Nazi spy!" snapped Fidelio Genovese. "Come on, let's play."

"Spy?" Terranova didn't make the connection. "What the hell has that got to do with sex?"

"Sex? What the hell are you talking about. Listen are we going to play *scoppa* or do we play with ourselves?"

"Go on, Terranova, tell us about the League of Nations," urged Lamantia.

"Yes, yes, tell us," insisted the excited redhead, Pietro Gagliolo.

"It's like this," began Lamantia. "All the rooms are named after a country. Inside each man gets fucked in the manner and customs specialized in each country. *Managghia!*" he howled gleefully sparked by fresh memories. "What a crazy dance-hall! It makes you wonder why you stay in one country when the whole world is waiting to delight a man's senses."

"Is that all? Is that all you can say? You get us all excited. You stop a good card game and you don't tell us the secret pleasures you yourself have experienced?" teased Fidelio, winking his eyes at the others. "*Allora*—tell us. Which country is the best, Terranova?" he asked with aplomb.

The lascivious grin disintegrated from Terranova's face. "*Capeeshi*, not all are pleasure rooms. Not to me, any way. The things some people do for pleasure shames me," he glanced uneasily towards the former priest, unsure of how far he could go in Santino's presence.

"Listen if you're concerned about me, Terranova. Forget it. I've forgotten more than *Madama* Neptune could tempt you hot studs with."

"*Allora*," began Terranova hesitantly. "One room's called Turk Arabia. Here a man can do the job on mares, sheep, goats anything he wants for as long as he wants." He gazed towards Calo Azzarello who sat back smoking with little reaction to all this immature talk. "Sometimes they let the animals do the job on women. Even children."

The men sat forward testily. Copulating with animals was nothing new, but to hear women permitted this activity piqued their interest. The thought of involving children in such games, however, appalled them.

"One room called the Vatican is filled with whores dressed like nuns, men dressed as priests . . . and those with loftier ambitions can even fuck a Pope."

"Very imaginative," snapped Santino dryly. The men laughed.

"Greece contains the homosexuals—younger boys, who sell themselves to the depraved Britishers. *Managghia*, those blokes really ring the cash registers for Greece. Me? I personally like France and Japan, where a man is a real man. Succumbing to the passions aroused in him he can be taken care of like a sultan." He leaned in and whispered in Fidelio's ears. Genovese's eyes lit up in amazement. "*Managghia!* Three women at once? How—how do you do it?"

"I don't have to," replied Terranova kissing his fingertips. "It's heaven, I tell you. Heaven."

Young Pietro Gagliolo, listening with both ears intent on the conversation, stroked the hard lump forming in his crotch. "Can we go there?" he asked his brother Uccidato.

The men laughed uproariously at the lad's excitement. Never mind that they, too, also felt the warmth of the erotic conversation. Across from them, Santino shook his head in mild amusement. Calo Azzarello, the flute-playing shepherd who considered most of the men, especially Terranova, highly immature, poured himself a cup of wine and, picking up his guitar, began to strum a tune, *Marching Son of the Bandits*, written by Athena. His melodious voice filled the grotto and echoed warmly throughout the air: "*It has been told there's a legend of one who comes from the mountains to the sea . . . In the dark of night, in eagle's flight, he fights to set his country free . . . Some call him the bandit, some call him the law; He's a renegade to the enemy, a hero to one and all he loves. He protects the rights of his countrymen. He received his guidance*

310

*from above. Some call him the bandit . . . some call him
the law. . . ."*

Santino entered into his log, this day in February, 1945:

Salvatore's idealistic views have altered considerably in two years. He discusses little with
his paladins, never asking, "What shall I do?"
He feels that a leader who consults his subordi-
nates is weak, ineffectual, and regarded by others
with contempt. He's more than a man to his
men. He's like a god, with the power of life and
death in his grasp. He's not hesitant to use force
or terror in enforcing justice. No one can say of
him his word is thin.

Yet in this strength is inner torment and conflict. In quiet meditative moments the youth,
Tori, stands in awe of this larger-than-life Salvatore, almost as if his accomplishments had been
attained by another—not he. I've heard him ask
himself, "Who am I to command so many men?
Who am I for the world to suddenly take notice
of? More important, how much longer can I
keep my men unified? How much longer will
they continue to follow me, with the rigid discipline I enforce upon them? How much longer
can we live as outlaws?" Those who know him
best believe that Salvatore wishes for little else
than to settle down, be granted amnesty for his
crimes, which he justifies as expedient acts committed in time of war, and continue with his own
personal future plans.

The idea of pardon obsesses Salvatore, now.
Through the counsel of older, somewhat distinguished men, wealthy nobles who've become enamored of him, and men in whom he places too
much confidence at times, he's come to believe
that such a pardon can only be achieved politically in these trying times. That if he offers his
services to some rising political party, the
freedom with honor which he seeks zealously
will be inevitable. It's been a period of great
frustration for this young man, who begins to
resent leading a life unlike the one he'd chosen
for himself long ago.

Power, influence and wealth mean very little
to Salvatore unless they can be used to help his

311

people. Lately a change has come over him. Gradually, without having spoken a word, he has stopped being an intimate friend to the men and has become their commander. They no longer walk up to him and joke, as they once did in the past. He's become a different man entirely.

Some call him the Bandit . . . Some call him the law. . . .

The next afternoon, February 4, Tori entered the Grotto d'Oro, one of the many caves they used when jockeying about the mountains with such ease.

"I've been looking all over for you," declared Santino. He handed him an envelope bearing the seal of the Duke de Gioia. "This came by special messenger. Our station in life shows some improvement, eh, Tori?"

Salvatore glanced at the seal, raised an eyebrow in playful speculation, and grinned. "The Duke de Gioia, no less?" he walked outside in the dazzling, crisp sunlight and sat propped up against the whorled trunk of an ancient olive tree. Opening the envelope, he read the contents three times, then, without expression, he replaced the letter into its envelope and tucked it into a breast pocket of an American general's uniform he wore. Noting the lateness of the hour on his gold watch, he picked up his binoculars and scanned the countryside.

There was no movement in the far distance—no signals either from Palermo or the Castellammare Valley. Scurrying over the rocks and craggy boulders with the agility of a lizard, he moved to a higher point on the slopes waved to the sentries. Their voices bounced back at him, "No one yet—nothing from across the mountains." Their upraised hands saluted him.

Tori half-heartedly waved back, and came off the rocks slapping his muscular thighs with impatience.

"Any signs of Vincenzo or the others?" asked Santino.

"No. They're long overdue," he replied, trying to suppress his concern.

"They can handle themselves. Don't worry, eh?"

"I should have gone with them. It was my affair," Tori replied cryptically.

"What's with the Duke de Gioia? Why does he contact you?" asked Santino.

"Tonight, at dinner, I'll tell you all."

Santino frowned. "I was planning to go to Palermo. There's talk of the new movement. It seems the Separatists are about to be sanctioned by the USA. I'm interested in learning why."

"The Americans plan to back the Separatists? But, why? Why should they?" It was Tori's turn to frown with puzzlement.

"I intend to find out in Palermo. There's been talk of a communist takeover in Italy. The Americans, gravely upset over this news, would prefer Sicily as an ally if trouble with Russia springs forth."

"Ah." Tori nodded. "That seems reasonable. Listen, before you go, I want you to post a letter for me."

"They want you—eh?" Santino smiled knowingly.

"Who?" he played dumb.

"Who? You know who. Why wouldn't they want you? You're their only hope."

"Why the hell do you ramble, *padre?* Stop talking like a woman."

"Say what you will. My guess is de Gioia's men will court you. There's talk of insurrection in the east," he cautioned.

Tori caught his glance. "How can that be? The Allied Control Council just transferred to the Italian government most of its authority in the liberated regions. They've been permitted to conduct foreign affairs, make diplomatic appointments, and enact legislation without the ratification of the Allies. Isn't that an indication the war will soon end?" he asked desperately—a bit too desperately.

"It would seem so, *amico.* "But don't build your hopes on it," he said quietly sensing Tori's despair. "There's much to be decided. It will take a long time before peace comes. Even then, peace won't end everything magically. You may have to remain the savior to our people for a long time to come. You're still the government in our province."

"What you're saying is that nothing's really changed in two years?"

Santino shook his head. "Only in our province, where you've been the law, are things better for the people. All over Italy and most of Sicily, the people are destitute."

"Are you telling me, *padre,* that I should spread out and promote my ideals to others?" Tori scowled darkly.

"Who, me? What would the mere historian to Salvatore know of such things?" he smiled irresistibly. "Too bad you can't light a fuse under the Big Four."

"Listen, *padre,*" said Tori in a fit of agitation. "I can only handle the matters that are Salvatore's. Let the Rome government tend its own business."

"It's you who appears most impatient," Santino said quietly and calmly.

"All right. All right! Impatient or not, if they don't hurry and correct things, the people will have lost their Salvatore."

Fifteen minutes later, Tori handed Santino a reply to the letter from the Duke de Gioia, sealed and addressed. "Make certain it leaves Palermo, today."

"To Francisco Bello. . . ." Santino read the name and address aloud.

"You know him?" asked Tori in mild surprise.

"He's the Duke de Gioia's man. Head of the new Partionist Party to replace Canepa, eh? What a laugh! Hah! Monarchists, Socialists, Separatists, what does it matter? They're all Monarchists hiding under the guise of Partionists. Mafia feudalists! It's still the same dirty old barn with a new coat of paint. The stink will return when the paint wears thin."

Salvatore stared quizzically and intently at the former Jesuit.

"What's it all about? Can you say, Tori?"

"Tonight, when you return from Palermo, come to my house. We'll talk. *Va bene?*"

Satisfied or not, he said, *"Va bene,"* and, once mounted, Santino rode off with a loud, *"Ciao!"*

The sound of gunfire exploded the air about him. He heard their wild cries. Tori ran out of the grotto and, through his binoculars, he saw his men herding hundreds of horses into the meadows below. Overhead, the sentries signalled an all-clear with ox horns. It was nearly sunset. Tori mounted his horse and headed into the draw below him to greet them.

"Where the hell did you find this bonanza of horseflesh?" he called.

Vincenzo grinned. "Go ahead, Duca, you tell him."

"No. You tell him," replied Duca with a hint of modesty.

"Someone better tell me!" said Salvatore, appraising the chestnuts, sorrels, mares, stallions, and geldings corraled behind the makeshift fencing with rapt astonishment and total bewilderment.

"We requisitioned them. Finished with our business in Mt. Erice, with time to kill, we ventured along the docks in Trapani. We saw American corpsmen loading and unloading equipment. Duca spotted these horses en route to Sardinia. Knowing our needs for such fine steeds, he simply requisitioned them. One look at the signature and the dock steward was so excited he threw in six cows, ten pigs, and his heartfelt thanks. Told us to make sure we gave his regards to the general."

"What general?"

"This one. "Vincenzo handed him copies of the expertly forged documents.

Salvatore glanced at the signature and burst into laughter. "General Patton! Didn't the fool know Patton left Sicily two years ago?"

"No, and I wasn't about to educate him, cousin."

It seemed that suddenly the fireballing sun exploded into a burst of blinding lights. And through the center of explosion came the most magnificent white Arabian stallion Salvatore had ever seen. Adorned with a silver-studded black saddle, it glittered and dazzled with such intensity that Tori was forced to avert his eyes.

With the sun at his back, Arturo Scoletti rode towards him on a most exquisite piece of horseflesh; a superb, powerful and compelling animal the color of muted pearl, with snow-white mane and tail, flaring pink velvet nostrils, and candy-glazed eyes the hue of anthracite.

"Just like the picture!" exclaimed Tori hoarsely.

"Just like the picture," agreed Vincenzo. *"Buon compleanno!"*

Tori couldn't believe his eyes. He always imagined owning such a piece of splendid horseflesh ever since he'd seen a painting of the mounted Napoleon by the artist Jacques-Louis David. He'd cut it from a book once and hung it on the wall of his bedroom.

"But, it's not my birthday—" he began, flushed with excitement.

"Well, we couldn't wait," replied Vincenzo. "Men like us have to act fast when the situation presents itself," he added. But Tori had already spanned the distance between him and the horse, and springing to the saddle, he spurred the animal into a wild gallop, wheeling him from side to side and putting him through a few fast-paced and expert maneuvers. The stallion obeyed implicity. They blended, horse and rider, into a magnificent rhythm as one powerful unbroken force. After several moments, Tori rode back into the draw and flung himself breathlessly from the horse, pausing to stroke the animal's head lovingly. He handed the reins to Arturo and embraced his cousin affectionately. He couldn't recall such excitement and fulfillment—such a glowing happiness.

"Thank you, Vincenzo, for all the thoughtfulness. Tonight you'll come to my house for dinner."

"Each night for two years I came to your house for dinner. Now, suddenly I need an invitation?"

"This is different." He waved the letter bearing the Duke de Gioia's crest under the other's nose. "This may be the good news I've been expecting, cousin."

"*Va bene.* I'll be there. *Allora*—news reached me in Trapani that Martino Belasci has been appointed Minister of the Interior in Premier de Aspanu's cabinet. He's moving fast, that one—eh?"

"And why not? My Godfather Matteo Barbarossa promotes him."

"You know this for a fact?" Vincenzo's mouth fell open in amazement.

"There's little I don't know, cousin. What's more, soon we will pay my Godfather a visit." He accepted the cigarette and match extended him. After he lit up he exhaled the smoke. "Did you handle that small matter in Mt. Erice?"

Vincenzo's smile disappeared. "I hope you know what you're doing, Tori. I've never seen a more sinister face than that *mafioso*'s," he cautioned. "*Managghia*, It took all my courage to put on a brave face and walk out of there when I finished. He's a fork-tongued viper, that Don Pippinu. You'd best steer clear of him."

"I know what I'm doing," said Tori. "I'm going to talk with my new horse while you clean up. I'll see you later at my house, *capeeshi?*"

"What will you call him?" asked Vincenzo, indicating the horse.

"What else? *Napoleono.*" Tori winked broadly at his co-captain.

Watching Tori ride off Vincenzo hoped the letter contained news to elevate Tori's spirits. Lately Tori had begun to evince an inner erosion of discontent with the life they were leading. Whatever it was that had been eating away at him had caused him to become more daring and audacious in coups against the *carabinieri*. Moreover, he'd become stricter with his men. The super-policing of the outlaws had begun to cause dissension among the men for the first time since they had organized.

The men had wondered what Tori expected of them, arguing they couldn't be the celibates Tori seemed to be. "We're virile men with healthy manly appetites. Why should we live like priests, without women?" They had lamented to Vincenzo as they burned under the rigid discipline and strict enforcement of morality imposed upon them by Tori.

If he lived to be a hundred, Vincenzo would never forget the humiliation he himself had received from his cousin Tori, recently. He'd suffered a *bastinada*, the pains of which had long since been erased, but the humiliation and the memory of his stupidity still lingered in his mind. Vincenzo, no angel, loved his sex life equally as much as, if not more than, the other men. God had endowed him with the virility of ten stud bulls. He wasn't ashamed to admit he loved to fuck. After all the abstinence imposed on him at Terra Diavlo he had a lot to make up—and he went at it like a champion, almost as much as Terranova.

Tori had warned him repeatedly to be careful, to play outside the province, and to take care that he told no one his identity or occupation. He'd been warned to be economical in his sexual relations because of his pressing health problems, but it had been to no avail.

Vincenzo had pretended to go along with his cousin outwardly, but inwardly never hearing a word spoken to him. His mind had centered on a particularly juicy morsel named Filomena, who had made him crazy over her, crazy out of his mind. Besides, Maria Angelica Candela had become so uppity with him she'd refused to tumble in the hay with him without benefit of a wedding ring. Vincenzo wasn't ready for marriage yet, so he had turned his attentions on Filomena. He had mentioned the girl to Terranova and his companion's expression had been one of farcicul disbelief. "That one has four legs, barks and says oink oink," the other Lothario had said. "I thought you had better taste."

Nevertheless, despite Tori's warnings that she was a known consort to *carabinieri,* Vincenzo couldn't get out of his head how *fantastico* she was in bed. And then one night it had happened. Irresistibly drawn to Filomena and her inventive ways, he had defied Tori one time too many. He had walked right into a betrayal. Four *carabinieri* had been lying in wait for him, and had dragged him from the house stark naked. Vincenzo had shaken uncontrollably as the handcuffs were clasped over each wrist and all the old horrors of *Terra Diavolo* had returned to shake him and fill him with the terrors he'd once lived through. He hadn't known that Tori, having already learned of the betrayal, had been waiting outside the whore's house with a few of his other men. They had moved in just before Vincenzo was thrown into the police van.

A shoot-out took place, three *carabinieri* lost their lives, one escaped, Miguel Scoletti had rushed into the girl's room, all the madness contained in him since his nightmare at *Terra Diavolo*, and holding his .38 calibre Mauser at the girl's temple, blew her brains out, shouting as he did, "*Death to the traitors in Salvatore's army.*" Something had happened that night to Miguel. Behind his dark, staring, catatonic eyes had hovered unlimited terror and violence, and a wrathful accumulation of loathing had been lying in wait, ready to unleash itself in the personality of a cold blooded killer. He'd been homosexually assaulted by Nazi prison guards at *Terra Diavolo*, and it seemed everything had come out at this particular time. Tori had had to send him away for a rest and some rehabilitation after this night.

And something happened to Tori that night. For in the senseless deaths of the *carabinieri* and the girls, which could have been avoided if Vincenzo had learned to exercise self control, he had seen what could happen if the men were permitted to go about without controls. That night he had taken Vincenzo home, tied him to a tree, and given him a *bastinada*, the likes of which his other paladins had never seen.

Later, Tori had helped Vincenzo down and nursed his wounds, with the solicitous and tender loving care he'd had given a brother. But he'd been firm. "If you ever permit your sexual passion to override caution, or place yourself or the lives of our men in jeopardy as you did this night, I won't end where I did tonight. You'll have me to reckon with, Vincenzo as you never had before." Then, as he had continued to nurse his cousin, he had grown emotionally overwrought and, speaking with a congested throat, he'd spoken with great affection and *molto dolore*, "Whipping you is like whipping my own flesh. I'd have preferred taking this punishment myself. But, you wouldn't have learned a lesson. While you are my second in command and owe a responsibility to the men, you must remember that women are our most dangerous enemies— even when they truly love us. Through them, we become vulnerable to betrayal and submission. When all this is finished, you can take all the women you want—a concubine if you will. But for now, until our roles have ended, you must exercise caution and intelligence."

Tori, who wasn't totally unreasonable, and understanding the physical needs of his men, had permitted them the companionship of women, but only under rigid rules. They could never be brought to a grotto or campsite used in their business, where they moved about or worked. Women, paid for by the night, were permitted into some sequestered place, blindfolded, where the men could partake of pleasure without danger of betrayal. If the men married, it was to be within a tightly knit circle of relatives or friends of the bandits themselves, with little or no publicity given the coupling or union.

Vincenzo thought back to a night, quite recently, when something had occurred which set him to wondering about Tori. He recalled that on one of their outings, the campsite had buzzed with gay activity on a festive occasion. Men and women had danced to the wild, sensuous music, some had made love, and all had drunk to their hearts' content. Near the fires a musician had struck up a fiery *tarantella* and Vincenzo, lured by his specialty, had fallen into a dancer's posture—arched back, shoulders and hips fixed—and begun his individual improvisation. Into the center of the activity he'd began pirouetting in and out of a moving line of hand-clapping, foot-stomping dancers, and, finding a suitable, lusty companion with smoldering dark eyes, he'd begun with her an interplay of female-male attitudes, set to the frenzied accompaniment of the stimulated musicians. The couple had become seductive and aggressive, and mimed a passionate jealousy between them; then they'd feigned indifference, even cruelty. For a time they had flirted outrageously, then, in tenderness had come the surrender. They had run the gamut of romantic feelings as if they had been truly emotionally involved; it was not unusual, after such a performance, for the dancers to get together for a romantic interlude. Such a stirring exhibition, too, was contagious and inspiring to onlookers.

On and on they had danced, whirling and twirling and snaking in a circle. The campfire had become a revolving kaleidoscope of oblique shadows and abstract forms, and stirring vibrations which electrified the air. Finally, Vincenzo had fallen laughingly in total exhaustion to the ground in an effort to catch his breath.

When he looked about for Tori's face among those of the spectators, Tori was absent. Vincenzo had searched everywhere and found him later, high on a bluff, outlined brightly by a full and enormous harvest moon in what appeared to be a poignant and private moment. Vincenzo had strained to hear Salvatore's words: *"I shall be avenged, Apolladora, mia. Never shall there be another for me!"*

Startled, Vincenzo had wondered. Apolladora? Apolladora who? Avenged? Upon whom? He had lumbered off the hill bewildered and taken aback. Who was Apolladora? Having never forgotten the incident, he had promised himself he'd one day ask Tori. To this day he

319

hadn't worked up the courage to ask, but he felt he must one day soon. Was now the time?

As Vincenzo made preparations, now, to ride to the house of his Aunt Antigone he considered the letter Tori had shown him. A royal seal—no less? He chuckled and hoped it was good news. He waved to Arturo Scoletti and called to him.

"C'mon, you son of a wayward tortoise, hurry up!" Mounting his black mare, he galloped ahead of Arturo, waving to his companions in the draw.

CHAPTER 24

Dinner that night at the house of his mother had been a mixture of business and pleasure and one of startling revelations. They were halfway through dinner when Tori noticed a tenseness in the air around him as the men, and his mother, waited to hear what it was that was chafing him so.

Finally Tori asked Santino, "Whats the word from Palermo?"

"Chaos," replied Santino in a candor. "Everywhere is chaos. In the elections Allies permitted all the political parties to register, and their shock at the results has left them stunned. The swing is decidedly to the left. The Reds must have infiltrated on the quiet, and suddenly, there they were in full bloom. I tell you, *amici*, everyone is shaking."

"What happened to Sicily becoming a state or colony?" asked Vincenzo idly as he devoured the succulent veal and peppers, rolling his eyes in appreciation towards his aunt.

"Talk is all it was. Talk," muttered Santino between mouthfuls.

"In any case separation from Italy is inevitable," stated Tori.

Santino shrugged. "Information I got today indicates the Palermo Grand Council, run by Don Barbarossa, is pressing for separation and autonomy. Their intentions are to form a Monarchy naming Duke de Gioia king. They are hard pressed to beat the Reds to power."

Antigone spoke up. "Russia may be one of the Allies, but at war's end there will be a mad scramble for power. Russia wants Sicilly. I fear the consequences."

"Why?" asked Tori.

"Why? Because, my son, our people are ready for anyone who promises better things than we've had in the past. At the end of the last war many soldiers returned with different ideas of how to live. They rebelled at the feudal system and refused to knuckle down to the old ways. When they learned they couldn't combat the system, some left, others remained. Attempts to take over uncultivated lands, theirs by virtue of the laws, were foiled by Mafia *gabellotti*. Rivers of peasant blood flowed in the wake of their dissent. It's still the same. Nothing has changed. Reflect on your own behavior. Haven't you all tried to change the old ways? You think it will do any good as long as the feudalists remain in power?"

The others frowned at her words, and Tori, who believed things had to change, brooded over her words.

"Shall I tell you what will happen? Sicily's conquerors—in this case the Allies—will turn their backs on her. They've a bigger job to finish—the war. They can't be bothered with us."

For a time they all tasted the new wine, with the exception of Tori. All made comments and passed judgment on it in a ritual-like activity. Tori waited until they were finished before he addressed Arturo. "What's the word from your sources?" he asked the jovial former strong man.

"A new Partionist movement is beginning, sponsored by the Allies, I'm told, all hush hush—an undercover cloak-and-dagger type of business," he replied.

"The Allies backing the Partitionists?" asked Tori, his fork in mid-air as his food was suspended in mid-sentence. "Is this the truth?" It was easy to see this news generated a great degree of excitement. Tori himself felt a new stirring in his stomach as something came together in his mind. He had already heard these rumors, and it seemed incredible to him that America would support the movement.

"It's what I heard," said Arturo. "Whether or not it's the truth depends on many things."

Tori addressed Santino once again. "What do your friends in Palermo say to this?"

"They were more interested in the Communist political strength spreading over the land. I, too, have heard such rumors. If it's important I'll check it out."

Santino gazed up into the eyes of Athena as she poured more wine. In the instant their eyes met, he read a message in them. Color rose to his face. Quickly he averted his eyes to see if they'd been observed. Excitement surged through him, at the same time he flooded with annoyance at the implications of such a look. Still, was it possible that she could care for him? He stole another glance—but by that time Athena had moved around the table, her eyes demurely lowered. Santino was elated. Blood pounded in his brain and his heart swelled with excitement as sweat poured from every pore in his body. Since before the war when he had preached from the pulpit, he'd been smitten with her beauty. Santino didn't know it yet, but he was deliriously in love.

"It's important," said Tori. "What the hell's wrong with you? Your hands are trembling, *padre*. Are you all right?" Tori studied him intently.

Every eye was upon him and Santino squirmed uncomfortably thinking they could read the truth in his eyes. "It's the wine. It's always heady when it's new."

Finally Tori unleashed the bombshell. "It's important because we've been approached by Francesco Bello and the Duke de Gioia to attend a meeting in Catania. The Partionists want Salvatore to support their cause." His voice, quiet and subdued, hadn't fully registered on the others, with the exception of his mother, whose face screwed up into a scowl.

Tori kissed his fingertips with a flourish, in full approval of her cooking. "As usual, Mamma, everything is delicious."

Antigone didn't acknowledge his praise. Her mind had stopped at the center of his announcement. "You won't go, of course," she told him. Confused by the message in his eyes she faltered. "Will you, Tori?" She studied him inscrutably as the others grew silent and motionless.

Tori broke the tension with a gentle reprimand. "What do you think?" he asked his paladins. "Here, I'm hailed as the King of Montegatta and my mamma treats me as if I were not yet toilet trained."

The others laughed in good spirits along with Tori. Antigone said nothing. She entered the pantry and returned with a large platter of *pinolatti*—deep-fried confections shaped like pine needles, dipped in honey and sprinkled with cinnamon and topped with powdered sugar. She placed the plate before Tori. "It's a trap," she said, *sotto voce*.

Again in the silence, the men refrained from speaking. They devoured the entire plateful of confections in a reverent silence, after which they extolled praises for the deli-

322

cacies. They sat back patting their stomachs, complaining they'd made gluttons of themselves.

"I said, it's a trap," Antigone persisted.

"All right, Mamma, what makes you certain it's a trap?" Having already sent his reply to *Capitano* Francesco Bello, he wasn't ready to reveal his position as yet.

"Have I taught you nothing, Tori? You can't trust the nobility," she retorted. "They've been unsympathetic to the peasants' cause for centuries. Hah! What irony! They want you, Salvatore, a peasant, to come to their aid! *Butana u diaoro!* Without you they can do nothing. They'll use you, make no mistake about it, to do all their dirty work, all the low, degrading, marauding and killing necessary to promote their cause so they won't soil their dainty hands. Yes, my son, they'll use you to be their right arm. But, clasped tightly in their left, they will keep in reserve the power to annihilate you. The entire nobility is full of duplicity, treachery—and a highly perishable loyalty. At the first sign of trouble, their loyalty to you will thin out and dissolve. Then it will be you whom they'll sacrifice on their altars of gold." Antigone's voice contained no arrogance, no repudiation, no egotism. She simply stated what she believed to be a self-evident truth.

Once again the room grew pregnant with silence. They studied Antigone, noting her great face and luminous eyes. They acknowledged her words, weighing them carefully. Hadn't history already proven them true?

Vincenzo, who used no cream or sugar, stirred his black coffee absently and continuously. Santino rolled a lit cigar back and forth between thumb and fingers, flicking ashes from it from time to time in a nervous gesture. Holding a few walnuts in the palm of his hand, Tori crushed them open and sorted out the meat from the shells, popped them into his mouth, and allowed the shells to crumble off his hands onto the dish in front of him. Arturo simply sat forward, his elbows on the table, his hands supporting his chin. They hung on to every word Antigone spoke.

"It matters not to these feudal *latifondisti* which way the votes go as long as they can eat on their silver and gold encrusted plates, as long as they can sip their wines from imported crystal and are permitted to keep their bellies fat and their perverse concubines intact. For these pleasures, they would sell their souls!" She continued in an articulation not lost on the others.

"Do you really believe it matters to them whether the peasants who till their lands starve or die? Do you think

323

they care if the less fortunate remain ignorant, without education? Haven't these past few years proven my point. They are obtuse and insensitive where the problems of the peasants are concerned. Who among them released their hoarded grain? None of them!"

"As usual, *Signora*, you speak with Solomonic wisdom," said Santino. He turned to Tori. "What, in your opinion, is so special about the Partitionist movement? Doesn't it breed monarchy? Haven't we had our fill of monarchy, the empowered nobility and their corruptive practices?"

Vincenzo spoke up. Been silent for the most part, his Vincenzo, been silent for the most part, his mind on other matters, spoke up. "They want you, Tori? All these land barons want you? These *pezzenovanti*, high in government want you on their side? Bandits, no less, to become their allies?" He couldn't handle the convoluted logic of diametrical opposites forming a symbiotic relationship.

Tori raised a gentle brow and shrugged imperceptibly, an enigmatic smile playing faintly across his lips.

"What's so surprising in that?" asked Arturo. "Even Garibaldi, while employing a strategy aimed at unifying the two Kingdoms, found it necessary to make deals with men he'd normally been repelled by—those *mafiosi*, that 'honored' brotherhood."

Tori's eyes snapped open. Without moving his head he fixed stern, disapproving eyes on the former carnival man. The room became electric. Suddenly Arturo, realizing what he'd said, flushed and squirmed under Tori's cold eyes. Antigone took her cue. "What Arturo just said reinforces my earlier statements. The defense rests her case."

Vincenzo, nonetheless played with the idea. "It's a great honor to be summoned by such men of stature, no? They must respect you substantially, cousin." He nodded as if to himself. "Power such as ours can't be ignored. With it comes respect, no matter who controls it. It carries a great deal of dignity which God knows you've deserved by all the deeds you've masterminded. "Listen, cousin, I'm not as smart as you or the *padre* here, but, I think it's an honor to be approached by such men. At least hear them out."

"No! No! Not if they want my son to clean out the septic-tank conscience of their minds!" snapped his aunt, with fiery eyes blazing at him. She turned to her son, imploring him. "No." She took a new tack with him.

"I know how you must feel. Resplendent and bursting with pride to have been called upon by these titled landlords to help solve their problems. You, with the red blood of peasants running through your veins, with only a limited education, must feel exhalted and puffed up with a deceptive feeling of importance to have been called upon by these titled men of dubious worth. But mark my words, Alessandro. It is you who are the important one—not they. Here in our world, which you command and control, is where you belong. Here, you reign supreme. I ask that you consider my words before making your decision. Then I'll be satified you've used your own will to guide you.

"I can't confine your thinking only to what I've learned in my lifetime, for you were born in another time. Let me only impart to you this wisdom, as old as time itself, which hasn't been altered by generations of distorted thinking. Once you agree to do their dirty work, it will be you, labeled with their crimes and deeds, who shall pay the penalty, one way or another. And it shall be you whom they'll dispose of, at their convenience. Each time these noblemen look upon your countenance and see, reflected upon it, reminders of their own vile and contemptible deeds, you shall be marked for death; these grand feudal lords can't tolerate constant reminders of their own malevolent and iniquitous crimes. I beg you, my son, stay here where you're a king among your people. Here, you know at all times what the highest of peasants think, for you are superior to him in knowledge, education and intelligence. If you choose to walk among barons, dukes and princes and condescend to become their puppet, forever, you shall be to them, the lowest of low. . . ." Antigone wasn't finished. "They boast of generations of knowledge, intelligence and royal breeding in their blood and bones. Yet, among them is more immorality, more duplicity and cunning—more irreverence to God in one noble head, I say, than in the minds of ten thousand peasants."

Tori laughed at the concern in her articulate eyes. eyes.

"Why such a sad face, Mamma *bedda?* Don't you know they'd have to get up very early indeed to fool a man who never sleeps?" He laughed again, trying to infect the others with a gayer spirit, even though his heart wasn't in it. "Besides, I've already sent my reply to his *elegance,* the Duke de Gioia, and to his puppet, Francesco Bello."

They were stunned—all of them. They looked expectantly at him. Antigone knew the look on his face. Now, she waited to hear the words.

"I informed his excellency that the city streets are too slippery for my horse!"

325

"*Bravo*, Alessandro," cried Antigone.

"*Bravo!*" the others echoed her words.

In the excitement, Santino hugged Athena, who stood at his side watching her brother, anxiously waiting for his reply. The room filled with shocked silence. Every eye was upon Santino, and he blushed a cherry pink.

"Forgive me," he apologized to the mildly astonished matriarch who exchanged glances with her daughter. "I meant no impertinence. I was carried away by the good news. . . ."

Athena lowered her thickly fringed lashes, so the delight in them wouldn't show. *He must feel something for me*, she told herself. *I hope. I hope. . . .*

Tori observed both Athena and Santino in silence. "Are you feeling any better, Athena?" he expressed his fraternal concern.

Blushing at the attention, she muttered. "I'm fine. It's nothing."

"What did the doctor say?"

"He says it's nothing!"

"Nothing!" exclaimed her mother. "This nothing causes her to bang her head against the door when the pain grows intolerable! These doctors aren't worth their salt. Nowadays they dispense aspirins if you can't have a good bowel movement."

"*Padre*, take Athena to Palermo," Tori said. "Make sure she sees a specialist. Talk with him. They won't double talk you. I want to know what ails my sister. You tell him, she's the sister of Salvatore. Spare no expense. I want her well." He leveled his dark eyes on the former priest.

"It's difficult to find good doctors," said Arturo.

"We'll find out what's ailing you, what's causing so much pain" Tori told his sister. He was astonished when Athena angrily spun around and left the room.

A loud piercing scream interrupted further comment. Athena rushed into the room, breathlessly. "Tori! Mamma! Someone come quickly! There's a giant beast in our back yard!" she exclaimed.

Guns drawn, the men ran towards the rear of the house. Tori first to reach the door, opened it, peered into the darkness, turned, and grinned impishly. He beckoned the others and slipped his Browning back into its holster. "Come, Mamma! Athena, come see the giant beast," he said smiling.

Napoleono had jumped the side fence, entered the yard

and stood contentedly nibbling leaves from a huge, spreading fig tree at the rear of the terrace.

"Look, Mamma. Isn't he beautiful? Vincenzo and the other men gave him to me today. He is like the one in the photograph, with Bonaparte." He stroked the stallion's head, nuzzled his own face close to him.

Vincenzo turned on the courtyard lights illuminating the stallion. Antigone froze. The words—those irrevocable words flashed across her mind: *It shall be a white horse reined in silver profusion. His horse and bridle must be protected by the sign of earth and fire."*

Donna Sabattini's voice pierced her consciousness; she paled and felt faint, as tiny bubbles of perspiration erupted on her face. There was no mistaking the *strega's* prophecy, she told herself in those next few moments.

"Don't you like my horse?" asked Tori grasping her arm to steady it. "Mamma, what's wrong with you?"

She averted her eyes. How could she tell him. Everything inside her wanted to blurt out the whole story, but all she could manage when she regained her composure was, "Yes, Tori. It's a fine horse. *Cento anni.* May you both live a hundred years." She walked to the stallion's side and stroked its mane with trembling hands; then, turning quickly, she fled into the house. At any other time she'd have been ecstatic over the Arabian, for her love for horses was known to her family. Knowing this, the others exchanged bewildered glances.

"What will you call him?" asked Athena nuzzling the horses head.

Tori grinned. "Napoleono."

"I had to ask," she replied knowingly.

A few moments later Antigone returned to her son's side. She raised the Eye of God amulet and positioned it around his neck.

"What's this? What's this, Mamma? An amulet from you?" He winked at the others and, holding it away from his chest, he examined the disc carefully. He was partially amused and a bit irritated at the incongruity of her act, so opposed to her general lack of belief in such things.

"Don't ask," she retorted with unmistakable petulance. "Just wear it for me and don't take it off." She ran back inside the house, hoping he wouldn't question her. Moments later, when she heard the commotion outside, she ran out to investigate, and found the men huddled about the lone figure of a boy.

"Tell me what you're doing hiding in the bushes?" demanded Tori.

"I'm here because I admire you and want to join with your gang," replied a young lad, Danillo, the son of a war widow—himself a petty thief, with the slick ability to squirm in and out of scrapes.

Everyone but Tori laughed at the youth and gave him courage. "There's nothing for me with the other boys my age. I want to be near the great Salvatore!"

Tori stared at the lad with the proper amount of menace. "Go home, Danillo. Don't let me catch you where you don't belong again." Not for one minute did he believe the lad. He boxed the boy's ears, led him off the property, and gave him a playful boot in the butt. "If I ever see you here again, I'll use my gun. You hear?"

Since Tori's affection for children was such, his men thought it strange that Tori should be harsh and punitive with the lad. Their silence was an indictment. Danillo, thinking he'd put one over on Tori, left the premises. He didn't take the threat seriously and convinced himself that it left the door open for his next try at gleaning information for which he was to be paid a considerable sum.

Staring after him, Tori let his face grow implacable. Hard lines set in around his lips, and they drooped somewhat in brooding. "Now, they send babies to spy on us," he told the others. "Has he ever been around here before?" he asked his mother.

"I'm not sure—" Antigone shook her head.

"From now on, try to remember anyone you might see around the house who has no business here. No matter what reason they give to you, let me know who they are."

"Yes, my son," she replied dutifully. *Now it begins,* she told herself, trying to control the squeamishness that wrenched at her stomach.

An hour later, Tori stood in solitude at the Temple of Cats, aptly named by the ancient Romans who'd brought snow leopards and mountain lions to the area to guard their women during summer retreats and vacations away from Rome. Long after the Romans had abandoned Sicily to her next conqueror, alley cats had begun coming from all the neighboring villages to congregate at this spot around midnight. By morning they'd disappear as mysteriously as they'd appeared. The inability of anyone, including the proficient storytellers who had perpetuated the tale, to give a satisfactory reason for the continuing phenomenon gave rise to a superstitious belief that the small alley cats came in search of the spirits of their "ancestors," the lions and leopards who once had prowled the area in dignified majesty.

As Napoleono roamed the temple floor, unrestricted, Tori smoked a cigarette, seated on a boulder, staring out at the villages below. The presence of Danillo, spying on him, had provoked a bitter despair in him. When would the treacheries end? There seemed no relief in sight.

The new government formed recently in Rome had dissolved in a twinkling. What Tori had started two years before had stretched into a long, arduous task, filled with constant dangers, violent jealousies, hatred and disagreements which he'd kept in check only by employing an iron-fisted discipline. What he'd embarked upon, thinking it would only be a temporary expedient, had already consumed too much of his time. How much more could he endure of this demanding role into which he'd eased himself? Where could he go from here? His people were well fed. Crime had dropped to its lowest rate in the history of his province. What more could he do until the war ended? He was overwhelmed, considering these dilemmas.

But, there was more provoking excitement in Tori. For two years he'd been secretly considering an important move, and finally he'd made the decision to meet with his Godfather, Don Barbarossa. He'd planned what he'd say and do, and now that the decision had been made he grew apprehensive and trembled with an inner excitement, much like the one he had felt when he'd received Napoleono. How many tims he had contemplated the encounter, only to tell himself that he didn't dare present himself to so powerful a dignitary until he himself had attained a certain degree of importance! Would the Don know him? he wondered. Had he recognized the name *Salvatore* in the papers? So many men in Sicily shared the same name and bore no relation to each other, it was possible that the Don wouldn't associate the name to that of his own Godson.

God Almighty, how exciting it would be for him to meet so fantastic a man of legend, he told himself. In any event, it was time for Tori to bring to fruition certain carefully laid plans, and he needed his Godfather's influence to harvest his meticulous strategy.

His thoughts trailed to his mother's indignation earlier at supper and he concluded that, as usual, she was correct in her assessment. But Tori also concluded that she didn't understand his thinking, nor the intricacies of politics. Couldn't she understand that for Tori to secure the amnesty he sought, he had to align himself with a powerful political party? Who could be more powerful than the former Monarchist, who'd formed a new coalition under the Partitionist banner?

Tori felt that he'd employed superb strategy in declining Captain Bello's initial proposal; it would only make him appear to be more vital to their plans. Besides, he'd become enough of a warrior to know their plans would fail without the support of a powerful guerrilla army—and the only such phenomenon in Sicily was Salvatore. He smiled and moving forward on the boulder, the amulet around his neck bounced about on his chest.

Tori caught it and, holding it a few inches away from his eyes, he struck a match on the stone so he could examine it better in the glow of light. What the hell had possessed his mother to give him this chatelaine? He removed it from around his neck and peered at it in the light of the full moon, and for no reason at all fastened it on Napoleono's bridle paraphernalia, allowing it to rest on the horse's forehead between its large eyes.

That night riding back over the twisting roads to his house, Tori wondered how *Capitano* Bello would react to his message. Surely, he'd be outraged, incensed, and filled with the usual mortification any of the land barons felt in having to consort with a mere peasant. He laughed aloud, knowing full well that the class-conscious constipation suffered by those men in the baronial circles would grow increasingly unpleasant when they read the reply they got from a mere peasant. He felt a sense of exquisite amusement as he pictured the fatuous nobles poring over his letter.

CHAPTER 25

" '*The City street is too slippery for my horse!*' Indeed!" roared Captain Francesco Bello aloud to himself. "Damn Salvatore! Damn the Duke de Gioia! Damn the whole Partitionist party and their muleheaded myopia!" Offended by the bandit's impudence, he slapped Salvatore's letter furiously against his thigh and paced the floor of the magnificently appointed, Moorish-influenced salon like a tiger at bay. He moved with the pretentious *panache* of a Nutcracker Suite soldier, dressed in his spanking new, royal blue serge uniform with mirror polished buttons and gold braid. Pausing momentarily before a roaring fire in the open hearth fireplace, he attempted to ward off the chill of the rainy night as he awaited the arrival of his host, the Duke de Gioia.

Outside, torrential rains splashed noisily against stained glass windows and the blustery winds, rising in ferocious intensity, denuded nearby citrus and filbert trees in its wake. Startled by the mighty force of the elements, Bello paused to listen to the eerie sounds. He asked himself, as a sinking depression engulfed him, why he had accepted this role. What minor flaws in his own character had induced him to subject himself to all the travail meted out to him as the new head of the Partitionist party?

Stuffing the offensive letter into his tunic, he reached for a nearby brandy decanter, poured himself a stiff drink, and quickly gulped it down. The blazing trail of warmth, shuddering through him, felt good. He dragged a high-backed Emperor's chair closer to the fire, plunked himself down in it, stretched his long legs, and allowed his arms to fall slackly over the arms of the carved rosewood. For a time he concentrated on the fire, fascinated by the myriad designs reflected by the flickering firelight on his black shiny boots, Mellowed by the brandy, warmed by the fire, and still despondent over his involvement, Bello became reflective.

He thought back a few months to a time shortly after New Year's in January of 1945 when there had gathered in his baronial estate in Caltagirone, southwest of Catania, a distinguished brood of politicians—influential Monarchists, representing a cross-section of the new movement favoring Sicily's separation from Italy who wanted no part in the growing threat of communism. These men, loyalists, considered themselves patriots; above all, however, were feudalists who staunchly wanted to cling to what had been theirs for centuries. They were men who'd continue to hold back large areas of Sicily from cultivation if it meant littering the street with corpses of all the peasants who dared buck their system. Having turned a profitable trick with Fascists and all previous conquerors for centuries, these breed of men, out of greed, would secure themselves, in the uncertain future, by grabbing the power wherever and from whomever they could.

An underground guerrilla movement, fostered by the Allies and later abandoned by them due to the swiftness in which politics fluctuated daily, had attracted the attention of many politicians who held high hopes in the mad scramble for power when Sicily became an independent state. Leadership in this movement changed periodically and would continue to change. Due to the unsettled conditions and chaotic state of Sicily's future, countless ambitious men, prepared to outguess History, were also prepared to shift loyalties from party to party, depending on which side showed the greatest potential and wielded the greatest power.

These men, a portion of them, had gathered in Bello's drawing room that day, having appointed as their spokesman a certain Baron Ermano Mattinata. He was a dark-skinned, ferret-eyed man whose black and piercing eyes seemed constantly to calculate a man's net worth. With all his wealth he always appeared dowdy, in a crumpled suit with a vest that rode up on him and always needed to be jerked into place, despite his thin, scrawny frame. This penny-pinching noble, well known for his niggardliness, spoke with supercilious pomposity. Like every man there, the Baron ruled his lands with a savage despotism and maintained a tenacious hold on his lands. They'd do anything, these landowners—anything, just to keep the status quo. To keep their bloodied hands manipulating the levers of their locomotives of oppression was all they lived for.

Tugging primly at his vest, Baron Mattinata had set aside his wine glass on that eventful day, stood up, and cleared his throat. His fists, balled tightly at his sides as he addressed Bello, should have given the lawyer insight into his perennial plea of penury. "My dear Bello," He had raised his voice to a high falsetto and unballed his fists. He slipped them into the high pockets of his pants and parading like a stiff-backed ostrich before his companions, winking cagily at some, nodding to others in a conspiratorial manne, he then showered his attention on their host.

"We've come to you out of respect *Avvocato* Bello," he began in a fawning manner which irked Bello. "You seem to have found a magic formula in keeping an orderly estate. Since you control your peasants well, you know what our problems are. It's simply marvelous, my dear Bello, how you've kept your peasants from claiming uncultivated lands. You see, we've been watching you."

Francesco Bello, a tall, slim man cut an imposing figure as he stroked his drooping moustache and nodded in silence. He swelled with pride at the formidable gathering of nobility under his roof. That they'd collectively seek his service for some small business venture impressed him

332

increasing his feelings of self-worth. He kept his eyes on the manipulative Baron nonetheless.

"You're well known to us," the Baron said, "respected for many shrewd business manipulations and, of course, for your political successes. All of which qualify you, my dear Bello, for the honor my associates and I intend to confer upon you." The Baron enumerating the salient points of his proposal. However, his duplicity and guile were so obvious to Bello and in a way insulting.

Too many compliments unnerved him and Bello braced himself. He took a good look at the distinguished gathering and he knew for certain they wanted something more than a mere favor. He wondered what it might be just as the Baron's voice sliced into his thoughts again.

"A month ago, Canepa, a feisty, silver-tongued orator whom you've no doubt heard of . . ." said the Baron, wiping the dry corners of his lips with his fingertips. "As scandalous as it is to speak of, this former leader of the Separatists was recently exposed as a communist! A communist, dear Bello," he blustered on tactlessly.

"Canepa a communist? No!" Bello feigned astonishment.

"Dear Bello, how we all wish your words were true," wailed the Baron. None of us were aware of his shady background. We gave him free rein to do as he wished to promote our aims. Money! Supplies! Information! We backed this traitor to the end! What we were prepared to do for him! You wouldn't believe!"

"I've heard many things about Canepa," said Bello vaguely. An eccentric—But it's definite he's a Red? It's certain?"

"Certain? Dear Bello, it's past history now. All the time he planned to do us in! Imagine? He used *our* money, *our* backing, just to get himself fixed up good with the Reds!"

"Where's Canepa now?" asked Bello pointedly . . . and with good reason.

"I can't answer you, my dear Bello. It's none of my doing. . . ."

"Nevertheless, *my dear Baron,* he's dead! Is he not?" he asked cagily.

"Then, you know? . . ." The Baron's eyes darted towards the others.

"It was an excellent hoax to keep his death a secret so as not to split up the factions, my dear Baron. But it was bound to leak out." Bello, a professional lawyer, knew the cat-and-mouse game well.

"It's none of my doing, believe me, Bello. I don't involve myself in such lowly acts," said the Baron. "I only handle diplomatic matters. . . ."

"How was it that none of your associates detected the truth of Canepa's politics? *We* recognized his leftist leanings long ago. Weren't you aware this man Canepa was once certified insane and locked up in an asylum? Didn't your people check into his background?" demanded Bello with dripping sarcasm.

"We knew he'd been with British Intelligence in 1943, and that he'd carried out a successful sabotage mission against the Germans near Syracuse. He parachuted to Northern Italy and organized the Canepa Brigade against the Reds! Even the Americans were favorable to Canepa! And with sixteen guerrilla bands ready to follow his orders—wouldn't you have been impressed?"

Bello shrugged. "The man was born of insane courage!"

"Insane courage? *Managghia!* He had to be insane to think he could fool the British, the Americans, *and* the Sicilian land barons! His plans were to seduce the Sicilian land barons, then, demand their lands or their heads! What a catastrophe! Oh, what a catastrophe that would have been!"

"Managghia!" exclaimed Bello. "What a special brand of guts that took!"

"Guts? You just said the man was insane! Demented—no? No one in his right mind would play three sides against the middle! Satan finally caught up to him!"

"You're telling me the Sicilian land barons had nothing to do with his death?"

"My dear Bello, between the British, Americans, and Russians, we Sicilians are lowest on the totem pole of worth. Canepa's communism didn't conform to Communist party lines. A separate Sicily, they felt, would be dominated by the Allies, and of necessity would be Anti-Russian and Anti-Communist. Canepa's treachery was leaked out through the Ministry of the Interior. We assumed that many red faced officials had decided it was best for all concerned if Canepa were eliminated. . . ."

Bello suggestedly knowingly. "That he was—wasn't he?"

Baron Mattinatta glanced uneasily at the others. "I repeat it wasn't *our* doing.

"What happened to the sixteen guerrilla bands?" asked Bello abruptly. Are they still available?"

The Baron's eyebrows twitched nervously. He shrugged. "It's my understanding they scattered, fearing the same betrayal as Canepa's."

Bello stroked his moustache thoughtfully. "This is a most difficult and weighty assignment you wish upon me," he began with noticeable reluctance.

"If we didn't consider you capable we shouldn't have come this great distance to pay you our respect. . . ." The Baron's hopes accelerated.

Bello shook his head dubiously. I'm afraid this will require considerable thought and study. I'm no military man. You all know that, don't you?" He didn't wait for an answer. "I can see the merit of Canepa's plan to employ guerrillas. It's the only way of demolishing government troops and *carabinieri*. . . ." Bello strutted before his captive audience in his elegantly tailored grey suit. He expounded pompously, as if he possessed the experience of a commander in Caesar's Legions. "Victory could be achieved using Pacino's bandits in the east and employing the strength of—what's his name—in the west? . . . Ah, yes, Salvatore! And mind you I'm no military strategist. . . ." Bello was impressed with his own reasoning.

"We want no common criminals to fight our cause. . . ." argued the Baron.

Palermo's Mayor Tedesco spoke up and, with perhaps the most prophetic statement of his career, he declared, "Salvatore's no common criminal! He's one of a kind!" He received scathing looks from most of the men. "You must admit—he's most unusual. There's been no one else like him. . . ." his voice dropped and he sat back, recoiling from their coldness.

Why a man of wealth and talent as Francesco Bello, a reputable landowner and lawyer with a successful practice, should abandon his professional leanings and expose himself to the perils presented as head of the Partitionist party was a mystery to his closest friends. Bello, certainly not the man Canepa had been, knew nothing of guerrilla warfare or military stratagems, but he possessed a special brand of courage, talent as a persuasive orator—and a driving ambition which dimmed his perspective. His insatiable vanity, and a superego that doted on the attention given him by these class-conscious, arrogant feudalists and Mafia Dons brought him to accept his role as captain of the Partitionist Army and plunged in valiantly to promote this venture.

There followed moments of sobriety when Francesco considered he was daft for permitting himself to be seduced by these crafty serpents. The months following his acceptance had proved trying and frustrating. There were too many people to be pleased in his pupet role as yes-man to a baronial circle of eccentric, petulant and irrational politicians. A man oriented in military protocol might have been more forceful, and less inclined to put up with their childish demands. Unfortunately for Bello, he was to learn, soon enough, that these bird-brained men whose heads soared above the clouds of reality wanted expedients for which they weren't prepared to pay.

"My dear Captain Bello," Duke de Gioia's voice interrupted Bello's reverie. "How good to see you again," The corpulent noble entered the salon on the arm of his mistress, *Principessa* Gabriella Rothschild, a slim, fashionably dressed, disdainful blonde, whose presence infused the air with fragrant perfume.

Bello rose to his full height, forced a pleasant smile on his face, clicked his heels together and bowed. He kissed the *Principessa*'s hand and embraced the Duke with the proper decorum. "My pleasure, Excellency."

The amenities over, Bello lost no time in explaining his mission. Reporting Salvatore's reply gave rise to his annoyance that this uncouth upstart of a bandit should have answered his five-page communique with a one-line sentence.

"My dear Bello, why do you fret? Relax. You don't find *me* upset by the antics of this *contadino*, do you?" The Duke moved laboriously towards his mistress, seated next to him on the silk damask sofa, he lit her cigarette and smiled at her in a secret way that annoyed Bello.

"Why do I fret?" asked Bello. "I'll tell you why. Look at this!" He tossed Salvatore's letter to him angrily and watched as the Duke fastened his *pince-nez* glasses onto his bulbous nose.

The Duke glanced disdainfully at the crude foolscap paper and the one-line reply and permitted the letter to flutter to the floor. He sighed with an attitude of boredom. "Why do you let yourself be inconvenienced by this lowly peasant? Why you need this arrogant, publicity-seeking plebeian, this son of a common sheepherder, is beyond me." The Duke, puffing on his thin cigar, dabbed at a few ashes on his vest.

Gabriella avoided eye contact with either of the men. She sipped her drink, appraised the diamonds on her fingers and wrists, and kept her thoughts to herself. Reflected in her azure eyes was an obvious boredom of long standing, one she didn't bother to obscure on occasion.

"You don't mean that the way I think you do, excellency," said Bello with narrowed eyes.

The Duke exasperated. "I meant it exactly the way I

said it. Wherever I go the subject of this peasant Salvatore monopolizes the conversation. I tell you, I'm bored with him. Bored—bored—bored!" He was panting noticeably. The Duke was fastidiously dressed, sporting elegant jewels that were somewhat offensive to good taste in wartime. This indolent noble had been courted by Don Barbarossa into thinking he'd be the ideal king in the future monarchy of Sicily, unaware that the Don considered this laughable lump of a man, with his outlandish white wig, only as a front; an ideal puppet to sit on the throne and disguise the *real* monarchy of Matteo Barbarossa. Earlier when he had confessed to Bello that he was bored, bored, bored, he meant exactly that, for the enticement of reigning as King of Sicily had been stretched over too long a period of time. He'd lusted after the throne, but it had become too elusive. He had tasted its heady elixir for so long and it had grown flat, and he needed continuous doses of flattery and reassuring praises to revitalize and rekindle his interest.

When he had first received Don Barbarossa's *communiqués*, the Duke had been in Switzerland, sitting out the war. He'd met Gabriella there in a Swiss chalet. Having considered the Don's proposal, he concluded it was only fitting that if he were to occupy a throne, he should have a princess at his side to reign as queen.

The two years in which the Duke had been forced to play a waiting game before he could be crowned King of Sicily, had grown tedious and too exacting to him. Recuperation from Canepa's treachery, painfully slow, had resulted in damaged pride—and in untold shame. Ridicule had been hurled upon him by his colleagues. Now, they weren't ready to fully trust another man. He had become cautious in his dealings and jaded in his attitude towards Bello, and an invisible barrier of hard-nosed skepticism had sprung up to disconcert the Captain. This finite comparison to Canepa, totally unfair to Bello, had greatly encumbered her progress. Having given him *carte blanche* to promote the Partitionist plans, the Monarchists now set up obstacles detering the former lawyer at every turn.

Bello stood before the floor-to-ceiling fireplace, staring glumly into the embers, sullen and downcast. Watching him, the Duke felt his temper abate. Perhaps he'd been too harsh on him. After all, it hadn't been his fault that the Kingdom had proved too slippery to grasp for the time being. Every monarch in history had kept at his side a faithful captain, a personal paladin in whom he confided.

Why wouldn't Bello be such a man, to inspire me, thought the Duke. He expressed himself in modulated tones, and addressed his captain.

"Try to understand, Bello. I come from a long line of nobles used to consorting with kings, emperors and presidents." It's degrading to be constantly reminded that some pubescent, publicity-seeking peasant, a depraved and immoral brute with no respect for law and order and who probably copulates with animals, is a man with whom men of our calibre must deign to deal with. . . ."

Gabriella's usually expressionless eyes, a pale azure, smoldered into angry sapphires. Across the room, her eyes met Bello's. They both flushed hotly, but for different reasons. Swiftly, she lowered her gaze, broke eye contact with him, and discreetly once again kept her thoughts to herself. Not Bello. He burned. He took umbrage at the Duke's insipid, double-domed, and thoughtless remarks. Bello, himself the son of peasant stock who had wisely turned into merchants when they could no longer tolerate the despair and suffocation of spirit brought on by oppressive nobles, felt insulted. Having only recently become a part of this political clique, he knew, despite the wealth he'd amassed, that he'd never be fully accepted as one of them. *Well, fuck it,* he told himself. *I'll have my say and if his fucking excellency doesn't like it—he can stick it!*

"He may be that and everything else you say, including a filthy degenerate, although I'd consider it most unlikely, Excellency," said Bello with the bit in his teeth. "But this pubescent, publicity-seeking plebeian, as you see fit to call him, controls the western section of our country! The sooner you and the other noble Monarchists recognize the fact that we need the strength of this powerful young Sicilian, who champions his people, the sooner our cause will be victorious! Are you aware that Federal officers no longer go through Salvatore's territory? That an *entente* exists between the security police and this unique bandit? Whatever remains of the *carabinieri* are under his rule and protection!"

"My dear Francesco, don't upset yourself," suggested the Duke. There's plenty of time. Relax. Pour yourself a drink. Brandy?—*Strega?* Help yourself. . . ." He gestured apathetically towards the glittering sideboard of sparkling crystal decanters and opalescent Venetian glass. "Then we shall sit down and discuss this situation like civilized men. . . ."

Resolute to the point of bullheadedness, Bello clenched his teeth and bit back the desire to tell off this overstuffed popinjay. Damned pretentious nobles! All alike! No concept of reality lodged in their antiquated brains! They're more ludicrous than any breed of men I've met, he cursed inwardly.

Principessa Gabriella Rothschild, a German Jewess who had escaped Hitler's wrath by fleeing to Switzerland, glanced at Bello in mock amusement. She could read his mind, for his thoughts draped his face like a week old laundry hung out to dry. She smiled internally. Children! All of them! These Sicilians played games that children would have abandoned long ago. She turned her attention to the ornate music box placed gracefully on the carved rosewood table next to her. With her long red-lacquered fingernails, she toyed with the switch and finally pushed it into motion. She languidly watched the small figures of cupids and dancing maidens revolve below a figure of Venus, curtsy, and whirl about on a track to the accompaniment to the habañera from *Carmen*. Her sardonic and amused eyes met Bello's and held.

Sharply annoyed by this intrusion into his thoughts, Bello cast a meaningful glance in her direction, then walked to a sideboard to pour himself a drink and refresh those of his host and hostess, wondering still as he did why he had let himself get talked into this thankless position.

"I'd hoped we could settle the matter of Salvatore," began Bello, crossing the room and seating himself opposite the Duke. "If we don't encourage his participation, we may as well abandon our plans."

De Gioia sighed heavily. "You won't permit me to enjoy your company without talk of this infernal bandit! Very well, tell me what you have in mind. . . ." The Duke's eyes never wavered from Gabriella.

"Since the stubborn billygoat refuses to come to us—I propose we go to him!"

Reluctantly, de Gioia removed his eyes from the girl. Glancing sharply at Bello he said imperiously. "Are you mad, my dear man? Are you positively senile? We'd be the laughing stock of Sicily!" The Duke tried in vain to lift himself out of the deep-cushioned sofa. After several attempts, Bello moved in and pulled him to his feet. Once erect, the grossly obese de Gioia, suffering from a malady called pure, unadulterated gluttony, paced painfully and laboriously about the room, fired by Bello's proposal.

"*Allora*—we shall have to become a laughing stock if it will win us Sicily!" Bello said firmly. "The establishment of a Sicilian monarchy, with full autonomy, will take all the military strength we can muster! Without it we haven't a whisper of a chance! None at all! It's obvious we need Salvatore more than he needs us, and I advise you to keep that fact uppermost in your mind!" he said with enough innuendo to cause the Duke to stop dead in his tracks and glance swiftly at him. Bello grew bolder. He added, "Regardless of what Don Matteo Barbarossa tells you!"

Their eyes locked and held, in duelistic silence. Watching them, Gabriella felt a rush of admiration for Bello whom she had considered to be a fatuous and over-ambitious marionette, nauseatingly condescending in his earlier poses. What a revelation! She felt like saying, "*bravo!*" Of course she didn't.

"We'll have to get full approval for this insanity!" said the Duke testily.

"Why? Why can't we tell them *after* we've effected a meeting with Salvatore? No one need know. If he refuses—there'll be no bitter vetch to swallow from our associates. If he agrees, we'll have cause to celebrate . . . *Pero*—I think we have the honey that will attract this pesky *zanzaro*, this mosquito who seems to irritate you to distraction," said Bello craftily.

In the silence, only the tinkling sounds of the music box permeated the room. 'Trust me, Excellency. With Pacino and his men in the east working in coordination with Salvatore in the west, we'll control the vote and rid ourselves of the Italian military police and government soldiers." Bello sipped the rest of the brandy and smacked his lips as his old confidence returned. The gouted Duke, with his swollen ankles, waddled about the room, wiping the perspiration from his cherubic face and pursing his lips in thought. He stopped at the ornately carved oaken table, opened a humidor, and offered a Havana to Bello, who accepted it with aplomb. For an instant Bello held his hand in the air, listened to the music and moved it rhythmically like a conductor in accompainment to the Bizet time.

"It's been a long time since I've enjoyed one of these, Excellency," Bello sniffed the cigar appreciatively and bit off one end; then he removed a candle from its holder and lit first the Duke's and then his own cigar. Outside the storm had risen; the rain and winds could be heard swooshing through the nearby trees.

"I love the rain—don't you?" Bello's voice filled the room. "Where was I? Oh, yes; Salvatore. We shall make him an enticing offer. Full commission as Colonel in the Partitionists' army, and complete amnesty for himself and his men if we emerge victorious. I understand this alone would be inducement enough. You see, he's obsessed with the idea of a pardon. I promise you, Excellency, Salvatore shall become a willing participant in our plans, a facile tool we can manipulate in any direction we choose. All bandits become as asses tied to the sun, once impressed with their own authority." His meaningful eyes shaded with subtleties only a crafty serpent could understand.

The Duke's grey eyes hung low in their sockets and grew heavy-lidded. He understood perfectly the treachery couched in Bello's words. It now became the Duke's pleasure to refill Bello's drink. Now they understood each other. He handed the glass back to his guest.

"To us," said the Duke, flushed with diabolical glee.

"To us!" echoed Bello, swelling with pride.

"By all means, to us," muttered the *Principessa*, who wasn't a princess at all, and had adopted the title in Switzerland to impress the other class-conscious prigs. She raised her glass towards them and smiled complacently. Inwardly she filled with contempt. They're both idiots! They talk as if they have cotton brains! If this man, Salvatore is half the man they say he is, he'll see through their deceit before they flick an eyelid. . . .

In recalling the photos she'd seen of Salvatore, and reading of his exploits and sheer daring she thought; *Now, here's a born leader! A real man! Just for once, I'd like to meet a real man! Just once.* . . . Her eyes lit up with such bright intensity that she caught the Duke's attention.

"Well, Captain Bello, it appears the *Principessa* must agree with our plans; see how the anticipation of such a proposal has stimulated her. . . ." Beaming with pleasure, he waddled to her side, bowed stiffly from the waist, kissed her hand, and patted it affectionately. "What a pleasure you are to me, Gabriella. . . ." His eyes filled with desire.

She would have liked nothing better than to clear his impression of her in that instant; instead, she lowered her eyes reservedly.

Captain Bello frowned. Discussing such vital plans in the presence of a third party, and a woman at that, left him disturbed. He sipped his brandy in silence, and kept his thoughts of her to himself, however benign or malignant her influence with the Duke might be.

Later that night, after Bello had retired, Gabriella sat at her dressing table, preparing for her hour of intimacy with the Duke. In her early thirties, she looked twenty two. Attractive, slim-figured but with ample bosoms, she had soft full lips which could turn petulant, even cruel on occasion. Her expressive eyes turned mysteriously blue or green at

341

random. Staring at her image narcissistically, she wondered why, of all the men she'd met at that Swiss chalet near Zurich, had she permitted herself to be seduced by Duke Federico de Gioia. Of course she knew the answer to her own question. She sighed deeply and considered it.

Twice her age, dazzled by her withdrawn charm, the Duke de Gioia had considered her, at first, to be a whorish bitch with insufferable airs of grandeur that somehow satisfied a masochistic quirk in his nature. On her he had showered costly gifts and extravagances that would have delighted a Lucretia Borgia, and through the art of costly persuasion he encouraged her to accompany him to Sicily, where he confided, he would soon be crowned king.

Carrying forged papers, her rapidly diminishing funds nearly gone, Gabriella, in a moment of black despair, had been forced to make a quick decision. It wasn't until she had been carefully tucked in the Duke's villa in Catania that she had revealed she was a German Jew who had escaped her homeland before Hitler had murdered six million of her kind and another six million other humans. The Duke had had his personal reasons for not caring what she was, of course.

Repulsed at first, by this giant of a man, she had later temporized and convinced herself she could have done worse. Anything was better than encountering Hitler or his dreaded SS men, she had reasoned. Now she suddenly found herself at the center of what promised to be a hotbed of political insurrection, in a foreign land, led by bloody nincompoops! She had never quite fathomed what the Duke's politics really represented. One day they were Monarchists, the next day Socialists. Then then became Separatists, now they were Partitionists. A late rumor, however true it might be, was that America was committed to back the Partitionists in their break from Italy, the Italy that had suddenly become an abomination to the Allies and had sprouted Communist horns—a fact which didn't set right either with the American, British and French, or the Sicilian feudalists.

Exposure to Hitler's brand of politics, she felt, qualified her to pass judgment on these hotheaded Sicilians, who by comparison to the Nazis were ridiculously naive. It would have accomplished nothing if she had deigned to tell Federico her views, for she learned long ago, a woman was sensible if she kept her thoughts to herself—particularly in Sicily, where she discreetly concealed any display of brain power. A glance at her five-carat diamond solitaire and her platinum and diamond bracelet convinced her she hadn't fared too badly. What the hell—

If she bided her time, she was thinking, the Duke would soon be dead. His overweight condition, his overtaxed heart, and the ills that plagued a man besieged with gluttony were horrendous. It was a miracle he'd lived this long. Not that she cared. If she had had her way, she would have preferred him dead. She hated him; she hated him in the same way she hated all men. But for Federico she reserved a particular loathing.

Wistfully she disrobed, slipped into a black sheer peignoir, and mentally prepared herself for the coming ordeal. Thank God, she only had to please Federico once a month. Thirty days each month she spent in dread of the moment to be spent in intimacy with him, and prepared herself as one might for an execution block or a chamber of horrors. At sixteen Gabriella had been mistress to a sadistic and cruelly inclined man; that had lasted until she was twenty-one, when finally she had worked up guts to escape his brand of torture—nightly torture, with her limbs tied to the bed, spread-eagled, whipped and beaten, burned with matches around the vagina, where the odor of burnt hair had sent her lover off into spasms of orgiastic pleasure. Nightmares, grotesque nightmares, she had taken in her stride until she had numbed herself into insensitivity. Lash marks had criss-crossed her body constantly; even now, after all these years, she bore faint scars. She'd never seen her youthful breasts without gnawed teeth ruts or purple weal marks until after she escaped the German's house. After that nothing a man did to her, or requested she do to him, had fazed her. Having been through the worst of it with the Nazi sadist, anything short of sadism had become a blessing. She had numbed herself to the grotesque sexual aberrations of men.

The first time of intimacy with the Duke, he appeared at her bedside without his toupee, wearing a stocking cap. Very well, she thought, some men wear socks to bed. What's wrong with a stocking cap? Due to his monstrous obesity, the only manner in which sex was possible with him was to mount him, or to engage in oral sex. Oral sex, because of its expediency, suited Gabriella. She could finish him off, drain him sufficiently, and cease contact with him, all in less than three minutes. Warned by doctors that his heart couldn't stand too much strain, Federico tended to space his sexual activities far enough apart to allow him to recuperate from the exertion.

On that first night, as she had moved her hands expertly

343

over his limp penis, she learned that by swearing at him, calling him vile names, she could excite him more readily, she had complied with his request, and when he had called to her, *"succhiare a' mi . . . succhiare a 'mi . . ."* she had obediently buried her head in his crotch and commenced her oral manipulations. Just a moment before ejaculation, eyes glittering maniacally, he'd torn off his stocking cap and pulled out tufts of hair from his head and stuffed them into his mouth! . . . .

Gabriella, who had thought she'd known every form of sexual perversion and all manner of deviants, had nearly choked on the yellowish, pale viscous substance that had spurted from the Duke's penis. Violently appalled by the scene she had vomited convulsively, and it hadn't been until the next morning that the dry heaves had ceased. His candy, perfume, messages, and other baubles had been rejected adamantly, and instantly returned to him. She had refused all communication with him and kept to herself in the Swiss Chalet. Finally, he had sent her a magnificent diamond and platinum bracelet and pleaded with her to listen to his story. The costly gift had weakened her resolve. She had permitted him to come to her suite, where with tear-filled eyes he had related his tale.

The Duke, it seemed, suffered from a form of trichophagia—an abnormal desire to break off one's hair and eat it during sexual release. It had all begun, he'd told her, when he was a small impressionable child. His mother, an Austro-Hungarian, with whom he had formed an abnormal attachment, had missed city life, her own Budapest, and the gay life of northern Italy. The Duke's father, away from the estate for so many long months of the year, had caused a terrible restlessness in the Duchess. She'd fondle her son during his bath, caress him and stimulate him more than a ten-year-old should be stimulated, and force him to watch her masturbate on occasion. Just before she climaxed, she would reach out for young Federico, grasp his head and hair with clutching fingers, and pull tight until she satisfied herself. Once, she had noticed his penis had erected from the erotic stimulation. Angry at what she deemed his indecent reaction she had grabbed at him and actually pulled out chunks of his hair. Whatever had caused him the further excitement—pain or whatever—he ejaculated. Further excited by seeing her son's semen, the Duchess had begun to copulate orally with him. At the point of her own arousal, before orgasm, once again she had pulled out chunks of his hair, and it had become his sad pattern of sexual fulfillment for life.

Tears had rolled down his punchinello face, and he had wept with bitter shame at his confession to Gabriella. He had begged her forgiveness, and promised her the world, if she'd tolerate this quirk in his sexual nature. She took her time deliberating, and, after weighing the factors, she had reasoned that the world was full of lunatics and madmen whose brains were scrambled, and as long as he didn't harm her—what could she lose? Once assured that she'd be rewarded amply for her attention and services, with priceless baubles, she had relented on the ground that she empathized with his problem. Coveting the gifts, she had begun with fierce determination to set them aside, and, as they accumulated, she had found herself waiting for the day he died, for he had provided generously for her in his will. Or, if that took too long, she'd told herself, she'd soon have enough set aside at war's end to go anyplace and live however she chose in luxurious comfort. . . .

"Ah, there you are my sweet, Federico," she purred seductively as the enormous blob of a man entered her boudoir, dressed in an elegant robe of Chinese silk with a stocking cap to match. "Come, I've been waiting anxiously for you, my sweet," she said in a deep, throaty voice, and, floating about the room like a graceful dancer, she began to dim the lights so she barely saw him. It eased the trauma. So did the champagne.

"My dearest," he began. "Would you mind if we put this off until tomorrow night? This chap Bello has tired me. His insufferable suggestions that this peasant, Salvatore, has so mesmerized his people that we are now dependent on him has filled me with such repugnance. . . ." He patted her head affectionately. "My dear you look positively ravishing tonight," he whined. "I had so looked forward to this night with you." Visibly petulant, he stuffed a chocolate cream into his mouth, from a small dish she kept at her bedside for him.

Loathing every moment spent with him, she dreaded the thought she might have to reenforce her courage for another twenty-four hours. Her belly tightened with revulsion. No! By all that was holy, nothing would deter her from getting the disgusting ordeal over with.

She reached out under his fat belly, pulled his limp sex organ from beneath his robe, through his pyjama fly, and began to knead it gently. Rewarded by a slight tremor, she felt more encouraged. It should be easy tonight.

"You mustn't allow this social frog, Bello, to interfere with your pleasure, my lord." she purred, leading him to the oversized bed, by his penis. "Why must you endure all this depressing nonsense? It's you who'll be King! You allow him to croak at you too often! You have needs which must be satisfied—no?" She pushed him down on the bed, where he sighed heavily and lay back, cooing, contentedly.

"My little pigeon, only you understand me. Oh, lucky was the day we met. . . ." He reached to squeeze one of her breasts, a small gesture of compensation for her service.

"Lie back, you fucking prick, and do as I say!" her voice rose and grew dominant and scathing. "You vile son of a whore! Bastard son of an oversexed whore!" she rasped like a raging fishwife.

"Yes! Yes!" he cried, his penis springing urgently to life. "Tell me what I am! I'm all those things you say! I'm no good! I'm a sow-fucking male whore, a craven and depraved humpbacked whale! Fuck me! Suck me! Shit all over me!" His voice was frenzied, his stocking cap falling off.

Gabriella knew her craft well. "You're so rotten the vultures turn away from you! I shall order six of my most disgusting slaves to defecate on your enormously fat belly, pee over you, make you eat their cunts, you screeching son of a bitch, lower than the whores of Satan. . . ." For an instant her voice was muffled by a gurgling sound as she finished him off. It took three minutes.

She helped him to his feet, coaxed him out the door, and accepted a small jewelled box. "Thank you my little pigeon," he said in a dazed breathlessness, with a dopey expression in his gazed wild eyes. He looked perfectly ridiculous with his stocking cap angled rakishly, but his heart, beating too swiftly and his breath, coming in short gasps prevented him from lingering. She closed and locked the door behind him.

Thank God! It was over for a month. She ran to the bathroom, washed her face and hands, and rinsed her mouth out with lemon and water in an effort to rid herself of the taste and feel of him. She turned on the bath water and bathed, scrubbing every inch of her skin until she felt cleansed. In a warm woolen robe she felt better. She had shut her eyes when he had pulled at the tufts of hair. It was less traumatic for her. She couldn't stand the sight of that billiard-ball head, with its small patches of fine hair growing sparsely and at random.

Reaching for a comforter, she dragged it across the Italian provincial bedroom and spread it on the chaise longue.

She'd never sleep in the bed in which she seduced the Duke until after the servants changed the linens.

Gabriella lay back on the damask lounge, under the glow of the lamp light gazing appreciatively at the ruby and diamond earrings the Duke had bestowed upon her. *Not bad for less than five minutes of work,* she told herself. She fell asleep admiring the gems, filled with curious thoughts of this man Salvatore, who, with his spectacular panache, had unknowingly upset the wealthiest man in Sicily, without knowing it.

This Salvatore must be some man! . . .

She stared at a photo of him she had clipped from a newspaper and slipped into the small book on the table in which she made little notes to herself daily. What was there about him that made him so vital to his people? He was a mere man—wasn't he?

Just a mere man. . . .

CHAPTER 26

It had taken three weeks of careful and meticulous planning before Tori was able to go to Godrano. And then one day he was there. He and Vincenzo arrived at the spacious villa of his Godfather, and were met by a slouched-over, aged peasant caretaker who eyed them suspiciously when they stated they had business with Don Barbarossa.

"Park the machine by the stone wall," he muttered, gesturing with his hands.

Tori glanced about the estate with admiration. "This Godfather of mine lives like a baron," he said to Vincenzo. He was glad he'd thought to bring a special tribute befitting so important a man—a man from whom he had to elicit a higher tribute in return. The matched ebony Arabian stallions, with their sleek velvety coat and flashing coal black eyes, would be perfect. Tori had discreetly said nothing to his mother about this encounter, now he wondered how he'd go about effecting a meeting with a man he knew only through her eyes.

"Rumors are that he's richer than any of the *latifon-*

disti—and more powerful," said Vincenzo, holding his awe in reserve. "I believe it. I believe it," he added.

They parked the jeep, and walked towards the dome-covered walkway at the side entrance as directed. Their eyes busily assessing the lush citrus groves, ancient olive trees, and other crops in the meticulously farmed lands.

"You think he'll like the Arabians?" asked Tori.

"Are you crazy? What's not to like? You said he once bred horses, no?"

"Yes."

"Then, calm down. *Managghia,* I've never seen you so excited. He's only a man like you and me. And while we're at it, don't forget who you are. You're not a nobody—you're Salvatore!"

"Yes," said Tori, as if he needed this to reenforce his courage. He tugged at his jacket. "Do I look all right?"

"Perfect," replied Vincenzo shaking his head in tolerant amusement. "Especially in your general's uniform. He'll be impressed, you'll see. *Porco Dio!*" he exasperated. "All this preparation for a Godfather!"

"He's not just any Godfather. He's Salvatore's!"

"That's more like it!" Vincenzo grinned. "And don't you forget it!"

Tori grinned self-consciously and felt better.

Shuffling toward them came a large-framed man in his sixties, with snowy white hair and alert black eyes behind dark tinted glasses, dressed in shirtsleeves and dark trousers held up by a pair of cheap suspenders. Don Matteo, looking tired, somewhat lethargic and older than his years, his face slightly jowled with excess flab, turned toward them without expression or acknowledgement. He walked with a royal posture and, despite his obviously paunched stomach, moved with considerable ease. In his hand he carried a slender stick, which he poked into a profusion of rose bushes bordering the villa, giving the impression he was looking for something. Annoyed at the sign of guests, he moved forward toward the young men, busily engaged in his chore. He'd planned a short holiday and rest away from the busy Palermo duties, but now, with their presence, he abandoned all hope. Preoccupied with the roses, he made alternate grimaces of approval or disapproval, depending on what he found as he inspected the foliage. Within a few feet of the Montegattans, the Don straightened up and demanded with polite aloofness.

"Who are you?"

"We're waiting for Don Barbarossa," said Vincenzo imperiously. He disliked the old geezer on sight.

"I asked—who are you, not what you wanted," snapped the Don.

About to tell the old man what he could do, Vincenzo was held back by Tori's restraining hand. He faced the Don with dignity. "You will tell Don Barbarossa, that I am Salvatore, here to seek audience with him," he spoke with measured politeness.

Don Matteo spat into the ground. Livid at the obvious insult, Vincenzo made a rash move for his gun. Instantly Tori moved to deter his cousin from making the most foolish mistake of his young life. No bodyguards were visible, but he felt instinctively that dozens of eyes were upon them, with perhaps even more guns aimed at their hearts. He was right. At least six guns, hidden from sight, were trained on them at that moment.

"Salvatore *who?*" asked the Don, with noticeable disdain. None of the silent interplay was lost on him.

Vincenzo's anger boiled over. He tensed and glared hotly at the *capomafia*.

"Alessandro Salvatore, Godson to Don Barbarossa," said the famous brigand with aplomb. "Now take me to him and be done with it, old man."

Don Barbarossa took a long hard look at the youth through his bifocals. "Alessandro Salvatore—eh? Huh," he grunted. "Come with me."

Without courtesy, friendliness or recognition, and with an air of decided boorishness, the Don turned abruptly and led the way along the tiled loggia into the villa proper. Vincenzo made a lunge for him with an appropriate facial grimace. Tori stayed him and shook his head in warning.

Neither had ever been subjected to such total lack of respect. The King of Montegatta and his Prime Minister, treated worse than the lowliest of lowly peasants squirmed hotly, their Sicilian pride damaged. Through a series of facial grimaces and hand gestures, Vincenzo conveyed his disgust. Salvatore winked and urged him forward, keeping his own indignation to himself.

They walked through long corridors under domed archways, past diamond-shaped panes of color-stained windows, alongside tropical plants and saintly religious shrines, over the gleaming tiled floors. Their boots clacked with the rhythmic cadence of a tiger beetle's death dance. Somewhere an old Caruso record played "Vesti la Giubba." They were finally ushered into the Don's office, and the two young men gazed about in fascination.

349

Three walls were covered by a profusion of photographs of high-ranking British and American officers, personally autographed to Don Barbarossa. An American flag, draped carelessly over the bright yellow flag of the Mafia and the tricolored flag of Sicily, stood at the center of a collection of distinguished brass plaques and citations honoring the Don. On the fourth wall, incongrous to the decor, hung a portrait of the most astonishingly beautiful woman with pale blue eyes Salvatore had ever seen. The signature intrigued him: Marco de Leone. The Lion of Sicily was a painter? More remarkable was the fact that the art work should appear in the house of a *mafioso*.

"*Managghia!* What a beauty," whispered Vincenzo appraising the oil.

Tori agreed. His attention turned to the desk—an elegant hand-carved piece with four lion heads supporting each corner and the body of the beast forming graceful legs to support the desk. On it were scattered stacks of papers and a white onyx inkwell with plumed pens. Nearby stood an elegant art object, a snorting bronze bull with flaring nostrils and ferocious eyes, its head sharply angled, displaying curved and pointed horns. Tori stared at it in rapt fascination. He was so absorbed in the deep, coppery, blue-green-hued metal that he failed to hear his host's words until Vincenzo tugged at his arm.

"Sit down," said the Don, without finesse. "Sit down—"

Irritated, yet curiously fascinated by this iceberg of a man, his guests sat in stiff, high-backed chairs opposite the messy topped desk seemingly untouched in a years accumulation of clutter.

"My Godfather's servant, no doubt," whispered Tori.

"*Porco diaoro,*" hissed Vincenzo. "I'd like to give him a taste of my hospitality. Pig-eyed rhinoceros."

The Don poured three glasses of wine and lit a cigar without offering one to his guests. He puffed furiously on it until it was well lit. Through the cloudy mist of blue-white smoke, he stared critically at Salvatore. Behind his dark sun glasses, the probing black balls of his eyes studied the bandit with a fierce intensity.

So! This is Salvatore. Reports hadn't lied. Amazingly handsome chap with the charisma of a film idol, he told himself. What was it he had said outside? He is my Godson? *My Godson? Mah,* how the hell is he my Godson? *Managghia!* This is the surprise of all surprises. Who would have thought that the upstart King of Montegatta would turn out to be my Godson? The Don smiled internally, with delicious amusement. Wait until Martino Belasci hears of this! And that *fanatico*—Archbishop Voltera! Phew! With so many godsons, he had lost count.

Don Barbarossa placed the wine glasses before his guests. He raised his glass in a toast and muttered, *"Salute."*

Salvatore and Vincenzo were thoroughly confused.

"What's wrong? Don't you drink—either of you?" asked Don Matteo.

"We're waiting for my Godfather, before we drink," said Salvatore, containing his rage. He drummed his fingertips against his thighs.

"All right—what are you waiting for?" The *capomafia* raised his glass to his lips and drained the contents. He sat back in his chair and belched.

Salvatore's face turned beet red. A sidelong glance at Vincenzo confirmed his thoughts. Vincenzo had paled excessively. In the uncomfortable silence, Salvatore thought, was it possible this man was Don Matteo Barbarossa? *His Godfather?* He felt sick. Where had the glorified concepts of his illustrious Godfather gone? The dashing libertine? The daring renegade? The flamboyant bandit of Mazzarino? The legend of the man disintegrated before his eyes. Never had he felt so let down!

"I'm Don Barbarossa," the Don said finally, removing all doubts.

"Yes, of course. I didn't recognize you," muttered Tori.

"People changed. They grow older. Pictures in the papers are twenty years old," the Don found himself apologizing—and it angered him.

Vincenzo, blustery and red-faced, moved to the door. "I'll leave you both. You must have much to discuss. If you need me, chief, I'll be outside the door." He appeared to be unaffected by the *capomafia;* inwardly his guts writhed. *"Piacere,"* he said to the Don mechanically, and left abruptly, closing the door behind him.

Outside, in the corridor, Vincenzo leaned heavily against the door and drew a long hard breath. Whore of the devil! So, this was Tori's Godfather? He shuddered. The Don, to Vincenzo, was the embodiment of everything evil he'd ever heard of the old Mafia. Why, he wondered, does Tori get involved with these vile *mafiosi?* What was so important they had to come here? *Mafiosi* chilled his blood. Their power-saturated stares could reach inside a man, twist his guts, and render him impotent of courage and life. Quickly he walked outside to where the stallions were housed. He unloaded them, tied them to hitching posts, and stroked their manes compassionately.

"There you are, you black beauties. Breathe fresh air while you can. I don't envy you your new master," he told them. Suddenly he wondered about many things. Why his cousin found it necessary to keep this visit a secret from his mother. Why, after his apparent dislike of *mafiosi* in his village, did Tori confer with the biggest *mafioso* of them all? Godfather or not? His speculation mushroomed. How in hell had his aunt and uncle selected Don Barbarossa to be Tori's *Padrino* in the first place? Sensing eyes upon him, he glanced up as two—four—six armed guards came into his focus from various points. Uneasy, for the first time in a long while, he merely touched his head in a salute and retreated to a nearby *pergola*, where he sat smoking a cigarette in reflective silence.

Godfather and Godson studied each other in silent appraisal. "Who was he?" asked the Don, with obvious dislike for Vincenzo.

"My cousin, Vincenzo de Montana. My co-captain."

"Hah! *Si tiene molto superbo!* He's too impressed with himself. Too arrogant! Hot-headed. A whoremaster."

"He's a good man. Loyal. He knows how to get along," countered Tori.

The Don shrugged indifferently and chewed his cigar, and, for a time, made small talk. "How's your mother?" he asked, at a loss for what to talk about.

"Bene, grazie." Tori's tone matched the Don's in cool aloofness.

The Don's brows shot up. *Now he mocks me,* he thought. "And your Papa?"

"Dead these thirteen years."

Barbarossa made a half-hearted gesture of sympathy. "We all must die—no? Only this we know for sure. *La morte e sempre vittorio.* Death is always the victor." Driven by a natural impatience, the Don asked abruptly, "Well, Godson, is there something you wish from me? Money—a job? What can I do for my Godson?" He scratched his ear, stuck a stubby finger in it, and shook it vigorously, still perplexed at their relationship.

Salvatore sulked internally. *Bastard! He doesn't even know me. Damned if I present the Arabians to him. He leaves me no opening. Very well, I'll talk in terms he'll understand.* He crossed one leg over the other and patted his thigh, deliberating. "No," he said through clenched teeth. "I want no job, no money." He gazed about the room idly. "You have a beautiful place here in Godrano."

"*Va, va,*" began the Don impatiently. "You didn't come here to praise my house."

"En route we saw one of your richly laden caravans."

"Nor have you come to speak of my caravans, eh Godson?"

He fixed a defiant eye on the other and stated simply, "I came for a favor—a special favor."

"A favor?" A faint, smug smile moved across the Don's thick lips, and he lowered his eyes on the sheaf of papers on the desk. "What is this favor?"

"Don Pippinu Grasso."

Barbarossa glanced up. "What about Don Pippinu?"

Tori swallowed hard. He locked eyes with his host and replied firmly, "I want him killed."

The *capomafia* didn't bat an eyelash. He removed his dark glasses, cleaned the lenses with a handkerchief, and gazed into his Godson's eyes. Tori felt the impact of those eyes as many men before him had, and he trembled inwardly; yet he held firm with his own steady gaze.

The Don, seething inwardly, broke the contact by barricading his burning orbs with the glasses once again. "Why come to me? From what I hear, you're perfectly capable of handling your own contracts."

"Because you can do it in such a way that it won't be traced to me," said Tori nonchalantly, irking the Don.

If the *mafioso's* astonishment was pronounced, and if he was grossly insulted by such obvious lack of respect shown him in these past moments, he contained himself superbly. "If, in my younger days, I had dared to be as impertinent as you young, overinflated cocks are these days, I'd have been tossed out on my ass and made into feed for vultures." He sighed resignedly. "Times have changed, no?" Behind those camouflaging glasses, his black eyeballs chafed with indignation, and his blood boiled at the audacity and pure gall of the man, Salvatore.

"I'll waste as few words as possible. There was no way I could have approached you before, Godfather. As it is, I've waited two years before coming to you." Tori himself grew bolder, for the Don with his earlier statement, had led Tori to believe that he wasn't totally unknown to the *mafioso.* "You see, I know you've been a busy man, and I, also am not without responsibilities."

Seated in a leather upholstered swivel chair, one elbow propped up on the arm, with a hand placed meditatively over his lips, the Don controlled himself remarkably well. His eyes were on the cigar he rolled between the fingers of his other hand.

"What injustice has Don Pippinu done to you that you ask his life in return?

"What injustice? Shall I list them all? *Va bene*. He cheated my mother and family out of money justly due us. He murdered my bride—an innocent flower in the bloom of life—without compassion. He violated the code of silence, by falsely reporting me to the *carabinieri* on trumped-up and false charges. Because of him, I killed a man needlessly. And because of him I embarked on a life of crime."

"You killed one man? Hah," grunted the Don. "Only one man, eh? Salvatore," he said in a patronizing tone, "I've heard tell there is more than one scalp strung to your belt of victories."

Tori's eyes flickered in amusement. He was right: he *wasn't* a stranger to this conspiratorial old devil. *His bags flow to overflowing with countless tricks. Va bene*, thought Tori. "What I've done was forced upon me by the vile and contemptible acts of this worthless son of a pig-eyed whore, Don Pippinu," he declared, innocence and naivete in his voice.

The Don countered skillfully. "You, Salvatore, have the gall to come to me? You, who've been like acid to our intestines for nearly two years? You've no respect for authority—only your own. You confiscate our goods, kill our guards, cut into our pockets, robbing us of profits—and now you come for a favor! You who've taken the law into your own hands have the *fegato* to come to my villa and demand the life of a brother?" He smirked contemptuously and spat into a nearby spittoon, with apparent disgust. He sat back in his chair, a leer on his face, indicating he held the trump card. "If I so desire, I'd have but to press a button and my men would immobilize you, finish you off if necessary—and no one would be the wiser."

Tori's eyes were fixed in fascination upon the bronze bull, taken by its powerful form. He appeared impervious to the Don's threats.

"You don't believe me?" The Don was both annoyed and favorably impressed with Tori's cool manner. His hands moved over a panel of buttons on the desk.

"If you were serious, Godfather, you wouldn't have taken time to warn me first." Quicker than the eye could follow, he whipped out his Browning, laid it on the desk. "But—you'd have to be faster than me."

In that instant, Tori chanced to see several newspaper clippings, with photos of himself, staring back at him from

354

a corkboard on the wall behind the Don's chair. His courage mounted.

Don Matteo looked at the gun as he might a fly. New respect shone in his eyes for the young man. He listened with fierce intensity as Tori spoke.

"Between actual facts and the reported words stand miles of disparities and untruths. In my province, before I took charge, babies died before taking their first breath because their mothers were sick and diseased from lack of food. Would you suggest I turn my back on the graft and corruption imposed upon my people by foreigners? How can you—who profess to love Sicily—turn your back on your own people? You permit the land barons to grow fatter by aborting the land and squeezing it dry. You claim to be father to the peasants? Hah! Instead, like a judas goat, you lead them to slaughter. I tell you, Godfather, you'd best look to the future instead of the past if you care anything for this great land of ours."

"Slaughter, you say?" The Don nodded. "Perhaps. But isn't that what one usually does with animals—especially sheep? Lead them to slaughter?" he mocked his guest. The Don thought, if I didn't have more vital and far-reaching plans for this *capo de cazzi*, I'd fix his balls for good. Furiously chewing his cigar, he wondered why he was permitting this impertinence and this dialogue.

The insult hit home. Tori's fists clenched, but he was damned if he'd let the Don know it.

"Ah, Salvatore, Salvatore," lamented the Don with special theatrics. "You haven't learned, yet. Peasants are no better than animals. They live in filth, worse than the stinking Bedouin across the sea from whose bellies most of them sprang. They've no guts to assert themselves. Look at me! The son of a man considered the lowliest of peasants. Did I remain in filth and squalor? No. I rose above my fellow men to become *numero uno*. It's true. I killed, murdered, and robbed to make myself important in a land where the peasant has no chance." He snorted. "I learned a long time ago the peasants are content to flounder about in their own shit."

"They are uneducated—"

"You think I was educated? My schooling came from the hard knocks I got from trying to survive. Now I survive the way the *latifondisti* survive."

"We're not all cut from the same cloth—"

"Ahhh," grunted the Don making guttural noises deep in his throat. "My sentiments, precisely. Some men are leaders. Others are content to follow. Should the leaders

355

continuously provide for the followers? Let them eat bread from the fat of the land gained by another's sword? *Porca miseria!* That's crazy thinking. You breed communism as sure as the seasons change each year. Peasants have to learn to take orders and work—"

" 'For slaves' wages? Oppressed by your *gabellotti* and indifferent landlords, who consider them so much cattle fodder? Where is it written that Sicilians must be slaves of the Church and the feudalists forever? Is there never to be a Utopia for them?" retorted Tori hotly.

The Don's patience wore thin. He wanted to argue and enlighten this brash young man, but, knowing it would be useless, he remained silent.

Tori remained adamant. "Since the inception of time, Sicily's been a refuge for slaves and the downtrodden serf. The status of the peasant, the real backbone of Sicily, remains the same. He's unable to work for a decent wage. No one has done a thing to elevate him from his misery." Annoyed by the direction of the conversation, Tori thought to end the subject. "Certainly their grievances can't be solved here and now by either you or me."

The transition in the *capomafia* was instant, immediate. "Don't be too sure of that, my boy. Do you know who it is to whom you speak? The most powerful man in all of Sicily—that's who," he boasted. "Do you really know who I am?"

"Do you know who I am, Godfather?" asked Tori, reining in his anger.

"I know who you are. What we can do for each other is more important."

In that split second Tori experienced a peculiar sensation, one so inexplicable and profoundly disturbing to him by what he saw reflected in the Don's mannerisms, that he was left shaken for a while. It was all there, the well-modulated, power-saturated glance and voice, the eye movements all of it. It was all too familiar to Tori, as if he'd held a mirror up reflecting himself. . . .

Irked because he'd been somehow driven to boast before this Godson of whom he had no recollection except from newspaper reports and the data supplied him by his network and spies—and those raving idiots on the Palermo Grand Council—he tugged at his memory, wondering how in hell it was that he had come to be Godfather to Salvatore. He knew very few people in Montegatta. Now how in the name of a bloated frog had it all come about? How? He tried a new approach. "You say you've not touched one of our caravans?"

"I've had no need to, yet, Godfather."

"You've a slick way with words."

"Why should what I do explode your corpuscles?" He took time to light a cigarette.

"Besides," added Tori, "my time has been taken up maintaining law and order in my village. The law of Salvatore prevails now."

Tori manipulated the conversation, designed to impress the Don with the dual purpose of letting the other know where the real power lay in the west and that of letting him know that Salvatore's name carried much weight. Meanwhile Don Barbarossa, in his unique manner, permitted Tori to ramble. He listened, and by listening with all his senses he learned more than Tori intended him to perceive.

"Since you are so all-powerful, why not handle Don Pippinu yourself?" A gleam of diabolical cunning sparked for an instant in the Don's eyes.

"Due to the vast space of emptiness that's existed between us over the years, I've wondered how far the bond of Godfather and Godson stretches," Tori temporized, then added cryptically, "A man must close the books on bankruptcy and go forward."

"What the hell does that mean? Listen, I don't appreciate riddles. And don't be clever with me. I don't like clever men," blurted the Don tightly.

Tori, taking the bull by the horns, argued, "If I slay Don Pippinu, it would add another crime to the formidable deeds already attributed to me, one which couldn't be argued as an involuntary act in a court of law. It would always sting as a premeditated crime, done by my own volition. Don't you see? Don Pippinu remains the only creditor to be paid off before I can move forward. I believe in closing all the doors after each bit of business, Godfather."

The Don heard him, but he didn't believe his ears. Too many contradictions stuck out in the lad already, like a swollen jaw. What a strange man is this who speaks of courts and law. What the hell's wrong with him? What the *capomafia* didn't understand, he dismissed by a wave of his hand and insults. "Bah! Sicily's no place for cowards and malcontents, certainly not for men afraid to piss in daylight."

"To be called a coward by anyone else would have brought instant retaliation," Tori said evenly. "I'm sure you didn't mean those words." It struck Tori that the Don's education was limited, that he didn't understand words with double meanings, so he proceeded on a differ-

357

ent tack, measuring his words carefully and employing a sprinkling of guile. "I, also, have found people to be foolish. Peasants, for that matter, can be more wanton than landlords and as capricious as lawmakers—"

"Ah!" exclaimed the Don. "Marvel of marvels. Then you are learning." The Don sat back in his chair, smug in his conceit, while Tori said nothing. After a moment the tight-lipped Don said quietly," "And if I should comply with your bidding?"

"I shall be forever indebted to you."

Don Matteo's head angled sharply. His brows shot up in amazement and his eyes locked with Tori's. Moments passed. Neither moved a muscle or spoke a word. Across the room a small yellow bird flew in, circled once, and came to rest on an open window sill, chirping audaciously, demanding attention. The Don averted his head, pleased.

"Ah, there you are, little friend." From his desk drawer, he removed a small box filled with bread crumbs, and, walking towards the bird, he asked cooingly, "Where've you been, you little rascal? I miss you when I don't see you. . . ." The bird took a crumb from between the Don's fingers and chirped his little head off. "See how I've trained him? When I'm away, the servants feed the little beggar—but he sings only for me." The Don laughed in a surprisingly gentle manner. When the bird flew away, the Don returned to his desk and picked up on the conversation as if there'd been no interuption.

"Among us, young man, words of honor are not spoken or taken lightly. You've uttered some heavy words, here. There may come a time when, called upon, you must return the favor done for you. . . . You've asked me to turn against my own kind, a political associate with whom I find no quarrel. In the brotherhood we are all brothers of a unity—of one strength. . . ."

"But, I'm your Godson! An injustice has been done me!"

The *capomafia* stared sullenly. *Godson! Che Demonio!* How the hell did I become his Godfather? He felt plagued by the question, disgraced to admit he couldn't remember his own Godson. Certain things were considered sacred, and the Don wouldn't think of refuting him in the matter. This situation certainly put a different slant on the plans he had had in store for this cocks o' the walk, he admitted sourly. He watched the splendid young man sit down.

Mistaking the Don's silence for encouragement, Salvatore found himself relating the full story of Don Pippinu's treachery, of the subsequent fate of Apolladora. Still the Don made no comment. No indication of his feelings, one way or the other, were visible on his face. When Salvatore finished, he redirected his plea.

"You'll see that justice is done, Godfather? That Don Pippinu pays for his deception? That I, your Godson, shall be avenged?"

Silence permeated the room. Salvatore could hear the savage beat of his heart bursting through his chest. His words had evoked a series of mental images and he felt himself reliving the horrors following Apolladora's death. He could feel the sweat roll off him, the dampness of his palms, the rising excitement, as he waited for an answer.

Barbarossa shook his head dubiously. "I agree to nothing—*yet*. Don Pippinu is an influential man, with many important friends. He controls the vote in Trapani, Marsala, and Mt. Erice. What do you control? What can I get from you in return for so special a favor?"

Tori got the picture all right. He squirmed uncomfortably and slapped the side of his boot, crossed over one leg, lightly with his fingers.

"Do my words shock you?" the Don said. "Offend you? If so you'd better learn the gut level of political manipulations. Nothing is for nothing in this life." On his feet, the Don paced the floor, chewing his cigar thoughtfully. "You say the weights and measures were established in the time of your Grandfather?"

"Si. The Naxos family held the license."

"Naxos. The Naxos family. The Don dug into his memory. "Naxos?" He had come to a complete stop before the portrait of the young beauty, when suddenly it all came together for him. He spun around, stared at Tori as if for the first time. "You are the son of Antigone Naxos?"

"*Salvatore*. Antigone Naxos *Salvatore*," Tori emphasized.

"The son of Antigone Naxos," repeated the Don. *Son of my heart!* He stared with wonder, at the strong jaw line, the unmistakable handsome features, the clear-sighted eyes, sparking with life, the even white teeth, the full lips, the shape of which he hadn't forgotten in two decades. The look of wonderment on his face dissolved his previous icy detachment. He returned to his chair, stalling for time. Color rose to his face, and he tried to subdue the pleasure shooting through him. "Tell me, how is your mother? Are your two older brothers in your organization?"

"She's as well as one can be in these troubled times. My brothers were killed in the war. Only a younger sister and I remain at home." The alteration of the Don's personality wasn't lost on Tori; before him the precious icy wall of reserve had suddenly melted away.

"The son of Antigone Naxos," the Don muttered.

Tori wondered at his sudden loss of guile, at the sentimental melancholy he detected when he spoke the name, Antigone Naxos.

"When do you come to Palermo?"

"With a price on my head, I don't court trouble. In my territory I roam with ease. Outside my domain, if a curious policeman spots me it might prove embarrassing for me, lethal for him. I provoke no such encounters without good reason."

"That's the only reason?"

"It's enough. . . ."

The Don opened his desk drawer, selected six cards, and scrawled his signature across them and handed them to Salvatore. "Passes signed by the Minister of the Interior, countersigned by me. Now, you can travel anyplace without fear. If accosted, stop. Show your passes and the *carabinieri* and security police will not dare touch you."

"You control the *carabinieri* like you do the security police?" Salvattore gave him a cynical, speculative glance.

The Don smiled enigmatically. "Its luck you found me here in Godrano. I spend little time here. I'm always found at my *apartamento* in Palermo, where I work with the Grand Council and act as chief advisor to AMGOT . . ."

"Work? I understand you *are* the Grand Council!"

The Don fairly glowed under the compliment. He nodded. "It's important that we prevent the spread of communism. God help us if Russia conquers us! She'll control the Mediterranean for sure, and in no time—the world! Sicily must be free. Separate from Italy. We must govern ourselves. With full autonomy."

Salvatore shrugged. "I leave that to you politicians," he said shrewdly. "I've little interest in politics. At least not until I've studied law, and earned the degree which qualifies me to be a lawmaker. . . ."

Don Matteo glanced up from his desk with a look of profound interest. Was the lad mocking him? Was he expressing sincerity, or was he playing a game? What? His last two statements had been as provocative as hell—but were they true, from the heart, or deliberately designed to deceive? The crafty and cunning politician put Salvatore to the test. Scowling darkly he snapped with marked irritation.

"Being a Sicilian, in itself, qualifies you to become a lawmaker, Godson! I hope you aren't the idealistic

360

dreamer the papers print you to be. Experience in life and a knowledge of your people qualifies you—not what you learn in books!" He snorted contemptuously. The reaction on Salvatore's face puzzled the Don, and he continued to assess the true nature of the young renegade.

"Tell me, are you making jest with me with this apparent naivete? How could you have risen to such power, thinking asinine thoughts?" For a moment, the Don suppressed an internal smile. Was it just possible Salvatore wasn't fully aware of the power he wielded? Was it? Son of a bitch! This brigand was either a paradox or a simple phenonemon. Which? He decided to pursue the issue.

"You should *be* interested in politics. You, who command over five hundred men and influence thousands of people, should be vitally interested! What happens to our people shall effect you forever!" he insisted. Suddenly the Don, faltered. He stopped himself from projecting the role of father to son, and wondered at his having such a reaction to the bandit whose antics had caused him considerable distress among his peers. The ambivalence shook him.

Salvatore replied. "With such formidable politicians at the helm—like you—why should I interfere? How could I hope to know what it's taken you a lifetime to learn?"

Why do I feel that he mocks me? wondered the Don, who suspected most men. Having been taught the ropes early in life, the hard way, he couldn't accept a compliment without suspecting the motive behind it. Despite his feelings he found himself extending the lad an invitation which, later, upon reflection came to baffle him. In a sudden mad impulse he insisted, "You'll come to see me at the *Albergo-Sole* in Palermo. Use the passes and you'll be admitted without question. Hear?"

"The *Albergo-Sole?* At Allied Command Headquarters? Isn't it off limits to civilians?"

"Off limits to anyone but me. Not even Nick Gentile or Vito Genovese has been accorded the privileges given me. You'll come. At the noticeable reluctance he saw in his Godson's face he hastened to add, "When you come to Palermo next week, I shall show you how politics are born and give you my reply to your request concerning Don Pippinu Grasso . . . *va bene?*"

"I can't make a definite appointment, Godfather," replied the cagey bandit. I promise I shall come one day soon . . ." He rose to his feet.

"Smart lad!" nodded the Don. "You remind me of myself in my Mazzarine days when, I, too, trusted no one. . . ." He shuffled his feet along to the front of the

361

desk and did the unexpected. He embraced the young man affectionately and fairly glowed with charm. "You'll give my warmest wishes to your Mamma . . . *allora* . . . until we meet again. *Ciao*. . . ."

Tori holstered his gun casually. Earlier, when the air between them had been filled with venom, he had decided against giving the Don the matched Arabians, now he had better thoughts about the matter.

"*Managghia*, Godfather! I clearly forgot!" He tapped his forehead in a significant gesture. "I've brought you a tribute. A small gift, to help erase the long years of silence between us, with hopes we may restore the closeness our families once enjoyed.

As overwhelming curiosity overtook him, the Don set aside the countless plaguing questions with mixed emotions, he followed the youth outside. He did this only after he pressed a button under his desk, which signalled to his bodyguards outside the villa.

When Don Matteo first saw the breathtaking sight of matched horseflesh, he stopped in his tracks. Actually, he trembled with excitement at the sight of such perfect specimens. Stunned by the unexpected generosity, he couldn't find the words to thank his Godson. He didn't have to. Having already experienced such joy when Vincenzo had presented him with Napoleono, Tori knew his Godfather's thrill must be double that of his.

Several of the Don's men, standing in the shadows with poised guns, retreated at the silent signal they received from their Don. Watching Godfather and Godson, Vincenzo de Montana sensed a distortion. There was something wrong in this picture before him, he thought, despite the bond which appeared to have sprung up between them in his absence. He watched as they embraced in parting, and this display of questionable affection, no matter how sincere it appeared on the surface, didn't ease the cold terror in his heart.

Long after the Montegattans left, the Don remained with the stallions, bursting with pride to be the possessor of such magnificent beasts and wondering how Salvatore could have been persuaded to part with them. That "*the great Salvatore*" had, in the manner of a vassal, honored him with such a fine tribute assured Don Matteo that his position as the greatest of Sicilian overlords was indisputable. To be held in such high esteem brought a glow of satisfaction to him.

Back in his study, the Don reflected upon the events of

362

their encounter, and admitted he was awed by this young bandit leader who had caused a furor among the *latifondisti* and created a cult of hero worshippers among the noted journalists of the land.

Managghia! This Salvatore knew how to make himself remembered! Who could forget such a tribute? At least, the first step in the journey of many miles had been taken on this day, he told himself as he poured himself a cup of *espresso* from a pot a servant had brought in. In the future, they would become better and better acquainted, he promised himself. The *espresso* was hot, bitter and strong. He made a wry face and retrieved a bottle of anisette from the tray. He poured a spurt into the murky steam, recapped the bottle and sipped the hot liquid. He smacked his lips and uttered a loud, "Ahhhh." He spun his chair about and gazed out the window in a reflective mood.

Reacting to all men at a gut level, Don Barbarossa knew instinctively if a man was honest or dishonest; if he should be trusted or feared; if he was friend or foe. With Salvatore he was sure of nothing. Something complex in his nature, something with which he couldn't identify, left him feeling unduly excited. This was no ordinary young man. Behind the cool manner, polite self-assurance, he sensed a shrewd brain, a dogged refusal to be intimidated or impressed or detered from any but his own point of view. He reflected.

Porco Diaoro! he thought. *How the hell does he come to be my Godson?* He spent several moments trying to recollect all the Godsons he'd baptized during his reign as *capomafia,* and quickly abandoned the project. There had been too many. He proceeded, then, to the next logical step, he hoped might unravel the mystery—Antigone Naxos Salvatore.

Antigone Naxos Salvatore! What could she have been, then? In her early twenties? How could he forget?

Away from Palermo, on a holiday doing a little *caccia*—hunting—on the estate of a friend near Porto Tommaso, the Don had been riding without a bodyguard on this brusque day in February in 1922. Through ancient Greek ruins and prolific orange and lemon groves ripe with winter harvest, past *pagliai,* straw storage huts, he rode, spotting a nearby well, the *capomafia* had wheeled his horse about to sate his thirst. Curious, and cautious, and ever on the alert for his enemies, the Don dismounted, and with drawn guns searched the *pagliao* for interlopers. He peered about the shadowy interior, satisfied his fears were groundless; until suddenly, he chanced to see the huddled form of a young, frail woman, with haunting dark eyes, hugging her two small sons to her bosom.

When asked to identify herself, she first comforted her two sons and instructed them to remain inside, while she accompanied the stranger into the glaring sunlight. She had blinked her sensitive eyes at the brightness and shielded her eyes for a time. She begged his forgiveness for intruding on his property and, with quivering lips, explained she had no place to go. She had fled her village, fearing for her life and of her sons' lives, in the wake of Cesare Mori's holocaust. Mussolini's chief executioner, in his sworn attempt to liquidate all *mafiosi* in his all-out war on the Mafia, had invaded Sicily and was killing everyone in sight, *mafioso* or not. "Lined up like animals, the peasants have been shot indiscriminately in a mass murder by Mori's men. Everyone in Piana dei Greci, Villalba, Corleone, Montelepre and Montegatta has already taken to the hills!"

Had the stories been true, the Don assured her, he would have heard. His stern reprimand left Antigone dumfounded. His lack of concern sobered her. Hysteria was replaced by self-assertion. Noting his country-squire hunting habit, she presumed him to be owner of the estate she'd trespassed upon.

"I'm not demented, Excellency. I tell you I was witness to the depravity. I saw men and women and children, even priests, lined up in a row, while Mori's *squadristi*, with machine guns opened fire and massacred them. To cover their butchery, they dumped bodies into deep mountain crevasses to remain forever lost to their loved ones." She implored him not to return to the city. "There'll not be a Sicilian left in our land when this most obscene of obscenities is through. Only the powerful *latifondisti* have escaped his wrath." Antigone shivered in the cool breeze.

He studied her smooth, tanned face with its high cheekbones smudged with dirt, and looked deeply into her deeply concerned dark eyes. Beneath the veneer of nervous self-consciousness he saw a stunning woman. Having instructed her to stay well hidden, he promised to return later with food for the children and blankets to keep warm. He directed her to the nearby well, should they need water. She confided that she was uncertain of her husband's whereabouts. In the confusion they parted, and when she didn't find him at their house, she had taken to the hills to protect her sons.

He removed his jacket, insisted she wear it, and begged

364

her not to worry in his absence. From his saddle holster he removed a *lupara,* loaded it for her, and handed her a chamois pouch of pellets. "Use it if you must," he told her, swinging to his saddle expertly before riding off swiftly into the hills.

At the Duke's estate, the Don immediately dispatched a courier to Palermo to learn what, if anything, had transpired. He returned to the woman that night after dinner, with a basket laden with foods and supplies. Her face had been scrubbed clean. A thick shock of black hair hung loosely, like coils of ebony, about her shoulders, and she moved about with a certain unique majesty. He watched her feed the lads and taken not of the bond of love and devotion between them. After supper she wrapped them in blankets and put them to sleep.

Outside the *pagliao,* they had walked about in the early twilight in the beam of light cast by a full, silver moon. Already a canopy of stars glittering like chipped ice had appeared above. Antigone became awkward and self-conscious under his fixed stare. She thanked him for his generosity.

"You are a beautiful woman, *Signora,*" he told her. "You speak unlike most woman I have known—more like the nobility." She acknowledged the compliment, and noticed that the words didn't come easy to him.

"What will you do, now? You can't remain here for long. The workers are in planting. Its likely they'll be working this section tomorrow. You'll be seen. I am concerned for your welfare. Come with me and I will protect you," He found himself telling her. "I myself shall return to Palermo as soon as I learn what is happening."

"No! I beg you. You mustn't go. You'll be killed. Stay away from the city until this madman Mori and his villains return to Rome. This barbarian kills at random—without mercy!" she insisted.

Matteo Barbarossa, moved emotionally that a stranger should show such concern for his welfare, hadn't been able to restrain the desire rising from the pit of his stomach to engulf him at that moment. Something intangible stirred his senses; something reminiscent of the only woman he'd ever loved in his Mazzarino days. Something about Antigone had reminded him of his former mistress, Diamonte, and he thought despairingly of his empty, loveless life of recent years. His wife, with whom he'd rarely coupled, he'd loathed. Her ugliness and uncouth manners had forced him into a life of quiet desperation. Three years of marriage—and the three times he'd been intimate with her had

365

produced three daughters. He'd simply not been interested in other women until th ismoment with Antigone, who in an instant had become the *one* woman most men meet in a lifetime, and live to regret they hadn't taken more time to cultivate.

He turned to her, took her work-worn hands between his, and said, "Mori wouldn't dare touch me. Not one hair from the head of Matteo Barbarossa would he have courage to disturb," he proclaimed imperiously.

The color drained from her face. "Matteo Barbarossa?" The name alone evoked paralytic fear. Being in his company had had an even more staggering effect. She moved away from him, stared in disbelief. Her hands flew to her lips, loath to have spoken his name. *"Barbarossa? The Mazzarino?"* She continued to back away from him. The shock of meeting this legend face to face, the trauma of her frightening adventure, her weakened condition from lack of proper nourishment, or the combination of all three—had caused her to fall faint.

Matteo caught her as she fell, and laid her upon the ground. Quickly removing his jacket, he rolled it up and placed her head under it. He rubbed her hands, smoothed her forehead, and pushed aside silky strands of hair. She hadn't been the phenomenal beauty Diamonte had been—but what a great face. Strong, compelling and filled with love. One who saw her couldn't forget her, he'd thought.

"I don't mean to startle you, *Signora*," he apologized when she'd begun to stir faintly. "There is nothing to fear from me." He astonished himself with such gentleness. The need and desire to be tender had long since left him. "Will you believe me?" he asked, helping her to her feet.

"You must think me to be an imbecile. I've never fainted before." She grew reserved when she saw desire in his eyes. "I can repay your kindness by imploring you not to return to Palermo under any circumstance. You, especially will be murdered on sight. This Mori is psychotic—sick in the head. I've learned one thing in this life, you don't reason with insanity. That's why I fled my village when I saw such random killing." Her composure had returned slowly in bits and pieces.

"Thank you for your concern," he said, smiling a rare smile. "I'm too important to be touched and they know it."

Antigone in full admiration shrugged imperceptibly. "Do what you will. But, remember Mori is a madman. In his fantasy, all of Sicily is Mafia!"

They walked the full length of the path to the well and back, pausing to inhale the sweet heady aroma of the fertile earth and the fragrant scent of orange and lemon blossoms. They talked a bit; she spoke of her heritage, told him her ancestors came from the Island of Naxos, named for her forefathers. She spoke of her grandfather and father, who owned the weights and measures in Mt. Erice. Not once did she stop to look at him, or note the effect she had been having on the notorious Don Matteo.

"You really don't seem concerned about this Cesare Mori?"

"*Non é importanto ora.* It's not important at this moment," he'd said.

She tried once more to impress him with the gravity of the situation. "Under the direct orders of Il Duce to exterminate the Mafia, he performs mass murder on countless thousands of innocent people. In Palermo, warrents for every known *mafioso* have been issued. Village dons, their followers and hired killers are being shot on sight. I was told most had fled into the hills to escape this lord high executioner. You see, he means to liquidate all of us. The Mafia is just a pretext!" she said bitterly.

"It's not important, now," he had repeated quietly, as they strolled under the enormous moon.

She'd shrugged. *The man is fearless,* she'd thought. *Very well, at least I warned him. If he doesn't wish to believe me. . . .* She looked about her and inhaled the sweet smells of the night. "When the silver moon and bonanza of winking stars overhead light up these nights and the ruins of ancient civilizations come to life to stir your senses to remind you of long-ago empires and conquerors, you know it's time for planting," she said breathlessly. "Next to harvest, it has to be the most romantic time in Sicily. And did you know that in certain areas close to the gulf of Castellammare, legend has it that if you stand still long enough and set your mind to it, the sounds of far off trumpets heralding the approach of the glorious Roman Caesars and their centurions, who came to Sicily to frolic several months out of the year, can be heard?" Antigone had paused a moment to look at him.

He laughed easily. "In Sicily anything is possible."

She nodded. Suddenly they looked at each other in that marvelous, unique way that transcends all worldly affection, politics, religions, philosophy, and government—and all else that is but pure adornment. They met and touched at the depths of their emotions, felt a power greater than personal will, and stood suspended in a moment borrowed out of the time of man and both experienced an inexplicable miracle.

367

Neither had anticipated such an explosive encounter.

When it was over, and they no longer felt as shaken and breathless and full of wonder, Matteo left reluctantly for the villa, with the promise to return the next day. He thought of nothing else for the balance of the night. When he returned the following day, Antigone was gone. She was no where to be found. No trace of her or her sons had remained. For a time, the Don wondered if he had dreamed her. When he'd relived those moments in which he'd headed for infinity during their sexual embrace, he'd known she'd been for real. For a long time she had remained in his mind—a vivid reality. How could he forget his Grecian goddess in the moonlight with the soul-stirring name of Antigone Naxos, with whom he had made love against a background of ancient Greek ruins?

In Palermo, chaos existed. Many of the brotherhood had fled in the night, booked passage, illegal or otherwise, to other parts of the world, mainly America. Others had sworn allegiance to fascism or went underground.

Arrested by his own hand and knowing that prison would be the safest place for him, until the *fascisti* cooled off, he had spent a few years in the Mafia prison at Ucci-ardone, much like a rest home for erring executives. One day, two years later the Don had walked out into broad daylight, the entire file of his criminal activites tucked safely under his arm, never to be heard of again for twenty years.

Don Matteo poured himself another cup of coffee, lit up a fresh cigar and continued to reflect. He'd never seen An-tigone again. Yet this outlaw boldly claimed him as God-father. Why had the woman filled her son with such deception? Why? Why? Why? More peculiar to the Don was why he himself hadn't set the lad straight? He was never ever hesitant or vague with others. Surprised and annoyed at himself, he wondered why he'd been so benev-olent.

Don Matteo's soul retreated in confusion to the inner security of his usual craftiness, guile and treachery. In a few days he'd dispatch his trusted bodyguard, Mario Cac-ciatore, to locate Salvatore's mother and arrange a meeting to discuss the situation with her. He wondered—would she still remember him?

He swiveled his chair around, faced the wall containing the newspaper clippings, and stared at the photographs of the young outlaw. Sonofagun! This Salvatore was mer-curial—perhaps as impossible and unmanageable as he'd heard. But, like himself, he was a living legend, a man who had killed as many *carabinieri* as he himself had, if not more. No one had been able to stop him. Ambushes and traps set for him failed, and he always fought his way out of the tightest situations with uncanny insight. With no real military training of any kind, two solid years at fighting off these crack military police had earned him the name of Salvatore the Invincible. How incredible it was that Salvatore won coup after coup with unshakeable *panache!* Sonofagun! It was marvelous, how he had captured the imagination of over four million people! Don Matteo had to give him that much.

Images rushed at him, and suddenly he saw himself as he had been in the old days, as the redoubtable bandit of Mazzarino. These images alternated with those of Salvatore, and, superimposed over each other it became difficult for him to separate them. *Managghia!*" he declared. "It's like looking at a reflection of me in my younger years." Somehow, though, no suspicion entered his mind that he could possibly have sired this incredible phenomenon.

He poured himself a tumbler of wine now and flipped through a few pages of reports he had requested from his aide in Palermo. In moments his thoughts dwelled on Don Pippinu Grasso. How much of Salvatore's story could he believe? With two sides to each story, he promised himself he'd look into the matter, and resolve the issue.

Don Pippinu had grown influential and valuable to him these past few years. On the other hand, Salvatore's strength would be invaluable, in the days ahead, in his plans to control Sicily. Weighing the matter in his mind, he was surprised to see the scales tipped favorably to Salvatore. His mind made up, he summoned a servant. "Pack my bags. I'm returning to Palermo. Tell Mario Cacciatore to meet me there. I have a special job for him."

CHAPTER 27

No one had to tell Don Pippinu Grasso that Salvatore would retaliate in the unwritten law of vendetta for the death of Apollodora. What stuck in the Don's craw was the fact that no money had been found on the bastard. He hadn't considered that the *carabinieri* might be holding out on him, only that Salvatore had somehow gotten away with all that money. That Tori had become a branded fugitive who couldn't show his face for a time didn't pacify the Mt. Erice Don, or avenge the shame and disgrace he felt at having been duped by so young a man. A convoluted logic ate at him like a malignancy. Never mind that he'd been the wrongdoer and perpertrator of the first evil.

Six months after the culmination of the distasteful and shameful affair, newspapers carrying bits of information about the amazing feats of Salvatore caused the Don to regret the injustice he had inflicted upon the son of his third cousin. Extra guards posted around his villa, and at the countless business interests he owned, kept a sharp lookout for treachery. When a year passed and no troubles arose, he dismissed thoughts of retaliatory action with a boast, "Salvatore wouldn't dare touch Don Pippinu!"

Two years later strangers began to frequent Naxos Weights and Measures. Always courteous, respectful and with authoritative manners, these men, dressed like dandies, would ask, "Which one is Don Pippinu?" The clerks would point to their employer. "The fat one? The one who stinks like swine?" Flushed with embarrassment, the clerks, casting furtive glances in the Don't direction, would not. "Yes, the one who stinks."

Thereupon the strangers would study the *mafioso* inscrutably for a time, as if committing him to memory. They'd exchange secret grins before departing. Many people came to gape at the formidable Mafia Don, who'd grown powerful and despotic through his association with the reestablished Mafia. So, at first, the clerks thought little of these incidents, until one day, when they began comparing notes, and felt obligated to inform the Don of this curious group of strangers and their subsequent inquiries.

It never occurred to Don Pippinu that any of this might be Salvatore's doing so long after the fact. During his rapid growth in the war years he'd made many enemies. Many were jealous of his power. In lieu of these developments, however, he chose to confine himself within a small stall and barred windows resembling early day postal booths where dollars were exchanged into lira—and where guns were kept secreted in the event of a holdup. A rigged alarm could be activated by a clerk instructed to pull a cord under a counter if and when some stranger appeared making inquiries about Don Pippinu. Automatically a small light would blink on and off beneath the

Don's counter in the cage, affording him first view of the strangers. Off the premises, he was constantly accompanied by at least two imposing brutes.

Two years to the date of Apollodora's savage death, Vincenzo de Montana, Turridu Nuliano and Dominic Lamantia entered Naxos Weights and Measures. They walked directly towards the small money cage where the Don sat confined. A clerk pulled the cord. Instantly the light in the stall blinked on and off alerting the Don. He reached for the gun and was about to press another alarm summoning his personal bodyguards.

"I wouldn't do that, *Signore*," said Lamantia coolly. He stood at the side window, a gun aimed at the Don's head, some six inches from his temple. He grinned wickedly when the Don, startled, turned in his direction. Vincenzo and Turridu stood facing them at the front window.

"Don Pippinu," Vincenzo paused a moment. "I've a message for you." He went through a lengthy ritual, placing his gun on the counter, next to which he placed a sharp stiletto, a *garrote,* a smaller hand pistol, brass knuckles—and an envelope.

Watching him stealthily through lidded eyes, Don Pippinu maintained a well practised calm. Vincenzo took the small box from Turridu's outstretched hands and plunked it on the counter.

"Here, this is for you." He shoved the box towards him. "Go on—open it."

Shaking visibly, the Don fumbled with the wrappings. Opened, he removed a glass jar containing what resembled a human heart. He read the accompanying note: *"The heart of Apolladora never forgets. Neither does Salvatore!"*

Don Pippinu fell back in his chair, the sweat pouring off his face. The sound of their laughter echoed through the store as the bandits left Don Pippinu to mull over his surprise package and wonder at his ultimate fate. It didn't take long for it all to come together for the Mt. Erice Don.

The next morning, accompanied by four trusted guards, Don Pippinu took the first charter boat to Palermo. By noon they arrived in the capital city, hailed a taxi, and went to Nunzio's *Birreria* to meet with Don Matteo Barbarossa.

The Mafia figureheads embraced in brotherhood fashion.

"Don Pippinu. . . ."

"Don Matteo—I kiss your hand."

"You look good," remarked the *capomafia.*

"You say that when I've lost much weight over a calamitous affair that needs your expert counseling. . . ." He bleated like a crusty mountain goat.

After a lavish dinner in the usual custom, and after the amenities were finished, both *mafiosi* retired to the small office kept only for the *capomafia* to conduct special business in. The Don selected two or three bottles from a lavish sideboard of special wines, to which only he and Nunzio held a key. "What do you prefer, my friend? *Vino bianco, or vino rossa?*" asked Don Matteo graciously.

"I prefer red wine today," stammered Don Pippinu, wiping the profusion of sweat descending on his brow. He placed his grey fedora on the chair next to him and watched the *capomafia* decant wine from one bottle to another, then pour it into a crystal goblet for his pleasure.

"It displeases me to bring this matter to your attention," began the harrassed Don Pippinu. "With so many things on your mind, Matteo—" He raised his glass in a silent salute to the Mafia chief. He sipped the red wine, and Don Matteo relished the *strega*. Don Pippinu smacked his lips together appreciatively and, with a winning smile, he asked, "Is this new wine? Delicious."

Don Matteo shook his head. "Three years old. Now, what complication brings you into my presence? I am flattered you seek counsel from me."

"A favor. I ask a favor of you."

"Ask."

"The death of Salvatore!"

Don Matteo bit off the end of a Havana *Sigaro*, proceeded to light it without flinching a facial muscle. Through clouds of smoke he noticed the nervous drumming of Pippinu's fingertips on the table. Only four days had passed since Salvatore had met with him in Godrano to ask for the liquidation of the Mt. Erice Don. *Annunca*—things were boiling, eh?

"Why?"

"Why? What do you mean—why? I must give you reasons? Is it not enough I came in respect to ask this favor be done?"

Behind his dark glasses, Don Matteo studied the man who ranted as one in fever. He maintained his silence. However, Don Pippinu was incensed.

"When you need a favor, do I question my *capomafia*? I didn't follow in blind faith in the matter with the Allies?"

"You've become a wealthy man, Don Pippinu," stated the *capomafia*, simply.

"Are you weighing me on the scales of merit?" Don Pippinu was aghast. His dry voice hissed when he spoke.

"It's a request I can't grant without prudent deliberation. I suggest you reconsider. Is there no way to settle your differences with Salvatore?"

"Are you crazy? Since when does the brotherhood suggest embracing an enemy?" Don Pippinu, driven by some inner goading, grew incautious.

"Salvatore," said Don Matteo, "has suddenly become a resource of considerable power, one which could prove vital to the brotherhood."

"I don't believe my ears!" Don Pippinu shook his head as if to clear it of confusion. "Do I hear you straight? Are you siding with my enemy?"

"Anyone else but Salvatore and it would have been done," Don Matteo shook his head regretfully. "It's possible we'll need this bandit in the coming days. I am pledged to the brotherhood, Don Pippinu. Not to personal ambitions."

"—And I am not? Is that what you say? Haven't my actions spoken for me?"

Abject humiliation struck and stunned him. He remained in a near state of paralysis as Don Matteo temporized.

"Were you not aware of Salvatore's rise to power? Didn't it cross your mind that, with his indestructibility, the brotherhood might need him? We're desperate for his support, now that Canepa's proven traitorous. To employ the power of this peasant is the only way we can advance our plans for a separate Sicily. Reconsider, Pippinu. I beg you. Is there no way to make amends?"

"Are you telling me you deny my request?" Don Pippinu jumped to his feet, red-faced and swollen. With reckless fury running rampant through his body, he became uncontrolled and stupid. *"Allora,* don't heed my request," he challenged. "I shall withdraw my support. With it goes Trapani, Marsala, and the villages between." He snorted like a mad bull. "You side with Salvatore over your own kind?" He proceeded to grow more stupid. "I've not been sleeping these past few years. I, too, have grown powerful, more than you imagine. The Reds have courted me. I've but to nod and I could become more prosperous than you. Have I made one disloyal move? No! I've waited with a loyal heart beating in my breast until your dream of full power was realized, like a true *amico de amici,* a true friend to you and yours. And this is the gratitude I receive?" He mopped his dripping, sweating face.

"You jump to conclusions, *amico*," said the *capo* quietly. He offered him a cigar, and proceeded to relight his own, puffing on it until it was well lit, again.

"Then tell me what you intend, so we'll both know," retorted his guest, waving aside the mist of smoke.

Don Barbarossa, the picture of serenity, purred like a benevolent father. "It would grieve me, Don *Pippinu*, if I felt compelled to take your threats seriously." A hint of compassion flickered in his eyes as he calmly watched the other loosen his necktie.

"Listen, the word, *Don*, before my name permits me to kill—not be killed. And if you don't dispose of this brigand—he'll kill me." Don Pippinu belched without apology, and patted his stomach agitatedly.

"Why is he such a threat to you?"

"I've nothing to hide. He cheated me. That sonofabitch cheated me out of six thousand American dollars! Me— Don Pippinu! While I was in the process of trying to recover my money, some cheap little slut of a prostitute was killed for refusing to tell us the information we needed."

"How did the six thousand dollars get into Salvatore's possession?"

Don Pippinu paused to sip more wine. He wiped his face and neck again.

"I paid it to him—after he threatened me, mind you. . . ."

"How long have you leased the weights and measures from his mother?" asked Barbarossa easily.

Don Pippinu glanced sharply at the *capo*. His pig eyes narrowed in suspicion and his manner grew stiff and formal, as he fought for control. "Is there nothing that escapes you?"

"No. Nothing." Pouring more wine from the special decanter into the other's glass, Don Matteo glanced with tilted eyes at his guest.

Don Pippinu coughed and hawked up a mouthful of phlegm, which he hurriedly spit into a nearby spittoon. He wiped his lips. "He told me he was your Godson, that you had a buyer for the weights and measures, and he forced me into making a deal—on the spot!" He protested.

"You could have refused him until you checked with me. Instead you chose to remain greedy. You wanted the business and the money too!"

"Ahhhhh. . . ." uttered the suddenly enlightened Don *Pippinu*. No one had to tell him the *capo* had already taken a position. His eyes furtively glanced about the room. *How am I to get out of this place, gracefully, with-*

out further inciting the Capo? he thought. He attempted to disarm the other.

"*Allora*—the young goat *is* your Godson, then?"

Don Matteo filled with a restless impatience. "Who can deny a *Godson?*" He made a gesture of helplessness.

Don Pippinu, it appeared, couldn't halt the increased perspiration. While his nervousness increased, he continued to mop his brow. "I was a fool, I should have attended to the matter personally. . . ."

"Instead you went to the *carabinieri*, Pippinu. . . ." Don Barbarossa purposely averted his eyes. He didn't want to witness the demeaning, caged expression on the other man's face as he tried to squirm out of this. "This distresses me the most. Your purse has always lain too close to your heart!" His words seemed lost on Don Pippinu, who, before his eyes, began to change rapidly.

His face engorged to a purplish hue, his eyebrows twitched, and his loose dentures rattled incessantly. He slowly deteriorated. "My stomach feels upset. I should have taken bicarbonate of soda. Why am I sweating like a stuffed pig?" He asked aloud. His right hand darted to his heart in an effort to still the tachycardia, and he gulped at the air about him.

"Did the *carabinieri* give you your justice?"

"They gave me *cazzu!*" retorted Grasso stroking his underchin with the back of his fingers in typical gesture.

"They even kept your money—*pezzo de feci.*"

"They kept—*my*—money?" It no longer seemed to matter to him. He removed his jacket with considerable difficulty. Soaked, his shirt clung to his body like the wet diaper on a baby's buttocks. "Goddammit! It's too fucking hot in here," he muttered. Abruptly he stopped. "*Who* kept my money?" His eyes screwed up questioningly.

"When Salvatore was arrested, they took the belt from him containing the money."

"But they found no money!" he protested.

"And you believed them? The *carabinieri?*" Barbarossa spat into the spitoon in a gesture of contempt, and followed it with a suitable hand gesture.

Don Pippinu couldn't stop the profuse sweating. His head fell forward as if he'd been mortally struck. In the ensuing moments, he turned a sickly yellowish color as if stricken with jaundice, and he appeared to have aged ten years. He raised his head laboriously, opened the collar of his shirt, and stretched his neck above the collar. A strained, waxy glaze appeared in his eyes. He coughed in

375

frenzied agony, waved his hands in the air, apologetically for this confusing behavior.

Don Matteo's eyes contained polite and genuine concern for his guest's discomfort. He said softly and with compassion. "A true man of honor never weakens his position, or arms his enemy by an outburst of passion or fear. He fights his own battles, keeps his mouth shut, and he never—never—goes to *the carabinieri*." Barbarossa continued to smoke with a nonchalance that maddened the lesser Don. He removed his dark glasses.

"You believe—Salvatore!" he accused.

"I—*don't* believe the *carabinieri*."

"Matteo!" he shouted frantically. "I have never asked a favor of you!" He grabbed the *capo*'s arm and pleaded, full of anguish. "You must get rid of him before he kills me! I came to you in respect—you must do me this honor!"

"It's not possible. . . ."

"This is your final answer?"

Don Matteo removed his gold watch from his vest-pocket, snapped it open, and set it on the desk before him. Slowly, with deliberate movements, he raised his heavily lidded eyes and stared into the eyes of Don Pippinu without expression. At that moment, Don Pippinu knew. At that moment he read his sentence. At that moment, Don Pippinu realized he had been marked for death.

. . . *Misericordia!* And I, like a—*pezzo de shekko*—didn't realize this old judas goat was leading me to slaughter, he told himself.

Don Pippinu knew he was lost—that in a matter of moments his life would end. Yet, for some reason known only to himself, in a furtive movement, he carelessly reached into his pocket. Instantly, two men sprang from the shadows.

One man moved in swiftly and struck Pippinu Grasso in the face with a powerful fist. He went down like an ox under a hammer. Blood spurted from his face and nose.

"*Basta! Basta!*" ordered the *capo*. "He's done for, anyway. The poison will finish him off, soon enough." He looked down at the motionless form of Don Pippinu, who could still hear, for the poison hadn't begun to affect his senses. He shook his head in a gesture of resignation.

"No malice intended, old friend. It's like I said, for now we need Salvatore. But—if it will make you feel any better as you prepare to meet your maker, know that Salvatore's days are also numbered. What I've done is for the good of the brotherhood." He grasped Don Pippinu's shoulder firmly as if to give him heart. "You tell God, that Barbarossa says you are a first-class man. You hear? Barbarossa says you are A-one O.K."

Don Matteo picked up his gold watch, clicked the cover shut, slipped it into his vest pocket, and tossed his cigar into the spittoon. He put on his dark glasses, nodded to his men, and walked out the back room.

In the restaurant, he beckoned to Don Pippinu's men who stood guard near by. In an instant, tears flooded his face. He blew his nose and shook his head sorrowfully.

"Your boss has just had a heart attack! *Meskino— Povero meskino!* You will see to his funeral needs. . . ." He raised his dark glasses, shoved them back on his head, and wiped the real tears that streamed down his cheeks.

"We were such good friends," he lamented. He reached into his pocket and pressed a wad of lire into the hand of one of the men. "Give my respect to his family. And buy a large wreath of flowers in my name, *capeeshi?*" In a gesture overcome with emotion, he walked away.

"How fortunate Don Pippinu was to have a friend like Don Matteo." There goes a prince of a man!" The men disappeared into the back room to attend the fallen Don Pippinu.

CHAPTER 28

In Naples the *Carabinieri* High Command, having reached the limit of their endurance in the outrageous war declared upon them by the Sicilian, Salvatore, dispatched to Montegatta a man familiar with the area—a man with an axe to grind. The former Lieutenant Giovanni Franchina, now raised to the rank of *Maresciallo*—Marshal, the highest grade of non-commissioned officer, entered the shabby quarters of his new office and eyed the sorry mess with hypercritical eyes. The place, already a dump two years ago, would deteriorate the morals of a lizard, he told himself, containing his rage. Tossing his briefcase on the makeshift desk in the corner of the shambles of a room, he snapped on the desk lamp. He removed his uniform tunic and hung it meticulously on a wooden wall peg after first blowing the dust off the peg.

Earlier he'd met the skeletal remains of a highly demoralized squadron of officers who hadn't a full uniform among them. He had asked himself how this swarm of mice-like men could claim kinship to the glorious *carabinieri*. How could they have permitted themselves to fall into such utter disrepute? Two years before, the *carabinieri* in this province had shown some spunk; gusty, feisty men who knew their business and took pride in their professions. How could one peasant have intimidated them and created such a shambles of the men? How? Sonsofbitches! Those men had better shape up, or he'd send for a battalion to combat this indolence and inertia among these counterfeit military policemen.

Marshal Franchina removed from his briefcase a bottle of whiskey and a glass and poured himself a tumbler full. He disposed of it in two gulps, smacked his lips together, and waited to feel the whiskey's fiery warmth pervade his spirit. He inhaled deeply and studied his reflection in the mirror, before resigning himself to the business at hand. He removed from the brief a thick scrapbook containing an accumulation of data and personal notes collected over a two-year span on the brigand, Salvatore, sat down at the desk, scanned the contents.

At forty-one, despite his war injuries and those which he had sustained on his last stint in Montegatta, he was still in prime condition. Fierce dark eyes, suspicious and calculating, lurked behind dark-tinted glasses, and a sharp Roman nose dominated his features.

For some reason, he couldn't concentrate on the subject matter. His mind kept seeing images of those idiots outside. Earlier he stood before the police barracks in the village of Montegatta, a temporary shelter a short distance from the *questura* and the headquarters of the security police, unable to restrain his feelings when he addressed the men, who stood at attention.

"You're a disgrace! All of you!" He told the twelve men. "Why aren't you wearing the proper uniforms? Who's in charge here?" he demanded.

"Me, *'Tenente'* Paterno. I'm officer in charge," declared a slim dark-skinned man, better known as Birdeyes. He pointed a grimy finger at himself.

"Tenente' Paterno, eh?" Franchina had glanced scathingly at him. "Do you and your men always dress so disgracefully? And where are your horses?"

"The bandits confiscated them."

378

"The bandits confiscated them." mocked Franchina. "Just like that, you tell me! Have you no pride? Damn the devil! How do you expect to catch the bandits if you're so disorganized? What the hell's wrong with you, eh?"

Lt. Paterno's gaunt face burned with humiliation. "There's a war on, *Maresciallo*," he managed with thinning courage. "Things have been hard on us."

"So! You've permitted yourselves to be corrupted instead of honoring your uniforms. Is that it? It's all a part of Salvatore's deviltry, and you fell for it."

Glowering fiercely, the Marshal, in his spanking new uniform which drew envious glances from the officers, paced disgustedly before the staggered row of twelve motley men who, through a quirk of providence, had been supplied with the uniforms of perhaps six Indiscriminately distributed amongst them, the uniforms allowed six men to wear the trousers, while the remaining six wore the tunics with improper accessories. Six men wore left-footed boots, six wore the right. None wore a complete uniform. Another time, this grim-faced perfectionist might have found the scene hilarious, but only if the unsightly platoon belonged to another officer's detail.

"Impossible!" exploded Franchina. "How does it happen you haven't the proper uniforms? . . . I know . . . I know. There's a war on, and everything is scarce. Couldn't you have requisitioned them?"

"We did, *Maresciallo!*" Birdeyes held up three fingers. "Three times. Each time the bandits confiscated the shipments. Besides, for the amount of work we do nowadays, Salvatore told us we didn't need them. . . ."

"So! Salvatore's become your commander? . . . I should have had the lot of you court-martialled! You hear? Court-martialed!"

"*Managghia*," whispered one of the men to Birdeyes. "This new Marshal means business. He's not like the other fleet-footed chickens they sent us from Naples before . . ."

"*Attenzione!* . . . Attention!" barked Franchina. "Hear me well. I want you to know I'll not stand for gross dereliction to duty! In my entire career I've never seen such a shambles! You're a blot, a stigma on the very word *carabinieri!* If I had any sense I'd take the next boat back to Naples and let you rot in your own dung!" His shark-like teeth ground together and his drooping moustache twitched noticeably. "I'm here to do a job, and by Lucifer, the job shall be done! This arrogant bandit's days are numbered. No longer shall he bring dishonor to the Italian

379

Military Police. The *carabinieri* shall not be subjected to the contemptuous role of subordinate in this fiasco between peasant and law enforcement. *Capeeshi?* . . . All right, for now, you're dismissed! But, I warn you. Shape up or I'll send you to the stockade in the Palermo jail, where you can sit to your hearts content and contemplate this bandit whom you've permitted to heap destruction upon your heads. Tomorrow when you report for duty, you'll arrive—all of you—with clean uniforms! Boots and buttons polished like mirrors!" His booming voice, echoing through the *piazza*, was heard by inquisitive and bemused shopkeepers who clapped their hands gleefully at the distress of their enemies.

Eager to break rank and leave the Marshal's company, the men made haste only to stop and glance at Birdeyes with puzzlement in their eyes. Birdeyes understood their dilemma. "Uh—*Marasciallo*, how? We've only six uniforms between the twelve of us. . . ." He waited for a reply, standing rigidly at attention.

"Simple, stupid. Six of you come fully dressed. The others will wear their regular clothing until new uniforms arrive," exasperated the Marshal.

"If I may suggest," said Birdeyes listening to his disgruntled men, 'It's best you assign the uniforms. It may not seem a big thing to you. . . ." he moved in close to the Marshal and whispered confidentially. "The men love the uniforms. You'll cause dissension if they can't wear a part of it. Even a mere shoelace makes them feel special like they belong. . . ." Birdeyes squinted and blinked his eyes rapidly, trying to read Franchina's eyes behind those dark glasses.

Marshal Franchina, fascinated by the unusual eye movement watched him. "What's wrong with your eyes? Why are you squinting? What is it, do you need glasses?"

Birdeyes nodded. "I can't see far off, only close up."

"Son of a toad-mouthed vulture!" snapped Franchina with scathing irony. "Now I find these half-assed marionettes led by a blind man!" He strutted before the others, hands on his waist, challenging. "Go on. While I'm here you may as well point out the deaf and dumb."

They all understood the insult. What remained of their self-respect hung loosely by a slim thread. Only their stubborn pride had seen them through these trying times. Trapped in the area, they had been forced to accept Salvatore's law—which they had found to be fair. Their unconcerned government hadn't taken time to bail them out of the circumstances and misery they had endured, and hadn't even paid them liveable wages. Salvatore had kept a roof over their heads and fed them well. What did this overstuffed peacock expect? What could he know of the perverse conditions they'd endured? How dare he hold these men up to ridicule? Having stripped them of the last vestiges of their pride and self-respect, he had left them nothing. They were frustrated and angry when they strutted past him. Arrogant popinjay! Cockroach! Who does he think he is? One thing was certain, they concurred, he was different than all the others who had attempted to take command in Montegatta.

"We'd better not fool around," said Birdeyes to a few of the more disgruntled. "This one's a real adder, but we'll know in a week if it's real venom he keeps stored in his serpent's tooth—or mother's milk."

The bombastic Marshal, who'd made his first mistake when he insulted these diehards, retreated to his makeshift office to reflect on the insanity he had demonstrated in returning to this land of crazy buffoons and bandits.

After the near-fatal tragedy of the second bandit attack at Rigano Pass on his previous hitch in Sicily, Marshal Franchina had spent, long, painful months of recuperation. After devoting nearly half his life to his country, he had little to show for it, and now, he wanted to live—really live—not simply exist in hospitals for the balance of his days. But how? How could he make up for lost time? For the long, agonizing days spent in hospitals under the care of doctors and nurses? He had to begin all over again.

In two years he had nearly lost touch with the Sicilian scene. Technically the war had ended, but its devastating effects were all around him. Naples was a shambles, destroyed by both German and Allied bombs. Yet, through it all, Franchina marveled that the people had something else to occupy their minds, to set aside their misery, to allow hope into their drab and dreary lives. Some bright star on the horizon had made their lives worth living. The story of Salvatore, printed in the newspapers like some romantic love story in serial form, his exploits, his brave daring and audacious behavior had become the talk of the nation. And the people, secretly in love with him, actually prayed for him. Imagine!

Giovanni Franchina, no different than others who needed hope and inspiration, judiciously followed the printed articles, dimly aware that the name Salvatore belonged to a scoundrel he might have once captured if he hadn't been caught up in that vortex of human misery in

381

which a man wearing a *carabiniero*'s uniform was doomed.

Two months before his arrival back in Sicily, while lunching at Alfredo's on the Via Veneto in Roma with friends in Army Intelligence, he had overheard a chance remark. "Whoever captures the bandit Salvatore will make an international name for himself," said one of the officers. "And I daresay the bloke, without contest, will be able to write his own ticket, anyplace—any time."

This brief statement had set the ball rolling. At that moment, Giovanni Franchina knew his destiny. What a snap it would be! Who else but a man bent on vengeance—and familiar with the area and its people—should qualify for the honor? Franchina further bolstered his ego by deluding himself into thinking the task would be simple.

Marshal Franchina was back now, a different man: harder, tougher, more cynical with fewer scruples—armed for bear. Shocked to learn how much the area had become the dominion of Salvatore, and how different from the place he had remembered, he confessed the changes had alarmed him. Yet, hadn't he, too, changed? More exacting and less principled, only victory became meaningful to him. Promotion, higher pay, ample residuals, and an arsenal of retirement benefits were his ultimate goals. What better way to attain these than through national acclaim?

On March 15, two weeks after his arrival in Montegatta, the Marshal, who'd already shocked his platoon of incompetents by remaining in the village longer than they'd wagered he might, was about to make his second mistake. He dispatched two of his men to the Salvatore house to bring the women, the *Signora* and *Signorina,* to the jail for an informal chat.

Before the matriarch had left her house, signals sent from house to house had reached the edge of town and proceeded, with the aide of mirrors, ox horns and whistles, used by farmers, shepherds and merchants to arrive at the bandits encampment. Homing pigeons, released earlier, had swooped into their wooden cages alongside several grottos with pellets tied to their legs, containing the following message: *"Mother and Sister arrested by carabinieri. Come at once."*

Slowly, from house to house, man to man, woman to woman, a whistle, to the tune of a funeral dirge was heard, sounding much like the Bandits' Marching Song: *"Some Call him the Bandit . . . Some Call him the Law!"*

The hot afternoon sun scorched and bleached everything in sight to a blinding, eyeball-charring chalk-white.

Sparrows on overhead tree branches, struck by the abnormal silence, craned their necks, blinking nictitating eyelids as the Salvatore women passed under them. Both women, mother and daughter, with proud heads held high and impassive faces cast like stone, expressionless eyes fixed straight ahead, marched with a certain majesty, as if summoned by royalty, giving no outward indication of the inner dread they experienced.

Leaving their sanctuaries, the villagers came from all directions to trail behind at a respectful distance as the entourage made their way to the jail with their military escorts. Oh, the shame of it all! How dared this son of a loose-tongued idiot, Marshal Franchina, subject *Signora* Salvatore to such lack of respect? Wait until Salvatore hears of this disgrace. Herded into jail like common criminals! Tori will fix their tails!

The officers escorting the women found themselves sweating profusely. Having heard the signals, and aware of the increased tension among the people who followed, they braced themselves against the angry snorts and caustic remarks hurled upon them from all sides.

"You undersized pricks—you forget who puts food into your mouths! I wouldn't give a fig for your lives when Tori learns of your treachery! Bastards! He gave you enough rope, but don't be surprised if when the time comes your feet don't touch the floor!"

The policemen tried to remain cool even when a flowerpot came crashing down from an overhead balcony, missing them by inches. A growling dog, egged on by an irate mistress, charged at them chewing and snarling at their pantlegs. From another overhead balcony, a woman shook out rugs filled with dust and debris on them. Choking and coughing at the flurries of dust, the *carabinieri* brushed at their uniforms, their eyes flaring. One of the men turned around and, in a voice filled with supplication, shouted, "Don't you understand we're only doing our duty?" They quickened their steps and hurried the woman along. *"Avanti! Avanti!"*

So, thought Marshal Franchina as he watched their approach through the open grilled windows in his office, I've struck a sensitive chord, have I? In two weeks he hadn't seen one tenth the number of villagers that now gathered outside in the *piazza*. He smirked and seated himself at the desk, occupying himself with trivia by the time the women entered the room.

He rose to his feet, bowed slightly and slipped into his bright red tunic and with a bright smile tried to disarm the

383

women. "Please, *Signora, Signorina,* be seated. What a pleasure it is to see you both again."

Antigone and Athena searched his face keenly. Neither remembered him. Two years was a long time.

"—And you, *Signorina,* I've never forgotten the heart-stirring beauty of your person." He picked up Athena's hand and kissed it lightly. Athena withdrew it from him instantly, flushed, and lowered her indignant, startled eyes. She had no immediate recollection of him at the moment.

"I am Maresciallo Franchina, at your service," He clicked his heels, bowed once again. "You don't recall me? I was here two years ago—"

No recognition shone in their eyes. He moved back to his desk and sat down. "I thought it might suit all our purposes if we became better acquainted. Right off, believe me when I say I have no personal animosity towards you or this beautiful daughter of yours, *Signora* Salvatore. I have made it my business to learn all about you, and I know you are both good women, possessed with high moral principles and the normal seriousness with which you protect the family circle. Law-abiding and God-fearing women who, through circumstances not of your own choice, find yourselves pressed like stone weights, by the shabby antics and criminal tendencies of your son. My dear *Signora,* how could this have happened to you? An erring, misguided son must be a terrible cross to bear. Let me assure you, with my guidance, your son can be reformed. I'm well qualified to rehabilitate a criminal, help steer him to live a decent life, you see."

Franchina rose to his feet, slipped his hands into his high pockets and swaggered about the room. "I want you to feel free to talk with me, as if I was your confessor in Church—eh?"

On and on, in boring repetition, he rambled, boasting of his conquests, emphasizing that he captured criminals solely for the purpose of rehabilitating them and not purely for punitive measures. Forced to listen to his bombastic *braggadocio,* both women suffered indignities at the disrespect hurled upon Tori. Neither questioned, acknowledged, or repudiated Franchina's statements.

Beginning to show his marked annoyance, the Marshal sat down behind the antiquated desk, in an atmosphere incongruous to his flamboyance. Removing a cigar from the brass humidor on his desk, he lit it and puffed thoughtfully for a time, filling the room with blue-white smoke. His dark, glittering eyes studied the women critically. Imperi-

384

ous lowly peasants! He wagered they hadn't heard a word he'd spoken—and this infuriated him more.

"Understand, I mean no personal effrontery in asking you here to chat with me. But, I've a job to do, and by God, I'll leave no stone unturned until this dastardly son of yours is caught and properly punished for placing himself above the government. He was earmarked for trouble in 1943, I should have stopped him then."

The women gave no outward indication that they were affected one way or another by the Marshal's words.

"Very well, play your game of silence, if you will. I've presented myself to you in friendship and in respect—without malice, mind you, and in all humility."

The women maintained their stoical silence, without reaction.

"I beg of you, as a devout follower of Our Lord, and a good Catholic, if you care for your son's soul, plead with him to surrender himself to me. My promise to you is that I'll see he receives only a short sentence. Otherwise he shall face, not only the wrath of a stern government, but also the wrath of God. His outrageous crimes, the lives of the innocent men he's taken, and the countless riches stolen from the *latifondisti* and the government are enough to keep him in jail at hard labor for eternity. Unless—I intervene and beg the court's mercy. They'll listen to me."

Maresciallo Franchina stared at the unreceptive stone statues seated in his presence and lost his control.

"Do I have before me—illiterates? Mutes who can't hear or speak? Last time we met, you had no vocal impairment. Has your son's crimes rendered you both shame-filled and silent?" His voice boomed loud and clear. "Very well, refuse my friendship! When all hell breaks loose and your son is behind bars, where he rightfully belongs, don't come begging at my feet, crying, 'Have mercy! Have mercy!'" Franchina's speech fragmented, and, growing animated, he bellowed louder, "You're either made of iron or have no tongue! Which is it?"

No reaction flickered in either woman's eyes.

Franchina jumped to his feet, flung his cigar from him savagely, stomped noisily to the door, and, with glowing menace in his eyes, he jerked open the sticky door and held it open in curt dismissal.

Antigone touched Athena's shoulder lightly with her hand. They rose to leave. Dressed in perennial black, they adjusted black mourning shawls over their heads and prepared to depart. In passing him, she permitted Athena to walk first. She raised her dark eyes, glanced at the swollen face of the Barracuda staring stonily ahead, and paused momentarily.

"When the dust settles," she said calmly, "we'll see if you ride the stallion or the ass. . . ." Taking her daughter's arm, she walked out of the decrepit, bare-walled room, where broken water lines creased each ancient wall.

Outside the villagers cheered and shouted, *"Viva viva Salvatore! Long Live Salvatore!"* when they saw the women leave the jailhouse. They swarmed around the two women and several men instantly formed a guard around them, parting the crowd, making way for them to pass.

Through the open grilled windows of his office, Franchina watched the scene of his momentary defeat as the pressing crowds moved in to champion the Salvatore women. He wasn't so crestfallen that he wasn't made aware of the tight network of protection afforded Salvatore and his men by all the villagers.

"Whoring sons of Satan!" he exclaimed bitterly. "So, that's how it is?" He moved away from the window and sat down behind the desk. From a drawer, he removed the large scrapbook he had kept on Salvatore and for a time thumbed through it, searching for something which would give him more insight on the woman, Antigone Salvatore. She was no usual peasant, this woman. He made a note to learn more about this matriarchal power who couldn't be intimidated. Finally he slammed shut the scrapbook, reached for his tunic, and decided to make an inspection of the arms and ammunition reserves.

Nothing was as appalling and disgusting to the Marshal as his unit's puny display of antiquated revolvers and rifles, many of them rusted, broken and unkempt and totally useless. He picked up a revolver based on a Colt .45, a weapon made in the late eighteen hundreds, and watched the weapon come apart in his hands. Angrily he tossed it aside on a crude wooden table, and picked up a carbine that resembled a child's popgun. Thoroughly repulsed by it, Franchina tossed it quickly aside, as if he'd been contaminated by the shabby weapon.

"Where are the supplies I sent before I arrived?" he asked Birdeyes who watched him from a short distance in the supply room.

"Oh, those?" Birdeyes scratched his head thoughtfully. "Salvatore confiscated them. . . ."

Right then, if *Maresciallo* Franchina had had any sense, he'd have taken the next boat back to Naples, permitted the Montegattans to live as they chose, and thus preserved his sanity. But the hardnosed *carabiniero* hadn't been called the Barracuda for nothing. He had had two failures in Montegatta, and didn't relish thoughts of a third. He blinked hard, turned on his heels, and left the room, lips tightly clenched. Striding across the dusty courtyard with giant steps, he paused momentarily at the sounds of bleating oxhorns. His face flushed beet-red. A knowing frown creased his brow. Swearing under his breath, he scaled the last few steps, disappeared through the entrance, and slammed the door shut behind him. "Fucking bandits! I'll get 'em all!" he vowed aloud, more grimly determined now than before.

By the time the Salvatore women arrived back at their house on Via de Grande, Santino Siragusa and the Scoletti brothers were there, concerned over their well-being. "We received word of your arrest," he began unable to take his eyes off Athena's flushed features. *What a beauty,* he thought. *An angel. . . .*

"We're fine," replied Antigone, preparing the coffee for them. She walked to a sideboard and returned with a plate of *biscotti* and a bottle of *vino rosso.*

"This Maresciallo is not like the others they've sent," she began with a note of solemnity to her voice. "He's well educated, less inclined to intimidation. Athena recalls him now. He was in Montegatta the night Vincenzo's father was killed. He was the one who came looking for Tori after Nino Marino was killed." She poured the wine. "Please tell my son, this one will bear watching."

"Allay your fears, *Signora,*" Santino smiled before he sipped his wine. "What can one man do, eh?"

"What can one man do?" Antigone rubbed the knuckles of her fingers to stimulate their flexibility. "You ask what one man do, Santino? Some men in high positions have asked that same question about Tori. And I say to you—one man can move mountains, if such is his destiny."

Their eyes locked. Santino raised his glass in a toast to her. "I defer to your wisdom—as usual, *Signora,*" said Santino.

The Scoletti Brothers, nodding, sipped their wine. "You needn't concern yourself, *Signora,*" spoke up Arturo wrinkling amused brows. "The *carabinieri* have no arms, no ammunition, not even horses," he laughed. "Not even shoes with which to chase us. More important, the villagers, all loyal to Tori, will continue to protect us. They know Tori is a dedicated man."

Antigone studied them quietly. "How much longer will this loyalty last? The Montegattans haven't been put to the test yet" Their silence inspired further words of caution from her lips. "Despite what you think, please inform my son that this Marshal is different. He's a man who could sway many for such is the power of his oratory and conviction. This *Marasciallo* is *also* a dedicated man—dedicated to his own cause."

They understood.

"*Va bene*. We shall see each other then," said Antigone.

Both women watched the men depart through the rear terraces where their horses were hidden. Athena entertained a secret rush of hope at the thought of spending time with Santino.

". . . You want me to put *these* up, *Maresciallo?*" asked Birdeyes squinting closely at the *Wanted Dead OR Alive* posters for Salvatore and his men. He swallowed hard and read aloud: "*Reward: $5,000.00*"

"Is there anyone else here? Of course I want you to do it. Take some of the men and make sure they are displayed conspicuously throughout the village."

Birdeyes shrugged. There'd be hell to pay, but he didn't relish being chewed out by the Marshal nor did he appreciate the threat of court-martial. He picked up the posters and saluted his superior officer, smartly.

"*Aspetta!* While you're at it, stop at the post office and check to see if the supply of guns has arrived from Palermo. And for God's sake, be discreet! No one's to know the shipment contains guns . . . *capeeski?* I'll show these stubborn mules! All of these hard nosed, tough-assed peasants shall learn how the word of Marshal Franchina weighs heavy."

"*Sicuro, Maresciallo*. For sure!"

"Now we'll see some action! Pretty soon this village will take full notice of Giovanni Franchina! With no cooperation from the security police, I accomplished what no other *carabiniero* accomplished in two years. After this Friday they'll not forget the name of Franchina!' he boasted. "Are you still here? Be gone, *'Tenente!'*"

Birdeyes saluting, scampered quickly out of the office.

Marshal Franchina buttoned his tunic. Studying his reflection in the cracked mirror next to a wooden coat rack, he stroked his beard thoughtfully. "Marshal, you need a shave and a haircut," he told himself aloud.

Outside, in the brisk, cool, mountain air, he drew up the collar on his overcoat and headed towards the barber shop across from the Norman tower in the *piazza*. As busy as a squirrel storing nuts for winter, the Marshal had, quietly and without fanfare, made several trips to Palermo, where he had succeeded in obtaining over two hundred warrants for the arrest of Salvatore and his men, who along with a number of villagers were charged with murder, conspiracy to commit murder, aiding and abetting outlaws, robbery, theft, and the confiscation of government property.

Franchina had revealed to no one, not even his men, what he had planned for this coming Friday, and wouldn't until the last minute to ward off any possible betrayal or treachery. Oh, did it ever pay to grease the palms of these money-hungry, half-starved peasants. His affair with the widow Grissi, a willing paramour, had opened the door for him. Silent and unassuming, he had simply kept his ears and eyes open and his lips sealed. And it was all about to pay off.

Just as Marshal Franchina made way to enter the barber shop, he caught sight of Birdeyes running towards him. He reported that the weapon shipment hadn't arrived. Franchina, swearing under his breath, ordered the *'Tenente* back to the jail with instructions to go to the stage office and check with them on the arms shipment. He watched Birdeyes salute and depart.

It was 9 A.M. The Marshal glanced about the *piazza,* where some of his men were tacking up the *Wanted* posters. He noticed that several villagers were staring with in-born curiosity at the activity. Franchina, smiling inwardly with a smug conceit, nodded to a few villagers. Most stared defiantly, while others ignored him. Very well, he told himself, we'll see how they react to my authority after Friday. By Friday night they'll all taste Marshal Franchina's brand of justice.

CHAPTER 29

"*Buon giorno, Maresciallo,*" called Gaetano the barber.
"*Buon giorno.*" Franchina entered the barber shop.
"I'm ready for you," announced the short, stocky man with the red moustache, brushing off the first chair in the two-chair tonsorial parlor which filled in for the office of a dentist, a doctor and a chiropractor on occasion.
Franchina removed his overcoat, slipped out of his im-

maculate tunic, and carefully hung it on the wooden peg provided on the opposite wall. He unbuckled his cartridge belt and gun holsters, placed them meticulously on another wooden peg, and moved with ease and agility across the small rustic room, unbuttoning the top of his long johns. He nodded to Ignazio, the second barber and son-in-law to Gaetano, who worked on a client, buried under a steaming towel.

"A little chilly out today—no?" he asked Gaetano, making small talk.

"You northerners find it difficult to adjust to our violent climate! . . ."

"That's what it's called? A violent climate?"

"The Lord punishes us with inferno in the summer and flood in the winter. What else can you call it?" Gaetano poured hot water into the Marshal's personal shaving mug from the kettle on the pot-bellied stove, and whipped up the lather. Only the rattling sounds of a wooden brush handle, knocking about the crockery, were heard. Gaetano placed a towel around the officer's neck, lowered the chair to a horizontal position, and reached into a steaming container for a hot towel, wrung it out, and twirled it in the air about him. He tested it, then placed it on Franchina's face, leaving only a space for him to breathe. He proceeded to hum an ethnic ballad.

"I'm going to buy a radio one day, to soothe my patrons," said the barber, looking toward the second chair nervously. He nodded. Instantly Ignazio removed the towel from his customer's face and Salvatore, rising, flung the sheet from him. With the agility of a cat, he leapt soundlessly from the chair, and moved across the room. He slipped the Marshal's cartridge belt over one shoulder, removed both guns from their holsters, and in seconds had positioned himself a few inches away from where Franchina lay, comfortable and without suspicion. Tori, in a careless pose, one leg up on a chair, leaned his shoulders forward, one elbow on his knee, a gun grasped firmly in each hand and aimed at Franchina. Behind him, Arturo Scoletti took his place at the rear entrance and flipped a *"Closed"* sign into place in a window pane and locked the door. Vincenzo de Montanta guarded the back entrance. Tori nodded to the barber, who on cue commenced to play his part.

"*Allora, Maresciallo.* How are you coming with the bandits?" Gaetano removed the towel and applied a foamy coat of lather to the Marshal's face.

"Can't complain. Soon, now, I'll have them all in my coat pocket."

Nervously the barber swiped the Marshal's nose unintentionally with lather. *"Mi scusa, Maresciallo,"* he said apologetically, wiping the soapy foam from his nose. He shrugged helplessly at Tori in a gesture of apology.

"What if I don't fit into your back pocket?" asked Salvatore quietly.

"What's that? Speak up, man. I can't hear you," muttered Franchina.

Gaetano paused in his work to wipe beads of sweat from his brow. Alerted by the lag in conversation, the Marshal's black eyes snapped open. From his horizontal position he saw the barber's lips weren't moving. Yet, the same voice persisted.

"What if I don't fit in your pocket?"

Suddenly, as it registered, Marshal Franchina bolted up right in his chair, whipped off the barber cloth—and stared solemnly into the face of the young bandit and into the barrels of the guns aimed inches from his heart. Franchina recognized Salvatore instantly. With little time to reflect beyond the fact that the brigand had grown more handsome and matured in two years, he was shrewd enough to know that his life hung in the balance of this moment of truth. Since no flicker of recognition passed Salvatore's eyes, he chose to treat his obstructor with the cool indifference accorded a stranger. "Who are you?" he asked icily.

"W-who is *he?*" stuttered Gaetano with trembling lips. *"Maresciallo, this is . . ."*

"Silence! This isn't your affair!" ordered the Marshal.

"But *Maresciallo,*" insisted Gaetano.

"Sta zitto! Be still!" commanded the officer. All the while, his fish eyes hadn't left Salvatore's face. "I suggest you put those guns where you found them, young buck, before they get you into trouble you can't handle," he said.

Salvatore grinned. Aiming the hair-triggered automatics at a neat row of leather strops hung on individual pegs, suspended from a wooden beam nailed to one stucco wall, he squeezed gently.

Ping! Kapowee! Bang! Ping! Baroom! He shot each strop at dead center. Ricocheting bullets bounced aimlessly off the walls. Terrified, the barbers fell flat on the floor on their bellies and covered their ears protectively with their hands. Marshal Franchina didn't move.

"Fine guns, Marshal. Better than I expected. Since I'm a collector of sorts, I might just keep these."

"Whoever you are, don't incur my wrath. Just lay the guns aside and walk out the door or I shall arrest you."

"Bravo. Bravo!" Tori forced a tight-lipped laughter. Which?" Tilting his head in mock amusement, his eyes suddenly caught sight of the officer's new boots. *"Managghia!* Such fancy boots. Please, you will remove them."

"Now, look here, boy, set aside the guns and I'll make nothing of this foolish encounter." Franchina's courage took flight. He turned his back on the brigand. "Hand me a towel, Gaetano," he addressed the barber.

A swift bullet whizzed by Franchina's ear. Before the sound stopped reverberating in his ears, Frenchina glared angrily at his obstructor. His beady eyes on Tori, he reached up, touching his burning ear and felt the warm blood ooze between his fingers. He stared at the crimson splattered on them.

"You crazy, punk kid! *Tu si pazzu!"* he shouted angrily. The pain or fear he might have experienced easily turned into shaking outrage. He snapped a towel from the petrified barber's hand and placed it against his injured ear. It hurt like hell, but he wasn't about to indicate this to the arrogant, cocksure Sicilian.

"And now, if you please, the boots!"

"I refuse!"

"I only miss a target when I wish to—" Another bullet grazed Franchina's other ear.

The Marshal reached up and, found it, too, was bleeding. His courage slowly disintegrated. *Punk Bastard! I'll fix your hide!* Both his ears throbbed painfully.

"Now, the boots!" Tori said without amusement.

Red-faced, and livid, Franchina complied. He sat forward to ease the boots off, one at a time. He beckoned to the barber for help. Gaetano moved in swiftly at a nod of Tori's head and removed them.

"Perhaps we understand each other now?" Tori slipped the guns inside his belt, pulled himself up straight and tall. "I am Salvatore," he proclaimed in his usual panache.

"Fancy that. Next you'll say you're king of Sicily." the Marshal affected boredom.

"Not yet," replied the handsome Sicilian. "But the Marshal shows himself to be not without foresight. Consider yourself fortunate that you have found Salvatore in a charitable mood. Otherwise you'd have been dead. Consider this also. You will never show such lack of respect to the mother and sister of Salvatore again, or I will replace the flagpole at Bellolampo with your body until your bones bleach in the broiling sun and the vultures feast on your entrails. Without Salvatore's protection you and your bloodsucking, thieving *carabinieri* are nothing!"

"Nothing—like Gucci and Molino?" Franchina was a brave fool that day. When Tori glanced sharply at him, trying to recollect the officer, Franchina spat at him. Tori's indulgent smile evaporated. Arturo moved in swiftly with drawn guns. Vincenzo's dark eyes froze, and he moved in towards the Marshal, filled with menace. Gaetano and his brother backed away from the activity; their eyes bugged from their heads as they watched first one, then another.

"Vincenzo, the Marshal's boots are of no use to us without his uniform. Do your stuff," said Tori, a wicked gleam in his eyes.

"Remove your trousers!" Vincenzo ordered.

"You wouldn't dare!"

Tori removed his Browning from its holster and shot over the Marshal's head nearly parting his hair down the center. Franchina, aware he'd reached the limit—both his and Salvatore's—stood up. He unbuttoned his fly and let his trousers drop. Laughing at the ridiculous figure of the officer in long johns with drop-down bottoms, Vincenzo moved quickly and collected all the clothing, including the ornately decorated tunic and overcoat. Stripped of his impressive uniform, Franchina appeared as silly as most self-conscious, disconcerted men might in such circumstances.

"*Ciao, Maresciallo!*" Tori bowed lightly and gave him a mock salute.

"Don't be smug. We'll meet again. I promise, I shall bury you."

Tori turned to him questioningly. "Would you care to make the appointment now, or another time?"

Franchina replied. "There'll be plenty of time, Sicilian. Since you took my clothes, what say you leave me a smoke at least?"

"Give the man a smoke," he said to Arturo. Sonofabitch, how he hated such men—yet this one had guts. He made the connection in that instant. "So! It's Lieutenant Franchina!" Everything came back to him vividly in his mind now, all the events of those bitter September days in 1943. He bowed grandly.

"You know, Salvatore, one of us must die. I've vowed to capture you."

Tori took a moment to light a cigarette. Through the inhalations of smoke he studied the man. Both Vincenzo and Arturo stood like statutes. Was the man daft to talk such boldness? Why didn't Tori finish him off? Vincenzo eagerly fingered his gun. Arturo's gun was still in his hand and his grip on it tightened firmly. The barbers, petrified with fear, huddled in the corner of the room.

"Let me finish him off, now, chief," said Arturo a bit too eagerly.

"No, we're not murderers." Tori stopped him.

"Hah!" Franchina's snort evolved into contemptuous laughter. "Not murderers? What happened to all those officers your weapons destroyed—an act of God, I suppose?"

"So, you're the skunk they buried in my mountains? The stench has been unbearable, *Maresciallo*, but at least now you've been sniffed out." Tori had learned much in two years. Most important was never to let your enemy know your intent. And Tori knew this man would be his enemy to the end. Not for one moment did he consider Franchina a fool. A man who'd return to this territory, after two years away from it, had to be as dedicated as his mother had suggested.

"And now that my enemy has declared himself, we shall leave you to contemplate your own fate, *Maresciallo*." Tori tossed a roll of money to the barbers. "For the damage. *Va bene?*"

"You should have disposed of him." Vincenzo told him outside as they mounted their horses. Arturo concurred with him.

"He's just lucky he didn't call me a son of a whore! I'd have had reason to kill him, then. But we're too close to our goal, cousin. I want no more problems. Especially not from a dedicated *moffetta*, a skunk."

They swung to their saddles and waved to all the villagers who cheered them as they rode out of the square. "*Viva! Viva* Salvatore! *Viva!*"

Inside the shop, the dedicated *carabiniero* stood watching the bandits through the large picture window, one towel held up to each bleeding ear. The barbers craned their necks to watch the activity, unable to conceal their glee, as the villagers tore down the "Wanted—Reward" posters. In thinking Salvatore had displayed a gutsy manliness, the barbers ignored the fact that the Marshal had also showed bravery in defying Tori. Turning from the window they caught the cold hostile look in the eyes of that foreigner, Marshal Franchina. No fool, this Marshal had seen through their sham earlier. Now, in his eyes was the fury of Vesuvius.

I'll fix their hides, Franchina swore to himself in those

moments. *We'll see who has the last laugh! Arrogant peasants! Bastards! They'll all feel the bite of my bullets one day.*

"Go fetch *Tenente* Paterno!" he commanded the youngest of the barbers. "Tell him to stop at my quarters and bring me suitable clothing. If either of you repeats what happened here today, I'll personally hack off his balls and let a jackass mount him! *Capeeski?*"

Two days later Tori and Vincenzo eased their horses off the ridge near the Grotto Esmeralda, one of the highest and most remote of the caves they used, and broke into a wild gallop across the buckwheat terraces as they prepared to descend the mountains. A blinding flash of light, directed at them, caused Tori to pull up sharply on the reins of his horse with terrific force. Napoleono protested, reared, and whinnied painfully at the bit in his mouth and snaked until his master comforted him. Tori glanced questioningly at Vincenzo. Both searched the area for the sourch of the mirror signals. A paint bleating of ox horns followed.

"What is it? Who's signalling?" Tori brought the binoculars to his eyes.

From the South came a single rider at breakneck speed.

"I've been searching all over for you!" called Arturo Scoletti breathlessly. He unscrewed an oxhorn amulet from a chain around his neck, removed a coded message from it. "Santino sent me, said it was urgent."

Salvatore studied the message. Decoded it read: *"Friday night, this week, Marshal Franchina plans a surprise for you and your men. Use caution. Warrants have been issued for two hundred men including you."*

He handed the note to Vincenzo. "It seems the *Maresciallo* wants blood. Ours!"

"So—the skunk already sprays the air with his stink!"

"It makes him easier to track down—no?" grinned Arturo.

Tori didn't take the matter as lightly as did his paladins. He wheeler *Napoleono* in closer to his co-captain. "Very well, cousin, the Marshal means business. And for business we ride to Palermo. To the *Albergo—Sole.*"

"Your Godfather?" Vincenzo tried to hide his dismay. Mere mention of the *mafioso* produced a black cloud over his mind.

"First, we go to my house, to change our clothes. Arturo, you ride back to the grotto. Tell Santino to meet me at my house at eight o'clock. By then we shall return.

395

Not a word about our mission—*capeeshi?* Not even to Santino."

Arturo nodded dutifully and rode off in the opposite direction.

CHAPTER 30

For a time early in 1944 there had been widespread belief that the war in Europe was nearly at an end. Allied armies expeditiously zoomed through the warring arenas, almost unopposed, to the Rhine. The optimistic and confident American War Department issued orders to divert supplies from Europe to the Pacific theater. Denuding the European front in Sicily and Italy meant the army would have to depend on partisan forces and those involved in guerrilla warfare. It also means that these flourishing bandits would be furnished a larger quantity of weapons to make their work against the Germans more effective. These antifascist, anti-Nazi guerrillas began to show a marked inclination towards communism, a fact which served to disquiet the British and American Allies.

Faced with a dilemma if aid was given exclusively to communist partisans, America feared this would insure for them control of the nation's most important industrial and agricultural regions once the fighting had ended. America couldn't, and wouldn't, tolerate such a situation. Disguising U.S. outrage behind a mask of efficiency, the Office of Strategic Services formulated a plan. This plan, including a critical analysis of the Sicilian political involvement and the communist threat, was presented to the Joint Chiefs of Staff and General Eisenhower. Shortly thereafter, the OSS approached the Allied Control Council with the idea of placing the right man into a key position to indirectly oversee and direct the fate of Sicily. If Italy should swerve to the Left, a closer alliance with Sicily was imperative, a fact Don Barbarossa had perceived long before the Allies had considered the implications involved in such a move.

It was agreed that this unique and very special man would have to be exceptionally bright, tough, and highly skilled in political skullduggery; preferably a law school graduate with a political science background. He'd have to be a dedicated officer who'd carry out orders—a stickler in following a set rule, yet elastic enough to know when to make a right decision on his own. He'd have to be a colorful person, one who could fraternize with and win the confidence of an exceedingly shrewd and manipulative group of Sicilian politicians, yet remain a bulwark of strength against the opposition, not be intimidated by them. A man with a touch of Sicilian in his heritage, a fact the Sicilians would find appealing, would make him more enticing.

These requisitites, described to General George Patton one day by General O. Bagley, added to the qualifications the following: "This special officer would, of course, be responsible for performing a threefold mission; to secure accurate intelligence on the political faith of each partisan group, to prevent the communists from building an army with American weapons, and to build a strength of non-communist resistance forces."

"What you want is a combination of Flash Gordon, Superman and God," retorted the feisty, fire-tongued Patton. "Too bad I'm unavailable. You see I've a prior commitment to go fox-trotting with Hitler," he chuckled without a hint of modesty. He then proceeded to suggest the name of an extraordinary officer who "served me damned well in the North African campaign against Rommel."

The extraordinary man turned out to be Colonel Stephen Modica, a strapping man in his late thirties, a well-built, handsome man who possessed uncompromising standards, great personal integrity and high moral character; even more important was his strong background in Intelligence work.

There was no question that the Allies had miscalculated and underestimated the power and lure of communism on a defeated warring nation, and they soon awakened to the jarring fact that the plodding, well-organized communists had industriously planted seeds of discontent in the minds of those who had come to despise Mussolini's ideals and held no truck for the doctrines of Hitler. If they had been more aware of the enticements communism offered, the course of history might have changed drastically.

But, then foresight is a privilege only the gods enjoyed, thought Colonel Modica as he settled himself in the confines of his comfortable office at Allied HQ in Palermo, Sicily. He'd been pulled off the Trieste detail, where he had made extensive use of the indigenous underground resistance movements to sabotage the activities of the German and Italian armed forces in the occupied nation where he and his men had continued to stir up national unrest; these same skills were now to be employed against the communist forces in Sicily. In his capacity as advisor to the Palermo Grand Council, he served as a channel for communication and support from Allied powers.

From the beginning, however, what appeared to be a matter of routine operations began to evolve into a hopelessly and grossly complex situation. Trieste with its mushrooming network of international spies and double agents, now seemed like nursery school to Colonel Modica by comparison to the continuum of intrigues and counter-intrigues that greeted him in Palermo.

For over a year all the Colonel heard was talk, talk, talk! Very little action followed. His days and nights were consumed by endless arguments and drinking soirees with British officers and Sicilian patriots, while he simultaneous-ly tried to uphold the intricate and clandestine duties to which he was sworn to support. The pattern was endless, unprolific, and discouraging. Why had he agreed to direct this comedy of errors, with its unusual cast of volatile and highly emotional players who, if viewed in another light other than in the tragedy of war, could be characterized as laughable? The elaborately framed plots and counter-plots, designed by characters lifted out of the Middle Ages—characters whose philosophies defied the imagina-tion and boggled the mind—thwarted the American colonel continuously. The senseless and ceaseless activity of these men appeared to be geared for the utter destruc-tion of order—namely Colonel Modica's order.

The way he looked at it, Colonel Modica had a prob-lem—a big problem. It wasn't the communist threat, or the countless resistance groups with their underground army of drones, or the continuous uprooting of disloyal partisans who intimidated the formidable Modica. Nothing so simple. His was a whopper of a problem! Don Matteo Barbarossa. Code name: *Redbeard*.

The business of war wasn't frustrating enough, he had to be provoked to exasperation by this enigmatic and dy-namic powerhouse, this streamroller with political clout, a Machiavelli and a subtle, ever-constant thorn in Colonel Modica's butt—Don Barbarossa.

Colonel Modica hadn't been in Palermo ten minutes be-fore he had learned that Matteo Barbarossa was the big gun. Not the princes, barons, dukes, the politically-orient-ed Cardinal, the Archbishop, or the government offi-cials—none of them wielded the power. The real political

398

clout and muscle belonged to this aging, nondescript Mayor of Godrano, an outgoing, outrageous peasant, a fearless dynamo who had masterminded the art of pulling the right strings at the right time to orchestrate life and human emotions to march to the tempo he prescribed.

The Don's formidable presence, and his astute contributions during Grand Council meetings, had stirred Colonel Modica to intense curiosity. Modica's advisors hinted at Mafia relationships. They spoke sparingly of the Don's absolute powers before the Mussolini era, and assured the American officer that, whatever else Barbarossa might be, although there was no documentation to prove it, he was emphatically anti fascist, anti-Nazi, anti communist, anti socialist, and so anti-everything that it followed he could only be pro-Mafia and pro-Barbarossa. In 1944 the word Mafia meant little to Modica or the world. Sicilians who had lived under its iron-fisted dictates, however, were far more affected by the word.

How, wondered Modica, was he to learn anything about this mysterious Don Barbarossa with no supportive data to guide him? Goddamn war and all its complications!

For better than a year all his attempts to secure an appropriate file on the *capomafia* proved futile. The crux of Modica's problem was that he didn't know the kind of man with whom he was dealing. He found it worse than attempting to consummate clandestine relations with an angel in the dark of night—and awakening in the light of dawn to see reflected, on her countenance, the putrefying mass of sickness on the face of a diseased prostitute.

No doubt existed in Col. Modica's mind that these Mafia-Feudalists in the Grand Council intended keeping secret from the American Officer, what they knew in advance; who would control Sicily, and how.

"All I want is something—anything—whatever you can find on the man Barbarossa," pleaded Modica to his friend Captain Matt Saginor at the Rome office for USA Army Intelligence. For the better part of the past year Captain Saginor's apologetic voice had come over the horn. He hated to disappoint the colonel, but, he hadn't been able to locate anything on this apparent ghost who held the Sicilian sceptre in his tightly clenched, greedy fist. It had been a snap to locate a make on Vito Genovese and Nick Gentile, but, on Matteo Barbarossa he hadn't been able to locate a goose bump; not even a birth certificate or baptismal record—nothing!

A few weeks before, while he was in Palermo on business, Captain Matt Saginor had suggested to Colonel

Modica that he get assistance from the brass. Modica, having already taken that tack, had replied in all candor that he didn't appreciate doing business with the deaf. dumb and blind. Everyone of whom he'd inquired about the Don had seemed afflicted by the inability to hear, perceive or see. He had then showed Captain Saginor a sheaf of papers which he had removed from a desk drawer—communiques on the subject directed to the Army brass, including his former mentor General George Patton. Modica took the time to read a few of these gems to his friend. "This is from old Iron Jaws himself!" he nearly snarled at Saginor: *"Give Barbarossa whatever in hell he wants and let's get on with the fucking war! We've still got Hitler to cut down to fucking size!"*

Col. Modica flung first one, then another and another of these messages, all with similar instructions, at his friend. Saginor, a fiery redhead with a spattering of freckles on his face and arms, was unable to contain his amazement. His concern grew more obvious than his west Texas drawl.

"Good buddy, I hope you aren't headed for a court-martial. Look, Steve, off the record, let me advise you legally. It just doesn't pay to be a maverick when the brass tells you to bleat like a sheep. According to the terms of the North Atlantic Treaty, we're supposed to give 'em what they want. It makes no difference what you want for them. They gotta want it first. Heah? If none of them has the guts to give a holler and a hoot for what they want—it isn't your responsibility."

Watching his friend bridle with frustration, Captain Matt Saginor downed a few swigs of Scotch and found he couldn't hold back his concern. "Why are you making it a personal crusade. You've got no choice in the matter, buddy."

"You mean I'm damned if I do and damned if I don't?"

"Listen, you won't be here much longer. Why get so steamed up?"

"You know something I don't?" Modica had asked him, alerted by his remark.

"The President is dying. When he does, you'll be pulled off the Sicilian detail. Concentration's gonna center on Berlin. I've already got you keyed in to A.C.C. there. Our info is that before the month ends, Hitler and his supermen will be saluting Old Glory. Keep this on the QT. All the Chiefs of Staff are being hustled off to prepare a possible confrontation with Russia. We've gotten feedback, Steve. that Russia's negotiating a peace with Hitler."

Modica snorted. "Now it begins! No one listened when

news reached the French underground, nearly two years ago, that a possible Russian-German Alliance was in the offing. They called us crazy! You know how many good men died in that operation? Goddamn them anyway!"

"You and I and a helluva lot of guys knew we should have invaded France first. Why rehash it, Steve? Does it make you feel better to know you're right—*after* the fact?"

"Why rehash it? Why? Because goddammit, there's the devil to pay! We've stayed too long in Italy! Meanwhile Russia advanced in Yugoslavia, took over Bulgaria, and reigns supreme in Warsaw! Bastards! They have the gall to boast they did it by themselves! Russia's so swollen with self-importance, she'll tell the world she won the war singlehanded. You think America has the guts to tell her to go chase herself? Oh, no. The brass will find another excuse to play down her arrogance. 'We'll need Russia to fight off the Japs,' they'll tell us. And we'll go on playing the patsy, while the big wheels continue to make their power plays! Man! Who the hell knows what goes on?" he exasperated.

"Yeah," sighed Captain Saginor. "Who knows?"

"Meanwhile Sicily goes down the drain," reflected Col. Modica, crestfallen. "I told them there'd be an insurrection—that the Sicilians would annihilate each other. Somewhere, not from me, they got the notion that America stands behind them in this strategy. Now, we're going to let them down."

"The spoils of war, good buddy. Some win—others lose."

Just before Saginor prepared to leave to fly back to Rome, he voiced his regrets in not finding the time to stay for dinner. They were interrupted by the Colonel's military aide, Lieutenant Destro.

"Sorry, sir. I've been asked to remind you the Grand Council is waiting for you."

Modica nodded, grabbed his jacket, shook hands with Saginor, and embraced him affectionately.

"Stay cool, buddy," said the Captain noting the strained expression on his friends face. "Figure it's all in a day's work. By the way, I hear your hands are full of this Sicilian Robin Hood, eh?"

"Sicilian Robin Hood?" Modica frowned in thought. "What the hell are you talking about?"

"You haven't heard of the shoot-em-up guy right in your own backyard?" Saginor laughed and poured himself a stiff drink for the road. "Headquarters is going ape with all the press-pass requests. We're deluged with requests for interviews with him. Right square in the middle of a fucking war, this *bandito* takes over like gangbusters! Like gangbusters, buddy! Word's out that a motion picture company is seeking a permit to shoot a film about him! Is he one of the resistance groups?"

"Oh, yeah. Yeah, him," muttered the Colonel. In seconds he came alive. "Yeah! Him! Salvatore! Why the hell didn't I think of him before?"

Halted in his tracks at the pure look of fiendish delight on Modica's face, Saginor's face clouded with concern. "Steve! Look, man, don't do anything foolish. There's no time to defend you in a military trial, pal. And I'd hate for you to sit out the war in the brig!"

Colonel Modica waved him off. "Have a good trip." He shed his jacket, loosened his tie, and commenced shuffling through the drawers of his desk fully preoccupied.

Captain Saginor bit his lower lip and stretched it over his teeth, in reflected thought. "Steve, Gina's in Rome."

Modica glanced up. His heart flipped over, and color rose in his cheeks "How is she?" he managed with some hesitation.

"As well as can be expected. Any message for her? She knows I'm seeing you this trip." When his friend grimaced with annoyance, Saginor added, "Sorry, buddy, it slipped.

"I've nothing to say." muttered Steve, already lost in the project at hand.

About to protest, Saginor saw it was useless. "*Ciao*, good buddy. Maybe you could save one of those little Mamma Mias for me next time I see you. . . ."

For a few brief moments after Saginor left his office, Colonel Modica indulged in a few whimsical reflections of Gina O' Hoolihan. Thoughts of her, and the love they had shared, brought a wistful sigh to his lips. *Goddamn the war!* he thought. Everything had been so perfect for them, but with the war what could he have done? He had to break it off. Just as he did then, and would continue to do until the war ended, Stefano Modica turned his mind off all thoughts of romance—the lasting kind, anyhow—and turned it to the business at hand.

He forced himself to concentrate on the newspaper-clipping file previously compiled on the brigand, Salvatore. He ordered his aide to cancel the meeting of the Grand Council on any pretext, and didn't wait for Lt. Destro's sputtered protests. He thumbed through the clippings recalling what he'd told Matt Saginor earlier in his frustration.

"The fate of a country and its people rests on my conscience and all I see around me is crap. Deals upon deals are born every second of the day. Everybody's wheeling and dealing for Sicily except Sicily, herself. The people aren't represented in this fiasco. If only one of them, just one lousy Sicilian, came off the streets to tell me he either agreed or disagreed with these antiquated prima donnas of the Grand Council, I'd jump for joy. This Don Barbarossa stacks the cards, deals from any position in the deck, and always comes up smelling like roses. Damnit! He holds more trump cards than a boll weevil lays eggs."

Colonel Modica believed these words, despite their seeming futility. Studying these news clippings, Modica felt a stir inside him. Was it possible the answer might have been within his grasp all the time? That this Salvatore could be the voice he had wanted so desperately to hear? Why hadn't he come forward?

He read and reread the newsworthy items, which he had meant to read long ago and had kept tabling until he could find the time. Finally, now, he made the time. . . .

All this had taken place a week ago. Since then Colonel Modica's time had been consumed with petty annoyances and disconcerting problems, all of which centered around the inimitable Don Barbarossa. A curious twist of events had evolved since the last meeting of the Grand Council last Friday which had stymied the American. At that time, Don Barbarossa had stated with confidence that he controlled all the outlaw bands in Sicily. He promised he would personally assume their leadership in any possible confrontation with government forces. The instant it became evident that Sicily might have to fight for her independence, the Don stated that he objected to plans for an

Long ago Colonel Modica had pegged the Don for a insurrection on the basis that no one could predict the outcome of a revolution. He was one for keeping all things under control—*his* control. He had cited the Canepa *fiasco* as evidence of what lack of control could reap.

man who'd play three or more sides against the middle if it were to his benefit. Playing his hunch, he had put a tail on this redoubtable power broker. Two days ago, his spies had brought him puzzling information. Following the last meeting on Friday, Don Barbarossa was followed to the office of Chief Inspector Semano, where he had astonishingly revealed in detail a summary of secret Council business, presumed to be highly classified information. In addition he betrayed plans of the proposed insurrection planned by the newly formed Partitionist party. Colonel Modica was flabbergasted at the contents of the report.

True, the scope of their projected plans *was* broad and somewhat nebulous in these embryonic stages of development, but, *why* the Don had seen fit to bare the plans mystified the American officer. It was to have been a mock insurrection in which the real bandits, disguised as Sicilian patriots and college students, would be prepared, should the government troops create unexpected violence. This staged insurrection, tantamount to revolution, would in no way be as perilous or unpredictable as the real thing, the Don had explained to the Chief. "You'll kill two birds with a single stone. Catch the bandits whom you've had no success in capturing, and break up what appears to be a real revolution. Think of the feathers in your cap—eh?"

Colonel Modica wondered what the hell this sonofabitch was trying to pull off. If Modica had harbored any illusions, before this, that his own varied experience had taught him how to sniff out the skunks, the diabolical schemers or the scurrilous plotters, he now came to realize he had met his match. If he lived ten lifetimes, he'd never understand such a man. *How can a man get to know another*, he thought, *when his past history, swallowed by the jaws of deception, disappears like the thief in the night who comes unseen and unheard and leaves behind only a vacuum as evidence of his past?* It would have made no sense for the Colonel to report his findings to his superiors. He'd been made too cognizant of the broken record playing endlessly in his mind, *"Give the Don whateverinhell he wants!"*

Very well, thought Modica, I'll play as dirty or crazy a game as is needed. As a temporary expedient, he cancelled all Grand Council meetings at which his presence was needed. Concerned that his feelings might betray him, he simply stalled for time. Meanwhile all political machinery had slowed down to a halt. Harried calls placed to his office were ignored. He wanted no locking of horns with Don Barbarossa, not yet.

On this Wednesday, April 2, 1945, Colonel Modica sat at his desk, hip-deep in newspaper clippings of Salvatore. He had reread all the articles until he had formed a vivid impression of the renegade in his mind. What had impressed the American officer was the detailed account of all Salvatore's victories, and if you could believe the press, the bandit had had no failures. That was what made it so marvelous! Incredible to imagine. No wonder he'd appeared in print as an arrogant, self-assured young prince.

Only a man who'd never known defeat could assume such a posture. God! He was beautiful! To have burst on the scene with such spectacular verve and *panache* was short of miraculous in this way and age! But why had *he* been kept from Salvatore? Why?

Modica lit a cigarette with his lighter, and for several moments he continued to click it open and shut as he pondered the situation. Was it possible that Salvatore was a part of the plan Don Barbarossa had so laboriously embroidered to stage the coming insurrection? Modica's mind lumbered back to the first meetings of the Grand Council when he first arrived in Palermo. . . .

Click, Click. Don Barbarossa, without preamble had made their position quite clear. "It is the ardent desire of all loyal Sicilians that their nation become a State annexed by America," he had stated firmly. Or if that wasn't possible, would it please the Colonel to personally speak with the British Government to see if they might consider Sicily as a British Colony?

Click, Click. Alarming revelation at the registration of political parties in Rome, that the trend was pro-Left, had brought immediate reaction and a turnabout in their previous objectives.

Click, Click. "If it pleased the American Colonel, the Grand Council urgently presses for the immediate separation of Sicily from Italy. We further must insist upon full autonomy. Does the American Colonel understand Sicily will not permit the Reds in their land? Does he know the full extent of their displeasure if the Reds rear their ugly head in Sicilian politics? In lieu of all that's happened, the Colonel must understand the Grand Council's dilemma. Would it not be more beneficial to the Allies, if Italy swings to the Left, to keep Sicily as a friendly ally? With Sicily goes control of the Mediterranean." Control indeed!

Click, Click. Shortly thereafter, Colonel Modica had received a communique from Rome, substantiating the pro-Leftists leanings. In addition the message, crystal clear, left no room for conjecture. "Italy—pro-Left. Encourage Separatists and form coalition of all parties under one strength—the Partitionists. Imperative that you cooperate with Barbarossa. In case of trouble with Reds, we'll need friendly Allies. *Redbeard* is the only one who can pull it off." Signed, Gen. O. Baglev, Chief of Staff, OSS (*Redbeard Papers Detail*).

Click, Click. Another message followed. "OSS advises you Canepa affair backfired. Reorganize resistance groups.

Procrastination must cease. Full and complete data to follow. Get cracking!"

Modica tossed aside the lighter. That had been three days ago. All Modica had to do was tell Don Barbarossa to forge ahead with his plans. The U.S.A. would back him completely. It was that simple. Why couldn't he bring himself to issue these directives? Why the reluctance on his part? Why should he continue to give a damn? Saginor was right, he told himself. If the Sicilians didn't give a fig about their fate—why should he? Soon, with all this trouble brewing with Russia, he'd be immersed in another cause, too busy to concern himself with an apathetic people. No rationalization on his part could sufficiently ease the pain of conscience he felt. His thoughts were interrupted by the impatient buzzing of an intercom. He leaned over the desk, flipped the switch. A look of annoyance flickered in his eyes.

"Colonel Modica—what is it?" he snapped absently.

"A call from the lobby, sir. We've got a visitor," came Lt. Destro's filtered voice.

"Well?"

"It's the brigand, Salvatore, sir."

"Damnit, Lieutenant! You know the *Albergo-Sole* is off limits to civilians. Why do you bother me?"

"He has a pass signed by the Minister of the Interior. Demands audience with the Mayor of Godrano, Don Barbarossa."

"Who does?" preoccupied with his thoughts, he hadn't caught the name.

"Salvatore, sir."

"*Salvatore?*" Modica's eyes swept over the clippings on his desk. "Salvatore is here? At headquarters? Well, I'll be damned!" A look of ineffable delight crept into his eyes.

"Tell you what, Lieutenant," said Modica in a conspiratorial manner. "I want you to divert Salvatore to my quarters. You are to tell no one he's here. *Especially* Don Barbarossa. Got it?"

"Yes, sir."

While he waited for Salvatore, Colonel Modica's mind raced ahead excitedly as a plan formulated in his mind. Having come to look with great disfavor at the man, Don Barbarossa, Modica would have liked nothing better than to emulate Pontius Pilate, by washing his hands clean of the Sicilian affair. But apparently it wasn't to be. And now— this! The infamous bandit Salvatore walks into the *Al-*

bergo-Sole and demands audience with the very man who plans to betray him? Was this to be believed?

If the Don planned to seduce the bandits, how did he dare bring them into such formal surroundings? Modica couldn't begin to comprehend the complexities in either the man or the situation. A sharp rap at the door sliced through his thoughts.

Lieutenant Destro entered, saluted, and announced, "Colonel Modica. *Signore* Salvatore is here."

Modica glanced up. "Send him in, please," he said, acknowledging the salute.

Before he reached the door, it pushed open easily. Salvatore stood poised on the threshold, his dark eyes expertly scanning the room. Then he fixed on the well-tanned officer whose friendly blue eyes widened in astonishment when they took into focus the handsome, well-dressed youth in his dark tailored suit with his white shirt and tie, carrying a briefcase. He could have been a young lawyer or business man, but certainly too young to have attained such status, thought Modica. Damn, he was something!

"I am Salvatore," he said quietly.

"I am Colonel Modica," he said rising from his chair, with arm extended. "Please be seated, *Signore*." Modica spoke Italian with a tinge of a Sicilian dialect and tried to remain aloof as befitted his position. It wasn't easy.

"*Piacere, Colonnello*," replied Tori. He sauntered casually by the adjoining bedroom and bath in an attitude of silent appraisal, while he checked all exits and entrances for possible entrapments.

"You desire to speak with Salvatore, *Colonnello?*" he asked pleasantly.

"Yes, as a matter of fact I do." The Colonel extended his hand towards a chair.

Tori sat down stiffly and struck a pose of polite reserve.

"May I see your passes? It's a matter of protocal. You understand." Modica set aside his fascination.

Tori leaned forward slightly, removed the documents from his hip pocket, and handed them to Modica. "You may speak English. It comes easier—no? If I don't understand, I'll make it known."

Modica nodded, impressed. "Did His Excellency, the Minister, sign these passes for you personally?" he asked, scanning the passes.

"Not in my presence."

"I didn't mean that. Did the passes come from Belasci, or second-hand?"

"Your Sicilian isn't too clear. But to reply—yes."

407

He removed a thin brown *cigarillo* from a slender box. "Permit me to smoke, *Colonnello?*" His easy smile covered his nervousness.

Modica nodded, extended his lighter across the desk. "How *did* you come by these passes?" he persisted.

"*Managghia!* You *are* relentless. My Godfather gave them to me."

Modica lit his cigarette. "Godfather?"

Tori hedged deliberately. "Please put to me precisely what you wish to know. I can shorten this interrogation." He spoke slowly, carefully.

"That's considerate of you. Please state your business." Modica found it hard to be formal with the Sicilian.

"My business—with your permission—is with Don Barbarossa."

"I'm sure. But, with *your* permission, please state the nature of it."

"With *your* permission, it's private," he replied tactfully.

"You realize I can restrain you, instantly? You took a chance, coming here with a price on your head," Colonel Modica snapped.

A thousand thoughts crossed Tori's mind. Tense, he tried not to indicate his discomfort. Had he been so blinded by his Godfather's importance that he failed to exercise simple caution? "You saw my passes. Are they not in order?" Tori moved slightly in his chair to feel the security of the gun strapped to his inner calf.

"You are an enemy of the State. Presently, I *am* the State—over and above any jurisdiction enjoyed by the Don."

"So—I am at your mercy." Tori felt sweat pop on his forehead. Under his arms it ran in streams to his waist. "Is it your desire, *Colonnello*, to shoot me up? Before you reach that button on your desk, you'll be dead. I promise. I will take my chances with those three *soldati* who work outside your door and those three by the elevator. Make no mistake, you will not live to see my fate, if such is your intent." He smiled tightly.

A glimmer of astonishment crossed Modica's face. "You're concealing weapons, also?" He shook his head tolerantly. "I shall have to reprimand my men for such gross carelessness."

"Have no fear, Colonnello. It's not my intention to contest you in a duel. My feelings are that you didn't bring Salvatore to your office to arrest him," he said, exuding an outward glow of confidence that belied his inner feelings. Tori would have liked nothing better than to leave these alien grounds.

For reasons they both were later to wonder about, their communication was as instantaneous and mysterious as it was unmistakable, Modica found it difficult not to praise the young man whom he still couldn't reconcile in his mind as being the same one written about so glowingly. Finally, and with an irresistible impulse, the Colonel managed to express himself.

"You're everything that's been written about you and more. Your perception, which is astonishingly accurate, amazes me. You're right, I've no interest in detaining you or arresting you. My business is far more important."

"What sort of business does an American *Colonello* have with Salvatore?" Toni smiled.

Modica got to the point. "Why haven't your people come forth to voice their concern for the future of their country? Don't they care what happens in their lands?"

"With so many political jackals braying at your feet in the Grand Council, you need more to drive you crazy?" Tori shook his head temporately.

Colonel Modica laughed. "Political jackals, eh? You may be right. Perhaps that's why I question their qualifications as well as their aims." He fell into a more serious pose. "Doesn't the fate of Italy matter to you or your people?"

"Sicily—yes. Not so much, Italy."

"One goes hand in hand with the other, no?"

Tori shook his head thoughtfully. "Italy, to us Sicilians, was once a big love affair. In the beginning she was a goddess, someone to revere. A long time ago we came to see her as she's always been—a whore. She was never pure, never saintly, never perfect. She took too much from us—our hearts, our blood, our sweat, even our lands, and she has squeezed us dry. What can Sicilians do—run away? To what, another land? Another love affair to dissillusion us? We have been a lost people too long. We who remain in Sicily do so because we hold hope for her future. We thought, *America has come to her aid. At last there is hope for Sicilians*. But time opens our eyes. We see nothing is done. Nothing will be done. Perhaps it's because for too long our lands and our leaders offer us nothing but oppression. We have grown accustomed to it. . . ."

"There's a chance to change all that, Sicilian. You aren't forsaken, yet!"

"How? For centuries we've been a people with no voice in government. We're a conquered land. Always Sicilians

409

are subordinate to the conquerors. Others in government, foreigners, dictate our policies.

"And you don't question them? Challenge them to make certain they do what the people want and need?" He extended an ash tray to his guest.

"But no. How is this possible? Only in a democracy are such things possible." Tori flipped his ashes in the metal container.

"Men like your Mayor Tedesco can authorize the regimentation of mankind, promote his antiquated and insufferable ideas, and you Sicilians sit back and take it like the serfs of old?" disdained the Colonel.

"The mayor can promote all he wishes. Whether the people accept such stupidity is another thing. We have our ways of dealing with such foolishness." Tori boasted with schoolboy defiance.

"Why elect such men to office in the first place? Wouldn't it seem sensible to stop them before they spread such insanity?"

"Perhaps he represents the lesser of other evils. You think we have a choice? The Church pushes its candidates upon us. If the people wish to eat and keep their jobs, they vote the way the Church tells them."

"And you permit this?" Modica was appalled.

"But—what is this? You blame *me?* I have no control in the elections. Only in these extraordinary circumstances of war have I been able to intervene for my people." The young Brigand indicated his annoyance.

"I'm sorry, Salvatore." Modica faltered, confused. "What I've read and what I heard is all to the contrary. Are you not fighting the cause of your people? Are you not rebelling against an unjust government?"

"*Si!* Against starvation, graft and corruption—inflicted upon us by those men you Americans hired to enforce your laws. *You* made it a felony to transport food from one province to another thus making felons of every decent Sicilian. It's an unjust law, *Colonnello.*" He put out his cigarette and leaned back in his chair easily.

Salvatore spent the next half hour explaining the ways of the *carabinieri,* their oppression, and treacheries. "You created a nation of hunted criminals whose guilt was only to feed themselves and their loved ones. That's why I release prisoners from jail and burn their records—so they can live in peace without fear of reprisal. It was for no other reason. I, too, was forced into a life of crime by your unjust laws." He paced about the room easily.

"Is it therefore, not your concern to prevent leaders in

government from taking and taking from the people and never allowing them to live as human beings? Man was born free, to determine his own destiny. Shouldn't he have the right to elect his own leaders? Leaders who echo their voices? Such a cause should be wholly supported by all those close to the soil, the masses of the oppressed, for they are the ones who stand to gain." Modica watched Tori glance curiously at the maps strewn about the room.

Tori, no fool, grew silent and reflective. This wasn't strange talk to his ears. These words were like the cherished dreams of his childhood, when he'd been filled with idealistic hope. Angered at first, by the accusatorial tone, he retorted, "But—this is not my affair—" He stopped in mid-sentence and stared at the American, temporizing. "Are you saying that a mere peasant could choose a president—a Ruler?" His words, spoken softly, just above a whisper, were hesitant, unsure. "Someone like me?"

Modica nodded. "Right now you control your territory. You lead some five hundred men who do your bidding. Has it occurred to you if your people united for a worthy cause you could create the Sicily you dream of, the kind of government you desire? Even a democracy—for the people, of the people, and by the people? Yes, Salvatore, why not you? This is your country, your home, your people."

Unable to restrain himself, Colonel Modica didn't realize how far-reaching were these ideas he had implanted in the mind of this Sicilian. Later, much later, he wondered how he an American on foreign soil, despite the Occupation, dared suggest such inflamatory politics to a native. Yet, Goddamnit, it *was* his job to stir up unrest, wasn't it? Wasn't that his posture in this damnable war?

In the ensuing silence, Tori studied the American Officer with whom he felt such mysterious affinity. After several moments in which he drew his own conclusions, he asked Modica, quietly: "You mean . . . a revolution?" His eyes burned into Modica's, and he stiffened suspiciously at the direction in which the conversation was directed. Tori recoiled. He was in unfamiliar territory and this could very well be a trap, he reminded himself. These Americans were too disarming, too generous in their praises.

When he heard his words played back without guile, with unmasked innocence, Modica almost backed off. Fully committed and deeply entrenched in his work, he pushed on. "Damnit, Salvatore! How else can you help keep your country out of the hands of the communists? You don't want the Reds to take over your lands, do you?" He paused a moment. "Do you believe in destiny?"

411

The American leaned forward, his blue eyes fixed on the Sicilian.

"Does a Sicilian believe there's a sun?" Tori gave him the shadow of a smile.

"When I heard you were in the lobby, I moved swiftly. I had to meet you. If anyone represents Sicily—it's you. If anyone can tell me how Sicilians feel, what they think, what they need, it's you!" he said, impassioned. "I'm certain destiny had a hand in our encounter." Modica walked back to his desk and poured two Pernods. He handed one to his guest, flushed with excitement. Salvatore, with USA aid, could rise and conquer!

"Tori shook his head. "Grazie, *Colonnello*. I do not drink."

"Nothing?"

"Nothing." Tori explained. "I learned that the Great Alexander once killed his best friend under the influence of alcohol, and lived to deeply regret the act. If such a man was disposed to commit an act against his nature—what chance would I, a lesser man, have in keeping my faculties under control while under so potent an influence?"

Pleasantly surprised at the sobriety of his words, Modica pressed. "Ah, but then that raises the question: which nature is the true one? That which is inhibited, or that which becomes free of inhibitions when relaxed by an intoxicant?" *He's sharp and at least he's a thinker,* the Colonel told himself.

Silence. . . .

"You speak in . . . how do you say . . . *astrazione*—abstractions. I have no use for such talk. Who can prove there is anything but one nature in man? Wine or no wine?" A marked disturbance creased his face.

"Come now, Salvatore, you're Catholic, no? The Church itself speaks of the God in Man and of the demon, or devil, within, that refutes the urgings of God. That shoots your theory, doesn't it? There's your duality." He sat down heavily in the chair behind his desk.

"I don't understand—*shoots* your theory?" He was perplexed.

"Blows up. Disintegrates. In short, it renders your theory of a singular nature in man, incorrect. Theologians should know. It's their racket."

"With your permission. Translate in Italian. I do not understand your idioms."

Modica complied, and explained himself as best he could. "You see, we Americans don't really speak English, we use considerable slang, as you do in your dialect. You

412

know, you are something special? Terrific! Did you study formally? Here or abroad? What made you take up the cause of the peasant? Did it intrigue you? What?" He wasn't prepared for the subtle change in the brigand.

Tori appeared instantly withdrawn. He glanced swiftly at the officer and drummed his fingers nervously on his thighs, working up to a controlled anger.

"I, *Colonnello*, am a peasant, with no formal education. Tutored by my mother, a former school teacher, I was inspired to become a reader of books. I do not find it intriguing. I found it a bitter necessity to take up our cause. Each day I hope you law makers accelerate your labors and bring a much needed peace and prosperity to our people in their desperate struggle for survival."

"Now, hold on a moment, Salvatore. I meant nothing derogatory. The hell of it is, I find myself speechless at your accomplishments and the manner in which you speak. To say nothing of your command of my language."

"With your permission, what does the word *terrific* mean" asked Tori.

"It means what it means in your language, except, we Americans use it in the vernacular, meaning something unusually great, intense, extraordinary."

"Then, you did not mean to suggest I was a frightening, dreadful or appalling person?"

"Never!"

He relaxed and spoke the word several times. "Terrific. *Te-rrific!*" I like that word. You, also are *te-rrific, Colonnello*. Is that correct?"

"I thank you for the compliment. But, it is you who is more suited to such a word. You still amaze me."

"Why? You expected an inarticulate, lowly dog?"

"Certainly not that." Modica shoved the news clippings towards him. "I also read extensively. From what I've read here, your letters will one day become collector's items."

Tori shrugged off the compliment.

He felt inescapably drawn towards the American. They entered into a dialogue in which Tori spoke of his youth, his dreams, those of his people, conditions before the war, and what his plans for the future included. He discussed his fiery resolve to seek amnesty for his crimes.

Listening to him, the American grew more aware of the complexity of Salvatore's nature. Modica perceived easily the "larger than life" figure of a hero as it attempted to shrink into a smaller shadow of the man Tori wanted to be. He was puzzled. For a time Modica couldn't reconcile the bandit, Salvatore, with the youth, Alessandro, as if

413

they were two separate people in one body. He found himself wondering which of the two would emerge victorious in the desperate battle that raged in him. Nearly two hours later, Modica expertly directed the conversation back to where it nearly exploded earlier. Totally without guile, he asked. "What do you know about this man, Don Barbarossa?"

"My Godfather?" Tori picked up the globe paperweight from Modica's desk and bounced it in his hands. "He is some te-*rrrific* man, no?"

Stunned, Modica hardly believed his ears. "I don't understand. Barbarossa's your Godfather?"

"Yes—Why? Does it surprise you?"

The Colonel was appalled. What madness is this? he asked himself. Barbarossa plans to betray his own Godson? Recovering momentarily, he thumbed through the manila file, oblivious to the curious glances cast upon him by his guest, until he located the report which had trailed the skillfully deceitful *capomafia* to the Chief Inspector's office. He scanned the contents to assure himself there was chance for error. There was none. It was all there—every slick and cunning trick Barbarossa had employed.

The change in the American became too obvious. Tori felt uncomfortable. "Something is wrong?"

Modica hardly heard him. A fucking three-year-old dummy could have seen through the acrobatics of this cagey Sicilian mongoose, Barbarossa! Disgusted, Modica slammed the file shut. He reached for a cigarette, and, finding his pack empty, he crushed it into a ball in annoyance and tossed into a wastebasket nearby. Tori leaned in, a pack of Camels in his outstretched hand.

"Accept one of mine and I shall be honored."

The Colonel nodded absently, and reached for it. He lit it and puffed thoughtfully on it. Snapping out of his reverie, he waved his hands in the air about him apologetically. "Sorry if I seemed rude. Something struck me—nothing to do with you," he lied and changed the subject. "I mentioned earlier that I should like to become better acquainted with you. I feel in my bones that something important will come from our meeting. You understand?"

"I understand. Only our native tongue separates our thoughts from time to time." A polite smile played about his lips as he lit his own cigarette.

"I mean no offense," He liked Tori immensely.

"None taken." He spun the globe in his hands and gave it his attention for a short time.

414

Modica began to ramble. He spoke of his experiences with the Sicilians, how the intrigues annoyed him and provoked his integrity. "They amend their minds constantly, shift and change their ideals as promiscuously as a whore changes bed partners."

"Credit that idiosyncrasy to the constant changes forced upon us by our conquerors. I doubt that Sicilians can ever be what our hazy ideals tell us to be. But, one thing is certain: the allegiance and love Sicilians feel for Americans is irrevocable. Your leaders cannot accept what Sicilians feel in their hearts? That they desire to be a part of America?"

"If that was my dilemma, there'd be no problem. *My* problem is communism. In a matter of time your lands will be infiltrated with communists. Sicily, courted and wooed by them, will once again be raped by a conqueror and turned out to whore for them."

"Yes, it's true. Russia seeks control of the Mediterranean. We've known this for too long. Incredible that America permits her this vice."

"Russia has made giant strides in the past year. It's natural she wants to spread her spheres of interest," replied the American blandly.

"Why does she pluck such power from the United States? Why?" queried Tori.

"We cannot afford to offend Russia, since Hitler remains to be reckoned with. You forget we still have a date to go dancing with Tojo." Modica stared at the smoke curling from his cigarette.

Tori found this incredulous. "You risk the spread of a malignancy by not cutting out a small infection?"

Colonel Modica remained silent as he studied the noticeable changes in his guest. The color left Tori's face, then slowly reentered it, flushing crimson.

"So! Once again Sicily becomes a pawn, to be betrayed. America with a short memory, forgets her friends too quickly." Tori jumped to his feet agitated. "As long as there is breath in me, *Colonnello*, the Reds will not rule my country!"

"What would you have her do? Become a Monarchy once again? A republic? A democracy? Is she ready for any of these? Would you favor separation from Italy with full autonomy A regional Parliament set up here in Palermo?" Modica's eyes blazed blue fire. "I want to hear what the 'people's man' has to say! God Almighty! I want to hear! . . . Well—tell me. I'm waiting!"

Tori backed off. The waters were getting too deep. He didn't know the Colonel, knew less about his motives, and,

415

as most Sicilians were prone to do, he suspected double-dealing of sorts. Salvatore smiled easily.

"I'm no *politico*, to tell you what is best for my people. They want what any man wants—freedom, a chance to live decent lives without being robbed of respect. To work and support their families. The things morally due to humans. At war's end, I shall complete my education and study law, then perhaps I can tell you the kind of government my people need."

"What qualifies you to be so positive they don't *need* communism? Moments ago you were on fire, blasting the Reds! You don't make sense, Sicilian! How can you be so adamantly opposed to one issue and tepid on others?" He wanted to inflame the young man as he had earlier.

"Everyone says communism is bad! You yourself admit it. Why is America so against it? Our lawmakers are against it because it's always the same with new conquerors. Russia will break all the promises she now baits us with."

Colonel Modica realized at once he had a neophyte on his hands. Terribly let down, he sighed with abject futility. In the next half hour he learned why Salvatore had hedged. This unusual, complex youth who had become a national hero had somehow psyched himself into believing that he was nothing without a formal education. He was wrong. But, as long as he believed it, it would remain his truth.

Almost as if he read the Colonel's mind, Tori explained. "I've become what I am through the circumstances of war. Do not mistake yourself about my importance. I told you, half the stories written about me are grossly distorted, over-exaggerated. The other half are fanciful products of highly imaginative writers."

Modica disagreed. "A formal education makes neither the man nor the politician. It helps, but it's not the prime requisite. Don't delude yourself into believing such trivia, for God's sake. In the two short years of your career, whether chosen by preference or through circumstance, you have *become* Sicily."

"No, no, no, no. You give me too much importance. I am presently nothing more than an outlaw with a price on my head—some say a bandit, a murderer chased by the law, who seeks to collect on unpaid accounts."

"That might be true—but there's more you must take into account. Unless you, yourself, recognize and face your own potential, nothing will come of your talent. What you've done—what you've accomplished—is so stellar that nothing you can say will dull the deeds you performed."

"Did you go to college, *Colonnello?*" he asked with interest.

"Yes."

"What about this General Patton. Him too?"

"Him, too."

"And *Generale* Eisenhower. What of him?"

"Yes, but—"

"You see? Every man who hopes to lead men must be more knowledgeable than those who follow. It is his duty to know more than his men."

Modica exasperated, "There is a man warming up in the bull pen right now, who never had a college education. Soon he'll be President of the United States. He was a farmer—a peasant, like you, who believed in certain principles, and became a politician. Elected to the U.S. Senate, he supported President Roosevelt and became a Chairman on a special investigation committee where his fairness and integrity came to light. He was later nominated Vice President, and elected to office with President Roosevelt. Because of the President's failing health, he will be Commander in Chief—all without a formal education. There are many others like him throughout history. Not all leaders graduate *Summa cum laude.*"

"With your permission, *Colonnello,* I will take some coffee. It is strange to hear my name spoken in the same breath as that of a future American President."

Modica barked into the intercom. "Lieutenant! Send some coffee and refreshments to us."

"Yes, sir," came Destro's filtered voice.

Tori gazed with great interest at the box on his desk.

"So, Salvatore doesn't recognize the extent of *his* power?"

"It's plain to see I haven't the power of that small box. You talk into it and it brings you coffee?"

Colonel Modica smiled. "It's plain to me you don't know. Let me tell you, you pack plenty of power. Such influence, if channeled correctly, can move mountains!"

"I have no interest to move mountains, *Colonnello.*" Tori wagged a hand in the air.

"Don't misunderstand. I'm not speaking in the literal sense, only figuratively." The American officer moved towards the window and glanced outside.

"Then, speak in the literal sense so I understand."

Modica smiled. "I'll put it this way. If I were a betting

man, I'd put all my money on you." He turned from the street scene below, his eyes on Tori.

"*Your* money on me? I don't comprehend such words."

"What I mean is, I'd promote you, push you forward, permit you to speak on my behalf. For instance, if you ran for public office, I'd back you with all I have." He groped for the right words in Italian.

"Ahhhh! *Capeeshu!* You'd buy all the votes for me."

"Buy all the votes? I don't mean that at all."

"How else would I win the election?"

"This is the way your officials get elected?"

"How else? Here the priests and nuns go from house to house with food and small cash donations. They even promise jobs if you vote for the men they promote."

"I assure you that isn't what I had in mind. Col. Modica took time to explain himself, while Salvatore listened intently as a student might listen to his teacher.

Finally, Salvatore understood. He sippped a glass of water and temporized. "You'd back me with money, eh? If the *Colonnello* should do such a thing, he would be backing the wrong man."

"Again you underestimate yourself—"

"If the *Colonnello* were to back a man such as Matteo Barbarossa, in my humble opinion you'd be backing the proper person. Be clever, put your money on him." Tori tapped his forehead with his forefinger. "He is one *furbo*—smart man."

Colonel Modica held his breath. Time, and a totally disarming congeniality, had lured Salvatore into his lair, where had he proceeded to methodically and intentionally, yet unobtrusively, exact certain information, heretofore elusive to him. If Colonel Modica had spent ten years compiling a dossier on Don Barbarossa, he couldn't have uncovered such explicit information.

Salvatore resorted to what amounted to hero worship as he guided the American officer through the legendary Barbarossa's life and his spectacular climb from those early Mazzarino bandit days to the uncontested high position of *capomafia* of all Sicily. Tori led the Colonel through the countless coups and the terrorizing of his enemies to which Don Barbarossa had subjected any obstructors who stood between him and the coveted role of head of all heads in the Mafia hierarchy. He afforded Modica a bird's-eye view of the national political climate that spawned such a power broker. He posed a comparison between Barbarossa and his predecessor, the former *capomafia* Don Calomare, and described the shame, and humiliation he had endured during the reign of *Il Duce*.

"Very little is known about Matteo Barbarossa's activities during his twenty year exile underground," continued Salvatore. "He wasn't heard of much until you Allies landed in Sicily. You must be aware of the cooperation he extended the Allied forces at that time. What a man, eh?"

The Colonel had listened in rapt silence. Through it all, he was visibly disturbed by recognition of the fierce pride that oozed from Tori as he spoke of the *capomafia*. His first comment was spoken with brutal candor.

"It seems to me that you intend emulating this Godfather of yours, eh, Salvatore?"

Tori's expression froze. Momentarily puzzled, he thought over his words and wondered where the Colonel got such a notion. A flicker of annoyance crept into his eyes. Just as quickly, it vanished. "You overestimate me, *Colonnello*. No one could imitate the bandit of Mazzarino. Barbarossa, the most powerful man in Sicily, dethroned by Mussolini, returns to power twenty years later, to be recrowned as uncontested leader. . . ."

For fear of losing ground already gained, the American didn't bother to argue the point. They both sat sipping coffee, brought in moments before by Lt. Destro, and dunked a generous assortment of Sicilian cookies.

"The twentieth century, stillborn for half a century has a chance to come to life, Salvatore. But, first the feudal tyranny has to be excised—cut out. You understand?"

"And you think I can revive it? Restore life to my country?" asked the outlaw quietly.

Colonel Modica smiled. "Precisely."

They were interrupted by the buzzing of the intercom. Colonel Modica glanced at his watch, and snapped on the switch. Tori, flushed by the conversation, was taken by the box. He leaned in to listen to the gadget, a look of marvel in his eyes, as Lieutenant Destro's voice came through the "magic box."

"Sorry Colonel. It's Don Barbarossa. He's furious. Wants to know why you've seen fit to detain his guest. He's hot as a pistol, sir. What'll I tell him?"

Tori grinned amiably, his eyes twinkling in amusement. "You see, *Colonnello*? It's best you put your money on him. He knows everything—misses nothing."

Colonel Modica scowled. "Tell the Don—" he began,

"*Uhhhhhhuhuh*," Tori wagged a finger at him and shook his head playfully.

"Tell the Don," said Modica with visible restraint, "his

guest hasn't been detained. He'll leave momentarily." The Colonel, annoyed by the interruption, hadn't finished his conversation with the Sicilian outlaw, not by a long shot. He wanted less, however, to give the Don any insight into any plans he might be formulating, those in which Salvatore might play an important role. He moved swiftly. "Have dinner with me on Saturday or Sunday, Salvatore?"

Tori expressed mild pleasure. "Here?" he waved his hands about.

"Yes, of course. Unless you'd prefer some other place."

He smiled graciously. "It would be an honor if you would come to my house in Montegatta. I assure you safe conduct to and from my house," he added at the momentary hesitation he read in the American officer's eyes.

Colonel Modica suppressed a smile. "My concern wasn't for myself. Is it safe for you?"

"Salvatore goes where he desires—with little effort or problems."

"Very well, Sunday. What time?"

"You will come early and remain late. I shall show you some true relics of antiquity." Tori grew expansive.

"I would like that very much." He stood up and shook hands, and with an arm around Tori's shoulders, he walked him to the door. For an instant, he paused and faced the young man. His face grew somber.

"Be cautious, my friend. Trust very few men, in these times." He wanted to say "beware of Don Barbarossa," but didn't.

"Does the Colonel mean what I think he means?" Tori's dark, compelling eyes bore into the American's. "Perhaps if you were more explicit—specific—?"

"No. I can't be. But it might be wise to weigh every proposal with respect to its long-term influence. What I mean is—oh what the hell! You're a prodigious reader. Bone up on Machiavelli!" exclaimed Modica.

"Bone up?" Tori's eyes twinkled again in merriment. "What are you telling me? What is bone up?"

"Refresh your memory—familiarize yourself with a subject—"

"Ahhh. *Si.* I understand. My, my, what strange idioms you Americans use." He smiled, tucked the brief case under one arm, then said quietly.

"Throughout our conversation, I sense you wish to tell me something more than your words convey. Permit me to say, I am safe. My enemies are few. No one would dare harm Salvatore."

"It's not among one's enemies that treachery usually

420

springs," cautioned the Colonel. "I suggest you use discretion about our encounter. Until Sunday—"

"Unless I decide to start a revolution before that—eh, *Colonnello*," he laughed.

Colonel Modica's blue eyes froze into a fixed look of concern. He grew edgy.

"Never fear, *Colonnello*, I was making a joke on you. *Ciao*."

Long after the young rebel left, Colonel Modica contemplated him. He found it incredible that so young a man could have come to world-wide prominence in these troublesome times of war. He glanced through several of the news clippings, picked one out in particular and with interest reread the item:

"Alessandro Salvatore, inspiration to the young, represents immortal youth in a decaying old world. Young, idealistic, imbued with a quiet power never credited to youth, he stands opposed to an ancient feudal system which for centuries has kept his people ignorant, subjugated and confused. Before Salvatore appeared there was disunity, starvation, lack of pride, and a loss of hope among his people. This reporter, having spoken with the rebel leader, found him to be the embodiment of a modern day Robin Hood, but one who practices the doctrines of Aristotle, conquers in the manner of Alexander of Macedonia, and employs Nicomacean ethics. He demonstrates small patience with those learned men, who, proficient in knowledge and education, use these tools to break the backs of the less fortunate. In these troubled times, to have brought strength and unity to a broken, helpless people is short of miraculous. He announces to the world, in the same manner he announces himself: 'I am Salvatore, world. Wake up! Help my people to become whole!' "

Every article about him bloomed with glowing accounts of the flamboyant brigand. His had been a popular cause, picked up and given worldwide recognition by an adoring press. Most correspondents continuously stressed, like advocates pleading his case, that Salvatore's crimes had been of an involuntary nature, forced upon him by devastating circumstances and intolerable conditions in a country prostrated by defeat and occupied by numerous alien armies.

Most articles referred directly to his quest for justice, his intent to strike at the oppressors of the poor—the *carabinieri*, the feudal land barons, the insensitive government, and, of course the Mafia. In one article Salvatore was quoted as saying, "The Mafia, the enemy of the

people, is a corrupt institution that has kept them bound
in near-slavery to the feudal landlords."

Colonel Modica, his forehead creased in frowns, sat
back in his chair apparently disgusted. He read that statement several times: "The Mafia, the enemy of the people. . . . ?"

Yet the biggest *mafioso* of all time was Salvatore's Godfather!!! Barbarossa was Agathocles incarnated, the Prae-
tor of Syracuse, the King of Syracuse who intrigued with
the Carthaginians and ended up in full control of Sicily!
And Colonel Modica sought to challenge such a man? He
shuddered, then grew irate as he mulled over the situation.

"Sicilian intrigue be damned! Fucking Sicilian logic!
Nothing but contradictions and intrigues upon intrigues!
All of it be damned!" shouted Colonel Modica, in a voice
loud enough to fill his quarters.

While he sat stewing over the countless intrigues and
counter-intrigues, more intrigue, hatreds, jealousies and
vendettas were brooding in the political gardens of Sicilian despots like a blood-red flower waiting to burst into
nightmarish bloom out of the corruption, evil and malevolency of an ancient system that refused to lie down and
die and give up the ghost so that civilization could
progress.

CHAPTER 31

By the time Salvatore arrived at his Godfather's penthouse
he found the *mafioso* seated behind his desk, trying not to
show his displeasure. As soon as the amenities were over,
the Don asked, as if it didn't matter to him, what Tori had
experienced in the American officer's company: "Did the
Colonnello cause you inconvenience?"

"He was *simpatico*," said Tori unruffled. "Most cordial."

"You were there a long time. What did he want?"

"No—not long. Perhaps thirty-forty minutes—"

"Precisely one hour and forty minutes," the Don said
abruptly.

"So long?" Tori smiled tersely. He disliked being questioned. Having been his own man for a lifetime, he

strained in a subordinate role. He crossed his leg over the other and tapped the side of his boot. "The time flew."

"What did you speak about?" The Don grew impatient with such evasiveness.

"He inspected my passes. Asked how I came by them."

"And, you told him?"

"Naturally. Was it unwise of me to have done so?"

The Don wagged a hand. "It matters not. No one questions my authority." He strutted about the penthouse in his typical attire, shirt-sleeves and trousers held up by suspenders. He waved his arms about the room, expansively. "You see how they treat me, your Godfather? All this at their expense, for Don Barbarossa! Because he is *importante*—to the Allies." He moved back behind the ornately hand-carved oak desk, picked up a fancy humidor, and offered a cigar to his guest.

Tori accepted one. The Don helped himself before replacing the box. Each man lit his own smoke. The room filled with smoke spirals. Don Matteo shuffled to the window, pushed it open, and took several fresh breaths of air. Patting his stomach contentedly he returned to the desk.

"What else did the American discuss?" He pushed his dark glasses up on the bridge of his nose. Beneath his polite mask was a raging anger.

"We spoke of politics."

"What did you tell him?"

Tori shrugged indifferently. "I told him I was no politician. That he should speak of such things to a man more qualified, more experienced and far more astute than I—you."

"That's straight? You told him that?" he expressed his surprised pleasure.

"I told him when I graduated from law school, I'd be better qualified—"

"That nonsense again? Listen, you'd better learn quickly you can't remain a rabbit among foxes!" he snorted. "What else did you discuss?"

The *Colonnello* was surprised you are my Godfather."

"You told him that, too?"

"Was I wrong to have told him?"

"It's no business of the Americans!" He stopped when he saw a curious strained expression in Tori's eyes. The Don waved his hands apologetically. "No, it wasn't wrong. I have no reason to conceal the fact the famous Sicilian bandit is Godson to Don Barbarossa," he said acidly.

He was sharp. He was hard. He was cunning. He was

capomafia, not a cheap imitator of the dime-a-dozen *mafioso*. He was the original. The stamp of an absolute monarch was on all he said and did, surmised Salvatore as he watched the man. And he *was* exciting.

"Certain things are better left unspoken. If it's known you are my Godson, with a price on your head, it might prove difficult to grant you a favor. Be it as it may, nothing shall happen to you as long as I sanction your protection. *Capeeshi?*" He shuffled through a few papers on his desk.

"Might I point out, Godfather, I've done quite well—without your protection." It was the special look the Don gave him that made Tori wary. Godfather or not, he saw something in the older man's eyes which bordered on hatred and envy. He had no desire of letting that enmity grow, so he grinned and said glibly, with a forced sparkle to his eyes. "Unless that good fortune I've enjoyed has been extended under the invisible protection and shining shield of power by the noteworthy Don Barbarossa?"

"You'll never speak truer words," replied the Don, relaxing a bit. "*Allora*, how is your Mamma? You gave her my felicitations?"

"Not yet. I've had little time to see her, since we last talked. I hadn't planned on visiting you so soon. A matter has arisen which needs the guidance of a person of your experience to steer me properly."

A rush of conflicting emotions surged through the Don. He felt, at first, the same inescapable feeling he had felt when, as a youth, out of necessity, he had mastered the art of flattery and persuasiveness for gain. He felt as if he was being had and nurtured for another man's benefit. It was this continuous push-pull, a strange compulsion to refrain from dealing harshly with Salvatore which unnerved him and placed him continuously on his guard.

"Talk. Tell me what it is you want." He sat back in his chair like an Oriental potentate.

"To my province has come a certain *Napolitano*, a *carabiniero*, *Maresciallo* Franchina who caused me much discomfort. There is no real problem, yet. Word has come that Franchina plans an ambush on Friday night, two days hence. He's issued two hundred warrants for me and my men. How he has learned the names of these men baffles me, for it has been a secret, well kept for two years. Perhaps he has the employ of many spies." Tori glanced at the ornate silver service on the roll away cart. "With your permission, Godfather, I should like a cup of coffee."

"Help yourself. Why don't you take care of this Marshal, yourself? It would be an easy task to dispose of him?" he tilted an eye at Tori.

"With conditions as they are, it doesn't seem appropriate at this time to promote unnecessary bloodshed, just because some overly ambitious *carabiniero* wants to promote himself at my expense. This is a critical time for Sicily, and I wish to do nothing to bring unnecessary publicity upon my affairs." He poured hot coffee into the bone china cup and allowed his eyes to travel about the splendor in which the Don lived.

Don Matteo hardly noticed Tori sauntering about the room. His brain roiled with thoughts of this audacious Marshal Franchina. A complication of this sort would prove more devastating to his plans than any of Salvatore's. All he needed was a self-appointed, promotion-minded *carabiniero* to throw a monkey wrench into his plans! And why hadn't he been informed of these warrants? For him not to have been informed there must be some diabolical plot underfoot to undermine his own efforts. Burning inwardly he wondered who was behind Marshal Franchina?

"How did you learn of the proposed ambush?"

"I have my spies." He motioned to the room and its trappings. "The Americans respect you tremendously, Godfather," he said tongue in cheek. "There's not a newspaper account of your deeds, I haven't committed to memory," continued Tori.

Tori sat down opposite him. "By the way, Godfather, I notice there are no pictures of my baptism. Don't you have any? My own mother seems to have misplaced ours. I'm sure you have a token of that special day?" He studied his Godfather through casual eyes.

"You took the words from my lips. I, too, misplaced the photographs. Times were hectic. I jailed myself after Mori's trail of death struck Sicily, and I remained at Ucciardone prison for three years. By then my wife had vacated our villa in Monreale and we returned to Godrano. After her death, I had no desire to uncrate the boxes. They are in Godrano. I promise, one day I shall have my men uncrate the boxes and locate the photographs." He avoided Tori's penetrating eyes.

Unwittingly the Don had already told Tori what he wanted to know. As soon as he'd checked the dates involved he'd know the answers to the questions which plagued him since he met the Don. He hardly heard the Don's next words.

"Leave Franchina to me. Carry on as usual. The burr shall be removed from your saddle."

Va bene. Grazie."

"It's not necessary you thank me. It is now two favors done for you out of respect. Remember, when the time comes, a favor shall be expected from you." It was the look in his eyes that jarred Tori.

"Two?" Tori was puzzled. "I don't understand—" It suddenly came to him. "What I spoke to you about in Godrano? The matter of Don Pippinu. . . ."

". . . has already been done."

"Already?" Tori was impressed. "But, how? When?"

"Not important. What matters is you've been avenged. Don Pippinu was a cheat, a disgrace to the brotherhood." The Don savagely tore the cigar from his lips and flung it into a spittoon. "We don't earn our respect through dealings with such a fool, a common gangster who would bring us shame, dishonor and disgrace."

"What would you have done in his place?"

Almost against his will, Don Matteo found himself responding to his Godson's question, and, in so doing, taught Tori a lesson he'd never forget.

"I'd have struck a fair bargain with you. No doubt you'd have settled for a lesser figure than the one you quoted—no?"

"Perhaps."

"Allora, with gentle persuasion, I might have encouraged you to accept even less. But—it would have been a bona fide deal. A deal in business is a deal, one which cannot be broken. If a man's word is like water, no one will trust him. If loss is suffered due to a man's inability to bargain wisely—it's his misfortune and must be erased from mind as a bad experience from which a wise man would profit. To be cheated is unpardonable. The test of a real man is at the center of bargaining. Don't you see? It's no different than the results in a prize ring. It isn't always the most powerful man who wins. The best trained fighter, using special techniques, who knows his opponent's weakness, more often emerges victorious."

Struck by the Don's words, Tori experienced a peculiar sensation as if for the first time he had been given insight into the extent of his Godfather's power. He spoke politely. "I am deeply indebted to you for having helped me avenge a terrible and inhuman act." As he spoke a tremendous weight lifted from his shoulders, gave him peace. Apolladora's death had been avenged. Tori rose to

426

his feet, prepared to take his leave, but the Don didn't acknowledge his move.

"How many men are in your command, Godson?" he asked softly and portentously enough to cause the hairs on Tori's neck to stand up. . . . *Two favors done of you. Favors will be asked in return. . . .*

Sensing what was coming, he shrugged noncommittally. "I have no figures at my disposal." He brightened and tried a new tack. "I forgot to ask. How are the Arabians? Have you named them, yet? Will you breed them?"

"Don't be clever. Just answer." He cleared his throat. "How many?"

"Two—perhaps three hundred. Why?"

Don Matteo grunted. He knew the figure exceeded six hundred. "If you are needed for a special job, how long would it take you to prepare your men?"

"A *special* job?" Tori's throat constricted. "Salvatore works for no man."

"No one but me. How long?"

"You are attempting to solicit the services of Salvatore as if he was a common criminal."

"How long?" insisted the Don as if he hadn't heard Tori's words.

"Less than a week," he replied against his will. "Four days if necessary." He balled his fists tightly.

"Two—perhaps?" The Don suggested with cunning, as he padded over to the silver service and helped himself to coffee and a plate heaped with *biscotti*. "You didn't taste these, Godson. Help yourself. *Sonnu delizioso.*"

Salvatore stiffly declined. He wanted out. Uncomfortable and seething with anger at the obvious lack of respect, he wanted to leave before he said anything to destroy their relationship.

"No?" Don Matteo shrugged. "*Allora*—before you leave, you'll be contacted soon, by—uh—uh. . . ." He placed the coffee and cookies on his desk and searched his trouser pockets for some article. "Ah—here it is." He sat down in his chair and read the name aloud: "*Capitano* Bello. That's it. This new leader of the Partitionist Party will contact you shortly. He's empowered to make you a proposition. Complete amnesty for your crimes and those of your men. In addition to the rank of *Colonnello* in the Partitionist Army, he shall offer you a political appointment, one to your liking, I'm sure. If the Partitionists prove victorious in their new government, you'll be handed the double post of Chief of Police and Minister of Justice. *Va bene?*"

Tori's face drained of all color. *How the hell does he know? Did he also know that Bello had already contacted him?* Was he needling him for information? Tori drew on all his resources to keep silent and listen. *You don't play games with this deadly viper unless you know all the ground rules,* he told himself, as his sixth sense came into play, alerting him.

"What's wrong, Godson?" The Don peered through his bifocals, noticed the pale face and tightly drawn lips bordered by a thin white line.

"Nothing. I missed lunch today. Perhaps I'll take a *biscotto*." He used the next few moments to compose himself.

"You will accept the appointment. Check with me all orders you receive from anyone in authority. *Capeeshi?*"

"If I decide against the offer?" Tori posed the question, prepared for the reply.

"You won't." Don Barbarossa slurped the coffee noisily.

"No one tells Salvatore which decisions to make."

"Except me." The Don dunked his *biscotto* in the coffee and brought the soggy confection to his lips before it disintegrated. He reached for a serviette to wipe his lips.

Tori measured his words carefully and spoke evenly so as not to be misunderstood. "I move only upon my directions. No one else's. Salvatore is puppet to no man." Godfather or not, *capomafia* or not, the man must be set straight.

The Don finished his coffee as if he hadn't heard a word. He pointed to the chair. "Sit down. Let's talk man to man. Peasant to peasant. Eh? Between us shall be no manure." He shook his head and reflected. "You know, you're a stubborn, mule-headed ass."

"The first lesson you must learn is never to turn down an offer until you've examined every angle. There's always time to refuse. Always leave yourself open for negotiations. Look to the future, to long term benefits. The difference between the nobility and the peasants is that peasants live only day to day. The nobility looks to the day, but plans also for the future. *Capeeshi?*"

Tori's mind blocked at the indignation he felt. "How dare you speak to Salvatore as if he was an ignorant child?"

The Don suppressed a twinkle in his eye. "You told me you wanted to end this career of banditry?" The Don played his trump card. "Well, to get something you must part with something. In this case you work for the Partitionists and earn your freedom. When victory is obtained, you shall enjoy an exalted office in the administration." The Don continued to dunk and eat all the *biscotti* on the

428

plate. "I can never get enough of these. They are my death. My death!"

"You make it sound uncomplicated. From whom would I take orders?" asked Tori, dropping his anger, a notch.

"Whoever issues the orders, you will not make a move until you clear it with me. That way I can keep my eyes and ears open for possible treacheries."

"Treacheries at your level? My, my, I thought only the savage peasants resorted to treacheries."

Their eyes met and held for an instant. "You've made many enemies, Salvatore. Many enemies," said the Don, evenly.

"Along with many friends," he retorted with marked irritation.

"Ah, si, friends," snorted the other. "Friends whom you've bought with generosity and kindness, who would sell your friendship in a moment to the highest bidder."

"You know all the answers, don't you, Godfather?"

"All the answers. Questions, too. When I led the Mazzarini we were real bandits, not this child's play which converted you to a national hero. Tell me—of what are you a hero? Of the reporters who seek your favors so they get rich writing about you? You are a hero on paper. You know what it means to be a paper hero? *Cazzu!* That's what! You know what they do with yesterday's newspaper? That's right. They wipe asses with it. And don't you forget it. I never set out to be a hero—dead or alive. You must take chances, *Capeeshi?*"

Don Barbarossa picked at the anise seeds stuck between his teeth and glanced slyly at his mercurial Godson, knowing he had snared his prey. "Don't answer me today. By next week, if you can find two good arguments against accepting the commission, come talk with me." His deceptive voice sounded placating.

Tori endured the scathing soul-ripping to which the Don subjected him to in complete humiliation. Never had he been spoken to in this manner. There had been no strong male figure in his life to excoriate him and peel back his defenses as this man had done. He also recognized the psychology behind the words and felt himself drawn to several half-truths the Don had brought to bear. A deep silence fell between them. They looked at each other without blinking; Salvatore, hostile and stonelike in features; Don Matteo, with the inert expression of a preying mongoose before the strike.

Don Matteo broke the connection. *"Va bene.* Come, we'll drink a toast."

"You have a short memory. I don't drink." Tori's words came dangerously close to severing the cord.

"Perhaps if I didn't drink as much, my memory might be as long as yours." The Don's meaningful glance left little to the imagination. "But you're right." He forced a light laugh. "You young bloods are far sharper than old codgers like me. If we don't keep in step with the times, we'll be put to pasture."

Godson or not, this young punk would be taught a lesson. The Don's eyelids grew heavy with displeasure. Whatever other plans he might have for this impertinent cock would have to wait. The political plans he held for Salvatore superseded his own personal displeasure. "You'll be contacted shortly, Godson."

Tori's fists were clenched so tightly he found it difficult to open them and shake hands with the Don before he departed. When he did, he was disgusted to find the handshake limp and without character.

He found Vincenzo at the whorehouse, Neptune's Daughters, a place overrun with soldiers and sailors, properous prostitutes, and pimping waiters, all busy making deals faster than an auctioneer calls for a bid. They left and had dinner at Angelo's on the Via Maqueda. Tori was unresponsive to conversation. He kept replaying Colonel Modica's conversation and that of Don Barbarossa's over in his mind.

"It's not among one's enemies that treacheries spring. . . ."

Weigh carefully the proposals made to you. . . ."

"Bone up on Machiavelli. . . ."

On the trip back to Montegetta, these words of caution cut into his memory, too sharply for comfort. He wasn't so naive that he didn't know the Colonel had tried to tell him something about his Godfather. What?

In recollecting how insulting his Godfather had been and how he boldly and with confidence had overstepped his position with him, he grew fiercely indignant.

"Botta de sanguo! You'd think I was his son, the way he spoke to me!"

"What the hell you talking about, Tori? You're acting like a crazy man!"

"On the contrary, cousin. For the first time in my life, I'm probably sane. I'm beginning to see things in their proper perspective. And you can bet one thing's sure. "I'm going to bone up on Machiavelli! *Capeeshi?"*

"You're crazy! That's what. You're crazy! You know

what I think cousin? I think you need a woman! A real woman—and bad! What do you say we turn around and go back, eh? *Managghia*—I found me some woman tonight. Phew! What a woman! She makes all the others look like amateurs.

"*Te-rrific!*" said Tori laughing aloud. "*Te-rrific!* Stop the car!"

"You mean it?" said Vincenzo, his eyes sparking with excitement. He braked the car to the screeching sounds of burning rubber.

"Go back to Palermo, Vincenzo, but not to Neptune's Daughters. To the Library, cousin. To the Library."

An hour later, armed with as many books as he could find on the subject of Machiavelli, they returned to Montegatta. That night, Tori poured over *The Prince* by Niccolo Machiavelli, and a whole new world opened up for him. So, he thought, the end justifies the means, eh?

More than any other precept contained in the book was the amazing insight his own mother had into Machiavellian politics—almost as if her words had been uttered verbatim from the text. She was some woman, he told himself.

CHAPTER 32

Athena sat primly in Dr. Colassamo's waiting room, wringing her hands, unable to shake the feeling that surged through her. She hadn't meant to eavesdrop, but the door was ajar and the nurse had left the outer office. When their voices, Santino's and the physician's reached her and she heard the verdict, she felt a sensation of helplessness surge through her at first, then, relief to have confirmed what she'd guessed for a long while.

Inside the doctor's office Santino sat rigidly erect, his face considerably pale. "A brain tumor?" His voice above a whisper grew thin and distant. "A brain tumor. Is that what you suspect?"

"Yes. yes!" retorted the brusque young doctor, who'd been pushed into revealing more than he intended. He strode a few feet from his desk and stared down out the window into the crowded streets below. "There's no point in either alarming the family or minimizing the situation until we're certain."

"A brain tumor!" Santino repeated the alien words.

"*Allora, Santino, basta!* Don't work yourself up. You insisted on knowing my suspicions. If it proves true that she has a tumor," he said returning to sit behind his desk, "Allow me to stress a caveat. We won't be able to determine if it's benign or malignant without proper tests."

"Doctor, you don't understand. She's the sister of Salvatore."

"I don't care if she's the sister to God! I can do nothing in war time."

"He'll spare no expense to see she gets the best of care."

"*Managghia!* Money's not our problem. War's our problem. Our biggest obstacle is that we have no equipment for diagnostic study, no specialized medical men, and fewer medicines. The Allies bring in their own medical staff and paraphernalia for use on their own men. I've been promised new equipment. . . ."

In her attempt to tune out the doctor's words, Athena vaguely heard him instruct Santino to take along a prescription for pain and to be on the lookout for the various symptoms he'd described earlier. There was something said of an electroencephalograph to study her brain waves. But he didn't have to say more. Right then she knew her time on earth was measured.

Santino's voice cut into her thoughts. "What can we do *dottore?* We must save her."

"What's the sense in my talking? You haven't heard a word I said!" The doctor returned to his desk and began to scribble on a desk pad.

"This is a prescription for medication. She is to take it once every four hours—and only when necessary! Understand that! I caution you to be on guard for other symptoms—any changes contrary to her usual nature. Promiscuity, careless morals—foul language—you know."

"*Dottore!* This is a fine, decent woman of whom you speak!" he glared angrily. "A fine, respectable woman from a moral family! Not what you think!"

"*What I think?* What the hell does what I think have to do with brain tumors and their varied symptoms?" Dr. Colasamo wagged his thumb and fingertips, held together in typical gesture. "I'm telling you a person's behavior alters considerably with the slightest pressure on the brain! Inhibitions disintegrate gradually in some instances, and

432

patients will do and say things they normally wouldn't do. Symptoms vary with the location of the tumor. . . ."

The doctor resumed his writing. "We need an electro-encephalograph to study her brain waves. We haven't the equipment! Now, if this Salvatore can conjure up an EEG machine, we'll be that much closer in discovering what causes the *Signorina* such *maldolore!* He tore off the sheet from his pad. "And mind you I said, we'd only know what it is—not find a cure! A cure is something else!"

"Through the Americans—perhaps?"

"That's your best chance! Someone at AMGOT Headquarters or through the local ministers in the Defense office. . . ."

Santino Siragusa left the doctor's office with the weight of the world on his shoulders and Athena at his side, unaware that she'd heard the doctor's words. She attempted to elevate her spirits and coax his into a more gayer mood.

"We don't have to return so soon, do we, Santino? I'd like to walk for a spell along the Corso Vittorio Emmanuale. We're but a short distance from the Garibaldi Gardens. Let's go and see the fountains and flowers. Perhaps a walk along the waterfront will inspire us. I see so little of the ocean."

He nodded numbly, hardly seeing anything or anyone. As they approached the Quattro Canti, the picturesque crossroads of the Via Maqueda and the Corso Vittorio Emmanuale, the heart of Baroque Palermo, Athena glanced all around her, and remarked, "We're either the most religious people in the world or the most wicked. Do you realize how many churches there are in Palermo?"

Santino, absorbed in his painful thoughts, said nothing. But he took time to look at the cluster of antiquity around them. To the south of the main thoroughfare stood the Royal Norman Palace, with its seventeenth-century courtyard where a magnificent staircase led to the *Capella Palatina*, a jewel of Arab art of colorful mosaics on a golden background that glittered in the mysterious half-light above the royal apartments, all decorated in a Baroque and neoclassic decor. The red domes and luxuriant tropical vegetation of the enchanting cloister of the Church of *San Giovanni degli Eremiti*, also built by Roger II, evoked a delicate image of some distant corner of the Orient. Close by the twelfth-century cathedral, majestically arrayed in fortress-like dignity with lofty Gothic towers which some late restorer had bastardized by incorporating upon it, among other monstrosities, an 18th Century dome.

"It's all so breathtaking," whispered Athena. "Although I've seen it all before, it still takes my breath away."

Santino took her hand and led her through the *Piazza Pretoria,* past the Tuscan Renaissance Fountain where flocks of doves cooed and fluttered in a mad clatter, then, they continued on past the facade of the Town Hall and the *Palazzo del Municipio* until they arrived at the *Piazza Bellini* where the breathtaking Martorana Church stood with its Norman bell tower and a huge mosaic of Roger II. It was the most magnificent Arab-Norman structure in all of Palermo, and Athena's favorite spot.

"May we go in for a moment, Santino? I'd like to offer a prayer for my brother," she said.

He stared at her with a peculiar sadness, nodding. Better she should offer a prayer for herself, he thought. Inside, they both blessed themselves and genuflected before a glittering altar. While Athena said her prayers, Santino offered his and lit a candle for her life. Watching her quiet, solemn figure kneeling, Santino's throat constricted. The doctor's words echoed through his mind, and he felt himself go weak. He was almost harsh with her when he took her small thin hand in his and went back outside into the brilliant sunshine.

A *potpourri* of all that ever was and is, Palermo greeted them on all sides. No matter where they walked, inside or out, in these creations of previous civilizations were to be found specters of a glorious and in some cases, a bloody, tortured past. Once they were back on the Via Roma, Athena asked him a question he'd never explained to anyone. "Why did you abandon the priesthood?"

"I left, that's all there is to it," he growled at her.

"No secret love—no paramour?" she persisted.

"Is that why you asked?" He smiled in spite of himself. "Sorry to disappoint you."

"I'm not disappointed. I'm glad," she giggled.

Santino said nothing. They passed hordes of street urchins, American Soldiers, British Tommies, and shabbily-dressed old men who talked with animated gestures and stopped periodically to stare with inbred curiosity at the American soldiers. Even as they unbuttoned their flies and urinated into the gutters they would tip their caps with a free hand and with toothless grins shout out their greetings, *"Buon giorno,* Joe!"

Standing on the corner waiting for the jeeps to pass, Santino caught a glimpse of Athena; she was so beautiful it took his breath away. She turned and catching the strange look in his eye, she baited him.

"What's wrong? Surprised to find I'm a woman? You always treat me as a child," she said pouting. "Look at me. Am I not desirable to you?"

Santino walked on ahead of her, red-faced and somewhat embarrassed.

"Aspetta!" she called after him, tugging at his arm to detain him. She was out of breath. "See?" She turned her head in profile from side to side. "See—I am a woman!" Athena smiled provocatively as though she had no cares. She twirled about for him, and the soft folds of her simple cotton frock billowed, whirled, showing trim legs. Amused, curious onlookers paused to watch them. "Really! Look!" She allowed her hands to outline her trim figure and caress her waist and hipline in a voluptuous manner.

Filled with awkward embarrassment, Santino avoided the all-knowing, smiling eyes of the more permissive libertines, who winked playfully at him. He grabbed her unceremoniously by the arm and yanked her alongside him. Made ill at ease by the emotions that sprang in him, he grew more flustered.

". . . I'm really a woman!" she laughed at his self-consciousness.

"I never thought otherwise!" he blurted, angered by the attention given her.

"Then, why haven't you talked with me? Do you find me attractive?" She pouted with the petulance of a seductive barmaid. "How stupid of me. Perhaps you don't share my feelings?"

"Managghia! These Americans drive worse than the Italians!" he shouted and held on protectingly to her as a jeep sped recklessly by them. He made a facial grimace at the driver who shouted an obscenity at them.

"No! It's nothing like that. If you want the truth, I've been enamored of you for a long time. At *Terra Diavolo* I thought of you, constantly. . . . Thought about you? Hah! I couldn't take you off my mind!" His face turned shades of pink.

They both stopped in the middle of the sidewalk to stare at each other in that glorious excitement of new lovers.

He told her. "I wondered about you, and I thought, Athena's growing into womanhood. . . . You are the most beautiful woman I've ever seen. . . . Your dark eyes of fire burned into my soul, and I believed with conviction that you had bewitched me! Took possession of all my senses. Then, I'd remember, I'm ten years your senior, and I'd dismiss you from my mind." He took her arm and steered her on.

"Holy Blessed Mother incarnate! Imagine! *Ten years older than I!"* She mocked him and made a clucking sound with her tongue. Her dark teasing eyes lit up in merriment.

"In truth, Santino, sometimes I think you act ten years my junior!"

She slipped her arm through his and walked to the *Piazza Marina* with the Garibaldi Gardens at its center, where they both walked in silence for several moments. To the right of the *Piazza*, the *Palazzo Chiarmonte* was visible in all its 14th-century splendor. Opposite, from Palermo Harbor, the fresh ocean breeze refreshed their senses and they simply walked about in appreciation of the fertility of greenery they seldom saw in and about Montegatta. For Athena it was all paradise, a Utopian setting, and she basked in it.

"Hello baby," said a few American soldiers in passing. They appraised Athena's beauty with open-mouthed expressions.

Santino glared at them. *"Allo bebee!* What is this?" he retorted angrily. "Go on. *Vatini!* Get lost!"

"No offense, *paesano*," they called and rushed on, about their previous business, filled with the exuberance of soldiers on leave.

"Bastards! They have no respect! What do they think you are?"

"A woman." she said simply. "Which is precisely what I am. Only you seem blind to the fact," she replied. "They are just lonely soldiers looking for a friendly face. There are so many of them." she said glancing about the busy *strada* filled with milling crowds of the military who occupied their lands.

"It's difficult to believe the war is still on and has turned into such a terrible one. We're lucky, I suppose, we didn't experience the genocide that's occurring in Germany—so many Jews meeting their death in those reported atrocities. Do you think it's true—what they say? Or is it propaganda?"

"At this point no one knows what's true or untrue. At war's end, when all the powers begin to divide the spoils; when they are forced to take an accurate inventory, the world will separate fact from fiction. . . ."

"You mean like the stories about my brother?"

He was noncommittal as he led her to a nearby bench, several feet away from the statue of Garibaldi. She was so beautiful, thought Santino. His spirits soared, and for a moment it seemed nothing could dampen this day. Again the doctor's words echoed through his mind, though, and he felt a quiver through his heart.

"What do you think of all the publicity Tori receives from the world," she repeated interrupting his mood.

"In what way?"

"Every way."

"What's more important, Athena, is *his* reaction to this concentration of spotlights focused on him. . . ."

"I'm gravely concerned," she said quietly.

"Why?"

"It frightens me, how he basks in it. This kind of attention can intoxicate a man worse than alcohol. It can fill him with a false ego and deceive his judgment. History has been written with the blood of such great men who surround themselves with *yes* men, who scatter and run the other way at the first sign of trouble. Invariably the hero falls to shame and disgrace, having been betrayed by those same men for whom he fought. None of his virtues is ever remembered. . . ." She glanced at him in a premonitory manner.

"Promise me, Santino you'll always remain at Tori's side! Be that solid foundation he can come to depend upon, to help him uphold his true philosophies and remain true to his ideals. . . ."

He saw the frantic concern in her eyes; felt the tightening grip of her strong slender fingers upon his arm, as she implored him. He wanted to tell her—no one told Salvatore what to do. Salvatore was his own man, and she shouldn't fear for him. But he couldn't. Instead, he nodded resignedly, gently took her hand from his arm and clung to it with both his strong hands.

Birds twittered overhead in the poplar trees in the well-manicured garden and the traffic from the street seemed muted and distant.

"For so young a woman you have remarkable depth." He felt a surge of pride as he spoke the words.

"Am I not my mother's daughter? Santino," she said suddenly, "Marry me!"

His face turned berry-red, and he was momentarily at a loss for words.

"Don't think about it. Let's go and get married. Perhaps at St. John's we'll find a priest who'll marry us today!"

"Today? Now? This very instant?" He composed himself and smiled at her impulsiveness. "You'd break your mamma's heart. It's a day every mother looks forward to, Athena . . . you should realize that."

"Then, let's rush home to tell her. . . ."

"*Aspetta, bedda,* lets talk about this. Listen, to me . . . I've nothing to offer. I'm not even the right man for you. You deserve a man of substance, a wealthy man who can give you things, make your life easier, shower you with perfumes and luxuries a great beauty like you should have. . . ."

She laughed a zany kind of humorous laughter. "Oh my dear Santino! You aren't impulsive at all—are you?" She plucked a nearby rose and smelled it.

"Athena!" Suddenly he recalled Dr. Colassamo's warning. "This isn't like you at all! In the past two years we've hardly exchanged a dozen words between us. Now, you're chattering like a silly cuckoo-bird! You're a different person entirely!"

"I *am* different, you silly ass! I'm in love with you. For so long, I've ached for you and I've never found the opportunity to tell you. You've been so occupied with Tori and the others. If I wait any longer for you to come forward and declare yourself—I'll be dead!" She twirled the rose in her fingers.

"Athena!" he reprimanded. His heart felt strangled. "Don't talk such foolishness!"

"Foolishness?" It was her turn to stare at him. "What— that I love you? Or that I'll be dead?"

In a sudden movement, he reached for her and pulled her close to him. He held her so tightly she could hardly catch her breath. They could hear the other's heart pounding furiously, unmindful of the smiling, gaping, and several shocked passersby. Flocks of pigeons hovered close by, ruffling their plumage and cooing incessantly. The multi-shaded pink to ruby roses, genuflecting in the morning sun, shed tears of early morning dew from their velvety rolled petals, and the world continued to move for the lovers.

They parted slightly and gazed into each other's love-filled eyes. Taking courage, Santino kissed her gently, until the response in his manhood stirred and became erect with desire. He sprang back away from her body, so she wouldn't guess how deep his desire for her could be. His face grew tell-tale, and when he found courage once more to look at her, she smiled in an all-knowing, feline exaltation, to mock him.

"Athena!" He reprimanded in embarrassment.

"Si," she purred softly.

"You're shameless."

"I know. I know."

"It's time to take you home."

"No. Not now. I'm having such a good time. Besides, you didn't answer me. Will you or will you not marry me?" She paused. "There might not be enough time for us," she whispered.

"What's that supposed to mean?" He felt a sting of anguish.

"I heard the doctor. The door was open." She turned away. "Is that why you won't marry me?"

Santino felt limp. His heart nose-dived. He turned to her, cupped her lovely face into his hands, and turned it towards him. His soft voice cradled her. "The doctor said nothing to influence me against a decision of marriage."

"Then you will?" she grinned happily. "You will? Santino—you will?" She took his hands in hers, pulled him to his feet, and turning in a circle, they danced a jig. He fell into her mood of wild and gay abandon with a youthful exuberance that spurred him into cartwheels of ecstasy. Her lustrous and clean dark hair swung freely about her shoulders as prisms of sunbeams danced on her anthracite tresses like iridescent star points. In those moments she became the embodiment of her favorite Grecian goddess, Psyche. Graceful and lithe, with dark exotic eyes filled with the spirit of eternity, she gazed at Santino, bursting with happiness, because, like Psyche, she had found her Cupid.

It was love! Every breathless, numbing, heartfelt moment catapulted them into that world of perfection reserved only for lovers.

And now to break the news to Signora Salvatore and to Tori, himself. . . .

While the lovers were discovering each other, Tori arrived home, at the house of his mother, where he had planned to meet Vincenzo to prepare offensive tactics against Marshal Franchina's planned coup that evening.

Antigone placed a hot cup of coffee before him on the table as she watched him devour a thick slab of *ricotta*, freshly made by the cheesemaker down the street. She stroked his forehead and pushed back a loose curl from his face.

"What are you doing home this time of day? I see something unusual reflected in those brown eyes of yours," she said quietly.

"I've never been able to fool you, have I?" He wiped his lips with a napkin, opened a fresh pack of cigarettes, lit one, and puffed thoughtfully for a time. He leaned forward in his chair, crossed a leg over the other and watched the smoke from his cigarette curl upwards. "I'm waiting for Vincenzo. We have business in Monreale." He sipped his coffee. "Before he arrives, I wish to ask you several things." He set the cigarette in the ash tray his mother provided. "Why is there no baptismal picture of my Godfather and me? You have one of Filippo, Marcos, even Athena—where's mine?"

"Why do you ask now, after so many years?" Her face became colorless. "Why are you curious?"

"Nothing. It's nothing," he said. He didn't want to hurt her in any way. Then, as if he couldn't resist, he asked. "When did my Godfather baptize me? What date?"

She glanced sharply at him, and sipped her coffee.

"Well, I might as well tell you, Mamma. I met my Godfather—the other day. . . ." He searched her face for some tell-tale sign—something.

Dying inwardly, she reached for the bottle of anisette. She steadied her hand, poured a little into her coffee cup, and recorked the bottle.

"What did he have to say, after all these years?"

"He sends you his respect and best wishes for your continued health. . . ."

"He—uh—remembered us?"

"Why wouldn't he?"

"I mean—uh—after all these years. Some twenty-four years. You'll be twenty-four pretty soon . . ." She stirred her coffee. Her throat constricted.

His features remained impassive. "Not for six months. . . ."

"Of course. I'm not thinking." She picked up her mending basket and began nervously to sort some of his socks.

"When was I baptized, Mamma?" he asked gently.

"*Managghia!* Alessandro! Is it necessary that you know right this moment?" she snapped irritably. Her face filled with color. "I'm sorry. Forgive me. I'm nervous and worried about Athena. She's in Palermo with Santino at the doctors!" Anything to change the subject, she thought.

"Alone, with Santino?" he scowled. "That's a fine thing! My sister, unmarried, in the company of a single man!" He was outraged. "How could you have allowed her to go? *Mizzica!*" he wailed at her obvious lack of discretion. *"Me fa scomparire!* You bring embarrassment to me!"

"Stop being a fool. *Che se testardo!* She's in good hands and you know it! I never knew you to be so old-fashioned! Now, let's get back to you!" she looked unwaveringly at him. "You were nearly a year old. It was sometime in

440

1923. I'll have to find your baptismal certificate for the exact date. Do you have to know right this minute?"

He shrugged nonchalantly. "Did my Godfather play an important role in my early life? I don't really remember him—not at all."

"Why?"

"It's uncanny how much alike we are. I didn't notice it when I visited him at his villa in Godrano—"

"His villa?" She grew unduly excited and set aside the mending basket.

"Vincenzo and I went to Godrano on business. Then two days ago I met him at the *Albergo-Sole* in Palermo. That's when I noticed the similiarity. . . ."

She jumped to her feet. "What business do you have with the *capomafia?*" Her whole body trembled with a rage, a violence he'd never seen before.

"Mamma!"

Her face contorted angrily. "What business? Tell me!"

"Mamma!" he grew alarmed. "Stop! Why are you working yourself into such a frenzy?" He grabbed her shoulders and shook her gently, at first, then more vigorously. Finally he broke her mood. Her dark eyes, fixed, stared as one in shock. She inhaled long breaths until she calmed down.

"What business do you have with a *mafioso?*" she asked.

"None," he lied and averted his head.

"Do you know what it means to get involved with these 'men of respect'?"

"But . . . I am involved with the greatest of all, aren't I? My Godfather?"

"But . . ." The protest died on her lips. How could she tell him? "Because he is your Godfather doesn't mean you must emulate his ideals or share in his politics. You have a well developed mind of your own, a brilliant one with great potential, my son. I beg you do not permit anyone or anything to persuade you to change your ways."

"What makes you think I'd do that?"

"Oh—I don't know. I don't know," she retorted. "What business do you have with the *Mafia?*" she asked again, sharp and unrelenting.

His reluctance to reply accelerated her fears. This approach to her son was all wrong. She brushed aside a few wisps of gray hair from her face. "Tori, perhaps it's time we have a serious talk," she began. "I see I've neglected a portion of your education. It never occured to me they'd be reborn again. Let me explain about these men. Then, like everything else you've accepted from me, I know you'll weigh my words and come to your own decision in whatever you are involved in." She held back a rush of tears.

"The *Mafia* is unlike anything you've ever studied in the countless books you've read. The *mafiosi* are a breed unto themselves. Once you take or give anything in their name, you belong to them for life. If you accept an ounce of flour they will exact from you, a ton. Give them a thimble of your blood and soon they'll demand your entire circulatory system, veins and arteries included. One never wins with them."

"Now, you tell me! Why pick a *mafioso* in the first place to be my Godfather?" he asked testily.

Their conversation was interrupted by Vincenzo's arrival. He came charging in the rear door of their house, bringing with him the Salvatore mail he'd picked up in the village post office. If he noticed any tension between them he gave no indication. After kissing his aunt affectionately, he sat down at the table next to Tori and accepted the coffee his aunt placed before him. He sniffed the air gingerly. "Do I smell fresh bread?" he asked.

While Vincenzo and his mother extolled the virtues of fresh bread and *ricotta,* Tori brooded over his recent involvement with his Godfather, aware that the situation took on a more ominous significance than he'd bargained for. He fell into a pit of uncertainty. Oh, he'd been avenged all right, but, at what price? How naive he'd been to think the Don had performed such a special service for him because of the Godfather—Godson relationship. *Porca Miseria!* What an *embroglio!*

Tori's men were waiting for him at the Grotto Bianca. He faced them with a wry smile and a terse voice. "Tonight you'll all do what you usually do on a Friday night. Should anything unusual occur, you are to drop everything and ride swiftly to the Grotto Persephone—not here. Take all usual precautions that you aren't followed."

He broke the men into squads, giving these men detailed instructions for stripping the Grotto Bianco of all traces of their occupancy. "Transfer all supplies and the arsenal to Persefone." He directed his next words to Gambo Cusimano his armorer. "I dislike giving you this extra work, *amico,* but, until we know what this *zanzaro* —mosquito—is up to we shall have to endure these small inconveniences."

To the Nuliano and Gagliolo brothers, whom he instructed to guard all entrances to the Grotto Persephone, he said, "Shoot to kill anyone who comes within shooting distance, if they fail to give you the coded password."

The men moved swiftly and silently to carry out his orders, filled with brooding and conjecture. This had been a first! The first time since they organized that any *carabiniero* had signed warrants for any of them. Franchina's recent activities had left most of them numb and shaken. Their criminal records had long since been destroyed. Who then, who had submitted the names of the four paladins of the Inner Circle, and the names of the men stated on the warrants? Their names, well guarded, had been known only amongst themselves. It followed then, that someone among them was a spy! It was cause enough for each of the men to view their associates with grave suspicion.

"Allay your fears," Tori told them. "I'll find out how Marshal Franchina suddenly got so lucky! And when I do—" He paused, looked at each of them gathered about him in the light of the bright sun, and removed his Browning from its holster. He pulled out the clip and held it up for all to see. "This gun clip is reserved for our betrayer! I promise! I, personally, will empty all fourteen shots into his guts!" he shouted dramatically.

Not one man among them disbelieved the sincerity of their leader, for Salvatore always kept his word.

Maresciallo Franchina, preparing to annihilate Salvatore and his men in those lonely hours just past midnight, preferred capturing them alive. With this consideration in mind, he had secretly procured the cooperation of the Monreale, Borgetto, and Partenico offices of the *carabinieri*, swelling his own squad of twelve men to nearly fifty well-armed horsemen.

His plan was straightforward and neat. The men were to meet under the Norman Tower in the *piazza*. There he'd break them down into small squads and progress to the proper locations, disarm the rebels, arrest them and jail them.

Maresciallo Franchina was no fool. He gave his men no information in advance. He knew that, for the sum of money he paid spies to report activity of the bandits, another man could pay that much and more for knowledge of the Marshal's plan. It wasn't without reason he kept the proposed coup, quiet.

At a quarter to midnight, nearly fifty strong, the mounted *carabinieri* converged quietly in the *piazza*, where in view of the Norman tower, Marshal Franchina instructed his men in their duties. Hardly finished detailing their orders, Marshal Franchia paused in mid-sentence, cocked his head to listen. Before he reacted to the sounds of motorized vehicles approaching the village square, his men reacted with puzzled expressions on their faces. Their horses, skittish, danced about nervously. Headlights shone first. Suddenly, they were surrounded by a horde of security police; some in jeeps, others in police vans, and a few mounted on horseback had arrived from Palermo and converged upon the village, locking the *carabinieri* into the square. Against the background of shocked faces and a pandemonium of honking car horns, spooking horses, and disgruntled, protesting military police, the bandits, expecting some unusual activity, jumped out of their warm beds and escaped to a predestined rendezvous.

The bedlam in the village square grew uncontrollable. In the melee, a special courier dispatched from the Palermo Central Office of the Italian Military Police searched frantically in the mob for Marshal Franchina. Caught at the very center of the tumultuous hordes, the Marshal, locked in tight, was unable to move his horse. Apparent on his face was the frustration he felt over this unexpected development.

"Maresciallo! Maresciallo!" called the courier loudly hoping to be heard above the din. He wheeled his horse into the turbulence, waving his orders in the air over his head. "I must see you, *Maresciallo!* It's urgent!"

"Yes! Yes! I'm over here, shouted the Marshal catching sight of the courier, "What is it?" Caught like a fly in a tangled web of irate horsemen, he strained to maneuver his horse about. A ghost couldn't have squeezed its way through the hundreds of men that spilled into the confined *piazza*, preventing any escape.

"Important message from headquarters!" called the anxious courier a few horses away.

The Marshal managed to sidle his mare in closer to the messenger and, stretching over the horse of another *carabiniero* he snatched the communique from the other's outstretched hands. Saluting halfheartedly, the courier was more concerned in finding avenues to unweave his way back through the congestion.

Even before Marshal Franchina glanced at the communique, he knew. By damn, something was amiss. At that moment with the message unopened in his hands, he sat in his saddle, a sinking sensation at the pit of his stomach and he knew. Somehow, someway, his plan of capture had been betrayed. A mule's brain could have discerned the treachery. He glanced at the artfully planned congestion,

444

his eyes narrowing to slits. Burning with anger deep inside him, his face remained expressionless. Finding a small opening in the tightly packed horde of men and animals, he backed up, wheeled his steed around and headed towards a flickering lamppost at the edge of the square.

As the dim amber glow of the lamplight barely lit up the message and the contents were made apparent to him, his face contorted into a mask of fiery emotions. His black eyes burned like live coals, his jaws jerked in spasms, and murder flooded his heart. If anyone had seen this Barracuda gritting his teeth, they would have recognized his fierce and relentless dedication to a cause to which he'd become addicted.

Contained in the message was the order for his immediate transfer out of the territory of Salvatore, to a new post in Messina, across the island. The order, dated two days prior, invalidated his present commission and subjected his activities to strict regulations which would, if he persisted, be construed as performance conducted against orders, he would then be subject to fine, imprisonment, demotion, or all three.

Marshal Franchina stuffed the message into his tunic and stared dispassionately at the thickly congested mob, who looked like ants converged upon a plate of honey. He quickly dismounted, tied his horse to a hitching post, and propelled himself through the skittish horses and motorized vehicles crammed in tightly around him, and, amid the raucous shouting of men, the impatient beeping of car horns, and the intermittent protestations of high-strung horses, he snaked his way towards his office.

Inside the sanctuary of the small working quarters, the Marshall, trembling with livid rage, removed a whiskey bottle from a desk drawer and, pulling out the cork with his teeth, he spat it across the room. He lifted the bottle to his lips and gulped the fiery liquid greedily until his senses were shocked and he felt its burning inner glow searing his intestines.

In that moment, Marshal Franchina swore another oath to capture the bandit Salvatore, regardless of the power he wielded and despite the protection he received in the hierarchy of the provisional government. It didn't take a scholar to realize such cooperation, given to Salvatore by the security police, came from a highly placed politician. Who it was—that was another matter. One day he'd learn.

He moved close to the open-grilled window and surveyed the fiasco of the tangled knot of men. He shouted irrationally. "Fuck you! You all took orders to get into this mess! Now, go find the same runted prick of a sow's whore to get you out of it!" He paused to guzzle more whiskey.

His eyes fell upon the thick scrapbook compiled on the activities of Salvatore. "Fuck you too, you King of the peasants' scrapile!" he shouted. "Just remember one thing. Franchina never loses! One day, somehow, someway, someplace, I'll get you, Salvatore! You hear? Franchina will tie your ass to the sun!" He swilled more whiskey and launched into a fist-waving lecture on courage, loyalty to the nation, and determination. He was still ranting when a bullet exploded through the window and tore into his shoulder.

No one knew exactly what had happened or how, or even why. But when the other *carabinieri* saw Marshal Franchina come raging out of the office, shouting the battle cry to commence firing, they drew back, stared around them, and wondered how in the hell they could raise their arms against the security police, formidable and imposing as they were.

"*Avanti! Avanti!* Fire, you miserable stinking cowards!" screamed the Marshal. He ordered his men to shoot anything that moved. They didn't.

But by then, the security police had begun to back away and out of the *piazza*, and in moments the area cleared.

"*'Tenente* Paterno!" shouted Franchina. "Get your miserable sons of whoring turtles to give those devilish dogs a round of bullets, or I'll have the lot of you court-marshalled for disobeying orders!"

By then, the *carabinieri* stood silent, down to the last man watching the antics of this bullet-crazed officer, with the gleam of a madman shining in his eyes. He had collapsed in a rage, and was carried off by four of his men, still raving maniacally. "Sound the call to arms, Bugler! Fire, men! Fire faster! Faster! I'll have the whole lot of you court-martialled!"

"Poor creature," they whispered among themselves. "The man's gone crazy! Absolutely, crazy! Some bullet must have deranged his brains!"

'Tenente Paterno dismissed the men and told them to return to their posts and not to worry about Marshal Franchina's threat. "The Sicilian sun has fried his brains, you can be sure. Marshal Franchina is in no condition to resume this command. My report will indicate, you all followed orders *perfettamente*."

He winked at his men and disappeared inside to observe Marshal Franchina's behavior. What a report he'd make!

plate. "I can never get enough of these. They are my death. My death!"

"You make it sound uncomplicated. From whom would I take orders?" asked Tori, dropping his anger, a notch.

"Whoever issues the orders, you will not make a move until you clear it with me. That way I can keep my eyes and ears open for possible treacheries."

"Treacheries at your level? My, my, I thought only the savage peasants resorted to treacheries."

Their eyes met and held for an instant. "You've made many enemies, Salvatore. Many enemies," said the Don, evenly.

"Along with many friends," he retorted with marked irritation.

"Ah, si, friends," snorted the other. "Friends whom you've bought with generosity and kindness, who would sell your friendship in a moment to the highest bidder."

"You know all the answers, don't you, Godfather?"

"All the answers. Questions, too. When I led the Mazzarini we were real bandits, not this child's play which converted you to a national hero. Tell me—of what are you a hero? Of the reporters who seek your favors so they get rich writing about you? You are a hero on paper. You know what it means to be a paper hero? *Cazzu!* That's what! You know what they do with yesterday's newspaper? That's right. They wipe asses with it. And don't you forget it. I never set out to be a hero—dead or alive. You must take chances, *Capeeshi?*"

Don Barbarossa picked at the anise seeds stuck between his teeth and glanced slyly at his mercurial Godson, knowing he had snared his prey. "Don't answer me today. By next week, if you can find two good arguments against accepting the commission, come talk with me." His deceptive voice sounded placating.

Tori endured the scathing soul-ripping to which the Don subjected him to in complete humiliation. Never had he been spoken to in this manner. There had been no strong male figure in his life to excoriate him and peel back his defenses as this man had done. He also recognized the psychology behind the words and felt himself drawn to several half-truths the Don had brought to bear. A deep silence fell between them. They looked at each other without blinking; Salvatore, hostile and stonelike in features; Don Matteo, with the inert expression of a preying mongoose before the strike.

Don Matteo broke the connection. *"Va bene.* Come, we'll drink a toast."

"You have a short memory. I don't drink." Tori's words came dangerously close to severing the cord.

"Perhaps if I didn't drink as much, my memory might be as long as yours." The Don's meaningful glance left little to the imagination. "But you're right." He forced a light laugh. "You young bloods are far sharper than old codgers like me. If we don't keep in step with the times, we'll be put to pasture."

Godson or not, this young punk would be taught a lesson. The Don's eyelids grew heavy with displeasure. Whatever other plans he might have for this impertinent cock would have to wait. The political plans he held for Salvatore superseded his own personal displeasure. "You'll be contacted shortly, Godson."

Tori's fists were clenched so tightly he found it difficult to open them and shake hands with the Don before he departed. When he did, he was disgusted to find the handshake limp and without character.

He found Vincenzo at the whorehouse, Neptune's Daughters, a place overrun with soldiers and sailors, properous prostitutes, and pimping waiters, all busy making deals faster than an auctioneer calls for a bid. They left and had dinner at Angelo's on the Via Maqueda. Tori was unresponsive to conversation. He kept replaying Colonel Modica's conversation and that of Don Barbarossa's over in his mind.

"It's not among one's enemies that treacheries spring. . . ."

Weigh carefully the proposals made to you. . . ."

"Bone up on Machiavelli. . . ."

On the trip back to Montegetta, these words of caution cut into his memory, too sharply for comfort. He wasn't so naive that he didn't know the Colonel had tried to tell him something about his Godfather. What?

In recollecting how insulting his Godfather had been and how he boldly and with confidence had overstepped his position with him, he grew fiercely indignant.

"Botta de sanguo! You'd think I was his son, the way he spoke to me!"

"What the hell you talking about, Tori? You're acting like a crazy man!"

"On the contrary, cousin. For the first time in my life, I'm probably sane. I'm beginning to see things in their proper perspective. And you can bet one thing's sure. "I'm going to bone up on Machiavelli! *Capeeshi?"*

"You're crazy! That's what. You're crazy! You know

tures of the American officer with his camera, he enthralled Colonel Modica with stories of the legend of the temple. By the time Tori finished, the American officer close to the parapet of the temple, cocked his head to listen. His startling blue eyes impulsed in every direction darted here and there about him. "What's that?" he asked Tori. "That sound—what is it?"

Pivoting first, on one foot, then the other, he glanced in the direction of the Tyrrhenian Sea and strained to listen. Stefano heard a distinct sound of ancient trumpets echoing remotely in his mind; a strange, muted, cacophony of triumphant battle cries of another era. Puzzled, he looked in the direction of the plains below.

Watching him, Tori smiled good naturedly. "*Colonnello*, my friend, you're home at last!" Tori told him about the friendly demons of *Siculi*. Although he listened, Colonel Modica didn't seem to hear anything of earthly matters.

The American felt a strong gravitational force which compelled him to walk dangerously close to the broken parapet of the temple. Tori made no move to warn him or pull him back. And when his aide broke away from the others in an attempt to warn him, he was silenced by Tori who indicated he was safe from harm. The Colonel, enchanted by what was happening to him stared out at the vast vista at a scene to which only he seemed privy. He watched ancient warriors materialize before his eyes; he listened intently, with a pang of dismay, as the sound of trumpets faded dimly in his mind. When it was over, Colonel Modica said softly, "This could very well be the very place where the Cartheginians did battle with the Greeks for control of the Island."

"Bravo! You know your history. The rest is vivid imagination."

"Don't tell me it's my imagination. I can still hear the trumpets!"

"It's the only logical explanation I can give you. unless you believe in reincarnation."

"Do you?" The American still stared at the fading scene in an effort to recapture it. It was incredible what he's seen and heard. Damnit! He wasn't imagining things—was he?

Tori angled his head sharply and studied the Colonel with a reserve of cynicism. "Your American journalists compare me with conquerors of the past. They say I'm the reincarnation of this man or that man; Alexander, even Napoleon. And I have yet to do real battle! The principle might explain our friendship. Perhaps we knew each other

30   449

in another time in history? Is it possible our spirits transcended earthly appearances in recognition?"

Tori smiled as he watched the rise of awe in the American as he gazed about at their surroundings. "You Americans are not only *te-rrific* with your praises, but you are also enthralled with antiquity—no?"

"There's nothing like this in America. No glorious reminders of memorable and past civilizations staring at us each day. No remnants of previous cultures—except for the Indians to whom I don't relate much. But, my friend, it isn't for this that I've made a special trip to see you today." Modica sighed heavily, then, on a more somber note, he explained. "Salvatore, President Roosevelt is dead. Truman has just stepped into office."

Tori gave a start. "That's why you are leaving so soon?"

"I shouldn't be here now. I received orders to shove off today."

"What happens now?" Tori sobered at the implications.

"Who can tell? Rome's in a helluvan uproar. It's rumored that Hitler has locked himself in the Reich Chancellory. The Russians advance towards Berlin at an alarming rate of speed. I've a hunch the war will soon be over."

"Then, you'll not be able to stay for dinner?"

It took several moments for Stefano Modica to realize this day meant more to Salvatore than the status of war or the death of a foreign president. But, then—why not? This was Salvatore's life, and his world was Sicily. Twenty-three years old, and he hadn't begun to realize his true potential. Colonel Modica glanced over at his aide, who gave him the business with his eyes and pointed to his watch.

"I know. I know," he muttered to Lieutenant Destro. To Tori he apologized. "He's like a watchdog—an indispensible watchdog, however."

"About dinner—" interrupted Tori.

Colonel Modica shook his head. "There's no time. I couldn't leave without speaking to you again." They both lit up cigarettes and for a time stood in silence.

"This is a difficult posture for me," began the American. "I've never interfered in the destiny of another man. What's more I've argued with myself, telling myself that what you do is none of my business. What compels me to offer my two cents' worth of opinion is even more of a mystery to me, *amico*." He shook his head, suddenly confounded by his actions. "But, I'd feel worse leaving Sicily without taking time to tell you of the greatness I see in you. No, no, don't interrupt me," he wagged his hand at

450

Tori. "It took two days of courage to arrive at this decision. There's a role in all this that only you can play. Why or how you've been chosen by this mysterious force who propels our destiny is not clear. I'm certain only of what I've observed. You possess certain charismatic qualities, which, despite your protestations, have already marked you for a certain greatness, a destiny you can't escape." Modica paused. "Somewhere I read something by Shakespeare—*"There is a tide in the affairs of man, which taken at the flood leads on to fortune. Omitted, all the voyages of their life are bound in shallows and miseries. . . ."*

Tori shook his head and interrupted almost apologetically. "I fear you give me more importance than I deserve. In Palermo, I suggested that if you bet on me— you'd be making a mistake," he avoided the colonel's eyes and subtly changed the subject. "When you leave—who replaces you?"

"I had hoped it might be you," said Modica straight out.

Salvatore exploded. *"Managghia u diaoro!* Damn the devil! Again with that talk! You are some crazy man, *Colonnello!"* He studied the American officer, and cooled down, flushed with self-consciousness. "I can see by your face, you mean the words you speak. But still, I. . . ."

"I've never been more serious in my life."

Didn't you implant in the minds of your men, your basic philosophy of justice for all—an end to the gross inequities dealt your people? Isn't this the premise, the spark, which ignited the flaming heartbeats of your nation and brought you into world prominence?"

As Tori listened to Colonel Modica, it appeared that he tried to convince himself he was capable of being the creature the American painted so vividly with words. He felt the push-pull, the hesitancy, the insecurities rush at him. "But—we are a few dozen men. . . ."

"With many cooperative followers, Salvatore. This is no time for modesty."

"All right. All right, then, with many cooperative followers, but. . . ."

"Go a step further. Spread the same ideology to the people of your village and to those in surrounding villages. Do it in the same manner the corrupt clergy teaches them to believe that poverty's a blessing," urged Stefano.

Tori observed him through tilted, indulgent eyes. "A revolution again?"

"Off the record, damnit it, yes! If it takes a blasted revolution to awaken your people. Well, if it—" He

451

couldn't bring himself to say what he really felt, for reasons his military status didn't permit. It was frustrating. "Damn-it, Salvatore, no one has to tell you what must be done!"

Demonstrating great restraint, Salvatore flushed self-consciously, still unable to picture himself in the role the American had cast him.

"Again I say, I am simply an outlaw with a price on my head. I am no politician. My powers are limited only to my province. One day when my government returns to normal, I shall be a lawmaker—"

"No! *Now* is your time. Your life is at full tide—*now!* Recognize it and go on. What if your government doesn't return to normal? Sicily and your people will be lost. Stronger nations will gobble her up—and think what a waste! America will stand behind you if you oppose the Reds!" Modica tensed, he had to convince the Sicilian.

"America will stand behind Salvatore?" Such an incredible thought shook the Sicilian and sent tremors coursing through his body. Awed by both Modica and his words, Tori walked alongside of Stefano in silence as they paced the open aired temple. Inwardly he felt a rising excitement.

"Russia, eh? You think Russia will take over?"

"Who else? Red banners fly triumphantly in Rome right now," Modica retorted bitingly.

"Why? Who gives Russia this strength?" he cried softly. "Why does America give her this latitude—this liberty?"

Stefano understood his dilemma. He tried to explain.

"Until the Japs blew up that paradise in the Pacific, Hawaii, we were only allies to Great Britain, with little say about anything. Invading Italy meant we had to cut down on provisions to Russia. Soviet-Western relations suffered consequently. Our failure to open what Russia considered a necessary second front until late in the war caused a serious rift between us to widen."

Tori, considering the growing threat of communism, observed, "America will experience great difficulty when this ambitious nation decides to carve the spoils."

"No question," agreed Colonel Modica as he harked Tori back over Russia's enormous victories and brilliant military coups in the previous year. "Our actions in Sicily and Italy set a precedent in that a nation which liberates another determines that nation's political and economic future. Now, Russia watching with ferret eyes what other nations will do, is determined to capitalize on that precedent. You see, Tori, where America prefers a nation to rule itself—Russia doesn't. Hasn't she already dispatched her communists to infiltrate Italy! Hasn't she already seduced the people with unrealistic promises? After the *fiasco* of fascism, the Italians will try anything. In stages of negotiation it's easy to promise the moon. Delivery is another thing. I fear for Sicily! She is too vulnerable."

Tori realized how shrewd was his mother's thinking after all. The *Colonnello* had echoed her words, practically verbatim.

"That's why I persist in trying to make you come face to face with your potential. You must assert *your* wisdom and strength, now, at this crucial time in your nation's history. She needs you! No matter how inadequate your strength appears, it is more than enough. What you consider to be inadequacy in your mind is simply the lack of experience. Experience without theory at times can be more practical than theory without experience. Given time, they both work. Can you see this, Salvatore?"

"*Colonnello*, I could never take your place with the Grand Council! They'd laugh at me. They'd say, 'look at this *contadino*, this mere son of a lowly sheepherder trying to be a politician!' You forget, I am a peasant!"

Colonel Modica saw his dilemma. "I didn't mean that at all. God forbid you should take my place. I was forced to sit like a frozen statue while the combined forces around me plotted for Sicily's death, not life. But, so that you don't mistake my words, let me set the record straight. It'll take the courage and suffering of the peasant to lift Sicily out of her bondage—that, and the aid of a powerful nation—America."

Tori studied this man who stood in profile next to him. His visored cap was pulled down over fierce blue eyes. He had a generous face, in which was read many things. There was a candor and ferocity in it, and a respectful reverence that literate men often express for their superiors. Yet, it was a face that would commit murder and throw his life away for a friend. Strange, the affection Tori felt for this man whom he'd known for so short a period of time. Different than the closeness and affection and love he felt for Vincenzo, yet almost the same. He felt as if he'd known him forever. Tori spoke in perfect Italian.

"Please understand me, *Colonnello*—"

"Call me Steve, or Stefano."

"And you may call me, Tori. *Va bene? Allora*—Stefano, deception and shaded subtleties, calculated to influence my thinking are an insult to me. The convoluted logic of these three-a-penny politicians bore me. You think I would have patience to listen to their empty words? I would not be so patient, and I would not appreciate anyone to vote against my word if I believe I am right. For two years—I've brought no failure to my men. We've had few casualties. All this because I stand by my word. I am aware of my limitations, and know I am politically naive. Those crafty, two-tongued vipers, those sophisticated politicians, would crush me and scatter my forces to the four winds before I knew what struck me." He laughed easily. "I regret, Stefano, I am not this great man of power you see photographed in your mind. Not even with America's support."

They had walked the length of the temple several times and paused now next to the staggered scattering of pancake-shaped boulders stacked on each other, precariously. Modica glanced anxiously at his watch. Time was his enemy on this day. He despaired. "How can I reach you? How do I make you understand that this point in time belongs to you. The brass ring rests within your grasp. How do I convince you of your destiny, which I envision so clearly in my mind, and which remains a distant dream in yours? A man who's become front page news the world over? A man who controls half his nation? You, leader to an army of well over five hundred men, stand here trying to convince me you aren't qualified to lead your people, with or without the power of America?"

Tori's eyes lit up like blazing tourmalines glittering in the sun. "I can see, *amico*, you'll not let me off the nail."

"Hook, *amico*. Hook." Stefano slipped out of his uniform jacket.

"Si, hook. You will not repose until I am committed."

"If you don't, I can't leave Sicily in good conscience." The officer pushed back his cap, fanned himself and mopped his brow with a handkerchief. "How the hell do you tolerate this bloody sun? Damnit! You don't even wear sunglasses."

Tori laughed. "A Sicilian without sun would wither and die."

Stefano had removed from his jacket pocket a small box, which he thrust at Salvatore. "Before I forget," he began. "Something I bought especially for you. Accept it in the spirit of friendship and wear it in good health with my wishes for your good fortune and a long life, whatever you decide to do with it. Perhaps, Tori, one day after this war of the devil ends I'll return to Sicily and we'll both have a laugh over my emotional zeal. Your birthday is November? The papers mentioned it."

Tori, flustered and uncertain of himself, was about to

454

refuse the gift. He stared at the open box, containing a solid gold scorpion amulet suspended from a thick gold chain. He turned the amulet over and read the inscription: "To Salvatore; May the King of Montegatta rule Sicily wisely. 4-12-45 Colonel Stephen Modica."

"Truly I do not deserve such adornment. You give me too much importance, I tell you." Tori squirmed awkwardly and flushed uneasily.

Stefano craned his neck to bask in the slight breeze that whispered across the mountains from the sea, in relief from the inexorable sun. He opened his shirt, loosened his tie, and said simply. "I can only tell you what I see in you, Sicilian, what I know to be fact, regardless of your modesty. But, unless you recognize these things in yourself, all my talking won't move your mountain. When I get to where I'm going, I will write to you. Keep in touch with me, Tori. If you need me write me in care of Captain Matt Saginor, USA Army Intelligence." He scribbled the instructions on a small white card. "If you decide on revolution, I guarantee my government's support."

"I can say *te-rrific*, to such news?"

"Stefano smiled. "You can say terrific. Now, before I leave, I am forced by conscience to tell you that I know of your involvement with Don Barbarossa—his plans for you. I urge you, exercise caution in your dealings with him. These members of the Grand Council are not to be believed. Collectively they are an insidious force, damned near impossible to reason with, and dangerous."

"All of them?"

"All of them. Its a damn shame we didn't meet a year ago. God Almighty, this procrastination would have ended abruptly. Now, I leave, having done less than I intended. Listen, Tori, drive back to Palermo with me, and I'll requisition this jeep to you, to be used however you see fit. It's a shame to leave it behind, where the scavengers can pick it up for nothing."

"You have such authority?" Tori was impressed.

"I can do whatever I deem important for Sicily. You'd make more frequent trips to Palermo with a jeep at your disposal—no?"

"You won't give up on me, Stefano." Tori was immensely touched.

"Now I'm leaving, I have to abandon such thoughts."

Colonel Modica signalled his aide, in a gesture of departure as they walked towards the other men.

Ten minutes later as the AMGOT Jeep spiralled in its ascent towards Rigano Pass at the summit, Tori mentioned

Athena's physical condition as Santino had explained it to him. A fleeting image of Athena entered Modica's mind, with a flash of compassion. He'd met her earlier at the Salvatore house and remarked ardently over her incredible beauty. He indicated his heartfelt sorrow to Tori as he scribbled the name of an officer with the Medical Corps. "Don't delay getting Athena to see him. I'm not sure how much longer the Allies will remain in Palermo," he urged.

Tori, grateful for his suggestions, thanked the American. Then, feeling more secure with Stefano, he laughingly told him of the proposals made to him by the Partitionists and what they offered him if they were victorious.

The Colonel listened attentively, even as his eyes darted about the changing landscape. "And if the Partitionist plan fails, Tori? What then?"

"Exile in Brazil," replied Tori with exaggeraged eye gestures.

"So that's it! That was Barbarossa's trump card!" exploded the American. "He already had you wrapped up. What the fuck's his game?"

"Who tied Salvatore? What are you saying, *Colonnello?*"

"Wrapped up, *amico.* Wrapped up. Don Barbarossa— that's who. You already had a deal with him, but he plans to do you in—double-cross, *Capeeshi?* To shaft you, *amico,* is what he plans to do. Probably to annihilate you," he said acidly, scanning the arid mountains. No wonder his plans had been foiled!

"No." said Tori quietly. "No deals have been made with Don Barbarossa. What means this *double-cross?* This *shaft?* Annihilation I understand."

Colonel Modica explained graphically. As he did, Tori saw the doubt reflected in the officer's eyes and he repeated himself. "I promise you, no deals were made with my Godfather. No agreements. My communications have been solely with *Capitano* Francesco Bello."

A variety of mixed emotions charged through Stefano Modica in those next moments. Searching Tori's eyes, his inclination was to believe him. Yet, it didn't subdue the fires burning inside him as he recognized the diabolical machinations Don Barbarossa had implemented without his knowledge. It took him a few moments to unravel the Don's revolting schemings and plottings.

"Sonofabitch! Listen, I mean no disrespect towards your Godfather—I know how you feel about him, but—" Stefano was boiling made. "Goddamnit! You'd better know your Godfather pledged your services to the Partitionists,

456

and guaranteed the Grand Council full control of all guerrilla forces, including all the bandits and brigands, in the coming years of insurrection. Due to my official involvement, I was unable to be more candid when we first met. Now, I'm officially off the Sicilian detail. I owe no loyalty to Don Barbarossa—or the others. It's best you know the kind of people with whom you intend to have an affair."

It was a far different Salvatore who sat, grim-faced and tight-lipped, engrossed in the American's words, his thoughts roiling turbulently.

Colonel Modica rambled. "So the Partitionists made their move towards you? You know, of course, Canepa's a communist. A hard-core Red. No matter what he appears outwardly, and he's fooled a great many, believe my assessment. He's a Red agent. Be sure you tread carefully."

"*Allora*—you don't know?" asked Salvatore, his dark eyes clouding over.

"Know what?"

"Canepa's dead."

Modica's astonishment was instantaneous. He stopped chewing gum, rolled it into a ball, and tossed it out the window of the jeep. He turned his full attention on Tori. "When? How?"

"It's suspected he was liquidated by those higher-ups who felt secure in his death. Surely you knew?"

"The hell I knew!" he retorted angrily. "And *why* I didn't know is what nags at me now! Fucking Sicilian intrigue! I'll never understand it!"

"Yet, you desire for *me* to stand at its center?" Tori forced a cynical smile. "If a man with your credentials feels at sea with such politicians, what can a baby lamb do among such predators?"

"You've got the edge on me. You're Sicilian—one of them. You all think alike." He made a gesture of apology when he caught the wilting glance Tori tossed him. "Well-almost," he added. Inwardly Colonel Modica fumed.

"They kept it secret so as not to split the factions," mused Stefano.

"*Bravo, mi Colonnello.* Sicilian logic isn't so complex."

Modica's next gesture defied classification and produced a gale of laughter by Salvatore.

"That *sonofabitch* Canepa, playing three sides against the middle. Aided by both Allies and the Reds, while courted and spoon-fed by the Sicilian land-barons, the bastard was bound to emerge victorious." Modica concluded the man was a double agent, a fact he'd known for sometime. That the man's death hadn't been reported to him is what disturbed him.

"What happened to the sixteen guerrilla bands?" he asked.

Tori grew silent. "What else? They split up and disbanded."

"And all this without my knowledge or sanction," blurted the colonel. He methodically brought it into the open. "Well—it's happened, without me. The Monarchists and Separatists formed their coalition and under the guise of Partitionists, led by this man, Francesco Bello, they've made their next play. You, my friend, are next. They want you. Only with the aid of your guerrilla army do they stand a chance at victory. You see what I've been trying to tell you? You can't escape your destiny. I only hope, my friend, that you'll know how to handle these greedy vultures."

While Tori pondered the weight of his words, Colonel Modica's mind shifted into high gear. Now, he understood why Don Barbarossa had done an about face when Italy's politics swung to the Left. Any new government assuming control of Sicily, including the Reds, could conceivably pass new land reforms and pose a serious threat to the ancient island's feudal laws, a move neither the nobility or the Mafia could afford to let happen. The American and British allies were lax, but, not Russia. She'd never assume the pacifistic role of her predecessors. Pushing for separation from Italy, and demanding autonomy with a regional Parliament would insure that Sicily would remain in the hands of the Mafia-feudalists who had kept her in bondage for centuries.

Torn between the uniform of the U.S.A. and a peculiar loyalty to his unique Sicilian, who, if guided properly, could raise his nation out of the middle ages and break the chains that kept her shackled to its unholy past. Colonel Modica stewed uncomfortably. Loyalty to the American uniform won out. How could he possibly disclose confidential matters of his government entrusted to him as Top Secret, highly classified data? He'd sworn to uphold his allegiance to America, not Sicily.

Until the jeep arrived at Rigano Pass, where Tori dismissed his paladins who had followed on horseback, and kept only Vincenzo at his side, both men remained silent, each engrossed in their personal dilemmas.

Once past Bellolampo Barracks, where *carabinieri* saluted the official AMGOT jeep, unaware that it transported the infamous Salvatore, the passengers were greeted by the constant clamorous pealing of church bells. Faint at first, the sounds increased in volume the closer they got to Palermo.

"The news is out. By now the entire world mourns the death of our President," remarked Colonel Modica with an edge of sadness to his voice.

"All except for America's enemies," said Tori candidly.

Modica glanced sharply at him, then nodded at the intelligence of the remark.

As they approached the City of Palermo, Lieutenant Destro was forced to gear down in the abnormal traffic jams. City streets were congested with crowds of weeping pedestrians mourning Roosevelt's death. Allied staff cars whizzed past them in the other direction towards Palermo Airport. Pandemonium existed on all sides. The deafening sounds of the discordant church bells numbed their eardrums. Car horns bleated incessantly. People shouted incoherently and wailed like banshees. In some areas traffic had slowed down to a standstill. Civilians sobbed as they waved farewell to their G.I. friends. "So long, Joe!" "Cheerio, limey," they called to the British soldiers as they drove out by the truckload. Official flags and standards drooped in fatigue as lovers embraced tearfully and parted in sorrow. Women clung tearfully to the men in the trucks as they passed. Even the whores at *Madama* Neptune's, seldom seen by the public, were framed in the shuttered windows, waving and tossing flowers to the best customers they'd ever had and would probably never have again.

Lieutenant Destro eased the jeep into another stream of traffic and wormed his way past the Quattro Canti onto the Via Roma. In moments he pulled up before Allied HQ.

Colonel Modica suggested that Tori remain in the jeep until he returned with the proper official documents that assigned the jeep to him. He ordered his aide to scrounge up a staff car and both men snaked through the crowds who pulled at them, and fired countless questions at them. Colonel Modica waved them off politely and disappeared into Allied HQ.

Lieutenant Destro was the first to emerge. He made his way back through the pressing crowds to Tori's side and handed him the packet. He saluted the brigand and left. Several moments later, Colonel Modica emerged from the building and snaked his way towards the jeep where the Sicilians waited. Spotting him, both Tori and Vincenzo alighted from the jeep and headed towards him. They shook hands and embraced. It was impossible to be heard over the boisterous shouts of the crowd. If the Colonel had known it would be the last time he'd ever see Tori, he might have taken more time with him. But the war, a greedy mistress, had placed too high a demand on him. He moved towards the waiting staff car amid a shower of confetti and multicolored serpentine. He turned with marked hesitation on his face, as if he had more—so much more—to discuss with Tori. Glancing somberly at his friends, he waved and boarded the auto.

Salvatore, waving back to his American friend, experienced a sinking sensation in the pit of his stomach. Enveloped by inner depression, he failed to notice he'd become the object of attention among the hordes of people who began milling around him. It wasn't until he felt himself being touched and grabbed at that he realized what was happening.

"It's him!" shouted a bystander peering inscrutably at him. "It's Salvatore!" The people caught up the cry. "It's Salvatore! Salvatore! *Viva* Salvatore!" they cried and rushed at him like a giant tidal wave. Filled with adoration for their hero, they forgot their temporary woes, "Salvatore! *Dio de benediggi!*" They shouted. "God Bless you!"

Was it possible these accolades were for him? he asked himself. Infected by their contagious emotion, Tori stood up straighter, squaring his shoulders and nodding to them with the majesty and forebearance of a young prince, as confetti covered him like mounds of pastel snowflakes.

Watching him with amusement and a peculiar delight, Vincenzo was unable to measure the enthusiasm of the crowds as they closed in around his cousin. In those moments he seemed to have grown in stature, thought Vincenzo. He was struck by the nobility of his cousin's profile, by the bold manner as he strutted before the host of admirers waving to them, nodding and acknowledging their praises. In an agile move to protect Salvatore from the threatening mob, Vincenzo rushed to his side, ran interference, and steered his cousin to the safety of the jeep, before they could tear off his clothing.

"*Managghia!* cried Vincenzo breathlessly. "Did you see the way they grabbed at you! They couldn't get enough!" The gears ground raspingly and he managed to steer the vehicle away from the hordes of people, who having heard the cries, "Salvatore!" rushed at them from the *piazza* across the way. It took twenty minutes for Vincenzo to move out of traffic and snake his way back towards the narrow road through the Conca d'Oro valley.

"If I never hear another church bell in my life, it will be too soon!" said Vincenzo covering his ears. "This *Colonnello* Modica really gave this jeep to you to use?" Vincenzo thought the whole affair totally incredulous, the gesture too magnanimous to be sincere. "For nothing? What did you have to do in return?" He coughed slightly.

"Just promise I'd use it," replied Salvatore quietly as he gazed at the rich fertile valley of the Golden Shell. "He thinks I should get to Palermo more often." He glanced at his watch. "C'mon, cousin. Step on it. I'm dying of hunger. With all that good food waiting for us. . . ."

Coughing again, Vincenzo nodded and floored the accelerator, much to Salvatore's discomfort. He clung to the door handle in panic. Nothing shook him as much as his cousin's wildcat driving! By the time they arrived at the summit, Vincenzo's cough had become so intense, he stopped the jeep, got out and leaned against the vehicle until the convulsions subsided. He didn't let Salvatore know he'd coughed up an excess amount of blood. Totally drained of color he walked to the passenger side and forced a smile.

"You drive, cousin," he said weakly.

"Botta de sanguo! If you don't see a doctor, tomorrow, I'll personally knock you down, tie you and drag you there myself! Hear?" exclaimed Salvatore. "If I've told you once, I've told you a dozen times. If you want to be my co-captain, you've got to be well!"

"I promise. I'll go," replied Vincenzo too weak to argue.

Salvatore started the jeep and driving slowly, he filled with great concern over his cousin. He wanted to talk, to help him ease the discomfort, but he couldn't. He still entertained a terrible feeling of emptiness at the departure of Colonel Modica, as if a part of him had gone with the American. His mind filled with Modica's words, and his usual ambivalence grew deeper. And when his thoughts centered on his Godfather, Tori's features turned stony, his jaw set like iron. He could feel the strength of Hercules in him, but what to do with this strength? What?

CHAPTER 34

Shortly after dinner, Tori lost interest in the conversation in which the guests at his house were engaged, so without a word to either his family or his paladins, he quietly slipped away to the Mountain of Cats.

In the sun's final curtain of the day the mesa had transformed into a fiery copper sea of shifting bronzes, taupes and velvety-brown shadows in an effort to give light to the full moon soon to rise against a midnight blue sky. Star points lit up intermittently, clustering overhead like a comforter of lustrous diamonds so close he could almost touch them. It was times like these that he missed Appolladora most, and times like these when he found the memories of her fading more each day. Since her death had been avenged, it was almost as if the books were being closed on the subject, and he was helpless to do anything about it. Tori struck a match on a boulder to light a cigarette. The instant burst of orange-blue flames lit up his face to reflect a myriad brooding thoughts.

Was it possible, wondered Tori, that he could be the man Colonel Modica described? Was he truly blind to his own potential? When Stefano spoke to him, he felt like a Hercules. But, did he really possess such attributes of leadership? He blew out the match before it burned his fingertips. Instantly his imagination took flight. Like a camera, his mind began to absorb the images, and he saw himself dressed in judicial robes, walking tall and proud among his saw himself treated with reverence and respect. People asked questions of him and hung on his every word. peers. Seated next to the imposing men in government, he There he was, riding in an open limousine, the streets lined with crowds of admirers shouting *"Viva Salvatore!"* just as they'd done in Palermo. In another split-second fantasy he saw himself seated in Parliament, complimented and lauded by Minister Belasci.

Managghia, he thought as his mood broke and he laughed aloud at the absurdity of such thoughts. Just as quickly Tori sobered. There it was again, that deep voice inside him trying to shake him awake as it had so many times in the past:

Wake up, Tori. You heard the American Colonnello. Now is your time! If you don't take hold, Sicily will be lost. You've been a savior to your people these past two years. You can be the man Stefano sees. You are that man!

He reached into his pocket and pulled out the golden amulet, studying it in the bright moonlight as he dangled it a few inches in front of him. *"Il scorpione, eh?"* he muttered aloud. He opened the clasp and slipped it into place around his neck, allowing it to dangle freely on his bare chest under his open-necked shirt. On this night Tori found himself at the crossroads of his life, stirred by Stefano's words and disturbed by his Godfather's. His mind, burdened by confusion, wrestled for a time with both opinions, and he knew instinctively that this night would change the course of his life. He didn't know how he knew, only that he knew.

Colonel Modica'a attempt to warn him of Don Matteo's treachery, which at first he had found hard to believe, had caused him to reconsider his Godfather. Recalling with vivid clarity the expeditious manner in which he'd disposed of Don Pippinu and the swiftness with which the security police had sent Marshal Franchina packing, he now took another look at this illustrious Don Barbarossa. He recalled his first encounter with him, and carefully considered the cold, inhospitable treatment extended him until the name "Antigone Naxos" was mentioned. The instantaneous reaction by the *mafioso* was inescapable. Tori's thoughts spiralled and he grew visibly troubled.

It just isn't possible, he told himself, feeling the cold sweat break out on his forehead. As the thoughts jelled in his mind, every nerve and fiber in his being tried to deny it. He told himself to stop the wild imaginings, that, if he permitted his thoughts to continue in this vein, he'd destroy his mother by bringing shame and humiliation to her house. But, no matter how he tried to shake the feelings his mind refused to firmly deny the truth.

For a time he forced his mind to think of his meeting with *Capitano* Bello. He instructed himself to be certain to examine all proposals. Once again his mind drifted to Don Barbarossa's recent words. "You will accept Bello's proposal and report to me," he'd told Tori. Those words burned in Tori's mind, coupled with a powerful resentment. What right did his Godfather have to demand this of him? What right? He considered who had sent the Trapani newspaper to his house. It had to be the Don's way of showing the job had been completed.

The unfortunate part of this was that the article had fallen into his mother's hands, or she might never have learned about the death of Don Pippinu Grasso. A few days ago, on Friday, just before Athena had arrived home with Santino to announce their intention to marry, Antigone had been sorting the mail casually when her attention had been captured by the sight of the Trapani newspaper. Not until she'd placed the article before him, with the photo of the dead *mafioso* staring up at him, had he understood what had caused her face to blanch. His eyes had scanned the article. Only a few words stood out: "Former proprietor of Naxos Weight and Measures from Mt. Erice dead. Heart Attack. In Palermo on business with an old friend and colleague, Don Matteo Barbarosa. . . ." At that moment Tori's eyes had met his mother's, and she had known how compromised he was with Don Barbarossa. He could see it in her eyes. She had left him alone with Vincenzo and gone outside into her unprolific garden, moving mechanically from one lifeless plant to the next, muttering, "Everything in Sicily is dead. Why do I bother to restore life to these sterile, unyielding plants that get little help from the barren earth?"

More than the recent association with his Godfather, Tori suspected that something more profound disturbed his mother, but before he had time to sort out bits and pieces in his mind, Tori gave a start.

It happened so quickly that at first he was baffled. He peered about the moonswept temple thinking a joke had been played on him. The Siculi demons, perhaps? A few stray cats had begun to gather in their nightly ritual, their cries and near-human moans growing more abundant. Still he saw no one or nothing. "Who's there?" he called out feeling for his gun. Damn! He'd left his gun at home! He slipped down behind the boulder, crouching out of sight and felt along his inner calf inside his boot for the knife he kept secreted there, while his eyes pierced through the shadows at the perimeter of the temple. He heard a voice call to him—not the voice of the playful Siculi's, for sure. Now he moved behind the huge columns, retiring into the shadows. His sensitive ears listened for unnatural sounds, and his intent eagle eyes fastened on a moving dark form who approached, seemingly unmindful of any lurking dangers.

It seemed that every cat in the province had converged upon the temple, uttering near-human cries as they swarmed together for whatever mystic rites they embarked upon each night. In the cover of this activity and these distracting noises Salvatore moved effortlessly until he was upon the interloper. With sudden agility he leaped forward, took his captive unaware, and with his knife aimed menacingly at the other's neck, he pulled back his other arm into a brutal stranglehold. In the struggle the black scarf fell from his mother's head and he found himself staring into her terrified eyes. He released her instantly. Panicked at the close call.

"Mamma!" he shouted. *"Dio Buono!* I could have killed you! What are you doing here? I could have killed you!" he repeated. "I could have killed you!'" He was shaken considerably.

"Well, you didn't. So relax! Calm down!" sighed Antigone. She appeared more interested in the congregation of cats and the eerie sounds emanating from them. *"Allora,* my son. They really *do* come here at night? I thought it was just another fanciful tale of folklore." Absorbed by the mass of cats, she wondered, "Why do they choose *this* place, in all the valley?" Shrugging, she turned to her son, dismissing the phenomenon of the cats. "What are you doing here all alone?" she scolded. "You left a house full of friends to come here by yourself. . . ."

"I came to think on some matters. By tomorrow I must make several decisions. It's best you return to the house, Mamma. You shouldn't have come by yourself, unaccompanied? Come, I'll take you home."

"Tori," she restrained him. "We must talk." Her voice was firm.

"Si, Mamma."

"Don't tell me, *si Mamma*. It's time to talk. For a long time I've not felt the closeness we once shared. Did the *Colonnello* give you cause to worry?"

"No. He suggested that I take a more active part in Sicily's politics."

"Bravo Colonnello! Mark my words, he has sense."

Tori broke out in a sudden burst of temper. "Why does everyone insist that I have such exceptional potential? That they see powerful forces in me? They ask too much—"

"Because it's true. . . ."

They stared at each other in a total silence, for several moments.

"You think I enjoy this dedication of yours to our country and our people?" began his mother solemnly. "These past two years, I've been both proud of your brave deeds and paralyzed with fear that something would happen to you. That at some time you might not return to Athena and me. Daily we offer prayers to God for your protection. From the first, when I saw you take command over those men in the *maquis* I knew no words I could offer would prevent you from doing what you believed you must do. I convinced myself not to interfere, not to act maudlin, not to press on you like a stone weight, for it would belie every principle I'd taught you to believe in all your life. On the day destiny became your mistress, I knew not to compete with her, for mothers and mistresses are as incompatible as oil is to water. My days of tutoring you ended on that day. . . ."

"Oh, Mamma," cried her son sitting at her feet. "I'm not sure of my destiny! The *Colonnello* filled my head with so many pictures of what he sees in me. I'm confused. For the first time in years I don't know my own mind. I'm twenty-three, not fifty-three—I'm not a sage. What do I know?"

She stroked his head tenderly. "The chaos will settle. Like the swirls of dust that rise in the confusion of battle and fall into place, the answers will come."

"The American stirred feelings and images in me that in my wildest dreams I dare not believe possible." His anguished voice trailed off.

"Haven't I taught you from infancy—nothing's impossible? Give your youthful emotions time to catch up to a maturing mentality. That's all that's troubling you."

"I wish it were only that. What disturbs me are the blatant contradictions between what *Colonnello* Modica sees in me and what my Godfather tells me I must do . . ."

Antigone stiffened. In the moonlight her face turned to a sheet of colorless glass. "Your—uh—Godfather? What contradictions? What does he tell you you must do?"

"He makes me conscious of my station in life. Dictates my responses. Whom I should trust—whom I shouldn't! He assumes too much authority for a mere Godfather!"

Antigone swallowed hard. The moment had arrived to give her son the answer that would steer his course for the rest of his days. Difficult as it was, after hedging for several moments she couldn't put it off any longer. "Just where is it written on destiny's tablets that Don Matteo should direct your action in this life?" she asked imperiously. "You owe him nothing! It's been years since we heard from him! Now, suddenly, you permit him to dictate to you?" She glanced at him suspiciously. "He holds

466

nothing over your head—does he?" The dreaded question was out.

Salvatore rose to his feet and paced about the mesa. He lit a cigarette and puffed on it thoughtfully. For a time he studied the burning cigarette. Anything to keep from looking at his mother. "Why do you ask?"

"Do you want me to keep silent? Continue to think the black thoughts I've not been able to rid myself of these past two days?"

He didn't reply. He knew she was referring to the death of Don Pippinu.

"I won't ask again, Tori. I will only repeat what I told you then. If they own you—you'll never be free of them. You owe them a favor? They won't stop at one, or two, or three. If you don't comply with their requests—even their slightest whim—they will dispose of you. *Capeeshi?* That's all I have to say."

"You should have thought of that twenty-three years ago, Mamma *bedda*," he whispered, half afraid of her response. The words were out, and Tori was more surprised at his own daring, his lack of anger.

She turned to her son, gazing upon him in the moonlight with a majestic dignity, and sensed instantly that he regretted his words. No matter, it was time for Antigone to unburden her soul. It came to her—to continue the deception —but she lacked the strength, and desire to do so. Besides, if Tori had gleaned any of her teachings, he'd see through any further chicanery. "You know," she said, relieved that the dreaded secret was out.

Tori felt terrible—dead inside. Thinking it was one thing; hearing the truth was another. "Then it's true, what I've sensed intuitively?" His voice, barely above a whisper, tried to conceal his terrible inner trembling.

Antigone nodded.

"You could have told me before this."

"I had no idea he was alive until you brought home the newspaper headlines." And because he was silent, she told him of the circumstances of their meeting, of the troubled times, how hungry her sons were when the Don found them.

"I was only the seed of a passing interlude—not loved, not wanted." He was reasonably hurt, angry and humiliated, suffering countless imagined indignations.

"No. No, you're wrong, Tori. I loved you more than the others. No, no, it wasn't intentional, I assure you. You were all of my flesh, babes of my womb." she reflected. "Something about you was special, even from the start.

467

I gave more to you than I did to your brothers, because you demanded it of me. Deep within you, even as a child, was an intense craving for love, knowledge and attention. You took whatever I had to impart—don't you remember what an active mind you had and still do?" She paused a moment to brush away an errant tear that had spilled on her cheek. "Since I assumed your real father to be dead, why would I tell you his real identity? What purpose would it have served? After my husband died, your need for a father was even greater than in Filippo or Marcos, so, I invented Barbarossa as your Godfather. Was that so bad? I never dreamed there'd be a day of atonement," she agonized.

Her words only vaguely entered Tori's consciousness. His mind had ground to a halt when he realized that Don Matteo was his *real* father. It was a paralyzing thought, numbing his senses—too much for his confused mind to grasp. For several moments they sat in silence, each filled with personal torment to which the other couldn't relate.

"It would be frivolous, Tori, to confront him with this news," she said. "You don't propose telling Matteo?"

"I don't know." He waved his hands despairingly. "I don't know. I just don't know. To suddenly awaken and discover I'm not who I thought I was all these years."

"Tori! I implore you. Don't bend your mind to this moment. You are exactly who you've been all your life. A name doesn't modify the fruit. You are what you are and who you are, regardless of the name you're called. The greatest men in the world have been born out of wedlock."

Tori remained uncompromising in his silence. Unintentionally, he had tuned his mother out. He sat there interminably, shrouded in tormenting silence. When he snapped out of his debilitating thoughts, he was surprised to find no one next to him. Antigone, unable to communicate with her son, had left him and returned to her house. His rejection had filled her with shame and remorse. It had been difficult to face Tori in the dark of night. How, she wondered, could she face him in the light of day?

Tori didn't recall how long he sat under the rising and fading moon. As the stars disappeared into the pale light of dawn he experienced emotional upheavals, more torment and agony than he had since the death of Apolladora. *Goddamnit! If only I could get stinking drunk—it would help ease the pain.*

At first, Tori sensed an inner revulsion towards his mother, for bringing him to these ends—a malice that grotesquely twisted his inner tranquility and rendered him beyond reason. As common sense set in, he attempted to reconcile the disastrous thoughts fermenting in him, and much of the destructive emotions abated. What the hell was wrong with him? He must be losing all reason. Apolladora had been a prostitute, whom he had willingly forgiven and had been willing to marry. His mother made one mistake—and here he was, ready to crucify her! *Dio Mio!* he thought. *What hell she must have endured to keep me.* She could have aborted. God knows how many women used the poisonous method of stuffing parsley into their vaginas to abort! Not his mother! *Damnit, Tori, grow up! These things can happen. Who needs a father, eh?* Hadn't he done well enough without one all these years? Why cry over the lack of one—rather, the acquisition of one, now? He commanded himself to cease in this schoolboy's display of foolish emotion.

It was nearly 5 A.M. when Tori left the temple. The vagrant cats had already vanished as he made his way to the Grotto Persephone. Enroute, he admonished himself over the treatment he'd given to his mother. What was more, he came to an important decision. The secret his mother had carried locked tightly in her breast all these years would remain just that—a secret. He vowed he'd never tell another soul—not even his father, Matteo Barbarossa.

"Alessandro Barbarossa," he toyed with the name over and over on his tongue. "No! It can never be," he shouted aloud at the alien sounding words. "I am Salvatore! I can be none other!"

Tori never made it clear to himself why he intended to conceal his identity from his father, not even to himself. Perhaps it was a punishment of sorts he wished to inflict on the Don for not caring enough about the woman he had impregnated with his seed. It might have been punishment directed against his mother, both for the act and concealment of his father's identity. It might even have been punishment directed against himself, for being the bastard son of an arrogant blackguard. Whatever, Tori resolved to dismiss the episode from mind—erase it completely as if his mother's words had never been spoken.

Moroever, Tori grimly determined to pursue—and find—total autonomy from Don Barbarossa, regardless of the consequences. Never, as long as he lived would he willingly involve himself in any business with the redoubtable *capomafia*. By the beard of a whale's whore, he wouldn't!

He rode swiftly through the hills and reaching the Grotto Persephone, he dismounted and stroked Napoleono's mane, nuzzling him for a few tender moments. He thought of Appolladora, then of Maria Angelica whom he hadn't seen in a long time. He promised himself to visit with her one day soon. But, in his mind was riding something more important than the image of another human being.

The early morning sun had already spread a blanket of heat on the scorched earth. Tori walked to the edge of the grotto and saluted smartly to an invisible being somewhere out in the vast open spaces spread below him.

"Perhaps, *Colonnello* Stefano Modica, I will become the man you see through your futuristic eyes, after all."

He moved over the rocks, scaled the steep incline and headed for the shadowy caverns of the grotto, the only refuge from the raw lights of a devastating, colorless sun. This day promised to be a scorcher in more ways than one, he told himself, and disappeared inside.

PREVIEW

Appassionato
Vol. 2

by

Gloria Vitanza Basile

The following pages are a brief preview from
the opening chapter of Appassionato Vol. 2,
published by Corgi at the same time as Vol. 1.

As political pandemonium erupted in Rome following V-E day on the eighth of May and the Eternal City became a hot bed of intrigue, a mad scramble had been precipitated into a free-for all in which ambitious political lions scurried frantically about in fierce competition for control of the government. A King had abdicated, the son had been denounced, and the House of Savoy had come tumbling down into a downpour of total chaos. A dozen political parties vied for supremacy, and, as Colonel Modica had predicted, a people ravaged by war and infected by wide-spread starvation and misery—a people fully disgusted with the circus theatrics of Mussolini's dictatorship—were ready for anything. Never had the nation been more vulnerable.

By then, Salvatore had provided for his people by adhering basically to the fundamental principles of a long-ingrained feudal system in which anyone who could seize power had the right to govern and make laws to meet the situation at hand, without concern for permanency. According to feudal law, the ruler was unrestricted in his right to judge or interpret law, and those subject to his law had to obey regardless of other circumstances.

Guided by these simple, fast rules, Tori had saved his people. But now the war had ended. Caught on the one side by the still-growing needs of his people and on the other by the growing demands of his own morality, Salvatore found himself bordering desperation. Conditions had grown more intolerable, and he had made himself heard through frank and outspoken letters to the press, on the platforms open to him. "I had thought at war's end, my work would have finished. Instead I find conditions more appalling. We are enmeshed in a chaotic situation, with an ineffective government who cares nothing for its people and does little to resolve the problems besetting them. Unless measures are taken to ease the suffering, I shall be compelled to enforce my own laws just as I've done for the past few years."

Well, things didn't get better. And it seemed no one heard his loud voice echoing across the mountains and sea; nor were the voices of Sicily, coming from the Palermo Grand Council, heard as storm clouds of rebellion loomed on the horizon. Once again the voice of Salvatore arose, and was heard again in the press, "Sicily weeps at her own seduction, and, like a tender and compassionate whore, she permits herself to be used without compensation. When will she learn? When will she rebel against such treatment? Must she enforce so high a fee on her services that no one will dare molest her?"

If any one heard his cries, they paid no heed to these warnings. In the tumult and confusion as his nation underwent massive and reconstructive surgery at a snail's pace, Tori stood in his lair at the top of his golden mountains, watching with eagle eyes the silent panic that suffocated him and his people, and decided it was enough. It was finished. He had had enough. He would no longer wait.

This was the time of Salvatore. Now! The tide was in, and he had to move. It was a new Salvatore who became a willing participant in the seduction aimed at him by the Partitionist Party. Now, all was in readiness. He had finally agreed to rendezvous with *Capitano* Francesco Bello.

As the crusty, uniformed driver of an old, dusty prewar Mercedes limousine approached a cauldron-shaped meadow surrounded by four hills, thick with undergrowth and scattered with craggy boulders and desert sisal, he scanned a hand drawn map alongside him on the seat. "We're almost there, *Capitano*," he told his illustrious passenger.

"There it is, up ahead. The bridge. See it?" Captain Bello strained to see through the dusty windshield. All but prostrated by the intense heat, he mopped the sweat balls rolling down his face annoyed that he sweated at all. He squinted behind dark glasses at the sun-scorched, bleached countryside, finding the raw wilderness an abomination. He glanced behind him through a rear view window. "They're right behind us, Mafalla. You just go ahead, the car will follow."

In the car behind Bello's sat the financial power of the Partitionist Party, Baron Mattinata, that miser, that money-grubbing Shylock, that wretched skinflint whose purse strings were too close to his heart—a man who had made Bello rue the day he had formed an alliance with him. He sat stiffly with his two aides, glancing about the rugged terrain with marked scorn. The things he had to do for the Party!

The people he was forced to associate with were repugnant to him, and he showed it.

Vincenzo de Montana, seated astride his horse at the top of a lone hill, watched the limousines approach until they disappeared behind rock formations. He turned in his saddle, lowered his binoculars, and signaled Salvatore who stood nearby on Napoleono. Tori nodded, shaded his eyes, and scanned the nearby hills. A total of three hundred men on horseback remained motionless behind clumps of bushes and boulders on the three hills surrounding the ruins of a Greek theater, awaiting a given signal. Below them, positioned at either side of the bridge, the Scoletti and Genovese brothers, dressed in combat fatigues, held their trusty Beretta submachine guns in hand. The sweat poured off them profusely as their eyes scanned the roads up ahead.

Vicenzo raised himself in his stirrups, adjusted the binoculars, and, squinting into the sun's glare, called to Tori, "They're almost at the bridge." Tori raised his arms into the air. The sound of bleating oxhorns pierced the air. The men on the bridge, alerted, gripped their weapons firmly in hand and turned in the direction of the sounds. Lookouts signaled from hill to hill until the all-clear signal reached Tori.

Captain Bello, hearing the horns, leaned forward in his seat, peering expectedly about the area on either side of him. The occupants of the second car, like Bello, peered about and saw no movement except for the men on the bridge flagging them down. The autos geared down and came to a full stop as Miguel and Arturo Scoletti stood in their path, guns held in menacing postures.

Captain Bello conforming to the cloak and dagger procedures, was somewhat reluctant to slip the catch on his gold belt buckle and place his gun and holster into Miguel's outstretched hands. He tried to suppress his indignation when searched by Marco Genovese, by asking in near contempt, "Where is your elusive leader?"

"In due time, *Capitano*," replied Fidelio, handing his .38 caliber Beretta to his brother. He hooked the grenade, palmed in his left hand, onto his belt and proceeded to search Bello more thoroughly than his brother. Satisfied he nodded the *Capitano* on ahead. "Go on. Up ahead," he nudged him.

Miguel Scoletti, slipping the wooden end of a match stick between his teeth, eyed with noticeable envy the fancy uniform worn by the Partitionist, as he and Arturo made their way up the hill.

Captain Bello, gazing about this *terra incognita,* found himself bottled in a mesa surrounded by three hills. He saw no one in his approach to the point of rendezvous. But in the blinding white glare of the sun, he felt a thousand eyes upon him, watching him, sizing him up. He wondered about them, as they might wonder about him. He was unable to detect any movement anywhere. It was too still— too quiet—too awesome. Only the sounds of his footsteps on crumpled rocks crunched as he moved forward. He wondered at the extreme measures taken by Salvatore to rendezvous in such a God-forsaken place with heavily-armed desperadoes enforcing his wishes. Were these measures of pure desperation—or of solid strength?

Bello was led to a petrified plateau of antiquity—a theater carved from the rocks of centuries past. He gazed up at the two smooth pillars of stone marking the gateway to the ancient arena, marvelling at their incredible longevity. A colorless sun, expanded to its zenith, filled the arena with pulsating hot light. It was difficult for Bello to see beyond the radiations of heat rising off the broken clay floor. Even the dry, parching heat, bore the unmistakable stench of the ages.

"You will walk to the center of the arena and wait, *Capitano,*" instructed Arturo.

Bello nodded and strutted pompously to the center of the blinding sunspot whiter than the bleached stones of a skeleton. The staggering effect of the sun made him feel faint. *Porca Miseria!* Why the hell meet in such a savage setting—in this devil's inferno? He began to grow impatient at what he considered child's play. His dark eyes darted about the area trying to locate movement. Staggered about the circumference of this open-aired pavilion, stood runted stone pillars, like broken rows of teeth, spaced four to five feet apart, that once had zoomed skyward some thirty feet high.

In this dramatic setting, Captain Bello felt like an actor, spotlighted by a brash, cruel sun at center stage—without his lines. Where are the other players? he wondered, as the sound of oxhorns bleated again, much louder than before. His eyes were impulsed around him.

All at once the hills came alive. He saw hundreds of horses come into view at the upper level of the amphitheater. Bello turned slowly in a semicircle, his eyes darting all around him. He heard the crumbling sounds of horses' hooves as they struck against small rocks, shattering them into many fragments that bounced down the incline of rocky steps scattered along the side of a hill. A horde of men, converging on horseback, approached the arena from every direction.

God! What a picture, thought Captain Bello. He saw the glaring whites of their eyes; of both horse and rider reflected in the sun's brilliance. Salvatore's men were everywhere. *Managghia!* What a show of strength! If he hadn't seen it with his own eyes, he wouldn't have believed such an army existed. What a magnificent, awe-inspiring sight! Goddamn the devil—Salvatore was truly something else!

Under the deceptive glare of the fireballing sun, three hundred men had multiplied to three thousand in Bello's eyes. Within moments the horseback soldiers had descended the hills and come to a full halt, standing in a full circle around the outer perimeter of the theater, between broken pillars like a guard of honor. A silence fell over the ancient ruins. It was the most dramatic scene Bello had ever seen.

Salvatore, dressed in the beige uniform of a U.S. Army general worn under a white trench coat, came riding swiftly down one hill to the west of the tableland in a streak of blinding white light, like a lightning flash, on his spectacular white Arabian. He came at Bello galloping across the mesa, and stopped short a few feet away from the impressionable Partitionist leader. He sprang flamboyantly from his horse, and for a time the two men regarded each other in testy silence: one, the elegantly uniformed lawyer and wealthy landlord, the other, the virile young peasant with the uncannily dramatic flair and the formidable reputation.

"I am Salvatore," he finally announced.

"I am Bello," declared the other in the same authoritative manner.

Tori studied the colorful, uniformed politician and felt an instant, keen distrust of the man. Bello, simultaneously studied his host inscrutably and smiled internally at the general's uniform, polite mockery in his eyes.

Approaching them at a tranquil canter, a white scarf tied about his forehead, Indian-style, to catch perspiration, Vincenzo de Montana guided his ebony mare to a spot nearby. He stopped at a respectful distance, sized up Bello within the periphery of his gaze, and without obvious reaction formed a snap judgment, *this man is nothing!* Hunched forward in his saddle, he indolently crossed one leg over the saddle horn while his eyes actively skimmed the area, filled with dust and smells of sweating men and horses. Amid muffled sounds of squeaking leather saddles, clanking bridle apparatus, and of men and riders squirming uncomfortably in the stifling heat. Vincenzo strained catlike ears to hear the words spoken between Salvatore and Captain Bello, both of whom struck poses of nonchalance.

"We meet at last, eh, Salvatore? You can't imagine how pleasant it is to do business with a man so pleasing to the eyes. Most men in your profession are barbarians, *caro mia*. Uncouth barbarians," exclaimed Bello seemingly against his will. "I've waited so long to meet you. Now, finally we can make our plans known to each other. Speak freely, my dear man."

"Try one. They're American," said Tori, offering Bello a Camel. *God spare me from these supercilious fops and incessant talkers,* he thought as the slightest flicker of annoyance crossed his eyes.

Bello accepted one and flourished his lighter, lighting Tori's smoke first, then his own. He puffed on it and inhaled appreciatively. "Milder than Turkish, no?" After a moment's pause he continued. "Only last night I had a vision. Mind you—I'm not superstitious. But, I tell you, I saw this giant white eagle descending from heaven, holding in one claw, the sun. In the other—Sicily." He sucked in his breath dramatically. *"Allora*—can you imagine what went through my mind when I saw you descending those hills in a whirlwind like the white eagle of my dreams? Will it be you, Salvatore, who'll bring Sicily and the world to our feet?" Bello paused to watch the effect of his words on the bandit leader. Spurred by the astonishment he read on the face of his captive audience, he continued with added pomp and *panache*.

"Yes—I see it now, written—*blazed* across the sky! Destiny has brought us together for a purpose. To conquer Sicily. God willing, it shall be ours. The Partitionists shall become invincible!"

It was a foregone conclusion that from the beginning the temperaments of these two men, from different backgrounds, would be too incompatible. Each of them felt hardly anything but repugnance for the other. But, on Salvatore's part, this was quickly developing into hostility and gross displeasure. Bowled over by the man's gilt-edged oratory, Tori collected his wits. He did not smile. Generous praise and unnecessary flattery weren't the tools to exact his loyalty, especially not when employed by a man like Bello, who wore his feelings of superiority on his face as a leper wore his lesions for the world to recognize.

MADELAINA, Vols. 1 & 2 by MICHAELA MORGAN

Madelaina meant many things to men . . .

To Peter Duprez . . . she was a breathtakingly beautiful child-woman who blazed a sexuality that roused him till he ached . . .

To her father . . . she was a mystery; she gave up the life of a princess to become a passionate revolutionary and help the poor . . .

To Maduelito Perez . . . she was the woman he made love to in his dreams: for her he would become the greatest matador in the world . . .

To Pancho Villa . . . she was 'Little Fox', spirit of the Mexican Revolution. He would have given her all of Mexico as a gift . . .

Fiery freedom fighter, tempestuous lover and loyal friend in one desirable body . . . that was Madelaina.

0 552 10811 1   Vol. 1 – 95p
0 552 10812 X   Vol. 2 – 95p

MISTRESS OF DARKNESS by CHRISTOPHER NICOLE

Gislane was a mustee – a beautiful young girl in whose veins ran a sixteenth part of African blood. Living in England, she was free; under the laws of the West Indies, she was still a slave – subject to a life of degradation at the hands of the Carribean planters . . .

Intent on destroying the love affair between Gislane and his young cousin Matt, Robert Hilton, master of the vast plantations in Jamaica and Antigua, had her cruelly abducted and sent back to the horrors that awaited her in the Caribbean. Matt followed, back to the sugar plantations he hated with all his being; back to the heartless savagery of the white, wealthy owners and the suffering of their black slaves. But now rebellion was in the air – slaves were listening to the voodoo drums that called in the night . . . And as Matt journeyed throughout the islands searching for Gislane, he vowed he would fight to the last to abolish the abomination of slavery . . .

0 552 10517 1 – £1.00

A SELECTED LIST OF FINE NOVELS
THAT APPEAR IN CORGI

WHILE EVERY EFFORT IS MADE TO KEEP PRICES LOW, IT IS SOMETIMES NECESSARY TO INCREASE PRICES AT SHORT NOTICE. CORGI BOOKS RESERVE THE RIGHT TO SHOW AND CHARGE NEW RETAIL PRICES ON COVERS WHICH MAY DIFFER FROM THOSE ADVERTISED IN THE TEXT OR ELSEWHERE.

THE PRICES SHOWN BELOW WERE CORRECT AT THE TIME OF GOING TO PRESS (OCTOBER '78).

☐ 10421 3	THE PERSIAN RANSOM	*Evelyn Anthony*	80p
☐ 10667 4	SEVENTH AVENUE	*Norman Bogner*	95p
☐ 10204 0	THE HUNTING ANIMAL	*Norman Bogner*	75p
☐ 10632 1	THE KING'S BOUNTY	*Roy Clews*	95p
☐ 10633 X	YOUNG JETHRO	*Roy Clews*	85p
☐ 10584 8	MAVREEN	*Claire Lorrimer*	£1.25
☐ 10585 6	A VOICE IN THE DARK	*Claire Lorrimer*	70p
☐ 10494 9	LOVE'S AVENGING HEART	*Patricia Matthews*	£1.00
☐ 10651 8	LOVE'S WILDEST PROMISE	*Patricia Matthews*	£1.00
☐ 10737 9	LOVE FOREVER MORE	*Patricia Matthews*	£1.25
☐ 10652 6	RAFAELLA	*George McNeill*	95p
☐ 10665 8	THE PLANTATION	*George McNeill*	95p
☐ 10811 1	MADELAINA Vol. 1	*Michaela Morgan*	95p
☐ 10812 X	MADELAINA Vol. 2	*Michaela Morgan*	95p
☐ 10470 1	THE POWER AND THE PASSION	*Christina Nicholson*	85p
☐ 10797 2	THE SAVAGE SANDS	*Christina Nicholson*	95p
☐ 10538 4	DOLORES	*Jacqueline Susann*	75p
☐ 10029 3	ONCE IS NOT ENOUGH!	*Jacqueline Susann*	85p
☐ 08523 5	THE LOVE MACHINE	*Jacqueline Susann*	£1.25
☐ 07807 7	VALLEY OF THE DOLLS	*Jacqueline Susann*	95p
☐ 10215 6	THE BASTARD, Vol. 1	*Brigitte Von Tessin*	75p
☐ 10216 4	THE BASTARD, Vol. 2	*Brigitte Von Tessin*	95p
☐ 08481 6	FOREVER AMBER, Vol. 1	*Kathleen Winsor*	50p
☐ 08482 4	FOREVER AMBER, Vol. 2	*Kathleen Winsor*	50p

All these books are available at your bookshop or newsagent; or can be ordered direct from the publisher. Just tick the titles you want and fill in the form below.

CORGI BOOKS, Cash Sales Department, P.O. Box 11, Falmouth, Cornwall.

Please send cheque or postal order, no currency.

U.K. send 22p for first book plus 10p per copy for each additional book ordered to a maximum charge of 82p to cover the cost of postage and packing.

B.F.P.O. and Eire allow 22p for first book plus 10p per copy for the next 6 books, thereafter 4p per book.

Overseas customers please allow 30p for the first book and 10p per copy for each additional book.

NAME (block letters)..

ADDRESS ....

(OCTOBER 1978) ....